Slight and

By Shae

For my beautiful cousin, Bayleigh:

We watched you grow into a loving and confident young woman,

and now you watch us from above.

You are our angel, our guiding light,

and we love you with all of our hearts.

Table of Contents

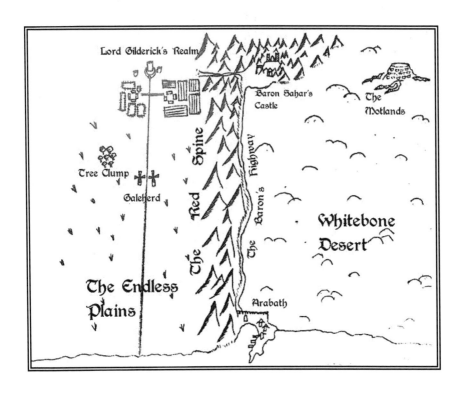

Lord Gilderick's Realm

Baron Sahar's Castle

The Motlands

The Red Spine

The Baron's Highway

Tree Clump

Galeherd

Whitebone Desert

The Endless Plains

Arabath

Prologue
Only a Messenger

It was the quiet hour before dusk. The sun slid between the horizon and the westward sky, moving as surely as an assassin's blade through flesh. And for a moment, the whole Kingdom was colored in red.

Winter was fading, spring was fast on its heels, and green, furled leaves had begun sprouting across the Grandforest's tallest limbs. Soon, the air would be filled with the songs of birds, and the ice covering the horses' water would finally melt on its own. But most importantly, the roads would be packed with merchants once again.

For one particular merchant, spring couldn't come fast enough. He'd just barely escaped the dinner table with his hide intact — and if he wanted to keep it that way, he knew he had to move quickly. He shuffled through a darkened hallway, nodding distractedly to the servants as he went, before he finally made it into the safety of his office. He closed the heavy oaken doors behind him and breathed a sigh of relief.

It was a small room: a desk, a chair, and a roaring hearth were about all that would fit into it. But it was sanctuary, nonetheless.

This was the one point in the Kingdom where the worries of the earth couldn't touch him. It was very likely that his wife nagged on, that she was still ranting to whoever would listen about how she'd have to run the house *all on her own* for the whole trade season. But in the heart of his office, he couldn't hear her. Nothing could trouble him — not even the grumblings of the servants, or the bickering of his sons.

No, the only sound was of the fire popping merrily in the hearth, and the only troubles were the sort that money could solve.

A pile of letters awaited him on his desk, and he'd been looking forward to opening them all day. He settled himself at his chair and retrieved a small, hand-carved box from his top desk drawer. It had been designed for quill and ink, but he'd gotten far more use out of it as a snuffbox. He tucked his pipe where the quill was supposed to fit, and in place of an inkwell was a packet of his favorite cherry tobacco.

He stuffed his pipe with a generous helping of the tobacco and traveled to the hearth to light it. Only when the air was sufficiently filled with the sweet aroma of the smoke did he open a letter.

This was how he preferred to spend his evenings: smoking, reading, and thinking. He read the message of the first letter — which was all business, mind you. There was absolutely no bickering and *no* weepy wives. The letter had come from a shopkeeper in Whitebone, who claimed that the Baron's craftsmen had raised their prices once again. And he wanted to renegotiate their bargain to make up for the expense.

The merchant chuckled to himself as he dipped his quill in ink.

My dear fellow, he began, *if we haggled every time the Baron upped the charge on his trinkets, we'd never make a deal. No, I'm afraid I must be quite firm on the previous price —*

"Evening, Randall."

The tail of Randall's *e* went shooting off across the page as he jerked. When he saw the figure standing before the window, his pipe nearly fell out of his mouth.

She looked like a highwayman, with her light armor and the mask that covered the lower half of her face. The armor was stained black and very well-made — the workmanship was nothing like the common bandit could've

8

afforded. She wore a short, red skirt over the top of her leggings, and the color matched the scarf behind her mask.

She might have been pretty. Her black hair, which hung loose to just past her shoulders, was so clean that it shined in the firelight. And her figure was certainly promising. But what little Randall could see of her face put any such thoughts straight out of his mind.

Her dark brows were so low that they nearly touched the tops of her eyes, and they were set at such an angle that it gave her a glaring look — one that made her stare all the more potent.

"What — what's the meaning of this?" Randall demanded, taking his pipe away so that he could frown at her properly. "Who are you?"

"Hmm," the woman murmured. She drew a small square of parchment from under the collar of her jerkin and opened it. After a quick glance, her eyes locked onto his once again. "You *are* Randall of Oakloft, are you not?"

"I am," he snapped, thrusting the pipe back into his mouth.

"Then I should think my meaning would be quite clear. I've come on behalf of Countess D'Mere."

Ah, *this* again. Well, he wasn't going to put up with it any longer — he was going to make himself very clear, this time. Randall took a long, steadying drag on his pipe. "This is about that blasted river bridge, isn't it?" When the woman nodded, he took another puff. "Well, I've already told her: I don't care if her convoys have to go a *thousand* miles out of their way — I won't have her trying to widen my bridge. It's good enough for my carts, and it should be good enough for hers."

The woman said nothing; she stared in reply.

Randall was starting to feel a little lightheaded. He supposed it was just the stress of trying to keep his words civil. He breathed in another lungful of smoke … for his nerves. "She ruined the Williamsons' land," he went on, determined to make his point. "And she never got it fixed. So you'll forgive me if I don't want her workers hacking up my bridge —"

"I haven't come to forgive you," the woman said. Her voice was muffled behind the slits in her mask, but it made her words no less sharp. With one hand, she crumpled the parchment and flicked it into the fire.

Her meaning became clear.

"It'll do you no good to murder me," Randall growled. He was far more furious than scared. The audacity of it all — the sheer, open-ended audacity! He was so angry that he'd actually begun to sweat. He brushed the dew from across his forehead impatiently. "If I die, the whole estate goes to my wife — and she'd rather stick her hand in the furnace than let anything happen to that bridge. Her pap built it, and that's all she's got left of him."

The woman's dark eyes bent into crescent moons as she ... smiled? He supposed that's what she was doing. But with that mask in the way, he couldn't be sure. The fumes from the smoke must've been burning his eyes. His sight was starting to blur.

"I'm not here to *murder* you," she said, as if it was a joke. "I'm only a messenger."

"Oh, really?" Randall wiped furiously at his stinging eyes. "Then what's ..." he coughed to clear his throat, which suddenly felt tight, "what's *that* all about?" he managed to sputter.

He waved at the deadly-looking blades she had strapped to each upper arm, and she touched one of them lightly. "They're for my protection, Mr. Randall," she said quietly. "The Kingdom is a dangerous place ... especially for a lady. No, I haven't come to kill you. And I haven't come to forgive you. I've come only to ask you to reconsider." She clasped her hands behind her back. "Will you sell your bridge to the Countess?"

"No," Randall said firmly. He coughed again, and this time it took him several moments to get the words out: "No, I ... won't! Now get ..." He coughed so violently that his pipe fell from his hand. It struck the desk, and the little glowing leaves spilled across its polished top. "Get ... out of my ... house!"

The woman nodded slightly. "As you wish." She was halfway to the window when she paused and held up a finger — as if she'd forgotten something. She crossed back to the fire and dipped her hand beneath her collar once more. This time, she drew out a vial of clear liquid.

"You don't mind, do you?" she said as she tossed the vial into the flames. "No, of course you don't. Enjoy your evening, Mr. Randall."

He heard the window open, but didn't watch her slip outside — his eyes were on the vial.

He'd stopped coughing, but only because his lungs had swollen shut. He couldn't catch his breath. The pressure in his head kept building. Randall realized that he wasn't having a reaction to the smoke at all — he'd been poisoned!

The vial — the antidote — he had to get it.

He tumbled out of his chair, dragging himself a pitiful few feet. Then his limbs began to twitch, and his whole body went limp. He managed to raise his head one last time, seemed to try to urge himself forward ... but couldn't muster the strength. At last, Randall went still.

And the Countess's message had been delivered.

Chapter 1
Two Thieves

Horatio put the letter down. He dabbed at the tears on his cheeks with a corner of his filthy apron, and smiled.

It seemed like only yesterday that Aerilyn was begging him to go off on a journey of her own. She was so wide-eyed, so wholly untouched by the world that Horatio had been reluctant to let her out of his sight. He didn't think he could have ever let her go, had he not been so thoroughly convinced that Kyleigh could protect her.

When she'd sworn to keep Aerilyn safe, he'd believed her. He certainly wasn't going to make a habit of trusting outlaws, but there was something in those strange, green eyes of hers that made Kyleigh trustworthy.

Well that, and he'd seen firsthand what she could do with a blade.

He picked up the letter again, sifting through the many pages that Aerilyn had managed to seal together for his favorite passage. It was hard to believe that the little girl who used to squeal about getting dirt on her hems had fought her way through a tempest — and a monstrous one, at that. But the picture Kael had drawn on the back of the page was very convincing.

The charcoal swirls of foamy waves and the jagged lines of lightning seemed to come alive on the parchment. They batted the tiny boat caught in the middle of them, ripped at her sails, tossed her about — and even though he knew how the story would end, Horatio found himself holding his breath.

For such a quiet boy, Kael certainly had a lot of talent.

No — Horatio was decidedly very happy for Aerilyn to be having her own adventure, and all seemed to be going well. The only truly troubling bit of news was how often this *Captain Lysander* fellow kept popping up in Aerilyn's letter. He seemed to haunt every paragraph: *Lysander* was so valiant as they sailed through the tempest; no finer *captain* had ever lived; there was nothing the *good captain* couldn't do.

And come to think of it, Horatio didn't remember Aerilyn mentioning what it was that Lysander actually did. He flipped the page over and frowned at the portrait Kael had drawn of him. He was handsome, to be sure — but perhaps a little too roguish to be a merchant. There was something about his grin that made Horatio uneasy ... almost like he should check his pocket for missing coin.

It was most troubling, indeed.

He was deep in speculation when the front door slammed open with such force that he nearly tumbled out of his chair. He heard footsteps racing down the hall and gathered his girth to meet them. "What in Kingdom's name — ?" Two boys turned the corner, struck Horatio's ample belly, and went flying backwards. "Steady on, lads! What's this all about?"

"It's the Countess!" the elder boy, Chaney, said as he shoved his younger brother away from him.

"And she wants to see Garron!" Claude added as he managed to untangle himself from Chaney's boots.

Horatio clutched his side. His gut was acting up again — a sign that trouble was about to cross his threshold. "Be off with you, lads. Go on — get back to your pap. And tell him not to come to the house until the Countess leaves."

The brothers' heads bobbed up and down as they tore off down the hall. When the back door slammed shut behind them, Horatio let some of the air out of his lungs. But it wasn't long before he heard something that made his stomach throb once again:

Two pairs of quick, graceful steps — two pairs of slippers striking the polished oak floor. And they were heading directly for the study.

Horatio shoved Aerilyn's letter to one corner of the desk and barely had a chance to turn around before the footsteps stopped.

Two women stood in the doorway: the first was a pretty young forest woman. Though she wore a tight-fitting red gown and lace, she stood with her legs splayed out — as if she was prepared to break her slippers on the shins of anyone foolish enough to attack her.

Her features were dainty, but her glare was not. The dark brows poised above her eyes matched the warning behind her stance. Horatio stood perfectly still as her gaze swept the room. When she was satisfied, she stepped to the side and allowed the second woman to pass through.

This woman was in her middle age, with long, golden-brown hair and eyes like ice. She carried herself in the same way a witch might have carried her impetus: moving gracefully, intentionally — and knowing full well the effects of the spell she cast.

Horatio's mouth went dry as Countess D'Mere tugged the blue silk gloves from her hands, one finger at a time. Her full red lips pursed when she turned to look at the empty desk. The arch of her neck began an S that followed the curve of her back … and downward.

"Where is Garron?" she said.

Horatio jerked his gaze from the depths of her neckline, and found himself caught in the snare of her crystal blue eyes.

Worry throbbed in his gut. She hadn't heard, then. He'd hoped the rumor would've reached her by now, if not by some loose-lipped sailor then by one of the other merchants. Every hold across the Grandforest had heard of Garron's death … though he supposed no one wanted to be the man who broke that news to the Countess.

Now she was standing in Garron's office, and Horatio knew he had no choice but to play the messenger.

He would have to choose his words carefully. If he didn't, his life could end swiftly. Oh, she wouldn't kill him immediately: the Countess was a patient woman. She might

14

feign some emotion. She might laugh or purse her lips. Or she might keep her face as smooth as her skin. He didn't know.

He wouldn't know until nightfall whether or not she was displeased. Even then, it would happen subtly — maybe as he drank his wine at dinner. Or perhaps he would fall asleep, never to rise again. These were the sorts of things that had happened to the other merchants. In taverns all across the realm, the truth was a dark joke:

If a dozen men died in the Grandforest, Countess D'Mere was behind roughly eleven of them.

As much as Horatio didn't want to speak, to keep the Countess waiting was just as dangerous. Somehow, he managed to pass the first sentence through his lips: "Have you not heard, My Countess?"

"Heard what?" she said, her voice suddenly as cold as her stare. "Speak up, cook. I haven't got time for riddles."

"Garron is slain."

His words came out loudly, blurted above the noise of his pounding heart. He hadn't meant to say it quite like that. And even after a long winter of mourning, the truth still stung his eyes.

The Countess spun to look at the desk once more — as if she expected to see Horatio proved wrong. As if she hoped to find Garron bent with his nose to his ledger, mumbling to himself as he once did, figuring the day's profit. "I see," she said after a moment. "If he *is* truly slain, would you mind telling me how it happened?"

Horatio told her everything he could remember about that horrible day in Bartholomew's Pass. He told her about the monsters that had ambushed them — the twisted creatures that were half man and half wolf. He told her about how Garron rallied the men together and saved their lives with his cunning. He told her the truth: that Garron fought till the end.

When he was finished, D'Mere nodded stiffly. She sat down at the desk, running her hand across its polished top. She traced the ink spatters and the little scrapes left behind by Garron's dagger — from the times when he'd opened a

15

letter too zealously. She seemed to be thinking very intensely about something, and Horatio had begun to wonder if his next breath might be his last.

He was quite shocked when she suddenly burst into tears.

The sobs shook her shoulders. D'Mere clutched a hand over her face; the skin went white where her fingernails dug in. Her breath came out thickly and in sputters — like a man choking on his own blood.

Horatio didn't know what to do. He glanced at the forest girl, who narrowed her eyes dangerously at him. So he kept his stare trained on the rug while the Countess collected herself.

It took her a moment to stop crying. But by the time she spoke again, all trace of sorrow was gone from her voice. "He died in battle," D'Mere said matter-of-factly. Then she smirked. "I always thought it would be the tarts that finally did him in."

Horatio returned her look with a cautious smile. "He *was* fond of a good pastry, My Countess. Especially the apple ones."

"Yes, with the sugar glaze on top." D'Mere's smile vanished as quickly as it'd come. "There are monsters roaming the Valley, you say? Beasts more wolf than man?"

Horatio nodded.

"Any idea where they might have come from?"

She was watching him, her eyes searching through the stubble and over every red blotch on his cheeks. But Horatio was no fool. He knew better than to tell the Countess that the wolves bore the mark of Midlan on their collars. To accuse the King of murder would earn him nothing but a trip to the hangman's noose.

He cleared his throat and said carefully: "None, Countess."

She watched him a moment more, her face completely smooth. Then she stood. "I just came to tell Gar ... well, I've finally secured the purchase of Randall's bridge. Once my

16

men have it widened, it should cut a considerable few hours from your journey."

Horatio was surprised. *"Randall's* bridge? I didn't think he'd ever sell it."

D'Mere smirked. "I didn't buy it from Randall — I bought it from his widow."

"I see." Horatio bowed as she swept by, but mostly it was to hide the worry on his face. "Much appreciated, My Countess. I'll be sure to tell the men."

"Very good."

As she turned to leave, Horatio glanced out the window at the falling sun. "It'll be dark in another hour or so. Will you not break your journey here for the night, My Countess?"

D'Mere tugged her gloves back on, glaring at her hands. "No — thank you. I'm impatient to get back to my journey. I'm afraid there's much to do."

Horatio stood uncomfortably as she smoothed the wrinkles out of her skirt. A heavy silence hung between them. It was the same air that might've hung between two thieves on the morning after a heist — now that they were forced to walk the streets in the daylight, and step over the shattered glass they'd left behind.

Horatio wondered if he ought to say something ... but in the end, he figured it was probably best to leave the buried things be.

He made to follow her to the door when the forest girl cut swiftly in front of him, shooting a warning look over her shoulder. Then D'Mere stopped abruptly in the doorway — and she had to come up on her tiptoes to keep from colliding with her back.

"What's become of the girl?" D'Mere said without turning.

Horatio tried to keep things simple. "I sent Aerilyn on a journey with some friends to the High Seas, My Countess. She's alive and well — and also quite taken with adventuring."

D'Mere spun, her eyebrows raised. "Oh? And which friends are these? Not that horrible fiddler, I hope."

"Eh, he's among them. But the whole lot's being watched over by a couple of fighters from the mountains."

Her brows climbed higher. "The Unforgivable Mountains?"

"Yes," Horatio said, wondering to himself what other mountains were worth talking about. "But she's in excellent hands, I can promise you that. The redheaded fellow is a sure shot, and the young woman can wield a blade better than a warlord. Between the two of them, I don't think there'll be — Countess? Are you feeling all right?"

D'Mere's face was suddenly the color of new-fallen snow. She gripped her middle and took an involuntary step backwards. "Yes, I'm fine," she said after a moment, though her eyes seemed distant. "I suppose I'm just a little sore from traveling. The boy had red hair, you say? And what about the girl — what did she look like?"

Horatio sputtered a bit as he tried to find the words to describe her. "Ah, well, she wasn't really *like* anyone I've ever seen, Countess. She had dark hair, green eyes — and the men spent more time staring at her than they did actually working." When the color left her face completely, Horatio's worry gave him the courage to speak. "What is it, My Countess? What's gone wrong?"

But D'Mere didn't reply. She turned and swept out of the room, the forest girl following close behind her.

Horatio listened to her footsteps as they went down the hall. The moment he heard the front door close, he stumbled over to the desk and collapsed in the chair, gripping his chest. It would be several long moments before his breathing steadied, and several moments more before the sick feeling in his gut stopped the bile from climbing up his throat.

But it would be many months before he found peace again. He didn't know what that look on the Countess's face had meant, but he couldn't shake the feeling that he'd somehow put Aerilyn in danger.

It would haunt him day and night.

****

The carriage rolled for three miles down the road before D'Mere found her voice. "It's her," she said, more to herself than anybody. "Aerilyn travels with the Dragongirl." The carriage bounced beneath her, jolting the end of her sentence.

"What does this mean, My Countess?"

Of course, Elena had heard her. She'd sat so quietly for miles that D'Mere had actually forgotten she was there. But when she looked up, she saw that the forest girl watched her calmly. The movement of the carriage didn't seem to bother her — she sat as neatly under the motion as she might've sat at a dining room table.

"It means we have to move quickly," D'Mere said. She mulled the problem over, watching as the trees whipped by her window. "I wish Reginald would answer my letter. I can't imagine what that fool has gotten himself into."

"I could find out, Countess."

"You might have to," D'Mere admitted. "But there's a task I need you to do first. The cook was reading something when we came in —"

"The letters were from Miss Aerilyn, Countess. I saw her name written on the envelope," Elena supplied.

"Good, I hoped they might be. I need you to retrieve them," D'Mere leaned forward, "tonight."

"Yes, Countess," Elena said, as if it was no more difficult a chore than running down to market. And perhaps for her, it wasn't.

Elena wore her pretty face like a mask, to hide the predator behind it. D'Mere watched as she stood and unbuttoned her skirt from her tunic, thinking how appropriate it was for a dress to be a cover for what lay beneath: boots, black leggings, and the two slender, deadly-looking knives strapped to the bands on her thighs.

19

Elena opened the carriage door and leaned out. D'Mere grabbed her before she could leap. "Return to the castle as quickly as possible. Time is not our ally."

Elena nodded. Then she sprang from the carriage like a cat out of a box, rolling gracefully, catching herself on her feet.

When D'Mere turned to watch her, she'd already vanished.

Chapter 2
The Endless Plains

Sweet mercy, it was hot — so horribly, insufferably hot. A drop of sweat raced from the top of Kael's head and down his nose. He tried to brush it away before it fell, but he didn't move fast enough.

When it splattered onto the pages of his open book, he swore aloud.

"You're right about that, lad," Morris said. The heat had settled in his throat, making his voice much croakier than usual. He fumbled with his canteen for a moment before he managed to get it wedged between his arms. Then he brought it carefully to his lips. "Sit up straight when you read, and you won't have to worry about the words getting all smeared," he advised, as he watched Kael dab gingerly at the wet spot with the hem of his shirt.

"I've tried that," Kael grumbled back.

By that point, he'd tried everything. He'd leaned against the wall for a while — until the cart rocked so violently that he smacked the back of his head. Then he'd sat with his knees pulled up to his chest until his legs cramped, and hunched over until his back hurt. He would've tried spreading out on the floor, had it not been packed full of tarp, tent poles, and supplies.

No, the only safe place to sit was along the cart benches — and there was hardly any room on those, either.

The benches were packed to both ends with pirates, and Kael saw his own misery reflected back on their salty, sea-hardened faces. It was hard to believe that they'd actually volunteered for this — fought for it, even. In fact, on the morning they'd left Gravy Bay, there had been so many volunteers that Captain Lysander had to draw the men's names by lot.

The pirates had whooped when their names were called. They'd kissed their families goodbye and marched proudly aboard *Anchorgloam*, rucksacks tossed over their shoulders.

"And what do you expect the rest of us to do, eh?" Uncle Martin had called as Lysander gave the order to set sail. He leaned on his cane and had seemed small from the dock, but his voice carried magnificently through the cool morning air. "I'm quite peeved about being left behind, I'll have you know."

"Just carry on pillaging," Lysander said distractedly, combing his wavy hair from his face as he ordered the sails into position.

"Just carry on —? How do you expect me to just *carry on*?" Uncle Martin bellowed, shaking his cane at them. "These are my countrymen — I have a duty to see them set free!"

"You aren't fooling anyone, father," Thelred bellowed back. "We all know what you're hoping to find in the plains, and it has nothing to do with your countrymen."

"Don't patronize me, boy! There's absolutely nothing wrong with wanting to see a giantess before I go blind." And his wide, swindler's grin had broken out from under his mustache as he added: "I hear they're every bit as enchanting as the average woman — only bigger! You wouldn't let your dear old papa perish without getting to see that, now would you?"

Despite Uncle Martin's numerous melodramatic complaints, Lysander forbade the pirates to follow them — warning that if he saw one of their sails on the horizon, he'd put a hole through it. And although they'd responded with a grumbled chorus of *ayes*, Kael had a strange feeling as they sailed out of the Bay ... like that most certainly wasn't going to be the end of it.

He wouldn't have been surprised if every one of those seadogs had his fingers crossed behind his back.

22

Now Gravy Bay was far behind them. They'd left *Anchorgloam* and the vast majority of the men in the docks of a small village, disguised as merchants. Then after two days of hard travel on foot, they'd crossed the border of the High Seas and wound up in the plains. From that point on, they'd had no choice but to pack themselves into the cart and try to stay quiet.

Gilderick's army patrolled the full breadth of the plains — and a crowd of travelers would certainly attract their attention.

Kael sat up and blinked, trying to give his eyes a break from all the reading. Captain Lysander sat across from him: the wave in his hair had gone limp with sweat, and his characteristic grin had been replaced by a determined frown. He sat rigidly on the bench, keeping his eyes closed tight and his arm clamped firmly around the woman by his side.

Aerilyn had the rings of her golden-brown hair piled on the top of her head in a skillful knot. She wore a man's tunic and breeches, but didn't complain about them as she once had. No doubt they were much cooler than a dress.

Even though the heat was enough to melt them together, Aerilyn leaned heavily into Lysander. She was fiddling with the buttons on her sleeves when she glanced up and saw Kael watching her.

She smiled — but it wasn't the same smile she gave everybody else. No, this smile was meant especially for him: it was a sad smile, a pitying smile. It was the same condoling look that every woman in Gravy Bay had been giving him all blasted winter. And he was growing rather tired of it.

He raised his book up and pretended to go back to his reading, blocking her face from view.

"How much further?"

The growl came from Thelred — the surly, clench-fisted pirate on Kael's left. The further from the seas they went, the more disagreeable he became. After a few hours of being trapped inside a stuffy, rocking cart, his temper had taken on a thickness of its own. Now it rose with the heat and added to the misery.

23

Kael flipped through his book until he came to the map of the Endless Plains. He'd scoured the mansion's library twice over, but hadn't found a more detailed map than the one in his favorite book: the *Atlas of the Adventurer*.

Because the land was so flat, the highway through the Endless Plains cut straight down the middle of it. They could go from one end of the region to the other without ever having to make a turn. He traced his finger up the road until he came to a small clump of trees — the only cluster large enough to be marked on the map.

"That's where we'll set up camp," he said, pointing to it even though he knew Thelred wasn't looking. He had his fists crammed so tightly against his eyes that he likely couldn't even roll them. "And that's just after we cross through the village of Galeherd. So we should get there a little before sunset, if our pace holds."

"Sunset?" Aerilyn looked shocked. "Oh, it's all happening so soon!"

At the sound of tears in her voice, Lysander's stormy eyes snapped open. He pulled her closer and planted his lips against one worried arch of her brow. "It'll be over before you know it, my dear. Kael has it all planned out."

"But what if something goes wrong?" she went on, twisting her hands into his shirt. "What if it takes ages? And what if I never — never —?"

"Do shut up." Thelred's eyes snapped open. They were bloodshot from having been pressed against his fists, and it made his glare burn. "Your constant moaning isn't helping anything —"

"You have no idea what it's like!" Aerilyn's tears turned hot and angry as they finally spilled over. "You have no idea what it's like to have your heart ripped out. So don't you *dare* —"

"All I'm asking for is one blasted moment of silence! Is that so much to —? What are you doing?"

Thelred tried to jerk his arm free, but Kael held on tightly. He pressed the tips of his fingers against the vein beneath Thelred's wrist and took a deep, relaxing breath. He let his memories of how sleep felt slide into Thelred, imagining that they flowed into his blood and made their way up to his head.

Sleep, he thought. *It's time to sleep.*

He let go as Thelred toppled forward. The pirate landed hard among their tent gear, and soon he was snoring peacefully. Morris kicked a bit of tarp over his shoulders before he turned his gap-toothed grin on Kael.

"Well done, lad. You're really coming along."

Kael had to admit that his powers of healing were getting stronger — and that probably had to do with all of his extra reading. In fact, when he wasn't lost in some book about the Endless Plains, he'd busied himself by reading every anatomy tome he could find. He was still nowhere near as accomplished as his grandfather, Amos, had been, but he was growing.

And the next time an innocent man was dying before him, Kael would be able to save him.

With Thelred asleep on the floor, there was a little extra room on their bench. Kael sat on his knees and tried to get a good look outside. A cage of rusty iron bars blocked the window, and he held onto them for balance. After a few uneventful minutes, he began to feel as if he was back aboard *Anchorgloam*, like he'd traded one ocean for another — only here the waves were made of grass.

"It'll look much nicer in a few weeks, once the green's come back to it," Morris said. They shared small halves of the window, and were stuck so close together that Morris's wiry beard tickled him. When Kael scratched at his cheek, he chuckled. "It wouldn't itch so bad if you'd grow your own."

"I can't," Kael muttered. "The hair doesn't cover everything."

"Well, that's just 'cause you're a young lad. You'll grow into your beard one day — and a lot sooner than you think."

Kael seriously doubted that. But it was far too hot to argue.

They rode along in companionable silence for a while — well, it was silent on Kael's end. Morris chattered on, but most of what he said was just to have something to fill the air.

It wasn't until he heard a strange, high-pitched noise that Kael made the effort to speak: "What's that?" he said, cutting over the top of Morris's rant about how Uncle Martin could make a fortune selling his grogs as rat poisons.

The noise was a rhythmic squeaking sound, like someone was opening and closing the hinges of a rusted door. Kael pressed his face against the bars and craned his head around to try and see what they were driving up on.

A large stone structure rose out of the earth in front of them, and Kael recognized it as a windmill. Two of its blades were broken clean off, and a third had lost its canvas. The fourth blade was broken in half and held on only by its sinew. The tattered canvas caught the slight breeze and rocked back and fourth, squeaking loudly through the still air.

Kael craned his neck over Lysander and Aerilyn — who were napping and using each other for pillows — to watch out of the opposite window. There was a windmill on that side, too, though it was in much worse shape: its whole top had been blown off, making it look like a busted clay pot.

"Galeherd," Kael said, matching the twin windmills to the ones sketched on his map.

"Aye. Or what's left of it, anyways," Morris amended as they passed a few houses with naught but their chimneys still standing. "Those mages really cooked them good."

"That's one thing I don't understand," Kael said, turning back to the window. "I thought the giants were supposed to be great warriors."

"They are, lad. Believe me, you'd rather fight a shark in the water than a giant on his plains."

"Then how did Titus defeat them, if they're so strong?"

Morris snorted. "Strength had nothing to do with it, lad. Titus marched through here with an army of *mages* — and even a giant's fury is no match for magic. Titus had them routed and clapped in irons within a fortnight." He groaned as he shifted his weight from one knee to the other. "I tell you, it was a dark day in our Kingdom's history when Crevan rallied the mages. We'd lived with the whisperers' protection for so long ... well, not an army across the six regions was ready to battle magic. Not a one."

Kael supposed that made sense. He was quiet for a long moment, just watching as the ruined houses drifted in and out of the window. Then a very sobering thought hit him: this was probably what Tinnark looked like, now.

He didn't like to think of his village lying in ruin. He didn't like to think about the fact that Roland's house was probably burned, or that all of Amos's tonics were smashed upon the ground, or that there was likely a huge, blackened crater where the Hall had once stood. He didn't like to think about those things, and so he didn't.

Instead, he grit his teeth and focused himself on the task at hand.

****

They arrived at the tree clump an hour or so before sunset. The driver led the cart into the thick of the trees, wedging it in as far as it would fit. Then the whole thing rocked as he leapt down and made his way towards the door.

Horrible, off-pitch whistling trailed the driver's footsteps. He seemed to fumble at the lock much longer than was actually necessary. By the time he opened the door, the men were already grumbling.

"Evening, gents!" Jonathan said, sticking his clownish face in to greet them. "Let's get those vittles burning — I'm not a moment away from eating my own boots."

"No, we'll get the camp set up first and *then* we'll eat," Lysander called from the back of the cart, where he was helping Aerilyn navigate her way over Thelred. "We may not be at sea, but I'm still the captain. And I say we ought to get some cover in place before we start lighting fires!"

After a long and painful discussion, they'd finally decided that Jonathan had to be the one to drive them across the plains: if any of Gilderick's men spotted them, Jonathan

27

was the only one clever enough to talk them out of trouble. Even if the soldiers didn't believe whatever harebrained story he came up with, he could always just whip out his fiddle.

And then whatever horrendous song he crooned would send even the meanest giant fleeing in the other direction.

Though they were confident that Jonathan could drive them safely through the plains, the decision *did* lead to one unfortunate side effect: the fiddler seemed to think that his newfound power gave him the right to be as annoying as possible.

Giving out orders was just the half of it. The first night they stopped, he'd very loudly exclaimed that he was far too tired to set up his own tent, and commanded that Thelred do it for him — which surprisingly, he did. Though *not* surprisingly, he built it up directly over a rather menacing nettle bush, and then he hid the mallet.

Jonathan slept outdoors until about the middle of the night, when a rainstorm forced him to take refuge inside the nettle-ridden tent. When he woke, he'd forgotten where he was and accidentally rolled over. It had taken him half the morning just to pull all of the thorns out of his rump.

Tonight, Jonathan declared that his bottom was far too sore to do any unpacking — but that still didn't stop him from being an arse.

He followed Lysander around for a while, repeating the captain's orders like an echo. When Lysander very calmly asked whether he thought he could still be obnoxious *without* his tongue, Jonathan seemed to get the hint. He amused himself for a while by sneaking up behind people and startling them with his horsewhip, but then he did it to Aerilyn one too many times.

She snatched the whip out of his hands and hurled it into the tallest tree, where it got stuck.

The pirates cheered.

"And how am I supposed to drive the cart without a whip?" Jonathan cried over their applause.

"You can't," Lysander said simply. "So I suppose you'll have to retrieve it."

Jonathan complained — until he was told that his other option was to help Morris scrape the calluses off the bottoms of his feet. It was amazing how quickly he was able to climb the tree, even with a sore rump.

They'd had a long day of travel and the night promised to be fair, so most of the pirates decided against setting up their tents: their bedrolls would do them for the night. Once the camp was made and the fires had been started, Kael volunteered to check and make sure they couldn't be seen from the road.

It was a mile's jog back to the highway, but he didn't mind it much — it felt good to be able to stretch his legs. He kept his eyes on the red, ridged mountains in the distance as he ran. They were marked as the Red Spine on his map, and though they were nowhere near as tall as the Unforgivable Mountains, they were a good deal longer. The whole range stretched from the sea and on, creating a natural border between the desert and the plains.

Once Kael made it to the highway, he turned — and was pleased to see how well their camp was hidden. The trees in the Endless Plains were particularly short and stubby, with their tops squished flat by what must've been the immeasurable weight of the sky above them. They were spaced far apart, but there'd been a large number of healthy nettle bushes growing underneath them. So as the pirates cleared a space for their shelter, they'd stacked the nettles up between the trees, creating a sort of makeshift wall to block their tents from view.

It wasn't perfect, but Kael didn't think a scout could spot them from the road. And it was far enough from the highway that the patrols likely wouldn't take the time to investigate it. Yes, their little makeshift village would be enough to hide the main party — while Kael and a small company of pirates wreaked havoc on Lord Gilderick.

Kael was nearly back to camp when he saw Aerilyn emerge from the nettle wall, a sack of vittles in one hand. She propped the other over her forehead, shielded her eyes against the falling sun, and had absolutely no trouble spotting him.

"I thought we might have a picnic," she called, when he was within shouting distance.

He didn't want to be alone with Aerilyn, not even for a picnic. He thought quickly. "Shouldn't you eat with Lysander? You won't see him again for a few weeks."

"That's what the night is for," she said, though she blushed magnificently as she said it. "No, I'd very much like to have dinner with you, if that's all right."

He grumbled that it was.

They arranged their picnic on the ground, sitting with their backs to camp and their faces towards the sunset. Kael was wary at first, but after several minutes of listening to Aerilyn's happy chatter, he began to relax. They gnawed on hunks of dried meat and chased their biscuits down with gulps from their canteens.

"Morris agreed to take me hunting tomorrow," Aerilyn said as she chewed. "I saw a few rabbits in the weeds earlier. After all of this salty fare, it'll be nice to have some fresh meat."

"Just be careful with your arrows. If you run out, it'll take Noah a few days to bring you more," Kael said. His biscuit got lodged in his throat, and it took him a moment to get it washed down. That seemed to be happening a lot, lately. Food just didn't agree with him. "You have to be especially careful with rabbits. It's easy to break an arrow on a rock —"

"I know all that. Stop worrying about me," she nudged him gently with her elbow, "you've taught me well."

He doubted that his teaching had much to do with it. Aerilyn was a naturally good shot, and once he'd convinced her to listen to her instincts, she'd become a pretty good hunter, as well. He knew she could keep the caravan fed.

They talked even after their picnic had vanished, trading thoughts as the shadows grew longer. And Kael actually began to think that he'd made it out of the woods.

But then came the dreaded pause — a heavy break in their words that Aerilyn didn't rush to fill. It hung there for a long moment, and he suddenly knew what was coming.

He tried to escape. "Well, I think I'll turn in —"

"I miss her, Kael." Aerilyn's eyes were distant as she watched the sun, like she was trying to strain them over the edge of the horizon to find their lost friend. Her gaze came back as she turned, and her eyes were hard by the time they found Kael. "I know you miss her, too —"

"I don't." He felt a wall rise in his heart at the very thought.

Lysander had promised that she would come back. And like a fool, Kael had believed him. For several weeks, he'd woken early and looked out of his window — hoping that he might catch her as she glided in from her journey, or perhaps spot an unfamiliar ship in the harbor. But he never did.

Still, he didn't give up his hope. When he found his window empty, he would search the mansion. He'd walk the hallways long before the servants rose, hoping that he might hear her voice coming from one of the many rooms. But the only sounds were the moans of an old house, and the heavy thudding of his own steps.

He even went down to the basement a few times, hoping to find her working at her forge. But it was always the same: the trough of fire was shuttered tightly, the anvil lay cold. What had once been alive and bright was now dark ... and miserably empty.

As the days became weeks, and the weeks became months, the truth began to crush him. It sat on his chest day and night, slowly pressing the hope from his heart. And he knew that if he didn't do something to stop it, the truth would kill him.

So he built up a wall inside his heart. He'd buried her behind it — he bricked up his memories of her and shored them against a corner of his mind. And that was precisely where he intended to keep them. That was precisely where he *had* to keep them.

But Aerilyn just didn't understand.

"It's perfectly fine to be upset," she said, placing a hand on his shoulder. "You have every right to be hurt. I know you care for her —"

"I don't."

"— but you're going to make yourself sick if you try to keep it in." She squeezed his arm tightly, and he bristled against her touch. "You *must* let your heart have its say, Kael. Let your feelings out. Cry about it —"

"I won't cry," he said, shrugging out from under her hand. "Where I come from, a wound that doesn't cost a man his life is something to be celebrated — not mourned. And she isn't dead," he got to his feet, "but she's never coming back. The sooner you understand that, the better."

He broke into a run, desperate to beat back a sudden swell of anger, and that's when he heard Aerilyn shrill from behind him:

"You're wrong about her — she *will* come back to us! She *will!*"

Kael couldn't tell her the truth. He couldn't tell anyone, because he was too ashamed to tell. But he knew without a shadow of a doubt that she was wrong — Kyleigh was never coming back.

And it was entirely his fault.

Chapter 3
Knotter

The dream faded like mist on a pond, slowly seeping back into whatever deep pool it'd risen from. Kyleigh was a traveler who arrived too late. She didn't see the mist rise, didn't know its meaning ... but she knew it was there. Her fingers curled and uncurled as the last tendrils slipped away.

Then she opened her eyes.

In the cool dark of the room, she realized what had happened: someone said her name. She waited for a moment to see if the call would come again.

"Lady Kyleigh?"

She wished the villagers would stop calling her that. She may have been a lot of things, but a lady certainly wasn't one of them. "Come in," she said, untangling herself from her covers.

"I dare not, my lady. It isn't proper."

She grinned as she felt around for a shirt, finally coming up with a slightly worn tunic, and pulled it over her head. It fell just shy of her knees, which was surely proper enough to go out in.

Her eyes adjusted quickly to the dark. She could see the shadows of the many objects scattered across the floor of her room. They were various bits of clothes and weaponry — projects she'd started, and never quite got around to finishing. There were simply too few hours in the day, and too little of her concentration to go around.

She blamed it entirely on the fact that she'd been cooped up all winter and fed far too well.

Kyleigh skipped over a pile of clothes and a rather menacing two-headed axe before she landed near the door.

When she threw it open, the man on the other side of it jumped.

He was a middle-aged fellow with a rather long face. He wielded a candle in one hand, and kept the other tucked behind his back. The pale glow from the flame made the shadows across his face even darker — and the disapproving frown he wore even more severe.

"My lady," he said, dragging his eyes from where they'd been glaring at the wrinkles on her shirt, "I'm sorry to wake you at such an odd hour of the night, but there is a matter in the courtyard that needs your attention. I'm afraid the gate is acting up again."

"Thank you, Crumfeld." She tried to dart past him, but he stepped in her way. "Was there something else?"

"I'm sure your courtly knowledge is unparalleled," he began — which was to say that it wasn't, "but it seems to me that the Lady of Copperdock shouldn't be wandering around outside of her chambers in little more than a nightdress."

Oh, Crumfeld. She tried to convince herself that she would miss him when she went away, but he was making it more difficult with every passing moment.

She had no idea where he'd actually come from. She'd simply skipped downstairs one morning and found a man dressed all in black, whipping Roost into shape. He got the cooks to serve dinner while it was hot, had the maids cleaning everything to a shine, and somehow managed to get the men working on the repairs to contain their messes — all with one arm propped smartly behind his back.

Though a good amount of grumbling came from several corners of Roost, no one seemed willing to do anything other than what they were told. Kyleigh thought it was rather funny to see her crew being made to behave — that is, until Crumfeld turned his impossibly keen eyes on her.

He said he was determined to make her into a proper lady. But from where Kyleigh stood, it looked suspiciously like he was just trying to ruin her fun.

His rules were ridiculous. Not only was she no longer allowed to dress however she pleased, she also couldn't wander outside of Roost without an escort — and was positively banned from leaving her kills at the kitchen door.

"But I like the way the cook prepares them," she'd said once, when Crumfeld caught her trying to sneak a deer carcass over the back wall.

He was far from sympathetic. "Then you will tell the lead huntsman what you want, and *he* will catch it for you. On days where you don't have any courtly duties, I may even permit you to join the hunt. However," and here he'd curled his lip at the badly-mangled deer, "I'll not allow the Lady of Copperdock to come scampering to the back door with a bloody carcass clamped between her teeth. And that's my final word on the matter."

She wanted to tell him that she didn't *scamper* anywhere, thank you very much. But his stern look made her think better of it. When he told her to kindly go upstairs and wash the blood out of her hair before dinner, she'd gone with a mumbled: "Fine."

But that wasn't happening today. No, Kyleigh was too peeved about her interrupted dream to let Crumfeld get the better of her. "All right," she said, pretending to turn back to her room. Then she spun around suddenly, slipping past him before he could block her.

"What are you doing, my lady? Come back here at once and put on some proper clothes!"

"Don't be ridiculous, Crummy. That'll take far too long," she called as she trotted down the stairs. "There's a nip in the air tonight, and I'll not make the men wait around while I cinch up my garters."

Crumfeld didn't believe in running — only in walking very briskly. So it wasn't long before Kyleigh outdistanced him.

Her bare feet slapped against the cold stone floor as she ran through the hallway at the bottom of the stairs. The gaping holes in the roof made it draftier than the average passageway, but she rather liked how it let in the sun —

though the light at this hour of the morning was more like a gray mist than anything. She inhaled deeply as she ran, and thought she could practically smell the hot, sticky afternoon hidden behind the cool dawn.

That was three days in a row, now. The slightly cooler winter was all but gone. By her guess, this meant her friends were already on their way to the plains. Change was coming quickly — and finally, at long last, it was time to do her part.

She'd been aching for an adventure all season.

The unfinished passageway spilled out into the great hall — a large, rectangular chamber with ceilings that stretched high into the shadows. Crumfeld hadn't quite decided on how he wanted to furnish it, so her footsteps echoed loudly against the bare walls. She slowed to a walk.

The guard at the front door spotted her from a long ways off and set about fumbling with the latch. He had to prop his spear up against his shoulder and work the mechanism with one hand — the other was wrapped tightly in a sling.

"There you are, my lady," he said as he succeeded in nudging the door open.

"Thank you, Gerald. How's the arm?"

He raised his busted limb gingerly off his chest. "Oh, the healer says the bones'll mend. And in the meantime, I'm to be careful about which wall I lean up against."

"Sage advice, indeed," she said as she passed him.

Gerald's face reddened considerably when she smiled at him, and his helmet nearly slipped off when he remembered to bow the way Crumfeld had instructed him to.

Kyleigh could feel his eyes on her as she made her way across the courtyard. She didn't think she would ever understand why humans used their eyes so often, when there were far more practical ways to choose a mate. If anything, her appearance should've been a clear warning to them: more often than not, the most beautifully colored creatures were also the most deadly.

Across the courtyard, Kyleigh spotted a crowd of men gathered around the front gate. The guards' swears pierced the cool quiet of the morning, and she heard a thumping noise as several of them kicked the gate. One familiar voice cut above the steady rumble of profanities:

"Where's that mage? Someone get his scrawny hide down here — and tell him I've got half a mind to blast those doors to splinters!"

A burly man popped out of the crowd and took a few stomping steps towards the castle. Even in the faint light, Kyleigh could see the bushy sideburns on either side of his boiling face.

He was in the middle of a rather colorful rant when he glanced up and spotted her. "Ah, sorry about that," he muttered.

She reached up to clap him on one of his thick shoulders. "No need for apologies, Shamus. I've heard far worse. Now, what's this all about?"

"That confounded gate has jammed itself again. We've got a shipment on the other side waiting to be let in, and I can't for the life of me persuade it to open," he said, shooting a dark look at the front door. "I'm going to get that mage up —"

"No, don't bother Jake," Kyleigh said as she headed for the doors. "He's already admitted that he doesn't know how to fix it. You'll only upset him."

Shamus snorted as he followed. "How can he not know? If I put a hole in something, I'd sure as high tide know how to fix it. If I built ships the same way that mage casts his spells, they'd sink in the harbor!"

Kyleigh didn't say anything — she knew he was just cross.

As the master shipbuilder of Copperdock, Shamus seemed to think he was required to work his fingers to the bone nearly every day. If there weren't repairs to be done, then there were bargains to be made and tight-fisted merchants to deal with. He packed so many of his waking hours to the brim that he was grumpy at the finish — and even grumpier at the start. Judging by the red lines across one side of his face, he'd only just peeled himself from bed.

When the guards saw Kyleigh coming, they let out a cheer. They moved to the side to let her through, flinging final curses over their shoulders as they went. She stepped up to the gates alone, rapped smartly against the left door, and waited. She didn't have to wait for long.

"Password?" a snide voice said.

There was a knot in one of the planks about halfway up, just over the top of Kyleigh's head. She always thought the lumps in the knot made it look a bit like a lopsided face: with one eye set high above the other, a jagged crack for a mouth and a slightly squished nose.

As she watched, one of the eyes cracked open and the mouth curled into a smirk. "Well, if it isn't the halfdragon."

No one was quite sure how it happened. As far as Jake could figure out, one of the spells he'd used to chop wood for the gate went slightly awry — and it resulted in the left door coming to life.

Not only could the door speak, but he also had control over the bolts. He'd already locked them out on several occasions, and had once slammed shut on Shamus's foot. The men un-fondly referred to him as *Knotter*, among other unrepeatable things.

"Hello, Knotter," Kyleigh said back, smiling pleasantly.

But he was on to her. "Come to scorch me again, have you?" Knotter said, twisting his eyes to look very pointedly at a small patch of charred wood near his bottom.

"That was a complete and total accident."

"No it wasn't! You're a bully and a monster — get off of me!"

Kyleigh ignored him, leaning harder against the door while the guards snickered. "Oh please. What are you going to do about it?"

"I'll swing open!"

"Good. That's precisely what I want you to do."

He sputtered for a moment. "I'll do it unexpectedly," he countered. "You'll go rolling down the hill — and the whole village will see what you've got under your skirts!"

She had to bite her lip to keep from laughing outright. She had no idea how someone as kind as Jake could've possibly conjured such a foul-mouthed apparition. "Let's talk about something else: why won't you let those merchants in?"

"Because they're hiding something," Knotter said, narrowing his eyes. "I can't actually see what it is, but why else would they try to deliver something in the dead of night?"

"It's dawn," Shamus hissed. "And they're hiding it for *us*, you great lump of tinder! We were hoping to sneak it in all quiet like," he explained to Kyleigh. "But then that termite-ridden tyrant had to go on and make such a hassle —!"

"Well ex*cuse* me," Knotter said. And if he'd had any limbs, Kyleigh bet he would've thrown in a sarcastic bow for good measure. "But if I hadn't been on my guard, this whole place might've gone up in flames —"

"*You're* going up in flames, if you don't open this instant!" Shamus bellowed over him.

Knotter gasped and looked down at Kyleigh. She shrugged. "I'm afraid it's true. If you're going to stop up our doors every night, I'll have no choice."

For the first time that morning, Knotter's obnoxious expression sunk back into his grain — replaced swiftly by a look of fear.

He had a good reason to be afraid. Jake had tried all manner of spells to disenchant him, and several more to try and blow him up. But thus far, the only thing that seemed to have any effect on Knotter at all was dragonflame.

Which was something Kyleigh had plenty of.

"You'll burn me alive?" he said dramatically, his eyes rolling back in terror. "You'd reduce me to cinders, even after I was trying to protect you?"

She inclined her head. "It's either that, or I'll have to put in a less-enchanted back gate."

The grain around his cheeks puffed out indignantly. "Well, I think I'd rather be burned than watch as another gate does my duty."

"Very well —"

"Ah, but that won't be necessary." Knotter scrunched up his face and the bolt slid open, seemingly of its own accord. "See?" He rocked backwards. "I'm opening right up." He made a face at Shamus before disguising himself as a normal knot once again — leaving Kyleigh to deal with the disgruntled merchants on the other side.

"What took so blasted long?" the first man snapped. He had the collar of his coat pulled up so high that he nearly brushed by without recognizing her. "Oh, Lady Kyleigh," he said, swiping his hat from his head. "I, um, forgive me — I wasn't expecting you to be the one at the door."

It had been several months since she'd tackled Duke Reginald at his own party — and Shamus had assured her that the *true* story never made it off the island. But even if the people of the seas didn't realize that she was the Kingdom's most wanted outlaw, they certainly gave her a wide berth. Even now, she couldn't help but notice how the merchant gripped his sword hilt when he greeted her.

Though she supposed it was possible that he'd just gotten wind of her blade skills: Shamus often visited the dock tavern, and it was no secret that a few tankards of ale could loosen his lips considerably.

"There's no need to apologize," she said, stepping aside so that he could enter. Four merchants stumbled in behind him, bent nearly double under the weight of a large crate. "Great skies, what have you got them sneaking in?"

"Oh, it's nothing," Shamus said, a little too casually. "Did you have any trouble finding the goods, Captain?"

He looked pointedly at the lead man — who was looking pointedly at Kyleigh's legs. A long moment passed before Shamus cleared his throat.

The captain jumped. He saw Kyleigh smirking at him, and red singed the skin beneath his whiskers. "Ah, so sorry. My mind ... ah, it wandered." he turned to Shamus, straightening his collar. "What was that you said?"

"I asked if you had any trouble collecting the shipment."

"Oh, not much. There was a *bit* of a scuffle. You know how those desert folk can be —"

"Desert folk?" Kyleigh looked at Shamus — who suddenly seemed very interested in checking the sturdiness of the crate. "What did you order from the desert?"

"I already told you — it's nothing. Now, why don't you go and catch another hour of sleep before sunrise?"

He tried to turn her away by the shoulders, but she broke his grip and wrenched the lid off the crate. She heard the captain gasp as the nails splintered from the wood, but she was too focused on the crate's contents to worry about what a spectacle she was causing. And judging by the reek of the captain's coat, he'd soon be drowning the memory in a flagon, anyways.

She pulled the first item out from underneath a thin layer of straw. It was a plain white tunic, made of a smooth material that she recognized immediately. "Silk shirts?" she said, doing a quick sum. "There's got to be nearly two dozen, here."

Shamus scratched at his head. "Aye, I got them for the men. I thought they might breathe a little easier in the summer heat — ah, since we've got so many repairs lined up, and all."

He kept his face suspiciously innocent under her glare. Kyleigh looked over his shoulder and searched the crowd of guards for an honest face. But there was none: just a lot of foot-shuffling and some vigorous nods.

She dug the shirts aside and found that the second layer was made up entirely of canteens.

"To save us some time," Shamus said, smiling as he grew more confident in his tale. "The men can carry them at their belts while they work, and they won't have to take so many trips down to the water barrel."

"I see. Well, I suppose that makes perfect sense," Kyleigh said, reaching in for the crate's final layer. "Hmm ... oh my — what's *this* for?"

Shamus balked when she drew the sword from its sheath. It was a scimitar, the curved blade favored by desert

41

outlaws. She spun it deftly in one hand and heard the wind whistle off its edge. "It's very well-made," she said approvingly. Then she leveled the point at Shamus's chest. "But what in blazes is it for?"

"Ah ..." He glanced over his shoulder at the guards, who tried very quickly to look bewildered, before he shot a pointed look at the captain. "I don't rightly know. I certainly didn't order them —"

"Oh, no you don't," the captain interjected, jabbing a finger at him. "Don't try and weasel your way out of our agreement! You *will* pay me, sir, or I'll spread word through every tavern on the High Seas that you're a thief and a timewaste!"

"Those sound like some grave accusations," Kyleigh said with a mocking smile, her eyes on Shamus. "Come clean, man — tell me what the swords are for. Do you plan to shave with them? Are your axes not as fun to swing about?"

Shamus glared daggers at the captain for a moment before he finally let out a heavy sigh. "All right, you've got me. You know what they're for."

Just as she'd suspected. Kyleigh thrust the scimitar back in its sheath and tossed it into the crate. "You aren't coming, Shamus," she said as she slammed the lid back over the top. "None of you are. It's far too dangerous."

Shamus made a frustrated noise. "But we can't leave you on your own, Lady Kyleigh. What sort of soldiers would we be, if we didn't follow you into battle —?"

"Obedient ones." She didn't like using the tricks Crumfeld had taught her, because they made her feel like a pompous git. But in this case, she had no choice. She arched her neck and tilted her chin — making it seem as if she looked down on Shamus even though he stood nearly a head above her. "If I'm to have any chance of reaching the Baron's castle alive, I've got to move quietly. And that's impossible to do with an army stomping along behind me — no matter how they're disguised," she added, when she saw the argument on Shamus's face.

He shook his head and started to say something else, but she held up her hand.

"Pay this man for his trouble." She turned to the captain. "And I'm afraid you'll have to take that crate back down to your ship. I won't let it sit in the courtyard to tempt my men."

The captain smiled as he bowed. "No problem at all. You'll never hear me complain about being able to sell the same shipment twice," he said gleefully.

Kyleigh passed a severe look around the guards before she headed back into the castle. She could hear Shamus arguing with the captain as she reached the doors:

"What was that? I gave you the look, man! How could you sell me?"

"How was I supposed to know? All I heard was that I suddenly wasn't getting paid —"

"You should've known I was only trying to cover my arse. Here — take your blasted gold and be off with you!"

Kyleigh sighed inwardly. She squished her toes into the ground as she walked, enjoying the cool relief of the morning dew. And she realized she would have to leave much sooner than she'd planned.

She couldn't give Shamus the chance to order another round of equipment and get the men rallied for battle. She wouldn't let them follow her into Whitebone — not because she feared being spotted, but because she knew how dangerous the journey would be.

Kyleigh was prepared to risk her own life, but she wouldn't cost them theirs.

Chapter 4
The Black Beast

It had been a long while since Death visited his dreams. Kael had hoped to never meet him again — for wherever the man in white appeared, trouble would follow at his heels.

He slid in while Kael's mind rested, in the moment when the dream world crumbled and gave way to inky blackness. He was a white smudge on the horizon — a something where there should've been nothing. And Kael knew it was wrong.

Death came closer, and closer. He drifted in like a fog across the seas. Soon, he was standing close enough that Kael could see his face — a face that looked so familiar and yet, he couldn't grasp who it was.

Then his heart figured it out.

The throbbing inside his chest was panicked. His heart shrieked, pushing against his ribs. It stuttered like a friend who saw danger, but was too terrified to point it out.

What? What? Kael heard himself say. He gripped his chest and peered at the man in white, trying to guess his face. *What —?*

Death's hand clamped over his mouth, firm and insistent. Kael tried to roll his head to the side, but couldn't break free. He couldn't draw breath. In his panic, he forced himself out of his dream, wrenched his eyes open and saw ... Lysander?

The captain was crouched over him; the worry on his handsome face showed clearly in the moonlight. He pressed one finger over his lips as he peeled his hand from Kael's chin. It was uncomfortably damp.

What? Kael mouthed. He realized that *he* was the one covered in sweat: it lathered his face, the backs of his knees and under his arms.

Lysander held his hands out in front of him, as if he was begging Kael to stay calm. Then he cupped one hand around his ear.

Kael listened. For a long moment, he didn't hear anything. Then soft footsteps came from his left and he turned in time to see Aerilyn kneel down beside them. It looked as if she'd gotten dressed in a hurry: she wore nothing but her boots and Lysander's white shirt, which covered her to the knees.

An object passed between them, and Kael heard the sly hiss of metal as Lysander drew his cutlass from its sheath. Aerilyn's quiver was strapped across her shoulders; she had her bow clenched in her other hand.

Their worry put Kael on edge. What in Kingdom's name was going on? He checked to make sure that his wallet of throwing knives was strapped to his upper arm. Then he began digging through his rucksack for his bow.

"Why'd you have to toss it the whole way out here, Dred?"

The booming voice came from just outside the bramble wall — so close that it made Kael jump.

An unintelligible reply drifted in from further out, closer to the highway. "Well, one of you sorry blisters might've at least come with me ... I *know* there are lions out here!" the voice snapped, after a second reply. "Why do you think I keep yelling? I want them to know that I'm not wandering around on my own."

Then came a sound that Kael most definitely didn't want to hear — not at this time of night, and certainly not so close to their camp: laughter. Several voices worth.

"Yeh, I hope His Lordship strips the meat off your back, Dred," the voice near the bramble wall muttered. "It'll sure hurt to laugh, then ..."

His words trailed off into a string of grumbles as he tromped closer. His footsteps were heavy. Each one sounded as if a full-grown man was driving both of his feet into the ground at once.

Kael motioned for his companions to stay back. He grabbed his bow and dug an arrow out of his quiver. Then he crept towards the bramble wall.

He was fairly certain he knew what sort of man lurked outside their camp — but he hoped that he was wrong. The brambles scratched at his cheeks as he pressed his face into a small hole between the branches. He squinted through the thorns ... and saw that he'd been right.

A giant stood outside of their wall.

The giants of the Endless Plains weren't *actual* giants, with toes the size of rum barrels and heads that scraped the sky. But they *were* exceptionally large men. As the giant wandered closer, Kael sized him up. If the top of his head reached the giant's underarm, it would be a close thing. But even more alarming than the giant's height was the thickness of his limbs. He might've been able to crush a slab of stone with his fist — or a man's head.

The giant stalked over to an object stuck into the ground — a weapon with a shaft as thick as a sapling. With one grunting tug, he wrenched it free. Dirt sprayed out in all directions as the weapon's blade came loose. It had a head shaped like a spear, winged on one side by a deadly axe blade. Kael recognized it as a pike.

For a man, a pike was an unwieldy weapon — better suited to defending bridges than close combat. But the giant spun the pike around as if it was no more burdensome than a sword, checking the blade for dents. Then, with a satisfied grunt, he turned to leave. And Kael breathed a sigh of relief.

Perhaps he breathed a little too soon.

He heard the stocky branches creak above him as a gust of wind blew through the camp — the first he'd felt all night. It whipped across the remnants of their fires, stirring up the scent of ash. Kael could only watch as a handful of little embers danced gleefully over the wall.

The giant froze as the breeze rattled against his armor. His shoulders stiffened, and he turned. His eyes were hidden beneath the shadow of his helmet, but his mouth had a suspecting, downwards bend. His thumping steps grew louder as he headed back towards the bramble wall.

Kael turned around so quickly that he nearly butted heads with Aerilyn, who watched intently from over his shoulder.

"Does he see us?" she whispered. Her voice was light enough that she could speak and not be heard, but Kael didn't trust his own voice. So he just shook his head.

He was about to signal for her to wake the others when he saw that the whole host of pirates was already awake. Most knelt in silent clumps, their hands resting on their cutlasses. Others were quietly packing their bedrolls, preparing to run like mad. Kael thought that might be a good plan.

"Is he gone?" Aerilyn hissed after a moment. "I don't hear him anymore."

Kael wasn't sure. He motioned for her to stay still and crept along the wall. He heard Lysander following at his back. The good captain's boots scuffed loudly through the dried grass and crunched every possible branch in their path. Kael was about to tell him to stop when an odd feeling struck him.

His hair stood up on end and his breath caught in his throat. The animal in him whispered to be still: danger lurked nearby. He pulled his arrow back on its string until he felt the fletching touch his chin. Then he turned slowly to his right.

There was a gap in the wall, here — a crack that the grasping thorns had carved out of the moonlight. Kael knelt to squint through it. He turned his head far to the left, and then to the right, but he saw nothing amiss. Perhaps the giant had turned back for the road. He *had* been worried about the lions, after all.

Kael was straining to see into the distance when something large blocked his vision. A giant's face met his, a gray eye rolled around in the crack. And in his surprise, Kael's finger slipped from the string.

There was a grunt and a loud *clang* as the giant's body hit the ground.

47

"What was that?" Lysander hissed. His stormy eyes flicked down to Kael's empty bowstring, and he groaned. "Please tell me that wasn't what I think it was."

"It was an accident — maybe he isn't dead," Kael said hopefully. But when he saw the giant lying on his back, motionless, with an arrow standing straight up from his head, he knew it was no good.

"We ought to start running, then."

Aerilyn, in spite of having been told to stay put, had materialized behind Lysander. "Start running for what?"

"For the seas, my love," Lysander said. He slipped past her and hastily whispered orders to the pirates. Bedrolls, cookware, and rucksacks went flying into the cart.

"But," Aerilyn split her glance between the packing and Kael, "what about the plan? I thought we were supposed to camp here while you —"

"The plan's finished," Kael murmured. He went for his own pack at a jog, with Aerilyn following close behind. "That giant wasn't alone — there are others camped near the road. I'm not sure how many, and I certainly don't want to find out."

"So? Maybe they won't come looking for him. You heard what they said about the lions."

"A man attacked by lions would've had time to scream. The giant I killed didn't make a sound. They'll come looking for him out of curiosity, and we haven't got the numbers to face them. I won't risk it." Kael shoved his bow into his pack. He'd begun to unbuckle his wallet, but a sudden realization stayed his hand.

"We still have the advantage of surprise," Aerilyn reminded him. When he didn't respond, she tugged impatiently on his sleeve. "Kael — we could take them. Their skin isn't made of stone, after all. And once we've killed them, we can bury their bodies out in the wilderness, or something equally clever. Granted, it would take a fair bit of digging. They *are* rather large —"

"If killing one man will draw out a patrol," Kael whispered, his mind made up, "then killing a patrol will draw out a swarm. No, if these giants disappear without any explanation, then Gilderick's men will come pouring out of the castle. They'll comb over every blade of grass and under every boulder — and it'll be midsummer before we have a chance to sneak back in."

"What?" Aerilyn eyed him suspiciously. "Kael, you aren't making any —"

He clamped a hand over her mouth and drew the *Atlas* out of his pocket. "I want you to keep this for me. Guard it with your life."

She took the book in surprise, turning its worn, leather-bound cover in her hands. "Your book? But it's your very favorite ..." Her shock wore off and her eyes snapped up to him suddenly. "No. No — I won't let you!"

She made to grab the front of his shirt when two stocky arms lunged out of the darkness and wrapped her up tightly. "Start screaming, lass," Morris warned when she struggled, "and you'll call the whole company down to slaughter us."

Aerilyn bit her lip tightly — but the look she gave Kael was every bit as painful as a slap across the face. He thought he might've preferred the beating.

"Do whatever it is you've got planned," Morris said with a stout nod. "We'll come back for you once things have cleared up."

For not the first time, Morris seemed to have guessed his intentions. But Kael shook his head. "I'll come to you. If I'm captured, it'll be much easier for one man to sneak out than for a dozen to sneak in."

"One *Wright*," Morris corrected him with a wink. "And don't you forget it."

Kael clapped him on the arm and turned to Aerilyn — who'd begun to tear up at the word *captured*.

"Please," she whispered. When Kael shook his head, tears slid unchecked down her cheeks.

He brushed them away and took her under the chin. "I owe you an apology — for the way I behaved at dinner," he added, when she looked confused. "You're a good friend to

49

me, and you know how much I hate having an unsettled debt. So I'll definitely be coming back," he smiled at her, "to give you a proper apology. And don't worry about me, all right? My heart's going to be fine."

That last bit was an outright lie, but he needed Aerilyn to believe it. He didn't want her crying over him anymore. She returned his smile weakly, and nodded.

When Kael glanced up at Morris, he caught the old seadog giving him a strange look. He blinked his droopy eyes and bent his neck, as if he was trying to drain water out of his ears. Then he shook his head roughly, and the look vanished. "Gravy guard your path," he whispered.

As Kael slipped away, all he could think about was that Gravy couldn't save him — not this time. There was a darkness in his heart that had been growing up in the place of his hope, a black beast that kept trying to strangle him with its wings. He'd been fighting it back all winter, shoving it aside as he focused on his plan.

But now that plan was broken, and the beast fed upon its ruins — growing stronger with every step: *Perhaps it wouldn't be such a bad thing*, it whispered, *if you didn't come back at all.*

Kael shoved the beast away. For all his many wounds, he still clung to a shred of hope. It was a ragged, miserable little thing — one glowing coal lying in a bed of dead ash. But he wouldn't let it go. He would hold it tightly to his heart, no matter how it burned him.

And the black beast would lie in wait.

****

Kael crept towards the giants' camp, stitching a plan together as he went.

The moonlight was proving itself to be his greatest enemy. He already felt like a black dot on a blank sheet of parchment *before* the moon dropped its infuriating beams on his head. Now he might as well be a beetle in a jar, for all he was hidden. Still, he did what he could to move quietly —

50

even if that meant crawling along on his belly a good portion of the way.

The giants were camped closer to the trees than he realized. So close, in fact, that he was surprised they hadn't heard their companion's body strike the ground. There were a half dozen of them — their hulking forms cast shadows out from their fire, stretching across the ground like blackened rays from the sun.

Kael was within throwing distance when he heard them speak:

"I'm sick of quail," one of the giants grumbled. "Sorry excuse for a mouthful, they are. I can hardly pick the meat off their wee little bones!"

"Try the rabbit," another one replied thickly, as if he already had a mouthful of hare rolling between his jaws. "You can always get a few bites off of them."

The first snorted in disgust. "Rabbits — there's hardly an ounce of fat on them! And you'd think, with those meaty little legs, that there'd be something worth chewing on. But oh, no." The fire hissed as he flung a clean-picked quail carcass among the embers. "I'll be glad to see the castle walls again, I can tell you that." His head swung to the left. "When are we setting out, Dred? I want a plate piled high with sausages and eggs for breakfast."

"We'll leave as soon as Grout comes back," a shadow replied — a shadow, Kael noticed, that sat taller than the rest.

"I haven't heard him squawk for a while," another voice chimed in. "The clodder probably got himself lost."

The others guffawed heartily at this for a moment. Then Dred cut back in. "Somebody ought to go look for him. His Lordship won't like it if we come back a man short."

The giant who'd been grumbling about the quail snorted. "Then it ought to be you — you're the one who tossed his weapon out in the empty, after all."

"You forget," Dred said slowly, a dangerous edge in his voice, "that I am Lord Gilderick's general — even while on patrol. So if I want to rip your head off and fling it out after that pike, all I have to do is say the lions got you. And not a man here will out me. Right, blisters?"

The shadowy heads stopped their gnawing for a moment and bobbed vigorously in agreement.

"See there?" Dred said smugly. "Now, I think *you* ought to be the one to check up on Grout. Think of it this way: the sooner you find him, the sooner you'll have your sausages."

The others laughed as the giant got to his feet. He snatched his pike off the ground and made a few idle threats to those laughing loudest. Then he turned — and nearly ran straight into Kael.

He aimed between the two crossed sickles on the giant's breastplate and heard a satisfying *thunk* as the knife struck true. Then Kael threw himself into the middle of the giants' ring.

It took him less than ten seconds to stir up chaos. He flung two more blades in opposite directions, yelling wildly as he went. Even the giants who weren't struck cried out in surprise and toppled over themselves just trying to get away. Then with a loud whoop, Kael bounded over the fire and dashed for the road — hoping that the giants would follow.

He allowed himself a triumphant grin when he heard them rumbling behind him. They roared at the tops of their lungs and flung their pikes at his heels, trying to pin him to the earth. But Kael was far too quick.

He wove a pattern any rabbit would have been proud of, cutting back and forth at such sharp angles that the pikes flew off course. When he chanced a look behind him, he saw that his patched-together plan had worked: the pirates' cart had burst from camp and was moving for the highway at full-tilt. A few moments later, and a cloud of pale dust billowed up as the wheels struck the road.

Yes, if he could lead the giants another quarter mile away, the pirates would be safe —

"Got you!"

Kael had been so focused on his run that he hadn't heard the great, loping steps of the giant behind him. He'd broken away from the pack and thrust the butt of his pike between Kael's shoulders — sending him straight to the ground.

Little rocks tore at his chin and the pads of his hands as he went sliding. Before he even rolled to a stop, his knees were beneath him. He was nearly to his feet when a boot heel slammed between his shoulders, crushing him back to the earth.

The thundering steps halted beside him. Kael grimaced as torchlight crossed his face. "What is it, Dred?" the giant who wielded the torch asked.

"Hmm." The boot dug uncomfortably against Kael's spine as Dred inspected him. "Looks like a mountain rat. Well," the pike's butt nudged through his reddish-brown hair, "half a mountain rat."

"Whatever it is, I want to be the one to kill it!"

Kael recognized the voice immediately and could hardly believe it when the giant he'd struck in the chest lumbered forward. He pulled Kael's throwing knife out from his breastplate with a grunt, then held it aloft. "Look at the size of this thorn! That's going to leave an ugly little scar, that is."

A second giant snatched it out of his hand and held it to the torch. "That's no thorn — it's a wee knife!"

Kael could see why the giants had mistaken it for a thorn: clutched between their thick fingers, he could hardly see the tip of the blade.

"It doesn't matter what it is," the first giant stormed. "That little rat meant to kill me, and so I mean to kill him —!"

"Stop your fussing," the torch-wielding giant growled. He switched the light to his other hand, and Kael saw the hilt of a knife sticking out from his shoulder. "I got bloodied, too. And poor Dingy — he took one straight in the rump." He gestured to the giant at his side — whose tight lips and sweat-beaded brow indeed reminded Kael of someone who'd taken an unfortunate wound. "Didn't you, Dingy?"

He nodded stiffly. "Somebody's going to have to help me pull it out. I'm afraid to reach back there."

"Oh, rumps and shoulders — I took one in the chest! So of any of you, I ought to — oof!"

His sentence got cut short by what sounded like the blunt end of a pike to the gut. "Shut it, you idiots," Dred growled. His boot left Kael's back and went under his stomach — flipping him over like a maid fluffing the pillows. "What are you doing in my plains, mountain rat?"

When Kael's eyes adjusted to the light, he got his first, horrifying look at General Dred.

He was a giant among giants, towering head and shoulders above the rest. His arms were crossed over his breastplate, twisted together like the knotted, bulging roots of an ancient tree. The shoulders that topped his barrel chest could've served for a bench in any respectable tavern. And all over, Dred's skin seemed to be struggling to contain him: stretching and straining over his muscles, thinned to the point that his veins popped out. But that wasn't the worst part.

Not even the shadows could hide the horrible scar that marred his features. It started at his upper lip — a crevice that ran along his cheekbone and stopped just short of his left eye. The depth of the scar warped his mouth, giving him the look of a man who had something rather unpleasant growing under his nose.

"You tried to kill us," Dred said, when Kael didn't reply. His eyes roved down to Kael's wallet of knives. "Did you kill Grout? Answer me, rat!"

Kael flinched as Dred kicked a large clump of dust into his face.

"Of course he killed him!" the giant with the chest wound piped in. He leaned forward and spat in the dirt near Kael's head. "He's a little monster."

"Someone ought to check in those trees over there," Dred mused. His eyes lighted on Dingy — who quickly shook his head.

"My rump's too sore, General."

"That's not my problem, now is it?"

"But there could be more of them! What if I wind up like Grout?" Dingy pleaded. When that didn't work, he changed tactics. "We don't have time to walk all the way back there. We've got precious few hours before dawn, after all. And if we show up late, His Lordship'll flay our hides."

He glanced at the others for support, and they quickly nodded. Grout's fate came second to a flogging.

"He's going to flay us anyways," Dred snapped at them. "We're going to turn up one man short —"

"Not if we bring *him*," Dingy said, thrusting a finger at Kael. "His Lordship always needs fresh beasts. And with the Duke's shipment running late —"

"Shut it." Dred fingered the scar at his lip, thinking. And Kael held his breath.

He could see the road from the gap between Dred's legs, and the cart hadn't quite made it over the horizon. A cloud of dust still hovered very clearly where the wheels had rolled by. If the giants turned back towards camp, they would see it.

Please don't turn, Kael thought furiously, trying to force his will through the iron plates of Dred's helmet. *Forget about Grout — head for the castle.*

After a long moment of thought, Dred took his hand away. He seemed about to speak when a strange noise cut over the top of him. It came from further up the road, away from the cart's path.

And Kael recognized the familiar, ear-grating sound immediately.

Chapter Five
A Fool's Help

"What in all clods was that?" Dingy hissed. He spun around, and Kael saw that he did, indeed, have a knife stuck in his right buttocks. He yelped when Dred reached forward and yanked it free.

"I'm not sure," Dred muttered, inspecting the bloody knife. He stiffened when a second note trembled through the air, more annoying and ghastly than the last. His knuckles whitened around his pike as he took a few halting steps forward. "Let's move out — quietly, now. And don't forget the rat."

One of the giants jerked Kael to his feet. "What's this?" His hand closed around the wallet of throwing knives and Kael heard the leather snap as he ripped it free. "No more pokey thorns for you," he said, waving the wallet in Kael's face. "Now get trotting."

Kael *did* have to trot to keep up with the giants' long strides. They moved quickly down the road — and every time a note danced through the air, they seemed to move faster. It wasn't long before the moon slipped beneath the clouds and hid the land beyond in darkness.

When the giants stopped to light more torches, Kael noticed that they held their pikes much tighter than before — and their heads never stopped swiveling.

"It's Scalybones," one of the giants hissed, when a particularly screechy noise came out of the scrubs to their left. "Oh, he's getting closer!"

"He's going to make shirts out of our scalps." Dingy had removed his helmet and was running a hand worriedly through his stark white hair. "Mum used to say — ow!"

Dred smacked him smartly across the head. "Scalybones is a myth — nothing more. And I'll prove it."

Without warning, he stomped over to the scrub bushes. Kael hardly had a moment to be worried before Dred jabbed the butt of his pike into the middle of them. There was a *thud* and a sharp yelp.

"Ha!" Dred reached into the middle of the bushes and flung the wraith out among them — lanky limbs and all. The giants swore and jumped backwards; several held their weapons protectively over their chests. But Kael was far more furious than scared.

Jonathan the Fiddler looked up at him sheepishly. An angry red patch was swelling rapidly over his eye.

"There's your Scalybones," Dred said triumphantly. "It's naught but a spindly little forest man."

"Ah, not *just* a spindly forest fellow," Jonathan sprang to his feet and drew his bow across his fiddle in a less-atrocious note, "a bard of the realm, at your service." He bent rather clownishly, swinging his arm out beside him in the courtliest of gestures.

Kael silently begged him not to overdo it.

"A bard, eh?" Dingy said, rubbing his sore rump thoughtfully. "We could use one of them. Lord Gilderick's hall needs music."

Dred made a frustrated sound and flicked one massive hand towards the road. "Then we'll let His Lordship decide what to do with him — if he doesn't mince us on sight, that is. Move out, blisters! We've got a long road and a short while before sunrise."

They forced Jonathan and Kael to the front of the line and set a fast pace for Gilderick's castle. Though they had to move at nearly a half gallop to keep the pikes off their backs, the giants were far from sympathetic: they lowered their weapons and made it clear that they would stop for nothing.

"We'll carry you in by your ribs, if we have to," one of them called, drawing a round of jeers from the others.

It wasn't long before the hard-packed road began to make Kael's legs ache. He could feel his boots rubbing large, twin blisters into his biggest toes. But he hardly noticed his discomfort.

He was still too angry with Jonathan.

What in Kingdom's name had he been thinking? It didn't matter what sort of evil awaited them in Gilderick's realm: giant warriors, witches, a vat of two-headed snakes — with enough time to think, Kael knew he could escape any cage they threw him in. But now that he had Jonathan tagging along, escape would be much more difficult.

He waited until the giants' chatter billowed up again before he shot the fiddler what he hoped was a dangerous look.

Jonathan licked his lips. "Now, now — I know you're upset —"

"Blasted right, I am," Kael snapped back. "You should've gone with the cart. I won't be able to save you if they take you into the castle. You *do* understand that, don't you?" he added, when Jonathan opened his mouth to retort. "This isn't going to be like sacking the Duke — there's no dancing in Gilderick's realm. And there's very likely no escaping, either."

Jonathan was quiet for such a long moment that Kael's anger cooled and he began to regret what he'd said. The giants had been about to turn around for camp, after all. And Jonathan's ruse had given the pirates the chance to escape. They might *all* be in irons, had he not led the giants away.

Kael was just about to apologize when Jonathan spoke: *"You're not stupid, Jonathan,"* he muttered, a small smile pulling at his lips, *"but you* are *a fool!* That's what Garron always used to say to me. He said I was one of those blokes who could never get his boxes stacked in the right order — and that I shouldn't be surprised when the whole lot came tumbling down on me. Maybe I should've gone with the cart," he touched the skin around his swollen eye gingerly, "but I couldn't leave you on your own. So come blisters or bruises or ole Gildepants, himself — you're stuck with me, mate."

"You *are* a fool," Kael said back. But he couldn't keep his face serious for long under Jonathan's silly grin. He broke into a smile — and punched Jonathan in the arm when he laughed. After a moment, their smiles turned serious once again. "I'm going to get us out of this. Somehow, I'll figure out a way to get us back to the seas."

"I know you will, mate," Jonathan said cheerily. And as his typical winking eye was already swollen shut, he just tilted his head to one side. "Though preferably in a way that doesn't involve a pair of coffins."

Kael promised that he would try.

****

Lord Gilderick's castle rose up like a boil upon the earth. Its red, rounded walls were swollen thick against invaders, its jutting towers stood high out of reach, and the front gate was sealed tightly shut. The way its massive beams and bolts crossed over each other made it look like a set of clenched teeth.

To the right of the gate was a large, squat tower — and judging by the mismatched color of its bricks, it was much older than the rest. The tower was connected to the castle by a covered passageway. Huge white clouds of smoke streamed lazily from its top.

If Kael blurred his eyes, he thought the whole thing looked a bit like a red skull smoking a pipe.

When they were a quarter of a mile from the grinning front gates, the road suddenly forked into three. The giants ordered them to a halt, and then began bickering amongst themselves about what to do with their captives. All the while, the sun crept closer to dawn.

"We'll take the bard to the castle," Dred finally said. His ruined lip twisted into a sneer. "If His Lordship doesn't like him, I'm sure he can think of something ... inventive, to do with him."

With a round of unsettling laughter, the others agreed.

"And what about the rat?" The giant with the chest wound narrowed his gray eyes at Kael. "We've already got a soul for Grout — we don't need him. Leave him in my charge for a moment, Dred. I promise I'll leave not a speck behind."

Kael met the giant's hard look with one of his own. For a moment, he was actually hoping that Dred *would* leave them alone. Morris had taught him well, and even a giant would have gaps in his armor.

But unfortunately, that wasn't what Dred chose. "No, we can't waste a slave — not even one as scrawny as *that*," he added, jutting his chin at Kael. "Take him to the fields, Dingy —"

"Why me?" he moaned.

"Because I order it." Dred coupled this with a sneer. Then he grabbed Jonathan around his belt and hoisted him to the top of his massive shoulders. As the giants sprinted away, Jonathan hung limply on his belly, bouncing up and down like a half-filled sack of potatoes.

Kael had hardly taken three steps before he found himself plucked from the road and draped uncomfortably across Dingy's shoulder. His armor bit into Kael's stomach, pinching him in places where he didn't think he'd had any skin to spare. He propped himself up awkwardly on his elbows, trying to keep the armor from biting him.

Half of his concentration was bent on not being jostled to death, and with the other half, he tried to get a good look at Gilderick's fields.

The *Atlas* claimed that the plains had the richest soil in the Kingdom. He'd found several drawings hidden in its pages: of green pasturelands, fields bursting bright with color, and orchards heavy with fruit. There had been giants in the drawings, too. He remembered the smiles on their painted faces as they worked the fields, sometimes hoisting monstrous vegetables from the ground, or wandering with their scythes propped across their thick shoulders.

But the fields he looked at now were nothing like the pictures in the *Atlas*: they were empty.

Large chunks of the earth had been scraped away, marring the land with a patchwork of dark, damp scars. The patches stood out like scorch marks in the dry grass, as if the whole land smoldered in ruin. Though he looked as far as his eyes could reach, Kael saw nothing green in sight: just dismal shades of black and brown.

The stars were still out, but several hulking shadows were already making their way across the fields to work. Kael recognized the thick limbs and plodding steps of the giants, and he knew that these must be Lord Gilderick's slaves.

He'd spent the winter reading the logbook they'd stolen from Duke Reginald. And from what he could gather, Gilderick had divided the giants into two groups: those who were willing to shed blood to join his army, and those who weren't. The giants who'd refused to join him had become his slaves.

Kael watched the slaves from around Dingy's massive head. Some of them hoisted tools across their shoulders, but even those with nothing at all still seemed to carry a burden: they were hunched over, their backs were like the curve of a bow and their heads were tethered to the earth — held down by some unrelenting string.

The giants who worked the fields had refused to bow to Gilderick, and so he'd bent them under his whips.

Anger swelled in Kael's chest when he thought of what a proud race the giants had been. He was determined to see pride straighten their shoulders once more. He would see them bent back — and Gilderick would pay dearly for what he'd done to the plains.

Kael was so caught up in his thoughts that it took him a moment to realize that Dingy had come to a stop. The road had finally ended in what looked like a small, dusty courtyard. Four identical barns hemmed its edges, forming an almost perfect wall. Something that looked like a small cottage was perched atop the roof of each barn. Their doors had been marked crudely with dripping white paint: *N, S, E,* and *W.*

Dingy was stopped at the barn marked *N*. His shoulder dropped suddenly, dumping Kael onto the ground.

"That had better not be for us."

A narrow flight of stairs led up the side of the barn and to the cottage perched at its top. The man who'd spoken stood on a small porch outside of the cottage, leaning against the rails.

He had a pinched face and a wad of something trapped behind his lower lip. His scarlet tunic was emblazoned with the gold, crossed sickles of the Endless Plains. Kael couldn't help but notice the wicked-looking black whip strapped to his side.

"You'll take what you're given and smile about it, spellmonger," Dingy growled back.

*Spell*monger? Kael had to bite his lip to keep from swearing aloud.

Why hadn't he thought of this before? Of *course* Gilderick used his mages for slavemasters — how else could he have hoped to keep the giants under control? So even if Kael hadn't been captured, his plan would've still fallen apart. The pirates wouldn't have been able to fight against the mages. He would've led them all straight to their deaths.

Kael wasn't used to being fortunate. He supposed that he should be grateful, but he was still too furious with himself to feel relieved.

"We won't get even an hour's work out of that rat," the mage complained, his lip tightening around whatever it was that he held against his gums. "I'm tired of getting all the cast-offs. Stodder thinks his *pens* are so much more important than everything else — and he sticks me with all the sicklings!"

Dingy smirked. "Well, if you're so upset about it, why don't you ask His Lordship for a better stock? I'll take you up to the castle, myself."

The mage's face, if possible, pinched even tighter. He leaned forward and spat in answer. A trail of brownish liquid landed near Dingy's boots.

He smirked all the wider "I didn't think so. That didn't work out so well for ole Ludwig, now did it?" Dingy shrugged as he turned for the road. "Put him to work, or throw him in the Grinder — the rat's *your* problem now, spellmonger!"

"Meat-headed oaf," the mage spat back, but Kael doubted if Dingy could hear it over the noise of his own chortling. "Finks!" The mage gestured to someone over Kael's shoulder. "You lost one of your beasts yesterday, didn't you? Why don't you take the rat?"

"An excellent idea, Hob."

Kael had hoped, as he turned around, that Finks wasn't going to look as wicked as he sounded. But for not the first time that day, he was severely disappointed.

Finks stood before the barn marked *W* — a slight man with hunched shoulders. His slick black hair was pulled back into a horse's tail, and bound so tightly that it stretched his skin thin across his temples.

When he spotted Kael, his lips parted into an impossibly wide grin. His teeth seemed too long and too numerous. His smile looked like the same one a serpent might've worn, had he found something to laugh at. And Kael shuddered to think about the sorts of things a serpent might find amusing.

Finks drew the black leather whip from his belt and swung it almost lazily in Kael's direction. The whip flicked out, snapping loudly at its end.

Something grazed Kael's shoulder. It was slimy, like the belly of a fish. The heavy, thick scent burned the sensitive skin on the inside of his nose. Without thinking, he scratched madly at the itch that sprang up where the spell had struck him.

Finks seemed to mistake Kael's annoyance for a grimace. His lips twisted higher about his teeth. "There's more where that came from, rat. You'll hurry up if you don't want another."

Kael followed him at a jog.

Finks led the way through the fields, and Kael's worry deepened with every step. Sneaking out of Gilderick's realm was going to be more difficult than he'd thought.

If the mages were in charge of keeping the slaves, it meant there would be plenty of spells to deal with. They'd probably use magic to seal the slaves' quarters. Would there be hexes on the doors, as there had been on the gates of Wendelgrimm? Would there be traps?

"One of my horses went lame yesterday," Finks said, interrupting his thoughts. He'd slowed his pace while Kael had been thinking. Now they walked side-by-side.

The stench of magic on Finks's breath was nearly unbearable. Kael turned his head away and focused on breathing in the smells of the earth instead.

Sunlight was beginning to creep across the fields, and he could see that the giants were already hard at work. Teams of three pushed plows back and forth through the earth: one giant guided it from behind while the other two pulled the blade along, doing the work of beasts. They leaned hard against their harnesses; their muscles strained through their ragged clothes as they dragged the plow forward. The lines they left behind them were as tight as the seams on a traveler's cloak.

Kael searched for a long moment, but he swore there wasn't a single horse in sight. Then he realized that Finks must have been referring to the giants as *horses*. He couldn't stop the anger from burning across his face, and Finks must've seen it — because he took it as an invitation to press on.

"Broke his ankle on a rock, poor little horsey." Finks swung his coiled whip through a clump of dried grass. "I tried to ... persuade, him to rise," his next swing bent the top of a weed, "but he refused. He just lay on the ground, moaning and carrying on. So I had no choice but to send him to the castle. Don't worry — I'm sure Gilderick will patch him up nicely."

And Kael was sure, if Finks kept talking, that the Kingdom would be short one annoying mage.

Fortunately, Finks's mouth closed over his long teeth and didn't open again until they stopped at a nearby field. This field was just as large and empty as the others. Two giants worked the soil alone, one guiding the plow while the other pulled. The blade must've been heavier than Kael realized: the giant in charge of pulling was bent nearly double. He dropped to all fours in places where the earth deepened, using the strength of his bulging arms to drag the plow forward.

Finks slung his whip and both of the giants' heads jerked to the side. They stopped their work and glared at him. Fresh red welts rose up across their brows.

"What is it, master?" the giant behind the plow said. He had a shock of white hair and limbs that were a little ganglier than the average giant's. Even though his mouth was serious, his eyes glinted like a man up to no good — which gave his words a mocking edge.

"I've found you a third," Finks said, shoving Kael forward with a thrust of his boot.

"That little thing? He'll be more a burden than a help."

"Don't try to make excuses, you lazy oaf!" Finks snapped his whip, and both giants winced as the spell struck them. "I still expect these fields to be plowed by sundown. And if they aren't, I'll bleed you. Understood, beasts?" He turned and marched away, his horse's tail flicking sharply across his back as he went.

For a long, icy moment, the giants stared at Kael. The one behind the plow leaned against it, his eyes glinting like a crow's. The second giant never moved. His eyes were set back so deeply that the ridge of his brow cast a shadow over them, masking the top half of his face.

Kael didn't have time for this. He didn't know how long it would take to plow the field, but staring at him certainly wasn't going to accomplish anything — and he had no intention of being flogged.

"What do you want me to do?" he said to the giant behind the plow. He wasn't sure if the second giant could even speak: his mouth was closed so tightly that Kael wondered if it'd ever been open.

"I don't know. What are you good for?" the giant behind the plow replied.

"I've never done any farming," Kael admitted. When the giant snorted, he added quickly: "But I've read all about it."

"Have you? Well then, by all means ..." The giant skipped out from behind the plow and bent his arms in a grand, sweeping gesture. "Lead us on, Lord Rat."

Kael wasn't surprised at his mocking. The *Atlas* had mentioned that the giants weren't very fond of outsiders. The few times in history when the giant clans had stopped fighting each other long enough to band together, it'd been to stop another race from sneaking in. They guarded their fields against invaders and chased all would-be settlers from their lands.

But Kael wasn't trying to steal anything from the giants. He'd been tossed into slavery right along beside them. He wasn't going to let himself be bullied for it. "Heckling me won't get the fields plowed any faster," he said, meeting the giant's glinting eyes.

"Oh no, you misunderstood me. I wasn't heckling you — I was just clearing a path. What with your book knowledge and all, I thought you might be able to teach *us* a thing or two."

He looked so sincere that for a moment, Kael almost believed him. Then the second giant spoke:

"We haven't got time for jokes, Brend." He grabbed another harness off the plow and tossed it at Kael's feet. "You'll pull alongside me, rat."

Kael shrugged the harness on as quickly as he could. It was far too big for him: the strap that was meant to go around his waist dangled almost at his knees. The shoulder straps felt uncomfortable as well, but he couldn't figure out why.

"Have I got this on right?" he said, hoping one of the giants would answer him.

"Most definitely," Brend said with a nod. "You just tuck that cord between your legs and pull it along by your important bits. That's always the most sensible way to drag a plow."

Kael's face burned as he turned the harness around. He hadn't realized that he'd had it on backwards. Brend could've just said as much.

"Ready, Declan?" Brend hollered.

"Yeh," the giant next to Kael said, answering with something that was halfway between a grunt and a *yes*.

Declan leaned against the harness and pointed his chin at the opposite end of the field. Kael mirrored him — and that's when he noticed something odd: Declan was easily the smallest giant he'd come across. He still stood over Kael, but it was by no more than a few inches. Perhaps he was only half-giant.

Kael looked him over quickly, but could see no other race in his features. Declan's hair was pure white, his eyes were stony grey, and his limbs were even properly thick. He was exactly like all of the other giants — only smaller.

"Ready, wee rat?" Brend called.

"Ready," Kael said. He wasn't entirely sure what he was doing, but he certainly wasn't going to ask Brend for help. He'd just figure it out as he went.

"And I'll tell you now, in case I don't have a chance to tell you later — I'm sorry if I slice you in half."

Kael spun around. Brend's face was serious, but his eyes were a joke. Kael couldn't decide whether to be worried or annoyed. And Brend didn't give him the chance to figure it out:

"Lead on, Declan!"

He charged forward, and Kael most certainly didn't want to be sliced in half, so he leapt to catch up. The plow was much heavier than he'd expected it to be. His skinny limbs shuddered at the end of the rope, and he knew he couldn't rely on his body's feeble strength to get the blade moving.

So he put every ounce of his concentration into pulling, using the power of his mind to steel his muscles and weight his steps. The blade moved easily — so easily that the sudden shift made Declan stumble. He caught himself on his hands and sprang back up to his feet. His heels almost nicked the tip of the plow blade as he leapt to catch up with Kael.

"All right there, Declan?" Brend called to him.

"Yeh," he grunted. He shot a glance at Kael — who kept his eyes purposefully forward.

Blast it all. He needed to be more careful. It was obvious that the giants thought of him as a weakling, and it would be best if they went on thinking it — because if they ever found out what he really was, they'd turn him over to Gilderick.

And there was no telling what would happen to him, then. But he doubted it would be pleasant.

Chapter 6
Mage Studies

After she'd uncovered Shamus's plan, Kyleigh realized that she would have to pack her things and leave Copperdock immediately. There were no two ways about it. So once the mess in the courtyard had been taken care of, she went straight to her chambers.

She found her armor crammed inside one of her dresser drawers. Crumfeld didn't like her to wear it around the castle, but she had far too much to do before nightfall to waste time worrying over Crumfeld. Besides, she could think much better if she was comfortable.

The blackened armor fit her like a second skin: the jerkin molded to her torso, the ridged gauntlets wrapped snugly about her arms, and the leggings formed to her shape. Because the armor was made of dragon scales, and not something burdensome like iron, the air came through it easily — which meant she never had to worry about baking alive.

In fact, it was practically as comfortable as running around naked.

She slipped on her boots, careful not to nick herself on the deadly spurs coming out of their heels. Then she began digging through her bed covers for the final piece.

He wasn't exactly a part of her armor, but her hip just didn't feel right without him. "There you are, old friend," she said as she fished Harbinger out from the foot of her bed.

The curved white blade glinted fiercely against the brilliance of the rising sun. He took in the peaceful golden light, swirling it across his surface until it began to look more like dancing flames. His voice was low and steady as he hummed against her grip.

Harbinger was a part of her. She'd forged him from her own scales. On the day he'd come out of the fire, and she'd held him for the first time ... well, that was the day that she began to feel like a true warrior.

She couldn't help but grin as his excitement thrummed against her palm. His voice made her veins tremble like fiddle strings. Harbinger was a bloodthirsty fellow, and he suited her.

She'd just gotten him strapped to her belt when someone knocked on the door: "My Lady? A word, if you please."

Kyleigh silently implored the skies for patience as she let Crumfeld in. "I've solved the problem with the gate —"

"I know, but now we've got a new one."

He seemed out of breath, like he'd charged up the stairs with his coattails on fire. A few of his hairs had even popped out of their usual slicked-back arrangement. But that wasn't the most alarming thing.

It took her a moment to realize it, but the potent smell wafting from him wasn't anything the cooks were preparing for breakfast: it was burnt flesh.

"What on earth have you gotten into?" she said, carefully pulling the arm he was trying to hide out from behind his back. The skin on his hand was red and raw. White blisters already sprouted up on the tips of his fingers.

"It's that mage," Crumfeld said, grimacing as she turned his hand over. "I only wanted to clean. He's been locked in his room all winter — Kingdom only knows the mess he's made. But he's hexed the door! When I tried to turn the knob, it burned me."

"Well, you're going to have to go straight to the healer."

"But my lady —"

"No, straight away, Crumfeld. I'm serious."

"Very well," he huffed. Then he noticed her armor, and he opened his mouth to protest.

"No — healer, first. You can fret about my outfit later," Kyleigh said. She turned him by the shoulders and marched him down the stairs.

****

Jake kept his room tucked deep into a corner of the west wing, up a poky flight of stairs and hidden in an alcove. There were other, grander chambers in Roost, but he'd insisted on that spot in particular because he thought he was less likely to be disturbed. And with the exception of Crumfeld, his plan seemed to be working perfectly.

Kyleigh stopped outside of the door. It looked safe enough: just a small, rounded opening about the size of a closet's. But she still approached it carefully. She didn't want to risk her hand winding up like Crumfeld's. Her armor could protect her against blades and arrows, but could do nothing against magic.

So instead of knocking, she raised her voice: "Jake?" Though she tried to keep her frustration hidden, the word still came out like a growl. She leaned as close to the door as she dared and thought she could hear papers rustling on the other side. "Jake — open up this instant."

"No!"

It was an oddly defiant reply, and there was a bit of shakiness in his voice. "Open this door, or I swear I'll kick it in."

"I don't care!"

It was obvious that Jake was upset about something, and she thought she might've been able to guess what it was. "Nobody blames you for what happened to Gerald," she said, struggling to keep her voice even. "It's not like you meant for the wall to disappear."

"But it did — and it's all my fault."

Poor Jake. He always meant well, but his spells rarely turned out the way he planned them.

The incident with Gerald happened two weeks ago, when Crumfeld had decided to add *cleaning* to the guards'

71

regular list of chores. They were none-too-pleased and complained loudly about it for days. So Jake had taken it upon himself to try and make their work a little easier.

He weaved together a spell that he thought might do the work of soap and a brush, then tried it out on a particularly filthy section of Roost: a wing that appeared to have been burned to the ground by invading armies and rebuilt several times over. The walls were streaked with black lines of soot, which Crumfeld declared to be unacceptable blemishes.

Jake's spell erased the soot on the first wall, and everything seemed to be working well ... except for one small problem: the wall *looked* like a perfectly normal, clean section of wall — but when Gerald went to lean up against it, he'd slipped straight through and fallen down into the courtyard below.

Luckily, a pelt merchant had just arrived at the castle and had been trying to persuade Crumfeld to buy the various furs he had for sale. Gerald crashed through the roof of the merchant's cart and spooked the horses pretty badly, but he'd walked away with nothing more than a broken arm and a hefty dislike of magic.

Things could've certainly gone worse.

"Gerald's on the mend," Kyleigh reasoned. "And I bought every ware that merchant had to offer in payment for the hole in his cart. So there's really been no harm done —"

"No harm done?" Jake bellowed through the door. "I've broken an innocent man's arm! He'll never forgive me for it."

"Oh, please — he brags about it every chance he gets. Not two nights ago, I saw him down at the tavern, wooing a pair of desert women with the tale of how he'd survived a blast from a battlemage."

There was a long pause on the other side of the door. "Well, that's not *exactly* how it happened," Jake muttered.

Kyleigh shrugged. "You broke his arm — he gets to tell the story however he likes. Now, won't you let me in?"

There was a great deal of huffing and tossing books about before the door finally swung open.

Jake was a skinny fellow. He wore wrinkled blue robes and a pair of round spectacles — which always seemed to wander towards the end of his long nose. And today, it appeared that he was in a rather foul mood: his thin lips were pulled into a frown.

"I'm a failure."

"Nonsense," Kyleigh said as she slipped past him.

"No, it makes perfect sense. I'm a mage who can't cast a proper spell. There's no clearer definition of a failure."

She thought carefully about what to say as she made her way to the one clean corner of the room.

Crammed into Jake's tiny chambers were a bed, several shelves of books, and a banged-up table that he seemed to be using for a desk. It might have been a decent space, if he'd kept it tidy. But instead, he had books littered across every spare surface: on the table, under the table, lining the windowsill, propped against his pillows, and covering the floor.

The books were all flipped open, lying on their spines like a flock of birds that had fallen from the skies. Some of the pages were badly stained, and they were filled to every margin with a strange, swirling language. It made Kyleigh's eyes cross just to look at it.

Navigating Jake's mess was a tricky patch of work. While it may have *looked* chaotic, the books were actually arranged in very specific circular patterns. The rings overlapped each other like links in a chain, connecting to form something like a net that covered the entire room. It would have looked very peculiar if Kyleigh hadn't known it for what it was: mage studies.

Long ago, she'd discovered that mages arranged their thoughts in the placement of their books. Every ring was linked to a specific study, which relied on an idea from the ring next to it in order to make a complete thought. It was all a very complicated, delicate process. If Kyleigh knocked one book out of place, Jake might lose a month's worth of work.

And she'd found out the hard way that nothing got a person hexed faster than ruining a mage's studies.

"Are you close to solving the great mystery of life, then?" she said as she skipped from one circle to the next. She landed lightly, careful not to nudge a single book out of order.

"Not quite," he mumbled as he closed the door. "Though I might've been a lot closer if that silly man hadn't wandered in here and ruined everything."

"Yes," Kyleigh said, as she finally made it to the clean spot next to the window. "Crumfeld showed me where you hexed him. His hand looked like he'd just taken it out of the oven."

Jake's mouth twitched slightly upwards. "Well, I've already told him that I don't want him in here. I suppose next time he'll listen."

Not surprisingly, Crumfeld and Jake weren't the best of friends. The first time Jake went out for a meal, Crumfeld swooped in behind him. He'd placed every book back on its shelf and swept every speck of dust out the door. When Jake returned and saw the damage, he'd blown a hole through the roof.

Kyleigh glanced up at the ceiling. She frowned when she saw the gray clouds that had suddenly gathered overhead. Fat drops of rain began falling from them as she watched. They struck the spell Jake had placed over the hole and went sliding harmlessly down the roof.

"Your barrier seems to be working well."

Jake made a scornful sound. "Of course it is — it's a shielding spell. Every battlemage can cast one."

"And your hex certainly worked on Crumfeld."

"Traps are the second thing we learn — right after the lesson on how to blow people up." He plunked down at the desk, removed his spectacles, and began to vigorously clean them on the hem of his robes. "I can also freeze your blood in your veins, if you'd like. Or strike you blind for a few months."

"Tempting ... but I think I'll pass," Kyleigh said lightly. When Jake didn't smile, she sighed. "This is my point: you aren't a failure. You've cast plenty of proper spells —"

"Proper, maybe. But they aren't useful." He slid his spectacles back on and pushed them up the bridge of his nose. He glared at the wall for a moment, his eyes flicked across the mortar lines as he gathered his thoughts. "I suppose I always imagined that things would be different, once I was freed," he said quietly. "I thought ... I *hoped* that the King had made me like this — that I was really a good man, but one just being forced to kill."

Kyleigh didn't know what to say, so she didn't say anything.

Granted, her hands weren't exactly the cleanest in the realm. Sometimes she would have nightmares about the battles she'd fought in, the friends she'd lost ... the many lives she'd taken. But those nights were few and far between. She supposed it was because she had the comfort of knowing that she'd *chosen* to fight. She knew in her heart that good men lived on because she'd had the courage to slay the bad ones.

But Jake's story wasn't like that — he'd had no choice. He spent nearly his entire life in chains, his body enslaved by magic. He killed the men he was forced to kill: first for the Duke, and then for the Witch of Wendelgrimm.

She couldn't imagine the sort of nightmares he must have, and so she didn't try to. Instead, she simply listened.

"It's me, though," Jake said after another long moment. "I'm a battlemage, through and through. The spells make sense to me. They come easily." His head fell into his hands, his thin fingers clutched tightly at his hair. "I'm a murderer."

Nope — that was enough. He'd slipped off the edge of reason and directly into a vat of nonsense. She wasn't going to let him feel sorry for himself.

Kyleigh hopped her way back across the room and grabbed him by the shoulder, careful to be gentle. Her strength was perfect for battle and hunting. But on more than one occasion, she'd accidentally broken a friend's bones by just squeezing too hard — and Jake's bones were thinner than most.

"Look at me." She waited until his eyes met hers. "Do you think I'm a murderer?"

"Well, no —"

"Do you think Harbinger is a murderer?"

He scoffed. "That's completely ridiculous. How could a *sword* be a murderer?"

"Exactly — he can't be. And even though he likes to think that he's got a mind of his own, he still swings when I tell him to." Jake could see where she was going and tried to argue, but she grabbed him under the chin. "The Duke and the Witch used you for a sword. But you aren't a sword anymore, are you?"

"No," he mumbled, when she raised her brows.

"That's right. You aren't a sword — you're a man. And a man who is more than capable of making his own decisions. You may have a battlemage's gift for war, but it's up to you to decide how you use it. Do you understand?"

He looked away. "Yes."

"Good. And I'll hear no more of this dark talk — it doesn't become you." She released him and planted her hands on her hips. "Are you still coming with me to the desert?"

He looked surprised. "Of course I am! I've been looking forward to it all winter." He straightened up, and Kyleigh smiled when she saw the inquisitive glint come back to his eyes. "It's supposedly the most uncharted land in the Kingdom. Three fourths of it is simply marked as blank space on the map. Even Baron Sahar doesn't have much control over it. His people simply live in tribes and keep to themselves. There's dozens of them, each with their own culture and language. Can you imagine? And there could even be dozens more that haven't yet been discovered — look here."

He reached over a ring of books and pulled a new one out from behind them. It was thinner than most and didn't seem to have a title. When he flipped through the white pages with his thumb, she noticed that every one of them was blank.

"It's a journal," he said, with a small smile that would've been a normal fellow's sharp-toothed grin. "I bought it from a vendor last week. I'm going to use it to record our whole journey — the lands we cross, the creatures we spot. Perhaps we'll even discover a new tribe."

Kyleigh laughed. "Well if we do, I certainly hope they're friendly." She glanced at the door before she lowered her voice. "It looks as if we're going to have leave sooner than I expected. Are you packed?"

"Are you joking? I've been packed for weeks." He shuffled through his papers for a moment. "But, ah ... I'm afraid I haven't been able to find us a very useful map."

"That's not a problem." Kyleigh tapped the side of her head. "I've got one right here."

Jake frowned. "That doesn't seem like a very sensible place to keep a map —"

"I know what I'm doing," she said firmly.

Well, at least she *hoped* she knew what she was doing. The truth was that Kyleigh wasn't used to being the leader. Any decisions she made were always hers to deal with, and if she got herself into trouble — well, she could always get herself out of it. But the thought having Jake along was beginning to make her anxious. She knew she would be responsible for his life, as well.

And she hoped she was up to the task.

Still, she wasn't worried about crossing the desert. That bit would be the simplest part of their journey, and she could certainly navigate without a map. Maps were for humans — a way to compensate for their duller senses. Kyleigh had no need of them.

"All right." Jake pulled himself to the edge of his chair and looked up at her through his spectacles. "I've got my journal, and you've got the map. So ... what are we waiting for?"

"Dawn," she said, stepping out the door.

She grinned when she heard Jake whoop loudly from behind her.

******

The clouds didn't relent their hold on the day, and evening seemed to come much more quickly than usual. Kyleigh finished packing and stuffed her equipment under her bed — where Crumfeld wasn't likely to spot it. Then she made her way down to the kitchens.

It was easily her favorite room in Roost. She could hear the sounds of pots clanging together from the great hall, the hiss of soup striking the fire, and the relentless tittering of the women in charge of dinner. The warm comfort of food wafted down the passageway, and Kyleigh's stomach had begun to rumble before she even opened the door.

Inside the kitchen was organized chaos. Women flitted here and there, hoisting sacks of flour over one another's heads and tossing potatoes wherever they were needed. Kyleigh ducked under a tray sporting the weight of a suckling pig, destined for the oven. She spun her way around a woman carrying a hot pot and helped a little girl retrieve a basket of apples from a high shelf.

By the time she made it to her usual spot, she felt as if she'd crossed a battlefield.

A round-faced young woman caught sight of her and smiled as she cleared a place for her to sit at the counter. "Evening, Miss Kyleigh."

"Evening, Mandy."

Kyleigh hadn't expected to make any friends among the women of Roost. Honestly, she found most women to be complicated beyond the point of frightening: their minds seemed capable of holding onto a dozen thoughts at once, and their emotions never trickled — but seemed to come only in torrents and floods.

The she-wolves in her pack had at least had some animal blood to temper them. But without it, a fully human woman could be rather ... wild.

78

Fortunately, Mandy wasn't like most women. She was calm-spirited and steady, and wise beyond her years. She was also the only person in all of the High Seas who would agree to drop the *Lady* from Kyleigh's name.

"What's for dinner tonight?" Kyleigh said as she situated herself on a tall stool.

"Venison." Mandy grabbed a nearby knife and began sharpening its blade against a whetstone. "The cook found your — ah, well, there was another deer found at the back door this afternoon, you see. And we didn't want to let it go to waste."

Kyleigh propped her fingers over her lips to hide her smile, nodding thoughtfully. She had a feeling that several nearby ladies were listening in, watching her like a clump of curious squirrels from the trees. "Yes, quite right. It's a shame that it's happened again — I wish we could keep the little blighters from leaping over the walls and breaking their necks."

Mandy struggled to keep her face serious. "Perhaps we ought to put a sign out for them, so they'll be sure to know the dangers."

"Brilliant. And we'll write it in *deer* so they'll be able to read it."

By now, the eavesdropping ladies were giggling into their aprons and giving themselves away. The cook shooed them back to their chores as she bustled over with Kyleigh's dinner.

"This isn't story hour — back to work, you lot! Those pies aren't going to bake themselves." She plunked a heaping plate of venison on the counter and said a quick hello — before she barreled off to scold some girls who were speaking *deer* instead of peeling apples.

"I'm afraid I get them into trouble with my nonsense," Kyleigh said as she cut into the venison. It was barely seared on top and raw in the middle — just the way she liked it.

Mandy smiled. "Oh, they don't mind it so much. They're fond of your nonsense: it's exciting to see the Lady of Copperdock behaving so poorly. You ought to see how they beam when the visiting captains grumble about how odd you are."

"I resent that," Kyleigh said around a mouthful of meat. "I'm not odd at all."

Mandy just smiled and shook her head. She pulled a bunch of carrots to her station and chopped them into neat, even slices — wielding her knife with all the deadly grace of an assassin. Kyleigh watched her for a moment, enjoying the spices the cook had rubbed into the venison. Then she had a thought.

"Would you like me to teach you how to use a blade?"

Mandy straightened up. "What ever do you mean?"

"Well, you know — how to fight. How to throw a punch and aim to cripple."

Mandy's eyes went wide and she clutched her bosom — as if Kyleigh had just suggested that they tie Crumfeld in a sack and toss him into the sea. "Oh, no. I don't think I should like that at all, miss. Fighting is a man's business."

Well, perhaps there were *some* things about Mandy that were a bit ridiculous. But Kyleigh was determined to make her see reason. "What would you do if a man attacked you?" she countered. "How would you fight him off?"

Mandy settled her shoulders and went back to chopping. "I like to think that I wouldn't have to fight — because there'd be some handsome young man who comes along and rescues me."

Kyleigh rolled her eyes. "That's rubbish, Mandy."

"No, it's *romantic*," she said, shaking her knife in Kyleigh's face. Then she flicked the blade to point to a goblet near her elbow. "Drink your tonic, miss. You're far more agreeable once you've had it."

Kyleigh's *tonic* was actually just warm, spiced wine with a few herbs thrown in. She normally didn't drink spirits, but lately it had become a necessity.

Her first few nights away from Gravy Bay had been complete and utter torture. She'd convinced herself that she was perfectly capable of settling her own heart. She had time on her side, after all. But her soul seemed to feel differently.

80

If Kyleigh ever managed to fall asleep, it was only to be jerked awake moments later — startled by the violent heaving of her chest. Gasps would rake her throat raw; tears pushed their way out and ran in burning lines down her face. She would wrap her arms around her middle, sometimes digging her nails in until she bled. Once, she'd screamed so loudly that Crumfeld had sent the guards to her room, convinced that she was being murdered.

Eventually, her chest would stop heaving and her sobs would quiet. But the next morning, she would be nearly too sore to walk. Her body would feel like someone had stripped off her skin and beaten her innards with poles.

It was on one such morning that she'd stumbled down the stairs and nearly run into Mandy — who'd taken one look at her before nodding knowingly. "I've got something for that, miss. You come see me after dinner."

Kyleigh did, and Mandy's spiced wine tonic had turned out to be just the thing to quiet her ... well, Mandy called them her *fits*. Kyleigh didn't know what to call them. All she knew was that they hurt worse than an axe to the face.

She'd just brought the goblet to her lips when the chattering in the kitchen came to an abrupt halt. The women were suddenly very focused on their chores — and very intent on not being noticed.

Kyleigh groaned when Crumfeld swept through the crowd and made a straight line for her counter. He had his bandaged hand propped against his chest and a rather peeved look on his face. She thought she might be in for it.

"But I don't want to eat in the dining room," she said as he approached. "It's lonely in there —"

"I'm not here about that," he said swiftly. "Though we *will* discuss it later. And in the future, I should like to see some vegetables on your plate," he added, wrinkling his nose at her nearly-diminished mountain of venison. He straightened his coat hems and glanced about him quickly. "There's a guest here to see you, Lady Kyleigh. I have him waiting in the library."

She sighed inwardly. It was likely just another merchant trying to get her to buy a dress. Or perhaps a curious noble here to see if the rumors were true — if Lady Kyleigh really *was* as beautiful as her manners were odd. There had actually been a few of those.

But as she rose to go deal with whoever it was, Crumfeld gripped her arm tightly — something he never did. So Kyleigh was already alert when he leaned forward and whispered:

"This man ... he is no ordinary man. He's dangerous, and my guess is that he means you great harm. Kill him quickly."

Chapter 7
The Lion and the Chandelier

Very rarely did Kyleigh ever get permission to kill someone. And she certainly never expected to get permission from Crumfeld — especially when he often complained about how difficult it was to get bloodstains out of the rugs.

So if Crumfeld was willing to risk irreparable damage to his furnishings, she knew the man waiting for her in the library must be very unsavory, indeed.

"After I present you, I'll find Shamus and have him bring the guard to your aid," Crumfeld said, straightening his collar as they arrived at the library doors. He cleared his throat and stepped stiffly inside — as if he was expecting to walk into a blast. "Lady Kyleigh to see you, sir," he said, with a great deal less than his usual pomp.

She strode past him, and he shut the door — leaving her alone with their unwanted guest.

Most of the rooms in Roost were completely unfurnished. But for whatever reason, Crumfeld had taken great care with the library. The small hearth was stoked to a blaze, the elaborate desk and its many compartments were swept clean, and every thread of the rug had been beaten free of dust. Even the lounge chair cushions were settled just so, with every stitch lined up with the pattern of the backing.

As if the room wasn't gaudy enough, he'd also taken it upon himself to hang an elaborate, gold-branched chandelier from the highest point of the ceiling.

It was all a bit unnecessary, in Kyleigh's opinion. The library should've been about books and little else. Towering shelves lined the whole room like walls but — to Crumfeld's constant dismay — they went mostly bare.

When she'd suggested that he fill them himself, his face had gone rather longer than usual. "You are the Lady of Copperdock," he'd scolded her. "The library should be your sanctuary. It is *your* duty to fill them as you please."

There were few things that exhausted Kyleigh more than reading. So if Crumfeld was waiting for *her* to gather books, he might have a several hundred years to wait.

She glanced about the room, and it didn't take her long to spot the man who'd managed to get Crumfeld's kerchief in a knot.

He was bent over behind the desk, inspecting the library's one tiny collection of books. He wore a stained tunic and breeches that were far too large — both sopping wet from the rain. His dark hair stood on end, as if he'd slung his head about to dry it. His feet were bare and caked in mud. She could see clearly where he'd roamed about the room, leaving filthy footprints across the stone and rug in his wake.

Well, no wonder Crumfeld was cross.

Kyleigh took a step towards him. "Can I help you?"

"An interesting collection, you have here." His voice was light, and the way he growled made it sound strange — almost like a purr. "I don't know all of the words," he continued, tracing one finger against the nearest spine, "but I think I know this one: *dragon*. And here it is again — *dragon*. Every book seems to have it. How interesting."

Kyleigh stopped. "Yes, I'm something of a collector," she said, more cautiously. She didn't like the direction this was heading, and her hand wandered closer to Harbinger.

Fortunately for him, the man turned slowly.

He was younger than she'd expected him to be — perhaps only a little older than Mandy. His skin was tanned like leather. His face was clean-shaven and his nose was straight. There was a considerable amount of arrogance behind his smirk. And his eyes ...

Wait — she knew those eyes.

Kyleigh took an involuntary step forward, squinting for a better look. The man's eyes were a deep, golden brown. They took in the firelight and somehow managed to mute it.

There was an unnatural focus in them, and a deadly sense of play. He watched her as if he had a hand about her throat — as if he were squeezing out her last breath and at the same time, trying to calm her struggling. As if she might as well just lie still, and accept the fact that there was nothing she could do to stop him.

Oh, yes. She most definitely knew those eyes.

"What are you doing in my territory, cat?"

He smirked as she stepped towards him. "Merely following some rumors ... I've come all the way from the Unforgivable Mountains, you know."

"Have you?"

"Oh, yes." He stepped to the side, dragging his feet obnoxiously against the rug as he went. "The birds have been growing ever more insolent. They've returned from their winters with fat bellies, and with their beaks full of tales. They claim that there is a beast in the Kingdom more fearsome than I."

"Only one?" Kyleigh quipped, and she was rewarded with a snarl.

"There is none greater," he growled, stopping his pace. He glared at her from under the lengths of his hair. "I make my home in the mountains when others would flee. I am the greatest beast in these lands ... and I've traveled all this way to prove it."

Quite suddenly, his clothes ripped apart and a blur of brown burst from the remains. She spun to the side and felt him whoosh past her, heard claws scrape against the stone floor — and when she turned, a full-grown mountain lion glared back at her.

He paced beside her, weighing her. Watching her. His powerful limbs curled beneath him, his tail flicked to the side. A purring growl came from deep within his throat. And then he lunged.

Kyleigh ducked under his grasping claws and rolled swiftly to the side, popping back onto her feet. The lion hit the front of the desk hard. He dug into its shining top to keep from flipping over. She grimaced as the wood screeched and splintered under his claws.

Crumfeld wouldn't be pleased about that.

The lion could only slow his fall — he couldn't stop it. His body fell behind the desk and for a moment, the room went eerily silent. But Kyleigh knew their game wasn't finished just yet. She kept her hands loose and slid one foot behind her for balance. The muscles in her back bunched up at her shoulders. She held her breath, tensed and waiting.

When the lion burst from his cover in a blur of teeth and claws, she was ready for him.

Taking her second shape was like stepping through a door, or cracking a joint: it took less than half a moment. She felt herself slide into her dragon skin and grinned when she saw terror widen the lion's eyes.

The scent of his fear filled her nostrils. Something like a hunger rumbled inside her lungs, and Kyleigh became too focused on her prey to remember not to cause a mess. She reared back; her horns scraped the top of the ceiling. Her wings unfurled as far as they could, crushing up against the shelves. A lounge chair sailed to the other end of the room as she snapped her tail about her.

The lion tried to change directions in mid-leap. His body twisted to the side and his limbs flailed madly in the open air. But try as he might, he couldn't stop himself, and he wound up crashing into the unforgiving scales of Kyleigh's stomach.

No sooner had he flopped to the ground than he tried to dash away, but she caught his tail in one of her massive foreclaws. Then she began dragging him towards her, slowly.

He hissed and slapped her arms with his claws. The blows he landed would've torn the hide off a full-grown deer, but Kyleigh hardly felt them. When the lion's claws glanced harmlessly off her scales, he began to wriggle desperately. Kyleigh tightened her grip and brought him to her face, holding him up by his tail.

She'd never liked cats. They were arrogant, spiteful creatures who claimed loyalty to no one but themselves. Cats preferred to crouch in the brush instead of meeting their prey outright. They went after young things, sickly things, and they had no respect at all for territory.

This cat was no exception. When he realized that his claws were useless, he roared defiantly in her face. And Kyleigh couldn't help it: she roared back.

He squirmed as her voice shook the room. The crystals of the chandelier tinkled as the deep tones made them quiver on their fastenings. She flung the lion away by his tail, and he struck the bookshelves hard. His body went limp as he fell behind the desk.

Kyleigh thought she'd accidentally killed him. And in her disappointment, she dropped back on all fours.

Her horns got caught up in the chandelier. Dust fell across her snout as it ripped from its fastenings, and she couldn't save it: the great, golden decoration crashed to the ground. The crystals shattered and went flying in every direction, spraying across the room like droplets of water.

Kyleigh hardly had a chance to groan before a voice cried out: "Enough! I yield!"

The cat wasn't dead at all: he was back in his human form, crouching behind the toppled desk. His eyes peeked out at her from over the top of it — the rest of him was hidden. "Mercy," he said, as he tried to rise. But he stopped and swayed, paling a bit as he gripped the top of his head.

Kyleigh arched her back. Her bones creaked a bit as they shrank, and her skin tingled as it slid back into place. The change always made her feel a little unsteady for a moment, as if she was returning right-side up after having gazed at the world upside down. But she'd had a lot of practice, and it only took a moment to get used to her human gait.

Her boots kicked up sharp bits of crystal as she strode to the front of the desk. Her fingers curled at her sides when she smelled the fresh blood that stained the cat's hair. There was a part of her that wanted to kill him, and the scent of his blood made it swell dangerously in her chest.

Half of her clamored for his death — and it *was* always rather satisfying to stomp on the head of an enemy. But that was an animal thing to do. And Kyleigh had been trying hard to live more like a human, which meant that she couldn't give in to her animal desires. No, she would deal with the lion in proper human fashion.

"Why should I offer you mercy?" she said, her voice low. "You've crossed into my territory without permission, entered my den without asking. You came here to kill me —"

"No, that isn't why I've come." He gripped the front of the desk and leaned forward. "I wasn't trying to kill you: I was testing you."

Kyleigh laughed. She'd almost forgotten how sly cats could be — especially when they were beaten. "Testing me, hmm? Then tell me: how did it go? Did you find your tail-lashing satisfactory ... or shall we continue?"

A playful smirk bent his lips. "You didn't defeat me. I just needed to make sure you were strong enough to serve my purpose." He leaned back and pointed his chin at her. "The birds called you a great white serpent ... but I can see now that you are much more. You are a dragoness."

"Really brilliant. What gave me away?"

He seemed confused for half a second, then he laughed. "You've spent too much time around the humans," he purred. "Methinks you're turning into one."

Kyleigh frowned. Now that they stood only a few paces apart, she got a better look at his eyes. There were none of the softening lines she found in human eyes, none of the thought or emotion. They were completely untamed — as untouched as the wildest corner of the Kingdom ... and as unforgiving as stone.

Now she understood why she wanted to kill him so badly: there was no human left in him.

"What happened to the boy?" she demanded.

The cat bared his teeth in a grin. "He was weak, dragoness. He entered the battle far too young, and I defeated him easily."

Kyleigh clenched her fists tightly, but managed to keep the anger off her face.

The magic required to become a shapechanger was particularly dangerous. After all, binding two souls into one body was no common spell: it required an offering of blood, and a ritual. And sometimes things went horribly wrong.

Only one soul could have control over their shapes, and if a man's soul wasn't strong enough to control the animal, then the animal would control *him*. Kyleigh was a woman who just happened to be able to take the shape of a dragon.

But this was a lion masquerading as a man.

"I'll admit that I did like one thing about the human: his name," the cat went on, smirking at the disgust on Kyleigh's face. "*Silas*. It's regal, don't you think? I took it for myself as a sort of ... tribute."

Though she found his smirk undeniably annoying, his confession made her think. "Silas?"

He nodded.

"You've given yourself a name?" When he nodded again, she crossed her arms. "That's odd. I thought you great cats didn't give yourselves names. I thought you just relied on your stench —"

"The name is for your benefit, not mine," Silas growled. "Every beast in the mountains knows me by my scent. You are unfamiliar with it."

"Still, it seems rather ... human, of you."

His upper lip pulled back threateningly over his teeth. "Humanity is weakness, dragoness. And you'll find no weakness in me."

Kyleigh wasn't convinced. She thought Silas might've been a little more human than he let on — which wasn't all that surprising, really. Cats tended to keep their pride in the most ridiculous places.

"I haven't traveled all this way to chatter with you," he murmured. His lip fell back and haughtiness smoothed his features once again. "It is a small matter, but —"

"Stop. Cover up."

He'd begun to slink out from behind the desk, and his clothes still lay in a mangled heap on the other side of the room. Kyleigh had no wish to see him naked.

Silas smirked at her. "My, my ... we *are* human, aren't we?" But he reached behind him and ripped a curtain off the window without a fuss. He fastened it around his waist as he spoke. "Humans are actually the reason I've come. They've been invading my mountains, and I want them gone."

"Humans have always lived in the mountains," Kyleigh said, narrowing her eyes.

Silas inclined his head. "True, but not quite like this. There is a vast gathering of swordbearers — all wearing a wolf upon their chests. And they've brought magic with them."

"Then they won't last long."

There was a force in the Unforgivable Mountains that bent its will against magic. Kyleigh had spent years wandering through the mountains — searching for a name she couldn't remember, bound by a task she couldn't forget. The rocks had sharpened themselves against her steps. She'd felt a mumbled warning in every breath of biting cold, and through the haunting, starless nights.

The magic in her blood quaked against the mountains' spirit, and it had taken every ounce of her courage to stay put. She knew without a doubt that she hadn't been welcome.

Silas's smirk disappeared, and his face turned serious. "I thought so, as well. But it's as if these shamans are imprisoned. I get close to them, sometimes." He smirked and looked to the window. His nose twitched as the rain pattered against it. "I can smell the fear on them, dragoness. I know they wish to flee, and yet ... they do not. What is it that keeps them bound to the swordbearers? I do not know." He turned from the window and fixed her with a defiant glare. "But their spells have left wounds on the land that will take lifetimes to heal. They've carved a great path from the bottom, and everyday it creeps skyward. It won't be long before they reach the summit."

This was the most troubling news Kyleigh had heard all season. She'd underestimated Titus, then. She thought the Earl of the Unforgivable Mountains would march just high enough to chase her down. Once she was gone, she thought he'd leave.

In all her years of hiding, she must've forgotten just how focused Titus could be. He wasn't content to stop halfway up: he wanted all of it. And it sounded as if he was using his slavemages to clear the way.

"They've stolen my hunting grounds, dragoness," Silas continued, breaking her from her thoughts.

When he stepped out from behind the desk, she couldn't even enjoy how ridiculous he looked with a flower-patterned curtain wrapped around his waist. She was far too concerned with darker things.

"What does this have to do with me?"

"Well, I don't *need* your help," he said with a shrug, half-turning from her. "However, as your strength would make things easier for me, I'm willing to offer you a place as my companion — but only until we have the mountains cleared out."

Kyleigh snorted. "Your companionship is hardly a prize. In fact, I think I'd rather have my —"

"Fine," he snarled, turning. "Help me chase the swordbearers off my lands, and I'll grant you a favor in return."

She didn't think a cat would be much use to her under any circumstances. "I can't help you."

He clenched his fists at his side — glaring like a child denied sweets after dinner. "Why not? My terms are fair enough, even for a human!"

"Your terms aren't the problem," Kyleigh said testily. "I haven't got the time to help you. I'm afraid I've got another task on my plate."

"What task?"

"It doesn't matter. All you need to know is that I'm far too busy —"

"Arrr!"

The library doors slammed open and Shamus burst through, followed closely by a small company of men. They brandished their swords and looked furious enough to go to war as they charged. But their boots skidded to a halt when they saw the ravaged state of the library.

In the silence of their shock, Kyleigh heard the sound of footsteps approaching — practiced and swift. She hardly had a chance to groan before Crumfeld stepped into the room.

"My lady! I've brought reinforce ..."

His words died. The silver candlestick he'd been wielding like a club slipped out of his hands and clunked to the floor. He saw the lounge chair first, broken and lying in a mangled heap with the stuffing spilled out of the cushions, and his mouth fell open. His eyes widened to take in the overturned desk, with its polished top all scuffed and scratched. He let out an indignant gasp when he spotted the curtain wrapped around Silas's waist.

But then he saw the chandelier ... and his shock sent him stumbling backwards.

"What — why?" he squeaked, slapping a hand to the side of his long face.

Kyleigh took a deep breath. "Things got a bit out of hand —"

"A bit?" he bellowed, his eyes wild. "A *bit?* Just — just look at what you've done! That chandelier took weeks to arrive!"

"Yes, I'm aware —"

"Well, are you *aware* that it was a special order from the desert? Or that the crystals were carved by hand to be perfectly equal in size and weight?"

"No, but —"

"But *what?*" he shrilled. He took a few stiff steps towards her, and Kyleigh leaned back. She'd never seen Crumfeld come so thoroughly unhinged. It was quite a fearsome thing to behold.

"Grab him, lads," Shamus said, and two guards wrangled Crumfeld by the shoulders. "Take him to his

92

chambers and have one of the kitchen ladies bring him up a stiff tankard of ale." Crumfeld slumped in their hold, shaking his head and muttering nonsense to himself, and Shamus frowned. "On second thought — make it a flagon."

When they'd dragged him away, Shamus's eyes flicked around the room again. He whistled. "If you don't mind me asking — what exactly *did* happen, here?" He glanced at Silas. "And what are you doing with a half-naked fellow in the library?"

Silas waved his hand. "It's not nearly as exciting as you think. Just a small tussle."

"Small, eh?"

"Yes. She's lucky I wasn't better prepared."

Kyleigh glared at him. "You're lucky I'm in a merciful mood." She turned to Shamus — who looked as if he was struggling to follow a foreign language. "Find our guest some accommodations for the night, will you? Someplace with holes in the roof, preferably. He's very fond of the rain."

"That won't be necessary," Silas murmured, sidling up to her. "I think I'll be quite comfortable in the stables."

Kyleigh narrowed her eyes at him. "Absolutely not."

"Why?"

"You'll spook the horses."

He was the picture of innocence. "My dear drag — ah, human female," he amended, with a quick glance at Shamus, "you insult me. I would never eat a fence animal. They're much too fattening."

She rolled her eyes. "Shamus — holes in the roof, puddles on the floor, and a lock on the door. You are to be gone by morning's light," she added to Silas, making her voice severe. "And if I catch one whiff of your stinking hide in my territory again, I'll wear your skin for a cape."

"As you wish," he said with a mocking bow. He was still grinning when the guards hauled him away.

****

93

They left before the sun. Kyleigh led Jake through the winding halls and across the courtyard with ease. It was the breath between shifts when the guards weren't at their posts, and so there was nothing but the fading braziers to see them off. Kyleigh hoped Shamus wouldn't flog the men too badly for letting her slip out unnoticed — she *did* have a rather unfair advantage.

They made it to the front gates without incident, and Kyleigh rapped Knotter awake.

"Mmm, what? What is it?" he murmured groggily. His wooded eyes creaked open and he frowned when he saw Jake. "Oh hello, father. Come to try and disenchant me again?"

Jake reddened — as he always did when Knotter mocked him. "Just open the latch, you stupid apparition."

Knotter's eyes widened when he saw Kyleigh in full armor. "Why? Are we under attack? Should I sound the alarm —?"

"No," Jake hissed, gripping his staff. "Can't you see we're trying to slip out quietly?"

Knotter's mouth bent into an obnoxious smile. "Ah, so it's finally official between you two, is it?"

"Open, or I swear I'll burn you to ashes," Kyleigh growled. Her ears twitched, straining over the sounds of the morning to pick up the muffled chatter in the distance. A new round of guards had approached the castle doors.

"Fine," Knotter said. He swung open just widely enough for them to squeeze through.

Kyleigh paused, an idea suddenly came to her. "When Shamus realizes that we've gone, he's going to send men out to find us." She glanced up at Knotter. "Any chance you might be able to jam yourself for a few hours?"

A look of delight crossed his face for half a moment, then it quickly faded into a frown. "Wait — is this some sort of test? Are you trying to trick me into jamming, just so you'll have an excuse to torch me? Because if you are —"

"It's not a trick — it's an order," Kyleigh said quickly, her eyes on the castle doors. She heard the soft clink of the latch sliding upwards. "I need you to jam so we'll have a chance to escape — and you're not to tell them anything, understood? Just slip back into your knot and keep your mouth shut."

He huffed. "Well, I don't relish playing the common bump —"

"But you'll do it anyways."

He gasped when Kyleigh kicked him shut.

She led Jake off the road and through the empty forests around the village. There was a ship waiting for them along a stretch of beach a few miles outside of town, and she'd promised the captain that they'd be there by dawn. But Jake was dragging his feet.

"Am I going to have to carry you?" she barked at him.

He let out a heavy sigh and jogged up even with her. His pack bounced and rattled with his run. "No ..."

"Stop moping."

"I'm not moping —"

"You are, and I won't stand for it. Your spell worked exactly like we needed it to: the canteens don't weigh us down at all."

Jake reached behind him, snatched a fistful of what appeared to be thin air, and shook it in her face. The sounds of sloshing water came from the empty space between his curled fingers. "No, not *exactly* — they've turned invisible!"

"Well, we'll just have to be careful not to set them down anywhere," Kyleigh said distractedly. She slowed for a moment and sniffed the air. A heavy, damp scent crossed her nose. It smelled a bit like wet fur. The forest was probably rife with sopping animals, after the evening rain. So she didn't think much of it.

They walked for a few minutes more — with Jake complaining loudly that he was snugly in the running for the worst mage of all time — before she smelled something she recognized:

It was the scent of pine ... and annoyance.

"Stop." She grabbed Jake by his pack and glared pointedly at a boulder up the path. "I thought I warned you to stay out of my territory, cat."

And just as she'd suspected, a tawny mountain lion sprang from his cover and landed gracefully atop the boulder.

Jake let out a sharp hiss of air and aimed his staff between the lion's eyes, but Kyleigh grabbed his wrist. "Believe me — he isn't worth the spell."

After he cleaned one of his massive paws for a moment, the lion dropped down behind the boulder. A second later, Silas's head and shoulders popped into view.

"Kingdom's name," Jake sputtered, with a glance at Kyleigh. "There're more of you?"

"More than you realize, shaman," Silas said lazily.

"Shaman?"

"It's what the shapechangers call their mages," Kyleigh said quickly. Then she turned her glare on Silas. "I'm going to think carefully about where to mount your head —"

"I'm not in your territory anymore, dragoness," he said, flicking his hair away from his glowing eyes. "I stopped smelling your scent a mile or so outside of the den. And you would do well not to threaten me, since I have decided to go out of my way to help you."

She snorted. "Unless you plan to fling yourself off a cliff, I can't see how you're going to help me."

"Ah, you can't see it *yet*," he said, smirking. "But you know as well as I that when Fate brings two paths to forge, we must be content to walk together. We must travel through the dark of the unplanned ... until Fate sheds her purpose upon us in glorious morning."

"I didn't know you lions were so poetic," Jake said. He sounded rather impressed.

Silas bared his white teeth in a grin. "How do you think I woo my mates? The females of my species are fond of pretty words — especially when the words shine light upon their beauty." He turned the full, haughty force of his eyes on Kyleigh. "So what say you, dragoness? Will you fight the path Fate has set you on ... or will you embrace me?"

Kyleigh had absolutely no intention of embracing him, and she growled at the thought. Still ... she knew they couldn't lose him — not at Jake's pace. Even if she told him he couldn't come, Silas would follow them anyways. But there was a fair chance that he'd turn on his tail the minute they reached the desert, anyways.

With all that fur, he wouldn't take well to the heat.

"All right, then." She turned to hide her smile and said: "Jake? Give him a pair of your clothes. It won't help us stay hidden if we have a naked man following along behind us."

Chapter 8
Gilderick the Gruesome

Kael was determined to keep his powers a secret. He was so much scrawnier than the giants that he knew it would only raise suspicions if he were able to keep up with them. He had to find someway to seem weaker ... but how?

As they dragged the plow down the field, he could feel Declan watching him. He may have been a great deal quieter than Brend, but his eyes never stopped roving: they watched from the deep cleft in his brow, hiding his thoughts in shadow. There was probably very little Declan didn't see.

So while Kael kept half of his concentration on pulling, he dug through his memory with the other half — trying to figure out a way to throw Declan off his trail.

He remembered the long, darks days of winter all too well. They'd seemed to stretch endlessly: every minute became an hour, and every hour became a day. He might've gone mad just watching the sun creep its way across the sky, had it not been for Morris.

The old helmsman must've sensed how his chest ached, because he filled Kael's days with as much training as possible. Morris taught him all sorts of different crafts, like sewing and drawing, and how to carve shapes from stone and wood. Kael's head was so packed full of information that he feared he wouldn't be able to remember it all. But now, just when he needed it, one of the lessons came back to him.

"Using your mind is all well and good — if you're only facing a scuffle or skirmish, that is," Morris had said one day. "But what if you ever found yourself in the middle of a real battle, eh? What if you were trapped, and had to fight for hours on end? You think your mind could last that long?"

Kael remembered shaking his head — reluctantly, because he knew how Morris would gloat.

"'Course it wouldn't! And you can't get a headache and go passing out in the middle of a battle — you wouldn't wake to rise! No, once your head gives up, you'll have no choice but to rely on your body for strength. Which is why we need to get those skinny little limbs of yours into shape."

So Kael had spent the better part of his afternoon hauling bags of sand from the shoreline, all the way up the hill to Gravy's mansion. He wasn't allowed to use his mind — and in order to keep him from cheating, Morris made him recite passages from songs and books while he walked.

It worked. Kael was so busy concentrating on which words came next that his body was left to fend for itself. He hadn't realized how often he'd been relying on his mind for strength. He supposed he'd been relying on it his entire life, because he hardly made it three trips before his legs turned to jelly and he collapsed.

But he wasn't discouraged. Knowing his weakness only made him want to work all the harder. The day might come when he needed strength, and he intended to have it.

Today, however, was a day when his weakness might serve him well. Kael started out small, letting the first few lines of the *Ballad of Sam Gravy* ring in his head. While he concentrated on remembering the words and the different changes in notes, his legs were left to walk on their own.

He could feel the plow's weight in every cord of muscle, in every quivering string of sinew. His boots slipped backwards and he dug his toes into the earth, pounding footholds out at every step. When the earth hardened, the blade got stuck. It jerked Kael and Declan backwards on their harnesses. They gathered their breath for a moment, and then they lunged forward — throwing their bodies against the plow until the blade popped free.

It was slow, backbreaking work. Kael lost track of how many lines they scraped. At one point, he felt the straps of the harness biting into his shoulders — gnawing with a thousand tiny teeth at his raw flesh. But he knew he couldn't stop.

Instead, he lunged forward with a determined grunt, pushing back against his pain, and his shoulders eventually went numb.

The sun blended with the sky, sweat trickled into his eyes and burned like seawater. He matched his panting breaths to Declan's. Sharp bits of earth ground their way under his fingernails, blistering them as he dragged himself stubbornly across the field.

"Supper time!" Brend called.

Kael didn't hear him. He tried to take several steps before he realized that he wasn't moving: Declan had a firm grip on his harness, holding him back with one hand.

"The day's finished, rat," he said. "You'll have to wait till tomorrow for more pulling."

Brend let out a bark of laughter — so sharp that it scared a flock of birds out of a nearby tree. They swooped in a disheveled crowd, squawking angrily to one another before they finally returned to their roost.

The giants ambled back towards the barns, with Brend talking loudly and Declan throwing in a *yeh* every few steps. Kael knew he should follow them, but he was afraid to take his harness off.

The leather was plastered very firmly onto his shirt, held there by thick layers of sweat and raw flesh. He decided it would only hurt worse if he dragged it out, so he pulled the harness off quickly — and grimaced when he felt a good bit of skin come off with it.

Kael's legs shook so badly that he could hardly stand still without falling over. The work had drained him of his muscles, his bones — everything. He felt like all that was left of him was an empty sack of pale skin.

With no small amount of effort, he urged himself into a walk. He followed the giants at the wobbling pace of a fawn, and it wasn't long before they outdistanced him.

The Red Spine had begun creeping in the deeper they got into Gilderick's realm. Now the closest mountains were only a little over a mile away. Sunlight brushed across their rifts, creating a pattern of red and shadow. The protruding cliffs caught the light and rent the orange and yellows, casting them along the waves of the stone. At a glance, the whole Spine looked like a wall of slow-moving flame.

It was so stunning that Kael was tempted to pause and watch it for a moment. But then he remembered what Dred's men had said about the lions, and he thought better of it.

By the time he arrived at the barns, most of the giants were already inside. A few loitered around the water troughs, taking long gulps and splashing the grime from their faces. Kael found a spot that wasn't too crowded and went to get a drink.

Dirt layered the bottom of the trough. It swirled around his hands as he scooped up a mouthful of water. It was warm, and little bits of sand stuck between his teeth as he swallowed, but that didn't stop him from gulping down several handfuls.

He was completely filthy. He stared at his rippling reflection for a moment and thought he could see a small trace of a mountain boy hidden beneath the dirt, but he wasn't sure. If he hadn't been able to feel it, he didn't think he could've found his nose.

In the end, he decided it might be best if he didn't wash. He remembered the welts that had risen on the giants' faces when Finks struck them. If he were ever struck on his bare skin, the lack of welts would only raise more suspicions. He thought a layer of dirt might help to hide it.

"Still alive, rat?"

Kael choked on his water. He hadn't been expecting a blast of Finks's rank breath. He was actually grateful when the water clogged his nose.

"Well, we'll have to do something about that." Finks grabbed the back of his hair and thrust his face into the trough.

Kael gasped — and a huge lungful of water rushed in.

Icy terror gripped him. His limbs froze as memories of the tempest rose up in his head. He swore he could feel the briny water swirling about him, sucking him downwards. The impossible weight of the ocean pushed on him, crushing him. He couldn't breathe, he couldn't breathe, he couldn't ...

Finks's voice shrilled inside his head: "I didn't even hold him down that long! The little rat just fainted."

The sharp toe of a boot jabbed against Kael's ribs. "Up, you!" another familiar voice said. Kael blinked back the heavy darkness and Hob's pinched face came blurrily into focus. He didn't look pleased. "You're lucky he's not dead," Hob snapped around his chew. "Gilderick would skin you alive if you cost us another one."

He spat, and the brownish spittle landed a hand's breadth from Kael's face.

"Back inside, beasts!" Hob lashed out in the direction of the barn — where several giants had been craning their necks around the door to watch. They popped back inside, and Kael thought he saw Brend's spiky hair among them.

Finks waited until Hob had stomped out of earshot before he put his boot in the middle of Kael's chest. "Well played, rodent," he hissed. Though fury burned his eyes, he broke out into an unsettling grin. "That's the second time you've bested me today."

Kael knew what he was talking about. At an hour before sunset, Finks had marched over to their field. Hob followed along behind him — a sinister-looking, many-headed whip clutched in his hand. Kael swore he saw sharp bits of metal glinting along the cords.

But Finks's serpent-like smile had begun to fade back the closer he got to their field. By the time he drew even with the plow, his mouth hung open in shock.

"Impossible!" he sputtered. He jogged along the field lines, looking for mistakes, and Hob grew cross.

"What? Did you drag me the whole way out here to gloat?" he fumed, thrusting a hand at their work. "So you're a few fields ahead of schedule — good for you. Waste my time again, and it'll be *you* that gets the whipping." Hob spat out a large clump of his chew on Finks's boot before he'd trudged away.

Now, Finks must've still been angry about the fact that there hadn't been a flogging. His boot pressed down harder, and Kael's shirt buttons dug uncomfortably into his chest.

"You think you're so clever, don't you? Well, mountain rats may be hardy little beasts, but we mages hold all the power. *I* am your master. And the next round," Finks warned, "will be mine."

He removed his boot and Kael got hastily to his feet — well, as hastily as he could with his sore limbs. He didn't trust himself to be able to take Finks's foul breath much longer: he'd lost control once before, because the smell of magic had driven him mad. And he didn't think tearing Finks limb from limb would help keep him hidden.

"Oh, and I feel I ought to warn you," Finks shouted as he jogged away. "You'll want to be *inside* the stalls, after the light dims. Horrible things happen to little beasts who don't make it into their cages in time."

Kael had no idea what that meant and frankly, he didn't care. If the stalls were where they kept the beds, he'd be there just as soon as he could.

The inside of the barn was much larger than he'd expected it to be. A wide aisle of packed earth split the barn down the middle, and a row of stalls lined it on both sides. Doors made of iron sheets stood to the side of each stall. They were nearly as wide as they were tall, but he imagined the giants' heads could still clear them.

A long trough had been set up in the middle of the aisle — stretching almost the length of the barn. From the way it bowed and waved in places, Kael guessed that it was the hammered-together product of several smaller troughs. As he got closer, he could see the weld marks clearly.

Someone made a loud, gasping sound, and Kael looked up instinctively. He wished he hadn't.

Brend had obviously been reenacting the incident with Finks. He rose from the trough with a gasp, his face plastered in whatever lumpy, porridge-like substance the giants had been eating. His mouth gaped open as he scrabbled at his throat. Then with a loud *thump* and a puff of dirt, he collapsed — his limbs sprawled out in every direction.

The giants behaved as if this was the most hilarious thing they'd ever seen. They laughed uproariously and slapped their meaty hands together. Several turned to sneer at Kael.

Had he been less exhausted, he might've been bothered by it. But as it was, there were only two things in the whole Kingdom that concerned him: the aching of his legs, and the rumbling of his stomach.

When Kael walked by, Brend made a show of twitching his limbs — flinging them about like a man in his death throes. His antics brought on another round of bellowing laughter, but Kael didn't even glance up.

He wandered the length of the trough, looking for a space between the giants' hulking shoulders where he might be able to slip in and get something to eat. At the very middle of the trough, he spotted a man-sized gap.

The space left a clear divide between two groups of giants: those on Brend's side talked loudly to each other as they scooped handfuls of porridge into their mouths, but the giants on the other side were far less social. Not a word passed between them — and that was probably because they had their heads buried in their food. They lapped at the porridge like dogs, coming up only to take breaths.

Kael squeezed into the gap — ignoring the looks he got from Brend's side of the trough — and brought a scoop of porridge to his mouth. It was grayish, lukewarm and slimy. But it didn't smell too horrible. He stuck his tongue out and took one apprehensive taste.

There were several different flavors mixed into the porridge. He chewed the lumps he came across and thought he tasted potato. There were some carrots, too. And a meat that he thought might've been pork — though it wasn't the thick, fatty cuts he'd enjoyed at Gravy Bay. They tasted suspiciously like the bits that most cooks tossed out.

Kael tried not to think about this as he swallowed. Instead, he convinced himself that the porridge was nothing more than a mushy helping of Tinnarkian stew.

He'd finished two handfuls and was going in for a third when a monstrous hand clamped over his wrist. By this point, Kael was entirely fed up. The giants could make fun of him all they wanted to, but if they tried to stop him from eating — well, that was going to be a problem.

When he looked up to say as much, the icy words died on his lips.

This giant was not like the others. Porridge ringed his mouth, dribbling from his lips and down his neck, where it crusted onto the collar of his ragged shirt. His skin was so filthy that his hair had actually begun to yellow. But the worst part, by far, were his eyes.

They were a stark, milky white — like the eyes of a man who'd been dead for a while. They hung still in their sockets; they didn't rove over Kael or even narrow in warning. So he was rather shocked when he was suddenly thrown to the ground.

"Argh!"

The giant bellowed as he stood over Kael. He seemed to be trying to speak, but his tongue rolled uselessly inside his gaping mouth. Finally, he seemed to give up on speaking and instead, raised his huge foot over Kael's head.

His meaning couldn't have been clearer.

Kael forgot about his aching bones and rolled madly to the side. He swore he could feel the earth shake as the giant's foot came down. He'd narrowly missed being crushed to death, and he realized that this wasn't a battle he was going to win. So he scrambled to his feet and tried to make a dash for the nearest stall — but the giant grabbed him by the shoulders.

With his arms pinned to his side, Kael had no choice but to fight dirty. He swung his leg up and caught the giant between the legs. It was a move he'd learned from Aerilyn — and one that had so far proven itself to be effective against men of all sizes. But even though his boot struck true, the giant didn't release him. He *did* stop roaring for a moment, and his dead eyes blinked slowly.

But in the end, the blow only seemed to make him angrier.

One of the giant's hands wrapped around his throat, and Kael's feet left the ground. He grabbed the giant's wrists, trying to hoist himself up and take the strain off of his neck. His legs kicked out wildly, his boots struck the thick meat of the giant's chest and stomach, but did nothing to stop him. If anything, he only squeezed harder.

There was no emotion in the dead whites of the giant's eyes — mercy least of all. Kael knew that if he didn't think of something quickly, he'd be killed. No one rushed to his aid. Not even Brend or Declan rose to help him.

Starbursts of black exploded across his eyes as the giant's grip tightened. He only had a precious few seconds of consciousness left. The giant raised Kael higher, lifting him until he could see the top of his yellowed head — and it gave him an idea.

He took his arms off the giant's wrists and balled his hands into a single fist. In his mind, he saw a mountain boulder. He clung to the image, remembering the smooth, unforgiving texture and the impossible weight. As he concentrated, he watched as his hands began to change: his fingers grayed, he could see cracks and crevices breaking out across his skin as his fist became like stone. His arms shook violently under the weight until he could no longer hold them.

His fists came down, and the giant released him.

Kael landed flat on his back. The wind left his lungs and he clutched his throat, feeling for any lasting damage. Fortunately, there was none — and for one brief second, he was relieved. Then he heard a groan from above him and looked up in time to see the giant lose his footing.

He swayed back and forth on his heels, his mouth open and listless. A stream of scarlet trickled from the top of his head and down his nose. His eyes rolled back, and then he fell.

It took the last of Kael's strength to roll backwards. The giant's head clipped the heel of his boot, but he managed to save himself from being crushed to death.

He lay on his back for a moment, massaging his sore throat and easing little breaths of air back into his lungs. He was none-too-pleased when Brend's face popped into view.

"Would you look at that?" he bellowed, rattling Kael's ears. "The wee rat's still got a bit of life left in him." He glanced towards the fallen giant. "Ah, the same can't be said for poor Casey."

"At least he'll finally be at rest now, poor soul," one of the giants said, and there was a murmur of agreement from the others.

Brend nodded slowly. He seemed about to say something else when the light in the barn suddenly dimmed. The fires of the torches shrank back, as if they'd been battered by a stiff wind. Then came a rumble of hurried footsteps.

"Grab his clothes, Brend!"

"All right."

Even though he was near to passing out, Kael still had the presence of mind to clutch his shirt tightly. He couldn't let the giants see his whisperer's mark.

Brend chuckled as he stepped over Kael to get to the dead giant. "Oh, your wee trousers wouldn't cover much."

Kael heard a ripping sound as Brend relieved Casey of his clothing. Then he headed for the stalls, nudging Kael with his foot as he passed.

"I'd get moving, were I you — you don't want to go all crispy."

That was the last thing Kael needed. He struggled to his feet, the world spinning around him. He'd just gotten his footing when the stall doors began to close.

They moved of their own accord, screeching down the rusted iron bars that served as their tracks. The taint of magic filled the room like a cloud. Kael managed to take a few steps before the smell finally overcame him. He fell on hands and knees, heaving against the horrible smell and at the same time, fighting to keep his dinner down.

He crawled for the nearest stall — the black opening shrank to hardly a crack as the door slid over it. He wasn't going to make it in time. There was nothing he could do.

Just when he'd resigned himself to whatever crispy fate awaited him, an arm shot out of the opening. A large hand grabbed Kael around the collar and jerked him to safety. His ankle struck the door as he was pulled through, pain shot up his leg, but he didn't care — he was safe. He looked up to see which giant had saved him, and was met by the stern face of Declan.

He watched Kael intently from the shadow over his eyes. There was a loud crackling sound out in the aisle, followed by a burst of blue light. But Declan never blinked.

"There goes Casey." Brend had been craning his neck over the stall door, watching the aisle. He shook his head as the blue light faded and dropped into a crouch. He flicked Kael's arm with the back of his hand. "Lucky for you that Declan thought to reel you in, eh?"

"Very lucky," Kael snapped back. "Especially since you left me to die."

There was a mocking edge to the hurt on Brend's face. "I thought you were right behind me — I swear it by the plains mother." Then his mask gave way to a smile as he punched Declan in the arm. "Why'd you have to drag him in *here*? You should've flung him into one of the Fallow stalls."

Declan didn't return his smile. Suspicion lined his face, bending his mouth more deeply than before. "No," he said slowly. "I think it's best if we keep an eye on this one. He's already proved himself to be the Kingdom's most interesting rat."

"What are the Fallows?" Kael said, quickly changing the subject. When Declan didn't answer him, he turned to Brend. "The giant who attacked me — Casey ... there was something wrong with his eyes. It was almost as if he was ..."

"Dead?" Brend said as he pawed through Casey's ragged clothing. "Well, that's because he *was* dead, wee rat.

Dead up here." He tapped the side of his head. "Why do you think we call them the *Fallows*? The ground's all tilled up, but there's not a thing left growing — if you know what I mean."

Kael wasn't sure he did. All he knew was that he didn't want to wind up like Casey. "What happened to him?"

"Gilderick," Declan grunted, his shadowed face still pointed in Kael's direction. There was a murmur of agreement from the other giants in the stall. "He sucks the soul right out of them, and leaves naught but an empty husk behind."

Kael wasn't sure he believed that. It was true that the Lord of the plains had a dark reputation, but he'd never seen anything like what had happened to Casey. It didn't seem possible for a man to be dead, but his body left to wander around.

When he said as much, the giants snorted.

"Gilderick is a monster." Brend's eyes glinted with what might've been scorn or fury — Kael couldn't tell. "He waits till one of us is injured or falls ill, and then he strikes. Many a good giant has been dragged from the fields, bleeding or sick. And they never come back the same."

"We aren't even allowed to *die* in peace," Declan growled. While the rest of the giants had crowded in to listen to Brend's tale, Declan hung back. He leaned against the far wall, watching.

"Do you know how he got the name Gilderick the Gruesome?" Brend said.

When Kael shook his head, Brend leaned forward.

"Well, during the Whispering War, he served as King Banagher's chief interrogator. Whenever they caught a rebel whisperer, they'd pass him off to Gilderick. They say he had a special room in Midlan — deep down in the belly of the castle. Only Gilderick and his subjects were allowed inside. They say you could hear the screams from the upper towers." Brend paused, and the silence in the barn made the crackling of the torches sound unbearably loud. "Gilderick wore a leather apron, smeared black with blood. And there was a bloody handprint stained into his doorframe, from where he'd lean out to tell the scribes what he learned.

"Everybody says he tortured them, but no one could ever prove it," Brend whispered. His gaze swept around the room for a weighty moment, and the giants leaned in. "The rebels would stumble from the castle a few days later, not so much as a scrape or a bruise about them. Then they'd wander out into the wilderness — never to be seen or heard from again. We can't *prove* that it's him," Brend's eyes flicked back to Kael's, "but we do know this: a man is never quite the same ... after an audience with Lord Gilderick."

Kael tried to shrug Brend's tale aside — but he didn't sleep well that night.

Chapter 9
The Head of an Arrow

Countess D'Mere's eyes hovered across the last page of Aerilyn's letter, moving in a slow, brooding line. Then she folded the parchment neatly and set it aside.

Elena had arrived back at the castle shortly after sunset, and now it was only an hour before dawn. D'Mere spent the night sifting through each one of Aerilyn's rambling notes, reading between the neat lines of her writing for the clues hidden just beneath. Her search had not been in vain.

Though she'd obviously tried to be cryptic, the truth still leaked out from Aerilyn's stories — escaping into the open space that the vagueness left behind. It was what she *didn't* say that most intrigued D'Mere. And that was how she came to learn of the Duke.

... Kael managed to get us into one of Reginald's parties! Well, we weren't exactly on the guest list — but Kael's very resourceful, and he thought up a clever way to slip us in. I can't say too much here, but I will *say that we accomplished a great deal more than dancing. I know you're dying to know more, but I simply can't tell you.*

All right, I'll give you one clue: a night at the inn won't cost you twelve silvers anymore. That ought to tell you everything you need to know ...

Oh, it most certainly did. And D'Mere was happy to hear it.

"Reginald has fallen," she whispered.

She said it so quietly that a dog lying beneath her chair wouldn't have heard it. But Elena's ears were far keener — she picked up D'Mere's words from the hearth.

"You mean he's been murdered, My Countess?"

She looked up from where she'd been tracing the lines of ink, and saw Elena sitting cross-legged before the fire. She still wore the clothes she'd traveled in, though now her scarlet corset was mud-stained and the toes of her boots were scuffed. Her back was turned so that she could watch both the door and D'Mere from the corners of her eyes. But the dagger in her hand held most of her attention.

It was entirely black, from pommel to tip. While she polished one dagger with oil and cloth, its twin sat sheathed on the ground beside her — both blades were nearly as long as her forearm.

D'Mere didn't ask if she'd had to use them ... but knowing Elena, she'd probably used them anyways.

"Not murdered," D'Mere said, answering her question. "If Reginald had been killed, there would have been a war — and no doubt those gold-mongering merchants would've tried to drag us into it. No ... more than likely, he's been captured." She flipped to the first page of the letter, prepared to begin her search again. "The only *real* question is: where are they holding him?"

"Would they not have left him in the island fortress, My Countess?" Elena said after a moment. She never took her eyes off the dagger — though her polishing slowed to a less-vigorous rate. "A rock floating out in the middle of the ocean would be difficult to breach. And they likely wouldn't want to risk trying to transport him anywhere. What is it that you're always muttering about the seas men?" She looked up from her work, her dark eyes lighted on D'Mere. "Something about the weather?"

"They only set sail in fair weather," she supplied. She was half-pleased with Elena — and half-troubled. Things would have been so much ... simpler, had she been as stupid as her brothers.

"Why didn't His Majesty tell us?" Elena went on, digging herself deeper. "Surely he's heard."

"Perhaps not," D'Mere murmured.

112

The walls of Midlan had gone strangely silent; its doors were sealed tightly shut. Even her spies were having a difficult time sneaking their way in. What few letters they managed to send were filled with all sorts of troubling rumors: tales of locked doors, closed passageways, and of windows being bricked shut. All of Midlan's armies had been called back to the fortress — where they'd disappeared behind the impenetrable walls.

All across the Kingdom, the question was the same: had the King gone mad?

If so, Crevan wouldn't have been the first. So many of the past Kings had fallen into madness that many believed the throne of Midlan was cursed — riddled with the spells of some ancient enemy. They said the halls were unnaturally cold, and the dungeons were rife with ghosts. D'Mere didn't know if the stories were true ... but she didn't think any amount of gold could've tempted her to find out.

"I know Crevan. If he knew one of his rulers had fallen, he would've called his whole army out by now," D'Mere said. She stood up from her chair and crossed to the map that hung on an otherwise-vacant portion of her wall. She followed the path of the High Seas and pressed her finger against Reginald's island castle. "But I've no doubt that he'll find out eventually. And if Reginald is still alive, the merchants might use him to bargain their way out — to put an early end to the war. We certainly can't have that, can we?"

"No, My Countess. The war needs to weaken the King."

Elena spoke from directly behind her. D'Mere hadn't even heard her move. "Precisely," she said, turning casually until both the girl and the map were in her vision.

"And the battle will draw him out of Midlan," Elena added. She traced her dagger's blade excitedly. D'Mere could hear the calluses on the tips of her fingers scraping against the edge. "It seems our plan will work even better than expected, My Countess."

D'Mere smiled.

Oh, clever Elena — calm, clever, and in control. She had always been D'Mere's favorite. After all, she'd outshined her brothers in every way: in stealth, memory, and wit. And while almost anybody could learn to kill, few were born to do it.

Elena had been born a killer.

D'Mere had entrusted her with her most troubling enemies, and the way she'd dispatched them was almost ... artistic. There was never a mess, never a struggle. Elena didn't waste time trying to create a scene, as so many of the others felt it necessary to do. No, she seemed to prefer subtlety and routine best of all: the utter shock of finding someone dead, having died doing something they did nearly every day.

Rabble-rousers would often disappear on their way to the village square to protest taxes. On more than one occasion, a property owner who was unwilling to sell his lands had fallen and tragically broken his neck. Randall had been her most recent target. His servants had discovered him dead on the floor of his office. The village healers claimed it was a trauma of the heart that finally did him in, a result of his unhealthy love of smoking.

It wasn't a grandeur death — it might've happened to anybody. No, it was the *timing* that made it suspicious. It was the way these sorts of things always seemed to benefit D'Mere that got people talking. And she rather liked that about Elena. In fact, it reminded her of another resourceful young assassin she used to know ...

But her pride could only go so far before it ran into her fear. Elena was no longer a little girl. She was very much a woman, now — and her powers were growing beyond D'Mere's control.

Our plan? *Our* was such a small word, and yet it had such potential to be deadly. It was the head of an arrow; the fully formed idea was not far behind. And if Elena ever thought to put any force behind it ... well, D'Mere's days as Countess would be shortened to an arrow's flight.

No, the hour had finally come. It was time to do something about Elena.

"I have a task for you," she said. She crossed over to her desk and felt Elena following silently behind her. "Obviously, we'll need to get to Reginald before the King does. He'll sing like a lark if Midlan captures him — and we certainly can't have that."

"It will be done, My Countess."

"Good." She pulled one of her desk drawers open and began to dig inside of it. "Oh — and take Holthan with you."

Elena inhaled sharply. "Don't you trust me to do it on my own?"

"*Trust* has nothing to do with my decision," D'Mere replied curtly. "After you've taken care of the Duke, I need you to go straight to the desert — which means I'll need Holthan to bring me news of your success. It's a job for two."

"Then can't I bring the others —?"

"The others are going to stay with me. You'll take Holthan, and you'll be silent about it. Understood?"

She thought she could practically hear the grate of Elena's words as they slid between her teeth: "Yes, My Countess."

A few moments passed where the only sounds in the room were the crackling of the fire, and of D'Mere as she shuffled through her desk — though she could feel Elena seething at her back. After a fair bit of digging, D'Mere found them.

They were tucked inside a box at the back of her drawer: three flat knives. Their blades were the length of D'Mere's smallest finger, not even long enough to be considered deadly. But when she held them to the light, she could see the faint purple poison that coated their edges.

"Be very careful with these," she said, handing them over to Elena. "This is not a poison you've used before."

She held them in her left hand, fanning out their blades in a macabre bouquet. "What is it, My Countess?"

"A special remedy, for a ... special problem." She stood and took Elena by the wrists, bending her head forward in confidence. "You see, for all of our careful planning, there's one pawn we cannot control," she whispered, making sure to keep Elena's eyes locked on hers. "Aerliyn mentioned that the Dragongirl has spilt from the main party. She may have been useful to us this time — but how much longer before she comes after me? How long will it be before she tries to cast me from my throne? She is a danger to us all, for as long as she lives." D'Mere took Elena under the chin and gave her a motherly smile. "That's why I need you to travel to the desert, where I believe she intends to strike next. Find out where Dragongirl is hiding ... and remove her from the board. Will you do that for me, my dear?"

Elena's face softened considerably. Her brows, usually stuck in downward slopes, bent backwards in dutiful arcs as she nodded.

D'Mere smiled and patted her gently on the cheek. "Thank you. Now, gather whatever supplies you need and let Holthan know of his duties. I've got to write to Lord Gilderick — he'll be pleased to know that I've accepted his invitation."

Elena stopped at the doorway. "I thought you said you weren't going this year."

"Well ... I've changed my mind," D'Mere said, flipping her hair over her shoulder. "Leave now, and travel quickly."

Elena nodded, slowly. She still looked confused as she closed the door.

The moment she was gone, D'Mere could hold it in no longer. She hurried across the room and tore through the piles of letters, flinging them aside until she came to the last one. She read the final sentence Aerilyn had written, hoping against hope that she'd somehow misread it. But she hadn't:

I can't tell you where we're headed next, dear Horatio — Kael said it wouldn't be safe to tell. But I can offer you a riddle: what's the distance of the sea, and what would the opposite of lavish be?

The Endless Plains.

D'Mere's heart began to pound as she grabbed a quill and parchment. She quickly scribbled a letter to Gilderick, her hands shaking all the while. The moment she was finished, she stood. Her nightgown swept out behind her as she paced, the soles of her feet were damp against the cold stone floor.

She didn't like this sick feeling, this sort of worry. She wasn't at all used to it — and to be perfectly honest, she never thought she would have to feel it. Her mind should be focused on more important matters, after all. There were far greater things at stake than the fate of a merchant's daughter who'd wandered so foolishly into Gilderick's realm ...

And then again, there was nothing greater.

****

Dark clouds gathered over Midlan in the early afternoon. They hovered above the fortress for an hour or so, swelling as they murmured their rumbling threats to the soldiers who wandered outside the barracks. At last, the clouds seemed to run out of things to say. And for a while, the grounds were silent.

Then they opened their gullets and spewed forth such a downpour of icy rain that every man went sprinting for shelter.

Argon watched it all take place from his window. He kept his chambers high atop one of the castle's smallest towers, and from there he had quite a view of the chaos beneath him. He could even hear the rhythmic *tink* of the rain as it landed on the soldiers' ironclad heads. Even though they'd just begun their shifts, they already had to pace across the walls to stay warm. It would be a wretched watch, and though Argon certainly pitied them, they would find no mercy from the King.

With every night the Dragongirl went unfound, Crevan slipped closer to the brink of madness. He traveled his own halls with his sword drawn and ready at his hip, a torch burning in his other hand. He slept in full armor. Not one week ago, Argon heard the servants claim that the King had ordered the windows in his throne room to be covered in mortar and stone.

He ate little; he drank less. And as far as anybody knew, he hadn't stuck his head outside since autumn.

Argon sighed heavily as he watched the guards — though his frustration was not because their clothes were already soaked through, nor that many of them would likely fall ill doing a task that could have waited for the rains to cease. No ... what worried him the most was something he couldn't seem to remember.

After a few moments of frustrated pacing, a shadow crossed over his window. He looked up in time to see the flutter of a sparrow as he rushed to find someplace dry to land.

Ah, now Argon remembered.

His ears were not as sharp as they'd once been, but he could still hear the many voices of the young mages who were camped inside his tower. With the King's mind weakening, the curse on their shackles began to wane. Crevan's orders didn't carry the weight they once had, and the young mages had taken the opportunity to wander from their rooms.

They loved to spend their days among Argon's books and instruments: studying, experimenting, and generally making a mess of things. Though there were far more char marks on his walls than there had been before, it made him happy to listen to their tittering. The young ones were often a danger to themselves, if they didn't get the proper training.

And speaking of the young ones — he'd promised to read something for them. *That's* what he'd been doing, before the vision struck him. He'd been leaning over his desk, his nose buried in a rather peculiar book.

One of the young mages had brought it to his office, claiming that he'd found it buried among the tomes in the King's library. He'd been afraid to open it, however: for some reason, he seemed to think it might be hexed.

Argon searched the tattered cover twice over for spells, but hadn't found anything amiss. The longer he studied it, the more curious he became, and it wasn't long before he'd decided to open it and read it for himself. This proved to be a more difficult task than he'd ever expect.

The book was old, and its pages were unusually thick. Most of the writing was faded to the point that it'd almost disappeared — but that wasn't why Argon was having a difficult time reading it.

No ... there was something odd about this book. It seemed like every time he sat down to read it, something happened to interrupt him: a knock at the door, or an small explosion from the next room, a fire that he had to put out. Not two minutes ago, he'd been reading along when a vision suddenly erupted across his eyes. Now he found he couldn't remember what he'd read.

In fact, he couldn't even remember the book's title.

He had to flip to the front cover again to remind himself: *The Myth of Draegoth*. Ah yes, *now* he remembered. It was a storybook — something a child might've read to escape his studies. The book was little more than the legend of how the first King came to be ...

Then why was Argon having such a difficult time reading it?

He cleared his throat and settled back down at his desk, determined to start where he'd left off:

From the bonds of magic pure and earth's most gleaming vein, the archmage did forge the King's salvation: a protection called the Dragonsbane.

Well, confound it all — none of that made any sense to him. He must've started in the wrong place. Argon flipped back to the beginning and was searching through the pages for a familiar line when the tower suddenly fell deathly silent.

All of the young mages' chatter had stopped. Argon could practically hear the rustle of their robes as they parted

— making way for the tower's unsavory guest. His familiar, dragging steps stopped just outside of the door.

The frame rattled and dust fell from the ceiling as he struck it hard three times.

"Come in," Argon said lightly, when the pounding stopped.

The door swung open and slammed against the wall. There was already a chip in the stone from where the knob had struck it on several other occasions, so Argon didn't worry too much about the damage.

The royal beastkeeper crowded through the doorway. He was a monstrous, bare-chested fellow, and today he wore breeches that had been shredded to the knee. Small tufts of white hair sprouted through the little patches of his massive head that wasn't covered in scars.

Upon his arm perched a stormy gray hawk. His head was slouched forward and his feathers were puffed out, as if he was trying to brace himself against the cold, even though the tower was comfortably warm.

The beastkeeper grunted as he held his arm out to Argon. The man couldn't speak. Argon didn't know why, but he suspected it had something to do with the scarred claw marks on his throat — the ones that started at his chin and raked their way down to his chest.

"One moment." Argon pulled a heavily-padded glove out of his desk drawer and slipped it over his hand.

He put his arm next to the beastkeeper's, and the hawk stepped obediently onto the glove. His talons left small, bloodied gashes along his bare arm, but the beastkeeper didn't seem to notice. Though his face was too mangled to show much of anything, Argon could read the worry in his one good eye.

"He isn't ill," Argon said quietly. He stroked the hawk's chest with the back of his forefinger, and his amber eyes hooded in content. "I've Seen what troubles him. He mourns for a friend."

The beastkeeper's shoulders slumped downward — Argon could see barely-healed bite marks on the left one —

120

and nodded. He knew the great creature Eveningwing mourned. Everyone enslaved by Crevan's spell had felt it when Bloodfang the halfwolf perished.

"But Eveningwing is a valuable spy," Argon said, guessing what it was that had led the beastkeeper to his tower. "The King wants him healed. But as his wounds are not of the flesh, he seeks a diviner."

The beastkeeper nodded, and the lumps above his eyes dropped low.

"I won't hurt him," Argon promised. "But it could take some time ... I trust he's been put into my charge?"

The beastkeeper nodded again.

"Excellent. I'll let you know when I figure something out."

With a final grunt, the beastkeeper made his way back through the tower to the winding staircase — scattering the young mages in his wake. Argon closed the door behind him. Seeing Eveningwing brought it all back: he remembered the vision he'd had just moments before.

There was trouble brewing in the plains, a boulder in the path that had to be removed ... calm waters that needed to be unsettled. He wasn't sure what it all meant, but Fate obviously had a plan — and Argon had learned long ago that it was best not to stand in her way.

No, he would play his part.

"I cannot raise the dead, little one," he said as he toted the hawk to his scrying bowl. "I'm afraid that a life once lost, is lost forever. But, perhaps there is a way to make sure Bloodfang's soul rests in peace. Of course ... I speak of vengeance."

At the sound of this word, Eveningwing's feathers came out of their ruffled state. They slicked down his back and flattened against his chest. His pupils sharpened into attentive dots. He was listening.

"Yes, I know the man responsible for Bloodfang's death. And what's more — I know where he's hiding." Argon brought the hawk up to his eyes, and normally, he would have held his finger up for emphasis. But one look at

Eveningwing's lethally curved beak, and he thought better of it. "However, if I show you how to find him, you must promise to keep this between us. The King can't know that I've sent you away, or he'll call you right back. So … will you keep it our secret?"

Eveningwing's head bobbed down — in the same quick motion that he might have torn flesh from bone. And Argon knew he'd been right to keep his fingers out of reach.

Though it was unlikely that Bloodfang's executioner would be so fortunate.

Chapter 10
No Ordinary Killer

Elena dragged her oars through the water slowly. She kept the rough shafts trapped against her palms, guiding the paddles in and out of the waves, coaxing the boat forward without so much as a splash.

The ocean was particularly still that night — which meant they would have to be particularly quiet. Elena matched her breathing with the steady ocean wind. Her companion followed suit, though his breaths were slightly heavier than hers. The rumbling in his chest sounded like the far-off beat of waves striking rock: a constant, deadly sound — a sound she had come to hate.

They rowed hard for Duke Reginald's island castle — two shadows balanced atop the quiet sea. A thin layer of clouds veiled the sky. Pale light peeked out for a moment before the dark covered it again, as if even the moon couldn't bear to watch their errand.

Elena bristled against the wet warmth as Holthan exhaled across the back of her neck. She knew he was doing it on purpose. There was nothing he loved more than to watch her squirm. He'd told her this, once. And though she knew she shouldn't give him anything to smirk about, she couldn't help it. One look from him, and her blood would freeze against her bones. It always did.

At last, the boat bumped softly against the island's rocky shore. Holthan anchored them to the rungs of an iron ladder before he stood. He leapt from the boat and onto the highest rung — a move that would have toppled Elena and flipped the boat, had she not braced herself for his weight.

"My lady?"

Holthan's hand appeared out of the shadows, but she ignored it. Instead, she pulled herself up along the slippery surface of rock, digging her boots and fingers into the crags until she popped up onto solid ground.

"Your mind moves so quickly," Holthan murmured as they crouched. His voice was slightly muffled behind his mask: a red scarf tied around the lower half of his face, with a black leather guard over his nose and mouth. His breath hissed as it passed through the slits in the guard. His dark eyes glinted beneath his hood.

Elena wore a similar mask — which she hoped made the look she gave him all the more sinister. "Keep your mouth shut until our task is finished. Or I swear I'll report you to the Countess."

Lines wreathed his eyes as he smirked, but he said nothing in reply. Elena glared at him before she turned her watch to the castle walls.

Whoever had been in charge of defending the keep hadn't done a very good job of it. The braziers were spread so far apart that they left a small patch of shadows between each one. Even the torches of the many pacing sentries couldn't quite uncover them. While the lights might've been enough to thwart an army, they were no match for someone of Elena's skills.

She made a dash for the first shadowy patch — sprinting until she could turn and plant her back against the wall. Holthan materialized by her side just as the sentry crossed above them. They had to stand with their shoulders crammed together for the shadows to cover them both, and Holthan had to duck his head. Once the sentry passed, they moved to the next shadowy patch, then the next. It wasn't long before they were standing with their backs to the westernmost wall.

The open sea stretched out before them, a dark and grumbling beast. Elena arched her neck back and watched the orb of a sentry's torch as it drifted overhead. The moment it passed, she nudged Holthan with her elbow.

He swept out into the light and began clearing weeds from the face of a sizable rock — one that looked oddly out of place next to the uniform cut of the wall. Elena thought she could make out the arch of a passageway hidden behind it.

She allowed herself a smirk. It was amazing what a few tankards of ale and a low-cut dress could buy. The merchant she'd met at the local tavern had been difficult to crack, at first: the solemn expression he wore made him almost impossible to read. But he seemed bitter about his lot, unappreciated and angry. The ale brought out his weaknesses, and all Elena had had to do was bat her eyes and listen.

"Our high chancellor is a fraud. I know those votes were tampered with," he'd stormed, after a particularly long drag from his tankard.

"By the pirate captain?" Elena murmured. She watched his lips waver along their solemn line — a line that his drink was beginning to soften.

"Yes. I'm sure of it." His gaze moved to her mouth as he wiped ale from his neatly-trimmed beard. "I told the others that *I* should've been chancellor. The votes were just supposed to be a formality — the office was mine by right! But did they listen? No!"

His fist slammed down upon the table. Elena reached across and wrapped her fingers about his wrist. She'd smiled sweetly as she felt his blood quicken its pace. "Then they're nothing but fools, and *you* are the clever one."

He returned her smile with a clumsy one of his own. Then it changed quickly into a sneer. "Yes ... yes, you're right. They'll get what they deserve. And it's only a matter of time, really — if marauders could break into the castle once, they can do it again. Someone's going to murder Colderoy in his bed, mark my —"

"Tell me more about the castle," Elena interrupted. "Why do you think it'll be so easy for thieves to break in?"

He smirked, and his once-sharp eyes fell hooded in spirits. "Because of the dungeon passages, my dear. The castle's first owner had his builders carve out an escape route, in case the fortress was ever under siege. But Reginald didn't think he needed it. He even tried to seal it up, but he did a sloppy job. Three strong men could move it easily."

And *that* was precisely the sort of information Elena had been waiting for. Once she got a few more details from him, it had been easy enough to lure him to a room upstairs — where she'd quickly clubbed him over the head.

She'd taken all of his coin and his fine leather boots with her. When he woke, he would think a thief had swindled him. Of course, the truth was far more sinister.

Now that they knew the castle's weaknesses, one stone was all that stood between them and a pathway to the Duke. Holthan had the strength of three men even on his weakest day. As he wrapped his arms around the boulder, his muscles swelled like bags of wetted rice — which was probably why he preferred to keep the sleeves cut out of his black armor.

The sword strapped to his back was nearly the length of an average man's spear. Firelight glanced it as he bent to ready himself to pull, but the blackened hilt did not wink back.

With a grunt and one swift motion, he rolled the stone free, turning it over on its side. Elena ducked behind him and slid into the passageway. She felt the hollow thud in her boots as Holthan allowed the stone to roll back into place.

Wet moss made their passage slippery. Elena was able to slide her way down most of the tunnel, but Holthan moved more slowly. She reached the iron grate several breaths before he did, and she took a moment to look around.

Fools.

There wasn't a single guard outside of the dungeon entrance. She stretched her neck in both directions, and when she was certain the hallway was empty, she waved Holthan forward.

He wrenched the grate from its hinges. Little white crumbs of dust showered down on him as he set it carefully on the floor. Then he climbed free and slunk towards the door on the opposite end of the hallway — the one that led back into the main castle.

Elena heard a soft click as he broke the bolt inside the lock.

While Holthan made certain they wouldn't be cut off from behind, Elena crept to the dungeon doors. The guards' noise came clearly through the wood: the loud slurping of that evening's dinner, the curses of men losing at cards, and the mutterings of those with nothing to do.

Holthan appeared beside her without a sound. His eyes closed as he pressed his ear against the door and listened. *Twelve?* he asked, using the hand signals the Countess had taught them. It was important that they keep as quiet as possible. They never made a sound that wasn't necessary.

Elena shook her head. *Fourteen. Two are sleeping.*

He listened for a moment more before he nodded. Then he raised his brows. *Ready?*

Elena ran her middle finger down the bandolier strapped across her chest, counting all seven of her throwing knives. She knew they were there, but for some reason it felt better to check before every fight. Her hands slipped past the leather gloves tucked into her belt. She didn't like to wear them.

The metal plates stitched into the gloves might've protected her hands, but the tightness of the leather strangled her fingers. She could work far more quickly, if her hands were allowed to breathe.

Once she was certain everything was in place, Elena grasped the hilts of the twin daggers strapped to her arms, and nodded.

Holthan's eyes lingered on her for a moment; she didn't like what she saw. But before she could start to worry, he spun around and kicked the door off its hinges. The loud crack of splintering wood and the startled gasps of the soldiers, the hiss of blades flying from their sheaths, the many widened eyes that locked onto hers — all made her forget the danger.

It was time to go to work.

Three of her knives brought the card game to an abrupt end. The men fell dead from their seats with their swords half-drawn. She spun under a fourth guard's blade and stayed in a crouch as Holthan answered. Once she heard the *thud* of the guard's severed head striking the ground, she sprang for the card table.

Elena used her hands to launch herself into a vault, landing directly in front of a fifth guard — whose momentary shock gave her the second she needed to draw her twin daggers.

Slight and Shadow, she called them — and they fit her better than any pair of gloves. She brandished Slight and kept Shadow tucked against her forearm. The guard sneered when he saw how small her blade was. He swung his sword for her middle, with all the force of a woodsman about to fell a tree. And Elena jumped.

She tucked her knees to her chest and his blade went whistling through the empty space beneath her. It was when she came into her landing that she brought Shadow out to play.

The guard never saw him coming — nobody *ever* saw Shadow coming. It was clearly a surprise when his shoulders locked at the end of his swing, and Elena cocked her fist to the side ... and Shadow's blade sprang out to kiss him across the throat.

His eyes were wide by the time Elena's feet touched the ground. She had to turn sideways to keep his body from crushing her as he fell.

A swarm of guards closed in on her. They tried to surround her, to overwhelm her with their numbers and force her to the ground. But Elena never panicked. Instead, her eyes sharpened. She focused on the man closest to her and used her ears to follow the others.

As she concentrated, the whole world changed: she saw no flesh, no faces — only blood and beating hearts. She imagined that the guards' limbs were made of steel, that their skin burned white-hot. She couldn't let them touch her. If they touched her, she would lose.

So she let the thrill of battle wash over her, let the heat run unchecked through her veins. Soon she was *Elena* no longer — but a living, breathing weapon. Her only purpose was to kill.

She sent the first man sailing with a thrust of her boot. Slight bit through the chest of another, and she spun — letting Shadow finish off a third guard who'd been sneaking in at her back. If she couldn't kill a man in one blow, she kicked him away, separating him from his fellows. It wasn't long before she'd broken their clump and had them organized into a single line.

Once they were forced to attack her one at a time, they died quickly.

Holthan took on all of the others. She watched for a moment as he spun through the crowd of armor and spears. The great sword he wielded wasn't like any Elena had ever seen: its blade was nearly an inch thick at its middle, and far heavier than the hilt. He wielded his sword with two hands — and blood trailed behind his sweeping blows.

Elena heard the twang of a bow behind her, heard the noise of wind whistling across feathers, and leaned backwards just in time to avoid the arrow.

She hated archers. They always stood at the back of battles, behind the protection of shields or the keep wall, and they picked off their enemies like vultures. When she turned, the guard who'd fired at her was fumbling with his quiver. She began a slow walk towards him.

By the time he had a second arrow trained on her chest, she'd closed half the space between them. His eyes narrowed as they locked on her heart. He exhaled, and then his arrow slipped from the string.

Elena sighed.

If she'd had a copper for every time a man had fired an arrow at her ... well, she probably could've built her own castle. She knew precisely when to turn, leaning so that the fletching brushed her chest as the arrow sailed by. It *thunk*ed into the back of an unsuspecting guard. She heard the sharp sound of iron striking stone as he fell to his knees. His gasps were cut short as Holthan's blade finished him.

The archer watched, horrified, over Elena's shoulder as his companion fell. It wasn't until Slight slipped between his ribs that his eyes shot back to her, and by then, it was too late. He was already dead.

The noise of hurried footsteps drew Elena's eyes to the ceiling. They clattered overhead for a moment, faded out, and she held her breath. Then came the noise of someone pounding on the hallway door.

She knew the time for play was over. Holthan would handle the stragglers — Elena had to find the Duke.

It only took her a moment to spot him: he had his face plastered to the iron bars of his cell door. His goatee had grown out into a full beard, the months away from the sunlight had paled him, but there was still a considerable amount of haughtiness in his eyes — and they watched her with interest.

His gaze flicked down to Elena's chest, obviously searching for an emblem or some clue as to who she was. But he found nothing.

"Who are you?" he demanded. When Elena didn't reply, his hands shot up to grasp the bars. "I don't know who sent you, but I'm worth far more alive than dead. Get me out of here, and I'll make you rich."

Elena stopped at the door, and Duke Reginald smirked.

"Yes, you heard me. I'll pack the whole bottom of a galleon with gold and jewels ... and your employer never has to find out."

He yelped and fell backwards as Elena's boot struck the door. The bolt snapped under the force of her blow, and she wrenched it open.

"You're making a mistake!" he cried, scrambling to his feet. "I'll make it so you never have to shed blood again —!"

"But what if I really, *really* like it?" Elena whispered. She watched as Reginald's eyes widened in recognition. "What if I don't want to stop?"

She pulled her mask down, then, because there was no point in staying covered any longer. Reginald's eyes swept over her, and then his face went scarlet.

"*You!*" he spat. "I knew there was something off about you — the whole lot of you! D'Mere was always going on about her little pets, but I was beginning to think that she'd made it all up. I must admit ... I never thought to look for you in her court." Greed shone behind his eyes as he took in the gory scene behind her. "D'Mere kept you close, then — closer than I ever expected. And I can certainly see why. You're no ordinary killer, are you?"

Elena didn't respond. She knew there was no point in denying it.

For some reason, Reginald seemed to think that knowing the Countess's secret gave him an advantage. "It seems a shame, to bind a woman of your talents to such pithy tasks. Set me free," he said, closing the space between them. "Ride with me to Midlan, and I'll speak on your behalf to the King. He won't let your skills go to waste. The Countess's plan is doomed to fail," he added, when Elena didn't respond. "I know how she's been scheming with the others. She even tried to drag me into it. But it won't work. And she's too stupid to figure it — gah!"

His body curled around Elena's daggers as she rammed them through his middle. "You would've done better to hold your serpent tongue," she whispered in his ear, "than to insult my Countess."

She pulled her blades free, and Reginald managed to land on his knees. He looked down at his wounds, grasped at them for a moment, but seemed to realize that it was hopeless. When he looked up at her, Elena was surprised to see defiance in his eyes.

"Too late," he muttered, coughing on a mouthful of blood. "She's got one, too."

"Who has what?" Elena said impatiently. The pounding on the hall door was becoming louder and more rhythmic: the guards were trying to ram it down.

Reginald managed a smirk. "The Dragongirl."

His words made no sense to Elena. They were probably only the ramblings of a dying man, but she remembered what he said — in case they meant something to the Countess.

She watched as Reginald toppled over, squirmed, and finally lay still. Then she sheathed her daggers and jogged out of the cell — where she nearly ran into Holthan.

He'd retrieved her throwing knives from the bodies of the card-players. *Is it done?* he asked, as she tucked the knives into her bandolier.

Yes.

Good. Follow me.

They left the way they came — slipping out through the grate, past the stone, and into the shelter of the night.

****

Once they'd made it back to the safety of the mainland, Holthan sunk their boat. They jogged into the woods, listening to the bells that cried out from the castle.

"What are they saying?" Holthan whispered.

Elena was in no mood to talk. "Figure it out," she muttered, moving ahead of him. "You were supposed to memorize the signals on the way here."

"Maybe I had better things to do."

"They're ringing about an emergency at the castle," she said shortly. "It's nothing specific — but you should stay off the main roads."

"Well ... why don't we just wait till morning?"

Elena didn't hear the darkness in his voice — she was far too busy thinking over the fight. Her muscles tensed as she remembered the precise angles at which she'd turned, the force she'd used to drive her daggers. She played it over, searching for flaws, and she didn't find many.

There were a few things she could improve on. But for the most part, it had all gone according to plan. Reginald had many enemies, and his wounds were common enough that any assassin might've been responsible. No one would be able to tie the killing to the Countess —

Holthan's hand clamped down on her arm, startling her. "Where are you off to?"

She broke his hold easily and darted for the horses. He obviously hadn't been expecting her to fight back — she usually didn't. Usually, the darkness in Holthan's eyes held her captive, and fear gripped her limbs like a vise. But not tonight.

Tonight, the thrill of the fight still burned in her veins, and it kept the fear from freezing her.

She'd just gotten her mare untied when Holthan grabbed her wrist and jerked her around. "Let go of me," she snarled. She tried to pull her arm free, but he was ready for it. This time, there would be no escape. "I have business in the desert," she reminded him, "and *you* have business in the forest. The Countess will want to know that we've succeeded —"

"The whole Kingdom will know by sunrise." Holthan pulled his mask down, and the dark hunger in his eyes matched the snarl on his lips. "No ... my business is with you."

In one rough movement, he ripped her mask away and locked his lips onto hers. He pressed down so hard — she knew her lips would bruise. She swore she could hear her ribs groaning against his hold.

But this time, Holthan had chosen poorly.

He hadn't waited until she was off her guard, or wandering alone in some unwatched corner of the castle. He'd attacked her while her blood was up. Through her eyes, he was nothing more than an enemy — just another lopsided match that she must find a way to win. So instead of squirming, she stood still.

She relaxed, and Holthan's mouth moved more boldly against hers. It wasn't long before his lip slipped between her teeth ...

Then she bit down. Hard.

He roared and tried to pull away, but she held on. Blood coated her tongue with a taste like metal. Her teeth went through his flesh and clicked together on the other side. Then his fist came out of the darkness and struck her in the face.

Her head snapped back and her mouth opened in shock as she flew to the ground. The whole earth spun around her, but she managed to pull herself to her feet. Holthan's moans came from behind her as she stumbled over to her horse. It was by sheer willpower that she managed to pull herself into the saddle — with one eye shut tight and her whole head throbbing in pain.

Elena pointed her mare to the south and left at a gallop. They tore across the countryside for several miles before the fire left her veins. It was nearly dawn when the full weight of what she'd done finally struck her, and she burst into tears.

Oh, it hurt to cry. Her whole face stung from Holthan's blow. Tears shoved their way painfully out of her swollen eye, the pounding steps of her mare jostled her throbbing head, but she couldn't stop. She realized that she could *never* stop. If she ever slowed down, if she ever tried to return to the Grandforest ... Holthan would kill her. He'd killed for far less. He'd killed just because he felt like it.

If she returned, not even the Countess would be able to protect her. No, Elena's home was lost.

This realization brought on another wave of stinging tears. What would Holthan say had happened to her? Would he tell the Countess that she'd been killed? Deserted? And what would D'Mere do without her? No one had been as vigilant as Elena. She didn't trust the others to keep the Countess safe.

But as the sun rose and warmed her swollen face, she realized that it was too late for regret. She couldn't turn back, now. She wouldn't be able to protect D'Mere any longer. The bile rose in her throat at the thought, but there was nothing more she could do ...

Wait — there was *one* thing, one last task to be done. And she intended to do it. She *would* do it, for the Countess's sake: Elena would find the Dragongirl, and she would kill her.

After that, she wasn't sure where she'd go. But there would be others across the Kingdom who would have need of her skills, and she wagered it wouldn't be long before she found a new home.

Chapter 11
Arabath

The fastest way to reach Whitebone was by sea. Kyleigh's little vessel followed the current south, and the days were mostly fair — but she still spent a good portion of the journey with her head over the railings.

The ocean was meant for swimming. It was unnatural to bob along on its surface, and her insides could never quite catch up. The movement wasn't so bad on a larger ship. But on this tiny merchant's vessel, she felt every buck and break. And her stomach heaved in constant protest.

"Look, dragoness," Silas murmured, tapping her on the shoulder as she voided the remainder of her breakfast.

"What?" she snapped.

Silas hadn't stopped chattering since the moment they set sail. He'd never seen the ocean before, and behaved as if nobody else on board had seen it either — calling out anytime he spotted so much as a weed drifting through the water, and exclaiming every few minutes that he'd never laid eyes on anything quite so bizarre.

Kyleigh was very near to giving him a closer look.

But this time when he pointed, she was actually excited by what she saw: a telltale shadow hung against the horizon, a sign that their journey was about to end. It was still too far out for human eyes, but she told Jake and Silas to start packing their bags. A few minutes later came the welcome cry:

"Land, ho!"

Her companions crowded in on either side of her, watching excitedly as the shadow in the distance took shape. Waves struck the beach and gave way to rolling hills of sand. The morning sun hid behind them, staining them pink with its rising glow. Tall, spindly trees grew like weeds along the shore. They were all trunk, with only a small gathering of leaves sprouting at their tops. But even that slight weight seemed to be too much for them: many of the trees were hunched over, slouching at such severe angles that they practically grew sideways.

The sleepy chime of a bell drew their eyes to the right, and Silas pawed at her arm again. "What is *that*?"

Not two miles away, a large gathering of rooftops towered above the dunes. When their ship crept around the next bend, an entire town blossomed out of the desert.

"It's the port city of Arabath," Jake supplied, since Kyleigh had a hand clamped stubbornly over her mouth. She was determined to hold onto the water she'd just swallowed.

Arabath was easily the largest settlement in Whitebone. Like all desert villages, it had grown up around a water source: a large oasis that pooled in the middle of town. The cool waters came from a spring deep beneath the sands, and many believed they had healing powers. Kyleigh had even heard of nobles paying large amounts of gold to have the waters bottled and shipped to their castles.

But that was before the Whispering War. Now the people spent their coin on armor and weapons — and cared more about *dodging* wounds than healing them.

The shelf of rock that jutted out from Arabath made a natural port, and the people of the Kingdom had been visiting it for centuries. They flooded in from every region, eager to spend their coin on the fine jewelry and glassware that the desert craftsmen were famous for.

They were so famous in fact, that Baron Sahar had stolen all of the best craftsmen straight out of their shops. Now he kept them locked in his mines deep in the eastern sands, where he forced them to work as slaves. His wares cost him nothing to make, and he sold them at exceptionally high prices. So Sahar had been living comfortably in his wealth for years.

But Kyleigh planned to change that.

Once their ship was tied to the docks, they were finally allowed off. Kyleigh had only ever seen Arabath from above — she'd never actually set foot in it. So she was surprised when a horde of merchants flooded the docks.

They swarmed the ramp, gathering so thickly that she had to elbow her way through them. They called out in the Kingdom's tongue, shouting high and low around each other, trying to be the voice that stood out from the crowd — though their accents were so thick that most of what they shouted sounded like gibberish.

Kyleigh pulled her hood over her head as she wove her way between them. She was determined to be careful, this time. Her long stay in the mountains hadn't dulled the King's memories: Crevan had already sent his army after her once, and if she was spotted in Whitebone, he would certainly do it again.

Last time, her foolishness had cost them the life of Garron the Shrewd. It was a mistake that haunted her sleep, a mistake that had made her realize just how fragile the lives of her companions were — a mistake that she would never make again.

So Kyleigh planned to keep her face hidden until they were well away from Arabath, out in the solitude of the desert.

As they filed off the ship, the merchants crushed in. Kyleigh shoved her way through them, dodging the various glittering trinkets they shoved under her nose, and balling her fists so they couldn't press anything into her hands. The stale odor of sweat and human filth hovered in the small pockets of free air; whatever array of spices the merchants had consumed for breakfast still clung to their breath and clothes.

She heard Jake cry out behind her and had to grab him around the wrist to keep him from getting swept away. After a few minutes of shoving and weaving, they popped out on the other side.

Silas wasn't behind them, and Kyleigh was afraid that she was going to have to go back in after him. But then Jake spotted him standing up the path. He was balanced on his tiptoes, his neck craning in interest above the crowd. His pants were tighter and a good inch shorter than they'd been before.

"What did I tell you about changing shape in public?" Kyleigh said when she reached him.

He looked away from where he'd been sniffing the air and fixed her with an unconcerned look. "That it's important that I not be spotted. And I wasn't." He pulled down on the seam of his breeches and grimaced. "Though I wish now that I hadn't changed. Things are beginning to get ... crowded."

While Kyleigh had been too sick to do much of anything, Silas and Jake had made good use of the journey south. Jake thought he might be able to create a spell that would keep Silas's clothes from ripping every time he changed, and Silas was happy to let him experiment. They practiced late at night, and where the merchants couldn't see them. The first couple of attempts caused Silas's trousers to burst into flame — and left the end of his tail smoldering.

But Jake eventually figured it out ... well, mostly. Silas could now change shape without losing his clothes, but they shrank a bit every time. By now, the hems of his trousers were almost to his knees, and the buttons of his shirt were strained tight.

"*Must* I wear them?" he whined, scratching piteously at his collar. "I could travel much faster bare."

Kyleigh waved a hand at the crowd. "Do you see anybody else running around the way Fate made them?"

"Well ... no —"

"And if *you* did, don't you think people would notice?"

"Perhaps," he said through gritted teeth.

"And if we get noticed," she pointed behind him, to where a cluster of guards were making their way towards the docks, "they'd probably want to have a chat with us. Of course, by a *chat* I mean that they'd string us up by our toes in the Baron's dungeon and burn the truth from our lips with red-hot coals. Is that how you'd like to spend your first trip to the desert?"

He glared at her.

She patted his cheek. "I didn't think so. Now, let's find you some more comfortable trousers."

They bought Silas a few more changes of clothes at one of the shops along the beach — and Kyleigh made sure they were especially itchy — before they wandered deeper into Arabath.

"Remarkable," Jake murmured as they wound their way through the narrow streets.

He had his journal opened and was already scribbling madly with a stick of charcoal. Though Jake was a clever creature, he seemed incapable of doing two things at once: in less than a minute, he'd already run into the back of a parked wagon, bruised his hip on a fruit stand, and nearly tripped over a wandering dog. Once, he'd been so focused on his notes that he'd made a wrong turn — and Kyleigh had to turn back to retrieve him.

"It *is* remarkable," Silas agreed. His golden eyes flicked every which way, and his nose never stopped twitching. For all of his talk about human weakness, he seemed rather interested in them.

Kyleigh had a difficult time not smiling as she watched him. She remembered her first trip through a human market, and all of the excitement of discovering something new: the many strange scents, the colorful tones of chatter, and the way the humans' faces moved. Their faces always seemed to be moving — and every slight twitch in their features carried a different meaning.

Setheran had begun to teach her what all of the expressions meant, but she never got a chance to finish the training. There was a lot about the humans that she still didn't understand, and on more than one occasion, it had gotten her into trouble.

Nevertheless, it was nice to have something new to learn. Kyleigh might've been old to the earth, but she was still young to the ways of men.

It was obvious that this was Silas's first time out among so many humans. Though she didn't know everything about them, Kyleigh knew a few things — and she knew Silas could get into trouble if she didn't keep an eye on him.

A woman slid past them, and his nostrils flared to catch her scent. Several brightly colored flowers were woven into the dark tresses of her hair. They gave off a sickly sweet aroma, and Silas leaned in to sniff them as she passed.

Kyleigh had to grab his collar to keep him from burying his nose into her hair.

"But there aren't any flowers like that in the mountains," he said, his eyes following after her. "I only wanted to smell them."

"Still — you shouldn't touch women who don't belong to you. If her husband is anywhere nearby, you'll be in trouble." Kyleigh bit back a smile at the confused look on his face. "Her *mate*," she explained.

"Stupid human customs," Silas said, with no small amount of disdain. "The females of *my* species aren't tied to anyone. They may go from one mate to the next as often as they wish."

"Well, we can't *all* run around with our tails on fire every spring — otherwise there wouldn't be any great cities like Arabath," Kyleigh quipped. "We'd all be living in caves and treetops."

"Boldly spoken, from the dark," Silas growled back. His gaze dug into the shadow of her hood. "You're lucky that I can't find your eyes to glare in."

"It *does* seem a bit darker than the average hood," Jake agreed. There was a smudge of charcoal on the end of his nose from where he'd had it buried in his journal. "I've often wondered about it. Is it magicked?"

Kyleigh shook her head. "A whisperer made it for me."

Jake's spectacles slid down as his eyebrows climbed. "Whispercraft," he murmured, and his mouth hung open even after he'd said it. "That must've cost you a fortune."

She shrugged, smiling at the memory. "Not as much as you'd think. The craftsman owed me pretty severely."

Silas stopped in the middle of the path, and Kyleigh had to leap to the side to keep from running into him. "Do you smell that?" he hissed, his eyes closed tightly.

It only took her a moment to catch the scent: meaty flesh roasting over open flames, thick skin packed full of spices — and crisping perfectly in the morning air. Kyleigh's empty stomach rumbled after it. Now that she was on firm ground once again, her appetite came back with a vengeance.

Silas took off at a run, with his shoulders arched forward and his neck bent on the hunt, and Kyleigh followed him without thinking — leaving Jake to tag along behind them. It was only after they arrived at the meat vendor that she heard the poor mage panting loudly, and realized that she'd let the smell of food get the better of her.

"Sorry, Jake —"

"You might've just *told* me that you were hungry," he gasped, planting his hands on his knees, "instead of setting off like that. I thought we were being chased!"

"It won't happen again," Kyleigh promised. She was more than a little embarrassed by the way she'd acted. They were *buying* their food, not killing it. She shouldn't have let Silas goad her into a hunt.

She looked up to chide him and saw that he was already standing at the meat vendor's table, watching as he turned a fresh leg of goat over a small fire.

"Easy with the roasting, friend," Silas said, his eyes on the meat.

The vendor smirked at him. He turned the leg twice, barely searing it. Then he handed it over. He looked rather shocked when Silas tore in.

"I'll have mine the same way," Kyleigh said, when she saw how much Silas was enjoying it. "And we'll buy all the salted meat you have prepared."

Most of what the desert folk ate came from the earth. There weren't many creatures that could survive the punishing sun, and so they usually did without meat. But Kyleigh couldn't do without it: her dragon half needed red flesh, and could survive on nothing else.

The vendor wrapped up their supplies without a word. Kyleigh wagered it would last them about a week — provided she could keep Silas out of it.

When the vendor handed over her barely-seared leg of goat, he watched as she bit into it. She could see his disgust clearly out of the corner of her eye, but paid him no heed. She was enjoying the spices immensely.

"And what about you?" the vendor said, turning to Jake. His accent was not as heavy as some of the others' had been. "Perhaps you would like yours a little bloody?"

Jake wrinkled his nose. "No, I'd very much like the blood cooked out of it, thank you." He watched the vendor work for a moment, then he drew out his journal. "How did you come to learn the Kingdom's tongue, if you don't mind me asking? Have you lived in Arabath all your life?"

The vendor shook his head. "Many of the tribes speak this language. We have hundreds of our own, and none would give up his native words to learn those of another. Your King's tongue belonged to no one, and so we agreed to learn it."

"I see." Jake's brows shot up, and he began to scribble furiously. *"And so the tongue that was foreign to them all became the language that united them.* Does that sound about right to you?"

He shrugged. "I do not care — so long as I am paid."

While the vendor finished roasting Jake's meal, Kyleigh kept eating. She'd just tore off a particularly juicy hunk of flesh when Jake tapped her frantically on the shoulder.

"Huh?" she grunted.

He bent down to her ear. "Don't look now, but I think we're being watched."

Kyleigh looked anyways.

He was right: a group of four desert men hung near a shop across the street from them. They had scarves wrapped about their heads and swords strapped to their hips. Their dark eyes blinked out unabashedly from their wrappings. They didn't seem to care that they'd been spotted.

"I think they mean to kill us," Jake hissed.

Kyleigh could feel their dark intentions even from across the path. It oozed out between their crossed arms, stabbed at her from the danger in their stares. "Yes, I believe they do ... eventually."

"Well, shouldn't we — I don't know ... confront them?" Jake muttered. He snatched his food from the vendor impatiently and pressed some coin into his hand.

Kyleigh wasn't too concerned about their followers. Granted, travelers *did* have a nasty habit of disappearing in Whitebone. She imagined it would be fairly easy to hide a body in the sand. But disappearances were bad for business, and Baron Sahar had done much to curb bandit attacks in recent years.

Now Arabath was thick with his guards. There seemed to be a pair of them for nearly every street. They patrolled the city openly, with the gold sun of Whitebone branded across their chests. Everywhere they marched, their eyes were peeled for mischief.

Kyleigh knew the desert men wouldn't risk attacking them in Arabath. So she told Jake to ignore them, and led her companions on with their chores.

They bought two weeks worth of spice rice from a vendor down the street. Silas made a face when Kyleigh handed him a sack filled with the bright red grains. "This is for prey, dragoness. You can't expect me to carry what I'm not going to eat."

"The rice will keep long after the meat's gone bad. If we run into trouble, you'll be glad you have it."

"But —"

She spun him around by the shoulders and stuffed the rice into his pack. "You'll carry what I give you, and that will be the end of it — or I'll make an end of *you*," she added, when he started to protest.

He clamped his mouth shut, though his eyes still glowed with a haughtiness that was every bit as insolent as a sharp retort.

As they moved on towards the edge of town, Kyleigh spotted a date vendor settled under the shade of a tree. She was a middle-aged woman dressed in a beautiful blue frock. The gold threads woven into her garb branched out delicately from the hems; they shimmered in the sunlight while she packed their dates.

She held the sacks out to Kyleigh, but when she reached to take them, the woman grasped her wrist. "You are being followed," she whispered. Her eyes darted over Kyleigh's shoulder, where the four desert men were feigning interest in some merchant's baubles. "I know those men — many travelers have died by their hands. You would do well to hire a guard."

Kyleigh was taken aback by the woman's kindness, and smiled at the concern on her face. "Thank you for telling me."

She paid with the last of their coin — silver worth more than three times the price of the dates. And the woman was so stunned that she didn't think to protest until they'd already disappeared into the market.

****

Arabath's back gate was actually only half a gate: one high wall protected the entrance to the Baron's highway, but the rest of the desert was left unprotected.

The highway was the only safe path through the desert, a natural shelf of rock that followed the path of the Red Spine. It wound from one end of the region to the other, keeping travelers safe from the perils of the burning wilds.

Rolling hills of sand stretched endlessly to the south and east. They shimmered against the rising sun, dancing excitedly as the heat warmed them. There was no wall set against this land, because there was no point in guarding it: only fools wandered out into the open desert.

"You're certain that you've traveled this way before?" Jake whispered, as they made their way purposefully towards the border.

145

Kyleigh sighed. "Yes, I'm certain."

"And you know where you're going, correct?"

"Correct."

She'd crossed the desert so many times that she thought she might've been able to do it blindfolded. Granted, that had been years ago, back when she'd traveled alone hadn't cared if she was spotted. Now that there were other lives depending on her, she was determined to do things carefully — even if that meant taking the long way around. She wouldn't take to the skies unless she had no other choice.

But even though Kyleigh could see things better from above, she didn't think she'd have any trouble leading her companions across the desert. Aside from a few villages scattered here and there, the land was completely empty.

How difficult could it possibly be?

Jake was silent for a moment. She could hear the squeaking of his sweaty palms as they twisted about his staff. "Remind me again why we can't take the road?"

Kyleigh glared in the direction of the gate. "Baron Sahar's highway is lined with forts — and each has its own price for passage. Merchants have lost a great deal more than their coin, along the way. Besides, the guards aren't likely to let me pass through like this," she said, tugging on her hood. "The minute I'm uncovered, they'll know who I am ... and our welcome will wear out very quickly."

"Ah, I see," Jake said, though he still looked rather put-off about it. "So you're certain you'll be able to navigate across —?"

"*Yes,*" Kyleigh said, throwing up her hands.

"Well, I only ask because people are starting to stare!" he hissed.

A number of small huts littered the rocky outskirts of Arabath. Desert folk milled around the tiny homes, stoking their fires and going about their chores. And many of them *were* staring.

Their gaping didn't seem to make Silas uncomfortable at all. In fact, he stared back with interest. "Why do they live out here, when there are far better dens in there?" he said, pointing back to the city.

"These are the un-favored," Jake mumbled. When Silas looked at him curiously, he brushed the sweat from his nose and tried to explain. "The culture of the desert revolves around the sun — they call it Fate's Eye, and believe that the sun favors some of them more than others. The favored ones live inside the city, while the un-favored must live on the outskirts."

"How are they favored?"

"It's hard to explain," Jake said, scrubbing his spectacles against his tunic. "But I think it all has to do with their skin. They believe that those born with darker skin are more favored, because it protects them from the sun. It's all tied into wealth and status — it's human business," he said bluntly, when Silas showed no signs of ever understanding.

"Humans," Silas muttered out the side of his mouth to Kyleigh. "And they call *us* barbaric. I'm glad I wasn't born here. I certainly would have been among the un-favored." He touched the back of her hand with his fingertips. "And it's a wonder they even let *you* inside the city!"

She shoved him away.

At long last, they reached the city's end. All that stood before them now were miles of fiery, untamed land. Kyleigh looked to the north, making sure that they were even with the Baron's highway. They would have to keep this path until the very last mile — then they would cut in.

She didn't know how long they'd have to camp in the Spine. They might have to wait for days, or even weeks. But above all, they needed to keep the Baron's castle in sight.

It was all Kyleigh's fault, really. After she'd burned Gilderick's castle to the ground, and after the incident with Sahar and the trolls, the two rulers had entered into something of an agreement. They blasted the mountains out from between them, forming a pass — and swore that if either of them was ever attacked, the other would come to his aid.

Kyleigh didn't know when Kael planned to launch his attack on the plains. But the moment Gilderick sniffed trouble, he would summon Sahar. Her friends couldn't possibly fight off two armies at once. So when Sahar's men left the palace, she would have to make sure they never reached the plains.

Their battle would seem small in the end, but if they could cause a little mischief, it might give their friends a chance to escape. And in Kyleigh's opinion, that would be worth every burning step.

"Those men are still following us," Jake said, with a glance over his boney shoulder. "What are we going to do about them?"

"We're going to lead them out into the desert," Kyleigh said simply, "where the sand will muffle their screams."

Chapter 12
Minceworms

They walked for hours, until Arabath and all of its lively comforts disappeared behind them. The sun climbed steadily higher, its light seemed to grow more powerful with every step.

The heat didn't bother Kyleigh: the scales of her armor reflected most of it, and the shadow of her hood protected her eyes. What she found to be more trouble than anything was the sand.

She'd had every intention of keeping them on a straight path. If they tried to weave around the dunes, the constant change in direction might force them to wander off-course. The smaller dunes were no trouble to cross — they took little longer than the average hill. It was when they came to the first reasonably-monstrous dune that her plan fell apart.

It rose like a mountain out of the desert; the gashes the wind had left in it were so deep that they came almost to Kyleigh's knees. But that didn't stop her from trying to lead her companions across it.

The sand slid out from under their feet, dragging them a half-step backwards every time they tried to lunge forward. More than once, Kyleigh lost her footing so suddenly that she had to catch herself on her elbows. But she kept her eyes on the crest, determined to reach it. Her muscles tensed at every slight shift in the grain, she wedged her feet deep into its slippery side.

"It's useless, dragoness!"

Silas was standing at the base of the dune. He must have lost his footing: she could see very clearly where he'd dug in all four limbs to try to slow his fall.

Jake had been less fortunate. He lay in a crumpled heap at the bottom, and the trail he'd left behind was more like a flopping fish's: choppy and wild, with the hard imprints of his body pounded into the dune at every few feet.

When Silas helped him up, an impressive amount of sand poured out the bottom of his robes. "I'm sorry — I can't make the climb," Jake panted. "We'll have to go around."

Kyleigh knew he was right. Even if they *could* manage to climb every dune in their path, they'd be moving so slowly that it wouldn't do them any good. They'd never reach the Baron's castle in time. She'd just have to keep an eye on the sun, then — and be careful not to get them turned around.

She sat down and was preparing to slide her way to the bottom when she spotted four figures atop a crest behind them. It looked as if they might be running, but the earth waved and shook so badly under the heat that she couldn't be sure.

In any case, it was obvious that they were gaining.

She rode the shifting sands to the base of the dune, using the weight of her pack for balance. "We can't stop here," she said, when she saw Jake settling down for a rest.

"Why not? This is as good a spot as any."

"Not quite." Silas watched the four bandits from over his shoulder. His eyes stayed focused on them as he spoke. "It would be best to meet our stalkers on even ground. If they attack us from a high point, it will give them an unfair advantage. I should know," he added with a wicked smile. "I've broken many necks that way."

Jake leaned away from him.

Kyleigh was surprised: she'd actually been about to suggest the same thing. Silas might've been a smelly cat, and she didn't trust him any further than the length of his tail, but perhaps he wasn't as worthless an ally as she'd thought him to be.

After they'd dusted most of the sand from Jake, Kyleigh led them through a gentler stretch around the dunes. They were able to follow along the ridged back of a drift for about a mile before it sloped down into a shallow basin.

The ground was hardened and cracked at the bottom — it stood out like a bald spot in the middle of the sand. Dunes ringed it on all sides, forming a nearly perfect circle. Kyleigh thought it'd be a grand place for a fight.

"Thank Fate," Jake said, when she ordered them to a halt. He sat down heavily — and then immediately sprang back up. "It's hot!"

Kyleigh laughed. "What did you expect, you silly mage?"

"Well, I expected it to be hot — but not *that* hot. It's like a bed of coals." He rubbed his rump for a moment, glaring at the baking earth. Then his brows began to slip upwards. "I wonder *why* it's so hot ...?" he murmured, crouching for a better look.

Kyleigh didn't want her rump to wind up like Jake's, so she sat on her pack. It was a bit lumpy in places, but there were certainly worse spots to rest and have a drink. They were stopped in the middle of the bald spot — where she could see all around them. She didn't want to give the bandits a chance to take them by surprise.

Silas paced restlessly in front of her, his eyes on the dunes. He kept his tension bunched up in the lithe muscle of his shoulders. His back was stiffened, his chest puffed out. His arms swung dangerously loose at his sides. Kyleigh swore she could see his every hair standing tall — even the fine, pale hairs on the back of his neck.

Excitement rose from him as thickly as the hot breath of the earth, and she began to catch it.

Her muscles tensed, her eyes sharpened. She could smell the sweat of the four bandits, drifting down from the other side of the dunes. Fatigue hovered over them like a cloud. Thirst pushed down on their shoulders. She could hear the hollow thud of desperation in their every step.

Kyleigh inhaled deeply. She caught the stench of their weakness, and her blood began to thrum through her veins —

"No," she said firmly. She pinched her nose shut and took a long drag from her canteen. Her animal half hissed and moaned when the water struck her innards, but soon fell quiet.

"No, what?" Silas said. He'd stopped his pacing and was watching her curiously. He smirked when he read the struggle in her eyes. "Why do you fight it, dragoness? Your senses are a gift."

"Only if they're used properly," she said with a glare.

Kyleigh couldn't remember who she'd been before the change — that memory was lost to her, trapped in a darkness so deep that she didn't think she would ever be able to find it again. But she'd learned much about being a shapechanger from the halfwolves who had taken her in.

The dragon she'd bonded with was a part of her soul, now — it would never leave. Even though her human half controlled it, that animal spirit was still inside of her. Sharpfang had warned her long ago that a shapechanger's war was never finished: if Kyleigh wanted to live as a human, then she must hold reason above bloodlust ... or risk letting the animal consume her.

Silas came closer, and she had to hold her nose again as his thick scent drenched the air. "Properly?" he said, half-growling. "Oh, you won't get far if you turn your nose up at yourself."

"I'm not turning up my nose," Kyleigh growled back. "But this isn't a hunt. And these aren't deer — they're men. If we must kill them, then I'd like to do it with honor."

Silas laughed in her face. "If we must ...? *Honor?*" He planted his hands on his knees and looked up at her through the crop of his hair. "Perhaps you haven't noticed, but they've been hunting *us* like deer."

"Yes, I know —"

"And the only reason they haven't killed us yet is that we've been outrunning them. Do you think they plan to kill us with honor?" he said, thrusting his hand back at the dunes. "If they mean to show us no mercy, then I don't see why —"

"It may be a lion's way to kill in cold blood," Kyleigh said, rising to her feet. Her anger must've been burning at the front of her glare: Silas stumbled backwards. "It may be a lion's way to stoop to his enemy's level, but that isn't my way. And as long as you follow me, you'll do things *my* way. Understood?"

Silas didn't nod. But he also didn't argue.

Her words would've never worked on a human. Humans were far too proud, and their instincts were muddled by their politics. But to control another shapechanger, Kyleigh had to be dominant. She'd seen Bloodfang do it loads of times with the other wolves. She knew that she had to stand up to Silas now and declare that hers was the only way.

If he didn't like it, then he was welcome to fight her for it. But it was obvious by how he kept his chin lowered that he wasn't keen to attack her.

So she watched over his shoulder as the first of the bandits made his way to the basin. When the bandit spotted them, he bellowed something to his companions. "We'll at least offer them the chance to turn back and live," Kyleigh said, as three more heads popped up over the dunes.

"Fine," Silas hissed.

Kyleigh stepped forward, and he crowded her heels. "Hello, there!" she called to the bandits.

They halted in surprise.

"I'm afraid it'll do you no good to rob us — we haven't got any coin."

"If you value your lives, you'll turn back now!" Silas added.

The bandits paused for only a moment. Then they advanced. The lead bandit shouted something in a foreign tongue, and the others laughed.

"What are they saying?" Silas pressed his chest impatiently against Kyleigh's shoulder, as if she was the only thing holding him back.

"I don't know, but it probably wasn't very nice," she mused. One of the bandits shot her a gesture. "And that *certainly* wasn't very nice."

"Can we kill them, now?"

When the bandits made the very serious mistake of drawing their swords, Kyleigh sighed. "I suppose we ought to. Let's get on with it."

Silas growled in delight and stepped out from behind her, his eyes locked on the bandits. Kyleigh turned to tell Jake to get ready, and saw that he was still crouched over the ground.

"Jake, we're about t — what in blazes are you doing?"

He had a vial in one hand and a long pair of tweezers in the other. With his tongue stuck out in concentration, he seemed to be trying to coax a small chunk of dirt into the vial. When he looked up at her, his spectacles nearly slid off.

"Sorry, I was just — there are some flakey bits sitting on top of the dirt, you see, and I thought they might be worth examining. I've never seen anything like it. They keep breaking, though. I'm having to be very careful —"

A roar cut over the top of him. The first bandit screamed as Silas burst into his lion form: "A'calla!"

"You go ahead," Jake said, waving Kyleigh forward. "I'm just going to finish up, here."

While Silas pounced on one bandit, two more charged around him — their eyes set on Kyleigh. She left Jake and went to meet them at a sprint.

Harbinger shrilled when she pulled him free; his voice trembled across her ears and set her heart to racing. The bandits slowed their charge when they heard him, leaning back in fright. And Kyleigh attacked.

She crossed swords with one bandit and sent the second flying with a boot to the gut. In two quick blows, Harbinger bit through the first bandit's blade. Its severed half clattered to the ground. He took a few more swipes at her before he realized that he wielded nothing more than the hilt.

Then she ran him through.

By that point, the second bandit had recovered from his fall and tried to attack her from behind. She spun out of his reach and cut Harbinger across his back, but his sword sprang up to block her.

Kyleigh knew then that she was dealing with an experienced swordsman. He glanced at the chip in his blade before his eyes shot back to her, and she knew he was trying to figure her out. He swung at her again, but his shoulder wasn't into it — he was holding back.

She ignored his feint and met him where he planned to strike: at her head.

Their blades locked tightly. Harbinger bit into his sword, peeling thin, curling strips of iron from its edge. The bandit's eyes tightened above his scarf, his arms shook against Kyleigh's strength, and she had no desire to make him suffer any longer. With one hard shove, she sent him stumbling backwards — and while he was off balance, Harbinger bit straight through his chest.

"Do we have them all?" Silas called to her. His head swiveled about as he counted the dead. Red stained the front of his tunic. "Where's the fourth one?"

Kyleigh spotted the fourth bandit quickly — sprinting his way over the dunes and back towards Arabath. She let out a frustrated growl. "That one was supposed to be yours!"

"How was I to know? You never said we were splitting them."

"When there's an even number, that goes without saying," she snapped as she joined him.

They watched the bandit cross over one dune and start climbing the hill of another. He had his back turned to them; Kyleigh could smell the panic on his breath. When he glanced over his shoulder and she saw his fear, she could no longer resist. She began walking towards him.

Silas followed along beside her, so close that their shoulders pressed together. His raw excitement spilled into hers, fueling it. "I'll race you for him," he said, baring his teeth in a snarling grin.

She grinned back. "Just try to keep up, cat —"

An explosion rattled the earth, cutting her sentence short. They watched as the whole top of the dune blew skywards, swallowing the bandit's body in a burst of orange flame. The dune showered back to earth in a stinging wave of sand, and Kyleigh thought she could see bits of the bandit's scimitar glinting among the debris.

When she turned, she saw Jake standing behind them, lowering his staff. He squinted as the last of the bandit fluttered to earth, his lip curled over his teeth.

"What?" he said, when he saw Kyleigh and Silas gaping at him. They didn't reply, and he huffed. "We couldn't very well let him get away, now could we? Especially after they saw *him* change shape."

He thrust his staff at Silas, who yowled and dropped to the ground.

"He's not going to kill you," Kyleigh said, kicking him in the rump.

"I might," Jake said glumly. "That's all I seem to be good for."

As they left, Jake looked back often. And darkness plagued his face.

****

"We need to find shelter, dragoness!" Silas hissed, tugging on the hem of her jerkin.

Yes — Kyleigh knew they needed to find shelter. In fact, she was so well aware of it that she didn't actually *need* to be reminded every five minutes. But that didn't stop Silas from pestering her.

"If we don't find shelter —"

"We'll be stripped of our flesh," she said over the top of him. "They'll gnaw us down to the bone, and leave our marrow to crisp in the sun!"

"I'm sorry — what was that?" Jake said, trotting up to them. He'd been lagging behind for hours, studying the dirt samples he'd collected. But at the mention of being devoured, it was amazing how quickly he closed the gap. "Who's going to be stripping our flesh?"

"The creatures that have been following us all day," Silas said impatiently.

"We're being followed?" Jake said, spinning around.

Silas grabbed the straps of his pack and bent him downwards. "Do you not hear them? The little voices beneath the sand?" When Jake shook his head, Silas released him. "Humans," he spat. His neck twisted about as he turned to glare at the falling sun. "Dragoness —"

"I *know*," she snapped back at him.

She'd actually been hunting for a spot to make camp for a good hour, now. The problem was that Jake couldn't climb any of the higher dunes, and a spot too close to the ground might very well get them eaten. She paused at the top of their next climb, scanning over the blistering landscape for a suitable place to rest.

"There's nothing but sand!" Silas moaned in her ear. "I was a fool to follow you out here — and now I'm going to be eaten for it!"

"Eaten?" Jake said, with no small amount of alarm.

Kyleigh ignored them. She'd just spotted a small drift in the distance — one that stood well away from the others, and just tall enough to keep them from harm. She left her companions and went for it at a run.

When she reached it, she dropped her pack at the dune's base and climbed its slippery side. It was much wider on top than it'd looked from a distance, which would suit them just fine. She balanced herself on the edge, and then slipped into her dragon form.

A good bit of the dune collapsed under her weight, sliding downwards as her claws dug in. She curled her tail up behind her for balance, and then she took a deep breath.

Every dragon had two sets of lungs: the ones they used to breathe air, and those they used to breathe fire. Kyleigh inhaled as deeply as she could, held her breath for a moment, and felt the click in her chest as the vault opened over her second pair of lungs. Heat bubbled from her middle, rising up her throat like bile. When the fire touched her tongue, she exhaled.

A river of yellow flame burst from her mouth. It followed the trail of her breath to the sand beneath her. She exhaled for as long as she could, tilting her head up and down, making sure that the whole top of the dune was covered. When she closed her mouth, the sand around her glowed red — like the fiery cap of a mountain.

"It's glass!" Jake said from behind her. He tried to sprint up the dune, slipped, and had to grab onto the spines of her tail to keep from tumbling down. He drew the vial of dirt from his pocket and shook it at his ear. "The flakey bits on top of the dirt — the thing that made the ground so hot — it was glass!" His smile faded and his mouth dropped open. "Good lord, the sun's even hotter than I thought it was. What have we gotten ourselves into?"

"We'll have worse than the sun to deal with, if this *glass* doesn't cool quickly," Silas muttered. He crouched at the base of the dune, his ear pressed against the sand. "The little voices are getting closer."

"I might have a spell to cool it — ah, if you'll help me up."

Kyleigh bent her head down and Jake grabbed onto one of her horns. She lifted him easily to the top of the dune. He seemed to think for a moment, muttering to himself as his staff hovered over the cap. Finally, he decided.

His staff came down and tapped the edge of the glass. The glowing red retreated from it, fading back like ripples in a pond. For a moment, the glass cap lay before them, clear and perfectly cool. Then for some odd reason, it started to crinkle — and wound up looking like a gigantic leaf of transparent, rumpled parchment.

"Huh," Jake said, staring at it. "Well, I don't understand *that* at all."

"There's no time for your wonderings, shaman." Silas scampered up Kyleigh's back — dodging swiftly when she bit at him. He leapt out into the middle of the glass and pounded down with his heels. It made a loud *thunk*, but didn't break. "Yes, this will do nicely."

"I still don't understand what the two of you are so worried about," Jake began, but Silas thrust a pack in his hands.

"You'll see soon enough. Why don't you get our dinner roasting while the dragoness and I set up the tents?"

When Kyleigh came out of her dragon form, she felt a bit dizzier than usual. She realized it was probably because she hadn't eaten much: between her constant heaving at sea and her scant breakfast, her stomach didn't have a lot to work with. And the cook in Roost kept her so well-fed that she supposed she must've gotten spoiled.

While there wasn't much that could chill a dragon's blood, the desert nights were cold, and Kyleigh feared her companions might freeze without a proper shelter. Their tents were small and fastened closed at both ends. She'd also brought along a bundle of animal pelts to line the floors.

It didn't take them long to set the tents up. Silas learned quickly: she only had to show him once. The glass was thick enough that they were able to drive the stakes in without cracking it. In fact, Kyleigh didn't think they even hit the bottom.

"The sun hasn't gone down, yet," Silas said, when she pointed it out. "Methinks you celebrate too quickly."

Kyleigh rolled her eyes. "Why don't you just admit that I saved your smelly hide and be done with it?"

"You saved nothing," he said haughtily, shoving a pelt into the nearest tent. "A few more moments, and I would have thought up an answer for myself."

"Oh really? And would that have been before or after you finished wringing your paws?"

"I wringed nothing —"

"You were mewing like a kitten."

He threw the pelt he'd been fumbling with onto the ground. "Lies," he hissed. "I do not *mew*."

Kyleigh shrugged. "I don't know ... I could've sworn I saw a tear —"

"What's that?" Jake said, cutting over the top of whatever nasty retort Silas had at the ready.

A strange, chirping had begun to fill the air, as if a large flock of birds was about to land on top of them. Voices joined the song by the dozen, growing louder as the last of the sun fell behind the barren hills. Kyleigh felt the earth quake as hundreds of eager bodies squirmed their way to the surface.

"Get back!" she shouted at Jake, who'd wandered to the edge of the glass.

"Do you not hear that —?"

Sand sprayed up in front of him and a white, wriggling beast leapt out. Kyleigh ripped Jake behind her and swung Harbinger blindly. There was a squeak, a shower of slime, and the two separate halves of a giant worm sailed past them.

One half stuck wetly to the top of Jake's boot. He slung it away and leapt back. "What is *that*? And why has it got so many teeth?"

"Minceworms," Kyleigh said grimly.

The heat in Whitebone was bad, and the sand made travel difficult — but the minceworms were the real reason nobody journeyed through the southern desert. The worms had white, fleshy skin and looked a bit like overgrown maggots. Thousands of razor-sharp teeth lined their gullets, and their mouths could stretch to fit around just about anything.

Kyleigh had once seen a swarm of minceworms devour a company of the Baron's guards — armor and all.

She heard the thumping beneath them as the minceworms tried to ram their way through the floor. Their hot breath fogged the glass, and their teeth squeaked wetly as they pressed their jaws against it. But fortunately, they couldn't get through.

For half a breath, Kyleigh thought her plan might actually work. But that was before she realized just how far the little blighters could leap.

"Get *back*," she said to Jake, when a worm burst from the sand and nearly latched onto his boot. She elbowed him to the middle of the camp, swinging Harbinger as she went.

At least when the worms landed on the glass, they seemed to lose their footing. Without the sand to grip onto, they flopped and squirmed helplessly, creeping forward mere inches at a time. Kyleigh hacked the ones that came too close, and Jake blasted them with spells.

"There's no end to them!" Silas cried. He wielded one of their pans like a club. A minceworm wriggled up to him, hissing furiously, and he squished it flat.

The worm's flesh stayed pressed down for a moment, looking like a berry crushed underfoot. Then it suddenly sprang back to life — and came after him all the more furiously. When Silas clubbed it again, the worm stuck to the bottom of the pan. He yelped and threw it away.

"We can't keep this up all night," Jake said. Sweat was already beginning to plaster his brow. "Even a mage has his limits —"

"I know," Kyleigh said, taking her frustration out on the nearest worm.

All around them, the sands had come to life. Pale bodies bounded up and out of the dunes, like fish riding the waves. Their chirping grew louder as they swarmed. She could smell their excitement. It was the same bloodlust she'd felt just hours before. Only now, the worms were the hunters.

And she was the prey.

"Ha!" Jake sent a fireball into a crowd of minceworms, and it worked rather well: the fire caught onto their flesh, racing from worm to worm like flame through oil, burning them up instantly. "It seems they're quite flammable ... wait, I've got it!"

Jake leapt forward and Kyleigh had no choice but to follow. He dragged his staff across the ground, muttering to himself, and fire sprang up in a trail behind him. Kyleigh moved with him, watching out of the corner of her eye for minceworms.

She hacked them away, sometimes cutting them straight from the air. The worms chirped and flopped after her; their fleshy jaws pulsed for her heels. She was so focused on not getting bitten that Jake had to jab her in the back to get her attention.

"Come on!" he said, waving frantically.

She dove between a narrow gap in the flames, and Jake quickly dragged his staff behind her. When she looked up, she saw that he'd drawn a protective circle around the whole camp, encasing them in a high wall of flame.

The few minceworms that tried to bully their way through the wall were burned up immediately. Their bodies burst into ash and the wind carried them away. After a few moments of hopeful circling, their chirping dropped in pitch — deepening to something that reminded Kyleigh of a disappointed grunt. Most of the worms sank back into the sands, leaving just a few dozen behind.

"Excellent," Silas said grumpily. "Now that we no longer have to worry about being eaten, I can enjoy my dinner."

"Finally decided to come down from the tent poles, have you?" Kyleigh retorted.

He hissed at her.

While Silas served himself some dinner, Kyleigh went after Jake. He knelt at the edge of the flames, inspecting the fire wall.

"A perfectly decent, proper spell," she said. "And it's done no harm to anyone."

Jake nodded out at the worms. "They might disagree with you."

"Well, they deserved it."

He laughed. "They *did* deserve it. Vile little creatures, aren't they? And yet ... I sort of find them interesting."

Kyleigh bit back a groan and instead, planted a hand on his boney shoulder. "You saved all of our hides tonight — mine included. And since that horrible little furball over there isn't likely to thank you," she jerked her chin at Silas, "I'll say it for him: thank you, Jake."

He nodded, made a great show of straightening his spectacles — and fought very hard to keep from looking too pleased.

Chapter 13
Lord of Southbarn

Escaping the plains was going to be a little more difficult than Kael had expected. Though oddly enough, it wasn't the guards or the mages that foiled him: it was his own blasted body.

Every inch of him screamed out in protest. Something like molten iron ran along his bones, burning him furiously with even the smallest step. He couldn't turn his head without hurting his neck, his shoulders ached too badly to raise his arms, and his legs — well, his legs just flatly refused.

He'd expected to be a little sore after pulling the plow, but nothing quite like this.

For days on end, things were the same. The stall doors screeched open at an hour before dawn, and Kael trudged down the aisle, past the giant-shaped scorch mark that Casey had left on the floor, and out to the water troughs for a morning drink. Then he followed Declan and Brend to whichever field they'd been assigned to plow. By the time they arrived, pale light had crept up over the horizon.

"Enjoy this sunrise, rat," Brend would holler, as Kael worked himself into the straps. "You'll likely not live to see another!"

The second full day of work nearly did him in. Kael's body was so beaten up that he had no choice but to use his mind to drag the plow. He figured that stumbling along on his sore muscles would make him seem convincingly weak.

It worked. Not only did they get their own field finished, they were able to help a neighboring team finish theirs. By the end of the day, Kael only had a very slight headache, and he was rather proud of himself. But his relief didn't last long.

The third day turned out to be the most difficult of all. Kael's body still ached, and his short night's sleep didn't give his mind enough time to rest. At just past midday, his head throbbed so fiercely that he had to give up on his mind all together. He pushed through the rest of the afternoon on nothing more than his aching muscles.

They were lucky to finish their allotted field that day.

No matter how hard he worked, or how long he rested, Kael could never seem to catch his breath. He found himself trapped in a cycle of sore limbs and headaches — a torment with no end. The days never seemed to grow any shorter, and the plow certainly never got any lighter. At some point, he even lost his boots: they sunk into a particularly soggy patch of field, and were never seen again.

Brend assured him that the bottoms of his feet would eventually harden: "A few weeks of this, and you'll be able to bend the pointy end of a nail back on its head!"

But Kael wasn't sure he would make it another day, much less a few weeks.

Time passed so slowly that he thought every day might've counted for two. The sun crept its way across the sky as they worked, baking the mud onto their skin and drying their sweat in salty patches. Then at night, Kael swore the moon must've sprinted from one horizon to the next. It seemed like his head had barely touched the pillow before Finks was lashing them awake.

But somehow, Kael managed to survive. By mind or body or sheer, stubborn will, he dug his heels into the earth and pressed himself on.

Slowly, his worries began to fade. Jonathan still hovered in the back of his thoughts; Kael knew that they still needed to find someway to escape. But the exhausting work of the fields calmed him. It covered over the black beast in his heart, and all of his troubles grew distant. They washed away with sweat, trickling in a steady line to the dirt beneath him.

Kael would let the earth hold his fears for the moment, and he would worry himself only with the plowing.

****

"Are you excited, wee rat?" Brend bellowed in his ear.

Kael *was* excited: the wagon that carried water barrels around to the fields had finally showed up. It was nearly two hours late.

The mage in the driver's perch had flat feet and a hunched back — as if he'd steered the cart for so long that he'd actually become a part of it. He stared blankly into the distance while they drank, his whip hanging limply in his hands. And he seemed entirely unconcerned with how thirsty they were.

Declan had just passed Kael the ladle when Brend's hand pounded down on his shoulder — sloshing nearly half of the water onto the ground.

"It's the last day of plowing," Brend went on, as Kael gulped down the remainder of his drink. When the ladle was empty, he reluctantly passed it off to Brend.

"Yeh, we'll be starting on the wheat tomorrow," Declan murmured. He raised his head to gaze around the fields, and the sun chased the shadow from his brow. Though his mouth stayed in a straight line, Kael thought he could see happiness in his eyes — though perhaps *happiness* was too strong a word. In any case, he didn't look as cross as usual.

Brend finished his drink and passed the ladle to Declan. He glanced up, but the water wagon mage just went on staring. So Declan dipped the ladle in among the barrels for a second drink.

Brend yawned and stretched his arms high over his head, and Kael caught a whiff of something unpleasant — a stench that probably had to do with the dark stains in the pits of Brend's shirt.

"Ole Hob is circling us again," he said, reaching over to bat at Declan.

They looked to where he pointed and saw Hob wandering on the edge of their field, the many-headed whip clutched in his hand. He walked back and forth down the rows, searching for errors in their lines, but he found none.

Though Brend was obnoxious in countless other ways, he did a good job of steering the plow. He hollered from sunup and on, ordering them to turn a bit more this way or that, shouting with hardly a pause until they scraped a perfect line. So Hob could search for a reason to lash them, but Kael knew he wouldn't find one.

Declan scooped out a second ladleful of water and passed it down to Kael. His eyes disappeared into the crevice of his brow as he glared at Hob. "He's got the wench-tongue with him."

"The what?" Kael said between gulps.

"That whip he's carrying — we call it a wench-tongue."

"Why's that?"

Brend pounded him on the back, and a good portion of Kael's next sip shot up his nose. "Because she'll bite you with every lash! There're little bits of metal woven into each strand. Makes for a mightily powerful bite, it does. But don't worry," he plucked the empty ladle from Kael's hand and went to fill it, "they're only allowed to hit us twice with a wench-tongue."

"Gilderick's careful with his stock," Declan said, in answer to the question on Kael's face. "He knows that every time one of us bleeds, there's a chance the wound will kill us. The mages aren't allowed to draw blood — unless we don't get our work finished, that is."

"Or if we're rebellious, or if we even *think* about trying to escape," Brend added with a snort. "They could flog us for anything and Gilderick would never hear about it. He hardly ever leaves his clodded castle."

"So why don't they?" Kael wondered. He knew for a fact that Fallon couldn't wait to strip the meat off his back — he'd told him so that morning.

Declan's mouth tilted into an almost-smirk: "Because His Lordship is a raving lunatic ... and they know it."

Brend let out a bark of laughter. "Not even being a mage'll save them. Take Churl, for example." He nodded to the water wagon mage, who still stared listlessly into the

166

distance. "I hear that he tried to sneak into the castle without permission, once — and Gilderick caught him. He's never been quite right, after that. But that's not the worst of it," Brend said, his eyes glinting. "Wait till you hear what happened to Ludwig —"

"Time's up!"

Churl had suddenly snapped awake. Now he slung his whip in wide arcs over their heads, his eyes wild with madness. "Get away, beasts!" he shrilled. "Get away from my cart!"

Spells lashed Kael's head and neck. He held his breath and threw his arms over his face, even though he knew it wouldn't do him much good. Brend tossed the ladle back into the barrel and they jumped quickly to the side.

A team of Fallows pulled Churl's wagon. When he cracked his whip over their heads, they tore off down the road in a panic — kicking up a monstrous cloud of dust in their wake.

"He's a bit off, that one," Brend murmured. He rubbed the side of his face, where a number of red welts had sprung up across his brow and cheekbones. "We'd better get back to the plowing."

Kael took three steps before he realized that Declan wasn't moving. Welts had sprung up on him, too — in a pattern identical to Brend's. But he made no move to soothe them. Instead, his eyes stayed locked on Kael's face. They roved over his sharp features for a moment, searching. And then they narrowed.

Kael turned away quickly, but he knew it was too late. Declan had already seen, even through the dirt and grime, that there were no wounds on his face.

******

By the time they returned to the barn that evening, Kael was too tired to worry about what Declan had seen. He shoveled a few handfuls of porridge down his throat and then retreated to the stall.

167

It was a small space. Perhaps at one point, it had been meant for horses. He wagered that about half a dozen giants could've squeezed into it comfortably. As it was, the stall was currently home to ten giants — and Kael.

Straw pallets littered the packed dirt floor. Many of them had been padded down with the ragged remains of filthy clothing. Worn shirtsleeves, the tattered ends of breeches and even a few pairs of gloves poked out from beneath them. The stale odor rising from the pallets was sharp enough to knock a man off his feet. Kael was always a little shocked whenever he walked into it.

But for all their peculiar scent, the giants kept their pallets tidy. They made them up every morning — fluffing the sweat-stiffened clothes with all the deft pride of chambermaids, arranging their beds just so.

Kael had thought it was a bit strange for the giants to put so much care into their living, when they lived so miserably. But then Brend had shouted something over dinner one night, and it made him think:

"The mages may call us beasts, but I say they're wrong — beasts don't have beds, after all!"

Kael had understood, then. He knew why the giants took pride in their bedding: they lived in barns, slept in stalls, and did the work of horses. There was so little left about them that was human, that he supposed having beds of their own made them feel like men.

Now, as he crossed the stall to reach his spot, Kael was careful not to tread on any of the giants' pallets. The space he slept in didn't have any bedding, because there wasn't any to spare. But he didn't mind it so much: his little patch of dirt sat at the back of the room, in a spot that wasn't too crowded. He wouldn't have traded the extra space for anything — not even a pillow.

For some reason, this spot had gone unclaimed. He supposed it was because the earth sloped down a bit there, forming something like a shallow bowl. The sloping earth would've been uncomfortable for the giants, but it suited Kael just fine. He curled up inside of the bowl, pressing his back against one lip and shoring his knees against the other.

It didn't take him long to fall asleep ... but *staying* asleep was another matter.

Kael dreamt that he was back in the Unforgivable Mountains. He ran along the forest trails at full-tilt, bow in hand. He'd been chasing something, and he was so focused on his prey that he forgot to watch the path in front of him. It wasn't long before he tripped on a rock and rolled down into a dark burrow.

Insects came out of the soil in a rush. Their black bodies were nearly invisible in the darkness, but he could hear them clicking to each other. They climbed across his ears and scurried down his back, their little feet dragged itching lines through his skin. All the while, they chattered:

Click click click click click ...

Kael woke with a start. He pawed at his face and rolled over onto his back, trying desperately to crush the bugs beneath him. Something was crawling through his hair. When he grabbed it, he realized that it was wet.

The things attacking him weren't bugs at all: they were drops of water. He looked up at the roof and groaned at what he saw.

No wonder the giants had avoided this spot — there was a leak in the roof! Muffled peals of thunder rumbled in the distance, rising and fading back like the snores of some enormous beast. Fat drops of rain slapped against the roof and slid through the crack above Kael's bed.

The crack was only about the length of his forearm, but the pressure of the gathering water bowed it out. A small waterfall poured from the roof, slapping down onto the stall floor. It quickly filled the shallow dip where Kael had been sleeping.

With his makeshift bed nearly submerged, he had no choice but to scoot closer to Brend. Only a thin sliver of dry space was left between them, and one of the giants had his massive leg sprawled out across it — cutting the sliver into a tiny square. So Kael was forced to sleep sitting up.

He leaned his back against the wall and comforted himself with the thought that things probably couldn't get any worse. Then, just before dawn, the roof collapsed.

Kael woke to a crash and a wave of muddy water that soaked him from head to toe. Apparently, the growing weight of the water had proven too much for the bowed-out roof: part of the beam had rotted and given way — raining chunks of wood and shingles down where Kael had been sleeping.

"Wasthat?" Brend's head shot up. His eyes were half-shut and bits of straw clung to his face.

"The roof caved in," Kael mumbled, trying to wring some of the moisture from his tunic.

Brend's lip puffed out in a sleepy frown. "Then stop jumping on it," he said groggily. His head sunk down, and soon he was breathing heavily once again.

Kael didn't get to go back to sleep. He was far too wet and cold to be comfortable, and his neck ached from sitting up. The stall doors opened later than usual: the sun was actually a respectable distance from the horizon when Finks released them.

"I don't know about you clodders, but I feel like I've had an extra hour of sleep!" Brend called, and the giants answered him with a yawning cheer.

Declan stepped around them and went to peer at the western sky. "More rain coming," he said.

And he was right. No sooner did they finish their drinks than another wave of rain came pattering down. "Back in your cages, beasts!" Finks cried. His face looked miserable beneath his oilskin cloak: shadows hung under his eyes, and his lips were bared away from his long teeth in a grimace.

As Finks chased them into the barn, Kael couldn't help but think that the spells coming off his whip were a little more potent than usual. "What's he so upset about?"

Brend shrugged. "Oh, he's probably just fussed over those long, lovely locks of his," he said with a wicked glance back at Finks. "Either that, or Churl didn't turn up to watch his barn last night. They hate it when he does that."

The barn doors slammed shut, and Kael had a feeling that they might be stuck inside for the rest of the day. At least they weren't trapped in their stalls: the doors stayed open, and they had the whole aisle to wander in.

"Why would Churl not turn up?"

Brend looked at him as if that was the most ridiculous question he'd ever heard asked. "Because he's mad — *that's* why! He doesn't remember that he's lord of Southbarn, so he doesn't —"

"Southbarn?" Kael said.

"Ah, that's right. We haven't introduced you to our little Kingdom. Well, since you show no signs of perishing any time soon, I don't suppose it'll hurt to — oops." Brend dropped his arm across Kael's shoulders with such force that it knocked him off his feet. "Sorry about that. I'm not used to having little chicken-winged fellows to talk to."

"You could be more careful," Kael snapped as he pulled himself from the ground.

"Yeh, or *you* could fatten up," Declan grunted.

Several of the giants chuckled at this. But before Kael could retort, Brend swept him under his arm. "Oh, don't talk about my wee rodent friend like that," he said, pawing roughly at Kael's curls.

The stench coming from under Brend's arm was so dense that it was practically a living thing. Kael slipped out from his hold and took in a breath of clean air. "What were you going to tell me about your Kingdom?" he said, before Brend could snatch him again.

Now that they had a free afternoon, Kael wanted to learn all he could about the plains. And Brend seemed to know a little bit about everything.

"Right. Well, we giants think of this as our own little Kingdom — we call it the Fields. Over that way is the Pens," Brend added, jerking his thumb behind him. "And inside the Fields, we have four castles, ruled over by four bumbling, magical lords: you've got Hob of Northbarn, Bobbin of Eastbarn, Churl of Southbarn, and Finks of Westbarn — that's where you live, in case you didn't know it."

"Surprisingly, I did," Kael said. He thought the giants' names were fairly straightforward and easy to remember. He tucked this information away and quickly pressed for more. "So if they've each got their own barn, why would the other mages care if Churl turns up or not?"

Brend bent down and pressed his hands to his knees, leaning over Kael as if he were a child asking after the color of the sky. "Well you see, wee thing — bolts and doors can't hold a giant. Not the normal sort, anyways. So the mages have got all of these little spells cast to keep us in." He pointed up to the ceiling, and his smile was so kind that Kael was almost certain he was being mocked. "Finks lives in that cottage above us, and every night, around the same time the fairies start sprinkling the dew, he locks us down — all magic-like. And if Churl isn't in his cottage," Brend spread his arms wide, "then the spells on *his* barn don't get cast. Which means —"

"One of the others has to do it for him," Kael finished, before Brend's mocking could go on any longer. He thought about this for a moment. "I imagine it would tire the mages out, having to watch two barns at once. I don't know much about magic —"

"Don't you?" Declan said. He was sitting down the aisle from them, his arms propped up on his knees. There was no telling how long he'd been listening in. "Why are you so interested in the mages, rat?"

Kael wanted to tell him to mind his own business, but he managed to hold the words back. "I just thought I'd learn about these things — seeing as how I'm going to be stuck here for a while."

Brend laughed so loudly that it drowned out anything Declan might've said. "That you are, wee rat. You'll make it out of here the same day we do: in a *while!*"

Kael ignored the many guffaws aimed in his direction and instead made his way to the stall. It was mercifully empty. He crept to the back wall and lay down in the only dry strip left of his bedding.

Light drops of rain thumped steadily overhead, their rhythm halted every now and then by a break in the clouds.

Water trickled down from the man-sized hole in the roof and pooled inside the shallow bowl, forming a little stream that ran under the wall and out into the fields. The noise of the rain relaxed him, and it wasn't long before he began to think seriously about taking a nap ...

A hawk's screech rent the air and Kael's eyes snapped open — just in time to nearly have them clawed out.

A barrage of feathers struck him in the head, knocking him blindly on his side. Two powerful wings beat him, talons tore at his shirt. He fell on his stomach and pulled his arms over his head — trying desperately to protect his eyes. Just when he thought he was in real danger of having an ear nipped off, the attack suddenly ended.

The hawk cried out again, though this time its voice sounded slightly strained. When Kael rolled over, he saw immediately why.

Declan stood before him. He had the hawk clamped tightly in his grip: one hand held it around the talons — the other held it around the throat. A large group of giants crowded the door behind him. Some popped their heads over the neighboring walls to watch. But none of them seemed keen to take a step inside.

The giants made a path for Brend, who paused in the doorway. "It's a crazed little thing, isn't it?" He bent closer to the hawk. "Mountain rat he may be, but he's still too big for you to go carrying off. Better snap its neck, Declan."

The hawk had gone quiet, its amber eyes slightly bugged out from the pressure of having Declan's fingers wrapped around its neck. But at the mention of being snapped, it began struggling wildly — squawking and flapping its monstrous wings.

Brend leapt back with a yelp. Declan had to whip his head to the side to avoid being struck. The hawk's talons squirmed against his grip, and that's when Kael noticed something odd.

He caught a glint of some object wrapped around one of the hawk's legs and he charged forward, bellowing for Declan to stop.

173

He looked surprised. When Kael reached for the hawk, he wrenched it away. "What are you doing? He'll cut you up —"

"I don't care — hold him still!"

The panic in Kael's voice must've startled him, because Declan didn't argue. He held the hawk steady, and Kael went to work.

Yes, there it was! A tiny shackle was clamped around one of the hawk's talons. He could see the milky white film of a spell covering the iron. He bent his head forward, shielding what he was about to do from Declan's searching eyes.

He took the talon in one hand and used the other to break the spell — pressing down with his thumbnail until the film broke. It was difficult because the shackle was so small, but he finally managed to peel the spell free. Then it was a simple matter of tearing the iron away.

He heard a soft *clink* as the shackle broke, and he stuffed it quickly into his pocket. Then several things happened at once:

Pain shot up Kael's arm as he came out of his trance. The hawk had scored him deeply while he worked, leaving a vicious-looking gash on his right hand. He wrapped the wound hastily in his shirt, cringing when he heard the giants gasp.

He thought they must've seen him break the shackle, and he knew he'd have to come up with an explanation. He was thinking furiously when something heavy struck the floor. There was a flash of movement as Declan shot behind him.

Then he heard Brend bellowing over the top of everything else:

"Plains mother — it's a barbarian!"

Chapter 14
By Way of a Giant

Kael looked up from his ravaged hand and saw that a boy had materialized in front of him. His eyes were the same solid amber the hawk's had been. A patch of stormy gray feathers sprouted from each of his elbows.

For a moment, the boy sat on the ground with a dazed look on his face. His eyes widened when he saw the giants, and he scrambled back against the wall.

"Kill it," Brend hissed, shoving Declan forward. "Don't let it get us!"

Before he could even take a step, Kael stood in his path. Anger drowned out the throbbing pain in his hand. "Try to kill him, and you'll have me to deal with."

Brend's face hardened. "It may wear a boy's shape now, but that's no human," he said, jerking his chin at the halfhawk. "He's a cursed monster, an empty vessel! Everybody knows about the barbarians: they're wicked men who've traded their souls for power. There's nothing but beast left in them —"

"You're wrong," Kael snapped back. He didn't know how the shapechangers came by their power, but he was certain they weren't beasts.

Declan stepped forward until there was hardly a hand's breadth between them. When Kael didn't budge, his face twisted into a scowl. "How can you be sure? How do you know that thing won't murder us the second it gets a chance?"

The words left Kael's mouth before he could think to stop them: "Because I knew one, once. We traveled together, fought together — she even saved my life. There was nothing but good in her. And she ... she became a very ... dear friend ..."

Kael's knees suddenly gave out. He felt strange, muddled — as if he'd just woken from a feverish sleep. His wounded hand was trapped beneath him, throbbing helplessly against his gut. When he tried to roll over, he found he couldn't remember how to move his legs. He was numb and listless — hurting, but too tired to cry.

Just when he thought he could stand it no longer, the weakness relented. He shook the numb feeling from his limbs and took his strength back. Air whistled across his lungs as he breathed in. It was like the first breath from out of the sea.

"Don't listen to him — he's all clodded," Brend said as Kael struggled to his feet. "The blood loss must have gotten to him."

Kael wasn't sure that was all there was too it. This was a different sort of weakness, one that frightened him even more than losing blood. For a moment, he thought he'd felt the black beast again. He thought he'd felt its jaws closing tight over his heart. He felt like it had almost killed him.

But even as he thought this, he shoved his fear stubbornly to the side. There were far more important matters at hand.

Though Brend tried to nudge him forward, Declan didn't move. His snarl was gone and his face was a careful mask once again. It looked ridiculous to see a man as large as Brend hiding behind one as small as Declan. But Kael was in no mood to laugh.

He turned and saw that the halfhawk was still crouched against the wall. His pupils sharpened when Kael stepped closer, but he made no move to run. "Does anybody have a spare tunic?" Kael said.

The giants met him with icy glares. No one was going to give up a part of his bed for a shapechanger.

Kael was in real danger of losing his patience when Declan broke from the crowd. He went to his pallet and dug around for a moment. "Here," he said, tossing a ragged tunic at the halfhawk.

176

His hand shot out with lightning speed, snagging the shirt between his curled fingers. Then he pulled it roughly over his head. The shirt must've been a giant's: the hem stretched well past his knees.

"What's your name?" Kael said, when the halfhawk made no effort to speak.

"Eveningwing," he muttered. Then his head shot up, and Kael flinched when those strange, piercing eyes locked onto his. "Yours?"

"Kael," he said, touching a hand to his chest. "What brings you to the plains?"

Eveningwing's pupils dilated and shrank as they studied his face, flicking quickly over his every feature. "I came to kill you."

The giants broke out in a chorus of mumbling. He thought he heard Brend hiss: "I told you so!"

But Kael wasn't alarmed. "Yeah, I'm not surprised. The King has sent shapechangers after me before."

His smile seemed to disarm Eveningwing, but only for a moment. He returned Kael's smile with a sharp one of his own. "The King didn't send me. I came here to kill you for myself — for my own reasons."

"I knew it!" Brend stormed. "What did I tell you, eh? There's no trusting them. We ought to have killed him when we had the chance."

Kael was slightly surprised by Eveningwing's confession. He was certain they'd never crossed paths before. What could he have possibly done to make the halfhawk his enemy?

"Why do you want to kill me?"

Eveningwing's face betrayed nothing. So Kael had no idea what he was thinking until he said: "You killed Bloodfang."

There was a jolt in Kael's chest at the sound of that name, a pang that made him choke on his next breath. Bloodfang was another memory he'd been trying to bury. He told himself over and over again that Bloodfang had wanted to die — Kyleigh had even forgiven him for it. But the guilt still haunted his heart.

"You're right," he said, not taking his eyes off Eveningwing. "I did kill him. And I deserve to die for it."

His black pupils sharpened into points, and Kael knew what was coming. He braced himself for the moment when Eveningwing would lunge at his throat ... but it never came. In another blink, his pupils were wide again, and he slumped back against the wall.

"I never had a flock of my own. Bloodfang was kind to me. Wolves are often kind — as long as you aren't hunting in their territory," he added with a smirk. "Bloodfang taught me many things about our people. He taught me to fight honorably. He told me to seek wisdom." Eveningwing sighed heavily. "Now I have found wisdom exactly when I didn't want to. I cannot kill you."

Kael had been trying to digest everything Eveningwing told him, but it was difficult: the halfhawk's tongue moved every bit as quickly as his eyes. "Why can't you kill me?"

Eveningwing rolled his head back, cracking his neck, and Kael saw that another patch of feathers sprouted from the base of his skull. "Because you saved my life. You've set me free. And by the laws of my people —"

"Stop." Kael held his hand up quickly. "I know what you're going to say, and I won't hear it. The debt between us is already settled. You came here to kill me, I stopped *them* from killing you," he waved to the giants — who, despite their suspicions, had begun crowding around in interest, "and then you decided not to kill me, after all. So everything balances out. There's no life debt between us."

Eveningwing blinked. "But there's still the matter of the curse —"

"Curse? What curse?" Brend said. He'd begun to slink closer, but at the mention of a curse, he leapt back. "You better not have brought any curses around here —"

"It's not that sort of curse," Kael said.

"Then what sort is it?" Declan stood with his arms tensed at his side. His gaze narrowed to burn a point through the middle of Kael's head.

He thought quickly. He couldn't let the giants know that Eveningwing had been magicked — that would raise all of the wrong sorts of questions. "It's ... more of a figure of speech," he said. An idea came to him, and he charged after it — hoping to mercy that Eveningwing would play along. "When a shapechanger loses a friend in battle, it hangs over him like a curse — um, plaguing him with grief. Until he can avenge his friend, that is. Then his grief is lifted."

There was a mumbled chorus of *ahs* from the giants gathered around him. They nodded to each other, their eyes widened in understanding. Only Declan still seemed troubled: he blinked furiously and scratched at his ear, a confused look on his face. But after a moment, even *he* seemed to believe Kael's story.

Or at least, he didn't say any differently.

"So your *grief* is your curse," Brend said. He watched for a moment as Eveningwing's head bobbed up and down.

"Yes." The halfhawk shot a look at Kael. "Though now I'm sad again because I have no way to repay you." He seemed to have another thought — one that was in no way connected to the first. His amber eyes flicked around the stall, over the rafters, along the wall and out into the aisle. "This is different from the other human nests I've been in. Why do you live here?"

Brend snorted loudly and shook his head at the other giants.

"We're stuck here," Kael explained. "It's like a prison."

Eveningwing's dark brows climbed high into the crop of his hair. Then for some reason, he began to squirm. "You're prisoners?" When Kael nodded, he broke into a wild grin. "*That's* how I'll repay you! I can set you free —"

"No!" Brend roared, and it was no joke: his foot came down so hard that it shook the dust from the rafters. "Try to spring us out of here, and I swear I'll kill you. I'll tan the savage leather from your hide —"

179

"He's only trying to help," Kael cut in. "Or are you too proud to take help from a shapechanger?"

"Pride has nothing to do with it," Declan said. He nodded to Brend. "Tell them."

Brend took a deep breath. The red retreated from his face, but the furious glint never left his eyes. "Gilderick keeps our women locked up in his castle," he said evenly. "We don't know where, and we don't have any way of finding out. But the important thing is this: if we try to rebel, Gilderick's sworn to kill them. For every man that escapes, he'll kill one of our sisters and hang her body in the Fields. That's why we don't care for outsiders — because outsiders don't care for us. What's it to them, if one of our sisters fall? They don't mind hurting us ... they'd do anything to save their own hides."

He glared, and Kael realized that the glint in Brend's eyes wasn't anger at all:

It was fear.

"Gilderick wouldn't really —" Kael began, but Declan cut him off.

"Oh, he certainly would. You weren't here the day the plains fell, rat. You didn't see how Titus's army slaughtered our parents. You didn't see how Gilderick sorted us out." His eyes slipped dangerously beneath the shadow of his brow. "So you'll just have to believe me when I say that he would — because he's already done far worse."

Kael's mouth went dry. He could practically feel Brend's anger burning behind his reddened face. All around him, the giants' breath blew out sharply, their nostrils flared. Even the rain sounded more malicious than before: it drummed in his ears, warning him.

But he didn't listen.

The giants might've thought that Kael didn't care, but the truth was that he cared very much. He wouldn't try to slip out now, not when it might cost the giants the lives of one of their sisters. But he also wasn't going to spend the rest of his life in chains.

180

No, this was just another rut in the path — a problem that he would have to solve. Kael realized that he wouldn't have a chance to go back to the seas. He wouldn't be able to rely on the pirates for help. From this point on, he'd be on his own.

It wasn't ideal, but he could do it. He'd *have* to do it. If he didn't figure out a way to free the giants on his own, they might all very well rot in their stalls.

"I think you understand now, wee rat. So I won't kill you outright. But know this: if I catch you trying to slip out of here," Brend smiled widely, "well ... we'll just tell Finks that the lions got you."

Kael shrugged. "All right. I won't go anywhere."

"Good," Brend said. Then he straightened up to look around at the others. "If there's going to be any plotting done, it'll need to be done a giant's way — and by way of a giant!"

There was a grunt of approval from the others. They crowded around at the door and poked their heads over the walls. Every pair of eyes was trained on Brend.

"Our Prince will have the answer. He's been thinking hard these last many years, and I feel he's close to making us a fine plan!"

Kael could hardly keep himself from gasping when the giants grunted in agreement:

Prince?

He'd read a little about the giants' government in the *Atlas*. They didn't have a class of lords and ladies, but lived scattered about in family clans. The clans warred amongst each other constantly: bickering over land, water, cattle — just about any little thing they might use to start a fight.

The only person who had any manner of control over the clans was the Prince. He alone had the power to collect taxes and call the giants to battle. When outsiders invaded the plains, it was the Prince who rallied the clans to fight. Some historians believed that the giants put the Prince's word even above the King's.

Kael was surprised at first, but his excitement quickly wore off when he realized that it didn't make any sense. "You mean to say that your Prince is *here*?" When the giants nodded, he still didn't understand. He thought they might be trying to trick him. "I don't believe you. Gilderick never would've let the Prince live — even as a slave."

The giants broke out in a rowdy bout of laughter, elbowing each other and pointing down at him — as if they could hardly believe such a silly creature existed.

Kael's face burned hot under their jeers, but he wasn't about to be defeated. "All right — who is it, then? Where's your Prince?"

"Here!" Declan said.

But before Kael could be properly shocked, the other giants began calling:

"Here!"

"Over here!"

"No — *I'm* the Prince today, you clodders!"

They dissolved into chuckles once again, and Brend goaded them on: "Gilderick tried to kill him, didn't he? He tried to wipe out the Prince's whole family! But that's the problem with the giants: we're *all* family. As long as there's a giant left alive, the plains will have a Prince. He's here among us," Brend said, sweeping his arms around. "One wee little Princeling cousin — a fellow so far down the line that not even the bloodtraitors could remember him. We've kept him safe all these years. And when the time's right, we'll put him back on the throne."

The giants let out a barking cheer, and Kael suddenly understood. "You wouldn't give him up."

Brend's mouth fell open in mock surprise. "He's got us figured out, lads — we'd better crush his wee head!"

Eveningwing sprang to Kael's side, shielding him with a feathered elbow. His sharp eyes stabbed at the giants, warning them. And their laughter dried up immediately.

"It's all right. They're only joking," Kael said, peeling Eveningwing to the side.

Well, he *hoped* the giants were joking. But with Brend, it was always difficult to tell.

****

That next day, the ground was still too wet to do any planting. So Hob ordered that the giants spend their time tending to the plows: they were to oil the harnesses, check the frames for cracks, and take the blades to the castle to be sharpened.

Kael was wondering how many fingers he might expect to lose when Hob shouted: "I need a team of beasts to go with Churl to the Pens — they've run out of straw for their blasted animals."

Brend and Declan's hands shot into the air. Kael's arm almost came out of its socket as Brend jerked his wrist skyward, volunteering him.

Hob's lips pinched around his chew. "A rat? And the two of you again?" He scanned the crowd, but none of the other giants raised their hands. "All right, I suppose you'll do —"

"No, you can't send *them*," Finks sputtered. He'd just emerged from one of the sheds behind the barns, a clump of Fallows in tow.

The Fallows stood pigeon-toed behind him. Their milky eyes sat dead, and their mouths hung slack. Each one had a shovel propped over his shoulder. Kael realized that they must've been going to dig a fresh latrine.

That was the one good thing about the Fallows: they did all of the tasks that nobody else wanted — like pulling Churl's wagon, and filling in the old latrines. And they never once complained.

They *were* a bit difficult to control, though. Even now, they didn't seem to notice that Finks had come to a stop: the Fallow nearest to him trod on the back of his heel, and he yelped.

"Back! Get *back*!" he screeched. He flayed them with his whip until they slunk away, then he spun back to Hob. "That little rat will be no good to you." His lips parted over his teeth in a sly grin. "Why don't you put him in my charge for the day?"

183

More than anything, Kael didn't want to spend his day digging latrines. The odor rising from the mire was so powerful that it singed his lungs. He always tried to keep his visits quick and to the point.

Fortunately, Hob was having none of it. "You're not the foreman, here — *I* am. And if I say the rat is fit enough to toss hay, then so he is. Now get back to your work."

Finks stomped off in a huff, and the Fallows trailed along behind him — waddling like a line of the largest, most unfortunate-looking ducklings Kael had ever laid eyes on.

As soon as Finks was out of sight, Hob chased them away with a few blows of his whip. Kael followed the giants to a shed behind Northbarn — one so large that it was almost a barn itself.

The shed was packed from floor to ceiling with straw. Declan handed Kael a tool that he recognized as a pitchfork. He'd seen pictures of them before, but never actually used one. He learned quickly that they were less a tool than a four-headed spear.

"Watch it, wee rat!" Brend called from over his shoulder. Kael stood back — but not nearly far enough.

Brend tossed a forkful of hay and Kael had to drop on all fours to keep from getting stabbed. "What in Kingdom's name are you —?"

"I told you to stand back," Brend said. He held his pitchfork out to Kael. "You see, what we do with these strange little things is scoop up great loads of hay —"

"I know what they're for," Kael snapped back. His hand burned furiously where Eveningwing had scratched him, and he was in no mood for Brend's heckling.

"Stand by the wagon and load the hay we toss," Declan said, jabbing his fork behind him.

Churl was parked a few paces outside of the shed. They'd taken the water barrels out of his wagon, leaving the bed empty. The giants tossed straw out in loads over their shoulders, where it landed in a neat pile in front of Churl. And it was Kael's job to scoop it into the wagon.

The shaft of the pitchfork had clearly been made for giant hands: try as he might, Kael couldn't get a good grip on it. His fingers stretched out until it pulled painfully on the wounded skin of his hand. The top end of the pitchfork was so heavy that he had to wedge it against his chest and try to lever it over his shoulder.

By the time he got the first load tossed back, most of the hay had slipped out between the prongs — dumping down upon his head.

Straw stuck in Kael's hair and to the sweat on his face. It fluttered beneath his collar and hung onto his back, itching him mercilessly with even the smallest movement. He shook the tail of his shirt, trying to force the straw out, but the sweat on his back held the itching bits to his skin like paste.

While Kael struggled, the giants made short work of the hay. He watched in amazement as they tossed heaping forkfuls over their shoulders. Their movements were deft and practiced: they bent over and around each other, turning like companions locked in battle. Brend's long arms hoisted high and up, while Declan launched bundles of straw in quick, heaving motions.

They had the whole shed cleared out in the time it took Kael to make a dozen throws.

"Shoo, wee thing!" Brend said, chasing Kael away from the pile. "This is a giant's work."

Once they had the straw loaded, the giants hopped into the wagon. Kael grimaced as the wheels groaned under their weight. They pulled Kael in by his belt, and he immediately wrapped his arms tightly around the wagon's rails. He'd seen Churl drive before, and he would take no chances.

Once they were all wedged in, Brend jabbed the butt of his pitchfork against the driver's bench. And Churl — who'd been staring fixedly at the clouds for quite some time — snapped to life.

"Move, move, *move!*" he squawked, swinging his whip in a flurry of lashes.

The team of Fallows roared and took off — sprinting down the road as fast as their thick legs could carry them. The wagon rocked dangerously as it bumped over rocks and divots; little bits of hay streamed out behind them. Kael's feet left the ground several times.

And had he not been holding on for his life, he probably would've been thrown to his death.

Chapter 15
The Scepter Stone

Across the main road from the Fields lay the Pens. They filled the land on the other side of Gilderick's castle: a patchwork of neat little fences that hemmed the earth into squares, each filled with an astonishing number of animals.

Kael had never seen so many creatures in one place. At first, he thought that all animals must live inside little paddocks, like the ones that dotted the Valley. Then he'd been surprised the first time he saw the pirates return from a raid with a large clump of cattle perched atop one of their ships. He remembered thinking how strange it was for so many great creatures to sit quietly, completely untroubled by the fact that they were trapped on a tiny boat.

He wondered why they hadn't tried to escape.

Now as he looked out at the Pens, he couldn't help but wonder the same thing. There were so many of them, and their fences were so small, that Kael couldn't believe that the animals hadn't tried to flee into the wilds. But they didn't so much as raise their furry heads to look at the lands beyond their fences: they were far too concerned with their grazing.

Herds of sheep wandered through the plots, their meaty sides covered in snow-white wool. They grazed contently on early shoots of grass while their lambs scampered about them on gangly legs — sparing with the tops of their hornless heads.

Kael held his nose when they passed by the pigpen. The stench rising up from the black mud was so potent that he could taste it in the back of his throat. He watched as several giants high-stepped through the filth, trying to corner some of the pigs.

Despite their enormous size, the pigs moved surely on their stubby legs. The mud coating their backs must've made them extra slippery: a number of the filthy creatures simply squeezed through the giants' arms and shot off in the opposite direction. After a considerable amount of chasing, one of the giants finally managed to grab a pig.

It was the size of a small bathtub. Kael watched in amazement as the giant snatched it up, hauling the whole squealing, wriggling thing over his massive shoulders. Though the pig fought desperately, it couldn't escape. It squealed all the more loudly as the giant carried it up the path, towards a second tower.

This tower was made of the same red brick as the castle, so Kael figured it must've been fairly new. There wasn't any smoke coming out of its top, but a large cloud of carrion birds circled it constantly.

He immediately felt sorry for the pig.

"We call it the Grinder," Declan said when Kael pointed it out.

His stomach twisted in a knot. "What does it grind, exactly?"

"Anything they toss into it — including nosy little mountain rats," Brend said. The wagon bumped to a stop next to another large shed, and he leapt out. "Now stand aside and leave us to our work."

Since Kael was next to useless with a pitchfork, he had no problem standing out of the giants' way. While they unloaded the wagon, he busied himself with trying to fish the straw from the back of his trousers. He wasn't very successful.

"That ought to do it," Brend said cheerily, slamming the doors shut.

Kael thought it seemed a bit pointless to drag a wagon-full of straw out of one barn, only to haul it across the whole region to have it stuffed inside another. "Why don't the Pens grow their own hay?" he grumbled, as he tried to coax a particularly stubborn piece of straw out from between his shoulder blades.

Brend sighed up at the clouds. "Spare me from the clod-headedness of manfolk. They don't grow hay in the Pens, because the Pens are for growing *animals*," he said, with over-exaggerated patience. "It's no small wonder you mountain rats have to scavenge for your food — you couldn't grow a weed in a pot!"

Kael glared at him. "You don't know anything about life in the mountains. You giants keep your food stored under the earth and tucked behind fences. You have no idea what it's like to track down a meal with tusks and teeth — to wake up every day knowing you might very well be eaten by your dinner. We don't *scavenge* for our food. We hunt for it. And I've killed bears bigger than you," he added, with what he hoped was a scathing look.

The giants glanced at each other — then they burst out laughing.

"Where's *that* wee fiery spark been hiding?" Brend said. "Had I known you were such a funny little fellow, I might've — oops."

His playful shove sent Kael rolling end over end, and Declan had to pluck him off the ground. "Steady, wee rat."

Kael jerked himself out of his hold and spun. He was entirely fed up with the giants: he was sick of being thrown about, laughed at, and called a *rat*. And he was about to tell them as much.

But when he turned, the look on Declan's face made him forget his words. He couldn't believe it: Declan was actually smiling. No, not just smiling — he wore a grin so ridiculously wide that it would've looked like a fool on anybody else. But on Declan ... well, it made him look like a completely different person. A much happier person.

No sooner did his grin appear than it vanished. Declan tossed his pitchfork into the wagon and walked off in the opposite direction, his fists planted firmly inside his pockets.

"I thought you rats were naught but slouch-shouldered clodders," Brend said, tossing his fork in next to Declan's. "But I have to say — I hate you less."

Kael frowned at him. "Less?"

"Oh, sure ... a *tiny* bit less," he said with a wink. "Now, you hang by the cart — and don't spook Churl. If you don't bother him, he'll just sit there and stare at the chickens. It'll give us a few minutes to ourselves." Brend slid around the front of the wagon, glancing up at the driver's seat as he went.

Churl didn't seem to notice. Instead, he sat limply on his perch, staring open-mouthed at the feathery inhabitants of the chicken coup.

They clucked and skipped about on spindly legs, deftly avoiding the men who tried to scoop them up. Kael noticed that they were men from the seas. And after having been trapped among giants for so long, he thought they looked ridiculously small.

He wondered if any of the seas men knew Lysander. At any rate, they might be nicer to him than the giants had been. He was about to walk over and talk to them when a familiar-looking shadow crossed his path.

He'd begged Eveningwing to leave him, to go out into the world and enjoy his freedom. But so far he'd insisted on staying put. He'd spent the night roosting in the rafters over Kael's head, and had left early that morning to go on a hunt. Now it looked as if he might be eyeing the chickens.

Roland had said once that hawks had remarkably sharp vision: "If you can see them, they're close enough to count your teeth."

So Kael looked up at Eveningwing and gave him a very pointed glare, shaking his head firmly. The hawk's gray wings tilted downward in disappointment before he glided back towards the Fields — as if he preferred not to be tempted.

Kael walked for a ways, just to make sure that Eveningwing wasn't going to try to circle back around. When he finally took his gaze from the skies, he spotted Declan.

He stood near a pen that was quite a bit larger than the rest, leaning against the fence with his arms crossed over the rails. He watched the creatures roaming on the other side of it with a look of longing on his face.

When Kael approached, he'd expected to see cows or sheep — something edible, at the very least. He was surprised when a group of young horses galloped by. They tossed their manes and snorted in delight, running in a line around the pen. Their legs thundered across the flat ground in a chorus of hooves.

The only horses Kael had ever seen had been either saddled, or tied to the fronts of carts. It was amazing to watch the horses move in a herd, free to gallop with no one to rein them in; free to buck and toss their necks without fear of throwing their masters. He'd never thought of them as wild creatures. But now it was hard to see them as anything else.

"Do you want to pet one?" Declan asked, when he saw Kael staring. Before he could reply, Declan stuck his fingers in his mouth and let out a sharp whistle.

A mare's head shot up immediately, her ears twitched for Declan. She shouldered her way through the crowd of her grazing fellows and trotted straight to the fence.

"This is Crispina," he said, reaching out to stroke her graceful neck. "Isn't she beautiful? She's got royal blood, you know. Her father was King Banagher's war-horse."

Kael didn't doubt it. With the height of her legs and her glossy black coat, Crispina looked every inch the royal horse. At Declan's urging, he reached out to touch her neck. He was surprised when her nose nuzzled the top of his head.

"She likes you," Declan said approvingly. "A horse can read a man's spirit better than any Seer. So if Crispina likes you, then I know you're decent."

Kael ran his hand along the white stripe between Crispina's eyes, and she snorted contentedly. "I didn't know the giants raised horses."

Declan's thick shoulders rose and fell. "Yeh, we've raised some of the best bloodlines in the realm. They're more like dogs to us, though — our arses are far too large to ride them."

"*You* can't even ride?"

He shook his head. "I may not be as tall as the others, but my bones are still made of stone. I'd squish their little hides flat, if I tried. And you wouldn't like that too much, would you?" he added to Crispina — who swished her tail in reply.

They stood in silence for a moment, petting Crispina while she nibbled playfully at their fingers. The young horses scampered around the pen behind her, chasing each other's tails. As Kael followed their merry game across the pasture, he spotted something odd.

An enormous stone stood out in the middle of the grass. It was easily the height of three men, and he bet it would've taken a ring of six giants to wrap their arms around it. The stone itself was pale red in color, with tiny flecks of black chipped into it. As the sun crossed overhead, the black flecks glittered under its light.

When he pointed it out to Declan, he sighed. "Yeh, that's the Scepter Stone."

"Is it magic?"

"No, there's no magic in the plains. Unless you count the skill of a giantess in her kitchens, that is," he amended with a small smile — a smile that quickly faded. "Come on, I'll take you to get a closer look."

They hopped the fence and walked out to the Stone. Declan said they couldn't stay for long: if one of the Pens' mages caught them among the horses, they'd probably earn themselves a flogging.

While Declan watched for the mages, Kael pressed his hands against the Scepter Stone. Its surface was smooth, as if the waters of some great river had shaped it. Warmth seemed to radiate from its middle. The little black flecks were a warmer than the rest. Though he felt as high up as he could reach, Kael didn't find a single crack.

"What was it used for?" he said as they hiked back to the fence.

Declan hoisted himself over the railings, while Kael slid in between them. "It didn't really have a use, not in the way you'd think. The Scepter Stone was more a symbol than anything."

"A symbol of what?"

192

Declan grunted and rolled his shoulders back, as if he wasn't all that comfortable talking. But Kael wanted to learn. So he waited patiently for a few moments, letting his question hang in the air. At last, Declan gave in:

"No doubt you've heard tales of the giants, and of our warring ways. The Kingdom is full of the stories. They like to paint us as bloodthirsty, club-wielding savages. Or stupid oafs." He glared out the side of his eye at Kael, as if he were expecting him to chime in with other offensive names.

But he only shrugged. "I actually don't know much about the giants. I've spent most of my life trapped on a mountain."

"Huh." Declan's face betrayed nothing as he went on. "Well, we *did* go to war more often than the other regions. The family clans used to get into all sorts of scuffles. They'd start out as small things, just an argument between two neighbors. But it wouldn't be long before we'd have ourselves a mightily thick battle."

"Why's that?" Kael wondered. "Why didn't the clans just settle things amongst themselves and be done with it?"

"We're not some region full of strangers — we're family. Every clan is tied together by some manner of blood," Declan said, picking at the rough top of the fence post. "If you got into a fight with a neighboring clan, there was a fair chance that you'd have a cousin or a grandpa fighting on the other side." He ducked his head a bit, and Kael saw that he was trying to hide a smile.

"That's why things would get so far out of hand. You'd ask to marry my sister, so I'd knock out a few of your teeth. Then your cousin would let his goats into my brother's crops. Next thing you know, somebody's plow blade would wind up at the bottom of the pond — it just wouldn't take long for things to go to clods." His head shot up, and he fixed Kael with a serious look. "But just because we fought all the time doesn't mean that there weren't any rules."

He waved his hand at the horse pen. "Anyone who stood in the shadow of the Scepter Stone couldn't be harmed. That's where the women and children would gather to wait out the fights. I traveled there with my mother once, as a wee thing." His eyes seemed to dull at the memory. "We waited there for many long days, picnicking and roaming through the Prince's lands. He let the clans fight for a while, but when it came time for the harvest and our fathers *still* hadn't returned, the Prince set out to bring them home. He rode from the castle gates with his mighty army at his back ... and he dragged my father and all my kinsmen home by their ears."

A floodgate must've opened over Declan's mouth: Kael had never heard him string so many sentences together, and he realized that he might never hear it again. So even though the questions pressed against his lips, he tried to sit quietly — just to see if Declan would say anything else.

"They tried to break it, you know," he murmured after a moment. Declan's eyes traveled to the Scepter Stone, and a hard smirk bent his lips. "When Titus captured the plains, he ordered the mages to cast a spell to crack it. They covered it in fire and ice, they tried to blast it down the middle — they even summoned great, snaking cords and tried to topple it over on its side. But the Stone stood firm." His lips tightened. "And we giants took it as a sign."

He said no more. And Kael couldn't think of anything to say in reply, so he kept his mouth shut. They stood in companionable silence for several moments before Brend found them.

"Oh no," he said, grinning, when he caught sight of them. "Declan hasn't been off on his tales about horses, has he? Talking about their shiny flanks and what-have-you? If he starts to bore you, wee rat, you can always just wander off — I know for a fact that he'll keep on talking to the wind."

Declan smiled and shook his head, but said nothing to defend himself. Brend went on:

"He can't help it, though. That's what happens when a fellow is born into clan Horseman. They'll chatter on about their prancing little pets till the earth goes blue. Whole armies have turned and fled, rather than be trapped in one of their tales — I swear it by the plains mother."

194

Kael turned to Declan and said: "Declan Horseman, is it?"

He nodded. "That it is, Kael of the Unforgivable Mountains."

****

With Churl content to watch the chickens, they were able to waste the whole day just walking around the Pens and looking at the animals. Brend knew many of the giants by name, and spent several minutes talking with each of them, asking about how they were getting on.

When the sun started to dip low, they hopped back into the wagon. As Churl hurtled them down the bumpy road, Kael began to think.

Declan's story burned in the front of his mind. He was determined now more than ever to find someway to free the plains. But he knew whatever plan he came up with wouldn't work — not unless he had the giants on his side. And it was obvious that they didn't trust him.

How could he possibly convince them to listen?

He was shocked when he suddenly found himself wishing for Lysander. Annoying though he was, the pirate captain would've known *exactly* what to do with the giants. He'd blind them with flashes of his white teeth and have them spun around so quickly that they'd lose track of their backsides. The giants would've followed him without even realizing it — and Lysander would've been long gone before they figured out that he'd swindled them senseless.

For some reason, this thought put a smile on Kael's face.

At dinner, he hardly ate. The thought of Lysander's particular brand of trickery was a loose thread — a path that led him straight to a tangled mass of ideas. There might be a plan in there somewhere, but it was too jumbled to tell. After a while, Kael was entirely fed up with thinking: he knew he had to stop agonizing over *every*thing and put just *one* of those things into motion. He had to give that thread a tug, and see what other sorts of ideas might pop free.

So as they sat at dinner, he did just that.

"I've been thinking a lot about your Prince," Kael said to Brend. He said it quietly enough that the other giants couldn't hear him. Though the noise at dinner was so loud that he probably didn't even have to lower his voice. "I think I might be able to help him with his plan."

Brend's head shot up from the trough. "What you have in mind?" he said, around a rather large mouthful of porridge.

Kael told him about Jonathan, and how they'd been captured together — though he conveniently left out the bit about the caravan of pirates. "So if I can find a way to reach my friend —"

Brend snorted loudly, spraying bits of porridge back into the trough. "How do you plan to do that, eh? Tie your message to a string and throw it through the castle windows?"

Kael gave him what he hoped was a disarming smile. "I *could* do that ... or, I could use the shapechanger."

It took a moment, but Brend finally seemed to catch on. He ducked his head down even with Kael's, and the mocking glint left his eyes. "You're going to have the wee hawk carry a message to the fiddler?"

Kael nodded.

"And what do you plan to tell him? You'd better not be plotting an escape."

"I'd have to be pretty stupid to try that — especially since you've promised to make a quick end of me." Kael's heart pounded in his throat, but he forced himself to smile when Brend nodded. He chose his next words carefully: "It seems to me that whatever the Prince has planned won't work, unless you find someway to free your women. You don't even know where they're being held. So if Jonathan could poke around a bit, perhaps even draw us a few maps ... do you think that might be helpful?"

196

Brend thought for a moment. He pawed at his chin, gazing out at the giants around him. He seemed to be torn, and Kael feared that he would refuse.

"If he could find out where Gilderick is keeping our women," Brend said slowly, "that would be a great help to us. We can't set a foot out of here until we rescue our sisters."

Kael knew that if anybody could find a roomful of women, it would be Jonathan. "I'm sure that won't be a problem. He's very ... um, observant," Kael said lamely. Then he got to his feet. "I'll send Eveningwing straight away, then."

Brend nodded distractedly, his eyes still roving around the giants. "All right, and I'll let the others know what you're up to."

Kael had made to walk away when Brend's hand clamped down around his wrist. He wore a scowl so severe that Thelred might've been proud of it.

"I'll be watching you closely, rat. If you try to cut our legs out from under us, then may the plains mother have mercy on your wee little head," Brend growled, "because I sure won't."

When Kael nodded, he let go — though he swore he could feel Brend's eyes scorching the back of his neck as he ducked into the stall.

He knew he was playing a dangerous game, but he didn't see another way around it. The giants might rot in their barns if they waited around for this mysterious Prince to rescue them. So Kael planned to take matters into his own hands.

He found Eveningwing roosting contentedly in the rafters over his bed. When Kael gave him his task, he bobbed his feathery head. Then he swooped out into the night, silent as a shadow.

Kael lay down on his little patch of dirt and listened as Brend told the giants what he planned to do. There were several who were heartily against it, and they spoke loudly. But in the end, Brend seemed to convince them that they had no other choice — and promised that they could break Kael's legs if he betrayed them.

And while he wasn't keen on *that* part of the agreement, Kael felt a slightly relieved when he knew that he would be allowed to carry on. He just hoped that Jonathan could stop being ridiculous long enough to find the women.

When the torches dimmed, the giants rushed back into the stall. Declan was the last to arrive. He stood in the doorway for a moment, silent and still. Whatever trust Kael gained that afternoon had obviously vanished: he swore he could actually *feel* Declan's gaze pressing on him, trying to crush him.

So he turned over quickly and pretended to be asleep.

It was near the middle of the night when Eveningwing returned. Kael felt something soft hit his shoulder, and when he looked up, the halfhawk blinked back at him from the hole in the roof. He ruffled his feathers in greeting before he disappeared again, soaring out into the darkness.

Kael felt around for the object that had struck his shoulder and came up with a leaf of parchment. It was rolled tightly around a lump of charcoal, held together by a small piece of twine. He rolled the parchment open and nearly grinned when he saw the wild, looping letters that covered the page:

Oi, Kael — so nice to hear from you, mate! I have to admit that I was beginning to worry about you a little. I stick my head out the window at least three times a day, trying to see if I can catch a glimpse of you. My eyes are sore from all the straining.

But just when I thought I might never see you again, I pop my head out and what do I get? A mouthful of feathers! Can't complain, though. I knew you'd find some way to reach me — never doubted you for a moment! Though a bloke in a nightdress is not at all what I was expecting.

I sent our new friend — Even-wings, was it? — off to the seas. He'll tell the pirates to go on without us. I expect they'll just pillage around a bit until we manage to spring out of here. And we will spring out, mate. Ole Gildepants doesn't stand a chance against us — we're the cleverest pair of villains this side of the seas!

Things are all well with me. Dred marched me up to meet His Lordship almost the moment we got inside the castle. "Whatever you do — don't look him in the eyes," Dred said to me. And I tell you, mate: when a bloke the size of a witch's shanty looks worried about something, you take heed.

Anyways, I stepped into the throne room, bowed and scraped my nose to the cobblestone like any bard before a Lord — though to be safe, I kept my eyes on his boots — and he ordered that I play something straight away. So I strung up the ole fiddle and played the most boring thing I could think of. You know, with flourishes and tremors and notes in all the right places. Awful stuff.

His Lordship must've enjoyed it, though — because no sooner was I finished than he said: "Kill the other one. I like this one better."

Don't get me wrong — I'm thrilled I got the job ... but I feel a little sorry for the other bloke.

Turns out that being a resident bard isn't as difficult as I thought it would be. It is *a touch boring, though. Gilderick doesn't seem to care what I do, just so long as I show up to play at dinner. I play for the guards every now and then, but mostly I just wander around the castle, looking for something exciting to get into. Gilderick's not much one for decoration and most of the doors are locked, but I* did *stumble upon a very promising mystery yesterday.*

I got a bit lost and wound up going through this long, poky old hallway. There was a door at the end of it — but of course, it was locked. I was just about to go back the way I'd come when I heard it: lady voices! Whole scores of them! I could hear them chattering and giggling on the other side of the door.

As you well know, I've always been rather good with the ladies. So I knocked and asked if they'd kindly let me in. When the door swung open, an old witch popped out. And I mean witch *literally, mate. She swung her ladle at me, screaming that men weren't allowed inside, and I swear I felt a zap on my rump. I charged out of there so fast that I nearly left my boots behind!*

Odd that you mentioned the lady giants — do you think that might be where Gilderick's keeping them? I swear I've walked the castle five times over, and that's the only place I've ever heard any ladies.

Well, it may be dangerous, and I might wind up with scorch marks on my rump, but I promise I'll do my best to get inside — ah, for the good of the plan, of course. I'll just have to charm my way past the old witch.

I've never tried my hand at map-drawing, but I suppose now's as good a time to try as any! In the meanwhile, take care of yourself, mate. I know just about every other word out of my mouth is a joke, but I get the feeling that there are some seriously spooky things going on inside the castle. I can't quite put a finger on what it is ... but I haven't slept a solid night since I've been here.

Chin up — and keep those wheels turning!

-Jonathan

Kael flipped the parchment over and took up the charcoal. He was so excited that he could hardly keep his hand from shaking as he wrote.

A locked door at the end of a long hallway — all he could think about was the smoking tower outside of Gilderick's castle. If the women were locked up inside that tower, things would be much simpler than Kael could've ever hoped for: they wouldn't have to storm the whole fortress, they'd only have to figure out a way inside that tower.

And with enough time to think, Kael knew he could crack it.

Chapter 16
Abomination

As they traveled deeper into Whitebone, Kyleigh kept track of the days by rations.

At dawn on the fourth day, they had no meat left — because try as she might, she couldn't keep Silas from pilfering it. She remembered the fifth day clearly, because Silas had spent it moaning loudly about how he was sure to shrivel up and waste away if he had to eat one more bowl of spice rice and dates. On the sixth day, she clocked him over the head and carried his unconscious form across her shoulders for miles, just to have some peace.

Then on the seventh day came relief.

"Stop. Do you hear that?"

She turned and saw Silas standing with his arms and legs apart. He stepped gingerly in a circle, as if he was trying to pick his way across a path of rusted nails.

"Kyleigh, please hit him again," Jake muttered as he caught up with them.

Poor Jake. After their first day in the burning sun, he'd woken with his face and neck covered in angry red blisters. Kyleigh hadn't thought to pack any ointment: the sun weakened her, but it never burned her skin. And Silas had just turned a deeper shade of brown. But Jake burned badly.

He'd been so miserable that he'd tried to heal it himself out of desperation. The result was that the hair on his face now grew twice as fast as it had before. And with the painful blisters still underneath, he couldn't shave. Six days later, he had a full, bushy beard.

"No, I hear something — little scratching sounds ..." Silas's voice trailed away as he sank into his lion form. He tore into the sand with his front claws, ripping it up onto Kyleigh in stinging waves.

She was too exhausted to pound him for it. Instead, she sat on her pack and felt around for the nearest canteen.

The skins kept the water cool, but their thirst drained it faster than the sun's rays ever might have. She'd been rationing her drinks, and the lack of moisture was beginning to take its toll on her body. She couldn't remember the last time she'd relieved herself.

"He's gone completely mad," Jake said as he plopped down next to her, shooting a look at Silas.

After a considerable amount of effort, Jake managed to find the top of one of his invisible canteens. He uncorked it, tilted it back for a drink — and poured most of the water straight up his nose.

"How close are we?" he snapped, wiping his face impatiently with his arm. He grimaced when his sleeve brushed across his blisters.

Kyleigh looked away before he could catch her eyes. "It shouldn't be too long, now."

"What does that mean? A day? Two days?" Jake made a disgusted face at the sun. "A week?"

"I'm not sure. I think we're close —"

"Not sure? *Close*? I thought you knew where we were going." When she didn't respond, Jake reached over and very suddenly pulled down her hood. "We're lost!" he said, when he saw her face.

She bristled against that thought. "We're not *lost*. I just ... well, it's a little more difficult to navigate than I thought it would be."

"But I thought you said you'd been here before?"

She hardly had a chance to open her mouth before Jake figured it out:

"You flew." In his shock, his glasses slid the whole way down his nose, and he made no move to push them back. "The last time you traveled to the Baron's castle, you *flew* there! You didn't walk. You have no idea how to navigate from the ground, do you?"

"Of course I know how to navigate from the ground," Kyleigh said defensively. She gazed around at the endless dunes, at the white-hot sky, and the realization began to creep in. "The truth is, I've never wandered through a land quite like this ..."

Her words trailed away as a wave of exhaustion swept over her. The sun may not have burned her skin, but it thwarted her in far more exhausting ways. In this empty land, her senses were next to useless: there were no scents to follow, no trails to pick up, and even a dragon's sight couldn't reach far enough to do them any good.

During the day, the horizon danced madly in the blistering heat — stacking the dunes atop each other, creating illusions of refuge to tease them. At night, the light from Jake's fire wall kept them from being able to see into the distance. They'd rise with the sun at their face, determined to keep it there. But by evening it would be hovering far to their left or right.

She had no idea just how many miles they'd wandered off-course. And the longer they stayed trapped in the desert, the more her strength began to fade.

Her blood had already begun to lose its magic. The sandy hills burned so hot during the day that Kyleigh swore she could feel the heat in the soles of her boots. The moment the sun went down, the hills turned cold — chilling her to the bone.

The hot, dry air raked across the insides of her nose every time she breathed in, and the skin cracked like the barren ground beneath them. Her nose had bled and dried several times over, and it wasn't long before she couldn't smell anything at all — not even Silas's stench.

All around them, the land was deathly quiet. Only the wind seemed to have a voice, and it never stopped speaking. Every gust of air carried little bits of sand in its folds, just enough to sting their lips and ears. It howled through the hollow hours of the night, blowing the tops off of the dunes and gathering them into new piles — so that by the time they woke, the land had completely changed.

They had no choice but to set out stubbornly at the dawn of each day … prepared to lose themselves to the hot, shifting world once again.

"It's not all that bad," Jake said. He must've seen the many frantic thoughts flashing behind her eyes, and now he was determined to solve their problems. "Let's see … ah!" He twisted towards her, planting his hands on his knees. "You could always go on a scouting expedition — you know, wing about and see what's out there. Silas and I would wait for you."

Kyleigh tried to smile, but the gesture pulled too roughly on the dried skin across her lips. "I can't, Jake. I haven't got the strength for a flight."

After they'd run out of meat, things had gone downhill quickly. Now her dragon half was starving.

It took all of her concentration to melt them a new glass shelter each night. Even at that, the lightness in her head often sent the world spinning. Her hunger was far beyond pain or a rumbling stomach — last night, she'd nearly passed out.

If she tried to take flight, she thought she might very well drop straight out of the skies. And who would look after Jake and Silas, then? No … she needed to save her strength. There was a cleverer way to go about things, and she was determined to figure it out.

Kyleigh looked to the north … well, she hoped it was north. In the desert, the sun seemed to spend an unnatural number of hours hovering at the top of the sky. It climbed eagerly to noon each day and then paused, as if the wispy clouds somehow held it captive. Several hours would pass where the sun hung directly over their heads, making any sort of navigation impossible. At last, it would manage to pull itself free — only to plummet beneath the horizon as quickly as it had risen.

"We ought to start cutting back towards the Baron's highway. I don't know how many nights of fire I have left."

"That goes for both of us," Jake muttered. A grim smile peeked out through his tangled beard. "If we don't get some food in our bellies, or find somewhere solid to plant our feet, we might as well —"

A scream interrupted him — a cry that Kyleigh recognized immediately. She spun to look at Silas.

He'd been digging while they talked. Sand coated his nose and powdered his coat, but all of his work had been worth the effort: he now had a lanky rabbit clamped between his pointed teeth. He pounded his front paws into the earth, jerking his head repeatedly at the hole he'd dug.

Kyleigh needed no translation.

She jumped into the hole and jammed her arm into the rabbits' burrow. It was a natural rock tunnel, a giant stone hidden beneath the sand. There was a whole family of hares hiding out inside the rocks, where the minceworms couldn't burrow in and get them. She grabbed a pair of flailing legs and yanked them free, flinging the terrified creature in Silas's direction.

Five hares flew out of the tunnel and into Silas's waiting jaws. There might've been more, but Kyleigh couldn't reach in any further. She sat back on her heels and turned to look at Silas. There was a brief moment when she realized that he could've gobbled the hares up as she flung them, leaving none for anybody else. But that fear passed when she saw him doing nothing more than standing protectively over their mangled bodies.

"Well done, cat. We'll have a feast tonight," she said.

Haughtiness flashed behind his eyes, but it was a halfhearted and exhausted gesture. He must've felt the weariness more in his animal form, as well.

Silas stepped aside, letting Jake wrap the hares so that they wouldn't spoil. A week ago, he might've snapped Jake's hand off at the wrist — or perhaps he would've already eaten him.

For a moment, Kyleigh was actually rather proud of Silas ... and she wondered if that meant she might be sun-stroked.

******

205

When evening came, they were all in high spirits. Kyleigh cleaned the rabbits and Jake cooked the whole lot with a hefty serving of spice rice and dates. They each had two heaping bowls full — though the way Silas and Jake carried on, passersby might've wondered if they'd had a few tankards of ale to go along with it.

"Oh, fantastic," Silas moaned, rolling over on his side.

Jake was doing a very off-key impersonation of Uncle Martin. He raised his invisible canteen in a toast. "To your health, Sir Cat! Had it not been for your keenly pointed ears and your keenly pointed teeth, we wouldn't have such fine rabbits to grace our pot!"

Silas wore a bearskin pelt like a cape, with its massive front paws tied in a knot around his throat. He bowed and swooped it out beside him. "I thank you, shaman. You could not have put your adoration in a more deserving direction. As for *you* ..." He fell on his knees next to Kyleigh. "I think I've earned a kiss."

"Not a chance," she said, shoving him away.

His glowing eyes widened pitifully. "Please? I've never had one before. I've often wondered why the humans find them so exciting."

"You know, I've never had one either," Jake said, looking up from where he'd been busily cleaning his spoon. "Why *are* they so exciting, Kyleigh?"

A memory that she'd fought for months to bury suddenly burned sharply against her lips. Heat sprung to her face. She found she couldn't think of anything to say ... and that *never* happened.

Fortunately, her companions were so flush with glee that they didn't seem to notice.

"Ooo, you've had one? Who was it from?" Silas said, creeping in closer beside her.

"Kael Witchslayer!" Jake shouted, shaking his fists at the crowd of minceworms that had encircled their camp. "And if he were here, he'd have crushed every one of you sorry little blighters with his bare hands!"

"Kael Witchslayer?" Silas growled, and Kyleigh knew he could sense how her heart thudded harder at the sound of his name. "Who is he? Another halfdragon?"

"No, he's a whisperer," Jake answered — which was a good thing, because Kyleigh doubted if she could've said it herself.

That memory was suddenly all she could think of. She was surprised at how well she remembered it: the feeling of his lips, pressed firm and confident against hers. The way his arm had wrapped around her waist, holding her tightly in the very moment when her legs went numb. She thought she'd felt a burning between them — a fire that arced from his heart to hers, a thrill he felt that set her soul ablaze ...

But then again, perhaps she'd only imagined it. Perhaps she'd wanted it so badly that it hadn't been *him* at all ... perhaps it was only her own thrill she felt ...

"Whisperer," Silas murmured. He closed his eyes tightly, and Kyleigh knew what he was doing.

It was a price all shapechangers had to pay: when their souls bonded, they lost a good portion of their human memories — and gained new ones from their animal halves. Kyleigh found it difficult to sort through them all, to remember which memories were hers and which were those of her dragon soul. Sometimes she would have dreams of lands she'd never visited, of battles she'd never fought in.

And sometimes, if she closed her eyes and concentrated, the memory she needed would come drifting out of the dark, swimming up like a fish to rocky shores.

She knew that was what Silas was doing. He was combing through his human memories, searching for the meaning of the word *whisperer*. And she hoped desperately that he wouldn't find it.

Then his eyes snapped open. "No ... not a Marked One," he hissed, glaring at her accusingly. "Dragoness, you know bet —"

"Are we going to play tonight?" Jake called from the edge of the fire wall. He twirled his staff in his hands, leveling it at Silas. "Or do you concede defeat?"

"I concede nothing," Silas said, rising to join him. But before he left, his hand clamped down on Kyleigh's shoulder — and his fingers curled tightly. "You and I will be discussing this later."

She glared at him, and he smirked back.

"Will you keep score?" Jake said to her. He propped a hand to the side of his face, pointed at Silas and mouthed: *He cheats.*

"I do not cheat," Silas said without looking. "Don't blame me for your poor aim, shaman."

After Kyleigh promised to keep things fair, the boys took their places at the edge of the wall. There wasn't much to entertain them in the evenings. Once the sun went down, the minceworms would come swarming out of the sand, trapping them inside their camp. But Jake had discovered a way to make the best of it.

He started sending fireballs out among the worms — purely for experimental purposes, he'd claimed. Silas laughed uproariously when the worms caught fire, and it wasn't long before he wanted a turn at it. They began keeping track of who was able to destroy the most of the horrible, squirming little creatures each night.

Then one of their shots had accidentally hit a minceworm full in the mouth. It swallowed the fireball whole and a second later, it exploded — putting out a burst of flame large enough to take out a chunk of the worms crowded around it.

And so Jake's experiments had dissolved into a game.

It was Silas's turn to go first. He took careful aim, holding Jake's staff and squinting with one eye until he found his target. "Fire!"

Jake muttered the spell, and a fireball shot out of the staff. It sailed over the wall and directly into the open mouth of a distant minceworm. A small explosion burst on the horizon, briefly lighting up the night — and sent several nearby worms sailing.

Silas cackled loudly as their flaming bodies fell from the sky. "That one was at least eight points," he said.

"*Eight*? You know, sometimes I don't think you even know your numbers." Jake did a quick sum on his fingers. "That couldn't have been more than five."

"You're both wrong — it's six," Kyleigh said. When Jake looked at her curiously, she sighed. "You counted the five that got their hides blown out from under them, but you forgot about the one he actually hit."

"Ah, you're right," Jake said, adding one more finger to his sum. "Six it is, then. And now it's my turn."

Kyleigh watched them for a while, doing her best to keep them both from cheating. But her heart just wasn't in it. After months of patching things together, of carefully stitching her frail hopes to a sturdy leaf of patience ... his name was all it had taken to pull the threads apart.

Just one mention of Kael, and she immediately grew restless. Her toes curled beneath her. She had to fight to stay put.

"Are you leaving?" Silas called as she made her way to her tent.

"Yes, I'm ... tired," she said. She thought her armor might be the reason her chest felt so tight. She'd sweated in it for days on end, after all. So she stripped off her shirt and jerkin and replaced it with a silk tunic. She kicked off her boots, but left her leggings — just in case she needed to get up in the middle of the night.

"Well, I think we'd all better call it an evening," Jake said loudly.

"You're just saying that because you're ahead," Silas countered.

"What? I would never —"

"Oh, save your words. You'll need them when I defeat you tomorrow," Silas added, with what she could only imagine was a toothy grin.

Kyleigh lay with her back against the tent wall for a moment, enjoying the softness and warmth of the pelts beneath her. She thought she had a pretty good chance of drifting off when she suddenly felt as if she wasn't alone.

She opened her eyes — and saw Silas lying across from her.

"Get out of my tent."

"Hmm ... no," he replied. "I promised we would talk. And so I mean to."

Kyleigh most certainly didn't want to do that. She tried to shove him out with her heels, but he knocked her feet aside. "Don't you have some licking to do? Or some fleas to gnaw at —?"

"Nothing is more important than what I'm about to say," Silas retorted. He slid closer to keep her from kicking him. "We're both alone in the world, dragoness — I, because I choose to be. And you, because you are a strange creature without any friends."

"Are you certain it's not the other way around?"

He smirked at her; his eyes glowed playfully. "I will ignore your insult —"

"How kind of you."

"— because I know that your strange, scaly heart is broken."

She fell silent.

He took a heavy breath. "And because we are both alone, it's my unfortunate duty to have to remind you of the laws of our people."

"I know the laws," Kyleigh growled. She hated rules. Rules were for people who liked to wear their breeches laced up too tight, and she loved nothing more than to break them.

But though she gave him a look that could've melted ice, it didn't stop him from lecturing her. "Then you know why I must speak with you — why I must stop your feelings for the Marked One, this *whisperer*, before they destroy you both." Silas sat up on his elbow. "If he were a regular brand of human, I'd tell you to take him to the forest and cast your lot at the Braided Tree — to perform the ritual, and hope to Fate that he's reborn a halfdragon. But he's not the normal sort of human, is he?" Silas's eyes stared a hole through her head, trying to pry reason from between her brows. "He's a whisperer. And you know as well as I that no man can survive Fate's dagger twice."

He held up his hand, and even in the dim light she could see the thin, white scar that cut across his palm. Her fingers twitched involuntarily for her own scar. It was the mark the ritual had left behind. Wherever Fate meddled, she always left a mark.

"Need I remind you why this is a problem?" Silas drawled, inspecting his scar, and Kyleigh got the feeling that he was enjoying himself. "Have you so easily forgotten the weight of the Three Tenets?"

No, she hadn't forgotten them — though most of the time she wished she could. But for some reason, it was as if they'd been scratched permanently into her skull. Even when she'd wandered nameless and naked through the woods, struggling to remember who she was, the Tenets still rang inside her head:

To take your own life is to forsake your eternal rest. To try to destroy your second self is to take your own life. And —

"*To bond with any but your own is Abomination,*" Silas whispered. "*And upon all Abomination, Fate will loose her brother — Death.* You see, dragoness? Your feelings for the whisperer are exactly that: an Abomination."

Kyleigh hated the Tenets. They were stupid, vague rules that could've meant a thousand different things to a thousand different people. "Maybe it's not an Abomination."

Silas narrowed his eyes. "But it is. It says so in the —"

"*Any but your* own," Kyleigh cut in. "It doesn't say anything about my own *kind*. Perhaps shape has nothing to do with it. If I'm for him and he's for me, then wouldn't that make him ... mine?"

Silas's laugh raked obnoxiously against her ears. "You shouldn't try to put words into Fate's mouth."

"Then perhaps Fate's mouth should've been more specific," Kyleigh said testily. "I know what I feel in my heart, and nothing is going to change that. Not even Fate."

"Are you willing to risk your own life to prove it?"

"Yes, and gladly."

"Are you willing to risk *his* life?"

The words froze on Kyleigh's tongue. She studied the high arches of Silas's brows. They rose higher in her silence. "It wouldn't be his life at —"

"Upon *all* Abomination, dragoness. Death would punish your little whisperer as swiftly as he punished you."

Kyleigh hadn't thought of that. But now that she did, the thought made her furious. "Get out," she snarled.

Silas shrugged. "As you wish." He crawled backwards out of the tent, but paused at the opening. "Remember, dragoness: we have a duty to protect those weaker than us — and unfortunately, that includes the humans. If you truly care for him, you should be careful not to lead him down such a dangerous path. And if you cannot control yourself ... then perhaps it would be best to separate from him, rather than sentence him to death."

Kyleigh went to throw a pelt at Silas, but he was already gone. She sank back down and propped her hands roughly behind her head.

Though she tried her best to ignore it, Silas's warning rang in her ears. It was no idle threat: she knew very well that Fate often punished the shapechangers who disobeyed her Tenets.

She remembered the stories Bloodfang used to tell the young pups to pass the long winter nights. Some of those stories were about the curses Fate had put on shapechangers who broke the Tenets. She remembered one in particular about a halfwolf named Bleakhowl, who'd been so distraught by his second shape that he starved himself to death — breaking the first Tenet. But Fate didn't let him perish: instead, she took away his human shape and forced him to live forever as a man trapped inside a wolf's body.

The story claimed that travelers could still hear Bleakhowl's woeful cry, on nights when the moon was full.

Kyleigh stared past the shadows in the tent's roof, thinking. Nothing could ever change what she felt. But she didn't think there was any chance Kael's feelings would change, either. He had that stubborn mountain blood running through his veins. Once he set his mind against something, that was it.

But if he ever *were* to change his mind ... then perhaps Kyleigh would have no choice. Perhaps it would be better for her to leave him alone than to put his life at risk.

She didn't know what to do. But she knew one thing for certain: in the end, she would do whatever was best for Kael — whatever that happened to be ...

No matter how badly it hurt.

Chapter 17
A Dagger in the Back

Elena waited patiently, frozen atop a nearby dune. Her legs were tucked beneath her, and her arms were balanced across her knees. She was careful not to budge.

She watched as the three figures within the ring of fire finally stopped their chattering. One by one, they slipped into their tents. Then she waited another hour, measuring by the rise of the moon. Her breath was so soft that she hardly felt it cross her lips. When she was certain the three companions were asleep, she got to her feet.

Their trail began at Arabath, where a woman who worked the date stand had casually mentioned that she'd seen three strange travelers enter the southern desert. She had wondered if Elena was part of their group, looking very pointedly at her blackened armor and the deadly knives strapped to her arms.

Elena had smiled, but she didn't answer. And the woman seemed to realize that asking another question might cost her more than a few dates.

"Four men followed them into the desert — men who had the blood of many travelers upon their heads. And they never returned," the woman had said. She raised her chin defiantly as she handed Elena her rations. "Their families went out to collect their bones in the morning."

Elena heard the warning in her voice, but it didn't trouble her. In fact, the date woman had been most helpful: now that she knew the sort of brawlers she was up against, she would take no chances.

Tracking the Dragongirl's party across the sands had been easy. The glass caps they'd left behind lit up like beacons when the sunlight hit them. Once she knew where they'd gone, it became a simple matter of catching up. Elena traveled at nearly twice their pace everyday — she had plenty of water and rations, and sleep was all she needed to replenish her energy.

The task ahead of her would be the most difficult of the journey.

The minceworms were creatures she knew little about. During her first day of travel, she could feel the worms rolling in the sand beneath her, following her steps. She left some dried meat behind, but when that didn't seem to tempt them, she tried something else.

One of the first lessons the Countess had taught her was how to quiet her steps. Elena could move silently, if she wished. And once she'd concentrated on stepping lightly, the minceworms stopped following her. So she supposed that it was the noise of her steps that had attracted them, and not the smell of her blood.

As long as she traveled quietly and slept perfectly still, the worms didn't bother her. Now as Elena jogged towards the ring of fire in the distance, her feet hardly brushed the sand.

The heavy footfalls of the Dragongirl's party had stirred the minceworms up to the surface. Elena strained her eyes in the darkness and wagered that there were close to three-dozen worms ringed around the glass cap.

The only way she could get close to the camp was if she timed her steps perfectly. She couldn't linger, and she had to be careful. If she so much as brushed a worm with the top of her boot, they would swarm — and she refused to die in the jaws of scavengers. It would be a humiliating death.

Elena picked up speed as she reached the edge of the worm ring, daring to dig her toes in a little bit deeper. She kept her eyes on the ground, searching for the bare patches of sand between worms, springing from one gap to the next. It took all of her concentration to keep her balance at every awkward landing. She kept her arms spread apart and the ring of fire in the corner of her eye.

When she felt she was close enough, she leapt.

Her arms stretched in front of her as she dove over the flames. She landed on her palms, rolled on her shoulder and popped swiftly to her feet. A shadow would've made more noise than Elena did.

The others had their flaps laced up tightly against the cold, but the Dragongirl's tent was wide-open. Elena crept towards it, her knees bent and her palms parallel to the ground. She moved on the balls of her feet and kept her muscles tensed: the Dragongirl had a fierce reputation as a swordsman, and she was determined not to become another victim of her blade.

As she crept closer, Elena prepared for the worst possible scenario. She planned through what would happen if she found the Dragongirl awake and waiting for her, or if she wore her armor and slept with her sword under her pillow. There were several dozen ways her attack might go wrong.

But when she ducked inside the tent, she saw that all of her worry was for naught.

The Dragongirl was sprawled out upon what looked like a blanket of animal furs. She lay on her back and had one arm stretched above her head. The other was tucked closely to her side. Elena paused at the tent's opening and quickly took in her surroundings: the white sword was sheathed and lay atop the Dragongirl's shirt and jerkin, well out of her reach. There weren't any other weapons in the room. Even if she *did* wake and try to defend herself, Elena would have the advantage.

She couldn't have planned it better.

There was a slight twang of regret in Elena's throat when she saw how beautiful the Dragongirl was. She hadn't expected her to be quite so lovely — or young. Her soft breath teased the strands of raven hair that fell across her face; her lips rested softly.

And with a sigh, Elena drew a knife.

It was one of the three poisoned blades that the Countess had given her, the one she'd kept tucked inside her gauntlet. Even in the pale light, she could see the dangerous film that coated the blade. The Countess's poisons had never failed her. Elena wagered that it wouldn't take much: just a shallow cut, just enough to draw blood, and the tainted blade would do the rest.

Elena placed the tip of the knife against the Dragongirl's smooth throat. With a deep breath, she went to flick her wrist across the vein beneath her chin ... but nothing happened.

She tried it again, but her wrist didn't move. Her arm suddenly felt numb, like all of the blood was stopped up and couldn't get to her hand. She squinted into the darkness and saw there were fingers wrapped around her wrist — and they were squeezing very, *very* tightly.

Her hand went numb. The knife slipped out of her grip. But before it could even strike the ground, she'd already ripped a second blade from her boot. When she looked up, the Dragongirl glared back.

Her eyes were open; the bright green of their centers blazed a hole through Elena. She tried to wrench her arm free, but the Dragongirl's grip was too strong. So she swung the poisoned knife at her face.

Elena hadn't felt the Dragongirl's feet in her middle — and by the time she realized what had happened, she was already sailing through the air.

Her body flew out of the tent and her back struck the glass floor. She sprang to her feet, but the Dragongirl jumped on top of her. She was much heavier than Elena had expected, and in her moment of surprise, the Dragongirl forced her shoulders to the ground.

Elena decided then that it was time to end the games. She drew Slight and lunged for the Dragongirl's heart.

With a twist and a flick of her arm, the Dragongirl dodged her blow and hit Slight in the hilt — popping him out of Elena's grasp. When she twisted back, Elena drove a knee into her ribs.

It was a move she'd used often. The angle and force of her blow should've been enough to crack the Dragongirl's ribcage. Elena waited for the familiar crunching sound, the feeling of bone popping against her knee. But it didn't come.

Instead, Elena felt as if she'd driven her knee into the side of a castle wall.

For half a breath, she thought she might be in trouble. Then the Dragongirl grunted, tipped sideways — and gave Elena the split second she needed to turn the tide.

Her elbow flew into the Dragongirl's ribs, into the exact spot she'd struck before. While she was off-balance, Elena grabbed her by the shoulders and used their difference in weight to shoot out from under her. The glass bucked and waved so badly that she flew off-course, almost missing her chance to grab Slight. She managed to get a finger on him before the Dragongirl kicked him out of her reach.

She grabbed Elena around one leg and jerked her backwards — leaving the other leg free to deal some damage. Elena twisted around and swung her foot in a deadly arc for the Dragongirl's face. It connected, and she fell.

Elena was on her in a second. She wrapped her legs around the Dragongirl's waist and squeezed hard — cutting off the flow of her breath and at the same time, pressing her organs painfully against her bones. Once she had her pinned, Elena drew Shadow.

The Dragongirl stiffened. Her green eyes watched Shadow's fall; hot blood leaked out from her busted lip. At the very last second, she jerked her head to the side with lightning speed. Elena grunted in frustration when Shadow missed her neck and struck the glass instead.

She leaned against the Dragongirl, using the weight of her body to hold her still. She had to hunch over to dodge the desperate flailing of her legs. Elena's next thrust would find its mark. She would make sure —

Pain ... and then a strange numbness began to creep across Elena's body.

It started at her hand — where a hairline cut on her knuckles bled freely. She felt the numbness ride through her bloodstream, weakening every limb and filling her mind with a dense fog. Her muscles lost their strength. She glanced down and saw the weapon gripped in the Dragongirl's hand: the last poisoned knife, the one she'd had hidden in her belt.

And it was perhaps because she watched the knife that Elena didn't see the Dragongirl's fist … until it was too late.

****

When she woke, Elena was confused. The Countess's poisons never failed: she ought to be dead. How could she possibly be alive?

Numbness still crippled her limbs and she didn't dare open her eyes. She could feel the rough bonds around her wrists and ankles. They were made of simple rope. She ought to be able to break them easily. She strained and pulled against them, concentrating on the feeling of snapping cord — a feeling she knew well.

But it was as if her arms couldn't remember their strength. No matter how she fought, her bonds held tight.

Frustration burned Elena's throat, but she swallowed it back. It would do her no good to start squirming and call attention to herself. She leaned heavily against what felt like a pole in the middle of her back … perhaps they had her tied up in a tent. She used the word *they* because she could hear three voices a few strides away from her. And from what she could tell, they were arguing.

"I can't believe neither of you heard me fighting for my life," a woman's voice said. It was rough and low — making her sound all the more cross. Elena guessed it was the Dragongirl.

"We had full bellies and warm beds," a man replied. He carried his words strangely, letting them roll off his tongue in a purr. "I don't think a thunderclap could've woken me."

"Oh? And how about a sharp kick to the rump?" the Dragongirl growled. "Did that work for you?"

He made an annoyed sound. "Well *obviously* it did."

"Fat lot of good the two of you are. What if there had been more —? Stop it, Jake!"

"I'm only trying to help," the man called Jake said. He sounded a bit hurt.

"It'll heal on its own. I won't look half as good with a beard as you do," the Dragongirl added wryly.

"Actually, I think I may have figured out what went wrong —"

"Hush," the first man purred, and Elena tensed as she suddenly felt the weight of eyes upon her. "I do believe our captive is awake."

Quick steps, and then a strong hand jerked Elena's head up by her chin. She realized there was no point in pretending any longer, so she opened her eyes.

The Dragongirl's face was close to hers, and she looked very cross, indeed. She had her dark hair pulled back in a pony's tail, though a few wisps still fell across her face. And those eyes — Elena swore she could see fire burning behind them.

"Who sent you?" the Dragongirl said.

Elena didn't answer.

After a moment, the Dragongirl's red lips bent into a smile. A thin cut split the bottom one, but it wasn't nearly as bloody as it ought to have been. Elena thought the wound looked at least a day old — but judging by the rise of the moon, she'd only been out for an hour. Maybe two.

How had she healed so quickly?

"Never mind," the Dragongirl said, as she followed Elena's searching gaze. "You don't have to tell me anything. I know you've come from Countess D'Mere."

She scowled to hide her surprise. "You're wrong."

The laughter behind the Dragongirl's eyes made Elena want to gouge them out. "Is that so? Then tell me: how is it that you've come to have mindrot poison on your blades? Only the Countess knows the formula."

Curiosity was making it more difficult for Elena to hide her emotions. She forced herself to shrug. "I often use poisons —"

"Not like this, you don't." The Dragongirl let go of her and leaned back. All of Elena's weapons had been spread out across the floor of the tent: Slight and Shadow, the band of throwing knives, and the three poisoned blades. "I d⟨..⟩t know how she tricked you into working for her, but let me offer you a warning: D'Mere is not at all what she seems. If she draws you close, it's only to bring you within range of her dagger. You've been warned," she added with a glare.

Then she grabbed one of the poisoned knives and held it up to her face. "D'Mere is also a very accomplished alchemist. I don't know exactly how mindrot works. The poison is useless against humans and mages, but if it's used on a whisperer ... well, the result is rather *crippling*."

A muscle in Elena's jaw twitched as she tried to keep her gaze steady.

"Once D'Mere discovered the formula, every weapon in Midlan was tipped with mindrot," the Dragongirl went on, studying the tiny knife in the dim light. "Some believe that the Kingdom would've fallen during the Whispering War, had it not been for D'Mere's poison."

Elena's throat was suddenly very tight. She had to work to keep the confusion from showing on her face. "Fascinating story," she said, as haughtily as she could. "Now set me free."

The Dragongirl's eyes glowed with her smirk. Elena winced when her fingertips brushed the swollen skin above her eye — the wound that Holthan's fist had left behind.

"There aren't many people who've had the honor of drawing my blood," the Dragongirl said, taking her hand away to prop her fingers against her busted lip. "You've been trained well. I don't think I'd ever like to meet the fellow who wounded you."

"Is someone wounded?"

A thin man poked his head into the tent behind the Dragongirl. Elena recognized his voice, and realized this must be the man called Jake.

Except for a bare patch around his spectacles, a tangled mat of hair covered Jake's entire face. He squinted at Elena's bruise. "I might be able to fix that ..."

He bent towards her, and his stench burned her nose. "Keep your hands off me, mage!" Elena shouted, struggling against her bonds. Anger flooded her limbs. If she could reach him, she'd rip his filthy throat out.

Jake quickly pulled his hand away. "I'm — I'm sorry, miss. I didn't realize —"

"Don't apologize to her. You've done nothing wrong," the Dragongirl said firmly, though she kept her sharp eyes on Elena. "If you raise a hand to him, I swear I'll call down such a fire upon your arse —"

"It's all right, Kyleigh," Jake said. He was hunched over to fit inside the tent, and had the long fingers of his hands clenched together. He looked pointedly at the floor. "I'm going to — ah, I'm going to make sure the fire's still lit." And he ducked quickly out the door.

The Dragongirl — Kyleigh — watched after him for a moment before she turned back to Elena. She was too weak to fight back when Kyleigh undid her first few shirt buttons and pulled it open. She figured it was too late to hide it, anyways. She flinched as Kyleigh traced the red mark on her chest, the one that looked like a dagger's scar.

"You *are* a whisperer, then. And your gift is war?"

Elena nodded. She suddenly felt a wave of hot tears pushing at the corners of her eyes, and had to bite her lip to keep them from spilling over.

The Countess had betrayed her. She'd sent her away with knives poisoned with the power to destroy her — and sent her to face an enemy that was well beyond her strength. There was no doubting it, no other way she could possibly explain it.

D'Mere had been trying to get her killed.

It shouldn't have surprised her. The Countess *was* a liar, after all. Elena would've had to use all of her fingers and toes to count the men she'd killed — men that D'Mere had been laughing with just days before. She'd seen the Countess smile as she slipped poison into a glass, or joke as she draped an arm about a merchant's shoulder ... all the while clutching a dagger in her other hand.

Yes, the Countess was a liar. She lied to everyone — even to the King ... but for some reason, Elena had never thought the Countess would lie to *her*. She'd never expected this wound, never seen it coming ... and she supposed that's why the old men called it a *dagger in the back*.

But no matter how it stung, Elena was determined not to let Kyleigh see her pain. Tears wouldn't solve anything. No ... there was a better way to settle the score.

Countess D'Mere would have to think very quickly indeed, to keep Elena's daggers out of her chest.

"Release me," Elena said. A new plan burned in her veins. She was already thinking about how she would do it, already planning her strokes. "I no longer have a contract to kill you."

"Well, that's a relief," Kyleigh said with a smirk. But she did as Elena asked: loosening her bonds until she could pull herself free.

"Hand over my weapons."

"Ask nicely," Kyleigh countered. And since she was spinning a poisoned knife so effortlessly between her fingers, Elena thought it best to do as she was told. Though she wasn't happy about it.

"*May* I have my weapons back?"

"Certainly — in the morning," Kyleigh added, when she reached for them.

Elena glared at her. "I mean to leave tonight."

"Then you must also mean to be ripped apart and eaten. The poison won't leave your blood for several more hours," she explained. "Until your whispering abilities come back, I'm afraid you'll be just as human as the rest of us. So, unless you want the minceworms to gobble you up ..." She jerked her chin across the tent, where she'd arranged the furs into a second bedroll.

Elena knew Kyleigh was right. There was no way she could hope to travel safely without her powers. She didn't want to share a tent with someone she'd just been trying to murder — it made the air between them a little ... uncomfortable. But the strength that usually kept her blood warm was gone, and the night was cold. So she would have to make do.

She curled up reluctantly on the other bedroll, lying on her back — so she could watch the tent's entrance *and* keep Kyleigh in the corner of her eye. She still didn't trust the Dragongirl. And the feeling was obviously mutual.

"I plan to keep these," Kyleigh said, holding up the poisoned knives. "So think carefully before you try to attack me." She turned over. After a moment, she glanced back. "And if you snore, I'll make you share a tent with Silas."

Elena didn't know who Silas was, but the way Kyleigh grinned made her think that she probably didn't want to share a tent with him.

Chapter 18
A Giant's Thanks

One morning, Finks woke the giants with a bellow. He swooped into the barn a little earlier than usual, flinging his whip about him and shrilling that the fields were dry enough for planting — so if they wanted to keep their hides, they'd better move quickly.

Once they'd gotten a few sips of water, Hob led them straight to a shed behind Westbarn. "No pushing, no shoving, and keep your blades pointed to the ground!" he snapped.

Kael thought the mages were being nastier than usual, but for some reason, the giants seemed excited. They grunted animatedly to one another as they crowded around the shed. Soon they were packed together so tightly that Kael feared he might actually be crushed.

Hob fiddled with the shed's lock for a moment, muttering curses to himself. When he couldn't get the key to work, he struck it with a spell. The lock fell into his palm, he tugged the doors open — and then had to spring away quickly to keep from getting trampled.

The giants rushed inside, squeezing through the doors so forcefully that the frame groaned in protest. One giant slipped in ahead of the others and emerged a few seconds later wearing a large cloth satchel across his chest. As he pushed his way out, Kael saw that he had a vicious-looking weapon clutched in his hands

He recognized it immediately from the pictures he'd seen in the *Atlas*. It was a giant's scythe — a weapon with a wooden shaft about the length of a spear and a curved blade at its top. There were worn, leather grips wrapped around the shaft in a couple of places, so that it could be wielded easily with two hands. The blade looked more like a sword than an actual scythe: it stuck straight up from the shaft, bent just enough to catch the backs of wheat.

Or a man's neck.

Kael imagined that the giants used their scythes for fighting as much as anything else. They warred so often that they'd probably leapt straight from their fields and into battle, so they'd needed a weapon that could fell both foes *and* crops.

With their scythes in hand, the giants looked more alive than Kael had ever seen them. Their backs straightened, and a fierce red burned across their cheeks. The dark rings seemed to fade from under their eyes as they studied their blades for flaws.

As giant after giant emerged from the shed, they smiled at each other — as if they all had a share in the same happiness. Kael watched them grin ... and quite suddenly, he felt a pang inside his chest.

He could see them, now — the shadows of the great warriors the giants had once been. He could imagine how they must've looked, all lined up together and prepared to defend their lands. They must've been a mighty, frightening force. And couldn't help but wonder how many armies had simply fled at the sight of them.

The crowd of giants shoved Kael forward, sweeping him helplessly into the shed. He took a satchel from a high shelf and grabbed a scythe off the floor. The weighty iron blade made it an impossibly heavy weapon. He wedged the scythe against his chest and stumbled outside as quickly as he could. The blade dragged along the ground behind him, and the satchel hung almost to his knees.

He was well aware of how ridiculous he looked, but the giants' heckling still burned him. They laughed as he walked by, elbowing their companions and pointing him out, so they'd be sure not to miss him. Their guffaws burned Kael to the tops of his ears. He was furious by the time he reached Brend.

"They're never going to stop clucking at me, are they?" he blurted out, shooting a glare behind him.

"Probably not," Brend said with a shrug.

"Why? I've pulled my weight, haven't I? I've done the same work as everybody else. I've even done some of *their* work — I've saved them from a flogging! And this is the thanks I get?"

"Thanks?" Brend shook his head. "A giant never offers thanks — he settles his debt in deeds. One day, they'll save *your* hide from a flogging, and it'll all be ironed out. *Thanks* are only for great debts, a debt that a giant has no other way of repaying. And even at that," he added with a wink, "most giants would rather die than ever have to give it."

Kael thought that was ridiculous. But before he could say as much, Declan cut in. "Tie your satchel up like mine," he said to Kael. He'd just emerged from the crowd and was working a knot into the straps, shortening them to a more manageable length.

Kael mirrored him, tying up his satchel until it hung at his hips. Then Brend led out, and Declan and Kael followed along at his heels.

"Let me see," Declan said, reaching for Kael's scythe. He studied it for a moment, his brows bent down tightly. "Hmm, oh that won't do. You've got a chip in your blade." He handed the weapon back. "I'll take you to the smith after we finish planting."

"All right," Kael said. For once, Declan wasn't looking at him. In fact, he seemed to be keeping his eyes purposefully on the road. Kael thought he might've been acting a little odd. But before he could wonder about it, Brend called out:

"Do you smell that, lads?"

Kael had learned — after a number of unfortunate incidents — to plug up his nose anytime that question was asked. And that went doubly for whenever it was asked by Brend.

"No, no," he said, laughing. He pointed up the road, where the smoking tower lay only a quarter of a mile in the distance. "They're baking the bread today." Brend inhaled so deeply that Kael could see his nostrils flare. "My, that takes me back. It reminds me of my dear, sweet mother ..."

"You shouldn't talk about your mother," Declan said, prodding him with the butt of his scythe. "You'll go all misty-eyed, and we've still got the wheat to plant today."

"You're right," Brend said thickly. And Kael was shocked to see that there were, indeed, tears welling up in his eyes. "I can't let the rememberings get the better of me. Someone's got to make sure you clodders get my wheat planted right!"

On their way to the grain fields, they stopped by Churl's wagon. The water barrels had been replaced with several barrels of seed. Brend filled his satchel halfway up, and then insisted on filling Declan and Kael's.

"That ought to get the field covered — you don't want to waste any of it. Now, come on," he barked.

Much to Kael's surprise, Brend was very particular about the wheat. He stood with his arms crossed in front of the field, and would only let certain giants join their team. "Get out of here, Taggart!" he hollered to one fellow who was making his way over. "I don't want you anywhere near my grains — go plant some turnips!"

Taggart didn't look at all hurt: he just shrugged and loped off in another direction.

"Cattleraisers," Brend said with a grunt. "Ham-fisted bumblers if ever there were any. They haven't got the touch for wheat. And if you start bumbling around," he added, shaking a finger at Kael, "I'll send you straight off to plant turnips. Don't think I won't."

Kael promised to do his best not to bumble.

Once their field was full, Brend assigned each giant to a row. Then he swooped down on Kael. "Our wheat grows in batches: the winter stuff's almost ready to be harvested, so now it's time to plant the spring seeds," he said, as he led Kael to a particular line on the field. "This can be your row for the day — the third from the right. Every field we move to, you'll just stay on this same row. It helps keep us organized. Have you ever planted wheat before? No? I didn't think so. Look here."

Brend flipped his scythe over with one hand, so quickly that Kael flinched when the blade hissed by his ear. There were a number of rings carved around the butt of the weapon. He'd thought they were some sort of decoration at first, but the rings were spaced too oddly to be a pattern.

He watched carefully as Brend traced one of the lines with the thick tip of his finger. "This is the mark for spring wheat — it tells you how deep you ought to plant it." He pushed the butt of the scythe into the moist earth, leaving a small hole in the mound. Then he sprinkled a pinch of seed into the hole and pushed the soil back over it with his foot. "See what I did? You don't want to press down too hard, now — otherwise you'll smother the little things."

Brend made Kael plant several patches — halting his work every now and then to bark that he was doing it all wrong.

"No, no! You're putting them too close together. You'll crowd them out." Then, when Kael began to space them a little further apart: "What are you trying to do — starve us? Give them that much room and we'll have a scant less than half of what we ought to."

When Kael finally got it right, Brend was rather pleased. He seemed happier that day than Kael had ever seen him, and he hardly stopped whistling for a moment.

"You were never this excited about plowing," Kael remarked. Though his planting was as good as anybody else's, the length of the scythe made it an unwieldy tool. Trying to dig a hole with it was about as comfortable as trying to eat his dinner with a spear.

Brend caught up to him quickly. "That's because we were plowing the vegetable fields," he said, as if it should be obvious. "It doesn't matter how many relatives we have in common: I may be half-Gardener, but I'm all Grainer at heart!"

"Brend Grainer?" Kael said, puzzled by the sound of it. It seemed odd for the giants to take their names from the crops they grew. Though he supposed it was better than having no name at all.

They'd just finished their second field and were moving on to a third when they saw Finks waiting for them. His lips parted in an unsettling grin as they approached.

"My, my — you're all doing so well today." And Kael almost expected to see his tongue flick out from between his long teeth as he spoke. "But I think we could do a little better. Let's play a game."

Finks's idea of a game was every bit as wicked as Kael imagined it would be. The giants walked the lines as they had before, but to make things more interesting, Finks trotted along at their backs — and swore he would mercilessly flay whichever one of them walked the slowest. "And I mean to do this properly, little beasts." He uncoiled his whip and stretched it taut between his hands. "No spells, just the hard bite of leather against your flanks. Let the game begin!"

"Yes, let it," Brend said. His eyes glinted as he leaned down the line to look at Declan — who nodded ever so slightly. "Pay attention, wee rat: we're going to play a little game of our own. This one's yours." Brend thrust his scythe into the ground, making a low, thumping sound.

Kael had no idea what that meant, but he didn't exactly have time to think about it. Finks hovered at his back — no doubt hoping that Kael's shorter stride would keep him well behind the others. And it did.

"Move those scrawny legs, rat!" Finks cried.

His whip came down, and the leather slapped against Kael's skin. The first blow shocked him: he arched his back away from it and nearly cried out. Then came the second lash, and the third. By the time the fourth blow fell, he was running back for the giants, planting as quickly as he could. But he couldn't catch up.

He was preparing himself for a fifth blow when he heard Finks laying into some giant down the row from him. He seemed to be struggling to get a hole dug, and his fumbling gave Kael the chance he needed to escape.

His back throbbed furiously where Finks had struck him. He swore he could feel the swollen tracks the whip left behind, rising up against his shirt. His skin stung and burned all at once, like some horrible little bee had gone and dragged its barb across his shoulders. But Kael was more furious than hurt.

His pride stung the worst. It was humiliating to be beaten by someone as evil as Finks — far worse than being struck by a spell. He'd felt defenseless as the whip bit him. The pain did what words could have done, what words *should* have done. The fact that he was beaten instead of ordered back into line made him feel less than human.

It made him feel like an animal.

No wonder the giants were a bit rough around the edges. They'd been whipped for so long that the blows ought to have broken them; they shouldn't be able to smile. They should've lost their pride long ago, given in to the whip — but they hadn't.

Behind every smile was defiance. Every joke was a rebellion. If Kael had been a slave for seventeen years ... well, he didn't know if he'd still be able to laugh like the giants did. And the next time they heckled him, he didn't think he would mind it as much.

As they continued down the field, Kael paid more attention to the giants' game. It didn't take him long to figure it out: the giants dropped back intentionally, in carefully planned patterns. No sooner did Finks lay into one giant than he would have to run to another, and often to opposite ends of the field. They kept him darting back and forth like a finger across fiddle strings, and each giant only had to take a couple of lashes apiece.

Kael had to admit that it was rather satisfying to hear Finks panting as he charged from line to line. His heavy breathing soon swallowed up his threats, and he could do no more than gasp curses between beatings. After the fourth time he'd sprinted completely across the field, Kael thought for sure that Finks would figure it out — but he never did. Perhaps Kael had misjudged him.

Perhaps Finks was the stupid kind of evil.

It wasn't long before they had him completely exhausted. He was so out of breath that he ran with his head tilted upwards and his mouth agape, as if he could somehow catch a lungful of air without having to actually make the effort of breathing it in. And while Finks suffered, Brend seemed to be thoroughly enjoying himself.

Kael watched him closely for a moment, and realized that Brend was commanding the entire prank. His whistling still carried on like a string of nonsense, but now there were subtle messages in the notes: when he struck a high note, or a steady low hum, a giant would obediently fall behind. Then he let out a warble that sounded like a bird's song, and Declan fell back.

But it wasn't just whistling. Sometimes when he would bend to drop some seed, Brend would have a different number of fingers propped against his scythe. These were signals, too. And the giants followed them dutifully.

At one point, Brend pretended to drop his scythe and then spent an obnoxious amount of time trying to pick it up. Finks caught sight of him and sprinted over, trudging across the high piles of soggy ground, murder in his eyes. But no sooner did he reach him than Brend had caught back up — and Declan was the one behind.

Kael waited until Finks had charged away before he elbowed Brend. "Did you come up with this on your own?"

He shrugged, but couldn't quite hide his smile. "Oh, sure. Are you surprised, wee rat? Didn't think the giants were good for anything but clobbering, now did you? Well, I ..." He leaned back to glance at Kael's shoulders, and his eyes widened. "I think your turn's over for the day, wee rat."

"Why? It doesn't hurt," he added quickly, when Brend shook his head. "It's all gone numb."

"A giant's hide is a mightily thick thing — we can shoulder the blows." He glanced at Kael's back again and whistled. "But that's not so for wee men. I can see the welts popping up through your shirt!"

"I can handle it," Kael insisted. He suddenly had an idea, and he wanted the chance to try it out. "If you take me out of the game, I'll just fall back anyways."

Brend was about to respond when Finks's shrilling voice suddenly cut over the top of him:

"Pick them up! Pick every last one of them up!" he cried, swinging mercilessly at the giant crouched at his feet.

It was Declan. The strap of his satchel must've broken: it lay on the ground and seed spilled from it, scattering across the dark earth. Though Declan tried to work quickly, his thick hands made things difficult. He shoveled through the dirt, trying to scoop the tiny bits of seed back into his pouch.

And Finks's blows kept coming.

Even from a distance, Kael could hear the leather slapping against Declan's flesh. He could see the angry red lines that blossomed across his head and down his neck. His teeth were bared against the pain.

Anger filled Kael like a red cloud, blotting out his reason. He didn't have a chance to plan anything out. Instead, he did the first thing he could think of: he reared back and threw his scythe as far as he could.

The weapon landed clumsily, skittering across the dirt. It hadn't gone as far as he'd wanted it to, but it still landed behind Declan — and that was far enough. Kael started walking, and Finks saw him.

"Where do you think you're going, rat?" he shrilled.

"I dropped my scythe," Kael said calmly. He walked at a leisurely pace, hoping to draw Finks away — and he did.

Finks charged, and Kael quickly drew up the memory of the mountain boulder again, imagining that the flesh on his back became like stone. He knew it was working because he could feel the extra weight in his knees as his skin hardened. When Finks's whip came down, it took all of Kael's concentration to keep the grin off his face: he could hear the whip slapping him, but couldn't feel it.

He bent to retrieve his scythe — and nearly cried out when Finks's whip struck him across the face. He hadn't been expecting that, and for a few seconds, he lost his defenses.

"Trying to be a hero, rat?" Finks hissed. He wrenched Kael's head back by the roots of his hair; a blast of tainted breath blew hot in his face. "Here — have a hero's beating."

Three blows landed across Kael's back before he managed to get his skin hardened again. His legs shook under the weight of his stoned flesh, making his steps slow and heavy. He kept his eyes straight ahead as he walked back to the giants. He could feel them staring, but didn't look at their faces. They were probably just laughing about how foolish he was, anyways.

But he didn't care. His effort gave Declan the time he needed to pick up his seed and tie the broken strap of his satchel into a fresh knot. Brend fell back to relieve Kael, and the giants continued on with their game as if nothing had happened.

At sunset, they plodded back to the barns in silence. Kael spotted Declan walking at the head of the line, and ran to stop him.

"My scythe," he explained, when Declan's brows raised in confused arcs. "You said you'd take me to get it fixed."

"Oh ... eh, don't worry about it," he grumbled, snatching the weapon from him. "I'll take it there, myself."

Kael was fine with that: he hadn't been looking forward to spending an extra hour at the blacksmith's. All he wanted was a quiet dinner and a long night of rest.

Unfortunately for him, dinner was far from quiet.

Kael's antics in the field *had* caught the giants' attention — but it wasn't the sort he'd been expecting. They didn't laugh at him or reenact his beating. No, what they did instead was far more annoying.

Brend told Kael's story as if it was the most legendary thing he'd ever seen. His voice carried through the rafters of the barn, rising and falling, drawing his audience in by the power of his words. While he spoke, the others listened silently — some with the porridge still hanging out of their mouths.

"Saved Declan from a hundred lashes, he did," Brend said. Though his voice was hardly a whisper, the giants could hear him clearly: the only noise in the whole barn was of the

Fallows as they snorted down their dinner. "That wee mountain rat — there, just as you see him."

Kael's face burned as several heads swiveled to look at him. This was the third time Brend had told the story, and it seemed to grow larger with every telling. He felt he ought to step in.

"It wasn't anywhere near a hundred —"

"Oh, don't be modest," Brend said over the top of him. He swept his hands over the trough in a wide arc, and his audience leaned in. "With one mighty heave, the rat tossed his scythe to the back of the field —"

"It didn't go quite that far," Kael insisted, but no one was listening.

In fact, somebody shushed him.

"He strode past that slick-headed mage, bold as a crow after crops. And when Finks asked what he was after, do you know what he said? *I dropped my scythe.*"

There was a round of appreciative laughter, and Kael winced has a giant's heavy arm plunked down across his shoulders.

"So Finks of Westbarn set upon him, striking with enough fury to split a man's hide. But this wee rat ... well, he took his beating without so much as a grimace."

"I grimaced quite a lot, actually."

"He stood there a full minute, blows raining down upon his reddened head. Never once did he budge —"

"What are you talking about? I got out of there as fast as I co — mft!"

The giant beside Kael clamped a hand over his mouth, giving Brend the chance to spin his wild yarn unhindered.

"He made his way back to us slowly, as if Finks's whip were no more troublesome than the bite of a fly. Then the rat took up his scythe and without so much as a grumble about his wounds, went straight back to work." Brend whistled, shaking his head. "I've not seen such a fierce look in a man's eyes — I swear it by the plains mother."

Kael was far more embarrassed by the giants' awe than he'd ever been by their teasing. He knew there was no point in trying to set the tale straight: no sooner did the giants cheer than they were begging Brend to tell it again.

He happily obliged — and rather than listen to how he'd survived four hundred blows to the head, Kael retreated to the stall.

Declan was already curled up on his pallet, his face turned towards the wall. He'd sulked for most the day, eaten very little dinner, and then disappeared as soon as Brend started telling his stories. He was probably just angry. It must've been humiliating for Declan, to have his hide saved by a scrawny mountain rat.

So Kael didn't worry too much about it.

Much of his sleeping space was still rather damp and covered in debris from the hole in the roof. But at least that meant he wouldn't have to worry about any of the giants flinging their limbs into his space. He was growing rather tired of being slapped awake in the middle of the night.

As he got closer to his spot, he slowed. It took him a moment of staring before he finally realized why his spot looked so odd: it had been taken. The debris had been cleared away, and a small pallet had been set up in its place.

After a puzzling second, Kael realized that the pallet must've been meant for him. It was so thin and short that it wouldn't have done any of the giants much good. But then who ...?

He turned back to Declan, and noticed that a good portion of his bedding was missing. His legs hung off the straw at his calves.

Kael stood still for a long moment. He knew very well that a giant's bed was his sole possession — the only thing he ever dared to call his own. And to think that Declan had given up a portion of his bed for Kael ... he didn't know what to say.

So he said the only thing he could think of, the only response that might possibly measure up:

"Thank you, Declan."

Chapter 19
The Grandmot

The sky was just pink enough to scare the minceworms back to their burrows when Elena bid them all farewell — saying that she'd rather strike out on her own than tie her lot in with a mage. And though that seemed to hurt Jake's feelings considerably, Kyleigh thought it was all for the best.

Once Elena was halfway to the dunes in the distance, Kyleigh turned to her next task at hand: discovering what it was that Jake was trying so desperately to hide in his pack.

"It's just an experiment," he grumbled. The pack squirmed a little, and he punched it roughly. "I'm trying to measure the effects of heat on minceworm skin," he explained, when Kyleigh narrowed her eyes. "We know how fire effects them. But I'm trying to deduce whether it's the light or the heat that keeps them hiding under the sand all day. Firelight doesn't seem quite bright enough to harm them, but the sun —"

"All right — which of you did it?"

Kyleigh was slightly grateful when Elena chose that moment to come storming back into camp. She knew how long-winded Jake's explanations could be. "Which of us did what?" she called as Elena approached them.

Good lord, that woman could melt flesh with her glare.

Her shoulders were stiff; her fingers curled into fists. An empty pack hung from her right hand. "Which of you did *this?*" she snapped, flinging the pack at Kyleigh's feet. "All of my supplies are gone. My rations, my water — everything!"

"Why do you think *we're* to blame?" Silas mumbled. He was lying on his back against the glass floor, smiling contently as the morning sun warmed it. "You left food out in the middle of the desert overnight. Did you not see the hundreds of hungry mouths waiting around our camp?"

"Yes, I saw them," Elena said, with over exaggerated patience. "But did you not see, *cat*, that my pack isn't torn to shreds? So unless the minceworms have discovered a way to work buckles and canteen caps, I'd say the head I ought to crack is somewhere amongst you three. Or perhaps I ought to just crack them all."

They hadn't been together an entire night, and Silas had already made Elena his enemy. When the morning sky was still dark, he'd snuck into Kyleigh's tent in his lion form and let out an ear-rattling roar. It startled Elena so badly that she'd nearly torn a hole in the tent's wall just trying to escape.

Silas had been chuckling about it all morning. Even now, his white teeth glinted as he grinned at her threat. "Well, *I* certainly didn't do it."

Elena spun on Kyleigh, and she shook her head quickly.

"I don't trust you," Elena snarled.

"Well, that's probably for the best," Kyleigh allowed. "But though I'm many things, a liar isn't one of them."

When Elena couldn't match her glare, she stomped over to Jake.

"Hold on a moment." He fumbled with the strings on his invisible canteens before he managed to pull one free. Then he held it out to her. "I didn't do it. But here — take this."

Kyleigh had to prop a fist under her chin to keep her mouth from falling open. She knew very well that the canteen he'd offered Elena was his last. And had she been a nicer person, the gesture might not have been all that astonishing. But as it was, Elena was about as nice as a cut under the fingernail.

She glared at Jake's hand. "Are you mocking me?"

"Not at all. It just *looks* like nothing —"

"So you've stolen my rations, and now you're content to sit back and laugh at me?"

"No, that isn't it." Jake got to his feet, and though he stood nearly a head over Elena, he hunched his shoulders forward and looked down at the ground. "I'm truly sorry for what happened to you. I'm only trying to help —"

"Don't apologize to her," Silas said, springing to his feet. He stuck his chest to Elena's arm and met her fiercely in the eyes. "The shaman is far too polite," he growled, "but I am not. Slight him again, and I'll chew you into pieces."

Elena glared daggers at Silas — who sneered defiantly back. And Jake, for whatever reason, looked remarkably close to tears. Kyleigh decided that now was probably the time to step between them.

She pushed Elena and Silas apart, with one firm hand on either of their chests. "I don't know what happened to your pack," Kyleigh said sharply, "but if Jake and I say we didn't do it, then we didn't do it. As for Silas —"

"You'll never know!" he crowed, laughing in her face.

Elena's hand twitched for one of her daggers.

Kyleigh grabbed her wrist. "Don't even think about it," she growled, shoving her back. "There's no changing what's been done, and we haven't got enough supplies to share," she added, with a pointed look at Jake. "So, you have two choices: follow us to water, or try to survive the journey back on your own. It's entirely up to you."

****

By midday, Kyleigh was beginning to wish that she'd just killed them all and been done with it. They had no meat for breakfast, and so Silas had gone back to being one high pitched and never-ending moan of despair. Jake still asked her a thousand questions every hour — none of which she was able to answer to his liking. But now Elena was there to make it all worse.

When Silas whined, she'd very tartly turn around and tell him to shut it — which would start a fist-flying argument that Kyleigh had to step in and settle. Then Elena complained

239

loudly about having to walk downwind from Jake, and he'd gotten rather hurt about it.

The next time Kyleigh turned, she spotted Jake several yards away from the main party, walking stubbornly in another direction.

So she made Silas and Elena sit with their backs to each other — and swore by the sky above them that if she had to separate one more fight, she'd reduce them both to smoldering craters. Then she went after Jake at a run.

"What are you doing, you silly mage?" she said when he was within shouting distance.

"I'm going home!" he snapped from over his shoulder.

"No, you're going east."

He stopped and squinted up at the sky. Then he spun around and with a good amount of cursing, began to walk in the opposite direction. "I can't take it anymore," he said as he drew even with her. He tried to push past her, but she wrangled him in by the shoulders. "Let me go!"

"Not until you tell me what's the matter," Kyleigh said, trying not to crush him as he struggled. "Was it what Elena said?"

"No," he snapped back. Then all at once, his anger deflated. "I don't like being a bother. Whisperers obviously can't stand the smell of me. That's part of the reason why I followed you out of Gravy Bay: I knew I was bothering Kael. He was nice about it, but I could tell that I bothered him. And I just ..."

"Yes," Kyleigh said after a moment. "He *was* nice about it. And do you know why that is?"

"No."

"Because, underneath that prickly skin of his, he's actually a very nice person." It was surprisingly difficult to talk about Kael. She tried to keep her voice steady, but for some reason, her chest was suddenly tight. What in Kingdom's name was wrong with her? She cleared her throat roughly and pressed on. "Elena, however, is not a nice person. She's a terror and a child — a spoiled ruler's pet who's been given everything she ever asked for. Believe me, I've seen her type before."

Jake shook his head. "No, you're wrong." He struggled again and this time, she released him. He dropped his pack on the ground and began to work the straps. "Here, I'll leave you with the cook pot and —"

The pack opened and a cloud of ash whooshed out, covering Jake's face and beard in soot. He swore.

"Perfect, just perfect," he muttered. His brows bent into a glare, but his spectacles were so filthy that Kyleigh couldn't see his eyes behind the lenses. "I can't believe I forgot about that blasted minceworm — now my experiment is ruined! See? You're better off without me." He ripped his spectacles off and began to polish them furiously against the hem of his robe. "Elena would be nicer if I wasn't here. If I stay, I'll only make a mess of things."

"Jake — she's treating you like one of her servants. She orders you about, tells you to walk so many paces behind her, to give up a portion of your water, and instead of standing up to her — you just let her do it!" When he shook his head, Kyleigh dropped down to face him. "You are *not* her slave, do you understand? So what if she has a problem with you? That's *her* problem — not yours. Silas and I don't put up with her nonsense, and neither should you. So the next time she snaps at you, I want you to tell her to shove —"

"Dragoness!"

Kyleigh jerked her head around to yell back at Silas, and instead saw something that made her heart catch in her throat.

A monster barreled up from the south: a huge, swirling cloud of wind and sand. It blotted out the sky behind it, swallowed up the massive dunes in its path. The storm rushed towards them in a perfect wall, breaking across the earth like foamy surf upon the shore — and they were nothing but tiny fish about to be swept away.

The storm stretched from horizon to horizon, thundering as it raced to devour them. It seemed to gain speed as it tore across the dunes; the sands caught in the gales thickened it, reaching up to cover the sun in a dense, brownish cloak.

Kyleigh knew there was no escaping it.

A blur of movement caught her eye, and she looked down in time to see Elena tearing off in another direction. She followed her sprint and saw that she was heading for an outcrop of gray rock in the distance — the only thing in sight that wasn't made of sand.

"Follow her!" Kyleigh shouted to Silas.

"What about the packs —?"

"Leave them! Go!"

The shrill in her voice seemed to convince him. He dropped on all fours and burst into his lion form. Kyleigh grabbed Jake by the hand and jerked him forward. She knew they didn't have much hope of making it to shelter before the wall overcame them, but at least they wouldn't be separated.

"It's a sandstorm!" Jake gasped as he struggled to keep her pace. "I was beginning to think we wouldn't see one. Is it true what they say? That sometimes the sand blows hard enough to strip flesh from bone —?"

"I don't know, and I sure as Death don't want to find out!" Kyleigh yelled over him. The storm thundered towards them, aiming to strike them in the side. She could feel its fury in the hot wind that cut across the nape of her neck.

Ahead of her, Silas had outstripped Elena by the power of his four legs. He was nearly at the rock shelter. Kyleigh reached with her free hand and pulled Jake's turban over his eyes.

"Unless you want the sands to scratch them from their sockets, you're going to have to keep them covered!" she said when he complained. "I'll guide you — trust me!" She got one last glimpse of their target before she pulled her hood over her eyes — and not a breath too soon.

The gales struck them hard, blowing them sideways. Jake fell and Kyleigh nearly tripped over him as she struggled to keep her footing. She felt as if she was trapped beneath the ocean, with the currents ripping her limbs in every direction. It wasn't long before she lost all sense of where she was, and the sand showed no mercy: it lashed her flesh, burning like flakes of hot ash.

She pulled Jake up by their clasped hands and heard him yell as she dragged him on. The fiery earth rose like floodwaters over their ankles and knees. As the sand tried to drag them under, they bent nearly double against the wind, fighting their way through the thick, burning drifts.

Grit caked Kyleigh's tongue. She felt as if every gasping breath she drew was half-sand. She didn't know how long they would have until they ran out of air. The shelter of the rocks was their only hope.

"Run!"

She pulled Jake into a desperate sprint. They moved quickly, jerking their legs stubbornly out of the drifts and dashing for a few steps along the shifting surface. Kyleigh wagered they would be at the rocks in thirty paces. Surely they could hold on until then.

She leapt free of another drift and went to take the next step, but her boot touched nothing. Her leg fell through an open space and dragged her body down with it. She was too shocked to let go of Jake. She heard him cry out as the weight of her body pulled him down.

The burning heat, the sand, the roar of the storm — it all suddenly disappeared, snuffed out as the earth sucked them downwards. Wind whistled across Kyleigh's ears and she dragged her elbow against the wall behind her, trying to slow their fall. The path curved, and she grimaced as her rump struck unforgiving stone. Then the tunnel spat them out.

Kyleigh slid until her back struck a wall, jarring her innards. Jake certainly didn't help things when he collided with her middle. She lay still for a moment, checking to make sure that she had all of her limbs. Once her arms and legs had all been accounted for, she looked to see where they'd landed.

Her eyes quickly adjusted to the dimness: gray walls of rock surrounded them. They must've fallen into some sort of cave.

Jake lay just in front of her. She reached out to make sure he was in one piece. When she gripped his shoulder, he didn't respond. She shook him gently — then much rougher when his body rolled limply to the side. "Jake? Jake!"

Her shout echoed sharply off the walls around them, but she didn't care. She pushed Jake onto his back and gripped his face between her hands. Hot, sticky blood stained the pads of her fingers. She felt through his shaggy beard and along his scalp until she finally found it: a gash the length of half a finger. Though it was no wider than a bootlace, the wound gushed blood at an alarming rate.

Something dug into Kyleigh's neck. She was so worried over Jake that she knocked it away without thinking. A second later, the pressure came again. And this time it was followed by a voice:

"What are you doing in our tunnels, outlander?"

Kyleigh turned — slowly, because she now realized that the object digging into her neck was the pointed end of a spear.

A woman's face was the first thing she saw. She was young. The black hair that fell just past her shoulders was held back by a silver clasp. Though her features gave her the same exotic look as a desert woman, her skin was almost the color of sand, the lightest brown Kyleigh had ever seen amongst the tribes.

The woman's stern look was tinged with surprise. Kyleigh guessed by the way her eyes wandered that she hadn't seen many travelers. "Why have you trespassed here?" she said again.

Kyleigh didn't have time to explain. "Do you have a healer? My friend's hurt."

The woman obviously hadn't been expecting a question. She eased back, and Kyleigh moved like a flash — ripping the spear out of the woman's hand and leveling it at her throat.

She was surprised to find that the shaft was made of metal. It was heavy, too. It didn't feel like iron, and wasn't as bright as steel. "Silver?" she said.

The woman nodded. She'd retreated back a few paces and was now standing protectively before the tunnel's opening. A dim light glowed behind her, and a little girl in a yellow silk dress clutched at her hand. Kyleigh thought the little girl's eyes looked strangely familiar. There was a depth in them that she recognized, and they held her with an odd power — almost as if they could see through her skin.

A memory flashed across the backs of her eyes. It darted by, teasing her with a flick of its tail as it swam away. The little girl's stare crept over her, and Kyleigh bit down on her lip. She was angry — not at the little girl, but at her stare. And something told her that she had a good reason to be upset ... but she couldn't remember why.

After a moment, the little girl blinked. The eerie depth disappeared from her eyes as she tugged on the woman's hand. A childlike excitement lined her smile. "Nadine — look!"

"I see, child," Nadine whispered back. She stared at Kyleigh, and the dark brows above her eyes tipped — from surprised arcs, to firm, determined lines.

Nadine was not dressed quite like the traditional desert woman. Her red silk dress had been altered to look more like a warrior's garb: one shoulder was bare, but across the other was a metal guard. Her skirt was cut to her knees and covered in heavy chainmail. She wore sandals on her feet, and the metal plates that wrapped around her calves protected her shins.

The gauntlets on her wrists were close enough for Kyleigh to get a good look at them. They had intricate designs carved into their surfaces, and the trail left a darker line than it would have in steel.

So, even her armor was made of silver.

"Why have we stopped?" a commanding voice said from deeper in the tunnel.

Nadine stepped aside, and another woman slipped out from behind her — placing herself firmly between Nadine and the little girl.

The hair on this woman's head sprouted short and wild: it stuck up in every direction and glinted strangely in the dim light. It took Kyleigh a moment to see that most of what she thought was hair was actually an astonishing number of tawny feathers. They'd been woven carefully among the dark strands, until most of them stood up straight. Kyleigh thought the feathers made the woman look slightly ruffled — like a barn owl caught in a gale.

A soft rattle of armor came from the tunnel behind them. Kyleigh took a protective step towards Jake when she saw the small force of spear-wielding guards gathered behind Nadine. One of them craned his neck over the crowd. He broke out into an excited grin when he saw Kyleigh.

"Dawn Hessa's vision has come to pass, Grandmot," he said to the feather-haired woman. He pointed his spear at Kyleigh and called behind him: "One more deserving has fallen into our path. Nadine will be spared!"

His announcement set off a round of muffled cheers from the other guards. More smiling heads popped over the Grandmot to get a good look at Kyleigh — who was trying desperately to wrap her head around the strangeness of it all.

They were deep underground. There shouldn't have been anything but rabbits and crawly things where she stood … and yet, there seemed to be a whole race of people living in the tunnels. She'd been certain that humans preferred to live in the open air.

Though, she supposed she'd been wrong about them before.

The Grandmot was the only one who wasn't smiling. "Hold your tongues," she snapped, and the guards immediately quieted. Her eyes shot to Kyleigh.

They were dark and set far apart. Her nose and lips stretched almost to a point, and her stare seemed to lurk behind them. It gave her a cunning look, one that reminded Kyleigh a bit of a fox.

The Grandmot's eyes flicked over her for half a breath, and then she spun back to the guards. "It is true that a stranger has fallen among us. But how can we know if she is more *deserving* than Nadine?"

Kyleigh had almost forgotten about the little girl. But at that moment, she suddenly leaned out from behind the Grandmot. Though her voice was small, the whole company leaned in to hear her:

"Surely one who trespasses upon our lands is the most deserving."

All heads turned to the Grandmot. Her face twisted up about her eyes, and the expression she wore was a strange mix of emotion. She might've been angry, or perhaps even upset. Kyleigh couldn't quite read her look.

The Grandmot had heavy, silver loops hanging from her ears. When she shook her head, they *thwap*ed against her jaw. "I cannot argue with Dawn Hessa's vision," she finally said.

Nadine's mouth parted in shock. "But the lot has been cast! I must go —"

"Did Hessa not say your life might be spared, should one more deserving come to us? And I say one who trespasses upon our lands is more deserving! The outlander will serve as our sacrifice."

The Grandmot's words were followed by a metallic *clang* as the guards drove their spears against the rock.

Had Jake not been so badly injured, Kyleigh might've objected to being a sacrifice. But she was no healer. She knew she couldn't save him. Her only hope now was to try to bargain for his life. So she leaned against the silver spear and forced herself to meet Grandmot's gaze with a smile.

"In need of a blade for hire, are we?" she said, with far more confidence than she felt. From what little she'd seen of them, Kyleigh got the sense that this was a rather proper brood of humans, a brood that would likely have a thick set of rules. So if she wanted their help, she knew she'd have to step lightly. "I'll tell you what I can do —"

"You have no right to address our Grandmot with your outlander tongue," Nadine said sharply, putting herself between Kyleigh and the Grandmot. "You will speak to me."

"I don't really care who I speak to," Kyleigh leveled the spear at her, "just so long as you listen carefully. Now, I have no idea what the lot of you are squawking about, but perhaps we might be able to help each other. My friend is in desperate need of a healer. Have you got one?"

"Yes, but *you* will have no need of them," Nadine said spitefully. "Where you are going, there will be no return. As for your friend —"

"Tell the outlander we will heal her friend, if she completes this task for us," the Grandmot said, waving a few of the guards forward to collect Jake. "Be gentle with him — he may be of use to us, should this one fail. And Nadine, you will take the outlander to her post immediately."

Nadine clenched her jaw tightly, but didn't argue. "As you speak, Grandmot." She slunk off into the tunnel without another word, and Kyleigh just assumed that she was meant to follow.

Chapter 20
Cave Trolls

A smaller, darker tunnel branched off from the main path, and soon Kyleigh was having to hunch over to keep her head from scraping against the ceiling. That's when she noticed that Nadine still had a few inches between the top of her head and the rock above her.

Odd ... she hadn't really thought of her as a short woman.

"Do you want your weapon back?" Kyleigh said. Nadine didn't turn around, but held her hand out behind her. She slowed her pace when Kyleigh passed her the spear.

"You are strange, outlander," she muttered after a moment. "My ancestors have spent centuries trying to find the light in the darkness. But you already see it clearly."

Kyleigh was still trying to figure out what she meant when she realized that Nadine's bright red dress had lost its color, and the world had gone entirely gray. They were in the pitch black, and her dragon sight had taken over. "Who are your ancestors, exactly?" Kyleigh said, trying to steer the subject away from herself.

"We are the lastborn amongst the tribes, the most un-favored. The others call us *mots* — a word that means *children* in many of our tongues. And though the name was meant to shame us, we now wear it proudly."

Kyleigh had never heard of the mots before. "How did you come to be all the way out here?"

Nadine shrugged. "There are many stories. The Grandmot says the first of our ancestors left the cities and sought fortune in the desert. Though the sun forsook them for their paler skin, the earth had pity on them. She took the mots into her arms and has held us ever since."

They were quiet for a moment. Kyleigh was still trying to get used to the fact that a whole brood of humans lived underground. *Under*ground. It was the strangest thing she'd ever heard of.

As Kyleigh watched Nadine, she noticed that the mot's back and arms were ribbed in lithe muscle. She carried herself on the balls of her feet and moved without a sound. When Kyleigh held her breath, the silence was almost deafening.

"You're a warrior," she guessed.

"Oh, I would applaud your wisdom," Nadine said dryly, "if I did not think the noise would alert our enemies."

Kyleigh laughed.

Nadine short pony's tail brushed the tops of her shoulders as she shook her head. "You are strange, outlander. Very strange, indeed."

The silence and the darkness didn't last long. Soon they stepped out of the narrow passage and into a hallway flooded with light. It was much wider than the one they'd just escaped, but for all of its size, there was only a very slim vein of empty space down its middle.

Dozens of campsites were crammed against either side of the hallway. Packs lay clumped together in neat piles, casting shadows across the row of bedrolls beside them. Soldiers slept in some of the bedrolls, but a good number of them were gathered around small, low-burning lights — which looked to be nothing more than a few hot coals glowing inside silver braziers.

Nearly half of the soldiers were women. All were dressed in red silk: the men had it wrapped about their waists, and the women wore a garb similar to Nadine's. But what made each soldier different was the style of his armor. Some were nearly covered in it; some wore only a few necessary pieces. And every inch of the silver was inscribed with delicate symbols.

The soldiers stared openly at Kyleigh, and several nodded to Nadine in greeting. When she turned to nod back,

Kyleigh noticed she had a small, silver hoop piercing the top of her left ear.

As they passed by, the soldiers rose from the camp and took up their spears. They began following behind Kyleigh in a swarm, tittering in a strange chorus of voices.

Her skin began to crawl. The mots' chanting was hardly any louder than a whisper, but the way it bounced around the tunnels made it seem as if their words were everywhere: behind her, before her — even inside her head. Though the tallest man among them was only just her height, Kyleigh kept a firm grip on Harbinger.

No matter what she'd promised the Grandmot, Kyleigh had absolutely no intention of being sacrificed. These passages were far too narrow for her dragon form, but if it came down to a fight, she thought she might still have an advantage: Harbinger could cut through silver just as easily as steel.

He wasn't particular.

"Make certain you are right with Death, outlander," Nadine said as they neared the end of the passage.

Kyleigh tensed. She raised Harbinger slightly out of his sheath. She could have him drawn in half a breath, if she needed to.

The curious tittering behind them grew to a steady rumble, quieting only when Nadine came to a halt. They stood at the mouth of a tunnel, which spilled out into a massive chamber.

Stone ceilings stretched into the shadows, sitting as tall as one of Roost's highest towers; the smooth, gray chamber was nearly as wide as the full circle of the castle walls. Thick beams of light filtered down from the many holes that peppered the roof. Kyleigh could hear the wind moaning as it blew across them.

The chamber looked as if it had once been a gathering place. Hundreds of chairs had been carved out of the stone floor, and they filled the room in tight rings — growing steadily smaller with every level, like ripples in a pond.

In the middle of the chamber sat a high-backed chair and a massive silver bell. The bell was perched on a short platform, and hung only a little taller than the chair.

It had obviously been a very important room, once. But the grandeur had long since faded. Now most of the chairs were missing their backs — some had been completely reduced to rubble. Even the grand chair in the middle had a jagged corner broken off its top. And the stench of death was everywhere.

Kyleigh wasn't sure how many hundreds of bodies littered the cold floor, and she didn't know if she had the stomach to count them. She saw bits of red silk here or there, but most of the bodies were of animal-like things completely covered in black hair.

One hairy body lay close to the entrance. A tangle of pointed teeth lined the creature's decaying mouth. She grimaced when she saw the huge, shovel-like paw that sprouted from the end of its arm. The paw was still stretched out towards the tunnel; the claws glinting at the end of it were short and thick — and strong enough to carve through stone.

Cave trolls.

"You must run to the middle of the room and ring the bell," one of the mots said, shoving a spear into Kyleigh's hands. "Do not try to abandon your task, or we will have no choice but to kill you. Our spearmen can split a grain of rice from one hundred footfalls away."

"Well *that* doesn't seem very practical at all. Wouldn't you rather use a spoon?" Kyleigh said as she quickly scanned the chamber's walls. There were a number of tunnels, each branching out in a different direction. She didn't know what would happen when she rang the bell, but it looked as if she would have plenty of options for escape.

The mot looked slightly confused by her joking. Then his face went stern. "You will not have time to make it back to shelter, once you have rung the bell. Go bravely, and may Death welcome —"

Someone darted past him, clipping his shoulder and cutting his sentence short. Kyleigh watched in surprise as Nadine leapt over the nearest bodies. She sprinted straight for the bell.

The mots cried after her, but Nadine ignored them. And no one seemed eager to try to chase her down. Instead, the mots filed out of the tunnel, shoving Kyleigh to the front of their ranks. They stood in a line and lowered their spears — obviously preparing for some sort of battle.

Nadine was nearly at the bell when Kyleigh managed to piece it all together. She thought she knew what would happen when Nadine rang the bell. She could guess the sort of creatures that would come charging out.

There was no way Nadine could outrun a troll. Her legs were too short, and she only had two of them.

Kyleigh sighed inwardly, cursing all brands of human pride. Then she tossed her spear to a nearby mot and set out after Nadine. She sprinted past the bodies and vaulted over the stone chairs, watching for danger out of the corners of her eyes.

Clang! Clang! Clang!

Nadine's spear struck the bell, and Kyleigh grit her teeth against the stabbing tones. She leapt over a particularly thick pile of corpses and skirted her way across a fallen pillar, finally leaping down to land next to Nadine — who looked rather surprised to see her.

"What are you doing?" she shrieked. "This is *my* fate! I was chosen for it!"

"For death?"

"Yes!"

"Oh, I'm sorry — did you *want* to die?"

Kyleigh had meant it as a joke. But when Nadine didn't respond, she spun around. The mot's face burned red, and she kept her features smooth.

"Why —?"

Howls bounced off the tunnels in front of them, cutting her sentence short. Kyleigh squinted into the darkness to try to see the sort of trouble they were up against.

Just as she'd suspected, trolls came pouring out of the tunnels — only, she hadn't been expecting quite so many. The horrible, hairy creatures spilled from the passageways like water from a leaky hull, moving in one great, furry wave to swallow them up. Their teeth glinted out from their jaws — jaws that could unhinge and stretch to nearly twice their normal size.

"Run, outlander, if you value your life!" Nadine said. She stepped forward and gripped her spear tightly. "Mine ends here."

Kyleigh had only had a few brushes with trolls, and mostly they'd been with the scrawnier forest trolls: the hairless little creatures that liked to keep their homes in hollow logs. She'd never battled an army of cave trolls. So she was rather shocked when the first one reared up and began to twirl a sling.

A rock flew out and shot towards them with deadly speed. Kyleigh heard it hiss past her elbow as she jerked to the side. "The trolls have *slings*?" she said, whipping Harbinger from his sheath. "Since when do trolls carry weapons?" Another rock whizzed by and nearly grazed her ear.

Blazes — the little devils had good aim, too.

The cave trolls' faces were split evenly between their gaping mouths and their large, bat-like noses — they had no eyes. The holes in the middle of their heads flared wide as they charged. When they caught the warm scent of the mots' blood, their barking grew frenzied.

Their cries bounced off the walls and down through the tunnels, calling others to the feed. Soon, the trolls' forces had swelled into a small ocean of furry, writhing black. For the first time in a long time, Kyleigh had to admit that she was outnumbered. There was nothing for it, then.

Though he complained loudly, she sheathed Harbinger and sprinted past Nadine — who apparently didn't want to be outdone. Kyleigh cursed when she heard the desert woman following close behind.

A volley of stones flew towards her. There was no way to dodge them without hurting Nadine. So with a roar, Kyleigh dove into her dragon form.

She heard the hollow thud of rocks as they bounced off her scales, and heard Nadine scream behind her. The trolls must've smelled the change in her blood, because sparks flew from their nails as they dropped on all fours and tried to skid to a halt.

But it was too late to run.

Yellow flame burst from Kyleigh's throat, reducing the first several rows of trolls to neat piles of smoldering ash. She turned her head from side to side, holding her exhale as she chased the trolls back with a steady, sweeping line of flame. The lucky few at the back of the charge managed to dash into the tunnels with little more than charred patches on their rumps. She could hear their screams of panic echoing off the walls — warning the others to stay away.

Kyleigh decided to let out a roar, just to see if she could get them to soil themselves. But no sooner had she inhaled than the world began to go black. The bits of rabbit she'd had for dinner were not nearly enough to ease a dragon's hunger, and her body finally gave out.

Her legs crumpled, her chin struck the ground. She used the last ounce of her remaining strength to slide back into her human form. She felt the cool stone press against her cheek ... and then the darkness rushed in.

****

When she woke, Kyleigh's first thought was that she must be dreaming. She blinked against the bright sunlight and turned her head towards a welcome sound.

No, she hadn't dreamt it. A stream of water trickled in front of her, a stone's throw from where she lay. It sparkled as it slid across the rocks and wove itself through a thick rug of grass. She reached out to run her fingers across the nearest patch of green, and discovered that her wrists were clamped together.

A shackle made of silver held them tight. There was no chain between the shackles, which meant she had very little room to squirm. When she rolled over, she found an identical shackle around her ankles.

What in blazes —?

"Hello, fellow a'calla."

She looked in the direction of the familiar voice and her heart leapt at the sight of Silas. He held his shackled hands up in greeting. A number of thick, purple bruises covered his face.

Kyleigh had never imagined that she'd be happy to see a cat. "Still alive, are you?"

He grinned. "You won't be rid of me that easily."

Kyleigh groaned as she forced her tired body upwards. Fortunately, there was something directly behind her that she could lean up against. *Un*fortunately, it was the bars of a rather large cage. They were seated on top of a small, grassy plateau, and seemed to be in the bottom of some kind of valley.

The valley was a little larger than the size of a small village. The ground was made up of different levels of plateaus, sitting like shelves across the earth. Crops sprouted up from most of the shelves — though there were a few that had goats grazing on them. Kyleigh's stomach rumbled at the sight of their fleshy legs.

If there hadn't been a blasted cage in the way, she would've snatched the fattest one right out of his pen.

But she was too weak to force her way through the bars, and it would do her no good to torture herself. So she tore her eyes away from the goats and instead, looked up.

Hundreds of eyes stared back at her, watching from the walls of stone that encircled the valley. Room-sized homes had been burrowed out of nearly every inch of the walls, separated from their neighbors by what looked like a mere foot of stone. The rooms spiraled in an unbroken line along the valley's innards, winding their way up the walls to the smooth top of the mountain.

Mots of all sorts peeked out of the open rooms. Some watched from their beds, others stood at the opening, and a rather brave group of boys sat on the very edge, swinging their legs over oblivion.

Kyleigh suddenly felt as if she was trapped in the middle of a gigantic beehive. "What's going on?" she said.

"Hmm?" Silas looked away from where he'd been staring hungrily at the goats, and gestured to the ground below them. "I believe they're deciding whether or not to kill us."

In the very bottom of the valley was a small circle of dirt. The space only looked big enough for five mots to sit comfortably, but she thought there might've been twice that many crowded into it.

She recognized Nadine straight away. She was seated in front of a few other soldiers on one side of the ring, while Hessa sat alone on the other side. And of course, the Grandmot was seated in the middle.

Though Kyleigh couldn't understand any of what they said, she couldn't stop herself from listening, either. The language the mots spoke was so fluid that it was almost musical. It even sounded lovely in the Grandmot's sharp voice.

With her ears still on their chatter, Kyleigh turned her gaze to the space directly in front of them. Her skin began to crawl.

A thick table sat before her, one made of beaten slabs of silver. The legs still gleamed like new, but the top of the table was stained beyond recovery — by what looked suspiciously like large amounts of dried blood. Several bowls had been arranged neatly across the table's surface. A number of instruments waited in a line near its head, sharp and twisted, each with a different gruesome purpose.

"Odd, isn't it?"

"What's odd?" Kyleigh said, tearing her gaze from the table.

Silas rolled his eyes, as if she was easily the slowest girl he'd ever had the displeasure of meeting. "Odd that we should be destined to die together: one proud King of beasts, and one lowly, hairless thing."

Kyleigh patted him on the shoulder. "Oh, come now, Silas — you shouldn't talk about yourself like that. I think you've got plenty of hair."

He made an attempt to look insulted. But in the end, he only smiled.

They leaned back against the cage for a moment, listening as the Grandmot made her speech. Hessa would break in every now and then, and Kyleigh couldn't help but notice how the people quieted at her voice. Even the Grandmot would fold her hands and listen patiently, as if she couldn't afford to miss anything the little girl said.

"Speaking of odd things," Kyleigh mused, "how on earth did you come to be here?"

Silas grunted as he shifted his back to a more comfortable position against the bars. "There was a cave in the shelter of rocks. I followed that stupid girl inside —"

"Elena," she corrected him.

"My apologies. I followed that stupid *Elena* inside," he said, grinning when Kyleigh struggled not to laugh. "Of course, she slithered off into the darkness at the first split in the road. I'm not sure where she went. Nor do I care. But I kept following the tunnel — ah, because it was cool, and I thought I could smell water."

"And did you find water?"

"I did, yes. It was a blue, shining pool of sweet water. And I could see little fishes swimming around in the bottom. I was trying to scoop one up when I was suddenly struck in the face." He grimaced, touching his bruises. "It shocked me, and I accidentally jumped back into my human skin. The next thing I know, all of these little humans are swarming about me, screaming *a'calla*. They clubbed me again, hobbled me, and carried me like a roasted goat into here." He waved his hand about him and made a face. "Wherever *here* is."

Kyleigh wasn't surprised that Elena had run off. Good riddance. "What about Jake — have you seen him?"

Silas's eyes widened, making him look the closest to *concerned* that he'd been since she'd thrown him across the library by his tail. "I thought he was with you."

She sighed. "He was, but then he got hurt ..."

She told him everything that had happened since the sandstorm, and he listened patiently. "Trolls?" he murmured when she was finished. "Well, that explains the stink I smelled on my way through the tunnel. Maybe that stupid Elena got herself eaten." He smiled at the thought. "Jake will be fine. I sense it."

Kyleigh sensed it, too. She just hoped their instincts were right.

"At least they gave me something soft to wear," Silas said over her thoughts. He pulled at the hem of his silk garment. It had no color, but was a plain, stark white. "This is much more comfortable than pants. I don't like having all of my —"

"Yes, I can imagine," Kyleigh said quickly. She turned her attention back to the circle in the middle of the valley, where the mots' tempers were starting to burn hot.

Nadine spoke now. Her voice was raised and her hands spread wide. The Grandmot leaned forward dangerously, as if she was just about to get to her feet — and the soldiers leaned back.

Kyleigh may not have understood their words, but she got the sense that the Grandmot didn't like Nadine very much. So if Nadine was pleading on their behalf, it'd probably only get them killed faster.

Kyleigh elbowed Silas. "I hope you're ready for a fight."

"Certainly, a'calla," he said with a smirk. Then he leaned forward. "Do you know what *a'calla* means? The men we slaughtered in the desert knew it, too."

Kyleigh sighed. She didn't know much of the desert language, but she certainly knew that word. "It means *the cursed*. The people of the desert believe that we had to trade our souls to necromancers in order to become shapechangers."

"And what is a necromancer?"

"Someone who practices dark magic — like raising the dead, and harvesting souls."

Silas raised his brows. "But that isn't true. Are humans in the habit of making up stories for the things they can't explain?" When Kyleigh shrugged, he let out a frustrated huff and fell back against the bars. "Stupid humans. Why don't they just let questions be questions?"

She didn't have an answer for that. Though she often found Jake's many questions to be annoying, there was a lot about human curiosity that she found rather ... endearing. Like the way Kael screwed up his nose when he was trying to solve a problem ...

"Look, dragoness."

She pulled herself away from her memories and glanced down at the circle. The Grandmot's hands were cupped over her head. She shook them, and Kyleigh's ears picked up a soft, rattling sound coming from between her palms. When the Grandmot opened her hands over the middle of the circle, a number of small bones fell out. Kyleigh had to strain to see them, but it looked as if there were symbols carved into each one.

The Grandmot leaned over them for a moment, and then she took to her feet. She spread her arms wide and spoke loudly to the people waiting in the hived houses:

"The runes have spoken!" she declared.

No cheers followed her announcement; the people remained eerily silent. Without another word, the council began trudging up the hill towards the cage.

Kyleigh reached instinctively for Harbinger — but he wasn't there.

Her heart began to thud inside her chest. She looked frantically about the cage, but didn't see him anywhere. Her eyes shot across the valley, combing over every shelf and grassy knoll.

And that's when she noticed the weapon strapped to the Grandmot's hip.

Chapter 21
Nakedness

"Think carefully before you act, a'calla," Nadine hissed as she put the key into the lock. "If you are not careful, your life could end swiftly."

Kyleigh wasn't listening. She watched as the Grandmot wrapped her sly fingers around Harbinger, and he let out a piteous moan.

Kyleigh bit down on her lip. The others couldn't hear Harbinger's plea: he spoke only to her. He begged her to do something — to fight for him, to take him back. She gripped the cage bars tightly. Her blood swelled as she tried to control herself; it pushed against the sides of her head.

"Please, outlander." Nadine was taking her time with the lock, turning it slowly while her eyes stayed locked on Kyleigh's. "If you attack, they will kill —"

"I'll take my chances," she growled.

Taunting lines creased Grandmot's mouth as her lips bent into a smirk. She knew very well what she was doing — and she was doing it on purpose. A scheme flicked across her fox-like eyes as she watched Kyleigh struggle. Like a bird feigning a broken wing, she was trying to goad her into an attack.

And what would the Grandmot do if she *did* attack? Use her own blade against her?

That thought made Kyleigh's blood burn all the hotter. She could feel it scorching the underside of her nails as she tightened her grip around the bars. She didn't think she could've been more furious — not even if the Grandmot had ripped her arm off and slapped her with it. She couldn't remember the last time she'd wanted to kill somebody so badly.

"Please." The word sounded odd on Nadine's lips, and by the faltering in her eyes, Kyleigh knew it wasn't a word she used often. "Please, outlander," she said again. "I have paid dearly for your freedom. Do not cast your ransom to the wind —"

"Stop!"

A familiar voice rang out across the valley, more powerful than Kyleigh had ever heard it before. The mots gasped in their hived houses as Jake stumbled out from a nearby tunnel. He seemed to have just escaped from the healers: his bandages were only half-wrapped, and a whole gathering of blue-robed mots grasped at his heels. They seemed to be trying frantically to coax him back inside, but he was too tall for their reach.

He moved unsteadily out into the grass and raised his staff high overhead. When he brought it down, a noise like the deep boom of a drum filled the valley.

The blast from his spell knocked them all off their feet. Nadine slammed into the cage, her mouth parted in a surprised O. The Grandmot and all of her guards went rolling down the hill. Kyleigh and Silas were thrown to the back of the cage — where they collided painfully with the unforgiving bars.

"Those are my friends," Jake roared, leveling his staff at the Grandmot. "And I won't let you ... I won't stand by ... and ..." He teetered dangerously, and Kyleigh feared that he might fall and hurt himself. But the blue-robed mots rushed in and caught him gently on their palms. "I won't ..." His head sagged backwards, and his body went limp.

Kyleigh watched as the mots rushed him back inside the tunnel, carrying him across their backs like an army of ants. She shook the door of the cage, but it was still locked. "Where are they taking him? They'd better not hurt —"

"Silence, a'calla!" the Grandmot snapped. One of the guards pulled her from the ground, but she didn't thank him — her eyes were on Nadine. "Did you know one of them was a spellweaver? Have you deceived me?"

Nadine shook her head. She brushed the dirt from the back of her dress and gathered her spear from the ground. "I had no idea, Grandmot —"

"Lies!" she spat, the tawny feathers trembling furiously on the top of her head. "You must have known. Why else would you have traded so much for their lives?"

"I must claim fault for that, Grandmot." Hessa was quickly plucked from the ground by a nearby guard. She had a smudge of dirt on her cheek, but made no move to wipe it away. She clasped her hands in front of her pleadingly. "It was I who told Nadine to buy the a'calla. I closed my eyes and saw our people's lands reclaimed, our fires burning brightly once more. And I thought ..."

Hessa's deep gaze roved from the Grandmot's furious, red-tinged face to the many watching eyes above her. "I believed there was something more to the a'calla than what we could see. Now we have a spellweaver in our midst." She smiled shyly as she turned back to the Grandmot. "Perhaps it is as you always say: we should never turn aside a gift until we understand its meaning."

The guards murmured in agreement with Hessa, nodding to her. The Grandmot clutched tightly at her robes. For a moment, she looked off-balance — as if she'd stepped into a hole. Then her face went dangerously smooth. "Very well. You paid me a fair price, Nadine. The a'calla and the spellweaver are yours by right. The guards will follow you to claim the rest of your payment. Come, Hessa."

The Grandmot held out her hand, and Hessa took it obediently. As she marched across the valley, Kyleigh couldn't help but think that the Grandmot's feathers looked severely ruffled.

That thought might've put a grin on her face, had she not been so worried about Harbinger. His moans faded as the Grandmot carried him away. Kyleigh stared after him until he disappeared into the tunnel, fighting not to cry in the silence he left behind.

She'd always thought humans were a bit ridiculous for how they blushed at nakedness, how they saw it as a

264

shameful thing. To her, there was nothing shameful about running around in her skin. But now ... well, she was beginning to understand.

It wasn't their *skin* the humans were ashamed of — it was their vulnerability. They kept themselves covered in order to hide their weaknesses. Without Harbinger at her side, Kyleigh felt empty. She felt exposed and humiliated, vulnerable to every slight. She felt ... naked.

The lock clicked and Nadine opened the cage. She freed their hands and ankles, leaving the shackles on the floor. Then she stepped to the side. With one hand on her spear and the other propped on her hip, she waited.

Kyleigh realized that she was being given a choice: she could behave, or Nadine could crack her over the skull. The sharpness in her stare was like the edge of a razor. She'd seen Kyleigh collapse in the arena. She could guess how weakened she must be.

Her dragon half stirred inside her chest, demanding vengeance. And though Kyleigh wanted nothing more than to snap the Grandmot's villainous neck, the thought of Jake made her think better of it.

"What do you plan to do with Jake — I mean, the spellweaver?"

"The healers have agreed to deliver him the moment he is ready," Nadine replied.

It was with no small amount of anguish that Kyleigh finally stepped outside of the cage. Deep in the pit of her heart, she knew Harbinger would be all right. He would find his way back to her.

Eventually.

****

The mots' home was indeed like a giant beehive. The tunnel they followed led out of the valley and to the foot of a giant, sloping staircase. The staircase spiraled up the inside of the mountain, wrapping behind the honeycombed rooms and winding its way in great circles to the very top.

It was a hot and stuffy passage. The steps were well-worn and rather slippery, in places. But the most unsettling thing about the long journey was the staring.

Each room had a silk curtain draped across its front like a door, and some of them were pulled tightly shut. But most were cracked open or hung unabashedly to the side, so that the many curious residents packed within them could gape at Kyleigh and Silas as they passed.

And none of them spoke a word.

"What do the colors mean?" Kyleigh said, lowering her voice when she heard how it struck the walls.

"What colors?" Nadine said over her shoulder. She was using her spear to help pull herself up the steps. It clicked rhythmically against the ground as they climbed.

"The colors on your clothes and curtains."

"Ah, those are the symbols of our classes. Those people of green are our farmers — because of the life they give us. Blue represents healing springs, and so our healers have chosen it for themselves. Warriors wear red ... for the blood we have spilled."

"What about the yellow?" Silas pressed. "And why does this *Grandmot* wear black?" He stared openly at the people they passed, meeting their eyes with interest. He even craned his neck to try to peer behind them and see into their rooms. Once, he leaned in so close that a whole family of mots squealed and jumped back behind their curtains.

Nadine turned so they could see her pursed lips. "The Grandmot is Fate's messenger — she alone bears the power to interpret the secret groans of the earth. She is most blessed of us all, and so her robes are black. Hessa wears yellow because of the dawn she represents. One day, when our Grandmot passes, Hessa will take her place as our guiding mother."

Kyleigh was slightly taken aback. "A woman is your leader?"

"Of course, outlander," Nadine said with a heavy sigh. "From *woman* is where all life stems. We are closer to the earth than men, and have a wisdom they do not. We are much better suited to leading. No — no more questions." She held up a firm hand. "Save your breath for walking."

It turned out that Kyleigh needed every ounce of her breath to make it to the top. For the first time in a long while, she felt the human ache of weakness. Her dragon's strength had waned to the point where she could hardly feel it. Human stubbornness was the only thing that dragged her to the top.

When Nadine finally split from the stairway and into a room, they followed her without question.

"Oh, there *is* a Fate!" Silas said as he crumpled onto the ground. He panted heavily, leaving a dark ring of moisture on the stone near his lips.

The floor felt cool beneath her feet, and Kyleigh was tempted to join him. But instead, she stepped over his sweaty body and took a good look around the room.

There wasn't much to it. A small bed of pelts lay in one corner, and it seemed to be made up of everything from goat to fox. Nadine went directly to the barrel on the opposite side and drew a half-empty sack from behind it. She handed it to the guards that had followed them up the stairs, and they left without a word.

Nadine went back to the barrel and spooned a ladle full of water into two clay bowls, which she handed to Kyleigh and Silas. They gulped their drinks down without taking a breath. Nadine seemed to be fighting back a smile as she poured them a second.

A silver brazier sat to one side of the room's large window, which spilled out into the dizzying drop below. Kyleigh leaned out of it and saw small dots of people moving across the valley. The wind kissed her face, and she breathed it in. She would've liked very much to drop out of the window, spread her wings and swoop up to the sky. But she didn't think she had the strength to pull herself out of a fall, just yet.

Instead, she traced the sparkling stream of water from where it pooled in the valley floor, up the crooked, wet line that streaked down the walls, to a rock at the top of the lip. It looked a bit like a broken egg.

"A spring," Nadine said when she asked. "We will have to hike there tomorrow to refill our water barrel." She watched Silas gulp down another bowlful and smiled wryly. "Or perhaps we will have to go tonight."

"I have a question," Silas interjected. "I could've asked it earlier, but I didn't want to be rude —"

"And you also didn't have the breath for it," Kyleigh added.

He scowled at her. "I had plenty of breath. And I still have breath enough to bite you, dragoness." Then he turned back to Nadine. "Did I hear you say you've ... *bought* us?"

Nadine nodded. "It cost me my entire fortune. The Grandmot owns all three of my goats, now. And I just gave my seed rice to the guards." Her eyes were distant as she watched out the window. "So even my poor fields will lie empty."

Her accent was thick. Kyleigh thought she could hear traces of the song-language in her voice. She *felt* the sadness in Nadine's words, even before her mind had a chance to sort them out. They fell like rain striking the rock: muted, and without hope.

"But I trust Hessa," Nadine went on, a bit of her strength returning. "So if it is my fate to watch over the a'calla, then I will bear it proudly."

"Huh." Silas narrowed his eyes. "Well, I'm afraid you've wasted your goats — I cannot be bought. I belong to no one."

Nadine shrugged. "Then I suppose you can return to the Grandmot. She wanted to split you open on an altar while you yet lived, and remove your insides one at a time to purge your body of its cursed soul."

Kyleigh choked on her water. "Would she really have done that?"

"I have seen it done before." Nadine sat cross-legged on the ground and gestured for them to join her. "I know you are a'calla," she said, her sharp gaze locking onto each of them in turn. "But you are in my charge. So I will try to help you fit in here the best you can. What you need to understand first," and here, she looked pointedly at Silas, "is that without my protection, they will kill you instantly. The runes have fallen in your favor, but they cannot keep you safe from the others' hatred."

Silas raised his hand. "And what are *runes*?"

"Shards of magical manure that mean absolutely nothing whatsoever," Kyleigh supplied.

"That is false, a'calla," Nadine said with a glare. Then she turned to Silas. "The runes speak the will of Fate — they carry her messages to us from the great beyond. The Grandmot alone knows their tongue. She reads their will and interprets it to us."

Kyleigh didn't say anything. She'd heard about this sort of thing before: of runes and tealeaves and pictures drawn in chicken blood. Very little of it had any meaning. The shapechangers believed that Fate had a will for all living creatures — but it wasn't anything they could *read*.

Fate's will was an instinct, a change in the weather or a hum on the wind. Kyleigh had felt it once before: it'd been like a hand in the middle of her back, shoving her on, steering her down a different path. The paths Fate chose for her were never simple, and there was always a great deal of mischief along the way. But she thought that might've been how Fate preferred to speak.

She certainly didn't sit around all day whispering to runes.

Silas seemed to feel the same way. He burst out laughing, and Nadine's face crumpled into a look of such hurt that Kyleigh couldn't stand it. She elbowed him sharply.

"Ouch! What?" he hissed. Silas followed her glare to Nadine — and for once, he shut his mouth. "My apologies," he grumbled, when Kyleigh dug her elbow in deeper. "I shouldn't laugh at such stupid — ow! I mean, at things I don't fully understand."

"It is forgiven," Nadine said, with a wave of her hand. "Our customs must seem strange to an outlander."

"Yes ..." Silas seemed on the verge of saying something else, but a sharp look from Kyleigh changed his mind. "Well, now that we're all settled in — when do we eat?"

Nadine lowered her gaze. "I do not know. I have surrendered all of my food to the Grandmot."

Silas raised his brows. "But isn't there someplace where we can trade for supplies?"

Nadine shook her head. Her smile was harsh when it finally cut across her lips. "Not so long ago, there were paths we could take to reach the seas. We would trade our silver wares for all we needed. But now trolls have come up from the north and taken over our tunnels."

Realization finally dawned upon Kyleigh. "That room we fought in, the one with the bell ..."

Nadine nodded gravely. "Most of our city is underground. Only the farmers used to live on the surface. But now that the trolls have run us out, we have no choice. We have had to dig new homes out of the mountain." She collected their bowls and stacked them neatly. "We have been locked out of our city for months, and our supplies are running low. When the soil dries up, so do our stomachs."

Shame spread like cold wind across Kyleigh's face. Nadine had little to her name before they arrived, and now she had nothing. What could she possibly have to gain, trading her family's fortune to spare the lives of strangers? Though Kyleigh tried to find an answer, the smooth calm of Nadine's face was impossible to read.

Well, in any case, perhaps they might be able to help her.

It took several moments of pointed glaring before Silas finally groaned and got to his feet. "Where do the goats come from?" he said as he stretched his neck.

Nadine looked confused. "From our families. The herds are passed down —"

"Right," Silas interrupted. "But if I wanted to find a *new* goat, where would I look?"

"There are deep cracks gouged out of the earth all around our mountain," she said, spreading her hands. "And at their bottoms, the underground water is close enough to form pools. The wild goats often go there to drink."

Silas nodded and turned to leave, but Nadine sprang to her feet.

"You will not be able to reach them, outlander," she called to him. "In all of our time here, we have only managed to capture a few that wandered too far up. The path into the ravines is much too steep for human tread."

"Ah, but not for the a'calla," Silas said with a grin.

****

Silas returned a few hours later with a goat draped across his shoulders. He plopped the carcass down at Nadine's feet and began to busily lick the blood off his skin.

Nadine stared at the goat incredulously. "Where — *how* did you manage this?"

Silas clutched a hand to his chest and said, with an obnoxious moan: "It's the dreaded curse of the a'calla, to be able to find red meat wherever it hides!"

Nadine didn't glare at his teasing. Instead, she held out her hand. "I thank you."

Silas stared in confusion until Kyleigh gestured for him to take her hand. He squeezed her fingers once and quickly pulled away, like he thought she might be trying to trick him. "You're welcome," he growled.

Nadine smiled, and it was a rather pleasant smile. Then her gaze went back to the goat. "I wish you had not killed her. I would have liked to use her for my farm."

"*Farm* ..." Silas closed his eyes, mouthing the word. "Ah," he finally said. "You wish to have some goats to save for later? Well, the next time I go out, I'll try to catch you a live one. Though they're much more difficult to carry, when their little legs still have some flail in them."

Nadine laughed — and her laugh was every bit as pleasant as her smile. Kyleigh felt the weight of her own heart lifted by it. Even Silas stopped grumbling long enough to smirk back.

While Kyleigh carved the goat up, Nadine worked with the silver brazier next to the window. There was what looked like an armful of pebbles sitting inside, glowing red like embers. Nadine blew gently on them for a few moments, and they suddenly burst into flames.

"There is a lake of fire deep in the belly of the earth, and its waters flow like liquid flame," Nadine explained when Kyleigh asked. "We harvest these rocks from along the shore. They can hold their fire for months. But over time, they get smaller. Many of these started out as the size of my fist," she said, waving at the brazier. "But soon they will be diminished to ashes. And when that happens, we will no longer have a fire to warm ourselves by."

"Can't you just harvest more?" Kyleigh said as she handed Nadine the first chunk of meat — which she stuck to the end of her spear.

"We have been trying, but the trolls are keeping us from it," she said darkly. The meat hissed as she held it over the flames.

"Yes, and what exactly are the trolls doing here? This isn't their territory," Silas murmured.

Nadine looked surprised. "How do you know this?"

"Because they haven't had time to mark it properly. Had they been here for long, the tunnels would reek of troll. But I only caught a faint whiff."

"Well, you are right: the trolls do not belong here. They tunneled into our lands from their burrows in the north."

"But why would they flee their dens so suddenly ...?" Silas's question dissolved into a purr as he turned to gaze out the window. His eyes closed as the soft glow of the setting sun crossed his face.

Nadine shrugged. "I do not know. But they chased us out of our great hall a few months ago — blocking the fire lake and many of our underground homes. They have also likely destroyed our mushroom fields," she added with a sigh. "I have missed having mushrooms."

Kyleigh thought for a long moment. "But what was the point of ringing the bell and drawing them out?" she said, when she couldn't untangle it for herself.

"The Grandmot believes that is our best plan of attack. We must chew them off one bite at a time — much like how the worm consumes a carcass."

Kyleigh wondered if the Grandmot had ever actually *seen* a minceworm strip flesh from bone. Probably not, since she seemed to think that it was a slow, patient sort of process. The mots didn't have time to play stones and spears: they were starving. They needed to shove the trolls out of their lands — and quickly.

But it would do no good to talk badly about the Grandmot in front of Nadine. There was no point in upsetting her further. So Kyleigh kept all of the dark thoughts about trolls to herself.

Once their bellies were full of goat, it was amazing how quickly sleep came for them. As the sun dipped below the valley's teeth, they collapsed on the bed. They'd meant to divide the pelts into separate bedrolls, but after Silas fell asleep in the middle of them, Nadine and Kyleigh had no choice but to curl up on either side.

It had been many long years since Kyleigh had slept in a pile. Humans were so fond of their separate spaces that she'd all but forgotten the fuzzy comfort of her pack. But with Silas's warm body next to her, and Nadine's soft breath setting an easy rhythm for her dreams, the longing came back to her quickly.

This would be the best rest she'd had in many years.

****

It was near the middle of the night when a rough hand clamped down over Kyleigh's mouth, startling her from her sleep.

Her eyes adjusted quickly to the darkness. She lay still as a familiarly-severe brow line came into view. One brow sat slightly higher than the other, swollen by a greenish, fist-sized bruise.

Elena pressed a finger against her mask's breathing slots as she loosened the hand on Kyleigh's mouth. She crept towards the doorway, swift as a shadow, motioning for her to follow.

"Absolutely not," Kyleigh said loudly.

Silas jumped and Nadine bolted upright, wiping impatiently at the sleep in her eyes. When she saw Elena, she dove for her spear. And Elena's daggers came flying out of their sheaths.

"No, no!" Kyleigh leapt over Silas and used Nadine's spear to push her against the wall. "Put those knives away, madam," she growled over her shoulder to Elena. "I promise you that we aren't in any danger."

After a sharp look, Elena flicked her daggers in an arc and sheathed them. She pulled her mask down. Underneath, her mouth was bent in a snarl.

"Oh, I was so *hoping* you'd find your way back to us," Silas muttered. His arm draped over his eyes against the sudden light as Nadine stoked the brazier.

"Shut up, cat." Elena turned to Kyleigh. "We shouldn't waste any more time. Come with me — I've found us water and food in the tunnels. We can get a full day's rest and be fully supplied for the journey home."

"Go home, then," Kyleigh said with a shrug. She took the bowl Nadine offered her and sipped the water, letting it soothe her dry throat. When she looked back up, Elena was still staring at her. She sighed. "Yesterday, you were all peeved with us because you thought we'd stolen your supplies. Now you've found some fresh ones. So go pack your bags and be off —"

"I'm afraid the sandstorm may have covered the safe path you left through the desert," Elena said quickly. "But I think there's a way through the tunnels to the seas."

Kyleigh didn't understand her pleading look. "Well ... all the better. You can go through the tunnels without having to suffer the sun."

274

Elena's lips parted — as if she wanted very badly to say something, but couldn't quite muster the strength to do it. So, Silas did it for her:

"You're afraid of the dark!" he cried, cackling as her face flushed red. "I can't believe it — an assassin who's afraid of the dark! Ha!"

"No, it isn't the *dark*," she snapped at him. She turned her head towards Kyleigh, but kept her eyes trained on the ground. "There's no sky, under there. I don't like having the pressure of the whole earth sitting above my head."

And for the first time in a long while, Kyleigh felt sorry for her. She offered Elena a drink and put a comforting arm about her shoulders. "We'll make it home someday, I promise. But for right now, things are a bit … complicated."

"How so?"

Kyleigh smirked. "It's a long story."

They spent the rest of the night telling Elena everything that had happened to them in the last chaotic hours. She took one dagger out of its sheath and twirled it about while she listened. Kyleigh found it hard not to be distracted by how easy her movements were.

For some reason, it made her miss Harbinger all the more.

"I have no intention of being anybody's servant," Elena said when they were finished.

"Good, because I do not think I can afford you," Nadine replied with a wry smile. She held her hand out. "May I?" And to Kyleigh's great surprise, Elena handed her the dagger. Nadine turned the blade over in her hand, studying how the light slipped across its blackened edge. "Outlanders and your strange weapons," she said, shaking her head. "How many different kinds are there?"

"Several," Elena replied, with the closest thing to a smile they might ever expect.

Silas hadn't been at all interested in contributing to the story, so he'd gone back to sleep. He woke as he rolled over onto his side, and groaned when he saw Elena. "Ugh, are you still here? I thought you didn't want to be a slave."

"I don't."

"Well, then why don't you go away?"

She frowned at him before she took the dagger back from Nadine and slid it into its sheath. "I'm not going to share a space with the cat," she declared as she stood. "I'll come back when I feel like it."

"Oh, goodie," Silas muttered.

And she kicked him in the rump on her way out.

Chapter 22
Holey Roofs

Days trailed by, and Kael's body began to get used to the work.

For weeks on end, he'd felt as if he had rocks sewn under his skin. Fist-size lumps formed on the back of his calves and the tops of his arms, and they rolled uncomfortably across his sore muscles. For a while, he'd been afraid that they might actually burst from his skin.

But planting wasn't nearly as difficult as plowing had been, and after a few days of lighter work, he began to notice a change: his legs no longer shook when he put them down, he could turn his neck without grimacing. Slowly, the rocks shrank down to something the size of pebbles — and with his body healing, Kael had more energy to plan an escape.

He paid close attention to the spells Finks had placed around the barn. He watched as the stall doors closed one night and saw the milky white film of a spell stretch over the iron, weaving around it in tight lines. It caught the whole door up in something like a spider's web. A single loose thread popped free from the end and tensed, trembling, as it pulled the door forward.

Kael followed the thread upwards and watched as it gathered in a bunch with the threads from other stalls at the top of the ceiling. They slipped through a dark crack in the shingles and stayed there, hanging lightly in the still air.

He realized that Finks must have the threads connected to him somehow. And if Kael tried to tear through them, he'd probably be able to feel it immediately. Finks would sound the alarm, and the giants would be routed before they even had a chance to fight.

Kael knew he couldn't free the giants with the mages hovering over them. There must be some way to get around the spells ... but how?

He was deep in thought one night when Declan came in and interrupted him. "That healed mightily fast," he said, glaring at Kael's wounded hand.

The slash that Eveningwing's talons had left behind was too deep to heal on its own, and Kael feared it might become infected. So he'd been healing it a little each night, sealing it closed until all that remained was a white, jagged scar.

He hadn't realized it, but he'd been scratching at the scar while he thought. He tried to stuff his hand away, but it was too late: Declan had already seen.

"You're fortunate that it didn't get rotted," he said slowly. "*Strangely* fortunate, I'd say."

Declan had been questioning him an awful lot, lately. While Kael's antics in the wheat fields had earned him something like a warm indifference from the other giants, Declan had become all the more reserved. If Kael ever felt himself being watched, he never had to look far before he'd spot Declan, eyeing him from a corner of the room. He followed Kael around like a gaping, cross-armed shadow.

And he was growing rather tired of it.

"Fortune had nothing to do with it. I kept it clean, is all," Kael said shortly.

"Hmm." Declan shrugged and slouched over to his pallet. He didn't say anything else, but Kael felt as if his ears were pointed towards him, straining to hear his thoughts.

The wind blew high overhead. It brushed across the hole in the roof and made a low, drawn-out whistle. Brend groaned as he stepped into the stall.

"We're in for a long night, lads. With that clodded wind humming every five breaths, we're not likely to get an hour's rest between us."

"Why don't we just tell Finks there's a hole in the roof?" one of the giants said.

"Nah — he won't do anything about it. The mages are a bit … touchy, about holey roofs. Especially after what happened to ole Ludwig," Brend said, a mischievous glint in his eyes.

Kael recognized that name immediately, and he was determined to hear the story. "Why? What happened to Ludwig?"

Fortunately, Brend was always eager to tell a tale. He plopped down cross-legged and the others crowded in. "Ludwig used to be the head mage of the Pens," he began. "I never spent much time over there myself, so I can't really tell you what he was like. But the rumor goes that ole Ludwig had a leak in his roof, and though he'd written to the castle several times for repairs, Gilderick never sent anybody out to fix it. One day, he got so fed up that he marched straight to the castle —"

"Nobody goes up to the castle without permission," one of the giants piped in. "Not even the mages."

"Then why did the guards let him through?" Kael wondered.

"Oh, they'll let anybody through the gates," Brend said with a wave of his hand. "They like to see what sort of horrible punishment Gilderick will come up with for trespassing. But we're straying from the tale." He propped his massive arms on his knees. "So, Ludwig marched up to the castle — to Gilderick himself — and demanded that the roof be fixed. And you know what His Lordship did?"

Kael shook his head.

"He shoved Ludwig into a cage and hung him up in the castle courtyard! *A few days of this*, he said, *and those holes will start to look a lot smaller.*"

The giants laughed, but Kael wasn't sure he believed them. Brend *was* given to tell tales, after all. He had to work hard to keep the skepticism off his face. "I see … and then what happened?"

Brend shrugged. "Gilderick said he'd be released in a couple of days … but Ludwig never returned. Though we *did* spot a swarm of crows hovering over the castle a week later. I'll bet Gilderick forgot about him."

That didn't make any sense to Kael. "But why would he waste one of his mages?"

"Eh, I suppose he figures if he loses one, he can just send out some of the guards to watch us. He's always hated the mages. If you ask me, he's just jealous — I'll bet he wishes he could cast spells." Brend shivered. "Gilderick with magic. Now *there's* a thought that'll keep you sleepless!"

The giants chuckled a bit before they drifted off to their pallets. It wasn't long before the noise of snorts and grumbles filled the barn, and Kael knew they'd they fallen fast asleep.

But he couldn't relax. The puzzle of what to do about the mages stuck to the front of his head, keeping his eyes peeled open. His mind spun so quickly that he thought he might be in real danger of losing it.

He was just about to roll over when something *thunk*ed onto his shoulder. Eveningwing had taken to roosting in the rafters above him. And even though they told him not to bring his kills inside, sometimes he would sneak in a rat or two. Kael reached behind him, preparing for the worst, and was surprised when he grasped the end of a rope.

It trailed upwards and out of the hole in the roof. Eveningwing the boy watched him silently from where he was crouched on the shingles.

"I can't." Kael had to raise his voice to be heard over the giants' snoring: "I promised I wouldn't try to escape."

"We aren't escaping. We're exploring," he whispered back. "Come on."

After a moment, Kael decided that it couldn't *hurt* to look around a bit. He never really got a chance in the daytime, what with the mages roaming about and Declan watching him constantly. Besides, he thought the night air might help clear his head.

He pulled himself carefully up the rope and out onto the roof. The heat of the afternoon still clung a bit to the evening. His collar was damp by the time he made it to the top.

Eveningwing dug into the front pocket of his dirty tunic and handed Kael another roll of parchment. "This is from your fiddler friend." He broke out into a wide smile. "I like him — he's amusing."

"He is, at that," Kael muttered, stuffing the parchment into his breeches. He didn't know when he'd get a chance to read it, now that Declan hovered over his shoulder at all hours of the day. "Are there ... there weren't any other letters, were there?"

Eveningwing bit his lip. Then he shook his head so vigorously that Kael expected to see him lose bits of his hair.

He tried to hide his disappointment.

When Eveningwing returned from the seas, Kael had been hoping to hear some news from the pirates: perhaps a note from Lysander, filled with far more questions than any useful information. Or at the very least, a scolding letter from Morris — one made much less severe by the fact that it had been written in Aerilyn's neat, curling letters.

And then there ought to have been some news from Aerilyn, herself. He thought she'd be worried over him, and he'd been expecting a packed-to-the-seams message from her, most of all — an envelope spilling over with a volume of her letters.

So it had hurt when Eveningwing returned empty-taloned.

"Where are we going?" Kael said as he coiled the rope.

Eveningwing shrugged. "Wherever you please. I'll watch the skies. Though ..."

"What?"

His strange eyes flicked over Kael, as if he was trying to interpret his expression. "I'm unsure — the voices usually tell me where to go next. But now that the shackle is gone I don't hear them. I don't know if I should make a suggestion. Or perhaps I should leave it to you. Or perhaps we'll both —"

"Just tell me what's on your mind," Kael said, before the poor boy could confuse himself any further. "Tell me what you're thinking about right now, at this exact moment."

"I ate a rabbit today."

Kael blinked. "All right ... but what about where we plan to go? Do you have anywhere in mind that you think I ought to look?"

Eveningwing's head bobbed up and down. He pointed across the dusty courtyard to Eastbarn. "See the little light outside the door?"

Kael found the lantern and nodded.

"There's a light outside of every door — except for one." He squirmed excitedly, smiling. "Do you think that might be something?"

"You know, it just might be," Kael said, with a smile of his own. "Lead the way."

Eveningwing took off immediately, changing shape and leaving his tattered shirt behind. Kael rolled the shirt up tightly and held it aloft. He flinched when Eveningwing swooped down and snatched it; the wind coming off his powerful wings blew Kael's hair back.

He moved cautiously at first, worried that there might be some guards patrolling the road. But he supposed if there had been, Eveningwing would've warned him. Soft beams shined down from the moon, and they were a welcome change from the boiling sun. It wasn't long before Kael was sprinting through the tall grass, enjoying how it felt to be able to run as fast as he pleased.

It didn't take them long to reach the Pens. Most of the animals were nestled inside their barns for the night. Some slept on four legs out in the pasture, their necks hung down and their tails swished contentedly as they dreamed.

Four barns stood out in the moonlight. They were identical to the ones in the Fields and arranged the exact same way: in a large square, with a patch of dust between them. Each one of the barn cottages had a lantern glowing on its porch. Only one doorway was darkened, and he thought he might've been able to guess who that cottage belonged to:

282

Ludwig.

Eveningwing drifted over to it and landed silently upon its roof. The moonlight glinted off his eyes as he twisted his head towards Kael, ruffling his feathers expectantly.

Kael knew he shouldn't. There could be all manner of spells guarding the cottage, after all. But he was too curious to listen to common sense. He headed towards the barn, his heart thumping excitedly in his chest.

His breath quickened as he reached the foot of the stairs. He climbed them one step at a time, concentrating on moving as lightly as he could. The crickets' song grew to a steady hum, matching the wild pace of the blood that hissed through his veins. His ears thudded with the frantic grunting of the frogs:

Turn back ... turn back, they seemed to croak.

But Kael didn't listen. He made it to the top of the stairs and paused at the cottage door. There was no spell wrapped over it, of that he was certain. So if there wasn't anything keeping him out ... why wasn't he moving?

His heart climbed up his throat until it became difficult to swallow. The sweat around his neck suddenly felt cold.

Turn back ... turn back ...

A dry, rustling noise drew his eyes to the roof. Eveningwing was perched over the door — the feathers on top of his head stood up impatiently.

"All right," Kael whispered, so lightly that it was hardly a breath. He swallowed his heart back down and pushed on the door.

The cottage hadn't been opened in a while: dust rained down from the ceiling as the door swung inward, falling so thickly that Kael swore he could hear it strike the ground. He went to take a step inside and the shadow of his curled hair moved slightly.

That's when he saw it.

A white string lay across the floor — stretched so thinly that he might've mistaken it for a cobweb, if he hadn't known it for what it was. He followed the line of the spell out the door and saw it reach towards the neighboring barn. He thought immediately of what Brend had said about Churl: that sometimes he didn't show up to watch his barn, and one of the other mages would have to do it for him.

Someone else must've been watching Ludwig's barn, then.

Kael knew he'd been incredibly lucky. Had the moon not been full, he never would've seen it. A large part of him hissed to leave it at that — to turn around and go back the way he came. But curiosity clung to him like grass beneath his shirt, itching all the more furiously as he looked about the room.

Moonlight fell from the peppered holes in the roof. He saw a small bed, its sheets yellowed and stiff with dust. A dresser leaned against the wall, slightly cockeyed on a broken leg. A short desk sat across from the bed ...

And there, sitting on top of the desk, was a book.

It was covered so thickly in dust that Kael might not have seen it, had the shadow cast by its spine not given it away. He couldn't help himself — he had to look.

He stepped quickly over the cobweb spell and made straight for the desk. The dust clung stubbornly to the wet on his palms as he brushed it away, revealing a tome bound in black leather. There wasn't a title on its front. When Kael turned the book over to check the spine, the entire front cover fell off.

Whoever owned it last hadn't taken very good care of it. He hated to see any book ruined, even the exceptionally boring ones in Amos's library. He picked the cover up and was surprised to find a loose leaf of paper beneath it. His first thought was that the whole blasted book must've been coming apart in pages. But when he looked closer, he saw that it wasn't a page at all.

It was a letter, folded over and sealed with wax. There was no name written on it, so he had no clue who the letter had been meant for. He realized he would never know ...

Unless, of course, he opened it.

Kael broke the seal with his thumb and unfolded the letter. His eyes followed the hurried words through the moonlight:

I'll admit it — I never believed Churl when he said there was something suspicious about Lord Gilderick. Vile, depraved, contemptible — yes. But suspicious? *I hardly thought so. He's been quite out in the open about his black-hearted humor. One can't really have any suspicions about it.*

But Churl didn't listen. He went up to the castle to poke around and got himself tortured. I suppose that's what happened to him. There weren't any wounds on him, but now he carries on like such a madman that there really can't be any other explanation.

Poor fool. Had he kept his wits a little longer, he might have been able to claim the reward he earned — the one I now plan to take from him.

He returned from the castle, wild-eyed and muttering gibberish, and thrust this book into my hands. I don't know why, but I hid it from the others. And now I'm so glad that I did. The giants are far too stupid to read, so I'm convinced that Churl must have stolen it from the castle library, from Gilderick's personal collection. From the moment I read its title, there was no mistaking what it was: the literature of the enemy!

What purpose Gilderick might have in hoarding it, I do not know. But this is a serious offense against the crown. If I am able to turn Gilderick over to Midlan, I might earn my way out of this boiling grass bowl. It shouldn't be too difficult to capture him: one netting spell ought to do the trick.

Though I am confident, I am also a cautious man. If you are reading this, it means something went horribly wrong. My advice to you is to burn this cursed book and flee as far as your legs can carry you — if you are free to do so.

If not, may Death find you before Gilderick does.

-Ludwig

Kael read the haunting words once more, slowly piecing the mage's story together. There'd been more to it than a leaky roof — much more, by the sound of it. He wondered what sort of book might call down the wrath of the King. And more importantly: who was *the enemy*?

He knew that if he wanted answers, he'd have to open the book. He sat Ludwig's letter aside and turned the first crackling page. The second page was blank, as well. But he found the book's title scrawled across the third:

The Dreadful Journeys of Ben Deathtreader.

Well, it was no small wonder that Ludwig thought the book was cursed. As if the title weren't hair-raising enough, the words themselves had a darkness to them: every letter was drawn sharply, every line pressed down and slashed across the page. It made the words look rather ... sinister.

Kael was deciding whether or not he should turn the next page when a noise drew his eyes across the room.

A man dug through the dresser behind him. When Kael saw the black pants and scarlet tunic, his heart very nearly leapt out of his chest. But then he noticed the gray feathers sprouting from the back of the man's head, and realized it was only Eveningwing. He must've found the clothes stashed inside the dresser: now he was opening and closing the filthy drawers so zealously that Kael thought for sure someone would hear him.

"Quiet!" he hissed, waving for him to stop.

Eveningwing's hands dropped obediently to his side. He stood, fidgeting for a moment. His head flicked quickly towards the dresser, then back — as if he was trying his best not to look. His head swung back and forth several times before Kael finally hissed:

"For mercy's sake, what is it?"

"I found a knife." Eveningwing pointed at the top of the dresser, where the curved end of a blade glinted in the moonlight. "Do you want it?"

"Sure." Kael caught the knife by its handle. It was simply made, with an iron blade and a hilt carved from bone. "Sit there and don't move," he said, pointing Eveningwing over to the dusty bed. "This will only take a moment — I'm going to read Jonathan's letter while I have the chance. And then we ought to get out of here," he added, with a quick glance at *Deathtreader*.

He scanned Jonathan's note. It was mostly about how he still hadn't been able to charm his way into the ladies' room. The margins were packed full of woeful poems, each more miserable than the last.

Kael didn't have time for Jonathan's nonsense. They were trying to escape, after all — and he didn't care if the fiddler felt like *a rose with all thorns and no bloom*. In fact, it took a considerable amount of effort to keep himself from crumpling the letter and hurling it out the door. He opened the second leaf, hoping that it would be more useful than the first.

This bit of parchment had been filled with crude drawings of the castle. It was easily the worst map Kael had ever seen: the hallways were wavy and uneven, the doors were often too big for the walls they sat in, and absolutely nothing was labeled. He didn't even know which way to hold the page.

So he wrote, in very large letters, for Jonathan to label everything as precisely as he could — and urged him to find a way into the tower.

Nothing I plan will work, he added, *if we aren't able to free the women.*

He turned to hand Eveningwing the letter, and saw that he wasn't sitting on the bed. He'd wandered over to the desk and was thumbing his way through *Deathtreader*. His amber eyes flicked across the tattered pages, widening in interest as they scanned the sinister letters.

Kael was furious. "I told you to stay p ..."

His words trailed away as he caught a glimpse of something out of the corner of his eye. He'd forgotten about the cobweb spell. Now the thread shimmered in the moonlight, catching the beams as it trembled back and forth — moving, even though the air was still.

Kael shoved the letters into his pocket, his heart hammering. "Did you touch the spell?"

Eveningwing looked confused. "No. Maybe. What spell?"

Kael pointed to it and Eveningwing dropped down on his knees, squinting at the floor. "I can't see it. I don't have mage's eyes."

But Kael didn't hear him: he was far too busy staring in horror at the orange light that had suddenly materialized outside the cottage door — a light that grew steadily brighter as someone plodded up the stairs.

Chapter 23
Scalybones

There were no other doors out of the cottage, and the holes in the roof weren't nearly large enough to climb out of. Kael searched frantically for a means of escape, but they were completely trapped — cut off by whoever was coming up the stairs.

"Hello?"

Kael froze when a pale face appeared in the doorway. A mage in nightclothes glared sleepily about him, waving his lantern halfheartedly in the darkness. After a quick moment, he seemed to give up. With a sigh and a muttered string of curses, he reached to close the door.

Eveningwing, whose face was still inches from the dusty floor, chose that very moment to let out a loud sneeze.

"What — what was that?" The lantern light swelled to a blaze as the mage leapt inside. He saw Kael immediately — standing in open-mouthed shock before the desk — and a tail of fire erupted from his fingers.

Kael acted quickly. He leapt in front of Eveningwing and hurled the curved knife in the same breath. Fire washed over him, the taint of magic burned his nose. He gasped against it for a moment.

Then he caught the smell of something far worse.

His knife had struck true. The mage's lantern hung limp in his hand. He pulled the knife from his chest and stood, gaping at it. Blood leaked out from his wound. The stench of magic filled the air like a cloud. Kael could taste it in his throat, on his tongue. He had to stop it. He had to stop that blood ...

The next thing he knew, Eveningwing's arm was around his neck. Kael couldn't breathe. He didn't know how long he'd gone without breathing. His limbs went numb and his head rocked backwards as his chin struck the ground. Only then did Eveningwing release him.

They were outside — he could feel dirt scratching at his face. The world spun as Eveningwing rolled him onto his back. Two amber eyes blinked down at him.

"You tried to — *kill* me," Kael gasped, clutching his sore throat.

Eveningwing shook his head vigorously. "No no — I saved you. You were killing him so loudly that I knew someone would hear —"

"Killing who?" Kael forgot about his pain and shot up to look in the direction Eveningwing pointed.

The mage's body lay a few paces in front of them. His lantern was shattered and lying on its side, its light extinguished. Kael could see the knife hilt sticking out of his chest. A dark puddle glittered under his torso.

Eveningwing crouched at Kael's side, his brows raised so high that they'd disappeared into the crop of his hair. "Now I see why you lied to the giants about freeing me — you're a Marked One."

"A what?" Kael said hoarsely. He still couldn't believe what he'd done. He stared at the mage, blinking furiously and hoping that it was all just a horrible dream.

"A servant of Fate," Eveningwing went on. When Kael still looked confused, he drew a line down his chest with the side of his hand. "You have the mark."

Kael's hand went to his chest instinctively. He could feel the red, raised scar even from under the fibers of his shirt, and he knew he'd been found out. "Please don't tell anyone," he said, trying to think of a way he might explain it clearly. "Bad things will happen to me if the giants discover what I am."

"Of course not," Eveningwing replied, sticking a finger to his lips. His eyes darted down to Kael's chest, and he fidgeted.

"Fine. But only this once," Kael muttered. He raised his shirt and watched the awe light Eveningwing's face.

"I've only ever heard stories," he said, eyeing the mark. Then he sat back and his face became serious. "I think Bloodfang would've been pleased. He would've wanted to die fighting such a worthy opponent."

Kael didn't want to talk about Bloodfang. His heart was still too raw. Besides, there were far more pressing problems to solve. He looked back at the mage. "What are we going to do with him?"

"I think you've killed him enough."

"No, that's not what I meant. We can't leave him out in the open ..." An idea came to him, and he pointed back to the cottage. "Get the sheets off the bed. I'll meet you back here."

"Where are you going?"

"To find some rocks."

He found several the size of his fist laying around the courtyard, and one the size of his head. He stuffed the smaller rocks into the mage's clothes, trying not to look at his wounds.

There were quite a few of them.

When Eveningwing returned, he pulled the blade free and offered it back to Kael. But he wouldn't take it. "Look at what I've done," he said, waving to the mage. "I completely lost control. There's no telling what horrible thing I'll do next."

"You weren't being horrible — you were protecting yourself. And me," Eveningwing added with a smile. But when Kael still refused, he stuffed the blade into his pocket, muttering that he'd hold onto it for a while.

They worked quickly: setting the mage on the sheets with the rocks and tying it up tightly. When everything was secure, they carried him to the latrines. Kael took the brunt of the weight while Eveningwing staggered along behind him and kept the mage's legs from dragging the ground.

Kael only had to follow the stench to find the Pens' latrine: it was festering line scored deep into the earth — as wide as a man, stretched the length of several giants, and filled to the brim with the foulest brand of filth that Kael had ever stumbled across.

On any other occasion, the smell alone might've sent them running in the other direction. But tonight, the latrine would serve them well.

They tipped the mage over the edge, and the filth immediately sucked his body down — stirring up such a horrible stench that it knocked Kael backwards. He felt his meager dinner rise up in his throat, but somehow managed to swallow it back.

Eveningwing was not as lucky: his rabbit came up so violently that he nearly tripped in his rush to get away. "Humans are so — filthy!" he coughed, dragging his sleeve across his mouth. "Why would you *pile* your waste? Leave it in the grass and let the rain take care of it!"

Kael managed to drag him away, but he still caught Eveningwing glaring back at the latrine every few steps, a look of disgust on his face.

****

Morning came far too early. Kael hadn't slept at all that night: his stomach twisted and bubbled, making any sort of rest impossible. He thought constantly about the mage — and about how foolish he'd been.

There was no telling the sort of chaos the mage's death would cause. What would happen when the others found him missing? Gilderick would probably ride down from his castle and begin lopping off heads immediately. Would he torture the mages? Flay the guards?

Or ... would he blame the slaves?

Kael's blood chilled at the thought. If that happened, he knew he would have no choice but to give himself up. He wouldn't let anybody else die for his mistake.

With that grim realization, he spent the night staring out of the hole in the roof, his ears clogged with the giants' contented rumblings. It was amazing how beautiful the stars looked, when he thought it might very well be his last chance to see them.

The doors screeched open at dawn, and Kael joined the silent line of giants as they plodded out of the stall. He was so lost in dark thoughts that he didn't notice that Brend had stopped — until he'd already bounced off of him.

"Steady, wee rat," Brend said as he plucked him from the ground.

None of the giants had made it out of the door. They were stuck in the aisle, crowded together and grumbling sleepily to one another. The Fallows shoved their way through, walking dumbly towards the exit.

Kael couldn't see over the wall of brawny shoulders in front of him. When he asked Brend what was going on, he shrugged.

"Eh, I can't see all that well. Just about the time I go to stand on my tippy-toes, the fellow in front of me has the same idea." He shifted his weight impatiently for a moment before he finally began shoving his way forward.

Kael grabbed hold of the back of his shirt and followed in his wake. Brend was not as thick as most of the others, so he was able to slide through the cracks between bodies. It didn't take him long to weave his way to the front of the line.

When he saw what awaited them, he let out a furious growl.

News of the mage's death must have already reached the castle. Now a horde of Gilderick's guards swarmed the area around the water troughs. They lifted things and looked beneath them, poked tentatively through the high grass with their pikes, and generally tried to keep their eyes away from the barns — where the slaves were growing restless.

They crushed together, leaning out as far as they dared. "Bloodtraitors," Brend hissed, loudly enough for the closest guards to hear him. "Blood-suckers and cowards, every one. Oh, what I wouldn't give for a go at them — any one of them! I'd thresh their flesh from their bones with my bare hands."

The other giants seemed to feel the same way. In fact, Kael thought the only thing that kept them from starting a war right then and there was Finks: he stood in front of the door, his legs splayed and his whip unfurled. Dangerous-looking blue light danced and crackled down the length of it.

Just when Kael feared the giants might surge forward anyways, two familiar figures cut in front of the door.

The first man was Hob. He spat in angry lines, waved his hands about, and nearly had to lean the whole way back to glare into the face of the giant he spoke to.

General Dred was just as hideous as Kael had remembered him. Though now he had a fresh purple bruise on his cheek to add to his horrible, lip-curling scar. "Tell me the truth, spellmonger," he growled. The sharp edges of his teeth poked out from under his warped lip, making him look more menacing than usual. "If you've figured out someway around the spell —"

"Then we'd be long gone by now, I can promise you that." Hob pulled on the sleeve of his tunic, revealing the iron shackle clamped around his wrist. "There. Satisfied?"

Dred's scowl deepened. "His Lordship demands an explanation, and I intend to get one."

"Well, then maybe he should've sent someone other than a stone-headed giant." Hob's mouth bent into a mean little smile. "Was there any evidence? Did Stodder leave a note behind? Think about that carefully, now."

It was obvious that Dred was desperate for help, because he ignored Hob's taunting and thought. "We found a smashed lantern and a puddle of blood in the courtyard," he said after a moment. "Maybe the lions got him."

Hob rolled his eyes. "Sure, they probably popped the door right open and dragged him down the stairs."

"Well, maybe he wandered out into the courtyard."

"Why would he do that? He knew there were lions!"

Dred turned to glare at the barn. "Maybe one of them did it."

Hob grinned — and spat a generous amount of his chew out between his front teeth. "The *slaves*? You think one of these slobbering oafs slipped his way out around our spells? That's got to be the stupidest thing I've heard since you opened your mouth. Oh no, General — it looks like you're stuck," he said gleefully. "Can't say that I envy you. *I* certainly wouldn't want to be the one to break the news to Gilderick."

For a moment, Dred looked as if he'd very much like to wrap one of his massive arms around Hob's head and pop it from his shoulders. But he seemed to decide against it. Instead, his lips twisted into an unsettling smile. "And I don't envy *you*, mage — whatever got Stodder is still out there. You'd better hope we find it quickly ... or you might just be next."

Hob's face pinched tightly around his chew. Finks, who'd been listening in, went slightly pale. And Dred seemed to think his work was finished. He ordered his men back to the castle with a wave of his bulging arm. He'd gone to stride off when Brend suddenly shouted:

"That's a right nasty bruise, *General*!" He thrust a finger at the mark on Dred's face and said, even more loudly: "See how His Lordship kicks his loyal dog?"

His shouting drew a round of raucous laughter from the giants in the barn. They whistled and slapped their knees, daring Dred to come closer. And unfortunately, he did.

Kael cringed when Dred stomped towards them. The knotted tangles of muscle that lined his arms bulged out, and his thick veins strained against their swelling. Brend should've just kept his mouth shut: there was no way they could hope to beat Dred, if he decided to pummel them.

Just when Kael was preparing himself to be snapped in two, Dred suddenly stopped. He stood an arm's reach from Brend, glaring at something behind them. After a moment, his warped lip fell back over his teeth and he spun away. It was only after he'd marched several yards into the distance that Kael dared to look back.

Declan stood behind them; his face was calm and his arms were crossed tightly over his hulking chest. He watched unblinkingly as Dred retreated. His stony eyes seemed to hang onto the general's back.

"So not today, then," he whispered, so faintly that Kael had to strain to hear him. "But someday soon, Dred. Someday soon."

****

Once the guards left the Fields, the giants went on with their chores as usual. Kael collected his scythe and satchel and followed his team down the road.

Relief swept over him like a flood. The knot in his stomach came unraveled, and he breathed as if a massive weight had just been lifted from his chest. No one seemed to think that the slaves had anything to do with Stodder's disappearance. In fact, it sounded as if they thought the very idea was impossible.

Kael knew he'd been incredibly lucky, but that didn't stop him from smiling.

All of the weariness left his bones. He swore the air smelled cleaner; the sun didn't shine so hot. Nothing could dampen his spirits — not even a beating from Finks could've wiped the grin off his face.

Speaking of Finks … he thought it odd that he hadn't already *gotten* a beating. He'd been assigned to oversee their team, after all. And usually anytime Finks was in charge, he'd flay them into a run. When Kael checked behind him, he couldn't help but notice that Finks looked rather distracted.

He walked carefully, as if the ground had spines growing out of it and he wasn't sure where to step. His head whipped to the left and right, and his eyes combed frantically through the high grass. He must've been taking Dred's warning pretty seriously.

When Kael pointed him out, Brend's eyes glinted so brightly that they practically put off a light of their own. "Oh, I can't pass this up — it's too good! What do you say we play a little joke on our favorite spell-flinger?"

Kael was certainly up for that. After he agreed to play along and look *mightily appalled*, Brend's mischief started up.

"Ho there, Declan — was that a full moon we had last night?"

Declan slowed until they were even. He caught Brend's look and nodded gravely. "Yeh, that it was. And now

296

all of our little seedlings have sprouted," he said, waving his hand out at the fresh green tuffs across the fields. "Some mightily strange magic must've crossed our lands last night ... and you know what that means."

Brend shivered. "Yes, but it gives me the tremblings to think about it! Dark things start happening when Scalybones comes to visit."

"Guard your scalps, lads," a giant in front of them hollered. "Or Scalybones'll strip them from you!"

There was such a convincing murmur of agreement from the others that it must have caught Finks's attention. He forced his way into their line, trotting to catch up with Brend. "What's this nonsense about?" he snapped, brandishing his whip. "If you're trying to use your tales to get out of work —"

"Oh no, master — it's no tale," Brend said, holding his hands up defensively. "Every son of the plains has heard of Scalybones. He wanders all across our lands, moving from well to well."

"He lives in *wells*?" Finks said skeptically. His lips parted in a serpent-like grin. "You giants really are the Kingdom's idiots."

"Scaly prefers the damp and the dark," Brend said with a shrug. "So the bottom of a well is the perfect place."

"But how does he breathe?"

"He doesn't need to. He's a specter."

Finks's eyes flicked tightly around the giants' circle, obviously searching for some hint of a joke. But they did a remarkable job of keeping their faces serious. "You're telling me that you believe a *ghost* is haunting your precious plains?" he finally said, with a heavy coating of disdain. "And you think he climbs out of his well at night to ... what? Scalp you?"

Brend sighed heavily. "I'm sorry, master. I shouldn't have troubled you with our stories. It's just that, after what happened to Master Stodder —"

"What happened to him?" Finks thrust his whip under Brend's chin. "If you know something, you'd better speak."

"I don't know anything in particular —"

297

"What *do* you know, then?"

Kael thought Brend was playing a dangerous game. Finks looked angry enough to beat the skin off his back — or worse, turn him over to Dred. He was trying to think of a way to get Brend out of trouble when Declan spoke:

"No man is safe, once Scalybones comes to visit," he said, as if it were as clear a fact as the color of the sky. "When we were children, men used to disappear from the fields all the time. They'd be swept away without any explanation — naught but a splatter of blood left behind. Things had gotten so bad that our mums wouldn't dare let us out after dark. When strange things start to happen, sometimes ole Scaly is the only explanation," he shrugged, "whether you believe in him or not. That's all Brend's trying to say, master."

"That is a *ridiculous* tale," Finks hissed through his teeth. "I know what you all are up to — you're just trying to find some excuse to laze about. And I won't have it! Now *move!*"

They sprinted away as the spells lashed them. But once their backs were turned, the giants were all grins. Kael glanced over his shoulder as he ran and saw Finks standing alone where they'd left him, his head still swiveling through the grass. His pace seemed to quicken as the giants outdistanced him, growing until he followed at an all-out run.

He may not have believed in Scalybones, but he obviously wasn't keen to be left on his own.

Chapter 24
A Warning

Time pressed them from all sides. With every passing hour, Kyleigh's heart was turned constantly towards the plains.

She worried for her friends day and night; she would've given anything to hear from them, to know for certain that they were alive. But for all of her worry, she had a feeling that everything was going to be all right. She *sensed* it — the feeling hung in her heart like the muggy promise of an afternoon storm.

And that promise was the only thing that kept her from doing something completely irrational.

Jake couldn't travel with his injuries, and so they would be forced to wait with the mots until he healed. Kyleigh filled the long hours of the day however she could — starting with finding someway to repay Nadine.

The mots didn't trade with coin: food was the only thing of any value to them. She quickly realized that the only way to restore Nadine's fortunes would be to fill her paddock and fields. So Silas spent several afternoons scouring the rocky crags around the mountain, tracking the wild goats.

When he finally discovered where they were hiding, Kyleigh followed him to their grazing grounds. Together, they managed to carry six of the squirming, bleating creatures up the side of the mountain to Nadine's farm.

It took them all night. They were both still weakened from their journey through the desert and by morning, they were completely exhausted. But when Nadine saw the goats, it made every cut and bruise worth the trip.

"I ... I do not know how to thank you," she whispered. She sat her spear down and clutched the rails of her little paddock, staring in open-mouthed wonder at the goats.

"They're scraggly little things," Kyleigh admitted. "We couldn't catch any of the fatter ones. I think that fellow over there might actually be missing a horn — oof!"

Nadine collided with her, jarring the end of her sentence. She squeezed Kyleigh tightly around the middle and thanked her several times. Then she pounced on Silas.

He spun, and she tackled him from behind. He yowled and tried to get away from her, but she stuck to him like a barnacle on the underside of a boat: wrapping her arms about his shoulders and her legs about his middle. He stumbled all around the plateau, trying desperately to shake her free.

"Dragoness — help me!"

"Absolutely not," Kyleigh said, laughing as he squirmed "You aren't in any danger, you silly cat."

"But what is this?" He shook madly, trying to throw Nadine off his back. "What does this mean?"

"It is an embrace — I am giving you my thanks," Nadine said. Soon she was laughing so hard that she lost her grip, and Silas was able to wriggle free.

"Well, next time you may thank me from a distance," he said haughtily. He took a sniff behind him and rolled his eyes. "Now I'm going to reek like *human* for the rest of the day!"

The small mountain the mots called home was perched atop a large source of underground water. A river flowed beneath it, and a spring trickled out from its top and drenched the mountain's steep sides in moisture.

The mots made good use of this: they cut their farms out of the mountain's sides, creating hundreds of little plateaus upon which to plant their food. The farms were stacked like shelves and covered the whole outside of the mountain. From a distance, Kyleigh thought they must look like the scales of a large, open-mouthed fish rising from the waves of sand.

Spice rice was the main staple of the mots' diets. Dangerous-looking red tufts sprouted from the ground in all directions, covering most of the fields. Kyleigh and Silas watched as Nadine traded one of her goats for a bag of seed rice, which she immediately passed off to a nearby farmer.

"He will plant it for me," Nadine explained, when she saw the curious looks on their faces.

"You don't work your own lands?" Kyleigh wondered.

Nadine shook her head. She pulled at the front of her red dress. "I am a warrior, remember? It is my task to protect our people from harm. That is my gift." She gestured to the many green-robed mots trekking through the plateaus above them. "Farming is their gift — and so I will gladly put my seedlings in their hands."

Silas looked down at his own garment. "And what does *white* mean?"

"Gift-less," Nadine said with a sigh. "Those who become slaves are thought to have lost their gifts ... otherwise, they would still be working freely."

Nadine wanted to check in on her goats before they left, and so they wound their way back up the slope to her paddock. When they arrived, Kyleigh was surprised to see that the goats were already being watched: the Grandmot stood at the paddock's gate, flanked by a handful of stern-looking female guards.

"What is the meaning of this?" The silver bangles on her wrist clattered together as the Grandmot thrust an arm at the paddock. "You were to surrender all of your animals to me, in payment for the a'calla. Have you cheated me?"

"No, Grandmot," Nadine said with a slight bow. "These are new goats, taken from the wilds —"

"Impossible! The wild goats are unreachable," the Grandmot said. She looked back at the soldiers — who fixed their icy gazes on Nadine.

"Not to the a'calla. I sent my slaves to gather them."

All eyes turned to Kyleigh and Silas.

The Grandmot's chin flicked back to the paddock. Slowly, her glare gave way to a sly smile. "This is not impossible, then. We have all heard tales of the a'calla's dark lust for flesh," she said to the guards. "They will have used their black magic to hunt the goats down." Then she raised her voice: "There is nothing in our laws against this. A mot has a right to grow her fortune from honest means. This is good for you," she added, wrapping her long fingers around Nadine's shoulders. "You are free to carry on."

The Grandmot strode off after that, and the guards followed dutifully behind her. When she waved her arms to the farmers, Kyleigh caught a glint of white at her belt — and she had to look away quickly.

It took all of her human reason to keep from grabbing Harbinger and flinging the Grandmot off the side of the nearest cliff.

****

At some completely ridiculous hour of the morning, Kyleigh woke to Silas's hot breath blasting across her ear:

"Dragoness!"

She rolled away from him and into Nadine — who yelped and punched her in the shoulder. "It's only me," Kyleigh said, pinning Nadine's arms down before she could strike a second time. Her eyes were so heavy with sleep that she could only hold them half open, but Silas wouldn't leave her alone. He shoved on her back, rocking her so violently that she finally snapped: "What? What in blazes is so —?"

"The goats!" he hissed.

It was the horrified look on his face that drew Kyleigh to her feet.

She followed him up the winding staircase to the top of the mountain. A wide lip encircled its top, forming something like a natural rampart above the valley. The guards patrolling the rampart looked to be well into their watch: several of them blinked and tried to quickly wipe the sleep from their eyes as Kyleigh passed.

From one side of the lip, they could see the mots' farms stretched down the mountainside. Silas pointed to

Nadine's, and Kyleigh gasped when she saw there were only two sleepy creatures left inside. The rest of her goats were missing.

"But where …?"

Without a word, Silas led her to the other side of the lip — where they could see clearly into the valley. Nadine had told them once that all of the lands in the valley belonged to the Grandmot, because it had the best soil. Silas seemed to be burning too furiously for words. He thrust a finger down at the valley's pens.

Kyleigh scanned over the Grandmot's herd and spotted a familiar, one-horned goat grazing among them. She couldn't believe it.

"She *stole* them," Silas hissed, his eyes bright with fury. "She crept into our territory and stole our goats with her shriveled little fingers! We should steal them back — and then eat one of *her* goats in warning," he added.

Kyleigh thought that was a pretty brilliant idea, and she wanted very much to do it. But eating one of the Grandmot's goats would probably just bring more trouble on Nadine. So she convinced Silas to sheath his claws and instead led him back to the room.

They woke Nadine, and her eyes were downcast as she listened. "There is nothing we can do," she said when they'd finished.

"There's plenty we can do," Silas growled. He leaned out the window, scowling down at the valley below. "My mind is already filled with ideas."

Nadine shook her head. "If you try to take them back, you will be breaking our law. And I will be punished for it. No one tends the Grandmot's soil," she explained. "Everything that grows on her land is a blessing from Fate. Her rice seeds are carried in by the wind, her fruit grows up on its own, and any animal that wanders into her pens is hers by right. If my goats have crossed to her lands," Nadine straightened up, "then it is because Fate willed it."

"Your Grandmot is a feathered thief," Silas hissed at her, his eyes bright with fury. "Can't you see how she's cheating you —?"

"She does not *cheat* me," Nadine snarled back, leaping to her feet. "My Grandmot was chosen for her lot, just as I was chosen for mine. Not all of us wish to live Fateless lives, *a'calla*. Some of us are brave enough to meet our fates, and to bear the dagger's biting edge ... whether it swings for our flesh, or in our favor."

Her look faltered for a moment. A strange light crossed her eyes, and Kyleigh thought she could almost smell the tears trapped behind them.

"If anything was taken from me," Nadine said roughly, "then it was because I deserved it. Now, I must see to my watch. Keep your heads far from trouble, a'calla."

Then she gathered her spear and went to take her turn on the ramparts, leaving Kyleigh alone to deal with Silas.

He blazed and roared for several minutes: crowing about how foolish Nadine was, how all of his hard work had been wasted — and he called the Grandmot all sorts of unmentionable things.

When he finally wore himself hoarse, he stalked towards the door.

"Where are you going?" Kyleigh called after him.

"To find more goats," he snapped without turning.

Even if Silas managed to cram the paddock full of the little creatures, the Grandmot would just keep stealing them. No, they needed to do something a little cleverer. The Grandmot needed to be warned. She needed to know that they were on to her — and that they wouldn't let her take advantage of Nadine.

They needed to stir up a little ... mischief. And so Kyleigh went out in search of inspiration.

She found Jake in the mots' hospital, and was pleased to see that his head was mending up nicely. A mixture of herbs and a pinkish, gooey salve had been plastered across his wound, tied down by a thick white bandage that wrapped around his entire head — leaving only his face exposed.

With his bushy beard stuck out in all directions, she thought he looked a bit like a wounded lion.

The healers refused to let Jake wander out of the hospital unattended. But it looked as if he was managing rather well. "Hand me that little knife over there, will you?" he said, holding his hand out blindly. A nearby mot rushed to slap it into his palm.

For whatever reason, the mots seemed to have taken a real liking to Jake. They followed him around in small herds, gasping excitedly when he cast even the most basic of spells. The healer-mots found him especially interesting, and they were always eager to help with his experiments.

At the moment, Jake was hard at work. He leaned over one of the tables, picking his way through a minceworm carcass. The poor creature had been split directly down the middle and opened like a book. Its separate halves were held flat against the table by a number of tiny nails — which made the whole thing look like a leaf of parchment covered in pointy teeth.

Jake appeared to be trying to coax a tiny, greenish-looking pebble from the pit of the minceworm's stomach. "There we are ... almost — ah!"

A squirt of foul liquid burst from the pebble and splattered onto the front Jake's robes. Kyleigh watched in alarm as the liquid began to sizzle. A tiny wisp of smoke trailed up as it ate through the fabric.

One of the healer-mots stood nearby, a bucket clutched in his hand. He reached inside and threw a clump of black mud at the stain, snuffing it out.

"Blast it all and again!" Jake moaned, slumping down into his chair.

Kyleigh slipped up to him, frightening the healer-mots to a corner of the room. They may have taken a liking to Jake, but they certainly wanted nothing to do with an a'calla. "Trouble with the experiments?"

"Yes," Jake sighed. He leaned forward and pointed at the greenish pebbles. There was a whole clump of them, hanging together in the bottom of the worm's gullet like a bunch of grapes. "I can't figure out why the minceworms have such combustible properties — why they explode when they swallow fire," he translated, when Kyleigh raised an eyebrow. "I think it might have something to do with these glands. They're obviously for digestive purposes. The liquid inside of them is quite ... corrosive."

He brushed the mud from his chest, and Kyleigh saw that his robes were peppered with tiny, ragged holes. "Have you tried putting them to flame?"

"That's the first thing I did," Jake said with a nod. "And they certainly shrivel up rather quickly, but they don't explode ..."

He leaned over, wielding a pair of tweezers, and Kyleigh stepped behind him to watch over his back. "Perhaps you shouldn't get your eyes so close —"

"Your breath!"

"Is it that bad? I *did* have cave fish for breakfast."

"No, it's not that," he said distractedly. Then he turned back. "All though ... yes. Anyways, I think you've helped me figure this out." He spun in his chair, and Kyleigh had to move quickly to keep his long legs from clipping her. "The liquid in a minceworm's glands must obviously be released prior to digestion — but it doesn't *stay* in liquid form. The worm's breath must act as a heating agent, producing enough warmth to vaporize it into a combustible gas." He sighed at the blank look on her face. "Like how the mist rises up from a pond."

"Ah, I see," Kyleigh said. "How are you going to prove it?"

Jake made a few hasty notes in his journal before he looked up. "Well, I suppose I'll need a live one." He turned to the healer-mots, who'd been listening curiously from the other side of the room. "Can we visit the silk farm again? I need a fresh worm — and some mint."

"Of course, spellweaver," one of the mots said. He scuttled over to a nearby shelf and selected a bowl from its top, which he presented to Jake with a bow.

He plucked a clump of small, green leaves from the tangle of stems and held them out to Kyleigh. She took them cautiously. "What's this for?"

"A *dragon's* breath should be deadly — a lady's breath should not," Jake said with a grin.

Kyleigh supposed he had a point. She chewed on the mint as she followed him out of the hospital, but she certainly didn't enjoy it.

The mots' entire city had been built around the great, underground bell chamber. It sat at the center, and all of the other chambers branched from it like the spokes of a wagon wheel. The farm mountain was just one spoke of the wheel — and fortunately for the mots, the northern passageway was the only path into it.

Guards stood outside its entrance day and night. If the soldiers camped in the hallway failed, they would hold the trolls back for as long as they could, giving the mots a chance to escape into the desert.

The guards' faces were every bit as cold and stony as the rocks around them. Kyleigh tried not to meet their eyes as she passed, but she could almost hear their lips curling up behind her.

They followed the healer-mots down a different tunnel. This one was so tight that Kyleigh felt the ceiling brush the top of her head, in places. Poor Jake had to stay hunched over much of the way. The tunnel curved and spilled out into a small chamber, one that was hardly the size of a respectable kitchen.

The only light came from the dim glow of the many braziers set up about the room. Hundreds of fist-sized holes peppered the walls and ceiling, making the whole thing look a bit like the inside of a giant sponge.

One of the mots waved them over to a brazier. Sitting next to it was a miniature silver shovel and a bucket of black pebbles. When Kyleigh bent down for a better look, she caught the musky smell of fence animal.

"Goat pellets?" she said.

Jake nodded, pointing to the mot. "Watch this."

The mot dipped the shovel into the brazier, filling it with burning rocks. Then he poured a bit of the goat pellets on top of the coals and blew on them, stoking them to a blaze. Smoke puffed up from the mixture. The mot held it up to one of the holes, guiding the smoke into it with his breath. After a few moments, he reached inside — and pulled out a large, floppy minceworm.

The creature hung limply in his hand. Kyleigh might've thought it was dead, had its white flesh not still been pulsing.

"How many do you need, spellweaver?"

"One ought to do it, thank you," Jake said, taking the minceworm from him. He held it up to Kyleigh. "Fascinating, isn't it?"

She leaned away. "It's certainly ... something."

"The smoke knocks them out — this one won't wake for hours. It's like coaxing bees from a hive." The worm flopped wetly as he shook it. "There's actually an awful lot about the minceworms' behavior that remind me of bees. For example: they line their nests with silk, but there aren't any eggs inside! It makes me wonder if the entire desert might be some sort of gigantic hive ..."

Jake's prattling went on, but Kyleigh wasn't listening. She never actually *planned* any of her mischief out: the ideas simply came to her, showing up suddenly in the oddest of places. She never knew what sorts of things were going to inspire her. But as she looked around at the silk farm, an idea suddenly struck her.

She had to fight very hard to keep from grinning as she followed Jake out of the tunnel.

******

When Kyleigh woke the next morning, it was to the force of a spear butt jabbing her side. Nadine's face came sharply into focus — and she didn't look happy. "What have you done, a'calla?" she hissed.

"Done about what?"

Nadine pointed to the window — where Silas was already crouched. He clapped his hands together gleefully. "Oooo, look at the guards running around! They're like worried little ants."

"This is nothing to laugh about!" Nadine snapped at him. Then she spun on Kyleigh, grabbing a fistful of her hair when she tried to hide her face. "Every last one of the Grandmot's goats has been eaten. Minceworms have found their way into her lands!"

"Well, then I suppose they're hers to keep, aren't they?" Kyleigh said with a grin.

Chapter 25
A Flock of Crows

When Kael returned to the stall that night, he was surprised to find Eveningwing waiting for him. The boy stood beside Kael's pallet, his hands clamped behind his back. He was obviously up to something, because he kept digging his toes into the ground.

Well, that — and he looked about as guilty as a thief caught in broad daylight.

"What did you do?" Kael said. He had to fight not to smile when Eveningwing's face reddened.

He bit his lip and stared very pointedly at the far wall. "I stole the book."

"What book?"

Eveningwing brought his hands out from behind his back and Kael's stomach flipped when he saw *The Dreadful Journeys of Ben Deathtreader* clutched in his hands. "I know most of the words. But I don't know them all," Eveningwing admitted. "My memory of them is ... fuzzy. I still think you should read it." He held the book out. "They're stories of your people."

"My ...?" Then he suddenly remembered what Ludwig had written, about *Deathtreader* being the *literature of the enemy.* And it struck him: "It's a book about whisperers?" he said, so quietly that Eveningwing had to lean in to hear him.

"Yes yes —!"

"*Shhh!*"

Eveningwing clamped a hand over his mouth. "I mean ... *yes,*" he whispered, glancing out the stall door. Fortunately, the giants were still at dinner. He thrust *Deathtreader* into Kael's hands and silently urged him to read it.

He didn't need much encouragement.

Even in Lysander's monstrous library, there had been very few books about whisperers. The King had ordered them all burned at the end of the War — and had made it a crime to own anything at all related to whispering.

Kael flipped past the slashing words of *Deathtreader*'s title and came to the first page. The whole book appeared to have been written in the same sinister hand, but the writing was uneven: sometimes the words were smaller, more concentrated. Sometimes the sharp loops of the letters dipped well into those beneath it. And in some places, it appeared to have been scrawled in a different color of ink — almost more like a journal than a book.

The reading started out more slowly than usual for Kael. It took him a moment to get used to *Deathtreader*'s peculiar style, but soon he no longer noticed the change in rhythm or ink. The words rose out of the book and seemed to take on a life of their own; the things they described filled his mind, as if he could reach out and touch them.

It wasn't long before he left the barn and the plains far behind him, and found himself lost — journeying alongside *Deathtreader*:

I am not your average adventurer. I'm not interested in rocks or trees or even treasures. No, reader — what interests me are mysteries: answers to questions so complicated, that few even think to ask them. And those who do are usually not brave enough, or skilled enough, to seek them out.

I am both.

Follow me to strange new lands, reader. Come face the monsters I have faced: beasts so terrifying that Fate herself dares not let them into this world, but keeps them trapped within our nightmares. Come walk in a realm void of sky, where even the most unassuming trinket might cause the whole world to collapse. And you will come to understand that doubt is the only death worth fearing.

What follows is an account of me — Ben Deathtreader — and the tales of my most dreadful journeys.

The mind is a house with many rooms ...

Kael pulled himself out of the book so suddenly that he nearly tipped backwards. He'd heard that phrase spoken before.

It seemed like ages ago, but Kael remembered it clearly: Morris had said the exact same thing, once. He'd been explaining the skill of mind-walking — a branch of healing so powerful, that allowed a whisperer to transport himself into the mind of another person. It was supposedly such a dangerous trick that Morris made him swear to never try it. And he fully intended to keep his word.

Kael looked up, but the stall was empty. Eveningwing had vanished. He'd likely set out to visit Jonathan, or perhaps he'd gone in search of a snack. Before Kael could wonder too much about it, the torches fluttered and dimmed. He had no choice but to stuff *Deathtreader* under his pallet and try to act as if nothing had happened.

A moment later, the giants flooded into the stall and began to settle down for the night. Brend had spent the whole evening telling the others about the joke he'd pulled on Finks. They chortled about it all through dinner — and had even come up with a plan to spread the tale amongst the other mages.

Everyone agreed that it would be a *mightily grand thing* if they could get all of the mages to think that Scalybones was after them.

Before long, the giants' excited whispers faded into grunts and snores, and Kael was left with little to distract him. He was exhausted; he knew he ought to get some rest. But *Deathtreader's* words raced unchecked through his head. Their dark mystery drove off his sleep, and he found himself longing to know more about mind-walking. His fingers itched to turn the next page.

After a few moments, a mischievous little voice rose up in his head: *You aren't really trying it,* the voice whispered. *And you promised only that you wouldn't try it, not that you wouldn't read about it. What harm could there be in reading?*

That was all it took to convince him.

312

Kael snuck *Deathtreader* out from the corner of his pallet and opened it carefully, so that the pages wouldn't crackle. His eyes flicked hungrily across the next lines:

The mind is a house with many rooms. Whether a man is rich or poor, it makes no difference. I have discovered a mansion hidden inside a hermit's skull: a beautiful, glowing world of warm fires, vaulted ceilings, and chambers grand enough to shame a King.

But inside noblemen's heads, I've often found the world to be disappointingly drab and simple — no more complicated than a hermit's hovel. I suppose if a man wants for nothing, he will dream of nothing. Though I can't prove it.

Regardless of the circumstances of our births, hidden within each of us is a world of our own devising: our minds. Every thought, desire, and even our unconscious dreams serve in its construction. It is a living thing. The pathways are ever-changing, new wings form the moment the old ones have crumbled, and the secrets — oh, the secrets scream out from the walls, trying to snare the unwary adventurer.

Do not follow their voices, reader. They mean to send you down a dark path ... a path from which you will not likely return.

Though the way be dreadful, I've walked the hallways of the heart. I've survived the maze of fear and discovered the Inner Sanctum. The steepest stairs I've ever climbed were not made of brick and mortar, but of belief. And if a man isn't firm in his morals, the climb can be most treacherous, indeed. There is no help for you, once you have entered. Even the owner will not know all of the dangers that await you.

For the mind is a house with many rooms — and we are merely its caretakers ...

Kael didn't know how many times he read *Deathtreader* — though when he woke the next morning, his face was plastered to its pages.

The stories were so complicated, so shrouded in mystery, that he couldn't quite piece them all together. Even if he'd read it a dozen times, he still didn't think he would have understood everything.

As Kael followed the giants out to their allotted field, *Deathtreader* consumed his thoughts. He was so wrapped up in his wonderings that he very nearly lost his head.

"Watch it!"

Kael ducked just in time: Brend's scythe hissed through the air above him, clipping off the top of his wildest curl. "Sorry," he muttered. He ran a hand through his hair, and the loose bits showered out.

"Don't apologize to me," Brend called over his shoulder. "It wasn't *my* head that nearly fell off!"

The giants moved in a perfect line across the winter wheat fields. Their scythes swung out from their middles in wide arcs, and heads of grain fell helplessly in their wake. Golden shafts toppled over onto their sides, falling with a final shiver, and it was Kael's job to pick them up.

His scythe skills had not improved. The weapon was simply too big around for his grip. His scythe had flown out of his hand on the first swing and wound up nearly maiming the giant next to him. So while the others harvested, Kael had been ordered to follow along behind them and tie the wheat into bundles.

It was an exceptionally dull task, and one that exposed far more of his neck to the sun than necessary. He straightened up for a breath, touching the burnt, red skin gingerly with the tips of his fingers. He'd been hoping that his freckles would eventually grow so numerous that they'd blend together, browning his skin like the sun had the giants'. But unfortunately, he seemed to have only two colors: white and red.

Kael knew he might very well get his head lopped off if he didn't pay attention. So he forced himself to stop thinking about *Deathtreader* and instead focused all of his concentration on the task at hand. He tried to keep his mind on the wheat bundles, he really did. But it wasn't long before he found himself distracted by something else.

He had to find someway to escape the plains. Several disappointing days had gone by, and he was beginning to think that Jonathan would never make it into the women's tower. It was frustrating, having to wait on him — it was like waiting for the rain to stop, or for a fair wind to blow.

And in the meantime, all of the excitement of the plains had thoroughly worn off. The work became tedious, the giants annoyed him, and his back ached for the comfort of a soft, clean bed. But until Jonathan could get a map of the tower, their plan was completely hobbled ...

Even as he thought this, he knew it wasn't entirely Jonathan's fault. Though he'd been wracking his brain for days, Kael *still* hadn't figured out a way around the mages. If the giants fought, they'd be blasted to smoldering bits. If they tried to sneak out — well, they weren't exactly light on their feet.

So far, Kael hadn't been able to come up with a single scenario that didn't end in a fiery death. It was a horrible, tangled puzzle. And it was beginning to wear on his patience.

He swiped the moisture from his brow and looked up to see how much more of the field they had left to go. That's when he spotted a lone figure working at the head of the line.

Declan moved through the wheat as if every shaft was his enemy: sparring with his invisible foes, stepping in complicated patterns and slinging his weapon about him with such force that heads of grain went flying in every direction. His movements were tight, practiced. There was little he did that didn't result in a large clump of wheat falling to the ground.

It gave Kael chills to watch. Now he believed what Morris had said about the giants. He thought he might've had a better chance against a shark than Declan.

A lonesome call drew his gaze to the skies. Eveningwing circled above them, watching for any stray rodents the giants might scare out of the field. No matter how many times Kael told him not to, Eveningwing always seemed to find them at some point in the day. He would glide above them, riding the gusts of wind, and try to be useful wherever he could.

Lately, he'd been watching over the cornfields. A flock of crows had taken up residence nearby, and they loved to follow the giants around on planting days: gobbling up the seed almost the moment it struck the ground. So Eveningwing had made it his personal duty to chase them off.

He flew by, tipping his wings to catch Kael's attention, and then dove towards the cornfields for a surprise attack. Frantic caws rent the air and dirt went flying as the great, black body of crows scattered in every direction. Their spindly legs kicked madly beneath their wings as they pumped themselves into the air. Eveningwing flashed through the crowd like a gray thunderbolt, nipping at their tail feathers.

The crows fled for the barn and huddled en masse on the roof — squawking angrily to one another. Their taunting chatter filled the air as Eveningwing circled overhead, but they didn't move. They seemed to realize that the halfhawk wasn't going to risk landing among them: once he left the air, he would lose his advantage. As long as they stayed put, the crows knew they would be safe.

After a moment, Eveningwing finally sailed off in a huff — screeching over the top of the crows' jeers. He may have been angry that his game was spoiled, but at least now the corn would be able to grow in peace ...

Kael stopped suddenly, the knot on his bundle half-finished. An idea glowed in the darkness, a strip of hot iron waiting to be forged. He turned it over, thinking furiously about how he would shape it. Then a memory pressed against the side of his head, pushing out against the iron like air from a bellows. It glowed so brightly that Kael had to shut his eyes against it.

Sweet mercy — that was it.

He didn't have to go to war with the mages. He didn't have to risk sounding the horn and starting a battle: he would *scare* them away, send them fleeing for the refuge of the castle like a flock of crows. Brend had already planted the seed. His tales of Scalybones were already being passed around the Fields, and it wouldn't be long before they began to take root.

All Kael needed to do was think of someway to bring the specter to life, and fear would do the rest.

The fires retreated, the iron cooled, and Kael was left with the beginnings of a very promising plan.

****

When their work was finished for the day, Kael practically sprinted back to Westbarn. He went straight into the stall and saw Eveningwing sitting in hawk form among the rafters. Kael thought he looked rather guilty, but it wasn't until he nearly cut his foot open that he realized why.

The hawk had once again been snacking where he wasn't supposed to: a pile of rodent bones lay beside Kael's pallet, picked clean and left sharp. But he was far too focused to be angry.

"Have you heard anything from Jonathan?" Kael said, prying a tiny bone from the leather of his foot.

Eveningwing's head bobbed up and down excitedly. He hopped in among the folds of his ragged tunic, which he'd been using as a makeshift nest. After a few moments of digging, he emerged.

He had a roll of parchment clamped in his beak, which he dropped into Kael's waiting hand. "Excellent — and we *will* be discussing this," Kael added, holding up the bone. "So don't think you've gotten off easily."

Eveningwing's head sagged low, making him look as miserable as a hawk possibly could.

Kael tore the parchment open in a rush, hoping to mercy that Jonathan had discovered something — *anything* — that he might be able to work with. His heart began thumping excitedly as he read the first line:

I've got some blistering good news, mate: I've made quite a bit of progress on our little pro —

317

"What's that?"

Kael jumped.

Declan stood in the doorway, his brows tipped low over his eyes. He jabbed a thick finger at Kael's letter. "I knew it. I knew you've been up to something — shooting off right after dinner, whispering to your feathered pet. Don't move."

Kael didn't. There was a darkness in Declan's eyes that he'd never seen before: it was as if the black of his pupils had spilled out into the gray. His stare had grown so wide that Kael felt as if there was no escaping it. He'd never seen a man's eyes do something like that. It wasn't natural.

When Declan leaned around the door and called for Brend, his voice sounded completely different — as if somebody else spoke for him.

"Uh, oh," Brend said as he approached. "Now Declan, remember to take deep breaths —"

"That rat's up to something," he growled. Veins bulged dangerously from his neck. "I don't know what it is, but I don't trust him one — omft!"

Brend threw a fistful of dust directly into the middle of Declan's face. It stuck to the sweat on his brow and lips. His eyes blinked out from it in surprise, and Kael was relieved to see they were a normal shade of gray once again.

"Better?" Brend said. He waited for Declan to nod. "Now, what are you all fussed about?"

"The rat has a letter."

"Does he, now?" Brend leaned around to grin at Kael. "Is it from your wee fiddler friend?"

"Yes," Kael said cautiously.

Brend slapped his hands to his belly. "Well then, you ought to read it to us over dinner."

It wasn't really a suggestion. Brend's eyes twinkled innocently enough, but Declan still scowled at him. If Kael refused, Brend might not save his hide a second time. So he had no choice but to trudge out into the aisle.

Brend made the announcement, and the giants crowded eagerly around him. They shoveled down their dinners as Kael began to read:

I've got some blistering good news, mate: I've made quite a bit of progress on our little project.

You remember that cranky old witch I was telling you about? It turns out that she's a bit keen on me — well, keen on my music, anyways. I swear I spent countless afternoons sitting outside that door, playing the most boring and perfectly-pitched ballads I could dream up. And ...

Nothing. Not a peep. Not even so much as a: "Clear off, or I'll turn you into a hoppy toad!" Not a thing I played seemed to interest her enough to stick her horrid little head out again. So I figured since I had nothing to lose, I might as well play what I wanted to hear.

Halfway through a terrible tune about an armless merman, I hear cackling through the door. And it was horrible, mate: worse than being tied to a chair with two Aerilyns at either ear — one squealing while the other sobs. I swear the whole door quivered on its hinges!

I made to bolt out of there when the witch grabbed me and jerked me inside. "Where do you think you're off to?" she said to me. "I want to hear what happens to that merman!"

So, I went on with the song — though it was difficult, I tell you. She screeched so loudly that I could hardly hear my own words. If I hadn't been able to feel my fingers, I don't think I could've finished it! But in the end, it was all worth it.

She slipped a key into my hand and said: "This'll get you into the tower any time, you handsome thing. Just don't tell His Lordship!"

I have to play a dirty song for her every time I go in there — she's filthier than I am! But you'll never believe what's inside that tower: it's a kitchen, mate! And not just any kitchen, but the most monstrous kitchen I've ever seen. There's two stories worth of ovens and cupboards, and a climb of stairs leading up from that. I can only imagine what else is up there.

But that's not the half of it, not even close. Guess who runs the kitchens? A whole stomp of lady giants!

Kael nearly leapt out of his skin when the barn erupted in roars. The giants grinned and shoved each other excitedly. Brend's bellowing rang over the top of them:

"I knew it! I knew they were all right!" He grabbed Kael by the front of the shirt, nearly dragging him over the trough. "Does he mention anything about a Clairy in there?"

Kael scanned the letter, then shook his head. "No. What's a Clairy?"

"What's a ...?" Brend snorted, but even his incredulity couldn't take the grin from his face. "*Clairy* is the name of my wee baby sister! She was only a babe when Gilderick took her. I left her in the arms of one of the older girls — Darrah was her name. She was our neighbor, and always a sweet girl ..." He cleared his throat and pulled roughly at his collar. "Anyhow, Darrah swore she'd look after Clairy for me. Will you ask the fiddler if he's seen them?"

"All right." Kael went into the stall and returned with the lump of charcoal and a clean leaf of parchment. "How do you spell their names?"

"Ah ..." Brend's face reddened as he glanced about the others. "We don't ... ah, that is, we never learned our letters." He cleared his throat and pounded his fist into his open palm. "And that's because we giants learn to read the earth and the skies. We haven't any use for *words*."

There was a round of proud grunting from the others. Then Declan mumbled:

"None of us can read. That's why the rest of the Kingdom takes us for stupid oafs."

The grunting died down immediately.

Kael didn't say anything. He could feel the shame burning across the giants' faces, and he didn't understand it. When he arrived in the plains, he'd known nothing about how to plow fields, plant seed, or tend to crops — things that all seemed to come so naturally to the giants. Though he must've looked like an idiot to *them*, he hadn't been embarrassed by it.

In his mind, there was no reason a man should be ashamed about something he could easily learn.

"You aren't oafs," he said firmly, letting his gaze trail all about the room. "So what if you can't read? You're clever in far more practical ways. I happen to know of several well-bred merchants who would pay good coin to learn your secrets," he added with a smile.

Slowly, the giants broke out into smiles of their own. Grins spread all about the barn. Even Declan's mouth bent slightly upwards for a moment — before he tucked behind his frown.

Brend clapped Kael on the shoulder — so roughly that it rolled him to the side. "Then we'll be sure not to sell our secrets cheaply," he said with a wink. "Now, ask that fiddler about my Clairy. And — and Darrah, if it's not too much trouble."

Kael wrote their names at the top of the page. "Does anybody else have a lady they'd like me to ask after?"

The requests came pouring in: sisters, friends, cousins — their names took up nearly half the parchment. And as Kael took them down, a quiet realization stirred inside his heart.

He was eager to get back to his friends, to see Amos and the rest of Tinnark rescued. But though the months had felt like years, he hadn't really had that long to wait. The giants had waited far longer than him. Even now, their faces lit up at the thought of just being able to *hear* of their loved ones — just to know that they were safe.

If Kael had to wait seventeen years to see Amos again ... well, he didn't know if he'd be able to hold on. His hope might fade long before then. And it was in that moment that he realized something odd:

Though the giants were large men, their strength wasn't in their limbs ...

It was in their hearts.

Chapter 26
A Good Hawk

So that was it: Kael's mind was made up. All he had to do was scare the mages into the castle, and the giants would be free to escape. If they moved quietly, they could pop the women out of the kitchen tower and be halfway to the seas before Gilderick noticed they were missing.

Granted, it wasn't the best plan Kael had ever come up with — there were still plenty of ways it could all go wrong. But at least it was a start.

The giants' tales of Scalybones proved to be a double-edged sword. While it was certainly entertaining to watch the mages jump at every slight rustle in the grass, it also meant that they never traveled alone. No matter where they were in the Fields, the mages always seemed to keep each other in sight. Finks rushed the giants into Westbarn the moment the sun fell and slammed the doors shut behind them. Kael could hear his boots tromping up the stairs almost immediately after that.

None of the mages wanted to be out after dark.

He knew trying to break into their cottages would be out of the question: they were probably all hexed, by now. Kael worried that he would only raise an alarm if he went sneaking through their doors. He might've been able to pick them off one at a time, had they not stuck so close together. While Kael liked his chances against one mage, a pair could be a problem. They might figure out a way around his powers, like the Witch of Wendelgrimm had.

Or worse, the one he didn't kill might escape and warn Gilderick that he had a whisperer on his lands.

The more he thought about it, the more Kael began to feel like he was stuck in the middle of a crumbling bridge. If he stepped on one loose stone, the whole thing might collapse. His plan could be ruined before it even began, if he wasn't careful. So he forced himself to be patient. He grit his teeth and stood perfectly still, waiting for an opportunity to present itself.

And at long last, it did.

One morning, he looked up from his drink and happened to spot Hob and Finks standing at the edge of the courtyard. They were in a heated conversation with a mage he didn't recognize: a small, sickly-looking fellow. There were dark circles under his eyes, and his hands shook badly as he brushed them down his tunic.

Kael thought the mages might be up to something. He slipped over to the trough closest to them, pretending to get a drink while he listened in.

"We can't take it anymore," the sickly mage wheezed. His skin seemed to have almost a greenish tint in the pale morning light. "It was hard enough when there were only three of us. But two mages for four barns? It's impossible! We can't keep it up."

Finks picked absently at something lodged between his long teeth. "I don't see how that's our problem, Doyle."

"It's certainly your problem," Doyle snapped back. "What happens if the beasts escape? Rebel? After Gilderick is done with us, the guards will string what's left up for the crows!" Doyle dragged one hand down his greenish face, his eyes wild. "Two barns, a dozen doors — it's too much. Gaff and I barely have enough power left to keep our beasts in line. If we can make it through the day without passing out, it'll be a close thing. A *very* close thing in —"

"Fine," Hob grunted from around his chew. He cut his hand through the air before Doyle could thank him. "But I won't have my men taking double duty the whole night. If there *is* something out there," his face pinched tight as he scanned the Fields, "we need to be strong enough to face it. Gilderick obviously isn't going to help us."

Doyle's hands began shaking all the more vigorously as he glanced about him. "Something's out there? What sort of something?"

Hob shook his head. "I don't know ... whatever it was that got Stodder." He turned to Finks — who'd been watching gleefully as fear spread over Doyle's face. "You'll go to the Pens at first watch."

His smile immediately vanished. "Why me? Why not Churl or Bobbin?"

Hob stuck out his lip. "I *will* send Bobbin — to relieve you at third watch. You're not to move until he comes for you. And you know very well why not Churl," he added with a snort. Then he waved Doyle away. "There you are. Problem solved. Now back to your Pens, you little boil."

Kael hurriedly dipped his chin into the trough as the mages walked by. But Finks spotted him anyways. "Get to work, rat!" he screeched.

The stench of magic on his breath was slightly muted by another foul odor ... one that Kael recognized immediately. As Finks chased him off, he couldn't help but notice that his boots made a wet, squishing sort of noise every time he brought them down.

Kael was puzzled by the time he caught up with the giants. "Why does Finks smell like pig dung?"

Brend exchanged a quick look with the others — then he burst out laughing. "Oh, I can't believe it! He's gone and done it, then? I'll admit, I never really thought he would."

"Would what?" Kael said.

When the giants saw the confused look on his face, the laughter started up all over again. Brend plunked an arm across his shoulders. "Well, I *might*'ve let slip that putting a handful of pig droppings in both boots would be enough to hide a man's scent from Scalybones," he admitted, his eyes glinting with his smirk.

"I hope Fate never learns of your deeds, Grainer," Declan said with mock severity. "Even the crows would hide from your mischief."

Brend shrugged. "Oh, Fate's right fond of my mischief. And the crows are just ruffled that they didn't come up with it!"

The giants wandered off down the road, laughing and carrying on, and Kael followed at a much slower pace. He realized that if he wanted a chance to stir up some mischief of his own, he would have to act — tonight.

****

Eveningwing woke him an hour before the third watch. Kael could practically hear his limbs groaning in protest as he climbed to the roof.

He followed the hawk's drifting shadow to the shed behind Northbarn. Armed with a bone he'd salvaged from Eveningwing's latest snack, Kael set about picking the lock.

"How do you know all of these things?"

Kael looked up distractedly. He was surprised to see Eveningwing as a human once again, wearing nothing but the black breeches he'd nicked from Ludwig. "I've spent a lot of time around pirates, lately," Kael explained. He felt around inside the mechanism for the tumblers, careful not to snap the bone. "You can't help but learn these sorts of things ... ha!"

There was a satisfying *click* as the lock sprang free. After all his time away, he worried that his skills might've gotten a little rusty. He still wasn't nearly as quick as Lysander, but he was learning. And he actually thought he was getting rather good.

He pulled the lock free and handed it to Eveningwing, who tucked it into his breeches pocket. "But you're a Marked One," he whispered. "I saw you tear my shackle in two. Why didn't you just break the lock?"

Kael felt around in the darkened shed, searching for tools. "I don't want the mages to know we've been here. If they see the lock's been busted, then they'll know that someone has broken in. But they'll be even more afraid of us if it looks like nothing has been touched."

325

"Why's that?"

Kael squinched up his eyes, trying to see something — anything — in front of him. But the darkness was far too thick. "Because they won't be able to explain it. There'll be no reason for why Bobbin has disappeared. It'll just be ... bizarre."

"That's silly. I'd be much more afraid of a predator than nothing at all."

"It's a human thing," Kael said impatiently. "We always have to have an answer for everything. And when we don't, we try to imagine one. Sometimes what a man can dream up is far more terrifying than anything he can explain. Now, where are those blasted shovels?"

Eveningwing reached past him and with no trouble at all, plucked two shovels out of the darkness.

Kael took the one he offered. "How did you do that?"

"It's a shapechanger thing," he replied. And even though Kael couldn't see his face, he knew the boy was grinning.

They jogged out to the main road, their shovels propped over their shoulders. On either side of the path was a shallow ditch, a pair of trenches that had been dug to keep the rain from flooding over it. The ditch wouldn't provide them with much cover, but it would be better than nothing.

Kael marked where they would dig with a line in the dirt, and then they got to work. Eveningwing wielded his shovel clumsily at first, but he learned quickly. Soon he was slinging chunks of earth so zealously that they wound up several feet behind him. Kael had to remind him to keep the dirt a little closer to the hole.

"What's it like to be a shapechanger?" Kael said. He was feeling good about their pace: they were already halfway done, and still had plenty of time to dig the rest. He saw no harm in talking.

Eveningwing straightened up for a moment. He appeared to be thinking. "Be more specific," he finally said.

"All right ... how did you become a shapechanger?"

326

Eveningwing's eyes closed for a moment. "I don't remember. Some nights I'll have dreams of a great battle. I'll see myself standing in a shadowy arena ... I think that might have something to do with it." He tossed another shovelful of earth to the side. "None of us remember exactly how it happened. Bloodfang used to say it was because Fate hid the memory from us — so that there would be no bitterness between our two halves."

Kael stopped digging for a moment. "Your two halves?" When Eveningwing nodded, it only gave him more questions. "What does that mean? I'm sorry if I'm bothering you," he added. "I just want to learn —"

"Your questions are welcome," Eveningwing said with a smile. "Most humans would rather kill us than talk to us. What your giant friend said is true: I *am* half beast," he admitted. "All shapechangers are bonded souls — one human and one animal. It's our binding that allows us to take each other's shapes. I — Eveningwing the hawk — am the one who speaks for us. But the boy I bonded with is still here." He tapped the side of his head. "We protect each other. I know the secrets of the earth and he knows the words of men. So we're able to live in both worlds. Does this make sense?"

Kael nodded, though now he had even more questions than before — and one of them glowed more brightly than all of the others. He could feel it sitting at the bottom of his heart, seething a hole through the muscle. But though it burned him fiercely, he simply didn't have the courage to ask.

"You said you had a friend who was a shapechanger?"

Kael nodded, his mouth suddenly dry.

"Why didn't you ask her these things?"

"I tried," Kael grumbled. "She wouldn't answer me. Anytime I brought it up, she'd get so stubborn about it. She was completely impossible, really. I don't know why she was so blasted protective ..." The world swam in front of him and Kael sat down hard. He forced himself to push all thoughts of Kyleigh from his mind. The black beast retreated, and his strength came back to him quickly.

"You miss her," Eveningwing said.

Kael knew it wasn't a question, but he shook his head anyways. "No, I don't."

"Then why do you smell so sad?"

He didn't have an answer for that. "Let's just finish this before Bobbin shows up, all right?"

Kael went immediately back to work. He could feel Eveningwing's eyes on him, boring through him — but he didn't look up. Eventually, the boy went back to his shoveling, and it wasn't long before their man-sized hole was finished.

They lay on their bellies in the ditch, watching over the road for Bobbin. Kael's stomach twisted when Eveningwing pressed the knife into his hand. "Don't let me lose control," he whispered. "I don't care what you have to do: punch me, choke me — just don't let me go wild again, all right?"

Eveningwing nodded slightly. "You're doing the right thing," he whispered back. "Any good hawk protects his nest from serpents."

Kael didn't feel like a good hawk. He didn't relish killing a man in cold blood, no matter how wicked that man might be. It didn't feel like a brave thing ... but he supposed it had to be done.

They saw Bobbin from a long ways off. He spent most of his time in the eastern Fields, so Kael didn't know much about him. Though he *did* have a very peculiar gait, and that was precisely how they recognized him.

As Bobbin traveled across the Fields, he seemed to jump or skip every few steps, wandering along like a man with a wounded leg. Every now and then, he would come to an abrupt halt and sling his whip at the grass — sending a blast of wind that parted it straight down the middle. He leapt back at nearly every sound; his head twitched away from the soft gusts of wind.

He was so worried about the noises around him that he wandered straight into their trap. Bobbin's odd, skipping gait made it difficult to find a clear shot. But when he stopped to inspect another clump of grass, Kael saw his chance.

The curved knife left his hand, glinting as it spun end over end towards Bobbin. He heard a faint gasp and a *thud* as the mage toppled over.

"Wait —!"

Eveningwing left the ditch like a shot, and Kael had no choice but to follow. Even wounded, Bobbin could be deadly.

He sprinted for the grass clump and prepared himself for a fight. But when they arrived, he saw the danger was over. Bobbin wasn't moving. Eveningwing knelt beside him and plucked the knife free.

"A clean hit!" he said excitedly. "I was worried about your weak human eyes. But you killed him perfectly."

The stench of Bobbin's blood was making Kael's vision slightly hazy. He pulled his shirt over his nose and grabbed the mage around the legs. "Get his arms — let's bury him quickly."

****

By the time the minceworms were finished with them, all that remained of the Grandmot's goats were a few horns and a pair of hooves. The worms couldn't burrow into the valley's denser soil. So when the sun came up, they shriveled to ash — taking every remnant of Kyleigh's mischief away with them.

The Grandmot made some long-winded speech about how it had been Fate's will to send the minceworms into her lands, and Kyleigh couldn't have been happier: she thought she might actually get away with it.

But by the time Nadine returned from her shift that afternoon, she was fuming. "I have been given the entire night's watch — and I must watch from the northern brazier. Its fire is out," she explained impatiently, when Kyleigh looked confused. "I hope you are happy, a'calla. Because of your meddling, I am going to spend my nights in the freezing cold!"

"At least you're willing to admit that it was because of my *meddling* that the Grandmot's punishing you, and not some great act of Fate," Kyleigh said lightly. "We're not going to let you freeze to death. I'll take the watch with you."

So that night, she followed Nadine up to the top of the mountain. The northern brazier was indeed burned out. And when the last of the day's heat faded, the cold slipped in.

Kyleigh's strength had been steadily coming back. She feasted on cavefish and wild goat whenever she could, and she was careful to stay in her human form — giving the dragon in her a much-needed rest.

The cold did not chill her as it once had. Her blood was getting its fire back, and her body put off enough heat to keep Nadine warm. At the middle of the night, Nadine sat down, claiming that she was only going to rest her legs, but it wasn't long before she fell asleep. Kyleigh sat next to her and kept a lookout for the Grandmot's guards.

With the brazier's fire burned out, there was nothing to veil the brilliance of the stars. They blanketed the whole sky, piercing the darkness with dots of quiet, shining colors. Their haunting light changed the desert: the burning dunes looked like drifts of new snow, the deep ravines became gentle rivers. The Red Spine was nothing more than a quiet shadow in the distance.

The mountains were closer than she'd ever hoped they would be. She thought they might've wandered so far off course that it would take a week to reach them. But from where she sat, she wagered it was only a day's journey over the dunes — a day and a half, at the very most.

"Hello."

Kyleigh tried not to look too startled when she noticed the young man sitting across from her. Had she not been so focused on the Spine, she might've noticed him sooner.

Fortunately, he didn't look as if he meant her any harm. He was bare-chested and wore a pair of black breeches. The dark crop of his hair shadowed his eyes, but didn't quite hide them. She saw through the amber rings and recognized their particular sharpness immediately.

"Hello, fellow sky-hunter," she said, smiling when she saw how the halfhawk's eyes brightened at her greeting.

"What brings you to these Fate-forsaken lands — and at such a peculiar hour of the night?"

She liked talking with other winged shapechangers: they saw the world from the same angle she did. And so few creatures were able to take to the skies that it was always nice to be able to talk with someone who understood.

This little halfhawk was no exception. He shifted his weight excitedly as she smiled at him, moving from one side of his rump to the other. "I've been speaking to the crows. They're always good for rumors." His smile flashed by as quickly as his words. "They told me I might be able to find you up here."

"I see," she said, though she was more than a little confused. "Why were you looking for me? And what's your name, by the way?"

"Eveningwing. Yours?"

"Kyleigh."

"A human name? That's good." He stared over Kyleigh's head for a moment, as if he was trying to think of how to arrange his next words. He scratched at his elbows, and she saw that a number of gray feathers sprouted from them.

A breath of air left her lungs, and her stomach dropped. "You were a slave of Midlan," she said, reaching for his arm. "The curse left its mark on you."

He watched calmly as she ran her fingers through his feathers. "Yes — though I was lucky to be freed before my two shapes got twisted together. That tickles," he added.

Kyleigh pulled her hand away, but it wasn't because she was tickling him — it was because she'd suddenly figured it out. She realized ... and yet, she almost didn't dare to say it. She didn't think she could bear it if she was wrong.

But she forced herself to ask: "Kael freed you, didn't he?"

Her heart leapt when Eveningwing nodded. She wanted to grab him around the shoulders and squeeze all of the air from his chest. She wanted to take to her wings and fly into the night, to let out a roar that would shake the entire

Kingdom with her joy and relief — but she didn't. Instead, she clasped her hands tightly and bit down on her lip.

Eveningwing read the desire in her eyes, and he grinned. "Would you like to hear his story?"

"More than I'd like to draw breath, yes."

He laughed. "Very well. I'll tell you ..."

Eveningwing's tale stretched late into the night. Kyleigh hardly breathed as he spoke of Kael's life among the giants, his battle with the mages, and his daring plan of escape. It sounded as if he was using every ounce of cleverness in that brilliant head of his, and as Eveningwing spoke of him, her chest swelled with pride ... even though she knew it shouldn't have.

Kael wasn't *hers*, after all. And he'd made it clear that he didn't want to be. She shut her eyes tight against the painful light of that memory. *Be proud of him as your friend,* she thought to herself. *It'll only hurt worse if you miss him as something he's not.*

Though he must have talked for hours, Eveningwing's story ended far too quickly. As the sun's bright shadow crept towards the edge of the horizon, it began to hide the stars from view.

"You knew Bloodfang, then?" Kyleigh said, watching the sky brighten. She wished she could hold back the sun.

Eveningwing nodded. "He was a good flockmate — he taught me everything."

"Well, if Bloodfang was in *my* pack and *your* flock ..." Kyleigh smiled. "I suppose that makes you my little brother."

He grabbed his knees and pulled them to his chin — as if that could somehow stop his grin from being so ridiculously wide. "I'd like that. I've missed having a family."

"Then it's settled."

They watched the sunrise for a moment more. Neither one of them wanted the night to end, but it ended all the same. Eveningwing got to his feet.

"I should go back — Kael needs me to watch the skies."

"There's nothing else you can tell me?"

Kyleigh's heart sank down when he shook his head. Somehow, it seemed to sit even lower than it had before. One final question weighed on her. It leaned heavily as she struggled to her feet.

"Why did you come find me tonight? Kael didn't send you ... did he?"

Eveningwing shook his head again, and she immediately felt like a fool. She should've known better than to ask. This disappointment was all her own fault. Would she ever learn?

"I came here because ..." He scratched at the feathers sprouting from the base of his skull for a moment, his fingers moving in a blur. "Kael's a good human," he finally said, leveling his chin at Kyleigh. "He's different from the others. And I just wanted to make sure that you weren't going to hurt him."

Kyleigh bristled at the thought. "I would never hurt him. I'd rather die than cause him any pain."

Eveningwing nodded. "I believe that," he said softly. He held a hand out to the horizon. "I believe it even more than I believe in the sunrise."

He left, then — promising that he would return if her friends needed her ... or if Kael fell to harm.

Chapter 27
A Monster in the Shallows

For some reason, Eveningwing's visit only made Kyleigh more anxious.

She was impatient to get back to her journey. Jake's head wasn't healing nearly fast enough, and she was afraid that they'd be stuck with the mots forever, just waiting for his stitches to come out. She knew she was being ridiculous, but that didn't make the time go by any faster.

It certainly didn't help when she discovered that everything in the motlands revolved around a strict set of rules. There were laws about where Kyleigh could be, when she could be there, and who she could be with. Every time she turned a corner, it was only to run into a pair of snarling guards. They'd cross their spears over her path and shout at her for breaking the rules.

Finally, Kyleigh could stand it no longer — and she swore that she'd trounce the head of the next little person who screamed at her. The guards gave her a wide berth after that, but Nadine still made her behave. So she sighed and resigned herself to her duties.

On bathing days, it was Kyleigh's job to walk Nadine down the long staircase to the bath. She was supposed to walk two steps ahead of her — so that if Nadine fell, she would land on Kyleigh and not on the stone steps.

She had a feeling that the mots used their slaves for a soft landing pretty frequently, if it happened often enough to be written into their laws.

The bottom of the stairway led into the underground portion of the mots' domain. It spilled out into something like a grand, circular hallway. The stone floor was cool against

Kyleigh's bare feet as she stepped to the side and allowed Nadine to take the lead.

The air was moist and smelled of earth. Kyleigh breathed it in as they walked, listening to how her breathing echoed softly against the ceiling. They passed an arched doorway, which Nadine said led into the Grandmot's chambers. A small company of male soldiers stood outside of it.

They nodded to Nadine as she passed. Kyleigh felt the soldiers' eyes flick across her body before they went back to staring purposefully at the opposite wall.

"I think you confuse them," Nadine whispered to her. "All they hear are tales of the a'calla's dark soul, and his hunger for red flesh. Your beauty has taken them by surprise."

Kyleigh imagined it *would* have been quite confusing, just to look at her. Perhaps if she strolled past them with a leg of goat clamped between her teeth, they might go back to thinking more about her dark soul — and less about her backside.

She had to bite her lip to keep from laughing at the thought.

The second archway they came to had a pair of female guards standing outside of it. When they caught sight of Kyleigh, one of them disappeared into the tunnel. She emerged a moment later, crossing her spear with the second guard in a protective X.

"You can enter when all the others have gone." Her gaze was rather flinty as she added: "They do not wish to share space with the a'calla."

It didn't matter which pair of women guarded the door, they said the same thing every time. Kyleigh was beginning to think that they were more interested in shaming Nadine than they were in being informative.

The women came out of the bath in a steady trickle. Most didn't even glance at Kyleigh, though a few threw haughty looks in her direction. Many of the younger women wore their hair in long, loose pony's tails, clamped down every few lengths by thick silver clasps. But most kept their hair cut short, trimmed to just under their ears. Hardly any of them had hair of medium length, like Nadine's.

Kyleigh wondered about it. But in the end, she decided not to ask. The length of Nadine's hair was likely some mark of shame, and she didn't want to risk upsetting her.

Several of the women had slaves in tow — Kyleigh recognized them by their white dresses. "Sometimes, if a family loses their fortunes, people are forced to become slaves," Nadine had explained once when Kyleigh asked. "They give up their freedoms, yes. But their masters are charged by law to keep them fed. So they do what they must to survive."

Blazes, even the other slaves looked at Kyleigh as if they'd very much like to throttle her. She waited patiently beside Nadine until the last scornful woman stepped under the archway. Then they went inside.

The area the mots used to bathe was nearly the size of Roost's dining room. The stone floor had a number of holes broken out of it: some were about the size of tubs, but most were large enough for four or five people.

There were small braziers glowing on the ground between the pools, and they produced enough light to show the bathers which paths were safe to walk along. Nadine wound her way down the path towards the back wall.

The water that filled the baths came from a slow-moving, underground river. The river flowed from the back of the room to the front, which meant that the waters furthest from the door were always the cleanest.

Because the mots' laws declared that only the Grandmot could wear black, Kyleigh wasn't allowed to wear her armor. She'd been forced to don one of the white slave dresses, instead.

Normally, she loathed dresses. She found them itchy, revealing in an insulting sort of way, and far too frilly. Not only did they offer no protection to her important bits, the skirts had a nasty habit of getting tangled around her legs. In fact, she thought she had a better chance of winning a fight naked than in a dress.

But she was surprised to find that the desert dresses were rather comfortable. They weren't frilly or itchy, and they were cut short enough that she didn't have to worry about them getting tangled. She supposed if she *had* to wear a dress, it wasn't too terrible. But she still couldn't wait to get it off.

The second they reached their bathing spot, Kyleigh pulled the dress over her head and flung it to the side. Then she leapt into the bath.

Warm water covered her ears as she sank to the bottom of the pool. She let the air out of her lungs in a stream of bubbles, making her body sink faster. Kyleigh loved the quiet comfort of the water, and envied the fishes for being able to breathe it like air.

She thought it might be worth the risk of winding up in some fisherman's net, just to know the underwater world as they did.

But Kyleigh was not a fish, and eventually she had to come back up. "This is, and without a doubt, my favorite bit of motdom," she said, pulling her hair out of its pony's tail. She arched her neck back and felt her muscles tremble as the warm water teased her scalp. "Though I don't understand why we've got to wear our undergarments to bathe in. It seems a bit odd."

Nadine dropped from the edge of the pool gingerly into the bath. The pale green glow from the water danced across her skin. "Only our husbands are allowed to see us unclothed, outlander." She crouched to scoop up some of the black mud from the riverbed and began scrubbing it on her limbs. "According to our law, if a man sees a woman unclothed and she is not his wife, his eyes must be plucked from his skull. They also cut out his tongue, so that he can never tell of what he has witnessed," she added. "Perhaps *you* might disrobe yourself for all who wish to see it. But beauty is sacred to us."

Kyleigh saw the tiny smirk on Nadine's lips and realized she was teasing. So she propped her elbows on the pool's edge and let the water carry her legs to the top — which put her feet squarely in Nadine's face. "I don't disrobe for *everyone*, I'll have you know. Just a special few."

She wiggled her toes, and Nadine lost the fight against her smile. She shoved Kyleigh's feet away. "Such insolence. I should have let the Grandmot split you open."

Kyleigh was about to retort when a familiar smell drew her eyes to the wall behind Nadine. She stared into the shadows, breathing in. The scent crept up on her, burning her nostrils like the spice of desert rice.

"Care for a swim, Elena?" she said to a patch of shadow that she thought looked suspicious. And to her delight, she guessed correctly.

Elena sauntered out of the darkness. She pulled down her mask, revealing the disappointed look underneath. "How do you know? How do you *always* know?" she muttered as she sat at the water's edge.

"I just get lucky," Kyleigh said.

Though she hated to admit it, Elena was turning out to be quite a useful ally. Her uncanny stealth and affinity for the shadows meant that she could lurk around nearly every corner of the motlands without being spotted, and she could turn any crevice into a hiding spot. She'd once dropped down from the ceiling and nearly frightened Silas out the window.

"I hope you have stopped your stealing," Nadine said, with a stern look at Elena. She brushed the wet hair from her neck, and Kyleigh noticed that she wore a ring on every finger of her right hand. They had thick, silver bands and were slightly pointed at their tops — which made her think they were more for cracking skulls than decoration.

Elena ignored her look. She drew a dagger from its sheath and spun it on its point. "I promised that I wouldn't steal from the farmers again, and I haven't."

Shortly after Elena arrived, crops began disappearing from their fields — along with pelts, various bits of weaponry, and several rolls of silk. Kyleigh suspected that she'd been building a nest somewhere in the depths of the tunnels, where she wouldn't have to put up with Silas.

The mots weren't pleased when they discovered that their possessions had gone missing, and they turned to the Grandmot for justice. That sly, feather-sporting fox had pinned the whole thing on Silas — declaring that cats were known to steal things, and that the mots should've known better than to let a thief into their lands. Poor Nadine had no choice but to slaughter one of her nanny goats and distribute its meat in payment.

After that, Elena had promised to stop stealing. But nobody really trusted her.

"What about the miners? Or the other warriors?" Nadine pressed. "You cannot just pick something out of a garden every time you are hungry. Come back to my home, and I will be happy to feed you."

"I promise I haven't stolen from any of the little people," Elena said shortly. Then she looked up, and there was laughter in her eyes as she added: "I've only been stealing from the Grandmot."

Nadine gasped.

"Well, then — that settles it," Kyleigh said, leaning back against the bath.

"That settles nothing!" Nadine brought her fist down, and Elena had to roll to the side to avoid getting hit by the splash. "You do not understand how serious this is. If you are caught, I will have no power to defend you."

Elena nodded, as if she understood. "Why does the Grandmot hate you?"

That was another of Elena's surprising virtues. She didn't seem to mind asking the questions nobody else would — because everybody else seemed to understand that some things were private. Elena, however, was often as blunt as her knives were sharp.

Nadine's mouth parted in surprise. "I did something I should not have done," she finally said. Her eyes were firm, but her voice wavered. "There was a time when I was an honored warrior among the mots. But when our people needed me most, I forgot my duties. I betrayed them. The Grandmot stripped me of my rank, and she was right to do so — where are you going?"

But Elena slunk into the darkness without an explanation. Her armor melded with the shadows, hiding her from view. A moment later, they heard the soft patter of footsteps cutting through the bath chamber.

Nadine craned her neck over Kyleigh's shoulder and her eyes widened. She leapt out of the bath so quickly that her feet hardly touched the ground. "What is it, child?"

Hessa rushed past the braziers. The yellow silk of her dress was wrinkled; strands of her dark hair had escaped their clasp. Nadine knelt, holding her arms open, and the little girl ran into her.

"I fell asleep — I had a nightmare," Hessa gasped. Then she began to sob, adding to the wet on Nadine's shoulder. Kyleigh climbed out of the bath and picked her dress up from the ground. She handed it to Nadine, who used the hem to dry Hessa's tears.

She whispered in the singsong language of the mots, holding her tightly. The way she carried her words gave them a soothing rhythm, like the hum of a lullaby. When Hessa quieted, Nadine took her under the chin. "Now, tell me what you saw, child."

"My dream was about you," Hessa whispered. "I saw you standing on the shore of a great river, watching over your herd. Your goats drank happily from the waters for a moment. But whenever you turned away, a monster would rise up from the shallows and snatch one of your goats. He ate them all, one by one. I tried to call to you, to warn you, but ..." she wiped miserably at her tears, "it was as if you could not hear me."

Nadine smiled softly. "I *always* hear you, child. No matter how much stone lies between us, I hear you like a spring inside my heart." She wrapped Hessa tightly in her arms once more. "But what you saw was only a dream: my goats are alive and safe. My servants watch over them for me.

340

Now, go back to your chambers before the Grandmot misses you ... she will not want to find you with me."

Hessa pulled away reluctantly, and there was such heaviness in their parting that Kyleigh could hardly bear to watch. When she returned Kyleigh's dress, their eyes met again.

The openness of Hessa's gaze startled her. She didn't guard her feelings, and she didn't try to hide. Dozens of lines crossed out from her pupils, bursting like a star into the brown ... and Kyleigh read the anguish in every one.

It was only after Hessa had gone that Kyleigh felt the wetness on her cheeks. She realized that she'd been crying. "Why do I get the feeling that Hessa is no ordinary little girl?" she said, quickly pulling her dress over her head.

Nadine gave her a long look. "You are right — she is far from ordinary. Now come, we have no time to waste."

She strode across the chamber, pulling on her dress as she went. And Kyleigh followed at a trot. "Where are we going?"

"To check on my goats." She paused just short of the door, out of the guards' hearing, and whispered: "I learned long ago to heed Hessa's nightmares. There is little she dreams that does not come to pass."

******

Silas was determined not to let the Grandmot steal another one of his goats, and so he'd appointed himself as their protector. Now he spent his days lounging next to the paddock, watching the farmers carefully whenever they came by to feed or water the herd. He would even get up two or three times a night, just to make sure none of them had *wandered* into the valley.

When Kyleigh and Nadine approached, they found Silas sprawled out on a thick blanket of grass next to the pen. His hands were tucked loosely beneath his head, and he seemed to be enjoying the sunlight immensely.

Kyleigh's shadow crossed his face, and his eyes snapped open. "Out of my sun, dragoness."

"We have come to check on the goats," Nadine said quickly. She stepped past him and leaned against the fence rails. Her fingers flicked over their heads as she counted them.

"They're all here," Silas drawled. He rolled, trying to get out of Kyleigh's shadow, but she moved in his way. "I'm warning you, dragoness — I've killed for less annoying things."

"Nadine's worried about her animals. And since you're her great furry goat-tender, I thought you might want to help her."

The edge in her voice was not lost on Silas. He got to his feet — but took his precious time strolling over to Nadine. "What are you worried about?" he said, leaning in next to her.

"I am not sure. It can be hard to see the meaning hidden in Hessa's dreams ..." A crease formed between her brows, and her eyes were distant. She muttered to herself for a moment, her fingers thrummed against the rails. "The water," she finally said, spinning around to Kyleigh. "The monster in the river ... the danger must be in their water!"

Kyleigh leapt over the fence. The goats scattered, bleating in terror at the smell of her. When she peered into the silver trough, the water sparkled innocently back at her. Nothing seemed amiss.

"Maybe it's been poisoned." Now that he thought his goats might be in danger, Silas was suddenly interested. He shoved in next to Kyleigh and scooped a drink to his mouth. He smacked his lips, his eyes closed as he tasted it. Then he shook his head. "No, the water's good."

Kyleigh thought for a moment, trying to remember everything she could about Hessa's dream. Then it struck her. "The monster was in the *shallows*, along the shore ..."

She brushed her finger against the floor of the trough and then stuck it to her tongue. Bitterness coated the inside of her mouth. She spat it out quickly.

"The *trough's* been poisoned?" When Kyleigh nodded, Silas tasted it for himself. His face burned red as he spat. "She tried to poison them! She tried to poison my little — *you*," he roared at a passing farmer. "My trough's been poisoned. I demand a new one!"

Before Kyleigh could stop him, he grabbed the end of the trough and hurled it, toppling the whole thing over on its head. Water splashed out everywhere. The trough struck the fence with a loud *clang*, and the farmers dashed off in opposite directions — running as if they thought they might very well get eaten.

While Nadine went to explain to the farmers what had happened, Kyleigh tried to calm Silas. Red crept down his neck and spread across his shoulders. He paced with his fists clenched, glaring furiously at nobody in particular — though Kyleigh knew all of his anger must be focused on the Grandmot.

She decided it would probably be best to try to distract him. "I must admit, I never thought I'd see you care about anything," she said, leaping back over the fence. "Much less a pack of horned prey."

Silas looked out at the goats. He tried to mask the softness on his face with a shrug. "I guard them like I would guard any meal. They are nothing but a dinner I haven't yet eaten."

Kyleigh wasn't sure she believed him. Now that she'd left the pen, the goats trotted eagerly up to Silas. Some nudged him with their horns, or stared affectionately through their strange, slitted eyes. One fellow started chewing on the hem of his garment, and he leapt away.

"Shoo!" he said as he retreated to the fence. "Go nibble elsewhere, you smelly little dinners!"

It took some convincing, but Nadine managed to get the farmers to trade her goats' trough for a new one — on the condition that Silas stand several yards away. Once the new trough had been set up and filled, Silas returned to his post. His glaring gaze was even more watchful, now. The

Grandmot's agents would have a difficult time slipping past him.

The afternoon was growing late, which meant that Nadine only had a few hours left before her watch began. She headed back to her room to get some rest, and Kyleigh followed.

"There's some Seer in Hessa's blood, isn't there?" Kyleigh murmured when they reached the stairs.

She'd sensed there was something odd about the little girl when they'd first met eyes, but it wasn't until after her dream that Kyleigh put it together. She remembered the peculiar weight of Hessa's stare; she'd felt it before ... but where?

When she forced herself to grasp for it, all she felt was anger. The memory must've been a bad one. Perhaps it was better if she didn't remember.

Nadine slowed her pace. Most of the mots were still going about their chores, so there was no one around to overhear them. "I see no point in hiding it from you any longer. Yes, Hessa is a Seer. But it is far more than that."

"Tell me, then," Kyleigh said. "Is that why the Grandmot chose her to be her successor?"

Nadine smirked. "Traditionally, yes — the Grandmots choose their own Dawns. But that was not so with Hessa: she was chosen by Fate. The night she was born, an owl lighted outside her family's window. We consider owls to be messengers of Fate," she explained. "That is why the Grandmot adorns her hair with his feathers."

"Is that what that is? Huh, I thought those might've grown in on their own."

Nadine swatted back at her. "Your teasing will get you into trouble one day, outlander." Though she smiled as she said it. Then she went back to her tale: "The owl perched on her family's window, watching with its all-seeing eyes. Her parents took this as a sign, and they sent for the Grandmot immediately. It was only after she declared Hessa her Dawn that the owl returned to the skies. We have never had a Dawn so young," Nadine said softly. "Our laws say that our Dawn must leave her family, and allow the Grandmot to guide her with motherly wisdom. But Hessa was too young to care for herself, and the Grandmot did not have time to raise an infant. So someone had to be assigned her protector.

"I was only a child — I was just beginning to learn the ways of the spear. But when the Grandmot lined all of the female warriors up, I was among them. She walked past us with Hessa in her arms. *She will know,* the Grandmot said to us. *Hessa will choose for herself.*" By this point, Nadine's pace had slowed to a stop. They stood outside of her room; she froze at the doorway. Her voice fell quiet: "When Hessa came to me, she broke out in a smile — the most beautiful smile. She raised her arm and held out her hand ... and I took it. And so I was chosen."

She turned around suddenly, and Kyleigh stepped back. "I raised her, I cared for her as a daughter. And that is where I keep her in my heart. Hessa has always known the future — even from the moment she was born. She knew how my life would unfold ... that is why she chose me." Nadine's gaze returned from the distance, and she batted Kyleigh with the back of her hand. "Now, I have told *you* something, so you will tell *me* something."

Kyleigh shrugged. "I suppose that's only fair." She followed Nadine to the water barrel for a drink. When she reached to retrieve the bowls, she felt Nadine's hand on the back of her shoulder.

"What is this mark?"

Kyleigh knew this question was coming. She'd known it from the moment she put on her dress and saw which of her shoulders was going to go bare. And even though she didn't want to talk about it, she felt she ought to give Nadine an answer.

"It's the dragon of Midlan."

"Midlan," Nadine said slowly. "Wait — that is the home of your tyrant, is it not?"

"Yes. Is that what you call him, then? Not *Your Majesty* or *His Royal Rumpness?*" She tsked in mock disapproval. "Such insolence. I ought to hang you by your toes."

Nadine snorted. "He is not *my* King." Kyleigh felt the pressure of her fingers against the dulled, scarred skin on her right shoulder blade; felt her trace the dragon's neck and follow the curve of its wings. "This is strange, outlander. Why did you do this?"

"I didn't do it. It was done to me."

"Why?"

Kyleigh wanted to lie. She'd always lied about it — because the truth stung too bitterly. Though she rolled her eyes at Silas and his proud ways, a small part of her knew how he felt. She'd been a proud creature too, once.

Perhaps she was still a little proud, because even now her fists clenched at the thought of telling the truth. She knew she wasn't really trapped with Nadine: rules or no, once Jake healed, she would leave. She was strong enough now to do as she wished. But once, not so long ago, she hadn't been strong enough. Once, she'd almost been doomed to the life of a slave.

She didn't want to lie to Nadine, not after she'd been so honest. So Kyleigh tried to explain it without having to go too far into the details. "This isn't my first time being a slave — which is probably why I'm so blasted good at it." She smiled when Nadine laughed. "I was the King's slave, once. And he branded my skin with this mark."

"How did you escape?"

Kyleigh had to steady herself against the memory. It was strange that an act so distant could still cause her throat to tighten — how one deed could bring the entire man into being. "I was bought by a very kind person," she said roughly. "And he promptly set me free."

That was how she would always remember Setheran: not as a great warrior or a fearsome knight, but as a kind soul — as a man who loved mercy ... and who'd taken pity on her.

Chapter 28
None Other Than Love

At best, Kael hoped that his latest attack might stir up a little mischief. What he got instead was full-fledged chaos.

When they realized that Bobbin had disappeared, the mages flew into a panic: they blasted through every patch of grass and rolled over every stone, scouring the Fields for his body. Guards poured out from the castle to help in the search, led by Dred — who'd acquired a rather nasty-looking black eye. They spent hours tromping every which way, screaming at each other, and generally trying to pin blame anywhere but their own hides.

It was nearly afternoon before anyone thought to let out the slaves.

"Oh, look at them squirm," Brend said gleefully.

They watched as a cluster of guards inspected a rather large, flat-topped stone. One guard pried it up with the sharp end of his pike while the other two stood with their weapons lowered — as if they expected a troll to leap out at them at any moment.

"I don't know," Declan murmured. A shadow crossed his eyes as he watched the guards poke tentatively beneath the rock. "That's two mages that have gone missing, now. There must be *something* that's getting them."

"It's ole Scalybones!" Brend said, chuckling.

They were supposed to be planting the cabbage. But since the mages were nowhere in sight, they were moving much slower than usual. Brend placed his seeds one at a time, with a good amount of back-straightening and joking in between, while Declan moved distractedly — his planting separated by long moments of staring at the Fields and muttering to himself.

For once, Kael was actually ahead of them. He thought it might be a good idea to keep his head lowered as much as possible. Declan might very well be able to read the whole story on his face, if he thought to look. But fortunately, the giant's eyes seemed to rove nearly everywhere else.

"You know Scalybones is just a tale —"

"But *they* don't!"

Declan made a frustrated sound. "Well, if Scaly is a tale and the mages are still disappearing, then it's got to be something real. And if that's the case, how long before whatever's out *there*," he thrust his scythe at the Fields, "comes after one of us?"

Brend made a face. "It'll have to climb through spells and locked doors before it can do that. It's probably only the lions, anyhow — they're thick this time of year. Any man who wanders out after dark deserves to be eaten. And what are you so grumped about?" He used his scythe to flick a clod of dirt at Declan. "Anything that's munching on the spellmongers is a friend of mine!"

When a few hours passed and they still hadn't found any sign of Bobbin, the guards marched back into the castle. One by one, the mages returned to their duties — and it wasn't long before Finks wandered up to them.

Kael thought they might all be in for a beating. Finks's skin was red and he had his long teeth clamped tightly on his lower lip. He threw a few halfhearted lashes at them, but mostly spent the day pacing around, scratching worriedly at the top of his head.

Brend couldn't contain himself. Sparks flickered behind his eyes as he planted, and Kael knew he must've been thinking up another wild tale. Sure enough, it wasn't long before Brend began to talk loudly about how Scalybones had it out for the mages.

"Don't you see? It makes perfect sense!" he argued with Declan. "Ole Scaly must've found some holes in his cloak after that last big rain —"

"Why would he care about the rain?"

348

"Because fresh rainfall burns his bones, you clodder! Everybody knows that," Brend said impatiently. He caught sight of Finks hovering nearby and lowered his voice. Kael nearly grinned when Finks wandered closer. "The skin of magefolk is extra oily, on account of all the magic in them. So it'd be perfect to keep out the rain."

"How many do you think he'll get?" Declan whispered.

Brend shrugged. "Who knows? He's had naught but giant skin for these last many years, and our hide is far more suited for breeches than anything. He might be weaving himself a whole new cloak, now that he's got so many nice, oily mages about." He spun to Kael. "And when the ground starts to harden, you'd better watch yourself: the skin of mountain rat makes for a fine pair of boots, on account of them being so particularly stubborn."

Kael did his best to look appalled.

Brend's wild tales grew faster than any weed, sprouting such a terrible fear amongst the mages that they actually began to go mad — and the next week passed by with hardly a dull moment.

It all started on a particularly hot and dusty day, when Churl screamed at the top of his lungs that he'd seen Scalybones hiding in the grass. He whipped his wagon into an all-out sprint for the barns, saw the cloud of dust rising up behind him, and thought the wraith was giving chase.

He leapt from the front of the wagon in a panic — and was promptly crushed to death beneath the wheels.

Without a whip to stop them, the Fallows tore straight through the courtyard and into the cornfields, nearly trampling the poor giants who were trying to weed them. They might've gone clear to the Spine, had the pond not gotten in their way.

The Fallows drove straight into the middle of it, and the weight of the barrels sank the wagon, burying it beneath the greenish waters. They managed to escape their harnesses, but made no effort to swim for the shore. For some reason, they didn't seem to be very fond of the water: they perched atop the sunken cart and flatly refused to budge

— swatting angrily at anybody who tried to swim out to them.

Hob finally had to use a spell to pluck them from the pond one at a time. The Fallows grunted and flailed their limbs as he carried them through midair, but the second their feet touched the ground, they went back to drooling contentedly.

Churl's death finally seemed to convince Gilderick that something needed to be done. He sent the guards to drag the wagon out of the pond, and ordered that a patrol watch the Fields day and night. They set up braziers on either side of the road and hovered constantly around the barns. There were so many torches lit that it was difficult to tell when the sun actually went down.

But for all of their caution, the attacks kept happening — and this time, the mages weren't the target.

After their first night on patrol, the guards seemed flustered. Kael managed to listen in and learned that a couple of men hadn't returned after their watch. Then they started patrolling in pairs — and began disappearing in pairs.

Kael's first thought was that Eveningwing might've been responsible. He often left during the night, and hadn't come out of his hawk form in days. Kael thought he might be hiding something.

"I only ask because I don't want you to get hurt," he'd said after dinner one night, while the giants were still eating.

Eveningwing cut his beak abruptly to the side — a gesture Kael figured was as good as a shake of the head.

But he still wasn't convinced. "I think it's noble of you to try and help, but we've been lucky not to be discovered so far. If guards keep disappearing like this, there's no telling what Gilderick will do. He might go mad and start killing the slaves off. You don't want that to happen, do you?"

Eveningwing's head dipped low, and the feathers on the tops of his wings bunched up miserably. Later that night, Kael heard the soft click of his talons as he hopped out onto the roof.

Though he'd adamantly denied that he'd had anything to do with it, after Kael's talk with Eveningwing, the guards stopped disappearing so rapidly. One or two would go missing every once in awhile, but it was a small enough number that it could be blamed on the lions.

****

With the mages' power weakening every day, Kael left his plan to simmer. The rains were coming more often, now. They drifted in from the seas and filled the afternoons with a soft, steady drizzle.

As the clouds swooped in, Kael watched them from a distance. Their gray, feathery tails would flirt with the Red Spine, fluttering halfway to its peaks before stopping suddenly — as if some invisible wall kept them from crossing into the desert. It was strange to think that the Endless Plains might've easily shared the barren fate of its neighbor: the Spine seemed to be the only thing keeping this land of plenty from becoming a land of waste.

When the rains began to fall, the giants had no choice but to return to their barns. There were so many eyes watching the Fields now that the giants knew better than to try to drag it out. The guards began closing in with the clouds, waiting for the first drops to fall — and then they'd chase the giants away with the points of their pikes.

Though Kael knew a rainy afternoon would give him more time to think, a large part of him felt as if he ought to be doing something — *anything*. Every moment he sat idle felt like a moment wasted. So while the giants lounged about and chatted, Kael began to pace.

"You won't get it off that way," Declan said. He sat with his back against the stall door and Brend sat across from him. They were playing a game that looked a bit like chess — a strategy game that Uncle Martin had taught him over the winter. Though the giants used a circle drawn into the dirt as a board, and pebbles for pieces.

"What are you talking about?" Kael grumbled. He was more frustrated with himself than anything. Gilderick's castle loomed in the back of his mind like a grinning vulture — circling him, waiting for him to make a mistake.

"Your beard," Declan said, nodding to him. "You aren't going to be able to scratch the hair off, so you might as well let it be."

Kael hadn't even realized that he'd been picking at his beard. But now that he thought about it, the hair *was* itching him. A thin dusting covered his upper lip, and he knew that bit wouldn't get any longer. It never did. The hair on his chin and cheeks was what worried him the most: it sprouted in determined patches — growing very thickly where it wanted to, and fading back whenever it pleased.

The result left him looking like a half-plucked chicken.

"Hmm," Brend said, peering over his shoulder at Kael's face. "I've not seen many, but that's the worst beard I've ever seen."

"Well, how do you keep yours from growing?"

Kael had noticed right away that none of the giants had a beard. There wasn't a hair on their faces, even though he never saw them shaving.

"Giant men don't grow much hair. We're born with all we'll ever have — and some of us have less than others." Brend reached across and tussled the top of Declan's head. "Look at that! Thin as a summer dew."

Declan knocked his hand away.

"Our women though, they've got mightily long hair. They weave it in thick braids down their backs." Brend stared at the game for a moment, and a ridiculous smile crossed his face. "The rest of the realm can all keep their frail little lassies — you've not seen *true* beauty until you've laid eyes on a giantess!"

A rumble of agreement followed his claim, and Kael suddenly realized that the other giants had begun crowding in around them, their separate tasks forgotten. Kael didn't like the way Brend's story was headed. He'd sat through his fair share of tales about women: from Jonathan's bawdy ballads, to the stories Uncle Martin told over dinner.

Try as he might to hide it, they always made him blush uncontrollably — which apparently gave the other men the right to heckle him for hours on end. He was convinced that Jonathan made his tales a little more colorful each time, just to see if he could get Kael to turn a deeper shade of crimson.

So as the story began, he'd prepared himself to be humiliated. But it turned out that that he worried over nothing. In fact, he tried not to laugh as Brend fumbled his way through a tale about a particularly busty giantess:

"And her hair was like — well, it was hair! And it was all clean and shiny, too. Not a touch filthy. Eh ... and she didn't have any warts to speak of. Her smile was nice — but not in the friendly sort of way. It was more like ... like ... eh ..."

"Sultry?" Kael supplied. He had to fight off his grin when Brend hurriedly jabbed a finger at him.

"Oh, yes — that sounds about right. So her smile was sultry, her hair was clean, and ... what was the other thing?"

"No warts," Kael said out the side of his mouth.

"Ah, right! She didn't have any warts. She might've had a mole or two, I don't know. We'll figure that out later. So, anyways ..."

Brend tried hard to tell a convincing story, but Kael had to clamp a hand over his mouth to keep his laughter back. At least he understood the giants' floundering: they'd been locked up for so long that they were probably the only men in the Kingdom who had less experience than he did.

****

A few days later, Kael's simmering plan boiled over.

Things didn't turn out the way he'd expected them to. Though the mages seemed to grow greener and more fearful with every passing moment, they still didn't retreat to the castle — which didn't make any sense.

If magic was the only thing keeping his slaves in check, why wouldn't Gilderick protect his mages? Why wouldn't he lock them up in his castle at night and keep them safe behind the reddened walls? It made no sense to leave them out in the open, to risk having them picked off one at a time. But that's exactly what he did.

And to make matters worse, Gilderick began to send his guards out into the Fields during the day, ordering that they watch the slaves. The guards swarmed about them thickly, pikes clutched in their hands. Kael thought the giants ought to have been worried. There were too few mages to go around, and if the guards decided to beat them senseless, it was likely that Finks and Hob wouldn't be able to reach them in time.

But instead of hunkering down and behaving themselves, the giants grew restless.

Hardly a day went by when threats and insults didn't spill over into a fight. The giants would gather in clumps on the edge of a field, taunting one guard or another by name. They'd remind him of the life he took to buy his way into Gilderick's army, bring his mother and sisters into it, and it wasn't long before he'd charge at them with his pike raised.

The slaves had no trouble beating the guards. Though their scythes were humble tools, they were also very effective weapons: they cut easily under the guards' pikes and popped them deftly from their hands. Then once their opponents were disarmed, the slaves pummeled them soundly with their fists.

Kael was convinced that the only thing that kept them from starting an all-out war was fear for their women — that, and killing a guard might just be the last grain that tipped Gilderick's scale from *mad* to *raving*. And nobody wanted that to happen.

Still, the giants didn't seem to be able to keep themselves from fighting. By the time Finks and Hob arrived to put an end to one scuffle, another would pop up in its place. After a long day of chasing the slaves, the mages would have to spend the night with their powers stretched between four barns. They were so green by morning that Kael thought every day might very well be their last.

For Doyle and Gaff, that day came at week's end.

An explosion rocked them out of their sleep one night, breaking so loudly over the empty plains that Kael thought the whole roof had fallen down upon them. The giants sat up on their pallets and waited. Every ear strained against the haunting silence of the night, trying to figure out what had happened. But they heard no answer.

In the morning, the mages were tight-lipped. They lashed the giants out of the barn and ordered them to go about their chores as usual. Kael knew something must've happened, but he likely wasn't going to hear it from the mages. So as he worked, he hung close to a patch of guards. He was able to stitch most of the story together by listening in on their chatter:

Supposedly, Doyle woke in the middle of the night and swore that he'd heard something scratching at his window. So he'd fled to Gaff's cottage in a panic.

When Gaff heard his door slam open, he thought Scalybones was coming to rip his skin off. He hit Doyle in the chest with a spell that exploded so violently, it blew the front part of his cottage off.

No sooner did Doyle's body land on the other side of the courtyard than the guards charged in. They saw Gaff, tangled in his sheets and tumbling down the stairs, and thought he was a ghost. It was only after they'd already skewered him that they realized their mistake.

Now that all of the mages at the Pens had been killed, Kael thought for certain that Gilderick would call Hob and Finks inside the castle. But he didn't.

Instead, he seemed to think his army could do a slavemaster's work just as well. One day, they saw Dred and a whole company of lightly armed guards marching towards the Pens — each with a wench-tongue at his hip.

"Gilderick won't beat them for nothing," Brend said, when several of the giants expressed their worry over dinner. "So as long as they keep their hands to their tasks, they'll be all right."

Kael couldn't help but think that he sounded uncertain, and the others must've felt the same way: the giants still glared daggers at the guards as they worked, but stopped trying to taunt them into fights.

****

The days turned sullen quickly. Not long after Dred had taken over the Pens, they heard the guards laughing about how he'd had beaten two slaves from the seas to death. The giants feared other killings would follow.

"No, that'll be the end of it," Brend tried to assure them, on one particularly soggy afternoon. "Gilderick's made his point, and he won't risk wasting another man."

As much as Kael wanted that to be true, he didn't dare believe it. He'd already made the mistake of believing he could handle the mages, and his meddling had only made things worse: Finks went to the Pens, and more guards were sent out to watch the Fields in his place. Hob's spell covered all four barns at night, and though the threads of his power were so thin they were practically invisible, Kael knew they would still serve their purpose well enough.

He couldn't get through the spells without setting off the alarm, and there were so many guards on patrol at night that he wouldn't risk trying to sneak out again. He was stuck, then — caught up in a problem he'd created. And the giants were stuck with him.

There was only one tiny crack in the miserable, worrisome clouds, only one small beam of light that could brighten their dark days, and it came from a most surprising source.

Kael never told Jonathan of their plight, and so his letters kept pouring in. His maps were much improved. When the giants fell asleep, Kael snuck them from under his pallet and read them by the moonlight, locking their every detail into his memory.

But useful as the maps were, it was actually Jonathan's rambling letters that Kael found the most helpful: the tales of

356

his exploits in the kitchen tower turned out to be the best salve for the giants' wounds.

Kael took to reading them over dinner, when the giants' spirits were all but crushed from the long day of lashings. The fiddler's merry accounts teased smiles onto their faces, prodding them with ridiculousness until he had them stoked into rowdy bouts of laughter:

Never thought I'd say this, but Uncle Martin was right: there's not a woman across the six regions that could hold her own against a giantess!

Believe me, mate — I've been all over. With most women, I'm hardly around them for a few minutes before I'm dealt a sharp slap about the ears. And for what, I ask you? A man can't help but admire certain things, and it's hard to be secretive about admiring said things when a man's got to tilt his chin down so far to do it. So when I set foot in the kitchens, I thought I might as well kiss the old ears goodbye.

But I'm pleased to say that I've been wandering around for days and haven't caught so much as a cross look. The ladies around here are so tall, that all the best bits are at eye-level. A man never has to worry about getting caught staring. All I have to do is turn around and — oops, there they are!

A roar of laughter shook the beams above them and nearly startled Eveningwing from his perch. Kael's face burned so hotly that he thought he was in real danger of setting his collar ablaze. He usually tried to read ahead and filter out most of Jonathan's nonsense. But that time, he hadn't been paying attention.

At least Brend wasn't amused. While the others chuckled on, he bellowed over the top of them: "That fiddler had better be watching where he looks! If his beady little eyes light on my Clairy — I'll tear them out!"

But fortunately, Clairy was one of the few lady giants that Jonathan hadn't been able to find. Though Kael had doubted in his ability to stay focused on much of anything, he'd actually done a fairly good job of finding the giants' loved ones: Clairy, Darrah, and a couple of others were the only ladies he hadn't checked off his list.

They might be in the upper tower, he'd written, after Brend had asked after Clairy for the dozenth time. *I'm not sure what they're hiding up there, but the old witch won't let me anywhere near it. And even the lady giants turn un-helpful when I ask. Tell your friend I'll keep trying, mate!*

Then one day, they finally got some news. Declan went into the stall after dinner and popped immediately back out. "He's found her!"

Brend looked up, a shocking amount of porridge clinging to his chin. "Found who?"

"Clairy."

"Clairy?" When Declan nodded, Brend shot to his feet. "Clairy! Oh, is she all right? She's not hurt, is she? Out of my way, you!" He bounded clear over the trough and shoved the giants aside, charging his way into the stall.

By the time Kael got there, it was so packed full that he had a difficult time seeing anything around the wall of bodies. He weaved his way forward until Declan pulled him into the corner, where he could see a bit more easily.

He caught sight of Eveningwing — who must've gotten dressed in a rush: he was shirtless and his pants were buttoned crookedly. He held a leaf of parchment in his hands and seemed to be looking frantically about him for Kael.

"Go ahead and read it," Declan hollered to him. "He'll never reach you, and Brend's trousers might split if you make him wait any longer."

The giants chuckled at this and a few reached over to slap at Brend — who indeed looked near to bursting. So with a smile, Eveningwing began. And Kael had a feeling from the first sentence that Jonathan's news was going to be trouble:

Fate must hate me. All my life, I've dreamed of winding up in a place like this — what bloke wouldn't want to be trapped in a tower filled with food and tall beauties? Free to wink in nearly any direction and catch a smile? Free to eat as far as his belly will stretch? I thought I'd have to die before I ever found a happiness like this.

But alas, no sooner did I find it than it was taken from me — stolen by a thief every man longs for ... and fears. Her hand has pierced the heart of both urchin and King, and now she's finally come for me.

I speak of none other than love.

Kael groaned. He knew very well where Jonathan's prose would take them, but the giants seemed oblivious. They were so captivated by the words that they hadn't heard the riddle.

And when he tried to warn them, they shushed him.

It happened swift as a crackle across the skies: one moment I was a humble fiddler and the next, I was struck — cast down upon my knees by a beautiful and fearsome sight. I turned, and she stood before me, her eyes snared me with a light I shall never forget — like two stars fallen from the night. Her hair wound in pale, crossing torrents down her back. Oh, even the rivers of the realm would blush at her curves!

She smiled at me, her lips parted like the rose in bloom, and her words struck my ears in the sweetest chord: "Ho there, wee fiddler. Care to help me start an oven fire this afternoon? That'll really set the old witch off."

Of course, I had no power to refuse her. A beauty and a prankster? Oh, Fate! Oh, skies! I can't explain it, mate — but I feel as if we're two patches sewn to the same shirt. We're a matching set, she and I. There's no hope for me now!

And — on a completely unrelated note, of course — would you ask that Brend fellow how he'd feel about having a handsome, pirate fiddler for a brother? Just like to hear his thoughts before I pop off and ask her.

It took Brend a moment to catch on. But when he did, he roared so loudly that Kael had to cover his ears. Poor Eveningwing burst into hawk form and shot out of the roof, leaving his breeches behind. The crowd of giants fled in every direction, scattering like bugs from the light. They dove for the safety of their stalls as Brend began to rant:

"Oh, no! He'll not be popping anything, that little snake. If he even thinks — why — I'll pop *him*! I'll pop his tiny little head from his shoulders — I'll pop the color straight out of his eyes!" Brend snatched Kael by the front of the shirt and hurled him from the crowd. "Tell him, rat — tell that fiddler what I mean to do to him! If he so much as *looks* at my Clairy sideways, I'll ..."

Kael spent a good hour pretending to write down every gruesome end that Brend promised Jonathan, should he try anything with Clairy. Though what he really wrote wasn't anything Brend would've been happy about.

He thought Jonathan's sudden love was actually a good thing. In fact, if he could get Clairy to trust him, she might just be able to sneak him into the upper tower. It sounded as if she was a rather resourceful giantess, at the very least.

Kael felt bad about tricking Brend, but he convinced himself that it was for the best.

Chapter 29
Dante

All of the long hours of the day ate away at Kael's plan. The passing time gnawed at it, chewing tirelessly until it was stripped down to nothing more than a thin, wobbling skeleton — a patchwork of hope held together by a single hinge:

If.

If they were ever able to slip past the mages, Kael thought he had a pretty good idea of how to free the lady giants. But that one little word — that *if* — grew into a wall so high and thick that he didn't think he'd ever be able to get around it.

He spent his days thinking about how to climb it. And at night, it tormented his dreams. He might've gone mad worrying over it, had it not been for *Deathtreader*.

Whenever he found himself at his wit's end, he would bury himself in *Deathtreader*'s words — drowning out the clamoring of his problems with one of the book's many tales.

He never got tired of them. Ben Deathtreader seemed to have been a very powerful healer, and he'd devoted his whole life to unlocking the secrets of the mind. But his methods were not boring, like Amos's had been. Instead of using herbs or salves, he used mind-walking to enter the minds of his subjects and cure them from the inside out.

His adventures were astonishing things. He'd once cured a man of a plague by chasing a horde of goblin-like monsters out of his left ear. When Deathtreader came across a woman who'd been trapped in sleep for weeks, he wandered through the corridors of her mind, opening and closing every door, searching until he found her locked up inside one of the rooms. He freed her, and she immediately woke.

But Kael's favorite tale was the last one — where Ben claimed to have gotten lost inside the mind of a madman:

Though hardly a moment passed in the world I left behind, inside this madman's head, the time felt like decades. I was trapped — nothing made any sense.

The stairs only went in one direction: some led up, others led down. To get upstairs on a downstairs stair, I had to walk backwards. If a door looked real, I found it was only an illusion painted on the wall. If a door was so crudely drawn that I was certain it was an illusion — it would open! The hallways would twist and turn, shimmering at their ends like the unreachable horizon across the seas.

And the walls ... the walls were eerily silent. The secrets did not scream out to try and deceive me, but seemed to understand that I would deceive myself.

I wandered for so long that I began to thirst — which I knew was madness, because the soul cannot thirst ... can it? Had I been trapped for so long that the walls were trying to draw me in with their silence? Did they seek to consume me, to plaster me against their sides and make me a part of this horrible world?

No — no! I would not let this happen. In my desperation, I began to think about the way I'd come in. I realized that I had dropped downward *— that I had* fallen *from reality and wound up inside the halls. So I knew that if I wanted to escape, the only way out was ... up.*

No sooner did I think this than a door appeared upon the ceiling above me. I did not question the absurdity of it all, or wonder why a ceiling would have a door — I wasted no time in opening it and climbing free.

Reality came back in a spin of brilliant colors. I found myself in my own home once again, my mad subject sat across from me — the food between us was still hot. I watched him devour his meal in silence, and thought what a shame it would be to house such a powerful secret ... and yet, never know it.

For it was inside the head of this madman that I discovered the key to all power, to shrugging off every limitation and seizing onto a whisperer's true potential: insanity.

Yes, reader — mad as it sounds, insanity is doubt's only cure.

Kael closed the book, his head still tingling with *Deathtreader*'s last, potent words — and nearly jumped out of his skin when he saw Declan sitting across from him.

"What are you reading?" he demanded. He jerked his chin at *Deathtreader*. "Where'd you find that book?"

"It's nothing — and Jonathan sent it to me," Kael lied. He tried to stuff it under his pallet, but Declan's arm shot out twice as fast. His thick fingers clamped down over Kael's wrist and he twisted, forcing *Deathtreader* out of his hand. "Give it back," Kael snarled.

But Declan ignored him. He flipped *Deathtreader* open. "Does Brend know about this?"

"No, because it's not any of his business."

Declan's brows dropped low, shadowing his eyes. "It's all handwritten ..." He turned the book this way and that. The dry pages hissed in protest. Then he snapped it closed. "Did you write this?"

"Of course I didn't —"

"I may not be able to read the words, rat," Declan growled, "but I can certainly read *you*. And I've been watching you closely from the day you stepped into our Fields." His lips curled over his teeth, like the warning of a cornered wolf. "I've tried trusting you, and it's only got us flogged. None of the others might be able to see it, but I do. I see everything. And I know you're hiding something —"

"I'm not hiding anything!" Kael lunged for the book, but Declan held it out of his reach. "Give it back — you're going to ruin it!"

"Is this some kind of letter? Have you been sent here to spy on us? Yeh, *that's* what it is!" he growled triumphantly, thrusting a finger at Kael — who'd looked up at the word *spy*.

363

Yes, he was technically spying — but not on the giants. And he might've been able to explain this, had he been talking to anybody else. But Declan was so eager to catch him in a lie that even if the truth had landed on the end of his nose, he still wouldn't have seen it.

So Kael didn't try to explain himself. Instead, he made a frantic lunge for *Deathtreader*. His fingers brushed the tips of the wrinkled pages before Declan jerked it out of his reach. Kael hadn't been expecting him to move so quickly. He fell forward — and accidentally grabbed Declan's forearm.

An image flashed before his eyes, startling him for a moment. But as the image began to take shape, Kael realized what was happening: it was the same thing that'd happened when Kyleigh showed him her memories. He realized that the image before his eyes must be one of Declan's memories — and he knew he should pull away.

But he didn't. And it only took a moment for the story to swallow him up.

He stood in the middle of the plains, a whole host of giants spread out around him. He saw the world through Declan's eyes, as if he lived inside his body. The giants he walked among stood together in neat lines, fully armed for battle. Kael was too short to see over them and when the lines grew too thick to weave between, he dropped on his hands and knees.

He crawled through a forest of massive legs towards the front of the line. He'd barely gotten a glimpse of what lay ahead when someone grabbed him around the belt and pulled him to his feet.

"Ho there, little Declan!" a deep voice boomed. "What are you doing the whole way out here? I told you to follow your mother."

The giant the voice belonged to had a deep-cut brow and a large, hooked nose. Even kneeling and hunched, he still towered over Declan.

"I came to join the fight, father." Declan's small voice rang confidently inside Kael's head. "I saw the banner of

Callan Horseman, and I knew this was where I ought to stand."

Callan's eyes were kind as he shook his head. "You can't fight with us today, son."

Callan's face came closer as Declan stood on his tiptoes. "Please, father. I may not be as big as the others, but I can still —"

"No, your size has nothing to do with it. Any man would be proud to have his son stand beside him in battle. But this is not a fight we're going to win."

"We aren't?"

This worried question didn't come from Declan, but from the man standing next to Callan. For some reason, he was so faded that Kael couldn't see his face, just the foggy outline of his body.

Callan turned to him, his eyes suddenly hard. "I've heard tales of these warriors — these *whisperers* who rebel against the crown. Steel means nothing to them. They wiped out half of Midlan's army with the flame from a single candle; they sunk the pride of His Majesty's fleet with a shirt button. Nothing can stop them, when they march as one. No, we'll not win today." Callan stood, and his voice boomed out across the sea of giants as he added: "But by the plains mother, we'll rattle them."

A noise like a thunderclap cut across Kael's ears as the giants rapped their weapons against their breastplates. Callan raised his scythe over his head, and with his every sentence, the giants rapped again.

"The earth will tremble where we meet. We'll clobber them so hard that their *souls* will have bruises. Oh no, they'll not soon forget the name *giant* — because we're going to carve it into their skulls!" Callan spun to the fields, and the fury of his thunderous words must've traveled the whole way to the seas as he roared: "For Prince, for clan, for homestead! *Charge!*"

The giants swarmed out to meet the whisperers — and in spite of his father's warning, Declan ran among them. The giant in front of him took an arrow to the helmet and fell.

With a cry that rattled Kael's ears, Declan picked up his scythe.

The rhythm of his charging steps matched the furious pounding of his heart. Declan's eyes locked onto the whisperer who'd fired the arrow, and Kael was surprised to see his mouth gape open in fear. When his second arrow flew wide, the whisperer turned and tried to sprint for his life ... but Declan caught him.

No sooner was one man dead than he flung himself onto the next. With every kill, the light seemed to dim and the noise grew louder. Soon, the world went black and the sounds of war raked against Kael's ears. He heard Declan's heaving, snorting breaths, heard the screams of the whisperers he met. And then very suddenly, everything went quiet ...

The darkness faded back as Declan's eyes snapped open, and Callan's monstrous face filled his vision. A large gash leaked blood down his forehead, and he looked worried. But when he saw Declan's eyes, he let out a triumphant roar.

"He's alive!"

Declan's breath quickened when a host of voices echoed his cry. Giants swarmed around him. Several reached down to clap him heartily on the shoulder.

"Fate's been kind to us today — we've beaten them back," Callan whispered. A shadow crossed his face for a moment, and his eyes hardened. "Your older brother fled, the coward! But I'll flay him on my own time. I'll not let him ruin your day."

The world spun as he hoisted Declan onto his shoulders, and Kael could see the huge crowd of giants gathered around them. There must've been hundreds of them — men from every clan. Their faces passed in a blur as Declan's eyes swept over them.

Kael saw two figures he might've recognized: they stood at the back of the crowd, and were far shorter than the others. But Declan's head spun away before he had a chance to study them.

"We've all of us been shamed today," Callan bellowed. "And I'm most shamed of all. For it wasn't your General who led us to victory, but this little fellow, here." He paused for a moment, and when he spoke again, his voice sounded much huskier than it had before. "From this moment on, we'll know him as *little* no more — but as Declan, a lion among men!"

The giants grunted and beat their scythes against their breastplates. They smiled up through their bruises and wiped the blood from their eyes with impatient swipes. But to Declan's ears, one small voice cut over all the rest:

"You did it, brother! You did it!"

There was a frustrated grunt from Callan as he bent down. "You too, eh? Do none of my sons listen to me?"

He fished a little boy out of the crowd and popped him onto his other shoulder. This boy was young, perhaps no older than six. He patted Callan's wounded head gently. "I *did* listen, father," he insisted. "I waited for the battle to end *before* I came out." Then he turned to Declan, his face open and glowing. "I saw you fight. You fought well, brother —"

The earth trembled as the memory shattered. The sky went black and the rain pounded him in lashing drops. He held someone in his arms — the same little boy as before.

The glow was gone from his face. His mouth hung slack. His eyes were empty. Kael clutched helplessly at the wound in the boy's chest, but it was too deep to mend.

Voices swam through his ears. He couldn't hear what they said. There was a rage building inside his limbs that he had no power to control. His ribs stretched against it, threatening to crack. His muscles swelled, trembling, screaming. Blood burned the backs of his eyes as he searched the crowd.

He found a face — his vision blurred so horribly that he could barely make it out. But he knew who it was. And he was going to pay.

Kael swung a sword at the man's face, screaming at the top of his lungs. He heard a satisfying shriek as the blade struck true. He lunged to finish him off, but strong hands held him back — a dozen of them, their fingers clamped around his arms and jerked the sword from his grasp.

Kael screamed. He screamed at the man he'd wounded, screamed until he could taste blood at the back of his throat: "I'm going to kill you! I'm going to kill you! I'm going to —!"

"Get out of my head!"

Kael's body flew against the wall, jerking him back into reality.

All of the wind fled his lungs. He heard the furious steps pounding towards him and he tried to run, but he wasn't fast enough. Declan fell upon him, wrapping an arm around his neck in a choking embrace.

"Get out of my head!" he said again, and Kael realized this wasn't Declan's voice at all — but a mad voice, a monstrous voice.

Kael's back thumped hard into the stall floor. Declan pinned him down with one knee. Thick veins bulged from his throat as he roared. His eyes were no longer gray, but a pointed black — like twin pits carved from the belly of the earth.

"Get out of my head!" Declan screamed. "Get out of my head!"

His hand was clamped so tightly around Kael's throat that he thought he could actually hear his bones bending backwards. He knew if he didn't do something quickly, he'd be crushed.

"Declan! What in all clods are you doing?"

Kael heard Brend's voice and cried for help. When Brend didn't respond, he began to thrash against Declan's hold, kicking his shins and pounding his fists into the tops of his bulging arms.

"Don't struggle, it'll only make it worse!"

"Then what am I supposed to —?"

But the second the air left his throat, Declan's hand crushed down tighter. Brend darted by and wrapped his arms around his middle. He heaved until his face turned red, but there was no moving him: Declan's eyes burned black as he watched the life slip from Kael's face.

The light in the stall began to fade. Darkness crept in. Kael raked through his memories and came across a mad thought, one last, desperate hope. He pressed his thumb into Declan's wrist and did what he'd done to Thelred — letting his memories of sleep slide into him.

Slowly, Declan's frightening eyes rolled back into his head, and he collapsed — landing squarely on top of Kael.

"What did you do?" Brend stood over them, pawing frantically at Declan. "You better not have killed him, you horrible little rat —!"

"I didn't!" he gasped, as Brend rolled Declan away. "I just knocked him out —"

"Well, you better not have killed him," Brend went on. He stuck his fingers against Declan's neck, feeling for a pulse. After a moment, he looked relieved. "You shouldn't have let him get so angry. He can't help it, you know."

"Can't help *what*?" Kael bellowed. He was still shaking. He'd thought for sure that Declan was going to kill him — no, not Declan: some black-eyed, screaming monster.

Brend's mouth sunk into a hardened line. "Declan's a berserker — but he can't help it, I tell you. His grandpa had it too."

"What in Kingdom's name is a berserker?"

"You know, one of the battle-mad." When Kael still looked confused, Brend sighed impatiently. "If Declan gets mad enough, he'll go berserk. His eyes'll go black, his strength will swell, and he won't know a thing he's done until he comes to. It's useful in battle, but dangerous if it gets out of hand. It's not common," he added, when he saw the worried look on Kael's face. "Declan is the only one of us who's got it."

Kael's head was spinning. He grasped at his sore throat and turned his neck to the side. That's when he realized that they weren't alone. Declan's screaming must've alerted the others: now the stall was completely packed full of curious giants.

"It's a shame, really," Brend went on. He grunted as he grabbed Declan under the arms and began dragging him towards his pallet. "All he ever wanted was to be the general — to follow in the steps of his father, Callan. And he *did* have a great mind for war. But the minute the battle struck him, he'd go berserk." He arranged Declan on his pallet gently, shaking his head. "A giant can't lead a host to war if he's too mad to give orders."

Kael knew the sort of madness Brend spoke about. It was the same thing that happened to him whenever he smelled a mage's blood. He couldn't help but think how miserable it must've been for Declan to go mad anytime he got angry. Kael was angry so often that he thought he might always be berserk, if he had it.

His throat still throbbed miserably, but he found he couldn't blame Declan for what he'd done.

"What'd you do to get him so fussed?" Brend sat cross-legged on his pallet, and his were not the only searching eyes on Kael.

He thought quickly about what he'd just seen, trying to find someway to explain it without giving himself away. "I ... I asked about his brother."

He jumped when the giants let out a collective gasp.

"Oh, no," Brend said, shaking his hands out in front of him — as if he might be able to stop Kael from doing it a second time. "Oh, you shouldn't have done that, wee rodent. No one asks about Dante. We don't even say his name."

"Why not?"

"He was Declan's wee baby brother," one of the giants hissed.

Several of them glanced at Declan, who was still fast asleep. The sorrow on their faces twisted Kael's stomach into a horrible knot. "What happened to Dante?"

Brend snorted and rolled his eyes, but a curious scarlet had begun to spread across his forehead. "Surely even the mountain rats have heard about how Titus forged the Five's armies."

370

Kael knew very well what Titus had done: he'd laid siege to nearly every village in the Kingdom, setting friend and kin against each other. Those who were willing to kill earned a place in the Five's armies, but were scorned as bloodtraitors by their people.

In a single act, Titus had set the whole Kingdom against itself — down to the last family.

"When the mages attacked us," Brend began, "our mothers and fathers met them bravely. But they were no match for the mages' spells. They were hunted down, burned to ash, every last one destroyed ..." He cleared his throat roughly. "It was Declan who rallied the children and gathered us at the Scepter Stone. It was the one place we thought no harm could reach us ... but we were wrong."

By this point, red singed Brend's face to the tops of his ears. Even the veins in his eyes looked bloodshot. "Titus tore our sisters away from us, and his army locked them inside the castle. Then he lined the boys up around the Scepter Stone. He gave every other one of us a sword, and the ones with swords were ordered to kill the giant on his right. I stood to Declan's right." Brend smiled hard. "I begged him to kill me quickly and be done with it — for Titus promised a mightily gruesome end to any boy who turned against him. But that stubborn clod wouldn't do it. Instead, he threw down his sword, stepped straight up to Titus, and what did he say, lads?"

"*My blood for their freedom,*" the giants murmured. Every one of their faces was as red as Brend's. The chilling look in their eyes made Kael's hair stand on end.

"What happened?" he said hoarsely.

"You know what happened." Brend's voice was hardly a whisper. "There were cowards in every clan — spineless clods who would've split a thousand hides to save their own. I won't tell you exactly how it happened, because it's not my story to tell. But I *will* tell you this: Dante was among those slain ... and believe you me, it's best if you never say his name again."

Chapter 30
The Razor's Edge

At long last, Jake's wound healed enough that he was allowed to leave the hospital and walk around on his own. He showed up at Nadine's door just as they were about to eat dinner. A smile peeked out of his bushy beard — which had grown so long that it stretched almost to his chest.

"It's about time you returned, shaman." Silas was trying his best to look indifferent, but Kyleigh noticed that the edge of his smirk was not quite as sharp as usual. The haughty glow in his eyes was almost forced.

Jake paused in the doorway. "Yes, well, now that I've finally been allowed out, I thought I might stop by and see you all. Also, I mean to shave." He held up the objects in his hands: a pair of goat shears, a bucket of mud, and a rather serious-looking razor. "I thought it might be best to be among friends ... you know, to help staunch the bleeding."

"We'll have cloths at the ready," Kyleigh promised.

Nadine led Jake over to the window and got him settled on one of her stools. It was so short that his knees came almost to his chest, and he had a difficult time deciding where to keep his elbows. Though he looked about as comfortable as a crow perched on the back of a spoon, he got to work immediately — clipping off his beard in thick, hairy strips.

As the beard shortened, Kyleigh thought she might actually be able to smell the happiness rising from Jake: it filled the whole room with a scent like cool wind across the seas, lightening all of their hearts. Nadine chatted with Silas, asking him all sorts of questions. But he didn't seem to mind — in fact, it looked as if he was rather enjoying the attention.

And Kyleigh leaned back against the wall, content to listen to the happy sounds of her companions.

For a moment, things were very nearly perfect. Then Elena showed up and flooded the room with her particular, spicy scent.

Silas groaned when he saw her. "No — go away."

Nadine swatted him with the back of her hand, and jabbed at him threateningly with her finger when he started to argue. Then she offered Elena a bowl of their dinner. "It is rice and dried fruit. I have mixed in a bit of goat cheese to temper the heat," she added, when Elena looked hesitant.

Kyleigh thought it might've been about the spice rice at first, but Elena wasn't even looking at the bowl: she was looking at Jake.

He happened to glance up and caught sight of her. His spectacles slid down his nose as he bent to gather his things. "I can leave —"

"No, you're going to stay put," Kyleigh said firmly. "As long as you insist on running around with sharp objects, I'm not going to let you out of my sight. Elena can stay and eat with the rest of us, or she can go sulk in the darkness."

And to her great surprise, Elena chose to stay.

They sat in a circle and chatted while they ate. The mots didn't use knives or forks, but ate their meals with their fingers. Jake couldn't talk and eat at the same time, and wound up getting most of the rice lodged in his half-trimmed beard. Silas, on the other hand, preferred to stick his face into the bowl as far as it would fit.

He gobbled up its contents and licked the bowl clean. Afterwards, he spent some minutes cleaning the debris from his face and hair with very cat-like swathes from the back of his hand — mumbling contented gibberish to himself as he worked.

Kyleigh had learned how to eat without spilling by watching Nadine. She expected Elena to fumble a bit, but she ate as if she'd eaten with her hands her entire life. Not so much as a grain of rice missed her lips. She said very little and kept her gaze on the wall, but Kyleigh felt as if she watched them all from the corners of her dark eyes.

Even after dinner was finished, Elena didn't leave. She sat quietly by herself in a corner of the room, polishing the glint back into her daggers. Kyleigh didn't want to leave her alone with Jake, but the sun was almost gone.

"We should probably head to your post," Kyleigh said to Nadine. "We don't want to give the Grandmot an excuse to salt your rice fields."

Nadine smiled. "I have no post tonight, outlander. These next days I will spend resting and tending to my armor, for my company is about to be called to take our turn in the tunnels. We are planning another attack on the trolls."

Kyleigh sank back to her knees. She hadn't been planning to stay this long. Their work in the motlands was finished: they'd restored all of Nadine's fortunes. She had enough rice to feed herself and, thanks to Silas, almost more goats than her little paddock would hold.

Now that Jake was finally healed, Kyleigh had been hoping to leave soon — tomorrow, even, if Jake felt up to it. But the thought of Nadine going back into the tunnels made her hesitate.

"They aren't going to force you to ring the bell again, are they?"

Nadine shrugged. "The Grandmot will cast the runes tonight, and the one whose name appears will be our sacrifice. If it is me, then that is well." She gripped Kyleigh's shoulder, and her smile was firm. "I promise you, I am right with Death."

When the last edge of the sun hovered over the mountains, it filled the whole valley with a warm, golden glow. Nadine gathered them at the window and drew back the curtain. They watched in silence as the Grandmot entered the speaking circle.

Hessa followed along beside her, and it made Kyleigh's stomach twist to see how the Grandmot's fingers twined around her little hand. For some reason, all she could think about was a spider — with all of its legs wrapped tightly around its prey, its pinchers waiting to begin the feed.

Kyleigh squinted, watching the Grandmot's sly eyes closely as she began to speak.

Her strange words echoed all around the valley; the bangles on her arms clattered together as she swooped them about. At long last, she drew the runes from a pouch at her belt. They rattled around in her fists for a moment. The valley was so quiet that they could actually hear the soft *clink* as the runes struck the ground. Then there was a long, weighty pause.

When the Grandmot spoke again, Kyleigh only understood one word, spoken like a bark at the end:

"Nadine!"

"Hmm, how surprising," Silas murmured.

Nadine stuck her chin out at him. "If that is Fate's choice —"

"It's not *Fate's choice*," Elena said, crossing her arms tightly over her chest. "It's the Grandmot's choice. She wants you dead, and she has the power to order it done. I've seen this sort of thing before." Her dark eyes roved to look out the window. "I wish you'd let me stick a knife in her."

"No knives," Nadine said vehemently.

"How about claws?" Silas interjected.

She jabbed a finger at him. "No. There will be no killing of the Grandmot. I know what you all are thinking." Nadine's eyes shined furiously as she swept her gaze around them. "And even if you are right, there is still this: our guiding mother was given her powers for a reason — for a purpose. However she chooses to use them, there is a purpose behind it. If my name is called one hundred times, it is for a purpose. You came to me for a purpose," she said quietly, and her eyes softened. "We are strange friends, but we have kept each other warm. And after so many months of darkness ... I feel you have given me light again. I feel I have found a new purpose, hidden in the strangest of places."

They fell silent. Not even Silas could think of anything to grumble back. Kyleigh thought she could feel the gratitude swelling inside Nadine's heart. It rose to overtake her, washing her in a warm, gentle tide.

She wasn't used to a human being so open with her emotions, and the sheer depth surprised her. She was struggling to think of something she might say in return when a soft noise drew their eyes back to the window.

Hessa had collapsed at the Grandmot's feet. She grasped at the hem of her black robe and brought it to her lips. Horrible, gut-wrenching sobs cut between her pleading gasps. Kyleigh felt her sorrow in the deepest corner of her heart.

"I could never do that," Elena said softly. Her eyes were wide, her face tinged with something between awe and fear. "I could never ... *beg.*"

When the Grandmot couldn't untangle herself from Hessa's grasp, she summoned the guards. Two women stepped forward and grabbed Hessa around the arms. As they dragged her away, the Grandmot turned back. Her eyes scanned the hived houses above her, stopping when they lighted on Nadine's.

Her feathers trembled as she raised her chin at Kyleigh. Her hand reached down to grasp Harbinger's hilt. He let out a woeful moan, calling for her.

Kyleigh's heart lunged after him. She grasped the edge of the window and had to use all of her strength to keep herself from leaping out. She spun away before the Grandmot could see her snarl.

"You'd leave that little girl without a mother?" Elena whispered. Her eyes were deadly calm as they lighted on Nadine. "What *purpose* can there be in that?"

Nadine said nothing. She stared down at Hessa, and her face twisted in an anguished knot as the guards dragged her away. The little girl hung limply in their arms for a moment, and Kyleigh thought she might've passed out. But then her eyes suddenly snapped open — and she broke free.

She charged past the Grandmot and stood in the middle of the speaking circle. Then she raised her hands to the sky and shouted something in the mots' singsong tongue.

As her words rang across the valley, the mots gasped. They broke their silence and began to titter furiously amongst themselves. Even the Grandmot looked shocked for a moment — before she grabbed Hessa and flung her back to the guards. This time, the little girl walked away on her own. And she kept her chin high as she went.

"What did she say?" Silas hissed, pawing at Nadine.

But she didn't answer him. Instead, she spun around. "I am going for a walk — alone," she snapped, when Kyleigh tried to follow her. Nadine kept her eyes forward as she marched from the room.

"I feel as if I've missed something," Jake said when she'd gone.

"It would take too long to explain, shaman. Go back to your trimmings," Silas murmured. Then he stepped close to Kyleigh, pressing his chest against her shoulder. "We have to do something, dragoness — not for the human, of course. I just don't like treachery."

"*Treachery* is the problem, is it?" Kyleigh raised an eyebrow at him, but he just glowered back. She realized that she'd never get him to admit that he actually cared about what happened to Nadine. Cats could be such silly creatures. "Well, I ought to be able to come up with some mischief. But we'll have to do something about those runes, first."

She glanced at Elena, who gave her a rare smirk. "That shouldn't be difficult."

It was all settled, then. Kyleigh lay back on the bed of pelts, her head swimming with a dozen different ideas — each more devious than the last. Silas sat down beside her, as if he somehow might be able to keep her on task by breathing into her ear. And Elena went back to her corner.

Jake had finished trimming the longest bits of his beard, and now had a thick layer of mud slathered over his face. He fumbled with the razor for a moment, struggling to pop it open. Then he jerked back when the deadly silver blade sprang free.

He stared at the razor for almost a full minute, flipping it over until the sharp edge faced his chin. He seemed to have

377

a difficult time deciding where to start: he turned the blade this way and that, like a man struggling at the keyhole.

Kyleigh was afraid he might cause himself real injury, and she was about to stop him. But Elena got there first.

"Hand it over." She snatched the razor from his hand and took the cloth from his shoulder — whipping it over her own. She knelt in front of him, but he leaned back.

"What are you —?"

"You obviously don't know how to handle a blade. And if you nick yourself, you'll stink up the whole room with your blood. Now, hold still."

Kyleigh made to jump to her feet, but Silas's arm stuck out like a bar across her chest. His glowing eyes watched them, and a curious smirk bent his lips. Kyleigh was so intrigued that she decided to wait — but she still kept a sharp eye on Elena.

Her strokes were swift and sure. She brought the razor down the side of Jake's face, leaving a line of clean skin behind her. As Elena worked, concentration softened her features: her mouth parted slightly, the harsh lines of her brows crept upwards. Her free hand rested gently under Jake's chin.

Kyleigh knew she shouldn't listen in, but it was obvious by the way Silas's head was tilted that he was already doing it. So she strained her ears in their direction.

"I'm usually not quite this hopeless," Jake said, as Elena paused to clean the razor. "But without a mirror —"

"Chin up," Elena barked, and he tilted his head back obediently. She began to scrape the stubble from his neck, working carefully. "I saw what you did, the day your friends were captured," she whispered. "You knocked the whole village off its feet with a single spell ... I had no idea you were so powerful."

Jake swallowed hard, and Elena took the razor away — so that she wouldn't cut him as his throat bobbed up and down. "I'm not powerful," he said scornfully. "I still carry a child's impetus."

"Why don't you make a new one?"

"I would, if I knew how to go about it."

"Aren't there books you can read?" Elena's mouth parted again as she concentrated on a tricky patch of hair beneath his jaw. "I thought mages were fond of learning."

"We are," Jake allowed. "It's just a rather complicated process. I doubt that you would even understand —"

"You're afraid," she said simply, cleaning the razor against the cloth. "You hold back your powers because you're afraid of the harm you might do, and you give no thought at all to the good."

Jake opened his mouth to retort, but she pressed a thumb against his lips, closing them. He blinked impatiently as she swiped at the hair beneath his nose. "I *do* think about the good," he insisted, the second she released him. "In fact, I think about it so often that it makes me miserable —"

"Why's that?"

"Because I'm *not* good! Don't you think I'd rather be the good sort of mage? I'd love to mix potions, or sell charms at the market — I'd even rather be one of those strange, hermit mages who live underground and chat with enchanted toadstools! But I'm not. I'm a battlemage. And blowing things up is all I'll ever be good for."

Elena finished the last bit of stubble with a few quick swipes. "So ... you're afraid of yourself?"

Jake huffed. "I suppose I am. What are you smirking about?"

She shook her head. "That's a stupid thing to be afraid of. *You* are the only person in the Kingdom that you have any control over. What you should be afraid of is the rest of us — and people like me, especially."

"Why should I be afraid of you? You're my friend —"

"What makes you think that?" she snapped. The softness left her features. Her eyes burned, and her brows dropped low.

Jake touched a hand to his face. "You helped me. That's something friends do —"

Elena pressed the razor against his throat, cutting his words short. Kyleigh smelled the danger and sprang to her

379

feet. She stepped behind Elena, putting her within arm's reach. If her wrist so much as twitched, even the minceworms wouldn't be able to find all of her pieces.

But fortunately for Elena, she didn't move. "I made it very clear why I did this, and it wasn't because I'm your friend, *mage*. I would still kill you if it suited me." She stood. And waving the razor furiously about the room, she added: "I would kill you all!"

"You could try," Silas murmured.

For a moment, Elena looked as if she might skin him then and there. But instead, she threw the blade down and stomped off into the darkness.

"No, wait — come back ..." Silas's words trailed off into a string of chuckles. "I can't even *pretend* to care about her without laughing!"

Jake said nothing. He stared at the empty doorway, one hand propped against his clean-shaven face. There was a look about him that Kyleigh didn't quite understand. But then again, magefolk were more difficult to read than the rest.

Jake gathered his things and said he was going to spend the night in the hospital: he suddenly wasn't feeling well. She supposed that might've had something to do with it.

Kyleigh and Silas waited up for Nadine. When she returned, they didn't speak — they simply got settled down for the night.

Sleep didn't come to her easily. Kyleigh felt herself stretched out between two worries: her worry for her friends in the plains ... and her worry for Nadine. Her thoughts pushed and pulled on her, stretching her heart thin as she struggled to find some peace.

When sleep finally did come to her, it wasn't peaceful at all — it was torment.

A horrible pressure suddenly crushed her from her sleep. Her muscles convulsed, writhing like snakes under her skin, twisting painfully in every direction. Something shoved against the backs of her eyes. It filled her head so tightly that she thought her ears might burst from the effort of trying to hold it in. A scream built up inside her chest, swelling until her throat ached.

Then it burst free.

"Dragoness!"

She was vaguely aware of Silas standing over her, how his eyes were wide with fear and how his hands hovered close to her skin, as if he was afraid to touch her. But she couldn't reach him. She couldn't stop her muscles from writhing, couldn't stop her nails from digging deeper into her flesh.

Tears streamed from the corners of her eyes, but they weren't the normal sort of tears: they seemed to burn everything they touched — her nose, her face, her lips ... and though they poured down, she couldn't seem to shove them out fast enough. Her throat stretched and ached, straining against them, throbbing with the promise of another scream.

Kyleigh's heart was the only thing in her body that seemed to belong to her, and it was as frightened as she was.

Just when she thought she might burst from her skin, she felt a pair of arms wrap gently around her shoulders. She was brought into the warmth, into a place where her tears could fall without burning. She felt a second heartbeat hum against her ear.

It was steady and deep. The rhythm matched the calming flow of the words — words that Kyleigh's ears didn't understand the meaning of, but her soul seemed to. Slowly, the aching left her body. All of the pain faded away, coaxed out by the words and the steady beat of the heart.

When Kyleigh opened her eyes, she realized that it was Nadine who held her. She held Kyleigh's head to her chest, and as the last of her song faded, she whispered:

"Hush now, there is no shame in your sorrow. I know what haunts you. I have cried those same tears ... perhaps my story will help quiet you."

Kyleigh was still too weak to respond. She lay in a sweaty, trembling mass in the middle of the pelts. Silas stoked the small brazier the best he could, though the feeble light of the pebbles was hardly enough to make any difference. He sat beside the window; his eyes were unmasked and wide as they stared at Kyleigh.

He didn't seem to want to be anywhere near her.

Nadine, on the other hand, settled Kyleigh's head into her lap. She felt the soft tug on her scalp as Nadine pulled the tie from her hair. Her fingers ran gently through the raven strands, and it calmed her.

Kyleigh wasn't used to having to be comforted. Very rarely was she hurt or frightened — and she'd never been wounded by something that she couldn't wound right back. But this was a strange enemy, one she couldn't defeat. She closed her eyes and let her ears tremble against the soft tones of Nadine's voice.

"My life has not always been how I wished it to be," she said quietly. "But I have had a good life. Hessa filled my heart with joy while I grew, and I thought I would never find a love more treasured. But when I was a young woman, I discovered a different sort of love.

"His name was Tahir." Her voice cracked a bit as she said it, but she cleared her throat roughly. "By the laws of my people, a woman may choose for herself when she is ready to marry — if she is ever ready at all. A man has no power to ask her ... except on one condition: if he saves her life, then he may ask. And she may not refuse him." Kyleigh could hear the smile in her voice as she continued. "I was convinced I would never marry. I thought my duty to Hessa would make it impossible. But ... I was wrong.

"Another tribe found their way into our tunnels one day, and I was called upon to fight them back. Our enemies were dark-fleshed men with blood on their faces. They wielded axes made of bone and rock. I underestimated their strength, and I was quickly thrown to the ground," she muttered. "Tahir ... he stepped over me, killing my attacker before my head could be crushed. And I knew I would be doomed to marry him.

"But he did not ask me." Her hand paused against Kyleigh's scalp, tickling her with its trembling. "When I asked him *why* he did not ask, he laughed at me. *You are Nadine, our*

Dawn's protector. I would not burden you with my love — but you may always hold it freely, and know that it was meant for you. It sounds more beautiful in our tongue," Nadine mused.

Kyleigh thought it sounded rather beautiful in the Kingdom's tongue. She couldn't imagine what it must feel like to have such words spoken to her ... and with a wrench of her throat, she realized that she might never find out.

She fought against a fresh wave of pain and focused herself on Nadine.

"Perhaps it was because he understood me so well, but I knew then that Tahir was my heart's bond," she whispered. "I asked him to marry me, and when he said again that he did not wish to burden me, I ..." She laughed, shaking her head. "I cut my hair! That is what all of our married women do: we cut our locks and put them in our husband's hands, as a symbol that our beauty will belong to him always. When I gave my hair to Tahir, I suppose he knew that I was serious. We were married and lived happily for several years, he and I — with Hessa as our daughter ... and then the trolls attacked."

Nadine's hand trembled again. Kyleigh reached up to her, and Nadine wrapped both hands tightly around her fingers.

"They came upon us swiftly, in the dead of the night. We were chased out of our homes. My first duty was to Hessa: I wrapped her tightly in my arms and carried her out here, to safety." She took a deep breath. "Tahir stayed behind in the tunnels. He led a company against the trolls, holding them back with the strength of his spear while the other mots escaped. They said he fought very bravely. If I have any honor left within our tribe, it is out of respect for Tahir. For I deserve nothing but shame.

"Long hours passed, and Tahir did not return. I was frightened for him. When Hessa fell asleep, I left her in the care of some of the other warriors and went into the tunnels to find my husband. I abandoned our *Dawn*," she said miserably. "I left Hessa's life in other hands — the very life I had sworn to protect with my own. And when I went into the tunnels, I saw that it was over ... that Tahir's men had been surrounded and swallowed up by the trolls. He was dead.

"I returned to the mountain, heartbroken. The Grandmot scorned me before our tribe for my betrayal. She took Hessa from me, and said I was not worthy to be the Dawn's protector. From that day forth, *she* would be the one to watch over Hessa — and I would not be allowed to see her again. These blows echoed through my heart like screams through the tunnels, for my soul was already empty." She spoke simply, as if this were a matter of fact and nothing more. There were no tears in her voice. "You asked me once if I wished to die, outlander — and now you know."

She placed a hand against Kyleigh's cheek. "I will not ask to hear who you cry for, but know that I understand. There are few hearts more desolate than mine. Sleep, now." Her thumb brushed a soothing line against Kyleigh's temple. "Sleep, and let the quiet of the night soothe your bones."

Kyleigh closed her eyes, but she couldn't sleep. Nadine's story didn't soothe her bones — it put a fire in them.

The mots were starving, they'd been driven from their homes, but the Grandmot didn't care about any of that. She'd grown to resent Nadine for the power she held — power that Nadine hadn't even thought about: Hessa's love. And she'd done everything she could to try to reclaim that power. She'd even used Nadine's grief as an excuse to take Hessa away.

But it was too late. Hessa already loved Nadine, already sought her wisdom above the Grandmot's. The only slight chance the Grandmot had to take her power back would be if Nadine was out of the way — lying dead in the depths of some tunnel. *That's* why the Grandmot hated Nadine. *That's* why she wanted her dead.

Well, as long as there was fire in her blood, Kyleigh wasn't going to let that happen.

Chapter 31
The Spring Sniffles

Things in the plains got steadily worse.

More guards came down from the castle, wielding wench-tongues instead of pikes, and they had no interest in being slavemasters. Whether or not the fields got planted wasn't any of their concern: they were out for blood.

They swooped in among the slaves, circling and waiting for a chance to strike. They walked the fields in groups, and would gladly pick off any man who strayed too far from his team. Giants were beaten senseless for walking too slowly, or being the last one out of the barn, or for no reason at all. One day, a giant was beaten so badly that he collapsed.

When the guards couldn't get him to rise, they threw him into the back of a cart and sent it for the castle.

Brend watched the cart roll away, a heavy fist planted on his chest. "Don't let him get to you, friend," he murmured. "May Death find you before Gilderick does." Then he dropped to one knee and ripped the next weed out of the ground with such force that it showered Kael with dirt.

They were deep in the vegetable patch, drawing out the many healthy weeds that had taken up residence amongst the beans and carrots. It was slow, tedious work. Kael knew that by the end of the day, every clump of grass would sit like stone, and their roots would feel a mile deep.

Some of the weeds were also rather vicious: the one Kael struggled with had a clump of tiny thorns hidden beneath its leaves, and it had already stung him once. He wrapped his fingers around a part he thought might be safe — only to find more thorns.

They bit into his fingers, but the sharp pain only made him angrier. He wrenched the plant from the ground with a roar and hurled it at the nearest guard. It struck his back with a satisfying *thunk*, showering bits of dirt and rocks into his armor. He spun, and murder lined his eyes as they lighted on Kael. But even though he clearly would've liked to beat him raw, he didn't move.

Declan worked a few paces away, and the guards went out of their way to avoid him. Even now, all he had to do was look up from his work and stare calmly in the guard's direction — and he immediately stomped away.

As soon as the guard was gone, Declan went back to weeding. He hadn't spoken to anyone since the mind-walking incident — not even to Brend. And Kael was slightly relieved.

He'd been so intent on discovering his secret that he'd expected Declan to out him the minute he woke up. Maybe he hadn't realized what had happened ... though he obviously knew that Kael had been inside his head — and that certainly wasn't a normal thing. The more he thought about it, the more he began to worry.

Why *hadn't* Declan told? What could he possibly have to gain by keeping Kael's secret to himself? As much as he wanted to believe that Declan wouldn't turn him over to Gilderick ... he didn't exactly trust him. He tried to watch, to peer beneath the deep shadow of Declan's brow for any signs of what he was up to, but he couldn't see a thing.

For not the first time that week, his stomach twisted into an uncomfortable, worried knot.

"What did you expect?" Brend muttered, when he saw the look on Kael's face. "Did you think he'd just open up and gab about it —? Ach!" He let out a loud sneeze, followed by a fit of violent coughs.

Kael reached over to pound him on the back, but Brend knocked his hand away.

"It's just the spring — ach — sniffles!" he gasped. When he caught his breath, he straightened up and cleared his throat. "I get them every year. It's nothing to worry about."

Kael wasn't so sure. He thought Brend looked rather pale.

******

Early the next morning, Kael woke to someone poking frantically in his ear. He batted the hand away and blinked back the fog of sleep until a very worried-looking Eveningwing came into focus.

"What is it?" Kael said groggily. "And what were you doing in my ear?"

"I was trying to be quiet," he whispered back. "I wanted to tell you something. But I wasn't sure where to poke —"

"Never mind," Kael mumbled, not wanting to try to follow whatever ridiculous path of reason the boy had come up with. "What did you want to tell me?"

"The swordbearers — the ..." he squinched his eyes shut tightly, "the *guards* — they're gone."

Kael sat up straight, rubbing impatiently at the sleep in his eyes. "What do you mean they're gone? They can't just be *gone.*"

"A great noise called them back to the castle," Eveningwing said, shifting his weight anxiously. "It sounded like a very large goose. Or perhaps a duck —"

Kael clamped a hand over his mouth as the cry of a battle horn trembled through the air. Its song was low and steady, a single note that had no meaning to him, but he knew very well might spell trouble.

"It was that," Eveningwing said when Kael released him.

"Are we under attack?"

"I don't think so —"

But they didn't get a chance to discuss it any further. The stall doors screeched open, and Kael hurried outside ahead of the others. He was one of the first in the courtyard. All across the Fields, the sprouts of fresh green lay sleepily in the earth, blanketed in a heavy layer of shimmering dew. His eyes combed across the thin morning mist, searching for a banner, or the telling glint of swords. But he saw nothing amiss — the land was quiet.

Kael still wasn't convinced. He spotted Brend crouched over one of the water troughs and went after him at a run. "Where are the guards?" he said when he reached him.

Brend looked up. His eyes were glassy and out of focus. He stared blearily at Kael for a few moments before he seemed to recognize him. "Ho there, wee rat," he mumbled.

His words trailed into a cough. It sounded as if he had a loose bone rattling inside his chest. When Kael asked if he was all right, he waved his hand impatiently. "I already told you — it's just the sniffles. Now, what are you shouting about?"

Kael hadn't been shouting about anything, but he lowered his voice and said it again.

Brend didn't seem too concerned. He glanced around at the empty land and shrugged. "Oh, Gilderick's probably just called them back for the Sowing Moon. He likes to keep his army close by, when others are around — and he knows we'll all behave because we don't want to get chosen."

Kael didn't understand three words of that. Brend wandered off, and he followed at a trot. "What's the Sowing Moon?"

"It's a festival," Brend said hoarsely. His brow creased in frustration and he cleared his throat. "It used to be a grand thing. All of the clans would gather together to celebrate the growth of their crops and the birth of their calves. There was food and drink, and games, too. A young man could win honor in the games," Brend smiled, "or the hand of the one he loved. See there?"

He held a finger up to the sky, where a faint outline of the moon still clung stubbornly to its perch. Its rounded halves were a bit uneven.

"In three days time, all of our crops will have sprouted and that moon will be full."

The Tinnarkians had always used the changes in the weather to mark their days, so it was strange to think that the giants followed the moon. Though Kael supposed it made sense: except for a light frost in winter, the weather in the plains was always warm and fair. Their days might run together if they didn't keep track of the moon.

"And you say that Lord Gilderick still celebrates the Sowing Moon?"

"Yes ... in his way," Brend said darkly. "Though he's twisted it to the point that hardly anybody can stomach it. Even the Five don't stick around —"

"Wait a moment," Kael interrupted, his heart pounding. "You mean to say that in three days time, the Five will be here? With their armies and everything?"

"No, it's not all that. Hardly anybody ever accepts — clodded leaky eyes!" Brend cursed, wiping them impatiently with the back of his sleeve. When he blinked, Kael couldn't help but think that his eyes were a little more bloodshot than they'd been before. "The Earl's usually too drunk to stay on his horse, and it's not nearly a grand enough event to interest the Duke. No, Baron Sahar and Countess D'Mere are the only ones who ever come out: he's here early, and she arrives late — both try to be gone before the games."

Brend had to cough a few more times before he found the breath to carry on. "I think Sahar only comes for the food. Desert fare is stringy at best, and Gilderick owes him a couple of castles. So the Baron stocks his larders a few times a year in payment. Gilderick's castle burned down *twice* — can you believe it?"

Kael certainly believed it. In fact, he happened to know the mischievous halfdragon who'd been responsible for the fires. He tried to steer the conversation back to the festival. "What happens at the games?"

Brend swallowed hard, and from the way he grimaced, it must've been painful. "I can't say, wee rat. All we know is that the day of the Sowing Moon, the mages choose a couple of slaves and send them up to the castle. They usually pick the sickliest ones, or some of those fellows from the seas. But the slaves that get chosen don't ever come back — not even as Fallows. I'm not sure what happens to them, but it can't be pleasant."

The information about the Sowing Moon was interesting, but Kael still didn't understand why Gilderick would risk leaving the slaves unwatched. Even the mages didn't seem too concerned: Hob stayed holed up in his cottage for a good portion of the morning, and only ventured out at midday. The whole thing made Kael uneasy.

The sun had begun to set when he finally got his answer.

A chorus of voices drew his eyes from the weeding, and he watched in amazement as a large procession of desert folk emerged from the Spine. He realized there must've been some sort of pass cut into it, a way to connect the desert and the plains — otherwise, the journey might've taken them several days.

There were dozens of desert folk, all traveling in a line. They carried heavy baskets across their backs, sunk low by the weight of glittering gold. The bright colors of their garments stunned the earth around them: brilliant yellows, fiery reds, and several shades of blues and greens. They clapped as they chanted, singing in a language that Kael didn't understand.

In the very middle of the line, eight guards held up something that looked like the top to a very fine carriage, supported by two long poles. The sunlight glittered off the carriage's gold trappings. Jewels winked across its surface, nearly blinding them with colorful bursts of light. Red curtains hid the inside of the carriage from view, but Kael thought he might've been able to guess who it carried:

Baron Sahar had arrived in the plains.

So *this* was why Gilderick had called his guards inside the castle. It wasn't that he needed the protection — it was because he didn't want the others to know of his troubles. If Sahar found out that Gilderick had lost nearly all his mages, how long would it be before the news reached the King? And once Crevan heard, Gilderick would surely be punished. He might even lose his position as a ruler.

So he'd had no choice but to call his guards away and carry on like nothing had happened. Kael realized that Gilderick would be vulnerable these next few days — which might just give him the chance he needed to fix things.

He was in the middle of trying to organize his thoughts when Brend interrupted him:

"Sun-loving sandbeaters!" He swayed a little as he stood, glaring at the desert folk. "They've got no business coming on our soil. By Fate, those mountains were put there for a reason — to keep you clods *out!*"

Though they were at least two bowshots away, he picked up a chunk of soil and tried to hurl it at them. It slipped out of his hand and plummeted straight to the ground.

The throw put Brend off balance. He stumbled backwards and likely would've fallen, had Declan not stepped up behind him. He caught Brend under the arms and led him to the edge of the field. "Sit down, rest your legs for a bit —"

"They've got no business!" Brend went on, his voice suddenly thick by what could've easily been anger or tears. "We should've been out by now —"

"Just calm yourself, try to take it easy."

But Brend would have none of it. When Declan finally got him to sit, he tried to rise by climbing up the front of Declan's shirt. "You were right — you've been right the whole while." He clung tightly when Declan tried to peel his hands away. "We're going to die like this. We'll be sent back down into the dust we've sobbed in!"

"You don't know that," Declan said, though now his eyes were wide with worry. "What's gotten into you? Are you sun-stroked?"

Brend's mouth opened as if he was about to speak, but the words never got out. His eyes rolled back into their sockets and his hands fell limply from Declan's shirt. Kael rushed over and caught his head.

He felt the alarming heat at the base of Brend's skull, and his stomach dropped. "He's got a fever."

"What do we do?" Declan's hands clenched and unclenched at his sides. His head shot to the left, where Hob was driving the water wagon towards them.

"We can't let the spellmonger see Brend — they'll take him to the castle!" someone hissed, and Kael realized that the whole team had gathered around them, staring worriedly at Brend. A crowd of giants would surely catch Hob's attention.

"Get back to work and try to act like nothing's happened," Kael said quickly. He sent one giant after some herbs from the garden and then left for the water troughs at an all-out sprint.

Hob was closer, but he thought charging the wagon would only raise more suspicions. He went from one barn to the next, searching frantically for something to carry the water in. He found an old bucket tossed out in the grass and could hardly believe his luck. When he tried to fill it, he discovered immediately why it had been thrown away: several large holes had been worn into its bottom, and they spat the water out nearly as quickly as he could fill it.

He plugged what he could with his fingers and held the bucket at an angle, keeping most of the water trapped inside. He moved at a trot and kept his steps smooth, trying not to slosh any of the water out. When he finally returned to the vegetable patch, he saw that the giants were clumped together again.

He swore.

"I told you to spread out," he hollered at them. "You have to listen ..."

But his words trailed away when a few of the giants stepped aside, and he saw that it wasn't Brend they were hunched over: it was Declan.

Three giants had fallen on him, plastering him to the ground with their bodies. He roared and squirmed against their hold, nearly breaking free. Two more giants had to jump in to keep him pinned down. His eyes were a deep, furious black.

At first, Kael didn't grasp it. "What happened?" He glanced everywhere for Brend, but couldn't see him. Then he saw the dust cloud rising from the road, saw Hob and the wagon heading straight for the castle — and with a horror that nearly sank him to his knees, he realized what had happened.

"They've taken Brend," one of the giants said, his eyes heavy with tears. "They've taken him to Lord Gilderick!"

****

It was almost dark before Declan tired himself out. Two giants hauled him back to the barn, holding his arms tightly behind his back. Even though his fury had drained his strength, he still had the energy to yell at them, and he ranted all through dinner.

He called the giants cowards. He said that if the ground was wet tomorrow, it was because their fathers were weeping in their graves. He said that their mothers would be ashamed of them. And the giants took their beating without a word.

They sat sullenly, and none of them took so much as a bite to eat. They slumped over the trough, flinching as if Declan's words bit through their skin. Several pressed the ratty hems of their shirts to their eyes, but no one spoke up against him.

Once Declan had the giants thoroughly beaten, he went after Kael.

"And *you*, you little rat —!"

"What have I done?" Kael snapped back.

He was just as furious about Brend as anybody else. He should've seen that he had a fever, and he should've done something about it. Had he not been so worried about his own blasted problems, he might've noticed it sooner. Now Brend was gone, locked up somewhere inside the castle — and he couldn't even send Eveningwing out to find him because the blasted bird had wandered off again!

But screaming at Kael wouldn't solve anything. There was nothing he could do, now — there was nothing any of them could do. They couldn't risk trying to sneak into a castle flooded with the guards of two rulers just to try and save one man. It would be folly. They might *all* lose their lives, and still fail to set Brend free.

But even though Kael knew this, it didn't stop Declan's words from stinging.

"What have you done? You've betrayed him — carved his heart out of his ribs!" Declan bit back his next words, and his face went dangerously smooth. "No, I shouldn't be blaming you. A rat's a rat, after all. He looks after his own hide, and he doesn't trouble himself with anybody else's. If there's anyone I ought to be angry with, it's me." The shadow left his eyes, and he fixed Kael with a look like stone. "I knew you were a schemer, but I thought you were a decent man. Now I see that I was wrong. I blame myself ... I should've snapped your filthy neck when I had the chance."

Kael went numb. He suddenly remembered that day in the wheat fields, when Declan had wanted to take him to the blacksmith to have his scythe fixed. He'd thought that Declan had been acting odd, and now he realized why: it hadn't been about the blade at all — he'd been trying to get Kael alone.

He'd been planning to kill him.

Declan stared him down. No one else would meet his eyes. And in their silence, he heard the truth. Kael's head suddenly felt light, as if it'd been filled with a cold, biting wind. He got to his feet and went into the stall without a word.

The night crossed overhead and the stars churned about the sky. Kael lay stiffly through the long hours of darkness, feeling the emptiness of Brend's pallet beside him. He shut his eyes against the moon's accusing touch as it drifted somberly through the clouds.

He kept reminding himself that he was doing what had to be done: the life of one man wasn't worth the lives of all the others. He'd chosen to do the wiser thing.

But wisdom was a sorry friend, that night. It whistled through the hollow of his heart, blowing neither cold nor hot — promising nothing but the chance to escape some greater ruin. And as the hour grew later, what he'd thought to be wisdom suddenly felt a lot like cowardice.

Perhaps Declan had been right about him, after all. Perhaps he *was* a rat.

Just before dawn, rain began to fall. Kael listened dully as it poured through the roof, as the sky shed the tears that he would not. He didn't move when the stall doors opened: the rain was falling too thickly now, and he knew that Hob would just send them back inside. It was going to be a long, miserable day.

When Eveningwing finally returned, Kael was alone in the stall. The halfhawk listened patiently as he told him what had happened. When he was finished, Eveningwing set out immediately — promising that he would scour the castle grounds for any signs of Brend.

Kael knew there was little hope for him now, and the others seemed to feel the same: the whole barn was eerily silent. The only noise was of Declan as he paced back and forth down the aisle. His quick steps were broken every now and then by a loud *clang* as he punched one of the iron doors. No one seemed to want to be the one to tell him that it was hopeless.

Dinner passed in miserable silence. The giants tried to get Declan to eat something. They stepped into his path and tried to force him to the trough, but he knocked them aside and kept pacing.

It was nearly time for the torches to dim when Eveningwing finally returned. He stumbled out of the stall; his hair dripped wetly onto his bare chest as he fumbled with the buttons of his trousers. When he looked up, Kael saw that his lip was bleeding. And he looked frightened.

"What happened to you?" he said, shoving through the crowd to reach him.

Eveningwing grabbed the front of his shirt. "I searched everywhere. I looked in every window for him. But I didn't see him. Then I was flying back here and I saw him walking down the path. I flew down to tell him that we were worried

— and he struck me." Eveningwing touched a hand to his lip. Confusion lined his face. "I'm not sure what I did."

"You didn't do anything," Kael assured him quickly. "Where is he now?"

"He's almost here."

Eveningwing glanced at the door, and dread began to boil inside Kael's gut. He tried to prepare himself for what he would see, but when the doors flew open, he still felt the earth drop out from beneath him.

Brend stood in the doorway. His arms hung limply at his sides and his mouth sagged open. He stared vacantly at the far wall. His eyes were fogged over and dulled — all of the glint and the mischief were gone from them ... never to return. For Brend was *Brend* no longer:

He was a Fallow.

Chapter 32
Across the Threshold

"Brend!" Declan charged down the aisle and tried to grab him around the shoulders, but Brend was too strong. He jerked himself free with an unintelligible grunt. Then he slugged Declan across the jaw.

The noise it made was like a slab of raw meat striking the tabletop, and Declan went down hard. Brend trudged past him without a second glance, his deadened face pointed for the Fallows' stall.

One of the giants helped Declan to his feet. "There's nothing you can do for him — he's gone."

But Declan didn't seem to hear. He stared after Brend, clutching at the thick red knot that had sprung up on the side of his face. Hurt filled his eyes from bottom to top. For a moment, it looked like it might spill over into tears.

Then the torches dimmed, and the hurt vanished — replaced quickly by a determination so fierce and dark that Kael could almost sense what was going to happen next. And he could do nothing to stop it.

Declan tackled Brend from behind. He was still lying flat on his stomach when Declan grabbed him around the ankles and began dragging him backwards. Brend grunted angrily, twisting and flipping like a fish caught on a line. His arms swung back, but he couldn't seem to figure out how to free himself. And with a mighty heave, Declan chucked him into the stall.

The giants inside bolted out immediately — some fled with bits of their pallets clutched in their arms, diving into the safety of the other stalls. When Brend tried to follow them out, Declan stuffed him back inside with a sharp thrust of his heel.

Kael, who'd been watching the whole thing with no small amount of shock, suddenly felt his feet leave the ground as Declan grabbed him and hurled him into the stall with Brend — who swatted him against the opposite wall.

He watched, dazed, as Brend tried to escape a second time. But Declan shoved him back. Then the doors began to close with a horrifying screech.

"What are you doing?" Kael shouted. "You can't lock us up in here — he'll kill us!"

"No, because you're going to fix him," Declan replied, kicking Brend backwards. When the door had closed enough that Brend couldn't escape, Declan tackled him again, this time wrapping an arm around his throat.

Kael saw a flash of movement out of the corner of his eye and turned to see Eveningwing slide in at the last moment. "No — get out of here!"

But it was too late. The door shuttered at the end of its track and Kael knew they were trapped — trapped with a roaring, dead-eyed Fallow who would rip them all to shreds the second he was free. He struggled viciously against Declan's hold and showed no signs of ever tiring, while Declan's face grew red, and his arms began to tremble with the effort.

"Fix him," he grunted, tightening his legs around Brend's.

Kael was furious. He pushed Eveningwing behind him and yelled: "How? How in Kingdom's name do you expect me to *fix* him? He's dead, Declan!"

"No he isn't —"

"Yes, he is! Brend's gone. He's not in there anymore — he's nothing but an empty husk. You said so yours —"

"He's not dead!" Declan cried. His eyes burned red with desperation, veins bulged from his neck. "He isn't gone. Not yet. He's just not right in the head, is all. And that's why you're going to fix him. You're going to get inside his head — just like you did to me. And you'll bring him back." He gritted his teeth tightly. The effort sent a tear burning down his cheek. "You know he's all I've got left ... he's my only family.

And if you don't help him," he choked, glaring, "then I swear we're all dead men."

His words were the words of a madman, the last request of a man so stricken by grief that he no longer cared if what he said made any sense. Anybody else would've slapped him across the face and told him so. Anybody else would've said that what he asked for was impossible — insane, even. But Kael was not like anybody else.

And he thought Declan's idea might be very possible, indeed.

All at once, *Deathtreader* was in his head, speaking as if he had the book opened in front of him: *I always start with the eyes*, it whispered. *The eyes are ever-open doors ... and the secrets of the mind lay just behind them.*

Kael looked at Brend's eyes. They were empty and lolling, yes — but not quite hidden. They weren't completely frosted in white like Casey's had been: he could still make out the pupil and pale grays.

He stepped up to Brend and grabbed either side of his face. The sudden touch seemed to daze him — and for a moment, he stopped fighting. *Then I lock eyes with my subject,* Deathtreader's voice went on. *I look deep into the black and imagine that I'm standing on the edge of a high cliff. The cord between us tightens, I feel the earth begin to slip away, but I do not fight it. Instead, I hold my breath and prepare myself for the plunge.*

Kael's hands began to tremble as he realized what he was about to do. No promise to Morris was worth a man's life. He'd had a chance to save Brend before, and he hadn't done it. Instead, he'd cringed in the safety of the barn and told himself that wisdom was more important than friendship.

Maybe it was. And if that was the case, then there was a very good possibility that Kael didn't have his boxes stacked in the right order. But he was all right with that: there were far worse things than being a fool.

So as he met Brend's eyes, Kael held on tightly.

And then the world slipped away.

****

Kael stood in a long hallway. It was wreathed in soft light and lined with sturdy doors. He realized that this must be the Threshold: the room at the front of the mind that Deathtreader said would lead to all others.

The hall stretched endlessly, disappearing into a black that he couldn't see beyond. He searched the walls for some marking or embellishment, any of the subtle clues that Deathtreader said to look for. But the walls were completely bare.

There must've been hundreds of doors, each carved from oak and set plainly into their frames. Where should he look first? What should he even be looking for? He had no idea what had happened to Brend. He had no idea where he might find out. What had he gotten himself into —?

Quite suddenly, the hallway began to blur and the colors waved in front of him, rippling like the reflection on a pond. He knew he was panicking. This was exactly what had happened to Deathtreader the first time he tried to mind-walk: he panicked, the world blurred, and he was spat straight back out. Kael knew if he didn't want to get thrown into reality, he would have to calm himself.

He breathed deeply, and the ripples began to fade. *I can solve this*, he thought to himself. *I can figure this out.* When the world was steady once again, he set out across the Threshold.

As he moved down the hall, he was careful not to open any of the doors. Monsters lurked in the Threshold — menacing beasts of madness and doubt. They would attack without mercy, and it wasn't just Kael they would try to devour: they'd feast on walls and doors, on morals and memories — anything they could wrap their horrible jaws around. And as they ate, they would grow stronger, feeding until they consumed Brend's entire mind.

Deathtreader had once let a monster of madness loose in a nobleman's head, and the poor fellow had wound up driving a dagger through his own heart to escape it.

So as Kael traveled down the hallway, he was very careful. He stopped and listened at the doors. Sometimes he would hear nothing, and sometimes he heard voices. They were memories, mostly — people and moments that Brend held dear to him. Kael knew they were only memories because they were spoken so faintly. According to *Deathtreader*, hopes and dreams were much louder.

"Come this way."

Kael jumped and spun around. It sounded as if the voice had come from right behind him, but there wasn't anybody there. "Hello?"

"Come this way," it said again, this time from down the hall. "There's something I want to show you."

Kael stepped forward. "Do you know what happened to Brend?"

"Yes, yes ... come this way. There are things you need to know."

He followed the voice down the hall, listening until it stopped. The silence felt strange to him. He wondered where his guide had gone. "Hello? Where are you?"

"Look in here."

A doorknob rattled on his left. He reached for it.

"Yes, yes ... you'll find your secret in here."

Mercy's sake — the secrets! Kael had forgotten about them. He jerked his hand back, his heart pounding. There was no telling what sort of horrible trap they were trying to lead him into.

He walked away, but the secrets kept calling to him. There were dozens of them, they talked over each other and seemed to grow louder with every step. He stuffed his fingers inside his ears and hummed, trying to tune them out.

He didn't know how long he searched, but he got no closer to finding Brend. The hallway never ended. The doors all looked the same — and with the secrets screaming at him, it made it impossible to hear what was behind them.

No clues lined the blank walls. He was far too terrified to open any of the doors. But even though he desperately wanted to panic and escape, he didn't. Brend was counting on him.

So he had to be brave. He had to press on.

He closed his eyes and began to comb through his memories of *Deathtreader*. Words and stories flashed across his eyes; he could practically hear the crinkle of the pages as he flipped through them. Then he came to the story of the sleeping girl, and he stopped:

She was not in our world and not in Death's, but stuck somewhere in between. I walked the Threshold twice over before I realized this, and then I felt like a fool. If she was not there or there, then she must be here*: in the mind with me. And if that was the case, then surely all I would need to do is —*

"Call her," Kael finished aloud. He didn't know if Brend was still in the mind or not, but it was the best idea he could think of. So he unplugged his ears and shouted: "Brend!"

Nothing. Not so much as a mumble came back to him. And to make matters worse, the secrets all began squawking "Brend!" as loudly as they could.

Kael tried his best to ignore them. "Brend!" he shouted over their chanting. "Brend! Brend! Br — oh, shut it! Shut up!"

He kicked the walls and beat them with his fists — which only seemed to amuse the secrets. They broke out in round of ear-piercing cackles, screeching all the louder when Kael began to swear.

He was thinking very seriously about finding a monster of doubt to devour them when a powerful voice shook the halls:

"Here!"

The secrets went silent, the light in the hallway brightened, and Kael knew it was Brend who'd spoken — he was alive!

"Where are you?"

"Here!" Brend said again, and something rattled loudly at the end of his voice.

Kael followed the rattling sound, calling out every now and then, listening for Brend's reply. He followed the noise to a door. When he called a final time, Brend's reply shook it soundly — jolting it on its hinges. He knew without a doubt that Brend was trapped behind it.

He grasped the handle, pausing as he remembered what *Deathtreader* had said about going through doors: *Once I decide to step in, in I must go. It's far too dangerous to linger in a doorway: it would be better to lock myself up with a monster, than have set it loose upon the world.*

With that steeling thought, Kael pulled the door open. He stepped inside and quickly slammed it shut. Nothing could have prepared him for what lay behind it.

The first thing he saw was Brend: his face was gaunt and pale, his limbs were thinner than Kael had remembered them being. Black, shining chords bound his arms and legs, holding them captive against a monstrous shadow.

The shadow was easily twice Brend's height and cut roughly into the shape of a man. Its flesh shined wetly and seemed to bubble up as it shifted its weight. The shadow's great limbs were connected to Brend's, and it wielded him like a child's toy: when the shadow stepped forward, Brend's leg rose with it.

Brend raised his head, and his chin trembled as he muttered: "Here ..."

Then his head collapsed upon his chest, and Kael watched in horror as the shadow swallowed him up. It pulled him into its folds and sealed his body away with a horrible, smacking sound.

The room shook as the shadow rolled its head back. The black lumps across its face became a nose and a mouth. From the top of its skull sprouted a familiar shock of hair. Then it clasped its hands above its head — and brought them down with a roar.

Fear sent Kael into a dive.

He narrowly missed being crushed to death. The shadow's arms came down, and he rolled away — grasping at his memories, trying to figure out what to do.

403

I would rather do battle in the mind than anywhere in the actual realm, Deathtreader had written. *For here there are no limitations of strength or flesh: I may wield any weapon I choose.*

That was it! He remembered the stories, now — of the times when Deathtreader had no choice but to fight. A man couldn't *carry* a weapon into the mind: he had to imagine it.

Kael's bow was the first thing that came to him. He gasped a little when he felt his hand curl around its familiar, worn leather grip, but managed to keep his concentration. The gray shaft sprouted from the grip, complete with its strange, curling marks. The string bent the bow tight. Kael reached behind him and felt the coarse fletching of his arrows. He nocked one swiftly and took his aim.

He didn't want to risk striking Brend, so he fired for the top of the shadow's head — and grinned when it struck true.

The shadow stumbled backwards for a moment, its large feet leaving a trail of sticky black goo behind, and Kael thought it would surely fall. But at the last moment, it regained its balance. Black tendrils sprouted from the shadow's head and wrapped around the arrow's shaft, sucking it down into the blackness — just like it'd done to Brend. Then the monster advanced.

Its gooey flesh quickly swallowed Kael's next two shots, and he realized that the bow wasn't going to do him any good. Perhaps if he hacked the shadow into pieces, he might be able to pull Brend free.

A sticky arm swooped over his head, and Kael didn't have time to imagine anything specific — just something sharp. He swung blindly above him and heard the shadow roar as a good portion of its arm fell away. He was surprised when he looked down and saw a giant's scythe clutched in his hands.

But his blow didn't stop the shadow's charge. The severed end of its arm melted and ran back into its legs, and a new arm sprouted up from the stump. Kael was so busy staring that he didn't see the shadow's other arm — until it caught him in the chest.

It felt as if he sailed backwards for a full minute. When he finally struck the wall, he collapsed in a heap upon the ground. The shadow's rumbling steps shook the floor as it hurried towards him, swinging its arms madly as it fought to pull its sticky feet free, closing the gap between them at an alarming pace.

Kael ached all over, but he dragged himself to his feet. Bits of the shadow stained his shirt. When he stuck his fingers to it, he realized that it felt more wet and slick than sticky. Almost like grease ...

An idea came to him, so swiftly that he didn't have time to doubt himself. The shadow's arm shot out to grab him, and Kael imagined that he was holding a torch. Heat crossed his hand as the torch flared to life. He grit his teeth and thrust the orange blaze into the monster's middle.

Fire burst from the end of the torch. It swarmed over the shadow's flesh, roaring as it ate. The flames fed greedily through the greasy layers. Great chunks of shadow sloughed off and struck the ground, where they were quickly burned away.

Though the shadow flailed its limbs and threw its body upon the floor, it couldn't stop the fire from doing its work. Within seconds, the monster had disappeared, leaving only a trail of smoke in its place.

Brend now stood alone in the middle of the room, alive and unharmed. He smiled as he took a deep, shuddering breath. Kael had made to run towards him when a great blast of wind threw him backwards. He rolled into the hallway and the door slammed shut behind him. He scrambled to his feet, prepared to charge back in ... but then he noticed something odd.

The Threshold had changed. Tapestries now lined the walls, filled to their ends with pictures of people, lands, and beasts. Shelves stood beside the doors, each one covered to the top with plain, sturdy trinkets.

Kael nearly cried out in relief.

This was how the Threshold was supposed to look. It was supposed to be bright and full. Brend's spirit must be free. He must've returned to the Inner Sanctum, the place Deathtreader called *the house of the soul*.

Kael's work was done, then. Brend was the master of his own mind once again.

There was a part of him that wanted to stay, to wander through the halls a little longer and discover all of the places that Deathtreader had spoken of. But Kael knew it would be wrong of him to stay any longer.

So he walked back down the hall, to the front of the Threshold, and went out the way he'd come.

****

"Kael!"

Footsteps slapped the dirt floor as Eveningwing rushed to his side. His body rolled over, and the earth ground against his back. Two worried amber eyes blinked down at him.

"Are you hurt?" Eveningwing said, his gaze flicking over Kael's face. "You fainted — I couldn't reach you in time."

Kael was thinking about how to respond when a very welcome voice growled in his ear: "Let go of my neck, you great filthy midget!"

Declan gasped and jumped backwards, letting Brend struggle to his feet. He rubbed his throat and gazed about him slowly, as if he was trying to figure out where he'd wound up.

Declan punched him in the arm.

"Ow! What's that for?"

"You gave us all a fright, you clod!" Declan said, though his grin didn't quite match the severity in his voice. "We didn't think you'd ever make it back to us."

Recognition crossed Brend's face, and for a heart-stopping moment, Kael was afraid he might remember. "Oh, *that*. That was just a wee fever — nothing to be worried about. I'm all well now." He took a deep breath through his nose. "See? The sniffles are all gone!"

Declan glanced in Kael's direction, but in the end, he seemed to decide that it was kinder to let Brend believe that he'd only been down with fever. "Whatever it was, we're glad to have you back."

Brend glanced curiously about the empty stall. "Where'd everybody go?"

"They spent the night elsewhere. No one wanted to catch your sniffles," Declan said. He curled up on his pallet, a wide grin still on his face.

Brend just shrugged. "Well ... I suppose that's fair enough."

Chapter 33
Unwary Revelers

Kyleigh wasn't sure what time she woke. It was still dark outside, but the air smelled a bit livelier — like the hours had tilted further from night and more towards dawn.

Restless knots bunched up in her limbs, and she knew she wouldn't be able to fall back asleep, so she didn't try. Instead, she crawled out of bed and went in search of something to do.

She was alone as she climbed down the spiraling steps, not even the farmer-mots had risen yet. She followed the winding paths through the mountain, her mind consumed with all she had to do. The next time she blinked, Kyleigh was standing in the hospital.

There was only one small light burning in the back of the room, and she went for it at a jog. It looked as if she wasn't the only one having a sleepless night: Jake sat alone at a small table, his head propped up against his fist. His journal lay open, but the charcoal sat unused next to his elbow. He tapped one finger against the large glass jar that sat in front of him.

A minceworm had been packed inside of the jar just as tightly as it would fit. The poor creature squirmed miserably against the glass walls, its skin made a squeaking sort of noise as it struggled to get comfortable.

"I thought they were more like bees," Jake muttered, when Kyleigh's shadow crossed over him. "But they've got these little pouches in the shallow parts of their stomach. Whenever they feed, half of their meal gets trapped inside that pouch. And then they try to take off." He waved his hand out in front of him. It was a halfhearted gesture. "They turn north — almost as if they've got very important business. I think they're trying to deliver that extra food somewhere. So they're not like bees at all: they're more like ants. I was wrong about them," he said with a sigh. "Turns out that I was wrong about a lot of things."

Kyleigh had a feeling that the slump in Jake's shoulders wasn't *all* about the minceworms. She sat down beside him and put her arm next to his. "It sounds to me as if you're a mage in desperate need of a task."

"Please, anything," Jake moaned.

Kyleigh hadn't been able to work out a plan on her own. She had lots of little thing buzzing around her head, but no way to tie them all together. And she wasn't sure which of them might be best.

Fortunately, Jake was rather good at that sort of thing. Kyleigh tossed out some ideas, and he got them organized — trimming the good bits up, while throwing the most dangerous ones aside. It wasn't long before they had a very roughly-drawn plan.

"It'll be like damming up a river," Jake said excitedly. There was a spark of new life to him now, an eagerness in his movements as he pushed his spectacles firmly up the bridge of his nose. "Here — I can show you on the map."

Kyleigh was slightly surprised. "When did you have time to draw a map?"

"I've been trapped in the bowels of a mountain for weeks: I've had enough time to write a book about the motlands, if I needed to." Jake looked at her curiously. "What have *you* been doing?"

She shrugged. "Eating, sleeping ... keeping Silas out of trouble. It's all very important business, I'll have you know."

"Indeed," he said with a smile.

He showed her the map, and it didn't take them long to figure out how to get the trolls taken care of. "There shouldn't even be a mess," Kyleigh said approvingly.

Jake nodded. "I think that'll be our best route of attack — as long as everything goes according to plan, that is. If not, things could end rather ... badly." He closed his journal, and his hand rested on the cover for a weighted moment. "I've been doing some research on trolls — oh, don't make that face," he said when Kyleigh groaned. "Fine. I won't go into the details. But let me just say that I believe this particular breed of troll comes from near the Red Spine. Desert folk have lived in that part of Whitebone for centuries, which would explain why these trolls have developed such human-like fighting skills. And as they likely didn't cross *over* the desert —"

"You think there might be tunnels leading from here to the Baron's castle?" Kyleigh finished for him. When Jake nodded, she felt relieved. "Well, that should clip a good bit of danger off our journey."

"Yes ..." Jake picked at his book for a moment, flicking his thumb absently against its spine. "You know, I've been thinking —"

"I'll try to hold back my complete and utter shock."

He made a face at her. "I've been thinking a lot about the minceworms, and I believe there might actually be a large, queen worm buried somewhere in the desert — much like there would be in an anthill. It would explain why there aren't any eggs in the separate nests we find, and why the worms carry part of their food north. And I thought, since we were heading north anyways, that we might be able to —"

"Find the queen of all minceworms and give her a poke? Absolutely not." Kyleigh had to fight hard not to laugh at how disappointed he looked. "Jake, even if we managed to find a jar big enough, I don't see how you'd cram her in it —"

"Joke all you want to, but this is important to me," he said, stuffing his journal roughly into the folds of his robe. "I've always dreamed of doing something like this: of discovering new lands, new species, a new people, even — and jotting it all down for somebody else to read. It's the mark of a good mage," he added, getting to his feet, "to be able to pass our knowledge down to others."

He made to stomp off, but Kyleigh grabbed the hem of his robes. "I'm sorry — truly, I am," she insisted, when he snorted. "I'm not used to having so many lives depending on me. I've never been the leader before, and I'm not sure I'm cut out for it. I suppose that joking about it is the only way I know to cope."

"I see." Jake sat back down. "Do you think that might be a species trait? Do all halfdragons use humor as a means for coping?"

"I don't — what are you doing?"

Jake had whipped his journal back out of his robes and was busily flipping through the pages. "I was so hoping we'd have a chance to talk about this. I've already got a space prepared — see?"

He held up his journal, and on one of the pages was a neatly scrawled title: *Conversing with a Halfdragon.*

"That way your name won't be out there for everyone to read," he explained. "We can keep things anonymous."

"Brilliant," Kyleigh muttered as she got to her feet.

"Where are you going? I thought we were going to have a talk."

"Not a chance. We've got loads to do, and only a little time to do it in."

Kyleigh left — grinning when she heard Jake's disappointed huff from behind her.

****

On the night before the battle, Nadine declared that she wanted to sleep outside. "I have spent so much of my life underground that I never thought to miss the stars. It is strange, but I think if I do not see them tonight, I will miss them."

So Kyleigh followed her out to the paddock.

With the sun gone, the farmers had all returned to their homes. The only noise was of the goats' sleepy grunts and the hum of the wind. They spread out on the soft grass, watching the stars as they wheeled overhead. The silence between them was light: Nadine seemed content to keep her fate pushed far behind her, and to focus on other things.

They'd only just gotten settled when a dark figure wandered up to them. The sharp lines of Elena's shoulders stood out against the glittering sky, as if she'd been cut from it, leaving a dark hole behind. When she spotted Kyleigh and Nadine, she raised her arm in greeting. There was a rather large jar clutched in her hand.

Nadine sat up. "Is that rice wine I smell?"

Elena shrugged. "I don't know what it is. But it smelled like liquor, and I thought we could all use a drink. I swiped it from the Grandmot," she added, when Nadine reached for it.

She hesitated for a moment — then quite suddenly, she snatched the jar from Elena's hands. She braced it against her lips and a little stream of wine trailed down her chin as she swallowed. "There is nothing more she can do to me," Nadine gasped, passing the jar off to Kyleigh. "So I might as well drink!"

"That's usually how I feel about things," Elena agreed.

They sat in a tight circle and passed the jar around. On its way down, the wine burned every bit as fiercely as the rice. But there was an earthiness to it, perhaps from the juice of fruits. The sickly-sweet grit coated Kyleigh's tongue, and by the time the jar came back around, she was ready to brave the fires once again.

She only took a few drinks — just enough to numb her fingers and toes. She knew she would sleep easier with the wine in her blood, but she certainly didn't want to overdo it. She'd seen the effects of spirits on unwary revelers, and had no wish to have her senses muddled.

But her companions must not have known the dangers, because they drank even after the wine had made them silly.

It turned out that Elena actually had a real smile hidden behind her terse lips — and a laugh, as well. Nadine spoke in her native tongue half of the time, and Elena answered her back with gibberish. They talked and joked as if they'd known each other all of their lives. Their spirits were impossibly high one moment, then they argued the next — only to burst out laughing once again.

Kyleigh leaned back on her elbows, content to ride along the bucking waves of their chatter. It was fascinating to watch humans like this. They worked so very hard to keep their feathers slicked back that it made her grin to see them come undone.

But as the night went on, their spirits waned. And their happiness dipped down rather suddenly into darkness.

Kyleigh listened, hardly breathing, as Elena told her story:

" ... I thought I loved him, but it didn't ... didn't happen like I thought it would. Is that what love's supposed to be like?" Elena said thickly. Her mask was gone, and years of hurt stained her face.

Nadine shook her head. She reached across and grasped Elena's shoulder clumsily. "That is not love — it is defilement. And in my culture, if a man defiles a woman, every member of her family may beat him with the backs of their spears — three blows each. Then, he is stripped naked and sent out to wander the desert at nightfall." She jerked her arm towards the Spine, so forcefully that she nearly lost her balance. Elena had to grab the front of her dress to keep her from toppling backwards. "If he survives the minceworms, then he has proven his innocence. But," she laughed, "it has never happened."

"I imagine that's a pretty effective punishment," Kyleigh mused.

Nadine held up a finger. "It is one of those rules that need only be broken once."

Elena stared at the desert, swaying a little under the effects of the wine. "Are all men such ... wolves?"

"No," Nadine said firmly. "They are not. My Tahir was a good man. He loved me truly, and he never left my side — even though ..." she choked and clutched a hand to her lips, "even though I am barren!"

She started to sob, then, and Elena cried along with her.

Kyleigh didn't know what to do. These weren't the sort of tears she was used to — the silly tears Aerilyn used to cry whenever she got her feelings hurt, or the sharp, final tears that flowed after death. These were tears that had been

413

buried, and buried deeply. They'd sat under years of pain and anguish, festering in the coldest chamber of the heart. Now they'd finally come bursting out.

And Kyleigh wasn't sure how to comfort them.

"You've been a good mother to Hessa," Elena said, squeezing Nadine's hands tightly. "I would've killed to have a mother as kind as you."

"And if I ever meet that Holthan, I will gladly beat him with my spear," Nadine promised. "The black will never fade from his bruises."

Elena wiped at her eyes. "That's the kindest thing anybody's ever said to me ..."

While they sniffled and dried their tears, Kyleigh quickly poured the rest of the wine into the nearest rice field. "I think we all need to get some sleep," she said, gathering them up. "We've got a long day ahead of us tomorrow."

"I agree," Nadine murmured.

Kyleigh lay back, and she was surprised when she felt Nadine bury her head against her shoulder. Elena stared at them for a moment, swaying. Then she tried to stand up.

Kyleigh grabbed her by the front of her jerkin. "Come here, you," she growled, pulling Elena down on her other side.

She struggled at first, but couldn't wriggle out from under Kyleigh's arm. In the end, she seemed to give up. It wasn't long before both women were breathing heavily into Kyleigh's neck. And the minute they fell asleep ... her own tears began to fall.

Her friends were such fragile things. She could've crushed them both on accident. Yet, they held so much hurt — more hurt than Kyleigh thought she ever might've been able to bear. She cried because she happened to want someone who didn't want her back. But these women had lost so much more. They'd endured so much more. And it had taken nearly an entire jar of wine to coax their sorrows out.

As the night stretched towards dawn, Kyleigh couldn't help but think that perhaps she wasn't as strong as she thought she was. She held her little friends tightly, and swore by the stars above them that she would protect them.

She couldn't wipe their hurt away ...

But she would live to make sure they were never hurt again.

****

Kael woke the next morning, and for the first time in a long time, he felt at peace. The weather was warm, but not unpleasant. The air was crisp, the breeze was gentle, and lively new scents blossomed from the earth.

Spring had been creeping up on them for weeks, and it appeared as if she'd chosen this particular day to make herself known. Kael looked out at the fields, at the land he'd once thought to be grim and barren, and marveled at the change.

Fresh life had sprung up where there'd once been nothing but scars. The lines they'd gouged into the earth were suddenly filled with green — brought back to life by the thousands of crops that sprouted along their backs. Green leaves unfurled confidently from their stems. They stretched out in every direction, reaching to embrace the sun. When the breeze brushed across them, they seemed to tremble with delight: as if everything on earth was new to them, and they still marveled at the wonder.

Kael was rather amazed, himself. He'd spent his whole life gathering his own food: trapping meat from the wilds, stripping fruit from the bush and roots from the ground. He thought his woodman's skills to be hard-earned and worthy ... but that was before he learned the skills of a giant.

Now his face burned when he thought about how he'd laughed at the giants' work, how he'd thought it to be simple and forgiving. There was an honor in farming that he hadn't quite understood, a patience that hunting didn't require. To raise life from a seed demanded much more than a bow: it needed a rough hand, a soft heart, and a constant hope.

It wasn't until he saw the earth breathe again that he realized this. And deep in his soul, Kael was proud to have sweated for it.

"Oh, look at the wee rat grinning!" Brend hollered.

He was standing up the path with Declan; they must've stopped when they realized Kael was lagging behind. Both wore smiles that he was certain held no mocking edge.

"You've started to take a shine to our lands, I can see it on your wee face," Brend continued as he trotted to catch up.

Kael stuffed his smile away. "No I haven't. It's just a pretty day, is all."

But Brend wasn't fooled. He slung an arm about Kael's shoulder and hurtled him into his side with surprising force. "Nonsense! We'll make a giant of you, yet."

He whistled as they wandered further up the road, trying to match the songs of the birds that passed overhead. His notes carried magnificently through unusual quiet of the morning.

Just as Kael had suspected, the guards still hadn't returned from the castle. Gilderick likely had them busy entertaining Baron Sahar and generally pretending that nothing was amiss. As an added relief, Hob had declared earlier that day that he didn't have time to drive the water wagon — so if the giants wanted a drink, they'd have to go back to the barns.

That suited them just fine. With all the planting finished, the giants spent the day wandering the fields, pulling up weeds, moving rocks, and enjoying the peace. Kael followed Declan and Brend around, helping wherever he could. Thick white clouds drifted above them lazily, and their shadows brought a long, welcome relief from the sun.

"It feels strange to work without a lash," Declan mused, tugging a healthy weed from where it'd been trying to hide between two carrots. "I keep expecting the sting to come at any moment. My back keeps twitching for it."

"The poor mages have got better things to worry about," Brend said. He shot a wicked look at Hob — who was wandering distractedly between the fields.

His fingers had scratched raw, red patches into the skin on his arms and neck. He looked about him as he walked, and his hand was clutched tightly around his whip. His chew sat in a forgotten lump between his teeth.

"Amazing what one little tale can do, eh?" Brend straightened up and glanced down the row. "Looks like there's just a few left, here. Want to head over to the radishes?"

Declan nodded in reply.

"All right, then. Finish this lot and then meet us over there, wee rat." Brend pointed to a neighboring field, and Kael nodded. Then the giants strode away, leaving him to his chores.

It was nice to have a few moments to himself. And weeding or no — he was planning to enjoy it. He'd just wrapped his hand around the next clump of grass when a familiar cry glanced the air above him. He looked up and saw Eveningwing circling overhead, but didn't think too much about it. He was probably just saying hello.

But when the hawk swooped down and batted the top of Kael's head with the thick of his wings, he had no choice but to look up. "What?" he hissed, as loudly as he dared.

Eveningwing came at him from the front, gliding straight towards him. An object fell from his talons a few feet away, and then he shot back into the air. When Kael saw what it was, he knew immediately that something was wrong: a note lay in the grass, bound hurriedly in cord.

They'd already talked about this. Eveningwing knew full well that he wasn't supposed to give Kael any messages out where the mages could see him. There must be some sort of emergency, then — perhaps Jonathan had gotten himself into trouble. Kael tore the letter open, hoping to mercy that it wasn't too late.

Jonathan's handwriting sprang from the page, though his words seemed more organized than before. His sentences were clipped tightly, and there were no poems or crude drawings scrawled in the margins. His message was earnest:

417

I finally convinced Clairy to sneak me into the upper tower — I found out that's where the lady giants keep their chambers. But it's not just that. It's horrible.

Clairy led me to her friend's room — a kind woman named Darrah — and she explained the whole thing: Gilderick's trying to breed a new army of giants, and he's using the ladies like cattle! A lot of the older women have already been chosen. Darrah was one of the first, and her belly was all swollen up to bursting.

I didn't know what to say. I was a bit shocked, to be honest — I couldn't believe that anybody could be so heartless. Not even Gilderick.

Then Clairy suddenly burst into sobs, Darrah teared up, and they finally told me the whole thing. Turns out that Gilderick's started choosing the women who'll be breeders on their eighteenth birthday ... and Clairy turns eighteen three days from now.

I'm sorry, mate — I know you've been working on a plan and all, but I can't sit by and let them take my Clairy. I won't do it. I'm going to think up a way out of here, and then she and I will leave tonight. We'll make for the seas, and I don't care how many guards Gilderick sends after us.

I'm writing to you so you'll know that I've gone, and you'll know not to worry after me anymore. I'm sorry if this ruins things, mate, but I've got no choice.

-Jonathan

"Eveningwing, get down here!" Kael hissed.

The hawk dived down quickly, hiding himself among the tall grass at the field's edge. Kael hurried over to him. He knew very well that whatever Jonathan had planned would never work: a witch guarded the kitchens, and it was likely that she used the same manner of spells on the tower doors that Hob did on the barns.

If they tried to slip out, the whole castle would hear of it in an instant. They would never make it out alive if they didn't have an army to block their escape.

418

Kael told Eveningwing all of this, and he told him to ask Jonathan to give him some time to prepare. "I'll have Clairy out before her birthday," Kael promised. "Once he agrees, I need you to fly to the seas immediately and tell the pirates that we plan to attack. They won't reach us in time to help with the escape," he said grimly. "But they might be able to hold off Gilderick's army in the wilderness ... if we can survive that long."

Chapter 34
Lake of Fire

The tunnels were dark and quiet, just as they'd been the first time Kyleigh walked them. Nadine traveled ahead of her, her shoulders bent towards her task. The swift steps of the Grandmot and Hessa's quiet sobs echoed behind them.

Elena had left without a word at first light; Silas was nowhere to be found. Kyleigh hoped they knew what they were doing, but she wasn't sure. She supposed that everything would work out the way they planned ... but if it didn't, they'd have to think very quickly. There'd certainly be no turning back, after this.

The thrill of the unknown, the weight of the risk — it made Kyleigh's heart beat excitedly. Her sight sharpened, her ears stood on point. She could hear the dry rasp of Jake's teeth as they scraped nervously across his lips.

It was midmorning, and Kyleigh wore her armor again. Nadine said it would only get her into trouble, but she didn't care: she certainly wasn't about to fight an army of trolls in a silk dress.

As they passed through the campsite at the end of the tunnel, the soldiers rose to greet them. There was pity on many of their faces as they nodded to Nadine.

The Grandmot followed them closely. It was obvious that she wasn't going to let them out of her sight, this time. She was going to make sure Nadine didn't walk out alive. "Form your ranks," she said to the mots, swooping her arms out. The wide sleeves of her robe made her limbs look like the wings of some giant, bangled bird. "Prepare yourselves for battle! Do not let Nadine's great sacrifice fall in vain — honor her with your spears."

The Grandmot wrapped her talons around Nadine's shoulders and squeezed tightly, as if she was trying to comfort her. But her eyes glittered with something that Kyleigh was certain wasn't tears.

"Yes, honor her," the Grandmot went on. They were almost to the end of the passageway, only a few dozen yards stood between Nadine and her fate. "Fight bravely, my warriors. Do not let —"

Clang! Clang! Clang!

The sharp, familiar tones cut through the passageway, and the Grandmot's mouth fell open. "Who rang the bell?" she squawked.

The mots seemed confused. Many of them bolted forward, and a wall of soldiers flooded the end of the passage, trying to push their way into the bell chamber. More soldiers crushed in from behind, trapping the Grandmot in the middle.

All of her composure vanished. She flapped her arms about and stomped her feet. "Turn back!" she shrilled. "We are not ready to face the trolls —"

"No! If we turn back, we will lose the passageway," Nadine cried. She held Hessa protectively behind her, their backs pressed against the tunnel wall. "The trolls will be at our doorstep —"

"Then we will push them back tomorrow!"

"We are not strong enough to push them back! If we lose this passage, it is lost forever —"

A chorus of loud barks echoed off the walls, and the soldiers began pressing forward all the more furiously. They were so crowded in that they couldn't lift their spears. The mots at the front wouldn't move: they were either waiting for an order, or frozen in fear.

And the barking was growing louder.

It was time for Kyleigh to put her plan into motion. She made to step towards Nadine when a swarm of mots flooded the gap between them, shoving them further apart. Kyleigh couldn't reach Nadine without crushing the mots in front of her, but the trolls would overrun them, if she waited much longer. She had to think quickly.

While the Grandmot shrilled for the mots to retreat, Hessa watched from behind Nadine's skirt. Her deep eyes wandered around the soldiers, studying their faces. Finally, they lighted on Kyleigh — who saw her chance.

She caught Hessa's gaze and mouthed: *The runes.*

Hessa's eyes flashed away, and Kyleigh was afraid she hadn't seen her. More soldiers weaved between them, blocking her from view. Kyleigh was trying to fight through the horde to reach Nadine when a little voice cried:

"Consult the runes!"

"Yes!" the Grandmot said, shaking a finger at Nadine. "We shall see what Fate decides."

The mots went deadly silent. They could hear the trolls racing towards them: their claws struck the stone, tapping like a fierce spring rain, growing more thunderous with every step. The Grandmot reached inside her pouch, felt around, and after a moment, her mouth dropped open.

"They — they are gone! My runes are missing!"

"Then we have run out of time." Nadine's voice carried through the tunnel as she cried: "We must fight! To arms, mots!"

No one seemed to mind that this order came from Nadine. Not a one of them spoke against her — instead, the mots cried out in answer. Those at the front spilled into the bell chamber, with the others shoving behind them.

The Grandmot was so busy trying not to get trampled that she didn't see Kyleigh until it was too late.

"I'll just take that back, thank you." She grabbed Harbinger around the hilt and ripped him free, snapping the Grandmot's belt. Then she sprinted down the tunnel — and laughed when she heard the Grandmot's angry scream.

In the bell chamber, the fight was already thick. Rocks flew from all directions. The trolls at the back of the horde used their slings to keep the mots at bay, while those closest to the front were forced to spar. They slung their shovel-like paws in mad arcs about them, swiping desperately at the spears.

A few of the mots got too close, and the trolls caught them in the chest. Kyleigh grimaced as their bodies rolled backwards. Some were even tossed clear over the heads of their companions.

Though the mots fought bravely, the trolls kept pressing in. It wasn't long before the bell chamber was packed full of black, hairy bodies; their stench filled the air. There were far too many of them, and more kept coming — pouring out of the tunnels in an endless stream of glinting teeth and claws.

Kyleigh had to act quickly.

Something brushed against her leg as she sprinted. She caught a brown blur out of the corner of her eye and her ears rang with a familiar roar. "Follow Silas!" she called to Jake, who panted along behind her. "Signal me when you've sealed up the tunnels!"

He nodded and loped away, struggling over bodies and toppled chairs.

Kyleigh never slowed down. She charged headlong into the fray, and Harbinger flew from his sheath, cutting through the first troll in their path. She nearly cried out when he sang in greeting. His voice echoed beautifully against the stone, rising and falling as he sliced his way through his foes. The tones of his song seemed to give the mots a burst of strength — while the trolls fell back in terror.

Nadine vaulted in beside her. She dispatched the trolls with quick, powerful thrusts of her spear. She goaded them with the tip until they wandered too close, and then she skewered them. Her weapon went through the center of their fanged mouths and came out their throats.

As they fought, Kyleigh watched for Jake out of the corner of her eye. She couldn't see him over the crush of bodies, but every now and then, a handful of trolls would go flying through the air, or suddenly burst into flame. And she knew Jake was behind it. He worked quickly, and it wasn't long before his signal came.

A tail of blue fire arced to the ceiling, filling the chamber with an eerie glow, and it was time for Kyleigh to do her part.

She'd been aching for this for weeks. Her dragon form had been wriggling inside her, teasing her like an itch she couldn't scratch. She sheathed Harbinger and arched her back, grinning as she felt her muscles stretch and pull, as her fingers became claws and her teeth grew pointed.

She didn't even have to breathe fire, this time: all she had to do was roar.

The trolls remembered her well. They yelped loudly at the sound of her voice and turned on their heels for the tunnels. They slammed against the opening, crushing each other as they tried to squeeze through. But Jake's shielding spells kept them out. There was only one tunnel that he didn't seal — and the trolls had no choice but to flee for it.

"Follow them! Finish them!" Nadine cried, as Kyleigh slipped back into her human skin. The mots were only too happy to obey. They knew very well where that tunnel led — and they knew the trolls had no chance of escape.

"Yes, finish them!"

Kyleigh turned and was surprised to see the Grandmot shuffling after the charge of mots, a spear clutched in her hands.

"Oh, *now* she's found her courage," Silas grumbled. He'd come out of his lion form and was grimacing as he pulled down on his breeches. His chest was peppered with angry red dots from the trolls' slings.

"Go stay with Hessa," Nadine ordered him, and he left without a word.

Jake and Nadine charged after the trolls, darting close to the grand chair in the middle of the room. As they passed by, a dark figure dropped out from inside the big silver bell.

"All right, Elena?" Kyleigh asked as she jogged by.

She rolled her shoulders back, and her eyes glinted above her mask. "It was a bit tight in there, but I'll be fine."

Kyleigh laughed as they sprinted after their friends.

The trolls had fled down a narrow tunnel. The deeper Kyleigh went, the more the air began to thicken. Soon an incredible heat filled the passage, tingling her skin. Around the next bend, the darkness gave way to an impossibly bright light — and then the passage spilled out into an enormous chamber.

The fire lake was exactly like Nadine had described it: as if the very waters were made of liquid fire. Black crusted over parts of it, as if the fires were so hot that they'd somehow scorched themselves. The black cracked in places, revealing swollen veins of angry red. Waves broke over the white-hot shores in brilliant oranges and yellows.

Kyleigh had never seen anything like it. The heat was so thick that she could practically hear it: it clogged her ears with a deep, contented groan — as if the earth was enjoying a warm bath.

The mots had the trolls pushed up against the edge of the lake. The trolls' barks were high-pitched and panicked as they fought for their hairy lives. They swung their paws desperately, trying to claw their way through the army of mots. Large, white-hot stones littered the shoreline, and the mots chased the trolls towards them with the points of their spears.

A few of the trolls accidentally stepped too far backwards, and Kyleigh could hear their flesh sizzling from the back of the room. When they yelped and sprang to clutch their wounded feet, the mots gave them a stiff push into the fire.

Though they were able to trap most of the trolls in, quite a few managed to squeeze through the mots' ranks and break for the tunnels. But they didn't get far.

Kyleigh and Elena were there to stop them. Harbinger bit eagerly through their fury necks while Elena's daggers flashed in and out. Her hands moved so quickly that Kyleigh had a difficult time seeing what she did — but judging by the amount of blood that followed her strokes, she was doing it well.

The first few lines of trolls got shoved into the fire lake, leaving the survivors no choice but to try to mount some sort of counterattack. The front row sparred furiously with the mots while the back row began hurling pebbles from their slings.

Stones flew from every direction, an endless volley hurled by a desperate force. The mots stumbled over each other, struggling to keep the trolls cornered. When they tried to shield themselves, the trolls broke free — shoving their way back towards the tunnel.

"Fight! Shove them back!" the Grandmot squawked. She'd found a rock to perch on, safely out of reach of the trolls' grasping claws. The feathers in her hair bounced wildly as she stomped her feet. "Do not let them escape!"

"We need another body at the tunnel," Elena grunted, burying both of her daggers into the chest of a fleeing troll. She pulled the blades free and kicked the troll's body in the path of its comrades — sending them all for a tumble. "Where's Nadine?"

Kyleigh had to get a few heads out of her way before she finally caught sight of Nadine. She stood near the edge of the battle. Her spear hung loosely in one hand and in the other, she clutched a troll's sling. Kyleigh called out to her, but she didn't turn:

Her eyes were on the Grandmot.

The sling spun around and around in Nadine's hand; her eyes narrowed on her target. And Kyleigh could only watch in shock as the stone left its sling.

Time seemed to turn back on itself. The noise of the battle faded, the stone whistled over the heads of the mots, streaking for its target — then with a loud *thwap*, it struck the Grandmot between her wicked eyes.

Her body went limp, and her eyes rolled back. She toppled over off of the rock and into the lake. There was a splash, a burst of orange, and then the fire swallowed her up. When Kyleigh turned around, Nadine met her eyes.

Her gaze was hardened and sure. She nodded once, firmly.

And Kyleigh nodded back.

"Out of my way!" Jake bellowed, waving his hands. "If you'll all just clear out for a moment, I can take care of this."

The second the mots leapt to the side, Jake slammed his staff into the ground. The earth in front of him buckled and snapped back under the trolls, launching them almost to the ceiling. They squeaked and flailed their hairy limbs as their bodies sailed through the air, but couldn't stop their fall. They plunged down into the fire — splashing like a handful of pebbles into a pond.

A small group of trolls had managed to climb up a narrow ledge over the lake. When they tried to hurl stones at Jake, he blew the ledge out from under them. They squealed in terror as they tumbled into the flames.

"Well, I think that settles it," Jake said. He turned too quickly and his spectacles went sailing off the end of his sweaty nose.

Elena stooped and caught them before they could strike the ground, moving so casually that Kyleigh had to wonder if she hadn't been expecting it. She cleaned the spectacles on the hem of her red skirt before she handed them back.

"Thank you," Jake said. He seemed very distracted as he slipped them on, and very nearly poked himself in the eye.

"We must return to our people," Nadine said. She glanced at the rock where the Grandmot had been standing, and her eyes were heavy. "It is time for our Dawn to rise."

The mots moved out. Some tittered happily about their victory, while others looked confused. Kyleigh didn't know if any of them had seen Nadine kill the Grandmot — but even if they had, they weren't saying anything about it.

They waited for the mots to pass by before they followed at the rear. "I thought you said there'd be no killing of the Grandmot," Elena muttered out the side of her mouth. When Nadine didn't respond, she pressed: "What made you decide to do it?"

"It was what you said about Hessa," Nadine whispered, her eyes distant. "I did not want to do it — and for

427

my betrayal, I know that I no longer deserve to live among the mots. But I could not leave her in the hands of that woman. Now Hessa will never be without a mother," Nadine added with a smile. "No matter where I go, I will carry her in my heart."

By the time they returned to the bell chamber, Hessa was waiting for them. She held hands with Silas — who looked rather frightened about it. His fingers stuck out straight and his arm was twisted away from her, as if he expected her to spring up and try to bite him at any moment.

Kyleigh laughed at the sight.

"Is it finished?" Hessa said, her eyes flicking worriedly over the soldiers.

"It happened just as you said it would," one of the mots called. "*Blood spilt upon the ground will rise into a red sun, and its light will chase away our shadows.*"

The others murmured in agreement, and Kyleigh realized those must've been the words that Hessa had cried out in the speaking circle — the ones that had made the Grandmot so furious.

Hessa nodded. Then worry creased her face again. "Who ...?"

The mots parted. Every last one of them turned to look at Nadine.

With a gasp, Hessa ran to her. They were quiet as they held each other, no tears fell between them. Then, just before they parted, Hessa whispered something to Nadine. She nodded.

"The outlanders must leave us, now."

Kyleigh felt it in her toes when Hessa met her eyes. She forced herself to nod. "Yes, I'm afraid we've got urgent business in the northern desert."

"Then you will not be going alone," Nadine said. She smiled as she leaned on her spear. "I will go with you."

The mots began to whisper. A few of them glared and tried to put themselves in Nadine's path. Hessa raised her hands to silence them. "Nadine is pardoned," Hessa said quietly. "She has played her part in Fate's plan, as we all must. Fate alone knows the ending to our story ... we can do nothing more than choose which path we will take to meet it. So what will you choose, mots?"

They looked bewildered. A woman near the front of the line spoke up: "We will do whatever you ask of us, Dawn Hessa."

She shook her head, smiling — and quite suddenly, she didn't look like a child anymore, but a woman prepared to lead. "There is much to be done. Our dead must be buried, our home must be rebuilt. But those are tasks for other talents. For you, my warriors, I have a different request. Two paths stretch before you: one sits in quiet, and the other in blood. Travel to the seas and trade for what we need to survive, or follow the outlanders on their journey — and you will find a wellspring to feed us all of our days."

The mots tittered for a moment, speaking over and around one another in the singsong tongue. All at once, they quieted. One mot finally stepped forward, and he spoke for them all:

"Then our path is chosen for us. We will travel with the outlanders."

As the soldiers readied themselves for the journey, Hessa bid them all farewell — standing on her tiptoes to hug each of them around the neck. When it was Kyleigh's turn, she held her a little longer.

"On the day you came to us," Hessa whispered, "I told the Grandmot that I had a vision of one more deserving who would come to take Nadine's place. And since you are so fond of trouble, I will tell you a secret: I lied." She pulled away, and a mischievous smile parted her lips. "That was not a vision at all ... but only a hope."

Kyleigh was surprised. And it was only after Hessa had gone to hug Silas that she realized she was grinning. As they left the motlands, she felt a peace inside her heart.

Hessa's people would be in good hands.

Chapter 35
If

By nightfall, all of Kael's momentary peace had vanished, replaced by a feeling that he was much more accustomed to: worry.

There was a chance that they might succeed. When he closed his eyes tightly, he could almost see it. If they were able to kill the kitchen witch, if he got the mages out of the way, if the giants went along with his plan, if the pirates ran like Death himself was snapping at their heels — there was a chance that they might all make it out of the plains alive.

He could almost see it, shining like hearth light through the crack in a doorway. And *if* they timed everything perfectly, they might just be able to slip through it.

If.

Kael ate little at dinner. The giants were livelier than they'd been in weeks, and they filled the whole barn with happy chatter. Though they were clearly thrilled to have Brend back among them, they did their best to hide it.

When they'd emerged from the stall that morning, Declan announced very loudly that Brend had recovered from his fever — and passed such a glare about the room that the giants had immediately gone along with it. None of them seemed eager to tell the truth, anyways.

And with Declan scowling at them, no one dared to ask how it'd been done.

Brend was enjoying the attention. Someone asked him to tell another story of Scalybones, and he happily obliged. Kael slipped into stall while the others were occupied, hoping to catch a few moments alone to steady his nerves. But it wasn't long before familiar, quick-strided footsteps came through the door.

"Is there something wrong, Kael?"

He'd had every intention of keeping his head low, but the sound of his name surprised him. He looked up instinctively — and Declan's eyes caught his face.

Blast it.

"I'm just tired," he grumbled, quickly burying his head once again.

A long, weighty pause hung between them, and Kael knew he was about to be interrogated. He'd begun gathering up his excuses when Declan surprised him for a second time.

"I'm not a man who says what he feels, and I'd never be grateful for my own life ... but I'm grateful for Brend's."

Kael's head rose ever so slightly. "Wait a moment — are you ... *thanking* me?" When Declan didn't respond, he couldn't help himself: he had to look.

Declan stood on the other side of the room, arms hanging loosely at his sides. He stared pointedly out of the hole in the roof, as if he meant to avoid having to come out and say it.

"Because if you are, I wouldn't consider it a debt —"

"Good, because it isn't a debt. It's just something that needed to be said." Declan's eyes snapped away from the roof and back onto Kael's — trapping him. "Now that I've told *you* something, is there anything you'd like to tell me?"

Kael realized that he'd been tricked again. He shook his head firmly, and Declan's gaze narrowed, crushing his lie before it even had a chance to escape.

But Kael didn't care. He rolled onto his side and was prepared to heartily ignore Declan when he questioned him. The questions never came, however. And it wasn't long before he fell into a fitful sleep. He tossed and turned through the better half of the night, until Eveningwing finally woke him.

The rough end of the rope brushed his shoulder, and he climbed it without thinking. It wasn't until he was already out on the roof that he thought to be surprised. "I wasn't expecting you until tomorrow," he whispered to

Eveningwing, who crouched next to the hole. "Were you able to reach the pirates?"

He lowered his head, and the crop of his hair shadowed his eyes. "Yes. The winds were fair today — they shortened my journey."

Kael shook his head in amazement, thinking how marvelous it must be to travel at the speed of a hawk. He saw Eveningwing about to pull the rope up and stopped him. "Let's leave it where it is. The giants sleep pretty heavily — I doubt anybody will notice it. And once we take care of Finks, we may not have time to get it set again. I'd rather not have to jump down and risk breaking an ankle."

Eveningwing's head jerked down in a nod. Then he took to the skies, and Kael followed in his shadow.

The braziers along the road glowed brightly. He set a swift pace for them, watching as the light danced along with the breaths of the wind. He was still several yards away when Eveningwing let out a soft cry.

Kael dropped to his belly immediately.

It took him a moment to see what the hawk had seen: a dark rider crossed between the braziers, his horse tread as silently as any cat. His armor was so blackened that not even the light could illuminate it. A red scarf was wrapped about his head, holding a black, slit mask over his jaw. His dark eyes seemed to reflect the lapping tongues of flame about him.

A noise on the other side of the road caught his attention, and he turned suddenly. There was a massive sword strapped across his back.

Behind the dark rider came a covered wagon, its canvas stamped with the great twisting oak of the Grandforest. A second rider passed it at a trot. This rider was much more slender than the first, and a tress of shining, golden brown hair trailed out from under the hood of her cloak.

Kael realized, with a worry that made his tongue stick to the back of his throat, that this must be Countess D'Mere — arriving late, just as Brend said she would.

The leafy heads of several small trees stuck out of the back of the wagon. They whispered dryly over the bumps in the road, bouncing under the weight of the fruit on their branches. Two boys walked behind the wagon, identical down to their strides. One watched the left side of the road; the other watched the right. Their hands never once left their swords.

That was the end of D'Mere's procession. No army followed at her back. Kael thought it strange that she would travel the wilderness at night, with so few men to protect her. They must've been far more skilled than he realized — D'Mere obviously wasn't worried about the lions, in any case.

Kael waited for Eveningwing's signal before he dared to cross the road. After a considerable amount of thought, he'd decided that it would be best to try to go after Finks that night. Hob would certainly have to be taken care of, but Finks was crafty. And Kael was afraid that if he gave the mage anymore time to protect himself, he might just slither away. And that could ruin everything.

No, he wasn't going to take any chances. Finks had to go first.

They arrived at the Pens without incident. Thick clouds had gathered over the moon, and there wasn't a guard in sight. But it only took Kael a moment to spot a new problem: the lanterns outside of every cottage were lit. He'd been right about Finks, then. The mage was already getting crafty.

With every lantern burning, Kael had no idea which cottage Finks might be hiding in. At least with a large part of its front missing, he could see clearly into Gaff's. But he sent Eveningwing to check the others.

The hawk circled the courtyard once, twice, tilting his wings and peering into every window. For a moment, Kael was afraid that he might be just as lost. But then Eveningwing settled firmly over Stodder's doorway, and Kael left at a trot.

He crept up the stairs, the curved knife gripped firmly in his hand. He would not have as much trouble with Finks as he'd had with the others: there was no doubting how wicked he was. Kael would sleep better every night hence, knowing that Finks would never harm another soul again.

His shadow crossed the porch, and perhaps it was because he was focused on moving quietly that he didn't notice anything peculiar straight away. The outline of Kael's head rippled over the wood, as if it crossed a puddle of water.

It looked odd. And his mind was still trying to grasp at *why* it looked so odd when he took his next step. His foot came down, and he felt the familiar, slimy back of a spell on his toes.

By then, it was too late.

A cloud of purple smoke burst in his face, blinding him. Then the whole porch shuddered and suddenly flipped up, launching him into the air. He landed hard on his back. All the wind left his lungs. He knew he was lucky to be alive — lucky that things hadn't gone any worse.

No sooner did he think this than a horrible, steady shriek cut through the air.

It sounded like a woman who'd just stepped on a mouse — a screaming alarm that he knew could be heard the whole way to the castle. With a desperate heave, Kael managed to pull himself from the ground.

The cottage door slammed open, but he didn't wait around for Finks. He didn't even wait for Eveningwing: he tore straight for the chicken coup.

The coup sat by itself in the darkness, out of the reach of the cottage lanterns. Kael leapt over the fence and ducked behind one of the little houses, watching Finks's shadowy form as he raced down the stairs. He went off in the direction of the Fields, and Kael breathed a sigh of relief.

For several long moments, things were quiet. He watched the skies, waiting for Eveningwing's signal — but the hawk never appeared. Minutes passed, and Kael began to get worried. What if Eveningwing had been captured? Had Finks's spell knocked him out of the sky? Was he hurt?

Kael realized he could hide no longer. He had to find Eveningwing.

He was just about to move when a pair of voices drifted in from the courtyard:

"It's about time you showed up!" Finks hissed. "I've got the murderer cornered —"

"How can you be so sure it's him?"

Kael grimaced when he heard Dred's voice reply, and cold sweat began to bead up on the back of his neck.

Finks made a frustrated sound. His steps grew louder as he stomped forward. "See those marks on the ground? Please tell me you see them. I know you giants are stupid, but surely you aren't blind."

"Watch your tongue, spellmonger," Dred growled back. There was a creak of armor as he bent to inspect the marks. "Yeh, I see them. They're little footprints."

Kael nearly swore aloud. In all of the chaos, he'd forgotten about the purple smoke. Now when he glanced down, he saw that it covered him from head to toe — and marked where he'd been with something like ink spots. He could see very clearly where he'd vaulted over the fence: an imprint of his palms stained the rails.

"Perfect," Finks said, with deliberate slowness. "Now, why don't you send your men in there after it?"

"All right. Follow those prints, blisters — and don't let the monster get away."

Kael heard the heavy, rattling steps headed in his direction, and he knew his time had run out. His only option now would be to try to outrun the guards. If he could make it to the pond, he might be able to wash off —

"We've got him! We've found the murderer!"

This voice belonged to Hob. He shouted from the other side of the courtyard, and the guards took off after him. "We'd better gut it quick. Don't let it get free!" Dred bellowed as he lumbered away.

Kael's breath caught in his throat. They must've captured Eveningwing.

He sprang back over the fence and went after the guards at an all-out sprint. If he acted quickly, he might be able to cause a distraction. He might be able to get the guards to chase after *him*, instead. And if he was captured, so be it. But they weren't going to gut Eveningwing. He wouldn't let that happen.

Kael turned around the next barn and found the guards crowded around Hob — who had his boot planted on the back of the man at his feet. One of the guards raised his pike above the man's head, and Kael cried out.

The giants leapt back for a second, clearly startled, and Kael tried to shove in between them. Someone grabbed him by the scruff of his neck and threw him to the ground; a monstrous boot heel ground into his back.

"*You!*" Finks spat. His lips pursed around the word, making his long teeth look like fangs. When his shock wore off, he blinked. "No, it can't be him —"

"Of course it's him!" Dred said incredulously, jabbing a finger at Kael. "Look at him — he's got that purple mess all over him."

"I can see that, you imbecile! But what I *can't* see is how one mountain rat managed to sneak through the wards of seven mages. You think that scrawny little thing has been killing us off? Been killing off your guards? I didn't think so," Finks said smugly, as his questions doused Dred's face in confusion. He turned back to the man at Hob's feet. "And *this* isn't any better," he added, with a sharp kick.

The man grunted in pain and began to squirm. The chains of Hob's spell tightened around his body, glowing red. The hiss of searing flesh filled the air for a moment, and then the man lay still.

Kael fought against the boot in his back, dragging himself forward, trying to reach him. When he saw that the man was too big to be Eveningwing, he was slightly relieved. But then his eyes wandered up, past the bonds around the man's mouth, over his hooked nose and into the deep cleft of his brow — and he found himself staring into the dazed eyes of Declan.

"They must've been trying to escape," Finks said, his gaze flicking between Declan and Kael. "They were always plotting, always scheming ... so *this* is what you were up to, eh? You thought because the guards weren't out that you'd have a clear path, did you?"

"If they were planning to escape, then why was the rat sneaking around your cottage?" Dred cut in. He jabbed Declan's limp body with the butt of his pike. "And this one might not look like much, but he's a killer." Dred jabbed him again. "Yeh, and killing's all he's ever been good for."

Kael felt his neck pop as Fink's boot pressed against his cheek. "What *were* you doing outside my cottage, rat? You'd do well to tell the truth," he added, unfurling his whip.

Kael couldn't tell the truth — the truth would get them both killed on the spot. So he thought quickly. "You're right. We *were* trying to escape," he muttered, after a moment of frantic thought. "I only went to the cottage because I thought it was empty. I was looking for supplies."

"I knew it!" Finks said triumphantly. He kicked a clod of dirt into Kael's face before he spun away.

"We ought to take them to His Lordship," Hob said, eyeing the castle. "Finks, you stay here —"

"Oh no, you don't," Finks said vehemently. "*I* caught the little beasts — and I'm not going to stand by while you take all the credit!"

"Well, seeing as how it's *my* spell that's got him bound," Hob said, nudging Declan with his toe, "it'll be me going up to the castle. I'll be sure and put in a good word for you," he added with a smirk.

The guards hoisted Kael and Declan across their shoulders and made for the castle at a march, leaving Finks alone to simmer.

As the first gray lines of morning crossed the horizon, Kael kept his eyes on Declan — who'd struggled until the spells finally burned him into passing out.

Declan knew that he'd had been hiding something. He'd known it all along. So he must've lain awake, waiting until Kael slipped through the roof. And then he'd used the rope to follow him out.

He wondered how many other nights Declan must've watched him. Perhaps he'd seen him leave every time, and wondered where he'd gone off to. Maybe he'd already figured out that Kael was the one responsible for the mages.

But if so ... why hadn't he stopped him?

They arrived at the castle gates a little before dawn. The towering front doors were already swung open. Each of its planks looked as if they'd been cut from the length of a single tree, held side-by-side with nails the size of Kael's fist. The wood must have been a gift from the Grandforest: there weren't trees that size anywhere in the plains.

A soft jingling noise and the patter of footsteps drew his eyes downward, and Kael saw that they were passing the Baron's servants. The desert folk were clearly on their way out: the baskets they carried were now empty of gold and packed full of food. A few of the servants cast nervous glances at Dred, but they didn't slow their pace. They must've been very eager to be on their way.

Kael caught the scent of fresh-baked bread as they passed, and wondered vaguely if Gilderick offered his victims a last meal. He seriously doubted it.

The castle courtyard was a wide, half-moon of dust. High walls encircled it, and they appeared to be several layers thick: three levels of ramparts were cut into the walls, and a narrow flight of stairs led to their top. The guards who watched the keep's entrance sprang to their posts at the sight of Dred. The doors swung open, and they stepped inside.

It was surprisingly dark. Even though the weather had been warm for weeks, the air inside Gilderick's castle was damp and cool — almost like a cave. The guards' heavy footsteps pounded through the silent keep, past empty chambers and bare corridors. At last, they stopped at a room with a little light in it.

The guard carrying Kael dumped him onto the stone floor. His groans were cut short by a new voice:

"Why do you interrupt me?"

Whoever asked this question did so as if there was a tremendous weight behind it — as if just the asking was going to force him to do something that they would all deeply regret.

Dred's massive shoulders stiffened. "We caught some of the beasts trying to escape, m'Lord"

Kael couldn't help himself: he looked up.

They were in a wide chamber that looked a bit like a dining hall. There weren't any decorations on the walls, no tapestries or merry paintings of feasts. There weren't even any windows — just a few candles melting miserably in an iron chandelier above them. The only thing that made Kael think of a dining room was the long table in the middle of it.

Glittering plates covered its every surface, piled high with food that smelled so delicious, his nose struggled to take it all in. He tore his eyes away from the feast and saw Countess D'Mere seated near the table's head. She picked halfheartedly at a plate of fruit with a golden fork. Even though she sat properly, her full lips were pulled into a sulking pout.

She obviously wasn't happy about Sahar's swift exit that morning, because it left her alone with the man at the head of the table — the man who must've been Lord Gilderick.

He was incredibly thin: the sharp edges of his cheeks cast a shadow down his face, and his spidery fingers sat curled on either side of his plate. He stared down at his meal, as if he was trying to will himself to scrape a bite onto his jeweled fork.

"Then why do they still have their heads?" Gilderick asked — again, like Dred was forcing him ever closer to the edge of a rather steep cliff.

"I thought you might want to," Dred glanced at Countess D'Mere, who was suddenly watching in interest, "um, punish them yourself, m'Lord."

"Ah." Gilderick's exclamation came out slowly, hissing as it crossed his tongue — like the first blast of air from an opened crypt.

His head began to rise, and Kael quickly looked at the floor. He remembered Jonathan's warning all too well, and he didn't want to get Declan into more trouble by meeting Gilderick in the eyes.

"Well, I suppose we've got a little time. We just started breakfast, after all. You haven't killed that other one, have you?"

"No, I've only got him bound, m'Lord," Hob chimed in. "He's not going anywhere —"

"Get out," Gilderick snapped, so suddenly that D'Mere jumped. "Go to the courtyard and prepare for the games."

Hob bowed quickly. With a flick of his whip, he released Declan from his chains and then scuttled out the door.

"I must admit — I'm intrigued," D'Mere said in the strained silence Hob left behind. She turned a lovely smile in Gilderick's direction. "It seems the plains have been more exciting than you've let on."

One of Gilderick's spidery hands twitched in her direction. His voice warmed a bit as he replied: "Oh, this sort of thing happens from time to time. The slaves just need a little ... reminder. Watch this." There was a creak as he repositioned himself in his chair. "I wish I had more time to think ... but with the Sowing Moon tonight, I haven't got the time. Just the usual dismemberment, I suppose — and start with the mountain rat."

"M'Lord —?"

"Do as I say, General," Gilderick snapped. "Kill the rat, and then wake the second one. I do so hate to kill them in their sleep," he said to D'Mere. "They go without a fuss, and it just doesn't seem right. A man ought to have a chance to scream when he dies. Go ahead, General," a gleeful darkness filled Gilderick's voice, "and see if you can't really get him to squeal."

Before Kael could think to fight, four sets of hands latched onto his limbs, pinning him against the ground. Dred's boot pressed down on his cheek. He squirmed furiously, but they held him so tightly that he couldn't break free. He looked around as far as his eyes could reach, searching for some means of escape.

And that's when he accidentally locked gazes with D'Mere.

She watched him curiously. There was a coldness in her eyes, a cool indifference. But there was also something else — a flicker between her brows that only seemed to deepen as she inspected him. Her gaze wandered the whole filthy, ragged, purple length of him before she finally leaned away, ducking out of his sight.

Kael gasped when he felt the sharp point of Dred's pike digging into the fleshy part of his arm. He clamped his teeth down tightly, almost biting his tongue. They could saw him limb from limb, but he was determined not to scream. He wouldn't give Gilderick a single ounce of pleasure —

"One moment, General." Gilderick snapped his boney fingers together and the pike immediately relented. "The Countess and I have just had a rather amusing idea. Instead of killing these poor fools outright, let's use them as fodder for the games."

"An excellent idea, m'Lord," Dred said with a bow, though he sounded as if he would've preferred an outright killing. "I'll just lock them up until evening, then."

Chapter 36
The Baron's Castle

They walked until the mots' domain ended, and then they had no choice but to climb through the troll tunnels.

"They've got a particular ... scent, about them, don't they?" Jake said. He stopped and pulled his journal out. "Would you say it was more *fetid*, or simply *pungent*?"

"How about *downright maleficent*?" Kyleigh said, holding her breath as she stepped over a suspicious-looking clump of rocks.

"It smells of death and dung!" Silas moaned. He shoved Jake forward with his elbow. "Keep walking, shaman. You'll have time to scribble later."

"*Death and dung ...*" Jake made a few hasty notes before he clapped his journal shut and pressed on.

The small army of mots traveled far ahead of them. Kyleigh could see the bobbing light of their lanterns as they popped in and out of the tunnels, scouting for the safest paths. The trolls must've dug their passages in a hurry: they weren't anywhere near as sturdy as the mots' had been. Some portions were completely caved in.

Every time they passed a pile of rubble, Elena gripped the sides of her mask and pulled it tightly against her face. "How much further? I hate it here — there isn't any air!"

"There is air enough," Nadine assured her. "Though it is certainly not the cleanest I have ever breathed." One of the mots called to her, and she broke from the main path, leading them down a much narrower tunnel.

Soon they were forced to walk one at a time, following the train of mots as the walls closed in. When Nadine held her lantern up, the rock took on a life of its own. Thousands of tiny gems glittered excitedly in the light, as if they'd been waiting since the dawn of the earth to show how they shined.

One vein to their right was particularly striking: it was made up of bright purple jewels, and their color gave the whole tunnel a soft, stunning glow. Kyleigh leaned in to look at them as she passed and was surprised to see that each one was almost perfectly square. Then the tunnel branched, and the purple vein went off in one direction while the mots stayed on the other.

"Huh, I wonder what gives them their shape?" Jake said. He stuck his head down into the purple tunnel. "Looks like there's more back here. I wonder how far it — oof!"

He tripped over his own feet and fell hard, knocking into the wall. A rumble sounded above them, as if some great beast was about to burst from the ceiling and attack them. Then rocks came tumbling down.

"Get back!"

Elena dove into the tunnel, and the last thing Kyleigh saw was Jake's spindly body rolling end over end as she knocked him aside. Large rocks struck the ground with a noise like a thunderclap, and everything went quiet.

Kyleigh shoved her way past Silas, and when she saw the debris, she gasped — accidentally inhaling a large cloud of dust. She had to cough several times before she could call out to Jake. "Are you all right?"

"We're fine," Jake grunted. The rocks had completely filled the tunnel's opening: there was now a large wall between them, and Jake and Elena were trapped on the other side.

"Hold on — we'll try to dig you free." Kyleigh only managed to move one rock out of the way before three more fell on top of it.

Nadine grabbed her wrist. "You will bring the whole earth down on our heads! We cannot dig them free. They will have to find their own way out." She leaned close to the wall. "Jake — there will be holes dug out of the tunnel in a few miles. The trolls will have dug them for air. Once you find one, use your magic to break it open and continue through the desert. We will meet you when we can."

"All right, that shouldn't be a problem," Jake said.

Elena moaned. "A few *miles*?"

"Think of it as an adventure."

"An *adventure* we wouldn't be on, had you kept your long mage nose where it belonged!" Elena retorted. Their words grew fainter the further they walked, and soon Kyleigh couldn't even hear them.

"They will be fine," Nadine assured her. One of the mots shouted something from up ahead, and she cried out in surprise. "There is an exit — not three miles from us!"

"Good," Silas snapped. He was trying to shake something foul off the bottom of his foot, but it clung on stubbornly. "The sooner we leave this wretched place, the better."

****

The exit the mots led them to was little more than a wide hole cut out of the ceiling. Even standing on Kyleigh's shoulders, Nadine was too short to reach it. So Silas had to give it a try.

"Quit your wobbling," he hissed. He dug his heels into her shoulders — a little harder than was probably necessary.

"Keep that up," Kyleigh growled, "and we'll see if you land on your feet."

Silas chuckled as he balanced himself. Then he stood up.

"What do you see?" Nadine called to him.

"Patience, mot — the sun is too bright. Let my eyes adju — ah!"

Kyleigh stumbled forward as the weight suddenly left her shoulders. She looked up just in time to see a pair of dirty feet disappear through the hole. "Silas?" She felt along the wall, trying to find a ledge or a foothold, anything she might be able to use to climb up. But the wall was completely smooth. "Silas! Are you all right?"

He didn't respond. She could hear muffled voices above them, and then the pounding of feet shook sand from the ceiling. Something dropped down into the hole, and she ripped Harbinger from his sheath.

"It is a rope!" Nadine said, stepping past her. She gave it a sharp tug, but the rope didn't budge.

Kyleigh stopped her before she could try to climb it. "Wait — we don't know what's out there. It could be a trap." She leaned back to look up at the hole, trying to squint through the blinding white of the sun.

A shadowy head popped into view. "Move your scaly hide, dragoness. You won't find a cleaner way up."

Now that she knew Silas was all right, Kyleigh felt a little easier. But she still insisted on going up first — just in case.

Once her head cleared the top of the hole, the sunlight nearly blinded her. They'd been underground for less than a day. But her eyes ached so sharply that she had to pause at the top of the rope to steady herself. She was feeling around for something she could use to pull herself free when a strong hand grabbed her wrist.

One man's strength wasn't enough to move her: it took several. Hands grabbed both her wrists, under her arms, the back of her jerkin — someone even snatched her belt. The hands dragged her roughly from the hole, and Kyleigh knew she could no longer afford to keep her eyes closed. She sprang to her feet and squinted against the searing light, forcing her eyes to adjust.

A ring of men stood before her. She saw the wraps over their heads and faces and realized with a jolt that they must be bandits. Harbinger shrieked as she drew him.

"Hold up, there! Don't start chopping off our heads just yet," the lead man said. She thought his voice sounded familiar, but it wasn't until he pulled his wrap down and his bushy sideburns sprang out that she recognized him.

"Shamus!" She's taken a step towards him before the realization hit her. "Didn't I tell you not to follow me?"

"Oh, aye."

"Then what are you doing here?" she growled.

His brawny shoulders rose and fell. "Well, we weren't *going* to follow you — honest," he added, when she narrowed her eyes. "You weren't supposed to be gone but a week or two. And when you didn't come back, well ... the lads and I thought you might need rescuing."

Kyleigh turned and saw there were close to forty men loitering behind him. Their blue eyes creased happily over the tops of their masks, and several of them waved to her in greeting.

She wasn't amused. "You could've all been killed —"

"But we weren't," Shamus interjected. A wide grin stretched between his sideburns as he added: "And that's not all — we're keeping the Baron holed up inside his castle!"

When he stepped out of her way, Kyleigh couldn't believe what she saw.

The tunnel path may have been dark and smelly, but the flat ground led them across the desert much faster than a path through the dunes. A few hundred yards away stood a monstrous fortress. It looked as if it had been carved straight out of the side of the Red Spine: the jagged teeth had been shaved down to form walls, and the sharp slope of its hills became thick, rounded towers. The keep's face was all that was visible of the main castle — the rest of it must've been hidden inside the mountain.

A tail of the Red Spine wrapped around it, forming a natural outer wall. Two doors had been set into its craggy front, each one standing the height of a small house, and made of what appeared to be solid gold.

The last time Kyleigh had been in Whitebone, it was under the cover of night. She hadn't noticed all of the fist-sized jewels set into the doors and along the walls. Now the sunlight glanced across them and blinded her with bursts of colored light. She could hardly get a good look at the ramparts, with the jewels blinding her.

And she thought that might've been the point.

"It was a great stroke of luck," Shamus went on. "We'd spent days sacking the forts all along the Baron's highway.

Granted, there weren't very many men on duty — but it was real delicate work. We couldn't let any of those sandbeaters escape and run off to warn the Baron! After a few days of fighting in this blasted sun, we were nearly dead on our feet." He beamed as he gestured towards the Spine. "Then we finally make it to the castle, and what do we see? The Baron, himself! He came right out of that pass over there and tried to sneak his way in, but we caught him —"

"Wait." Kyleigh grabbed the front of his tunic, jolting him. "You say the Baron was coming *from* the plains?" When Shamus nodded, she felt as if the earth had fallen out from beneath her. "Then we're too late! He's already attacked —!"

"No, it wasn't an *army* he had with him," Shamus assured her, catching onto her arm before she could sprint for the Spine. "It was just a bunch of servants and a handful of guards. Gilderick must've been having some sort of party," he mused. "Anyways, we attacked Sahar's caravan just the second they popped out of the Spine. He got away, but," Shamus grinned, "he had to leave all of his loot behind."

She followed his gaze and saw another group of seas men standing guard over what looked like some sort of golden carriage. Packed inside the carriage were dozens of large baskets. And packed inside the baskets, tight to bursting —

"Food!" Silas moaned.

Shamus chuckled. "Aye, we've been feasting all afternoon. Go help yourself to the vittles!"

Silas didn't need to be told twice.

Now that she was certain the way was safe, Kyleigh called down to Nadine, and told her to start sending the army up the rope. One by one, Shamus's men pulled the mots out of the tunnel, staring openly at their short limbs. They seemed to be extra gentle as they helped them to their feet.

"Small folk, aren't they?" Shamus said, watching as the mots joined Silas.

Kyleigh grinned. "Just stay out of spear's reach, and you shouldn't get hurt."

447

Not surprisingly, the mots were thrilled about the food. But they didn't attack it headfirst, like Silas did. Instead, they hefted the monstrous fruits and vegetables out of the baskets and brought them carefully to their noses, as if they weren't sure what to do with them. Someone found a thick loaf of dark, rich bread, and their eyes lit up like jewels. They passed the loaf around the circle, smelling its crusted top and chattering excitedly to one another.

"They know they can eat it, right?" Shamus said.

Kyleigh shrugged. "I doubt if they know what half of it is."

"Oh. Give that here, lass — and I'll show you how to crack it open."

Nadine handed over the melon she'd been inspecting and Shamus brought it down across his knee. The hard skin cracked and he pulled it apart — revealing the sweet flesh underneath. Then he showed the mots how to scoop it out with their fingers.

Nadine tried it first, and then the others dug in. They passed the halves of the melon around, taking small bites and grinning broadly as the flavor hit them. "I never knew food could taste like this," Nadine said, licking the juice from her fingers. "It is even sweeter than wine!"

Shamus seemed to be enjoying himself as much as the mots. He happily answered their questions and showed them how to open some of the fruits. Then he sliced up the bread and passed around a basket of apples, chuckling as he watched them chew.

"Dragoness!" Silas had been busily digging through the baskets, searching for something. When he found it, he broke off a hunk and tossed it at Kyleigh.

She could smell it as it sailed through the air. Her mouth was already watering by the time she caught it: salted pork.

After weeks of stringy goats and tiny fish, she swore the first bite of pork melted in her mouth. Usually, salted meats were tough and made her tongue curl up. But this bit was different: the thick slabs of fat between the meat had been rubbed in a blend of spices that made it taste as if it was fresh — and hot off the roasting spit.

"This prey is long dead ... but it doesn't taste like it," Silas groaned thickly, moving his lips around the large strip of pork he had clamped between his teeth. His arms were laden with great slabs of beef, smoked chicken, and a long cord of sausages. "It's like magic!"

Kyleigh took another bite. She remembered the flavor well, and knew the skill that had gone into preparing it. "A giantess made this," she said, waving the pork at him. "That's the only possible explanation."

"Aye, and speaking of magic," Shamus called, "where's that mage run off to?"

Between bites, Kyleigh told him of what had happened to Jake. Nadine kept assuring them that he and Elena would find their way out, but Kyleigh wasn't going to chance it. As soon as her belly was full, she was going to go back into the tunnels and try to find them.

"Oh, there's little hidey holes all around here," Shamus said, waving his arm out at the desert. They were camped in the shadow of the Red Spine, along the flattened ridge that served as the Baron's highway. The ground beneath them was mostly stone, with only a light dusting of sand on top. "I'll have the men spread out and look for him. If his head pops up, we'll snatch him," Shamus promised.

Kyleigh still wasn't convinced, but she also didn't want to leave her men unprotected in front of Baron Sahar's castle. "Don't you think it's strange that he hasn't attacked yet?" she said, staring at the golden gates.

"It's because he's scared of us," Shamus replied. "We gave him a good walloping, didn't we, lads?"

The men cheered, raising their scimitars over their heads.

Kyleigh knew that wasn't it. She'd seen the Baron's army before — up close, and on several occasions. And he certainly didn't like to let invaders sit on his doorstep. No ... knowing Sahar, he was likely just taking his time. He would probably soak himself in some rose-petal bath and wash the stink of the plains from his golden clothes.

Then he'd slip every one of those jeweled rings onto his fingers, perhaps even treat himself to a sprawling lunch — and then when he was good and ready, he'd send his army out to clobber them.

Kyleigh was thinking darkly about this when Nadine wandered up to her. "Would you like a bite?" she said, holding out a chunk of her bread.

"No, thank you. It'll just taste like dirt to me," she explained.

Nadine shook her head. "You are strange, outlander." Her eyes wandered over to the mountains that flanked the right side of the castle, and she tugged on Kyleigh's jerkin. "What is that place?"

All along that stretch of the Spine, ramps had been carved out of the red stone. Holes peppered it in clusters, as if it had been struck by a handful of giant arrows. Men in ragged clothing moved in and out of the holes, shoving small carts laden with dirt and jewels.

As Kyleigh watched them, she thought she might've figured out where the trolls had come from — they'd been driven out of their lands, as well.

"Those are the Baron's mines," Kyleigh murmured. She noticed that the guards who watched the miners were still going on about their duties, ignoring the small force that had laid siege to the castle. That, more than anything, told her that Sahar wasn't troubled over them.

As evening crept closer, her worry only grew.

At sunset, she began to hear the clink of armored bodies moving around inside the courtyard. It was difficult to count them by the noise of their steps, but she thought there might be close to a hundred soldiers waiting behind the golden doors. Sahar was about to attack.

There was no way her little army could hold their ground. They'd camped far too close to the castle, and hadn't left themselves a lot of room for an escape. Kyleigh couldn't leave Elena and Jake behind, and she couldn't risk the Baron's army leaking over into the plains — but she also wasn't going to sentence her men to death.

"Gather whatever supplies you can and head straight for Arabath," she barked. She began hoisting baskets and handing them off to whoever happened to be standing close by.

"Why would we leave? We've got such an excellent view of the castle," Shamus said, waving an arm in front of him.

But Kyleigh was in no mood to joke. She turned him by the shoulders and began shoving him down the road. "Any second now, the Baron's going to attack —"

"Then let him!"

"We're too few," Silas cut in. He stared at the gates, his nose twitching in the evening air. "I smell the stench of humans … and steel."

Nadine tossed a basket over her shoulder. "If we leave now, we may be able to outrun them."

"Oh no, we're not running anywhere!"

Shamus tried shoving Kyleigh back, but she was far too strong. When he tried to spin out of her reach, she grabbed him around the belt. As they struggled, the mots and the seas men looked on with open mouths, as if they were unsure what to do. And then a familiarly-exalted voice drifted through the air:

"I should have known it was you!"

When Kyleigh turned, she saw that Baron Sahar had finally emerged. He stood on the ramparts over the gate. His intricate robe glittered in the fading light, and his jeweled fingers sparkled as he waved to her.

"The Dragongirl, herself — standing on my steps," he went on. "I must say, I'll consider it a great honor to bring His Majesty your head."

There were few people who could make Kyleigh want to punch them simply by speaking, but Sahar was one of them. She'd always thought that he had an extremely obnoxious voice: he carried his words as if they were some sort of precious gift, as if everybody should be delighted to hear them. And they had a peculiar way of grating against her nerves.

Kyleigh was determined to shut him up. She pushed Shamus aside and drew Harbinger. "Make sure your eyes are opened, Baron — because my face will be the last thing you ever see."

She charged. And just as she'd suspected, Sahar wasn't going to wait on top of his castle to be an easy target for her flames: he nearly tripped over his fine clothes in his rush to get to the stairs.

"Attack!" he cried. "Attack her *now*!"

Kyleigh knew she only had seconds to act. Once the Baron's soldiers escaped the courtyard, they would scatter like ants from a hill, and she wouldn't be able to stop them all. No, she'd have to blast them quickly.

The golden doors began to open, and she braced herself for a fight.

Chapter 37
The Queen of all Minceworms

The walls were trying to crush them — Elena was sure of it.

She followed Jake along the twisting passageway, straining her eyes to see beyond the feeble, greenish light that spouted from the top of his staff. At every narrow turn, the walls brushed across her shoulders, tightening against them like a serpent's coils. Wet drops fell from the ceiling. They would strike her neck, startling her. She could do nothing as they slipped beneath her collar and trailed an unsettling line down her back.

Once, her boot slipped off the edge of a damp rock, and she yelped because she thought she was about to tumble down one of the black holes that lined the path. But her foot thudded hard against the solid ground, and her scream echoed off the walls — as if the earth was mocking her.

"How much further?" she hissed.

Jake was bent over, inspecting a cluster of delicate crystals that sprouted from the stone floor like weeds. "Hmm? Oh — I'm not entirely sure. It's hard to gauge how far we've gone, what with everything being so blasted dark."

"Can't you make your light any brighter?"

He inclined his head. "I *could*, though it tends to get a bit ... volatile, if I make it too bright. Sometimes it's better to err on the side of darkness." He looked back at the crystals. "I probably ought to take a sample of this. One never knows when one might stumble across it again."

He pulled a tiny pair of tweezers out of his pack and advanced on the crystals. Whatever he was about to do looked suspiciously as if it was going to take a while, so Elena decided to speed things up: she ripped the whole cluster out of the ground and crammed it into his pack.

"There you go. Now keep moving."

Jake seemed to think better of arguing with her. He moved out, heading in a direction he was *reasonably* certain was north. Elena didn't think that was nearly as comforting as being entirely certain. But what choice did she have? She could hardly muster up the nerve to breathe — much less to navigate.

The tunnel they'd been following finally ended, and they found themselves stuck at what appeared to be a dead end. But before Elena could panic, Jake discovered another passage.

It was little more than a narrow crack in the wall, so blackened that not even the staff's light could illuminate it.

Elena's limbs froze at the sight of it. "I'm not going in there."

"Well, you may not have a choice." Jake passed his light about the room, then he shook his head. "It looks as if this is our only way out. Come on — we'll travel quickly."

He was wedged halfway into the crack when he looked up and saw that Elena hadn't moved. Even if she'd *wanted* to, she didn't think she would've been able to convince her feet to step towards it. Her lungs tightened at the very sight of the crack, as if they were preparing themselves to be crushed.

"It's not all that bad." Jake was standing beside her, now. She'd been so busy staring at the narrow passageway that she hadn't heard him move. "I'm sure it's not even that far a stretch."

She stared at the crack. It seemed to watch her through mocking eyes and dared her to come closer. If they went inside, they might very well get stuck. Then they'd suffer for days as they slowly starved to death. But perhaps it wouldn't be *that* bad: perhaps they'd die quickly — perhaps the floor would simply fall out from beneath them, and send them tumbling down into oblivion ...

Her heart shuddered and tripped midstride. She realized that Jake had twined his fingers in hers. Their palms were pressed together, but he didn't hold her down. His grip was more comforting than demanding. She wasn't sure how to take it.

"One step at a time," he said, and his thin lips bent in the tiniest of smiles. "Do you happen to know how all of these tunnels were formed?"

Elena shook her head. And as Jake talked, he coaxed her forward.

"I've done a bit of research on the topic. Of course, there are a dozen different theories, but the one I think makes the most sense is that this was all once part of a great channel of rivers. They say the desert was every bit as fertile as the plains, at one point. But then the historians claim that the river dried up, and the entire region was left to bake in the sun. I don't think that's entirely true. I don't think the river dried up: I think it sank! Like the water beneath the mots' mountain, for example ..."

They edged their way through the crack, and Elena focused on Jake's chatter. It was strange ... but he didn't smell as foul as he once had. Perhaps that was because whatever lurked inside the tunnel smelled far fouler. Her hand was so sweaty that the magic in his skin didn't even itch her.

As they slipped deeper into the earth, she began to forget that he was a mage. It was easy to see him just as she saw every other man. And yet, it was difficult ... because he wasn't like any man she'd ever met.

"Ah, here we are!" Jake said, interrupting her thoughts. He pulled her through the last stretch of the tunnel and they popped out on the other side.

Elena stretched her arms as far as she could, but didn't feel any walls around her. Jake's feeble light seemed to make the darkness, if possible, even darker. "Do you see a light?"

"No — but that doesn't mean anything. Perhaps it's already nightfall," Jake said quickly. "In that case, there wouldn't be a light. Let's just see."

He stepped forward, and she caught hold of his pack. She wasn't about to be left alone in the dark. There could be holes in the floor, after all.

They only got a few steps in when a blast of hot air suddenly ripped across their faces.

"Ah, there — you see? Fresh a — ack!"

Jake doubled over as the horrible stench hit them. It smelled like a battlefield in the middle of summer's heat: thick with the odor of rotting flesh and curdled blood.

"Now *that* is fetid," Jake gasped.

Elena's mask was helping to block out most of the odor. She tried to strain her eyes in the direction the air had come from. "But if there's wind, doesn't that mean there's an exit?" She pointed Jake towards the ceiling. "Hold your staff up there."

He did, but the light was too feeble to reach the top.

"Make it brighter."

Jake grunted. "All right. But you'd better stand back — just in case."

Little beads of sweat popped up across his brow as the light brightened. It stretched towards the ceiling, trembling and waving like a soap bubble in a bath. Jake held the staff up as high as he could, revealing the long, ribbed passageway above them. Glistening wet clung thickly to its edges. Thousands of white stalactites grew sideways all around the walls ...

Wait a moment — stalactites didn't grow sideways.

"Ha! I can't believe it!" Jake said excitedly, even though his arms trembled under the weight of the glowing green bubble. "We've found her!"

"Found who?"

The light crossed deeper into the fanged tunnel, and Elena jumped backwards as the whole ceiling convulsed with a wet, smacking sound.

"It's the minceworm queen!" Jake cried.

Another blast of hot breath rocked them. Jake staggered backwards, and the green bubble quivered dangerously at the end of his staff. The minceworm queen hissed at the end of her breath, drawing in a fresh gasp of air. And the bubble suddenly popped free.

It floated upwards as the queen inhaled, drifting calmly through the dark passage of her open gullet, past her gleaming teeth — and into the depths of her gut.

Jake moaned as he watched the bubble grow smaller. "Oh, no. Oh, this isn't good. This is *not* good!"

He charged for Elena, and the terror on his face froze her limbs. He jumped on her, knocking her to the ground. Then he waved his staff and a blue wall wrapped around them, shielding them against the floor.

"Better hold on tight," Jake muttered in her ear.

She watched over his shoulder as the green bubble drifted all the way to the back of the queen's throat ... and then it popped.

****

Kyleigh's steps pounded in a fierce rhythm as she charged the Baron's army. She could hear her companions behind her, but they would never catch up. The golden doors opened and a horde of scimitar-wielding soldiers began to pour out.

She knew she didn't have another second to waste. Kyleigh slowed, concentrating as she arched her back and prepared to become a dragon —

A bright flash of light enveloped the entire castle. It was so fierce and loud that for a moment, she thought the sun had actually fallen from the sky. The insides of her ears nearly burst as the blast threw her backwards. She'd never flown through the air when she hadn't meant to, and was surprised at how badly it hurt when she finally struck the ground.

She blinked against the brightness. Gold leaves fell towards her, drifting down from where they'd been launched into the sky. They fell closer and closer, growing larger as they twirled and as the air shrieked off their sides. No, those weren't leaves at all — they were the Baron's golden doors!

Kyleigh ran for her life. The gates crashed into the ground, knocking her off her feet again as the whole earth trembled. Stones the size of men thudded into the ground behind her. Jewels rained down upon the sand in shimmering, stinging drops. Her companions sprinted back to avoid being crushed, and their mouths gaped open as they watched what was left of the Baron's castle go sailing through the air.

A monstrous tongue of green flame erupted from the ground, where the courtyard had once stood. It burned very brightly for a few seconds before it suddenly flared out, hissing as it disappeared. Now the castle walls were little more than a pile of rubble. All that was left of the Baron's great army were twisted bits of swords and armor.

Kyleigh lay still for a moment. Her ears rang the whole way down her neck. When she opened her eyes, Silas was standing over her. He pulled on her, trying to get her to look where he pointed. She couldn't hear what he said over the noise of the ringing.

He helped her sit up. When his mouth came close to her ear, she could make out his muffled words: "Look — look at the mines, dragoness!"

She did, and she saw that the miners were using the explosion as an opportunity to revolt. They swung pickaxes and shovels at the guards, chasing them out into the open desert. The mots arrived with their spears, quickly dispatching the few guards that had been foolish enough to try to stand and fight. As the guards fled into the desert, Shamus and his men sent arrows after their heels.

Kyleigh put her hand out to try to push herself up, and felt something sharp against her palm. It was a tiny pair of black crystals, grown together like two heads on one body. She normally didn't care for jewels. But her ears ached so badly that she wasn't thinking clearly, and she decided to keep it.

She tucked the jewel inside her pocket and dragged herself to her feet. Shamus headed towards her. He stooped to grab something off the ground as he approached. When he drew even with her, he pressed it into her hand. It was a charred, ragged piece of a golden robe.

"I guess this means the Baron's been taken care of," Kyleigh said.

Shamus's chuckle was still a little muffled. "Aye. There's not enough of him left to scrape into a bottle."

Kyleigh was just happy that her friends were alive. That blast could've easily taken them all out. "What happened?"

Shamus shrugged. "I don't rightly know. Why are you shouting?"

"Because I nearly had my ears blasted out!" she said, swatting him in the arm.

They approached the castle ruins carefully. It was still smoking in places, and there was so much rubble that it took them a while to get around it. Silas slipped into his lion form and leapt from pile to pile, edging closer to the center of the blast. When he reached it, he jumped back into his human skin so quickly that he nearly tumbled over.

"It's that stupid Elena!" he cried, clapping his hands together.

"Shut up, cat."

Kyleigh's heart leapt when she heard Elena's voice. She picked her way hurriedly over the rest of the debris and found herself standing on the edge of a giant hole.

Slabs of rock had collapsed into the hole, forming something like a makeshift ramp. Elena had climbed it as far as she could, but it looked as if she would need help getting over the rest: she held Jake's staff in one hand — while the mage himself hung limply across her shoulder.

"He's fine," Elena called to them. "He just passed out. Now get us a rope or something — I'm sick of being underground!"

Chapter 38
The Sowing Moon

The day passed miserably. The guards hauled Declan and Kael into the dungeons and locked them up inside a dampened cell — along with what appeared to be the cell's previous tenets.

Apparently, Ludwig wasn't the only captive that Lord Gilderick had forgotten about.

Kael swept the pile of bones to the side so that Declan would have someplace to sleep. Then he paced furiously inside their little cell, wondering what sort of horrible punishment Gilderick had planned for them.

An hour or so later, Declan finally woke. The thin burns that crisscrossed over his face and limbs weren't too blistered, and it made Kael wonder if Hob hadn't hexed him to sleep. But he was too angry to bother finding out.

"Why did you follow me?" he snapped, after he'd given Declan a very rushed explanation of what had happened to them. "Was it really so blasted important to find out what I was up to? You should've just trusted me! I hope you're happy, because now we're both trapped."

Declan didn't seem too concerned. He touched the burns on his face gingerly, wincing. "Oh, don't flatter yourself — I knew it was you all along." When Kael looked surprised, he broke out in a rare grin. "Seventeen years pass without trouble, and then this wee little mountain rat shows up — and suddenly the whole under-realm is clawing its way out to greet us? You weren't exactly sly about it. No, I knew it was you. And after what you did for Brend, I *mostly* trusted you. But I'm a curious fellow. I just followed you out to see how you'd done it." He leaned forward, and still grinning, he said:

"Now that we're both dead men anyways … I don't suppose you'd tell me?"

Kael glared at him. "No. And I'll take it to my grave, Horseman — just to spite you."

But instead of putting him off, this only made Declan smile all the wider.

There were no windows in their tiny cell, and therefore no way to guess how much time had passed. Kael tried to sleep, hoping that sleep would make the night come faster. But no sooner had he drifted off than a loud, booming noise startled him awake.

It was deep, like the call of thunder, and the ground trembled a bit as the noise faded. Kael leapt up and peered beneath the crack of the cell door. A few pairs of monstrous feet passed by, but they seemed to be in no hurry.

"What *was* that?" Kael murmured.

Declan didn't look too concerned. "Oh, the Baron's probably just blasting himself a new mine. He does that every now and then — he's always digging for his clodded jewels."

Kael hoped that was all it was, but he wasn't sure. His worry kept him awake, and his rump started to go numb from sitting on the stone floor. It was actually a welcome relief when the guards came for them.

The cell door opened, and Kael recognized the giant named Dingy standing on the other side. "Here," he said. He shoved some object roughly into each of their hands and then chased them out with the sharp end of his pike. More guards waited for them on the other side, and they herded them quickly down the hall.

The things Dingy had given them were satchels, the same rough-spun pouch that the giants used to plant their fields. Kael slung one over his shoulder and reached inside. In place of seed were a handful of dirt clods. Each clod was about the size of his palm. Some felt as if they had nothing in them, while others sat heavily, as if they were made of stone. He thought one might've felt strangely warm — almost hot.

He held the clods up to Declan, who shrugged. And then very suddenly, Dingy's hand clamped down upon his wrist.

"Don't you even think about it," he growled. "You put those back and don't let me catch you reaching in there again."

And because there was a pike digging uncomfortably into his middle, Kael did as he was told.

The guards hauled them out of the dungeons, through the dampened hallways, and stopped abruptly at the keep's front doors — the doors that would lead out into the courtyard. Kael couldn't see over the bodies in front of him, but he could hear Dred's voice booming clearly from outside:

"... you know the rules — this is your chance to climb the ranks, blisters! The last giant standing will earn himself a higher spot in His Lordship's army. And if there's a tie ... you all die!" There was a thunderous roar of approval from his audience and for a moment, Dred's voice was swallowed up.

Kael could hardly believe what he was hearing.

"We aren't going to be slaughtered," Declan hissed to him. "We're going to be given a chance to fight."

Darkness began to creep over his eyes, and Kael knew he'd have to think quickly. He didn't know what the clods in the satchels were for, but he didn't think this was going to be a normal sort of fight. If Declan went berserk, he might very well get himself killed.

"No, it's not a fight," Kael said, grabbing him by the shoulder. "Look at me. This isn't a fight — it's a game."

Declan looked confused. "A game?"

"Yes. They call them the Sowing Moon *games* for a reason."

"But you heard them out there. They mean to kill us —
"

"But in a clever sort of way," he reasoned, gesturing at his satchel. "These aren't your average weapons, are they? Of course not. And that's because we're not going to fight for our lives — we're going to *play* for them. Just follow my lead," he added, with what he hoped was a reassuring smirk. "I happen to be pretty good at games."

Kael had enough time for one deep breath before Dred cried:

"May the best giant win!"

The keep doors burst open and the guards shoved them outside. Kael stumbled into the courtyard to a thunderous roar of jeers. He couldn't believe how much everything had changed: the ramparts were packed like tavern benches, hosting what must've been nearly every member of Gilderick's army. The guards held tankards and thick legs of meat in their hands. They roared at him through their full mouths.

Lord Gilderick and Countess D'Mere were seated on the lowest rampart, poised in the exact middle of the courtyard's arc. Gilderick sat stiffly in a high-backed chair. He had a plain white handkerchief pressed over his nose and mouth — and wore a look that made Kael think he might've gotten a whiff of the latrines. Beside him, Dred stood with his pike clutched warily in his hands. D'Mere's twin guards stood unmoving at her back. There was no sign of the dark rider.

"What's this clodded madness all about?" Declan shouted, trying to raise his voice above the cheers.

Kael looked where he pointed and saw that the whole yard had been transformed — from an empty plot of dust, to something that looked a bit like a battlefield. Boulders and debris were scattered across it, and most of it was too tall for Kael to see over. The towering obstacles were bunched so closely together that they formed something like a maze.

"What are we supposed to do?" Declan said. He spun around in a tight circle, as if he expected to be attacked from behind.

Kael wasn't sure. He glanced all around the maze. Then a flash of movement caught his eye.

A guard sprang out of the rubble and clambered to the top of an overturned wagon. He carried a shield and wore a satchel across his chest. When he spotted Kael, his face twisted into a wicked grin. He reached inside his satchel.

A dirt clod flew out of the maze and struck him in the head. His eyes widened and froze. A patch of gray spread from where he'd been struck, down the side of his face and across his limbs. Half a blink later, he'd been turned completely to stone.

The crowd cheered.

When a second guard leapt out of the maze, Kael didn't have time to think: he grabbed a clod out of his satchel and hurled it at the guard. It flew in a straight line and likely would've landed true, had the guard not caught it on his shield.

For a split second, the shield turned to stone and the guard struggled to hold it up. But with a crack and a burst of light, the stone fell away, leaving the shield smooth once again.

"They're enchanted!" Declan hollered, his eyes wide.

The guard laughed at the stunned looks on their faces — then he made his throw. Declan grabbed Kael around the middle and hurtled himself behind the nearest boulder. A burst of fire erupted behind them.

"What do we do —?"

"Just keep moving!" Kael said over the top of him. "I'll figure something out."

Magic — *why* did it have to be magic? Kael's heart pounded as they ran. Even though the clods wouldn't hurt him, he still couldn't risk being hit. Once the spells touched him, everyone who wasn't blind would know that he was a whisperer.

His only chance to stay alive was to keep moving, and hope that the guards would eventually kill each other off.

They weaved a dangerous trail through the maze, never once pausing for a breath. Kael tried to listen for footsteps at every corner, but he couldn't hear anything over the roar of the crowd. And to make matters worse, the guards on the ramparts began to help the ones in the arena, pointing excitedly every time they spotted Declan and Kael.

Once, they took a bad turn and wound up nearly running into a guard from behind. He spun and threw blindly, but the clod slipped out of his hand. It burst on the ground between them, and a cloud of green smoke erupted from it. Kael shoved Declan back, lodging him safely behind a massive crate.

"What *was* that?" he gasped, wiping the dirt from his sweaty brow.

When the smoke cleared, Kael leaned around and saw the guard lying motionless upon the ground. His skin was swollen and green. His chest didn't rise. "It must've been poison," Kael guessed. "Better hold your breath the next time we're thrown at."

Declan nodded. "Sounds like a fair plan to me."

Kael leaned back against the crate, his mind spinning. The crowd was already pointing them out to whichever guard was on their trail, and he knew they'd have to move soon. He watched the eyes above them, watched where they pointed and how they gestured, and it wasn't long before he figured out their plan.

"They're trying to trap us," he groaned.

Somehow, they'd wound up inside a narrow passage, one so packed with debris that it formed something like an alleyway. Judging by the crowd's excited shouts, one of the guards was already upon them. They'd have to try to outrun him.

"Come on!"

Declan was still panting from their latest sprint, but he followed Kael stubbornly to the alley's end. That's when Kael realized that he'd made a second mistake: the only way forward was around a sharp corner, down a passage that elbowed out into the open maze.

There was no telling what awaited them around the corner — though he couldn't help but notice that the crowd above them had gone strangely quiet. They sneered down at Kael, and sat purposefully on their hands. It was very likely that a second guard was waiting to ambush them at the elbow.

Light flared up over Declan's shoulder. The guard who'd followed them down the alleyway had been creeping up on them, and he'd chosen that moment to attack. But fortunately for Declan and Kael, he missed.

Though *unfortunately*, the fire that burst from his clod caught viciously onto the wooden debris — and within seconds, the whole passageway was engulfed in flames. The guard swore and stumbled backwards to safety, but the damage had already been done: they were trapped.

Their only way out was around a corner that would almost certainly lead to an ambush. The fire's voice roared in their ears, the flames raced closer.

"We have to move —"

"Wait!" Kael grabbed Declan before he could bolt around the corner. "Not that way." He thought hard, and an idea suddenly came to him. "Lift me — do it quickly!"

Kael stepped into Declan's palms and the giant hoisted him above the wall. The crowd shouted in warning, but it was too late. Kael spotted the guard who'd been crouched, waiting for them at the opening. And he threw a clod at his back.

Blue lightning devoured him before he even had a chance to scream. He fell out of his armor in a pile of ash, and the wind scattered his pieces.

They burst from the alleyway, narrowly escaping the flames. The crowd booed as thick black smoke trailed up from the fire. It swelled to fill the air and blocked a good portion of the arena from view. Kael's eyes streamed against the fumes, blinding him.

He tried to follow Declan, but it wasn't long before he got lost. He went around the next corner at a sprint — and ran straight into a thick patch of smoke.

He gasped. The burning tendrils shot up his nostrils, doubling him over when they struck his lungs. He coughed madly, heaving — trying to force the smoke out. And while he struggled to breathe, a pair of rather large hands clamped down on either side of his head.

Kael's feet left the ground as his body was hoisted into the air. He hung by the weight of his neck; his arms were trapped over his head. He kicked out behind him, but his heels struck uselessly against an iron breastplate. A voice blasted across his ears:

"Come out, Declan Battle-Mad!" the guard said mockingly. "Come face me, you filthy blood-bather. Or I'll snap your rodent's furry little neck!"

Kael braced himself against the guard's arms as he spun, trying to keep his neck from breaking. With his hands trapped above him, he couldn't reach his satchel. He strained to see through the billows of smoke, searching for any sign of Declan. The pathways around them were empty. No cry answered the guard. For a moment, Kael thought he might very well be on his own.

Then a shadow caught his eye — a silhouette of a man burned through the smoke. He was crouched some feet away, perched on top what appeared to be a chunk of broken wall.

Kael didn't know if it was Declan or not. It could very well have been another guard. But he decided that he had nothing left to lose.

He stretched his hand out to the shadow, flexing his fingers, asking for something. For a long moment, the shadow didn't move. And Kael was afraid that he'd been left to have his neck broken. But then with a grunt, the shadow's arm came up, tossing a clod in his direction.

Kael caught it gently, careful not to break it. He hoped to mercy that the smoke would block what he was about to do from the eyes above him. Though he supposed that if he didn't act now, he'd be dead anyways. So he took a deep breath, reached behind him — and smashed the clod into the guard's face.

Green swarmed over his vision. The guard coughed and sputtered violently as the poison enveloped him. He grasped for his throat, and Kael fell to the ground. He lay there for a long moment with his eyes closed, not daring to breathe. Then someone grabbed him around the ankles and yanked him backwards.

"Steady, wee rat!" Declan said, half-laughing as Kael tried to pummel him away. "It's only me."

He pulled Kael to his feet — only to stumble backwards as a blast of wind swept across the arena. It extinguished the fires, carried the smoke up and out into the night sky. The crowd reappeared, craning their necks to see which of the fighters was left standing.

They booed at the sight of Declan and Kael.

"Quiet! *Quiet*, blisters!" Dred shouted over the top of them. He hurried down the ramparts behind Hob, who was busily putting out the last of the flames. A menacing company of guards followed at his back.

"I'm sorry, Kael," Declan whispered. His eyes were locked on Dred's. Black began to seep into them as the General got closer; Declan's voice grew more furious. "I'm sorry — but I might not get another chance."

Then without warning, he charged — flinging clods from his satchel as quickly as he could draw them. Terror filled Dred's mangled face as he held his shield up to defend himself. Clods erupted across it, spraying fire and poison in every direction. His shield turned to stone and for a moment, it dropped — leaving his head exposed.

Declan's next shot likely would've killed him, if Hob hadn't stepped in. Chains snaked over Declan, strapping his limbs to his sides. He toppled onto the ground as the crowd roared. His chin struck the dust hard.

Once his opponent had been safely hobbled, Dred suddenly found his courage. He stepped up to Declan and raised his pike overhead.

Kael reached into his satchel. Dred could try to bring his weapon down, but Kael's shot would reach him first —

"Stop." Gilderick took the handkerchief away from his mouth and stood calmly from his chair. His boney arms stretched out at his sides, making him look like some underfed gull.

Dred's pike hovered over Declan. "But, m'Lord —"

"Curb that defiant tongue, General. Or I'll feed it to the crows."

It was amazing how quickly Dred took his weapon away. He pawed nervously at his chin. "Please, m'Lord — I meant no defiance. Don't cut my tongue out."

"I didn't say anything about cutting it out," Gilderick said, and an amused smile stretched across his pasty lips. When his chin began to turn in Kael's direction, he quickly looked at the ground. "Odd ... the slaves have never won before. I don't think we have any rules for this. I suppose I could've offered you both a place in my army." His voice changed to point at Declan. "But I'm afraid your outburst is going to cost you dearly. Twelve lashes each — and then tuck the little beasts back into their barns."

All of the warmth dropped from Kael's face when Hob pulled the wench-tongue from his belt. Gilderick declared that Kael was to be whipped first — and for his outburst, Declan would be made to watch.

Kael hardly felt it when the guards tore the satchel off his shoulders and bent him over the nearest crate. A guard held his arms over the edge, leaving him no way to shield his back. They propped Declan up beside him. His eyes were still dark and crazed, and he bellowed unintelligibly into the chains around his mouth.

"Now, I trust there will be no more attempts to escape," Gilderick said from above them. "If there are ... you will not die quickly. I shall have plenty of time to think about how to drag it out. Hob — you may begin."

Kael closed his eyes tightly. He knew there was no way out, not this time. There would be no hardening his back against these blows. Every bite of a wench-tongue was supposed to draw blood — and if he didn't bleed, he'd be found out.

So he would have to grit his teeth and take it.

But as he watched the shadow of Hob's arm come up, fear suddenly gripped him. Kael realized that he didn't trust himself not to cheat. Every instinct in his body screamed for him to use his powers — to protect himself against the coming pain. He knew he wasn't brave enough to face the lashes on his own. And so, in the moment before the whip came down, he found himself thinking of her ... of Kyleigh.

It was so easy to draw her up. He felt as if she was branded into his memory, burned so deeply that he could never forget her ... he had no hope of ever forgetting her. He saw her smile, heard her laugh ... he remembered the way her eyes glowed in the firelight.

His strength began to fade as he thought of her, and the black beast rose up inside his chest. It wrapped its terrible wings about his limbs, strangled the cords of his heart ... and his sorrow finally crushed him.

The first lash bit easily through his flesh.

Chapter 39
The Dark Rider

Several long, dark hours passed before Kael finally woke. When he saw the familiar faces surrounding him, it was everything he could do to keep from crying.

He'd been hoping not to wake — to never have to see this miserable little stall or hear the giants' gruff voices ever again. He was hoping that the lashes had killed him. He was hoping not to have to live through the pain.

But not surprisingly, Fate had other plans.

Something cold dribbled onto the raw flesh of his back, burning his wounds like he'd rolled over into the fire. He yelped and sat up quickly — so quickly that the tender, ragged edges of his stripes tore anew. The world swam in front of him as fiery pain pulsed at the backs of his eyes. He swallowed the bile down and knocked away the hands that grasped for him.

"Lay back, wee thing," Brend said. "We've got to clean them, or they'll never heal —"

"I'll heal them myself," Kael snapped. He blinked the last of the little black dots from his eyes and saw the whole stall was gathered about him.

Brend crouched before him. The bowl of water he held looked tiny in his massive hands. Eveningwing sat back on his knees, twisting a wet cloth worriedly at his chest. A drop off fresh blood trickled down Kael's neck, and he eyed it.

"Don't —"

But Eveningwing's arm jabbed forward with lightning quickness, dabbing the blood dry before Kael had a chance to swat him.

"You're not helping things," Kael said, groaning as he reached back to feel the damage. His fingers passed over the

471

first wound, and he nearly passed out again when he felt how deep it was.

"You did a brave thing," Brend said. And for once, it looked like he meant it. "Declan's told us how you fought at the Sowing Moon ... how you've been fighting for us all along. I'll admit that I wasn't happy to find out about your fibbing," the severe lines of his brows bent up as quickly as they'd fallen, "but I can understand why you did it. I certainly would've tried to stop you, had I known."

Kael didn't know what to say to that, and he didn't exactly have the energy to think. So he just nodded and said: "Where's Declan?"

"Here," he grunted.

Two giants sat behind him, cleaning the red stripes across his shoulders. It was clear by how slowly they moved that they were trying hard to be gentle — though judging by the grimace on Declan's face, they weren't succeeding.

He ground his teeth against their next swipe. When they went to clean the cloth, he spoke: "My wounds aren't as deep as yours: a giant's hide is a mightily thick thing." Then his face suddenly crumpled. He bit down hard on his lip, and Kael was alarmed when tears began sliding from his eyes. "I did a selfish thing, tonight. For so many years I've carried this burden, and when I saw a chance to lift it, I took it without thinking."

He wiped impatiently at his eyes and signaled for the giants behind him to stop their cleaning. He took a deep, shuddering breath, and the whole barn fell silent. "But since you've shed blood for my hurt, I feel it's only right to tell you why I did it. I'm the second of three brothers," he began, keeping his shadowed brow cast down at the floor. "I was born a sickly child — smaller and leaner than the rest. My father, Callan Horseman, was our Prince's great General. There are as many tales of his courage as there are stones across the plains. And he deserved a far better son than me.

"As luck would have it, Fate had already given him an elder child — a son that was his match in size and strength ...

and an older brother that was everything I ever longed to be. You've likely already guessed it, but his name ... was Dred."

No, Kael hadn't guessed that. In fact, he had to clamp a hand over his mouth to keep it from falling open.

Declan's hands balled into fists. His voice fell rougher. "Even now, my gut burns with sick when I think about how proud I was of Dred. When I watched him beat the other lads at sparring, when he tossed full-grown giants over his shoulders like they were naught but wheat bales ... it was *pride* that flushed me red. That was *my* big brother, after all — the pride of clan Horseman." Declan's fists began to shake as he forced the next words out. "Yeh, I watched Dred with the eyes of any younger brother — looking up, longing to be able to reach the same heights as he.

"Now, I'm ashamed to think that I ever loved him." His eyes locked down on Kael's, holding him like a pair of desperate hands upon his shirt. "You already know about the day they discovered my ... my madness. When the rebel whisperers attacked us, I went against my father's wishes and fought. Dred turned and ran for his life — he fled to my mother's family, clan Goatherd. And they granted him protection from my father's wrath.

"But when the mages swept through our region, not even the Goatherds could save him. And though Dred was old enough to stand and fight, he fled with the children to the Scepter Stone." Declan's eyes burned red. His face contorted as if he'd just had a dagger thrust into his belly. "And now it's time to tell you about Callan's third son," he said, his voice hardly a whisper. "It's time you know about Dante.

"He was my wee baby brother, and a gentle soul." Declan stopped. He pressed his thumbs against his eyes so forcefully that Kael feared he would gouge them out. He breathed in across his gritted teeth, and when he looked up, anguish burned his face.

"You know what happened at the Scepter Stone — you know how Titus lined us up, how he set us against each other. I tried to stop it." Declan rocked forward, bracing his fists against the sides of his head. "But when I stepped out to face

Titus, I heard Dante scream — I heard him cry. I turned around, and I saw him ... I saw him ..."

Declan couldn't seem the get the words out. His fingers clawed the side of his face, scratching raw lines down his temples. Brend had to step in and grab his wrists to keep him from hurting himself.

"It's all right," Kael said quickly. "I know what happened to Dante. I saw it all — remember?"

"You don't know!" Declan cried. The rage in his eyes was not meant for Kael, but it made it no less terrifying. "You'll never know — not until you watch one of your brothers slay the other. Dred was the oldest. He was supposed to *protect* Dante. I trusted him!" He took his hands away from his face and crossed them over his chest. "But brotherhood never mattered to Dred. The only thing he ever cared about was his own hide. He drove a sword through Dante's chest — *my* sword, the blade I'd dropped behind me. If I hadn't set it down, if I hadn't let it go ..."

"He would've done it anyways," Brend said firmly, clutching Declan's arm. "Don't carry his evil on your shoulders. It's no fault of yours —"

"It is," Declan said darkly. He glared until Brend released him, then he went on. "He used our little brother's blood to buy his way into Gilderick's army, and I gave him the means to do it. I've sworn to kill Dred," he growled, "and I still mean to. As long as I've got breath in my body, I'll hate him. That's why I charged him tonight. And I'm not sorry for it ... but I'm sorry that I dragged you into it," he muttered, staring blankly at Kael's bloodied shirt. "You kept me alive in there, and that was a sorry way to repay you. I cost you your hard-earned freedom ... and I'll never forgive myself for it."

Silence hung over the stall so thickly for a moment that Kael almost forgot to breathe.

Then he laughed.

Or he started to, anyways — until the movement tore painfully at his wounds. So he settled for a hard smile, instead. "There wasn't going to be any freedom. You know that as well as I do," he said scornfully. Then he raised his voice. "When will you giants understand? You can't earn your freedom in this Fate-forsaken place. You can't wait for it, either. If you want to be free men — then you've got to take it."

He put his hands to his shirt, undoing his buttons as quickly as his sore back would let him. Brend watched him curiously. The giants leaned in. Eveningwing clutched his legs to his chest and grinned widely over the top of his knees.

"What are you doing?" Declan said, looking slightly alarmed.

An involuntary smirk bent Kael's mouth as he pulled the last button free. "You've told me your story, Horseman. Now it's high time that I tell you mine."

At first, the giants were shocked to find out that Kael was a whisperer. When he showed them his mark, every mouth in the room fell open on one hinge. There was a good amount of head-scratching and muttering, and a few of them wondered if he meant to kill them. The only one who didn't seem at all surprised was Declan.

He laughed like he'd just won a victory, jabbed a finger at Kael's chest and shouted: "I knew it!"

"What do you mean, you —? Well, then why didn't you come out and say so?" Brend grunted. He pawed through his shock of hair, and it was obvious by how clenched his eyes were that he was still trying to figure it out.

But Declan offered no further explanation. "I had my suspicions," he said with a shrug.

When Kael set about healing his wounds, it was all he could do to keep the giants from rumbling too loudly. He healed the bits he could reach, starting with the deepest patches. He didn't heal them all the way, but worked until he could move his arms and shoulders with only a little pain. The shallower cuts would have to wait: he knew he would need every ounce of his strength for the hours ahead.

It took a bit of convincing, but Declan finally let him seal up some of his gashes. His back kept twitching every time Kael would try to pull his skin together. When he growled for Declan to hold still, he growled back:

"What am I to do? It tickles."

As soon as he was finished, Kael told Eveningwing to go to Jonathan — and to tell him to get ready. He left in whirl of feathers.

Brend, who hadn't stopped fussing with his hair the whole while, overheard. "Tell the wee fiddler to get ready for what?" he blurted. His eyes shot frantically between Declan and Kael. "No more secrets — I want to know what you're up to, and I want to know it *now*."

So Kael told him everything.

Brend was heartily against his plan, and had started off on what promised to be a very fiery rant when Kael told him about what Gilderick planned to do with the women. Then he sat down heavily.

"Not Clairy ..." he murmured, after a long moment when he'd tugged so hard on his hair that Kael feared it might actually part from the roots. Then he shook his head. "I can't do it. I won't risk the lives of so many to save the comfort of one — not even one so dear to me as my Clairy," he said, though his voice broke miserably at the end.

"This isn't about Clairy," Declan replied.

He'd listened quietly as Kael told his story, keeping his thoughts hidden beneath the shadow of his brow. Now his eyes were raised and pointed directly at Brend — and there was a fire in them that Kael liked the look of.

"This is about all of us." Declan raised his voice, so that it echoed through the rafters and touched every stall. "This is about our chance at freedom."

"But what if it fails?" Brend whispered back. "We've had no part in the planning. We haven't had much time to think —"

"Then think of our little seedlings," Declan replied, gesturing towards the Fields. "They don't know when the rains will come, but do they hold out for a cloudy day? No, from the moment they're tucked into the earth, they put their roots down — so that when the rain falls, they're ready for it. Well, lads ... we've had our roots buried deep in our hope for years. And now the rains have finally come." He turned to

Kael; a fierce smile parted his lips. "I, for one, am ready to soak them up."

The grunts started in slowly, passed about from stall to stall. Then the giants began to roar. They beat their chests and their eyes caught like embers. It was only after Brend stood to quiet them that Kael realized he'd pressed himself very firmly against the wall.

He understood now why it had taken magic to conquer the plains: nothing worn or wielded by men stood a chance against the giants, once they'd been called to war.

"So it's settled, then? We all agree?"

The giants answered Brend in a single furious bark, so loud that it rattled the shingles across the roof.

"Very well." And Brend's lanky limbs seemed to swell as he said it, so that by the time he turned, he wasn't *Brend* anymore: but a towering giant warrior. "We'll follow you into battle, wee whisperer. Just tell us where to go."

The night was still young, but Kael knew the hours would pass quickly. He decided to let the giants figure out how to free the Pens on their own. They knew the land better than he did, after all. And he had no doubt they would be able to rally the others quickly.

Once he'd rushed through the rest of his instructions, he asked Brend to hoist him through the roof. "We'll be thinking hard," Brend whispered as Kael popped out into the night. "Fate go with you."

Kael didn't want Fate anywhere near him, but he nodded distractedly as he climbed free.

Hob's cottage sat on top of Northbarn, their neighbor to the right. As Kael picked his way towards it, he was careful to stay low and cling to the shadows. A small patch of clouds had swallowed up the moon for the moment, muting its light behind a thin veil. But they wouldn't hold for long, there was no telling when the moon might break free. And aside from those few wispy clouds, there was nothing but clear skies in all directions.

Kael had to move quickly.

He'd gotten used to having a pair of sharp eyes above him, but Eveningwing wasn't around to warn him of trouble, this time. So it took him a bit longer to reach Northbarn than he'd expected.

Once he made it to the foot of the stairs, he was ready — he couldn't afford to hesitate. Kael stopped, and allowed himself a deep breath. Then he grasped at his belt for the curved knife ... and his hand came back empty.

He nearly swore aloud when he realized that he'd left it behind. In all of the excitement of the evening, he'd forgotten to retrieve the knife from Eveningwing's perch. He wanted to kick himself for being so foolish, but there wasn't enough time. If he ran back now, Brend might be able to reach it and toss it out to him.

He turned to jog back to Westbarn — and froze.

There was a shadow in his path, waiting where there hadn't been one before. It stood so close to him that he couldn't see what it was, but he could certainly feel its hot breath on the top of his head.

"Come with me," a man's voice whispered.

When Kael didn't move, he felt a hand clamp firmly around his upper arm.

"You can carry yourself, or I'll carry you over my shoulder. Your choice."

Kael didn't have time for this. But he couldn't see very well and this man, whoever he was, obviously could. He realized he might lose every last moment of his precious time if he tried to fight him. So he decided to go along ... and he waited.

The man led him out into the Fields, dragging him roughly by the arm. They passed through the vegetable patch and into the corn, keeping well away from the road. Kael could feel the minutes slipping by with every step. He tested the man's grip, twisting his arm ever so slightly.

And it was twisted forcefully back.

Just when Kael thought he might have to risk trying to fight his way free, the clouds broke and moonlight rained down upon him. He saw the massive sword strapped to his captor's back, and knew immediately that this was the dark rider he'd seen traveling with Countess D'Mere.

But before he could think of how to disarm him, the rider spun. "You've caught the Countess's attention, whisperer. You ought to be frightened."

Kael tried his best to look confused. "Whisperer?"

Lines wreathed the rider's dark eyes. "Don't play stupid. I saw you heal yourself, and your little giant friend. The Countess has already left the plains and moves quickly for the forest. She sent me back to retrieve you."

It made Kael's gut twist to think that he'd been spied on, but he tried to stay calm. "What does the Countess want with me?"

"To use you, obviously. Healing is such a rare gift. You could do great things for her army. But first ... you're going to do something for me."

Kael watched — half in curiosity and half in worry — as the rider pulled his mask down. He stretched it gingerly over his nose and let it fall to his chest. The face beneath it might've been handsome at one point, but the swollen, festering cut on his chin marred his features.

It looked to be weeks-old and deep. The jagged line sat beneath his lower lip, so thick that it could've been mistaken for a second mouth. He *had* tried to stitch it up at one point, but the threads were so lopsided and uneven that they did little good. Amos would've been furious, had he seen them.

"Heal it," the dark rider said, "and we'll be on our way."

Kael was about to refuse when an idea struck him. "All right." He stepped closer and put one hand beneath the rider's wound. "Close your eyes."

"Why?"

"Because I can concentrate better if you're not staring at me." When the rider hesitated, Kael sighed impatiently. "Do you want it healed or not?"

"Fine."

The rider closed his eyes, and Kael aimed carefully. Then he sent his fist flying into the rider's chin.

It was a blow Morris had taught him, a blow designed to cripple an enemy with very little force. Kael knew he'd struck true when his knuckles connected, and the rider should've fallen unconscious. But instead of collapsing to the ground, he drew his sword.

Kael dropped to all fours as the blade swooshed over his head. A boot to the shoulder sent him rolling backwards. As the world spun, he caught a flash of steel — a deadly, glinting arc poised to fall for his middle — and he kicked up desperately, flailing his leg with all of his strength, his only thought was to get the sword as far away from him as possible.

His boot connected, and the rider grunted in surprise. Kael landed clumsily on his stomach. When he looked up, he saw the rider's hands were empty. Somehow, Kael's wild kick had managed to disarm him. He'd knocked the sword away, and for half a blink, he breathed a little easier.

But then those empty hands knocked him flat on his back.

Kael hardly had a chance to figure out where he'd landed before the rider was upon him. He tried to defend himself the best he could, watching out of the corner of his eyes for the rider's sword. If he could reach it, he might be able to turn the tide. It should've landed somewhere nearby, but the ground around them was empty. Where on earth had it gone?

Without a weapon, the fight quickly turned against him.

The rider's teeth shone wetly in the moonlight. Fresh blood dribbled out from his stitches. He grabbed a fistful of Kael's hair and with a painful tug, brought him up on his heels. "A nice thought," the rider growled, "but you missed. Let me show you how it's done." He jerked Kael's head back by the roots of his hair, exposing his chin.

The full moon hovered in the night sky. Its glowing skin ruled the stars, unhindered by the clouds. Kael stared up at it desperately. His eyes searched over the gray, quiet mountains as he struggled to free himself from the rider's hold. But any move he made was quickly countered; any small ground he gained was easily swallowed back up. Then, just when he thought the world was about to go dark, the moon gave him his answer.

A black shape crossed it; the pale light couldn't quite illuminate its steely surface as it flew overhead. The shape rose until it could go no further, then it turned and began to plummet towards them. It fell for the earth like a crow with a broken wing: spinning tightly, its beak aimed helplessly for the ground.

The dark rider's fingers curled tighter around Kael's hair. "Close your eyes, healer. You're going to have a nasty headache when you come to."

"I'm not a healer," he said back. And for a single grain of time, the rider's surprise put him off-guard. That was all the time Kael needed.

He pulled his legs up to his chest, putting his full weight on the rider's arm and jerking him off his feet. Kael slung the arm back behind him, a thrust of his boots helped the rider on his way, and he went tumbling overhead.

There was the fleshy *thud* of his back, a gasp — and then a sharp, hissing sound ... a sound like a plow blade cutting through the earth.

"I'm a Wright," Kael whispered, in the silence left behind. He allowed himself a few moments to catch his breath before he got to his feet.

The rider lay motionless on his back; his own sword was buried deep in the center of his chest. In his desperation, Kael must've kicked the sword a little harder than he meant to: it had gone sailing through the air, and the weight of its thick blade had dragged it back down to earth — point first. That must've been what had happened, it was the only possible explanation ... and yet, it seemed so very *im*possible.

If he'd had more time to think, Kael might've been able to figure it out. But time was slipping by too quickly, and he couldn't afford to waste another second.

One of the rider's arms hung limply across the sword's hilt, as if he'd been struggling to pull it free. Well, he would struggle no longer.

Kael closed the rider's eyes with the tips of his fingers and quickly searched his body for weapons. He found a long dagger strapped to the rider's hip. It was single-edged and sharp. He knew it was bad luck to take a dead man's weapon, but since rotten luck already seemed to follow him wherever he went, he tucked the blade into his belt. He was certain it would serve him well.

Kael sprinted back to the courtyard and this time, he knew what to look for. He tore the spelled trap off of Hob's front porch. Then he kicked through the door.

Hob bolted upright. His eyes widened when he saw the figure in his doorway and with a cry, he sent a spell hurtling for Kael's chest. The magic washed harmlessly over his body, itching as it passed. When the spell cleared, he made his throw.

Poor Hob died without ever knowing what hit him.

Chapter 40
A Bright Light

The Baron's fine furniture was scattered all about them, lying across the sand in pieces. The shipbuilders gathered it up like bits of dried wood and used it to build fires around the camp. Warmth chased the cold away and brought new, crackling life to their food. They spent the evening in high spirits, drinking and feasting on their spoils.

Most of the miners were eager to return to their families, and they headed down the highway without a second glance. Nadine was able to convince about a dozen of them to stay and fight.

"I have not heard much about these giants from the plains," she admitted. "But I have been told that they are taller even than the outlanders. I cannot imagine having to fight an enemy so large. We will need all the spears we can muster."

Kyleigh couldn't have agreed more. They'd been fortunate today, but even fortune wouldn't get them past Gilderick's army.

Her blood was still too hot to sit quietly, so she decided to take a walk around the camp. She smiled as she listened to the songs of laughter and happy chatter, the merry clinking of tankards and the murmur of contented chewing. It was strange, the sort of peace that seemed to follow a human battle. They seemed to grasp peace so quickly, so easily ... and not so long ago, she'd thought them to be ignorant for it.

The halfwolves mourned all death, even the deaths of their enemies. She'd thought her pack brothers and sisters to be respectful, and the humans to have respect for no one but themselves. But the more she fought along beside them, the more she'd begun to realize that the humans celebrated because they understood something the shapechangers did not:

For every wicked man that fell, a good man would be allowed to live freely.

Kyleigh thought about the miners who walked the Baron's highway now, thought about the lightness in their steps as they hurried home to their families. It was this new chance at life that the humans celebrated — not the death.

And she thought that was a rather wise thing, indeed.

On that particular night, there must've been some strange magic in the air: Kyleigh passed by one fire and was surprised to see Elena sitting next to Silas — and they weren't even throwing elbows.

Elena shook her hands over her head, and a rattling sound came from between them. "Ask me anything," she said loudly. "I am now the great knower of all things!"

"Hmm." Silas's eyes glowed as he thought. "Will I meet a pretty cat this spring?"

Elena opened her hands and a rather familiar-looking set of runes fell out. She pretended to study them for a moment. "No, I'm afraid you won't."

"What?" Silas leaned over in alarm. "Do they say *why*?"

Elena pointed. "This one here says it's because you're a twit."

He hissed at her.

A few paces away, she found Jake and Shamus. The master shipbuilder seemed convinced that Jake was ill, and had therefore insisted upon draping several thick pelts over his shoulders and settling him close to the fire. The poor mage was sweating by the time Kyleigh reached them.

"I already told you: I don't have a cold. It was a simple matter of overexertion," he said slowly, as if he'd already had to explain it several times. "I just miscalculated the reach and magnitude of the blast."

"Aye, a cold has a way of muddling a man's brain," Shamus agreed. He pressed a piping hot bowl of something into his hands. "Drink up, lad — this'll get you back on your feet."

And since Jake didn't seem to think explaining himself again was worth the effort, he did as he was told.

Except for a few scattered camps, the vast majority of their party was gathered around the mots. They'd formed a wide circle around one of the smaller fires and started what looked to be some sort of dance. While the mots around the circle clapped and sang, others danced in the middle. Their movements were graceful, but more sharp than smooth: they leapt about each other, moving their legs and arms in complicated patterns. The deadly grace of their dance made it look as if they were acting out a battle scene.

A few of the shipbuilders wandered too close, and Nadine pulled one of them into the circle with her. He struggled badly with the movements. The mots' song broke for a moment as they laughed at his efforts, then they picked back up, singing with one voice. Their song slowed as Nadine showed him the steps, gradually picking up the pace as he learned.

Another couple of shipbuilders joined their friend in the circle, but even those who weren't brave enough to venture in stood around the edge and clapped to the beat.

Kyleigh loved to dance. It was like speaking in a different tongue. She felt like the movements of her body could express all of the things that she couldn't quite think to say — like the dance could somehow speak for the muffled cries of her heart. And not so long ago, she would've joined in.

But she just hadn't felt like dancing, lately.

As she watched the mots clap together, the heat suddenly left her blood. She felt exhausted. It would do her no good to try to sleep with the noise of her companions all around her, so she plunked down in front of the quietest fire she could find and tried to calm her heart.

She pulled the little black jewel out of her pocket and turned it over in her hand. Its two heads caught the firelight, reflecting each tongue of flame as clearly as the surface of a mirror.

"Ah, that is a rare thing you hold."

Kyleigh looked up and saw a thin, middle-aged desert man sitting next to her. His eyes studied the jewel like a pirate might've studied a map — as if he already had a plan for it. "Are you a craftsman?" she guessed.

He nodded. "My name is Asante. May I?"

She handed him the jewel.

Instead of holding it to the fire, Asante turned and held it to the night sky. "This is starlight onyx — or a lover's jewel, as it is commonly known," he added with a sly look. "Its secret is something only the night may reveal. Here, see for yourself."

Kyleigh took the jewel and held it high above her. The night went through it, brightening its skin as not even the fire could. When the first star touched the jewel, it turned almost transparent: she could see the star's light sparkling clearly through the onyx.

"I've seen plenty of jewels with their own light," she said quietly, still marveling at it. "But I've never seen anything that could borrow light from the stars."

"It is a rare thing," Asante agreed. "And it is even rarer because you have found one grown into a pair. What you hold in your hand could feed a man his entire life. No, I insist you keep it," he said, when Kyleigh offered it to him. "It came to you, and you must find a use for it."

"I don't wear jewels," she pressed, trying to force it into his hand. "Please — take it for your family."

"I have no family. I have only my craft," he said simply. He closed her hand around the onyx, gazing at it one last time. "If you would offer me anything, then offer me this: whatever you choose to make with it, keep this pair together — do not sell them to two different merchants. They have been one since the earth was young." He squeezed her hands tightly. "It would be cruel to separate them."

Asante left, then, and said no more about it. Kyleigh lay back and propped an arm beneath her head. She stared dully at the night sky — and tried to lose her heartache among the stars.

****

When Hob died, his spells evaporated — and freeing the giants became as simple as opening the door.

Kael let the giants of Northbarn out first, and they immediately went to work. Some broke the locks on the sheds and distributed the scythes; others went around to the different barns, freeing their fellows; a small group ran off to nick the water wagon; and a few had the good sense to barricade the Fallows inside their stall — just in case.

Brend ran every which way, gathering the giants into groups and explaining to them what was going on. Kael had expected some manner of resistance: surely one of them would question whether or not rebellion was a good idea. But for some reason, no one argued with Brend. They drew up their scythes and stood silently by, awaiting their orders.

"How many do you want at the tower?" Brend said.

Kael suddenly realized that all eyes were on him. "Um ... ten ought to do it." His voice sounded incredibly loud in the quiet, but he pressed on. "We'll need two to pull the wagon —"

"Done," a pair of voices said. Two giants had already worked themselves into the wagon's harnesses. They grinned broadly at Kael.

"All right ... the rest will help lead the women back to the road. Those who can't run, you'll put in the wagon." He turned to Declan — who'd been following him closely from the moment he returned. "I need you to take a small company to the Pens. Wait for my signal before you start busting the locks. We've still got Finks to take care of, and he won't die easily."

Declan looked rather put off about being left out of the rescue, but he didn't argue. He must've understood the reason.

Brend, however, insisted on coming along to the tower. So Kael passed the rest of his orders out, and the giants moved obediently to their tasks — their hulking shoulders set in determined lines.

They'd hardly taken a step out of the courtyard when the moonlight disappeared. Kael looked up, and was surprised to see the once-clear sky covered in a thick mass of clouds.

"Our good mother has sent her lover to look after us," Brend said, smiling up at the sky. "He'll keep his head covered while it suits us. But the minute we need him, he'll be back."

A cool breeze brushed over them, stirring up the dust at their feet. And Kael didn't know if it was the wind or Brend's words that chilled him.

The clouds hid them as they made their way to the castle. Darkness covered the red walls completely, not even the braziers were lit. Apparently, the guards had gotten so lost in their tankards that they'd forgotten about their duties. Every one of them was likely fast asleep, wrapped tightly in a fog of ale.

They reached the kitchen tower without incident. Kael led the giants into the shadow of the wall before he let out a low whistle. His ears pricked against the night, listening for Eveningwing's reply. But it never came.

"What's keeping them?" Brend hissed.

Kael wasn't sure. When he chanced a look through the gate, he saw the door beyond was still closed. Jonathan was supposed to have the women gathered up by now. What could he possibly be doing?

Brend tested the gate with his heel. "She's sturdy, but we might be able to lift her enough for you to slip inside. It wouldn't take much of a gap," he added, with a glance at Kael's skinny frame.

He couldn't think of a better idea. And as the minutes dragged on and Eveningwing still didn't answer him, he began to think that it might be for the best. He was about to give the order when the door creaked open and a familiar, lanky figure popped out.

"Evening, gents!"

"Jonathan!" Kael reached through the gate to clasp his hand, and Jonathan grinned back. For once, his scruffy face was a welcome sight.

"I heard some whistling and thought I'd better take a look. Our little feathered friend has gone to raise the ole girl up," he said, slapping his hand against the gate. "It's a simple lever. We've seen the guards do it loads of times. It shouldn't take too — ah! There she goes!"

With a groan, the gate began to rise. It clicked and clacked along its chain, moving steadily upwards. Jonathan threw the door open and began waving the women outside.

The first giantess ducked under the gate, and Kael was taken aback by how tall she was. He'd expected the women to be larger than average, but never thought they would dwarf him as easily as the men.

This giantess kept her long white hair bound in a skillful braid down her back. Her skirt swept gracefully behind her as she sidestepped around Kael. "Watch out, wee thing," she said with a smile.

His face burned when he realized that he'd been staring.

Three women passed him before he noticed that their hands were full: they carried pikes, swords, bows and quivers of arrows in the cradle of their arms — which they deposited into the cart. Then a few seas women trailed by, carrying sacks heavy with vittles.

"Well, the guards all passed out after their drinking," Jonathan said when Kael asked. "And Clairy thought it might be a good idea to do a bit of raiding. The only weapons left are the ones the guards had tucked into their belts, and there's hardly a crumb worth munching on, in there," he added, jerking his thumb back at the kitchens. Then he sighed, grinning like a fool. "Isn't she brilliant?"

Brilliant, indeed. Kael hadn't even thought about raiding the armory or the larders. He would have to thank Clairy, when they met.

Everything went smoothly for a few moments, and Kael thought they had a real chance of escaping quietly. But when the gate reached the end of its chain, mayhem broke loose.

A steady, shrilling note cut through the air. It flew out into the night and covered the whole of Gilderick's realm in a never-ending scream of terror. The noise stabbed so mercilessly at their ears that Kael thought even a deaf man would've been able to feel it.

"You didn't kill the witch?" he shouted at Jonathan — who had his lanky arms clamped protectively over his head.

"That old bat must have woken up!" he cried, grimacing. "I *told* Clairy we should've put a few more herbs in her tea —"

"You can't just put her to sleep! I told you — you have to *kill* her!"

"What?"

But at that moment, a bright light flared up at the castle. The braziers burst to life and several monstrous shadows popped up around the walls. Torches were lit, someone let out a bellowing command, and the shadows began to cross the wall at an alarming pace — moving towards the covered passageway.

Kael turned and slung his arm at the giant in charge of the women. "Start running for the Pens! Go!"

He did, and the women who were able to run followed along behind him. Two had bellies so round that they couldn't make the journey, and Brend helped them into the wagon. "Is that all of them?"

Kael turned to ask Jonathan, but the fiddler had suddenly vanished. He'd slipped back through the doorway without so much as a warning, and Kael had no idea what he was doing. He was about to go in after him when a familiar screech sounded overhead.

He looked up and saw Eveningwing fighting above the passageway. Several guards sprinted across the roof, heading straight for the tower. Eveningwing dove in among them, beating them with his wings and raking their helmets with his claws. He managed to knock one guard off his feet and sent a second plummeting from the wall. But the others made it across.

There was a small door on the roof of the tower, one that would open into the kitchen's upper levels — Kael remembered it from Jonathan's maps. He could do nothing but watch as the guards scaled the remaining few feet of wall and reached the tower's top.

"They're going to cut the gate!" Brend hollered. "Is everybody out?"

Kael started to reply when he saw a giant down the road waving frantically. "The castle's opening up — they're sending out the army!"

"We've got to run!" Kael said to Brend. "Get the women back to the Pens — tell Declan that trouble's coming!"

He nodded and passed the order back. The giants strapped to the wagon took off at a sprint. The rest followed Brend at a jog, their eyes on the castle gates. When Kael stuck his head through the door to yell at Jonathan, he saw the fiddler was not alone.

He and another giantess were helping a second giantess down a narrow flight of stairs. Her belly was round and swollen beneath her dress. She moved as quickly as she could, but her face was white with the effort.

Kael swore.

The wagon had already left without them, and he knew they would never be able to outrun the guards at her waddling pace. What little hope he'd had of making it out alive was quickly evaporating. And they still had Gilderick's army to deal with.

He charged forward, prepared to carry the giantess over his shoulders, if he had to. But a noise stopped him short.

Clang! Clang! Clang!

Jonathan looked up, his eyes wild. "Eveningwing jammed the gate — they're trying to cut the chain!"

No sooner were the words out of his mouth than a horrible groan spun Kael on his feet. The gate snapped at its chain — and it began to fall.

The blunted bottoms of the gate's teeth stretched for the ground, trying to clamp down upon the clear night sky. Once the gate fell, there would be no lifting it. There would be no getting through it. They'd be trapped inside this tower, left to wait for whatever miserable death Gilderick had planned for them — provided the guards didn't skewer them first.

No, Kael knew that their only hope to live lay beyond that gate. And their only chance of escape was to keep that gate from falling.

There was no time to panic, no time to doubt himself — he simply did what had to be done. He threw himself between the ground and the gate. In his mind, he held a memory of the Scepter Stone.

He saw the mighty red rock of the giants — so tall and thick that not even the mages had been able to split it. He raised his arms over his head and imagined that he *was* the Scepter Stone. He saw his skin turn scarlet, bespeckled in black. He imagined that his arms hardened and his legs sank deep into the earth.

I am the Scepter Stone, he thought to himself. *Nothing can break me.*

He felt the thrum in his chest when the gate crashed down into his open palms, but his arms didn't shudder. His legs stood strong. For a few moments, he held the gate above him as if it was no more trouble than an open door.

Then his head began to ache.

He realized that he was exhausted. He hadn't slept in two days. He hadn't eaten. He'd been too busy battling in the arena, fighting the Countess's guard, and killing Hob to do much of anything else. And now his weakness was catching up to him quickly.

Pain glanced his skull so sharply that it felt as if an axe had split it in half. His arms began to tremble. The barely-healed wounds in his back tore anew, and hot blood trickled down his shirt. Dots of light burst across his vision, blinding him. His strength was draining fast — crushed out from under him by the impossible weight of the tower door. He knew he might very well kill himself if he pushed much further.

But he had to try.

Jonathan and the two women were almost there. If he could hold on for another few seconds, they would be free. He pushed back stubbornly against the pain, holding it at bay. The women passed him, then Jonathan darted by, and Kael could hold the gate no longer.

His head struck the ground hard, and a black cloak threatened to cover him.

No! he said to himself. *You can't pass out — you've got to get up! You've got to get the women to safety.* He bit back against the fiery torment that raged through his skull and worked his arms beneath him. He tried to rise — only to find that he couldn't.

The gate had come down on top of him, and now his head was trapped between the bottom rung and the ground. He tried to pull himself free, but the beam was wedged very firmly over his throat. Any other time, he might've considered himself lucky to be alive: a few inches were all the difference between being trapped and being crushed.

But with Gilderick's army unleashed, he thought he would've rather been crushed and done with it.

Dirt sprayed across his middle as someone slid in beside him. He heard a pair of hands scrabble desperately against the rung. "I can't lift it, mate!" Jonathan grunted. "Can you wiggle your head a bit?"

Kael wanted to scream at him — to tell him to get out of there and follow the women. But he could hardly think about speaking before a fresh wave of pain blinded him. He fought the blackness back a second time, struggling to stay conscious.

An explosion split the air above them. Kael felt it through his chest as it rumbled the earth. A burst of orange light burned across the doorway, and he saw Jonathan's worried face peering down at him. He had his head pressed against the upper rungs. Kael only got a quick look at him before he disappeared.

An ear-piercing whistle cut through the night, and then Jonathan hollered: "Oi! Some of you larger blokes come give me a hand — Kael's stuck!"

The earth shook again as several giants rushed to his side. More explosions rattled the ground, startling the dust from the archway. He heard cries and the sharp clang of steel coming from the castle gates. He tried to speak again, but had to shut his eyes when lights burst across them. He grit his teeth against the pain, holding it back.

When the lights faded, his eyes opened — and he was shocked to see a familiar, sandy-headed boy grinning down at him.

"Don't worry, Kael — we're going to pop you out of here," Noah said.

Noah? How on earth was *Noah* here? He should've been at least a day and a half away, traveling with the other pirates. There was no way he could already be at the castle. Perhaps Kael had fainted without realizing it.

But then a high-pitched shrill cut across his ears, erasing any doubt: "Kael! Is he all right? Oh, he's not hurt, is he?"

"No, he's fine —"

"He isn't *fine!*" Aerilyn cried. And Kael felt her hands tugging at his belt. "Oh, he's bleeding — and he's got his head stuck in a gate! Get him out!"

"Just keep those blasty arrows coming, lassie," Brend shouted. "We'll handle the rest. Ready, lads?"

There was a collective grunt in reply, and then a loud creak of wood as the gate began to rise.

"Heave, lads! *Heave* —"

"Pikes on the wall!" someone cried.

"No time — pull him out!" Brend grunted.

Two pairs of hands grabbed onto Kael's legs. He left a good bit of his skin behind as his body was dragged forward. A pike thudded into the ground beside him, inches from his nose. Another whistled over his head and he heard someone grunt in pain.

"Noah!" Aerilyn screamed.

"We'll take care of him — now *fire*, lassie!"

An arrow struck the tower above them and exploded. Pieces of brick rained down. Through Kael's foggy eyes, the chunks of the tower seemed to glide to earth as calmly as flakes of snow. He watched them curiously, but didn't have a chance to see them fall. Someone scooped him up, and the motion rocked his skull. Lights flared before his eyes. He fought them back.

And when he forced them open once again, he saw something that stopped his heart.

Noah lay in the arms of the giant next to him. A red, gaping hole split the symbol on his pirate tunic. He pawed at it desperately, trying to staunch the bleeding.

Kael could fix that — he could save Noah. He was certain of it.

One last time, he forced the darkness back. He pressed his hand against the hot wet of Noah's wound. He felt for the ragged edges of his flesh and thought hard: *You are cl ... clay ...*

Light — a light brighter than any he'd ever seen — erupted across his eyes.

And Kael knew no more.

Chapter 41
Where All Men Fall

Kyleigh woke to a strange feeling.

At first, she thought it might've just been from the vast amount of salted meats that she and Silas had eaten. But the longer she thought about it, the more she began to realize that she didn't feel too *full*: she felt empty. She felt as if she'd never eaten — like she didn't need to eat because there was absolutely no point in it. The light dulled and all of the color around her seemed to fade.

She forgot the sound of laughter. When she tried to remember it, all she could think of was the lonesome call of the wind. No matter how she begged them, her lips wouldn't bend into a smile. She might've propped them up with her fingers ... had she been able to move her hands. But instead, they lay limply beside her, as if her very bones had crumbled away.

It was fear that finally gave her the courage to stand. She had a horrible feeling that something was wrong.

The pass between the Red Spine called to her, and she went for it at a jog — skipping over the sleeping forms of her companions, moving as fast as her legs would carry her. She was so focused that she didn't see the man in her path until she'd already run him over.

It was Eveningwing. He sprang up from the ground; sand clung to the sweat on his chest and neck. He panted and grasped for her, tugging furiously on the front of her jerkin.

"Your Kael!" he gasped, shaking her. "Come quickly — your Kael!"

For the first time in a long while, Kyleigh was afraid.

A new instinct gripped her, a sense she never knew she had. The Spine loomed in her vision. Her wings beat against her head. She no longer cared if she was spotted. She no longer cared if she was in danger.

Something like a thread wrapped around her heart, ripping her towards Kael. She followed it over the Spine and across the plains. Four barns stood out sharply against the flat land, like footprints in the mud. Little fires danced all around them.

It was for Kael's sake that she dropped down into the shadowed fields. She'd left Eveningwing far behind her, she didn't know if Kael was among enemies or friends. She wouldn't land in full dragon form and risk starting a battle — a battle would take far too long, and she had to reach him quickly.

She'd hardly gotten her human legs settled beneath her before she sprinted towards the barns. Giants jumped from their fires as she passed, but she didn't care. Her eyes flicked over the many structures looming around her, and the thread wavered. Panic scraped against her chest as she tried to figure out where to find him.

"Kyleigh!"

Someone grabbed her arm, and she ripped it away. It wasn't until she was grabbed a second time that she recognized Aerilyn. Her nose was red and swollen, her eyes burned and her face was wet with tears. When she breathed, there was a different scent on her breath — one that was slightly muddled by another. This scent meant something ... but Kyleigh didn't have time to remember what it was.

She had to find Kael.

Aerilyn pulled desperately on her arm. "He's in here — oh Kyleigh, he's hurt so badly. We don't know what to do!"

As Aerilyn led her away, Kyleigh felt as if she walked through a nightmare. There was noise all around her, but she couldn't hear it. Light shined, but it brightened nothing. There was solid earth beneath her feet — there must have been ...

But for some reason, she couldn't feel it.

Familiar faces blurred out of the corner of her eye. More hands reached to grasp her, thumping hollowly against her flesh. She passed through wood, through steel, and then the thread suddenly ended, jolting her.

When she saw him, the world snapped back.

Kael lay in the corner of a horse stall, curled up on a pile of filthy clothing. He was exactly how she'd remembered him: his straight nose, his lips ... but there was something wrong with his brows. There was usually a little line between them, one that went deeper as he furrowed them. And they were usually always furrowed, even when he slept. He was always thinking about something.

But now his brows were smoothed — relaxed, even. And it startled her.

She dragged her eyes from his face and saw his tunic was shredded and soaked in blood. *His* blood. He lay on his stomach, and she saw that his back was covered in gashes — as if some monster had raked him with its claws. She stared, frozen, at the dried, black shores along his gaping wounds and the bright red pools in their middles.

"We haven't got a healer," Aerilyn gasped, wringing her hands. "Oh, I don't know what to —"

"Take his shirt off, little Declan," Kyleigh said. She looked to the giant who squatted next to Kael, the only one in the room whose eyes weren't filled with panic.

He held a bowl of water and moved a bloodstained cloth gingerly across Kael's back. There was a steadiness in his hands as he moved them, a desperation in the pressure he put on Kael's gaping wounds. But the line of his mouth was firm and strong. The calmness in his breaths soothed the panicked air.

She thought Declan looked more like his father now than ever. The deep cleft beneath his brows grew shallow as he raised them. "You remember me?"

Kyleigh thought that was an odd thing to say. "I try to never forget the men I've fought beside. Don't you remember me?"

"Yeh, but a man would have to be worse than blind to forget Kyleigh Swordmaiden," Declan grunted. He tore Kael's shirt open with a single, quick tug. As he eased the shirt over

498

his limbs, Kyleigh got a clear look at Kael's back. It was worse than she'd thought. So much worse.

She spun to Aerilyn and began ripping the laces off her gauntlets. "Help me."

Aerilyn undid the buckles along her jerkin while Kyleigh removed her gauntlets and belt. Every second they spent, the air in the room grew colder. She started to shiver. Time was running out.

"That'll have to do," she said, when she wore nothing but her leggings and breast band.

The cold had started to settle in her bones as she lay down next to Kael. Carefully, she pulled him into her. Wet warmth spread across her skin as she pressed her chest and stomach against his wounded back. She twined her limbs with his, molding them together, connecting them down to their fingertips and toes.

As she pressed her cheek against his neck, she caught his scent. He smelled like the earth after a steady rain. It was a good scent, a calming scent.

But it was faint — and fading quickly.

Kyleigh bit her lip hard and tried to keep her tears at bay. "No matter how I scream," she said around her teeth, "don't touch me. Don't try to pull me off of him. I won't be responsible for your deaths, if you try to separate us."

Aerilyn nodded. "We'll leave you alone." Then she turned and began shooing the others out the door. There were some protests, but the stall eventually emptied — giving Kyleigh the chance to concentrate.

The skin between them was the only thing that kept their souls apart. Kyleigh held Kael tightly and thought she could feel his spirit bubbling up to the surface. It pressed against her wherever they touched and slid between the tiny holes in her skin.

Her limbs went numb. She could no longer tell their bodies apart. They were one flesh: breathing together, hearts beating together.

And then came the pain.

****

Cold ... Kael was first aware of the cold. The hard earth beneath him ached with it, as if it had never known warmth. A gust of wind swept across his back. The cold was there, too — glancing his flesh with a thousand tiny knives.

And it was the shivering in his limbs that woke him.

Somehow, he'd wound up back in the Unforgivable Mountains. He'd fallen, though — through one of the great cracks the weather had rent into the mountainside. It was an easy trap to fall into, if a man wasn't paying attention. The cracks were often hidden beneath thick tangles of brush, lying in wait to gobble up unwary travelers.

But Kael should've known better. He knew he was lucky to be alive ... though when he saw the height of the sheer rock wall behind him, he didn't see how he could have possibly survived the fall.

He needed to find a way out, and preferably before the sun went down. How was he going to explain this to Roland? He'd be disappointed that Kael had let his attention wander. Amos would gripe about the fresh holes in his breeches.

Well, there was no point in putting it off.

Kael dragged himself to his feet, and was surprised to find that he wasn't in pain. He expected to be bruised and bloodied. He must've been very lucky, indeed.

There was no way through the wall behind him — his only hope lay ahead. A small river flowed through the bottom of the crack, its waters bubbled gently over the rocks settled within it. Beyond that river was another wall, and Kael groaned when he saw that it was every bit as tall and sheer as the one behind him.

He thought he might never make it out. Even if Roland sent the hunters to look for him, they would never find him here. How could he have been so foolish? Why hadn't he watched his steps?

But before he could get too furious with himself, his eyes caught something they hadn't noticed before: there was a crack in the wall across the river. It was so small that he'd likely have to crawl to fit between it. As he studied it, a gust of warm air breathed out of the hole. Even from a distance, he smelled the promise of summer riding along the gales.

Somewhere beyond that crack was a green land — an earth that the cold couldn't touch. All Kael had to do was cross the river, and he'd be free.

It didn't look too deep. He thought he might be able to reach the other side without getting his breeches wet. He'd taken one step into the water and was preparing to take a second when a strong hand grasped his shoulder.

"You shouldn't go that way, boy."

Kael spun around and cried in relief when Roland smiled back. He grinned through his grizzled beard and pulled Kael in for a tight embrace. His arms were stronger than Kael had remembered. His chest wasn't quite so boney.

"I thought I'd been a fool," he said, when Roland released him. "But if this crack managed to trick both of us, I don't feel so bad."

Roland laughed. "And you'd be right not to. Far more cunning men than you or I have fallen here," he said, waving his arm at the high walls. His smile changed, softening. "All men fall here, eventually."

Before Kael could ask what he meant, Roland clasped his arm.

"I've got some traps to run. Want to give me a hand?"

Kael hesitated for a moment. His eyes wandered to the crack across the river, his thoughts trailed to the green lands beyond it. "Shouldn't we press on?"

Roland saw where he was looking and shook his head. "I can't let you go that way, boy. I already promised your father that I'd keep you on *this* side of things."

He started to walk away, and Kael went after him at a trot. "My father? He was here?"

"Oh, I'm sure he was. But I'd already promised him long ago — back when you were just a little thing. Though," and here he smiled again, "I didn't quite realize what he was asking of me."

"What do you —?"

"Hush, boy," Roland whispered. His arm sprang protectively across Kael's chest, like he'd just seen a lion or a bear.

Kael froze. He knew if Roland could sense something, he ought to be still. He scanned the scrub bushes in front of them, searching for any signs of danger. And it wasn't long before a number of large figures crossed their path.

They were giants — dressed in rough spun clothes and marching barefoot across the rocky bank. What in Kingdom's name were *giants* doing in the Unforgivable Mountains?

"Watch carefully," Roland said, as the giants approached the river.

They stepped in one at a time. The river must've been deceptively deep: by the time the giants reached the middle, the water was up to their waists. Most of them sank even deeper. Kael could only watch as the river flowed over their heads, dragging them downwards.

The giants made no attempt to save themselves. Their arms didn't flail above the water, they never cried out. One moment they were crossing the river and the next — they were gone. Their large heads sank beneath the waves, and they never came back out.

Only one of them made it across. He stepped out onto the opposite bank and moved surely towards the wall, towards a refuge that Kael couldn't see. And then he disappeared.

"Ah, see there?" Roland whispered. "His deeds must've carried him on."

Kael thought that was a strange thing to say. Strange ... and yet, familiar. Roland had said something like that before, but it hadn't been while they were on a hunt — it had been in the Hall, when Kael was a child. Roland had been telling him a story about Death:

"Few things test a man like the savage back of a river," Roland had said. "That's why Death keeps a river at his threshold — it helps him sort everything out. You see, there's only one thing a man can take with him when he dies: and that's his deeds. He'll stand on them all his life, and in death he'll have them strapped to his feet. Good deeds rise up like walking stones across Death's river ... while the bad ones will cause a man to sink."

Kael's memory came back in a rush. He hadn't been in the mountains at all — he'd been in the plains. There'd been fighting and bursts of light ... Noah had been wounded.

Where was he? He needed to get back. His friends were in trouble — his task wasn't finished yet.

"Roland, I ..."

He stopped. Roland had wandered further up the path. When he turned, he crossed his arms over his tunic — a tunic that was as white as the clouds above the sea. It matched the white of his breeches, his boots ... and Kael realized that the man in his dreams hadn't been Death at all.

It was Roland.

"There now, boy. Don't you cry over me." Roland's rough hand clasped his shoulder, but Kael's tears continued to fall. They streamed down his face in miserable torrents, wetting the ground at his knees.

"You're dead," Kael managed to gasp out.

"That I am."

Roland told him everything that had befallen Tinnark — of what Titus did to the village, how many of the Tinnarkians he'd seen cross the river. He even told about how he'd been slain. And as Kael listened, his tears began to dry.

"But you wanted ... a woodsman's death ..."

Roland's hand tightened on his shoulder. "I died a *warrior's* death, Kael. That was a gift that I'd never dared to wish for."

This comforted him a bit, but Kael's thoughts quickly turned dark. "I promise you, I'll make sure Marc and Laemoth pay for what they did."

Roland glanced at the river. "Laemoth's already been paid back," he murmured. "And I'm sure you'll send Marc on his way — but when the time comes, all right? It'll do you no good to dwell on it. Don't let him gnaw at you."

Kael nodded. There was one other question he needed to ask, but it took a great deal of courage to force it out. "What about Amos?"

Roland shook his head, grinning. "He hasn't come through here. That clever old coot must've charmed Titus into keeping him."

Kael sighed in relief. For some reason, it made him feel a little lightheaded. He got off his knees and sat on his rump. Roland sat down beside him. "Am *I* dead?" he wondered aloud.

"Not quite," Roland said with a wink. "Otherwise, you'd be dressed like me."

Kael hadn't realized that he was still wearing the same tattered, filthy tunic and breeches that he'd been wearing in the plains. His eyes suddenly felt heavy. He tried to prop them open.

"How did you find me?" he muttered. The crack they sat in was rather large — he couldn't see the end of it. "How did you know I'd be here?"

Roland's smile was sad. "I didn't know. I just happened to be wandering by when this little brown-headed seas boy waved me down ..." He had to stop when Kael broke into a fresh wave of tears.

Anguish gripped him on either side of his head. It squeezed him, forcing all the wet from his eyes, but he felt no shame. There was no shame in these tears, not when he thought of the young life that had been cut so horribly short.

"Noah," he managed to gasp. He saw the boy's face clearly: how it had brightened at adventure, hardened as he fought. Even now, he remembered how Noah used to follow Jonathan around the ship, laughing at his mischief.

"You were asleep," Roland went on, once Kael had quieted. "That happens when a man is near to death, but not quite there. I told young Noah that I'd look after you, and I sent him on his way."

Kael glared at the river. "Did he ...?"

Roland nodded firmly. "He crossed over without a fuss — his boots hardly even got wet. He was a good one."

504

Relief covered Kael like a blanket, warming him against the cold. It was suddenly very difficult to keep his eyes open. He decided to lie down, just for a moment, and close them. "I don't want you stuck here any longer," he muttered to Roland. "I don't care what you promised my father — I want you to cross the river. I think there's a much gentler land on the other side ... the trapping will be better."

Roland chuckled. "I don't doubt it. And I promise that I'll cross — just as soon as you've gone back to sleep."

This was a comforting thought. With his last conscious breath, Kael whispered: "Do you think I would've made it?"

Roland sighed heavily. "The only man who knows the answer to that question is the man who's already standing on the other side."

******

He fought her. He always fought her. That was just like Kael: he never wanted any help, he never wanted anybody else to know his pain. But Kyleigh was stronger. When he tried to hide from her, she drew him out.

Her soul twined with his — holding him, comforting him. Slowly, his hard shell began to crumble away, and he spoke:

It hurt so badly, his soul whispered.

I know. Let me take it, Kyleigh whispered back.

An ache filled her head, throbbing in the beginning and stabbing by the end. Her eyes trembled in their sockets as the storm raged behind them. Then came the blows — blows she was familiar with. She felt the slap of the leather and the sharp, metal teeth woven into the lashes. They tore across her back, splitting her skin. She screamed as the blows fell, but not because it hurt: because she was furious.

Kael should've never had to suffer like this. These blows should've never touched him. She understood his pain. His soul spoke for him, sharing all of the torment and humiliation, all of the agony that she knew he would've never said aloud.

Hot tears of rage burned down her cheeks when she thought of how much he'd had to endure ... simply because she hadn't been there to protect him.

When his soul was finished speaking, he woke. He squirmed in her hold and she released him. He flopped over and grabbed her by the shoulders. His warm brown eyes were still glazed in sleep; she knew he was only half awake.

"Roland's dead," he moaned. "He's ... he's *dead*."

The tears that streamed down his face hurt her more than his wounds. She wrapped her arms around him and held his head to her chest. She ran her hand down his back, sighing in relief when she didn't feel any gashes. His body was healed, he was out of danger. And after a few moments, he quieted.

As she settled him back onto his pallet, she couldn't help herself: she kissed him on the cheek.

For a long moment, Kyleigh didn't move. Her skin was raw and bleeding. She could hear the sizzling of her blood as it trickled from the fresh gashes on her back. One drop crossed her shoulder and raced down her arm. She watched dully as it fell from the tip of her finger and onto Kael's chest.

Anybody else would've woken with a scream. Her blood was every bit as hot as molten steel: it could burn a man's flesh to blisters — she'd seen it happen before. But the fire in her blood could never harm Kael.

Though she'd felt this in her heart, it wasn't until that moment that she knew for certain. She wiped the red drop away, and Kael's skin was smooth and perfect beneath it.

If the dragons had a word for love, it would've been *valtas*. In human words, she thought it meant *the very deep*. Valtas was a blood oath — a connection that would never break. Two dragons who shared the valtas could feel the same pain, suffer the same wounds. But most importantly, the fires in their blood could never burn each other's flesh.

Her dragon soul remembered the valtas, but Kyleigh never thought she would feel it for herself. She was only half-dragon, after all. She'd chosen to live as a human, and she thought if she ever fell in love, that it would be the human

506

sort of love — the sort that wasn't binding. The sort she could escape from.

She'd always liked Kael, even from the first moment she'd held him. There were lights in his eyes that excited her, a depth that made her feel understood. He was different from the other humans, and she knew they would always be great friends. She would've protected him from all harm. She would've cared for him in his old age.

Yes, she knew from the beginning that she would always like Kael. But somewhere along the way ... her feelings must have changed. They'd grown quietly, creeping in from the edges to the very center of her heart. She hadn't realized just how much her feelings had grown, until the day she rescued him from the tempest.

She'd pulled Kael from the sea, felt him go limp in her arms, felt her own lungs tighten as he struggled to breathe — and felt a part of her life begin to fade with his. She realized that if she ever lost him, the sunlight would go gray. Her body would live on in a dark world, a strange world. A world that might last for a thousand years ... until the sun finally dawned on her last day.

Kyleigh had realized this as she pressed down on Kael's chest, as she'd breathed life into his lungs. But she hadn't wanted to believe it. She didn't want her life to be tied to anybody else's. She wanted to be her own creature — a free, proud creature. And for a few desperate moments, she'd been furious.

It was when he breathed again that everything changed ... it was when Kael opened his eyes that Kyleigh began her second life.

The same warmth coursed through their blood, the same breath filled their lungs. Kyleigh felt a thrill that burned to the tips of her fingers. These were new skies — the beginning of a strange, uncharted, and wonderful land. In all her many sunrises, she'd never felt her heart beat quite like this.

She had to wonder if that was the moment it truly began to beat.

For a while, she'd been impossibly happy. Then ... things changed once more. Kael was a human. He didn't feel the same way she did, and she thought — she *hoped*, that perhaps she'd been mistaken. Perhaps she'd only imagined that she felt a dragon's love for him. Perhaps it was only human love she felt, and nothing more.

But now, her blood proved her wrong. There was no longer any hope that what she felt for him wasn't valtas. She couldn't deny the truth, and she couldn't escape it, either:

Kyleigh loved Kael with both of her hearts.

Chapter 42
Squirming Hope

When Kael woke, he was alone.

He lay with his face pressed into his pallet for a moment, trying to remember where he was. When the familiar, stale reek of giant clothes filled his nostrils, it all came back to him suddenly: they'd been trying to free the women, Gilderick's army had attacked, and Noah ...

He knew that Noah was dead ... somehow, he knew. His eyes still ached from crying. He thought he could feel the dried trail down his cheeks, from where his tears had fallen.

Kael rubbed the soreness from his eyes and tried to focus. He saw that he was back in the stall, and he thought they must've failed. Gilderick must've captured them and locked them back up. But when Kael turned, he saw the stall door was open. Voices drifted in from outside.

Slowly, he got to his feet. He remembered that he'd been wounded, and that all of his gashes had torn open again when he tried to stop the gate. So he moved carefully, his face already pulled into a wince. He waited for the familiar sting of pain, but it didn't come. He reached behind him in surprise.

Though his shirt was torn, he felt no wounds. He twisted his back from side to side, testing his skin, and he realized that his wounds were gone. Somehow, he'd been healed.

What in Kingdom's name was going on?

Kael left the stall at a jog. Outside, there were dozens of large, sleeping forms gathered around low-burning campfires. The giants were curled up together, wrapped tightly in makeshift blankets of filthy clothes and potato sacks. He saw several long braids peeking out from the covers, and sighed in relief. At least the women were safe.

But mercy's sake — they snored just as loudly as the men.

"Kael!"

A shadowy figure hailed him towards Eastbarn, and then it slipped back inside. Kael walked through the doors, stuck his head into the first stall — and was met by a familiar, shining white grin.

"My dear boy," Captain Lysander began, when he saw the confused look on Kael's face, "you didn't *really* think we'd let you face the Lord of the plains all on your own, did you?"

Kael had to clench his fists to keep from swinging at him. A flick of movement drew his eyes to Lysander's shoulder, where Eveningwing was perched.

He ruffled his feathers apologetically, and Kael immediately understood. "You've been helping them, haven't you?" he guessed. "You led the pirates back to the tree clump weeks ago — *that's* how they got here so quickly." He turned his glare on Lysander. "And that's why the guards started *mysteriously* disappearing."

"Their armor is weak at the neck," Lysander said with a grin, but Kael wasn't amused.

"I told you to stay put," he growled, stalking forward. Another memory came back to him, and his anger blazed even hotter. "And I can't believe you dragged Aerilyn into this! How could you, when you knew very well how dangerous —?"

"Ah, now *that* I can't take the blame for," Lysander said, and his face became stern. "When Eveningwing told us you were in danger, we planned to set out immediately. Of course, Aerilyn wanted to come along, but I wouldn't hear of it. We'd been lucky to escape with our hides the first time. And I wasn't about to risk her life again."

Lysander clasped his hands behind his back and started to pace. Poor Eveningwing nearly toppled off his shoulder at the first quick turn.

"But there's no reasoning with Aerilyn, once she sets her mind on something. So I didn't try to reason. Instead, I led cabin, gave her a *proper* farewell," he added with a

510

wink, "and then I locked her in. I thought this sort of thing might happen eventually. I'd even had the men pack their steel codpieces, just in case. And I was certain they could hold her captive for a few weeks." Lysander's stern look melted into a smile. "But I was wrong.

"Not three days after we arrived at camp, Aerilyn found us. She dragged my entire crew in by their ears and flatly refused to tell me how she'd managed to escape — even though I asked politely. I suspect a mutiny," Lysander mused, though his smile didn't fade. "In the end, we wound up needing every sword. So I suppose it all turned out for the best." He leveled his chin at Kael, and his face went serious. "We've managed to free the Pens, and we've pushed Gilderick's army back into the castle, for now. But I suspect they'll attack us again tomorrow. Or today, rather — we've only got a couple of hours before dawn."

Kael was still furious with him for sneaking back into the plains, but there were far more pressing matters at hand. "Have we got a plan?"

Lysander shook his head. "*I* wanted to leave His Lordship to rot, but —"

"The giants can't be free, so long as our plains mother is in bonds," Brend called from behind him. His eyes glinted as they fell on Kael. "We'll leave the planning to you, wee Wright — since you're such a great schemer."

Kael didn't have energy to try and figure out if he was being serious. He saw the giantess sitting next to Brend, and recognized her as the one Jonathan had been trying to help through the gate. She had an open face and a soft smile. She leaned back against Brend, her arms propped across her rounded belly.

"You must be Darrah," he guessed.

Her smile widened. "That I am, wee thing. And you look as if you could use a meal. We've got the vittles stacked up over there." She pointed towards the aisle.

Kael leaned out and saw that the whole trough had been packed full of rations. Sacks stuffed with meats, cheeses, and breads filled it just as tightly as they would fit, and the rich smell of food thickened the air.

"Go and get yourself fed," Darrah insisted. "Don't be shy about it — you need to get some meat on those wee little bones!"

"They nearly fed us to death," Brend whispered. He groaned and clutched his belly. "I don't think I could manage another crumb!"

Though the food smelled delicious, Kael was too focused to eat much of anything. He grabbed a strip of salted meat and gnawed on it distractedly as he left to inspect the camp.

How large was the giants' army? Did they have any hope against Lord Gilderick? There were certainly more men than he'd expected ... but they weren't very well armed.

A few giants carried the pikes that they'd stolen from the castle armory. Most of them were armed with scythes, and some had even had to make do with pitchforks or shovels. A handful of giants *had* managed to pilfer bits of armor from the guards they'd slain — though most had scythe-sized holes punched into their breastplates. But they didn't seem to be bothered by their disadvantage.

At nearly every fire he passed, Kael saw giants sharpening their weapons. A few even hailed him over, and asked when he planned to attack. He heard the eagerness in their voices. Their mouths were set in impatient lines.

The giants' hearts were certainly ready for battle ... but would that be enough? He wasn't sure. Gilderick's forces were well-armed and well-trained. They were bloodtraitors: they'd already lost everything, and would fight like they had nothing left to lose.

Perhaps the giants loved their plains so fiercely that it wouldn't matter — maybe they'd be able to match the bloodtraitors' strength, overcome their pikes and armor. But Kael wasn't sure.

Worry sat so heavily in his gut that he thought the giants might be able to read it on his face. So he left the light of the fires and went in search of someplace quiet.

He found Thelred standing guard at the edge of camp, stalking a line around the barns. He spent most of his time glaring at Declan — who sat alone at the edge of the grain field, his scythe propped across his knees.

Not surprisingly, Thelred didn't offer Kael any sort of greeting.

"I'm not going to turn my back on that one," he said, jerking his head at Declan. "He's insane."

"He can't help it."

"You didn't see him fight," Thelred snapped, and Kael thought the anger in his eyes might've been tinged with fear. "He howled like an animal — he killed like an animal, too. I've never seen so much blood."

"You don't know anything about him. He's a good man," Kael growled. He started to walk away, then, because he thought that if he stayed another moment he might have to knock Thelred unconscious again.

"Men like that don't know friend from foe," Thelred called after him. "If you get in his way, he'll kill you."

Kael refused to believe that. Declan wouldn't hurt somebody he cared about, he would never go *that* mad — because if Declan was capable of killing his friends, it meant that Kael was, too.

His teeth clamped down hard at the thought.

A little further across camp, he found Aerilyn. She was crouched at the shed behind Northbarn, her bow in one hand. She had her enchanted quiver strapped across her shoulders — the one Jake had spelled to make her arrows explode.

Kael slowed his pace as he approached. From the sound of it, Aerilyn was in the process of voiding her latest meal into some unlucky nettle bushes. He knew that she would probably like some privacy.

"It's just all of the excitement catching up to me," she insisted, wiping the back of her hand across her mouth. Kael retrieved her canteen from the ground, and she took a long drink. "I've been worried about you for weeks! And then I finally get to see you again, and Noah ... Noah ..." She pressed her thumbs against her eyes, trying to stop the flow of tears.

"Lysander said that I'm not supposed to cry for him — he said Noah wouldn't have wanted me to cry. And I've tried not to, I really have, but ..." She wiped her eyes on her sleeve, and pointed her chin at Kael. "They've got his body in one of the barns. You can see him, if you'd like."

Kael shook his head. "I don't want to see him like that." He swallowed hard, but forced his next words out: "I'd rather remember him the way he was."

Aerilyn's chin quivered dangerously. Then quite suddenly, she flung her arms around his neck. "Oh, I've missed you so horribly. You always know just what to say. I'm glad you're all right, and that your wounds are mended ..."

Kael had forgotten about his wounds, and Aerilyn looked as if she'd forgotten that she wasn't supposed to mention them. Her mouth clamped shut, and her eyes widened for half a blink.

She grabbed his arm. "Let's go find Morris —"

"What happened to my wounds?" Kael pressed her. "How did they get healed?"

She dug something out of her pocket. "I've got your book," she said, stuffing the *Atlas* into his hands. "I kept it safe, just like you —"

"Aerilyn," he growled. "Just tell me."

But not even his glare could shake her. She gave him a defiant look. "I promised I wouldn't tell, and I won't do it. That's the end of it," she added, when Kael started to argue. "Now, let's go talk to Morris."

As he followed her away, his steps felt lighter than they had in months. There was a hope squirming inside his chest, wriggling like a new thing against the blackened shell of his heart ...

No, he thought furiously. *Don't even think it.*

And his tiny hope went still.

They stepped carefully over the many sleeping giants, and wound their way through camp a few times before they finally found Morris and Jonathan hiding out in Southbarn. Morris leaned up against the far wall, munching on a hunk of toasted bread. He'd lost both of his hands while fighting in the Whispering War, and kept his nubs capped in leather gauntlets. There was a long stick wedged into the straps of one of his gauntlets, and he had the bread stuck to the end of it.

"You done it again, lad," Morris said as Kael approached. He broke out into a gap-toothed grin. "I've got to stop being so surprised about it."

"What surprises me," Aerilyn cut in, "is *that*."

They followed her appalled look to Jonathan — who was sleeping soundly on the dirt floor, and tangled in the limbs of a rather stunning giantess. Bits of hair popped from her braid in wild, wavy strips. And even as she slept, her brows were arched in mischievous lines.

Kael realized this must be Clairy.

When he saw the swollen, fist-sized lump on the side of Jonathan's face, he *knew* it must be Clairy. "So I take it that Brend still hasn't warmed up to the idea of having a fiddler for a brother?"

Aerilyn shook her head. "If it hadn't been for the women, I don't think there would've been much left of him." She smiled and lowered her voice. "Darrah put her foot down, and I didn't think it would do much good — but Brend actually listened! In fact, he got rather upset. One word from Darrah, and his shoulders slumped. He looked as if he'd just been scolded by his mother, in my opinion. Can you believe it? A big man like Brend, being told what to do?" Aerilyn took a quick breath. "Anyways, Darrah made Brend apologize, and then she led him off. I believe Lysander has been distracting him with his pirate stories ... while Clairy keeps Jonathan out of arm's reach," Aerilyn added, pursing her lips at the sleeping couple. Her brows furrowed for a moment as she stared at them. Then with an exasperated huff, she threw up her arms. "Oh, I'll just go cross-eyed if I sit here puzzling over it!"

She marched away then, leaving Kael alone with Morris.

"Come here and have a sit," Morris said, thumping his arm onto the ground beside him. "I'd ask to hear how you managed it all, but I've already heard it told a dozen different times! The giants haven't stopped talking about you since the moment we got here. We only just now got them to settle down." Several crumbs went flying out of his bushy beard as Morris shook his head. "After hearing it for myself, I got to say — it's a touch insane, what you did."

Kael shrugged as he sat. "Sometimes insanity is the only cure." He turned to Morris with a smile — but he didn't smile back.

His mouth had dropped open, and his eyes narrowed in their pouches. "Where'd you hear that?"

Kael's stomach twisted. "I ... I don't remember, actually."

All at once, Morris began to blink furiously — as if he'd just caught a cloud of dust in his eyes. He wiped his ears with his nubs and shook his head. "There it is again! I thought I'd heard it before."

"Heard what?" Kael said. He was more than a little confused, and the look on Morris's face was making him uneasy. It was a look between surprise and fear.

"I suppose it's my own fault," Morris grumbled after a moment. His bushy brows snapped low over his eyes. "I thought you had a leaning for war, but I was wrong — you're more a craftsman than anything. Aye, only a craftsman could've managed it."

"Managed *what*?" By this point, Kael was fighting to keep his voice even. He didn't know why Morris was looking at him so accusingly, but it made him feel like a villain. "All right, fine: I lied to you. I read it in a book about mind-walking. Are you happy?"

Morris shook his head. "You don't understand, lad. Everything a craftsman makes will do *exactly* what he means it to. And words are a craft all their own — a skilled craftsman can even use words to bend others to his will. It's been done before. You've got to be careful about the lies you

516

tell," he muttered, looking away. "Otherwise, you might cause some real hurt."

At first, Kael didn't believe him. How could his words possibly control somebody else? Then he thought back to that day in the stall, when he'd lied about Eveningwing's curse. He remembered the look on Declan's face: he'd blinked and rubbed his ears just like Morris had. And then, his face had gone smooth.

Perhaps Kael *had* controlled him.

"I could hear it," Morris went on. "Your words had a ringing to them at the end — like a hammer striking the anvil. I knew it was some kind of whispercraft." He plunked a stocky arm across Kael's back, jolting him from his thoughts. "You're a smart lad, and I won't press you. A Wright's got to choose for himself the sort of paths he'll take. But you've got to be careful about what you read. And that goes doubly for anything written by Deathtreader."

Kael looked up in surprise. "You've heard of him?"

"Aye, he was a great healer, in his day. But he's dead now," Morris said offhandedly, as if he was eager to change the subject. "The only question you ought to be worrying about right now is how we're going to slip our way into Gilderick's castle!"

Kael had a few ideas. He worked his way through the different scenarios, planning what they would do if Gilderick came out to fight them, if he tried to surround them, or if he simply stayed holed up inside his walls. He wouldn't be able to survive a siege for very long: thanks to Clairy, his larders were empty. So he would have to come out eventually.

And when he did, the giants would be ready.

Still ... even though Kael thought he had a decent idea, nothing he'd planned so far had worked out the way he meant it to. Gilderick always seemed to do the most implausible things — the one thing he hadn't thought of.

So though he'd thought carefully, he knew he shouldn't celebrate just yet. He began to think of all the ways his plan might go wrong. "Lysander said you managed to free the Pens."

"Oh aye, that bit didn't take too long."

"Do you know if they killed a man named Finks?"

Morris squinted. "I'm not sure ... there weren't many that got away." He whistled and shook his head. "That Declan fellow — whew, I'm glad he's on *our* side!"

Kael nodded, trying to bite back his frustration.

It was possible that Finks had been killed, but he didn't know for sure. He realized he would never really know, not until he stared down at his corpse. But there was no point in worrying about Finks right now: he'd cross that river when he came to it.

"Do you know anything about Gilderick?" Kael said. He could see pale light filtering into the aisle. Dawn was approaching, and the thought of the coming battle made his worry bubble up. Perhaps if he knew a bit more about Gilderick, he might have a better idea of how to defeat him.

Unfortunately, Morris wasn't much help. "No one knows too much about him — even when he worked for King Banagher, he preferred to keep to himself. And we preferred to let him!" Morris shivered. "I saw him roaming the castle a couple of times ... people said he was a necromancer, or something. They thought he sucked the souls out of the rebels he questioned. I'm not sure, though. I don't remember ever smelling any magic on him."

Kael nodded. He didn't know what else he'd been expecting. He rubbed at his stomach, where his scant meal was beginning to churn. Jonathan and Clairy were still sleeping peacefully. Kael watched them for a moment, and listened to their steady breathing.

They'd come so far ... now he knew there'd be no turning back. If they failed, Gilderick wouldn't be content to simply lock them back up: he'd make them pay in blood. But the giants would never let him slaughter their women. No, they'd fight on to the last breath. If they failed today, there would be no tomorrow.

Kael suddenly felt as if all of the giants' massive weight had come down upon his shoulders. He'd led them into this. If they died today, it would be his fault — his, and nobody else's.

"I'm afraid," he whispered. And for some reason, admitting it aloud only made the weight crush down harder. He hardly felt it when Morris draped an arm about his shoulders.

"'Course you are, lad — I'd be worried if you wasn't! No man wants to go to war. But you know something?"

Kael looked up, and Morris's eyes twinkled in their pouches.

"Fear can't kill you. Oh, it can freeze you. It can scare you into giving up — but it can't kill you. What kills you are all the little things you didn't do because you were too scared to do them. It's the *regret* that gets you in the end." He squeezed Kael tightly. "So no matter what happens tomorrow, don't you ever regret what you did in the plains ... because you done a great thing, lad."

Kael wasn't sure about that. If he led the giants to their deaths, it wouldn't be a great thing. Noah was already dead because of him. He didn't think he could live with himself if he caused another life to end. He hoped he wouldn't have to.

But before he could slip too far into darkness, Lysander strode through the door. Eveningwing was still perched happily upon his shoulder — though it was likely that he just used the captain for a shield: when he came back into his human form, Kael planned to scold him.

"I've brought your weapons," Lysander said, handing Kael his bow and quiver. Then he pulled the wallet of throwing knives out of his pocket. "And I believe these belong to you, as well. They were among the things the women raided from the armory," he added with a smirk.

Kael got equipped the best he could. The straps on his wallet were broken, and he doubted they would be much good against the giants. But he tucked them into his pocket, anyways. "We ought to wake everybody up," he said, rising to his feet. "I don't know when Gilderick plans to attack, but we need to be ready."

Lysander grinned. "Oh, I don't think he'll be attacking for quite a while. There's a thick spring mist out there. A man can hardly see a hand in front of his — where are you going?"

But Kael didn't answer.

He sprinted out of the barn and heard Morris thumping along behind him. They tore outside, and stopped.

A white mist covered the Fields, so thickly that Kael swore he could feel himself breath it in. He *could* feel it: the mist itched the whole way down his throat and into his lungs. When he breathed again, he caught a horrible, familiar scent. His stomach fell to his knees when Morris cried:

"Magic! Wake up, lads — we're under attack!"

Chapter 43
A Battle for the Plains

No sooner did Morris speak than the mist evaporated. The earth drew it away, sucking it down like water through a crack. And as the mist disappeared, Gilderick's army sprang out to meet them.

With a thunderous roar, they charged. Their heavy footsteps shook the earth. Kael felt the insides of his head rattling as their feet struck the ground. Their eyes blazed beneath their helmets. They lowered their pikes, holding them out like the fangs of a furious, steely monster. A monster hungry for blood.

Kael saw them coming ... but for some reason, he couldn't move. He was trapped: held down by the hatred in their eyes, afraid to lift his feet because the earth shook too badly. Gilderick's army charged for him, and he could do nothing to stop it. He couldn't even run.

Someone sprinted past him, clipping him so roughly than he nearly tumbled to the ground. An inhuman roar raked his ears, a cry he recognized:

It was Declan. He raced out to meet Gilderick's army — a lone figure against one hundred pikes. The rising sun glinted off his scythe as he raised it, and his cry pierced the air.

He met them like a stone in a river's path, scattering the bloodtraitors to either side. They cried out and tried to leap away, but Declan moved too quickly. Weapons shattered. Splintered bits of pike went sailing through the air as his scythe came down. Armor screeched and groaned as he thrust his way deeper into the crowd. When he spun, scarlet ribbons flew up in his wake.

But Declan was so much smaller than the rest that it wasn't long before the bloodtraitors' towering bodies hid him from view. Gilderick's army swallowed him, and Kael forgot his fear. He wasn't going to let Declan be killed.

His first arrow flew wide, but his second got the bloodtraitors' attention. It sailed into the throat of the nearest man, and his body fell against the backs of his companions. When they spotted Kael, they came after him with a roar.

Blood pounded in his ears and his sight seemed to narrow as they charged. The blazing eyes that had crippled him before were suddenly nothing more than targets. Three bloodtraitors fell before he realized that he'd made a terrible mistake: he'd let them get too close. They were nearly within pike's reach now, and he didn't have a sword to fight them off with. The first bloodtraitor swung for his throat, and he threw himself into a dive.

There was a loud, metallic *thud*. When Kael looked up, he saw Brend standing over him — the bloodtraitor skewered on the end of his scythe.

"I've got you, wee rat!" he cried. Then he looked over his shoulder and bellowed: "The time has come, lads — let's take back the blood these traitors stole from us!"

Kael threw his arms over his head as the giants thundered past him. They were barefoot, carried scythes and pitchforks instead of proper weapons, and their clothes were so ragged that they could hardly stop the wind — much less an arrow. But when they bellowed, the bloodtraitors stumbled back.

The giants crashed into Gilderick's army, knocking the first line of their enemies to the ground. They swung their scythes in high arcs, brought their pitchforks down with deadly force. Under the fury of their blows, Gilderick's army faltered. They retreated a few hundred yards before the shock of the giants' attack wore off — and then they fought back.

A line of pirate archers joined Kael. They launched arrows over the giants' heads, trying to thin the bloodtraitors out the best they could. Most of the arrows clattered harmlessly off their armor, or stuck in their limbs — which Kael knew wouldn't slow them down. He watched as several bloodtraitors simply wrenched the arrows from their flesh and went back to fighting.

"I've got the women gathered in one of the barns — Morris is watching them," Lysander called as he sprinted by. "Now move your legs, seadogs!"

"You heard the captain — get moving!" Thelred shouted as he followed.

A small company of pirates hollered in reply.

They went straight to the giants' flank, where the bloodtraitors were trying to muscle their way through. The pirates arrived just in time, darting in and causing as much havoc as they possibly could. But their cutlasses were no match for the pikes: Kael watched in horror as several pirates were skewered through their middles and flung to the side, as if their bodies were nothing more than piles of hay.

"Help them!" Kael cried, pointing the archers towards the pirates. He yelled for Lysander to pull back, but the noise of the fight was too great. The captain couldn't hear him.

Bloodtraitors crushed against the pirates, trying to bully them into a corner, and Lysander was caught in the middle. His patched-up sword flew in and out as he fought to keep his balance. He was so focused on the enemy in front of him that he didn't see the pike at his back.

Kael had no choice. He went for Lysander at a sprint, but Eveningwing got there first. He dove down and dug his talons into the exposed flesh of the bloodtraitor's face. He screamed and clawed at his eyes, swinging his arms wildly, trying to swat Eveningwing away.

When the bloodtraitor turned, Thelred buried a sword into the small of his back.

"You have to retreat!" Kael shouted.

But Lysander was too busy exchanging blows to listen. Kael shouted again, and the captain just ignored him. So he sent an arrow into his opponent's throat.

"You have to pull back," Kael said, as the bloodtraitor crumpled to the ground.

Sweat matted the wavy hair across Lysander's forehead as he slung his head around. "Never! A pirate would rather die than —!"

An explosion cut him short. It hit the bloodtraitors in front of them and sent them flying through the air in pieces. The force of the explosion blew the pirates backwards. Lysander slammed into Kael, and they landed in a tangle upon the ground. When he finally managed to pull himself free, Kael looked up — and saw Aerilyn standing among the archers.

She already had a second arrow nocked. Her glare burned a straight, deadly line to Lysander as she took aim. "Get away from there, you bloody pirate!" she shrilled.

It was amazing how quickly Lysander sprang to his feet. "Retreat, dogs! Fall back!" he cried, waving the Lass in an arc. "I may rather die than run," he said to Kael as they sprinted away, "but when my wife swears, I've learned that it's just best to do as I'm told!"

Aerilyn sent another exploding arrow into the fray as they retreated, blowing half a dozen bloodtraitors to pieces. But even though her shots kept the giants from being overwhelmed, they were still losing: the bloodtraitors pushed back hard, and the giants couldn't protect themselves from the pikes. Kael saw several raggedly-dressed bodies lying in a heap upon the ground.

"Aim for the middle!" he cried to Aerilyn. "See if you can get them to scatter."

She nodded, and her next arrow flew in a high arc over their heads. Kael watched it climb, hoping the explosion would give the giants the breath they needed to push back. The arrow had begun to fall when a purple flash of light struck it — exploding it harmlessly in midair.

"What happened?" Aerilyn said, squinting after her shot.

Lysander waved his sword. "Just try it again!"

She did. And this time, the purple flash exploded the arrow before it could even finish its climb. Aerilyn stomped her foot. "Why isn't it working?"

"It's Finks," Kael said, his mouth suddenly dry. "He's still alive. Have the archers fire all at once," he shouted to Lysander. "He can't stop them all — Aerilyn's shot will have a better chance of getting through!"

"All right, but — where are you going?"

"To kill Finks!" Kael said shortly. He wasn't about to sit back and let that blasted mage ruin everything. No, he was going to make sure that Finks would never trouble them again.

The land around him was completely flat. There were no hills to climb, and no way to see over the mass of gigantic bodies in front of him. So Kael had no choice but to try to sprint around them. It wasn't long before a small pack of bloodtraitors caught sight of him and began to fling their pikes at his back.

He dodged them easily — slowing his pace as they aimed, and then tearing into a sprint when they threw. While the weapons thudded harmlessly behind him, Kael continued his sprint, watching out of the corner of his eye for Finks.

It looked as if the purple flashes were coming from the back of the army, from safely behind a wall of armored bodies. Kael was thinking about how he was going to get around them when he heard footsteps thundering at his back. Apparently, the bloodtraitors had gotten tired of trying to hit him: now they planned to run him down.

Their long legs cut easily through the gap. No matter how hard he sprinted, Kael couldn't lose them. He could hear their armor rattling with every step; hear their panting breaths as they chased him. He knew that if he didn't want a pike rammed through his back, he would have to turn and fight.

He looked to his left, where the thick of the battle raged on. The giants in the back of the fray were shoving hard against their companions, trying to force their way into the fight. Brend's face was so covered in gore that Kael didn't think he would've recognized him, had it not been for the shock of his hair.

His head popped up over the crowd. When he caught sight of Kael, he slapped the heads of the giants at his elbows. "Help him! Go help the wee rat, you clodders!"

The pack of bloodtraitors had chased Kael far away from the main army, and now they were trapped — cut off by a cluster of slaves. The giants dove into their path, scythes raised, and their attack gave Kael the chance he needed to escape.

A few minutes later, he'd nearly reached the edge of the battle, and that's when he spotted Finks. The mage had himself tucked safely at the army's back. Arrows flew overhead and he swung his whip, destroying them all in a wave of purple light. His skin was a sickly, yellowish green. His legs trembled weakly at his knees. Sweat trickled down the length of his horse's tail, leaving a wet patch in the middle of his back. But even though he looked near to passing out, he kept fighting.

He must've realized that his greasy life depended on it: if he was captured, he would certainly get no mercy from the giants.

Finks was so focused on the arrows that he didn't see Kael run in beside him. They were a stone's throw apart, well within Kael's range. He drew an arrow back and locked it on Finks's chest. Then his fingers slipped from the string.

At that exact moment, a bloodtraitor stumbled out of the battle, clutching his wounded arm — and walked straight into the path of Kael's arrow. His body struck the ground hard, and the noise made Finks looked up.

His eyes found Kael. Something wild sparked behind them.

He raised his whip and a tongue of fire raced down its length. He bared his many teeth in a wicked grin, and then he swung his whip over his head. A massive fireball erupted from the end of it, flying like a boulder from a catapult. Kael watched it sail upwards, high over the battle and into the Fields. He wondered where it could possibly be going.

He followed the fireball's path — and saw that it was headed straight for the barns.

"The women!" Kael's blood pounded in his ears, the force of his legs jarred him. He sprinted for the barns, screaming at the small company of pirates that stood watch in the courtyard. He was too far away to read their faces, but he could see their chins tilting upwards as the fireball arced through the air.

The pirates began to struggle against the barn doors, trying to heave them open, but Kael knew they would never get the women out in time. The fireball began to fall, and in a matter of seconds, the barns would be destroyed.

Something *whoosh*ed over Kael's head, sending him chin-first to the ground. He looked up and watched in horror as a second fireball cut in. It shot over his head and collided with Finks's spell — swallowing it up.

The two fires swelled into one massive, blazing beast. It seemed to grow wings as it soared away from the barns. The fireball tilted itself towards the battle, and made a straight line for Finks.

He sent a flash of light into the middle of it, bursting it before the fires had a chance to reach him. It fell to the earth in burning chunks, raining down among the bloodtraitors. They screamed, and several of them burst into flame. The battle slowed for a moment as the whole company turned towards the Spine.

"It's another one!"

Kael looked in the direction the bloodtraitors pointed, and what he saw nearly dropped him to his knees.

A familiar figure strode towards the battle. Kael recognized his thin frame immediately. He thought he could see the light glinting off his spectacles as he raised his staff.

"Jake!" he cried.

But Jake couldn't hear him: he was locked in a spell battle with Finks. They sent bursts of light flying at each other, trying to break through the other's defenses. Some of their spells exploded so violently that it made Kael's ears ring — and the noise sent the bloodtraitors into a panic.

"Run! Get back to the castle!" they screamed.

All at once, the whole army turned on its heels and tore for the safety of the castle. Finks had to give up his fight with Jake and run with them just to keep from getting trampled. The heat of battle caught in Kael's legs. He hadn't realized that he was chasing after Gilderick's army until the giants passed him up. They followed with a roar, swinging their scythes at the bloodtraitors' backs. The pirates cut the stragglers down with a volley of arrows.

But the bloodtraitors' fear carried them swiftly, and it wasn't long before they broke free. The first wave was nearly at the castle gates when another force struck them in the middle.

Shrilling cries rent the air, and Kael saw that a very strange-looking army had burst from the Spine and was racing for the bloodtraitors' flank. It was an odd mix of desert folk: some wore rags over their heads, while others were so small that he thought they might be children. He was still puzzling over it when he heard a sound that stole his breath.

An unmistakably-familiar singsong cry — a hum that trembled furiously across the cords of his heart.

Harbinger.

The song glanced across his ears, ringing as sharply as the blade's white edge. It swelled in Kael's limbs, filling him until he thought he might burst. He lost all feeling in his legs. He couldn't feel his arms as they swung out beside him, or his eyes as they cut through the crowd. His body went numb, and for a gut-wrenching breath, he feared he might crumble to the ground.

Then his heart brought him back to life.

The first beat echoed inside his chest, striking with such force that he nearly toppled over. His ribs rattled as his hope roared to life. It shoved hard against the calloused, blackened walls of his heart, shaking him with every throb. The thumping inside his chest rattled his breath, sending it gasping from his lungs. For a moment, he stood on the brink.

And then ... he saw her.

Kyleigh led the charge. She darted into the thick of Gilderick's army, Harbinger swinging furiously at her side — and Kael knew no more.

He grabbed a giant's scythe from the ground and hacked his way forward. Bodies passed him in a blur. Hot, sticky liquid clung to his shirt, but he didn't care. He ground his way through flesh and steel to reach her. Only when they stood side-by-side did the world snap back.

They hacked through their enemies. When a bloodtraitor swung at Kael's middle, Kyleigh cut his legs out from under him. Another tried to charge her back — and Kael sent his head flying. He watched her movements from the corner of his eye, darting in to block for her whenever she attacked. If there was ever a gap in her defenses, he was there to fill it.

No matter how the blows jolted his arms, he would keep swinging. No matter how the scythe trembled in his hands, he would hold on. No matter how weak he thought he was — he would be strong enough to protect her.

He would never let anything happen to Kyleigh.

A bloodtraitor sprinted by, and Kael swung for his back. But before his blow could land, Harbinger sprang up to block him, jarring his arms against its blunt side.

"They've got men on the walls — come on!"

Kyleigh dragged him away by his scythe. Pikes thudded into the ground at their heels as they sprinted out of range. Kael looked up and saw that the rest of their little army was already waiting for them. How long had they been defending the gates on their own?

"You little fibber!" Brend bellowed at him. He had a nasty cut over his eye, but that didn't stop him from grinning. "I didn't think your wee limbs could handle a scythe!"

Kael didn't have time to answer him. He ran his eyes over the giants' heads, trying to guess how many men they had left. Bodies lay strewn across the Fields behind them. And he saw many more piled up at the castle gates. Most were the ironclad bodies of Gilderick's soldiers, though he saw several ragged slaves lying amongst them ... and a few smaller forms of pirates.

When he saw them lying, broken and bleeding in the grass, Kael's knees began to shake. He might've collapsed under the horror of it all, had it not been for Kyleigh.

Her hand squeezed his shoulder tightly. The pressure reminded him that the battle wasn't over, just yet. There was still much to be done.

He searched the crowd for the faces of his companions, sighing in relief when he saw they were all there. Lysander and Thelred were scraped up, but otherwise unharmed. Most of the pirates had gathered behind them. Aerilyn jogged in from the Fields, the archers following along at her back. There was a determined set to her chin as she eyed the castle gates.

Brend and his giants had torn ragged strips from their tunics and were trying to bind their many wounds with makeshift bandages. Their thick fingers moved clumsily, though — and those with wounds on their arms had to try to bind them one-handed. That's when the little people from the desert stepped in.

They drove their spears into the ground and cut in among the giants. Their smaller fingers moved surely, and some even tore strips from their own garments to use as bandages. The giants hunched over and grunted as they worked, their filthy faces lined in surprised. Kael might've laughed at the sight of it, if he'd had the time.

"Are Morris and Jonathan —?"

"They're with the women," Thelred answered shortly, glaring up at the castle. "If things go badly, they'll be able to lead them out into the wilderness."

Lysander rolled his eyes. "Things aren't going to go *badly*," he said, with a sharp look at his cousin. Then he turned a tired grin on Kael. "We're ready when you are, Sir Wright."

"Hail, Witchslayer!" a number of gruff voices echoed.

Kael leaned around the pirates and was surprised to see that the men with rags on their heads weren't desert folk at all: they were shipbuilders. Shamus's wide grin stretched between his bushy sideburns as he raised a fist in greeting.

Battlemage Jake stood off by himself at the edge of the force, leaning against his staff. His spectacles slid down his long nose when he nodded.

There was only one person that Kael didn't see. "Where's Declan?"

Brend pointed behind him, and he turned.

Declan paced back and forth in front of Gilderick's castle. His bare feet dragged a line through the dirt path; his scythe hung poised at his side. His shoulders were bunched up tightly. His deep, gasping breaths made his chest swell to nearly twice its normal size.

And he was covered from head to toe in blood.

His head whipped around, and his bottomless black eyes lighted on Kael. "We've sent our enemies fleeing — we've got them trapped," he growled. "What are we waiting for?"

Kyleigh's shoulder brushed against Kael's as she shrugged. "You know, I'm not sure." She met his eyes, and he tried to keep his heart from flying out of his chest when she smiled. "What *are* we waiting for?"

"Nothing," Kael said. "Not a blasted thing."

Kyleigh nodded. And still smiling, she called over her shoulder:

"Jake? Get the door."

Chapter 44
Into the Keep

Jake's spell blew the gate wide open. The clenched teeth of Gilderick's front door burst into splinters, and chunks of his wall blew skywards. The minute the path was clear, Declan charged headlong for the castle — and the giants followed him with a thundering cry.

Kael knew the giants would keep the bloodtraitors occupied, but there were still other enemies they couldn't reach. "There's a witch in that tower over there," Kael said, waving to Jake. "Make sure she doesn't cause us any trouble."

Jake left at a trot, and the army of little people followed along behind him.

Aerilyn seemed to have appointed herself over the archers: she dropped her arm, and the pirates sent a volley of arrows towards the castle walls — forcing the bloodtraitors to duck. Without pikes to stop them, the giants leapt over the shattered gate and poured into the courtyard.

"What's our plan?" Lysander said.

"We can't let Gilderick escape." Kael turned to Shamus. "There's only two ways out of the castle: Jake has the kitchen tower covered, but I'll need you and your men to watch the front gates."

He nodded and quickly passed the order along.

"We'll follow you," Lysander said, when Kael turned to him. "We pirates have to stick together, after all. And I'm rather looking forward to seeing the look on Gilderick's greasy face when we sack him!" he added with a grin.

Kael turned to Kyleigh, who stood quietly by his side. "You know I'll come along," she said, flicking Harbinger in an arc. "I say we end this."

So with a cry, Kael led them to the castle gates.

They leapt over bodies and chunks of jagged rock. Once they were inside the courtyard, Kael slowed. He realized that the Sowing Moon maze was still set up: walls of stone and debris stood in their path. The giants clogged nearly every twisting passageway with their battle. There were so many bodies pressed together that Kael had no choice but to lead his companions down a much narrower path.

They sprinted to the end of one passage and a tumble of giants nearly blocked them in. Kael had to take them down a sharp turn to avoid getting caught in the scuffle. When they came around the next corner, they found a bloodtraitor waiting for them.

He charged. Kael nocked an arrow, Harbinger screamed from behind him — and then a brown blur shot over the top of their heads. Kael watched in disbelief as a tawny mountain lion slammed into the bloodtraitor, digging in with its claws and wrapping its powerful jaws around his neck. The bloodtraitor tumbled out of their path with a scream.

Before Kael could think to do anything, Kyleigh shoved him forward "Keep moving — there're more coming in behind us! He's on our side," she added, when she saw Kael staring at the lion.

He didn't see how a mountain lion could possibly be on their side, but he didn't have time to ask questions. They twisted their way around another curve, and three more bloodtraitors leapt out to skewer them.

It happened so quickly that Kael hardly had a chance to take it in: he heard the hiss of something flying overhead, and all three dropped to the ground — grasping at the knives buried in their throats.

Kael spun and thought he saw a flash of dark hair as somebody ducked behind an overturned wagon, but he couldn't be sure. Kyleigh shoved him on, and he forced his legs forward.

When they came to the charred passageway, he suddenly remembered how to get out. He retraced the wild steps he'd taken during the Sowing Moon, careful to avoid the grappling giants that tumbled into their path. He could hear Brend's voice bellowing over the fray:

"Finish them off, lads! Don't leave one of those spineless snakes alive!"

There was only one *snake* that Kael didn't want to meet in the maze — and that was Dred. He thought it was strange that the general hadn't shown up at the battle that morning. Gilderick was probably keeping him close. He wouldn't want to be taken prisoner, if his castle fell. And a battle with Dred would certainly give him enough time to escape.

Kael realized that if he wanted to reach Gilderick, he'd probably have to find some way to get through Dred. Though he didn't see how he was going to do it.

He pushed this thought aside as he sprinted through the maze. Instead, he focused on the twists and turns, keeping his eyes wide to the dangers around them. Then after several minutes of desperate weaving, they broke into the open courtyard.

Kael spun to make sure his companions were still following, and when he turned back around, the keep doors stood only a few paces in front of him. Unfortunately, the doors were shut tight — and barred by a small mountain of iron and meat.

Just as he'd suspected, General Dred stood before the doors. Half a dozen bloodtraitors gathered at his back, pikes lowered in a menacing wall. When he saw Kael, Dred's stony eyes widened in recognition.

"His Lordship should've killed you," he growled, his shredded lip twisting in a snarl. "But since he didn't, I suppose I'll have to do it for him. Make it count," he added, when Kael drew his bow. "You'll only get one shot."

One shot was all Kael needed. He locked onto Dred's left eye, and as the general lumbered forward, he prepared to take his shot —

"No!"

Declan strode out from behind a ruined stone wall, a small army of glaring giants following at his back. He was so covered in blood that his feet left a dark trail behind him. He had his scythe gripped in both hands, and gore trickled from the end of it.

His black eyes locked onto Dred. "No ... this one's mine."

With a howl he felt in his gut, Declan charged — and Dred's face went white with terror. He turned and ran for his life, leaving the other guards to fend for themselves.

Declan chased after Dred, and the giants fell on the remaining bloodtraitors, shoving them away from the keep doors. For a moment, Kael thought they might've actually won.

"The Fallows!" Brend called. He stood on top of a pile of rotted barrels, and he thrust his scythe towards the Fields. "They've broken out — the Fallows are coming!"

"What in blazes is a *Fallow*?" Kyleigh said, trying to crane her neck over the nearest bit of wall.

Kael's stomach twisted in a knot. "Believe me, you don't want to know. Come on!"

He grabbed her arm and pulled her to the keep doors. In two sharp kicks, she broke the lock. Kael shoved her through, and Thelred and Lysander fell in behind them. They stumbled around for a moment as their eyes got used to the damp gloom of Gilderick's castle.

"It's dark in here," Thelred grumbled. "Why is it so blasted dark?"

"Well, what did you expect? Did you think he'd have merry little lights dancing in the hallways?" Lysander said. He shoved the doors closed and wedged a nearby chair against the lock. "That's not going to hold for long. Let's get moving."

Kael couldn't have agreed more.

He led them through the passages, his ears pricked against the unsettling silence. Kyleigh kept a hand in the middle of his back, as if she was prepared to hurl him out of the way if somebody tried to attack them. But they walked for several minutes without a guard in sight. And Kael began to get worried.

"Perhaps he's gone," Lysander whispered. Even though they were alone, he kept his voice quiet — like he thought the halls might have ears of their own.

The hand on Kael's back twitched as Kyleigh shook her head. "No, he's still here. I can smell him."

"Then why don't you lead?" Kael said to her. His stomach flipped when she laughed.

"I would, if you were going the wrong way," she said quietly. "Keep moving — we're nearly there."

A faint light glowed at the end of one passageway, and Kael followed it to a closed door. Though he gestured for his companions to stay back while he opened it, they flatly refused.

"Then at least be quiet," he whispered as he turned the knob. "We may only have one chance at this." When they nodded, he shoved the door open.

A long hallway stretched out in front of them, and a man stood at the end of it. Kael already had an arrow trained on his chest before he realized that it wasn't Gilderick waiting for them:

It was Finks.

He stood guard before a second door at the end of the passageway. A purple, waving shield hovered in the air in front of him. "Your arrows will do you no good, rat," he hissed, his eyes wild. "You'll have to step a little ... closer."

Kael knew better than to do that.

But Thelred didn't.

He shoved past Kael, yelling at the top of his lungs and waving his sword through the air. Kael lunged for him, tried to snatch the back of his shirt, but he missed. "No! Don't —!"

An explosion shook the hallway. Thelred flew backwards, slamming hard against the wall. Hot, sticky drops sprayed in every direction. Kael stared at Thelred's crumpled body and for one heart-stopping second, he thought he was dead. Then he rolled over.

"My leg!" he screamed.

Lysander was already at his side. He'd begun to tear a strip from his shirt when Kael stopped him. "Let me. Kyleigh — watch our backs."

She stood bowlegged in front of them, Harbinger clutch in her hand — a hand that trembled as her fingers tightened around the hilt. Kael couldn't see her face, but he could see the red spreading across the back of her neck. And he could only imagine the sort of look she was giving Finks.

"Fix it!" Thelred screamed, grasping at his knee. His face was white with pain, and he grit his teeth so hard that Kael feared he might actually crack them. "You have to fix it!"

There was no way Kael could fix it. Thelred's leg had been blown off just below the knee, and now lay across the hall in pieces. The best Kael could do was try to stop him from bleeding to death.

"Grab his hand," he said to Lysander.

The captain wrapped both of his bloodied hands around Thelred's, and he squeezed tightly. "Steady on, Red. Let Kael stop the bleeding."

It only took him a moment to find the thick veins in Thelred's leg and to pinch them shut. Once the bleeding stopped, he helped Lysander pull Thelred up. "You won't make it out of the courtyard like this. Take him to one of the empty chambers and lock yourselves in. We'll come back for you."

Lysander nodded. "Do you hear that, Red? You're going to be just fine."

"*Fine*? My bloody leg got blown off!" Thelred snapped as he slung his arm about Lysander. Just before they limped away, he turned to glare at Kael. "You'd better make him pay — do you hear me?" Beads of sweat lined Thelred's mouth. His eyes threatened to roll back, but he forced them to stay forward. "Get him."

Kael planned on it.

He slung his bow over his shoulder and warned Kyleigh to stay back. Then he drew the dark rider's knife from his belt and brandished it at Finks.

The mage threw back his head and cackled. "Come on and stab me, then," he dared, his evil eyes glinting. "Come drive your little knife through my heart!"

Kael smiled. "All right."

He charged. The explosions rattled his ears. One, two, three — every trap he stepped on blew up in a wave of fire and smoke. The soles of his feet itched furiously. Blasts of wind blew across his legs, but did no harm. Flames licked his ears as he passed, but couldn't burn him. When Finks saw him burst through the final trap, he tried to run.

Kael grabbed him by the horse's tail and jerked him backwards, out from behind the protection of the shield. Finks squealed as he flew backwards — and fell straight into the tip of the dagger.

"You're the sixth mage I've killed with a knife," Kael said, as Finks wriggled hopelessly against the blade. "Perhaps you aren't as powerful as you think."

Kael twisted the dagger once, hard ... and then Finks went still. He threw the mage's body aside, turning when he heard footsteps coming up behind him.

"The giants have broken into the keep," Kyleigh said. Her green eyes flicked to the door in front of them. "Gilderick's in there — I can smell the evil on him. They'll probably want to tear him to shreds, but ..."

Her brows creased over her eyes, and Kael didn't understand her look. Kyleigh was either confused ... or worried. Perhaps a little of both.

"I don't trust Gilderick," she finally said. "He'll have something planned. So we'd better end this quickly. Are you ready?"

Kael nodded. He wanted nothing more than to have it all end, and he *would* end it: for Thelred, for the giants, and for all the friends they'd lost. He'd make sure that Gilderick rotted for his deeds — and he'd let the evil in the plains rot along with him.

Kyleigh threw her shoulder into the door, stumbling through when the latch broke free, and Kael stepped in behind her.

Gilderick sat in the middle of the room, his spidery fingers curled around the armrests of a blackened throne. His chin was pointed downwards, but when he heard Kael stomping towards him, his head began to rise.

Kael didn't look away. He wasn't afraid of Gilderick anymore — in fact, he wanted to see the look on his face when the arrow struck him. The lank mop of hair parted from across Gilderick's forehead, and two dark eyes met Kael's.

Even from a distance, he could see the many lines that fanned out from around Gilderick's pupils. They filled his vision, as if those lines were all there was to look at — as if his eyes were all there'd ever been to see.

Heavy footsteps pounded through the hall behind him, closing in. But Kael's ears clogged against them. The room disappeared, the castle, the plains ... even Kyleigh slipped away, tumbling into the dark nothingness that waited beneath him.

All at once, Kael lost his footing — and he fell headlong into another world.

Chapter 45
The Only Death to Fear

The world drifted in slowly.

At first, Kael thought he was back in Gilderick's throne room. But it was brighter here than he'd remembered. The stone floor pressed hard against his back, and his whole body ached — like he'd fallen from some great height and still had the wind knocked of him. The floor was covered in a thick layer of dust: it clung to the wet of his palms as he tried to roll over.

He ignored the creaking of his bones and forced himself to sit up. His vision blurred dangerously, and he had to concentrate to keep from passing out. Slowly, he managed to get his eyes to focus.

A wide stone chamber surrounded him. It was completely round, like the inside of a tower. Shelves of books wrapped around the walls and the many colors of their spines seemed to brighten the room all the more. He was certain now that he wasn't anywhere in Gilderick's castle. But then ... where was he?

Just in front of him was a landing of shallow steps — like the climb to a throne. But in place of a throne was a plain, oaken desk. Though its edges were smooth, Kael could see clearly where the desk had been shaped: it looked rough, like something Roland might've whittled for one of the Tinnarkian children.

There was a large book sitting on top of the desk — so large that Kael didn't think he would've been able to wrap his hand around its spine. A man sat at the desk, leaned over the book, and Kael recognized the greasy mop of his hair immediately.

"Where have you taken me, Gilderick?" he said, glancing around the room. His heart shuddered when he saw they were alone and in his panic, he tried to jump to his feet. But his knees gave out, and his legs collapsed beneath him. His whole body felt like a limp rag. He couldn't get it to do what he wanted. "Where's Kyleigh? What have you done with her?"

"Done with her?" Gilderick's face twisted into a smile. His skin hung loosely from his mouth, as if it'd been stretched across a bare skull. "I haven't done anything with her — ah, well, I suppose I left her behind. But the Dragongirl doesn't interest me. Her barbarian mind is too simple to be any challenge. No ..." His brown eyes flicked to the top of Kael's head and tightened, as if they tried to peel up his scalp. "You're the one I'm interested in.

"I admit that I misjudged you — I thought you were little more than rebel. But, after a bit of reading," Gilderick placed his hand on the large book in front of him, "I discovered that you and I are quite similar."

"I'm nothing like you," Kael spat. He didn't know where he was, but he was determined to get back to Kyleigh. He propped his hands beneath him and tried to pull himself up, but his elbows gave way. His forehead struck the dusty floor.

Gilderick ignored his struggle, turning one of the book's thick pages absently. "We're more alike than you may think ... we were both born poor and weak. Neither of us knew our fathers. And," he traced a finger down the page, "we've both lost our homes. I *chose* to leave. But you ... oh, that's tragic," he murmured, though he smiled rather widely as he said it. "Titus burned your little village to the ground, didn't he? This *Tinnark* that you remember so fondly?"

Kael's mouth went dry. "How do you know that?" When Gilderick didn't answer him, his eyes swept across the room. "Where am I? What have you done to me?"

Gilderick's spidery fingers twined together and rested upon the book — a book, Kael suddenly realized, that must've told him everything. With a sickening lurch of his gut, he figured out where he was.

"Done?" Gilderick's tongue clicked against his teeth. "Allow me to answer your question with one of my own: what's it like, to be conscious inside your own Inner Sanctum?"

Kael couldn't breathe.

He was trapped inside his own head — trapped with Gilderick. How was Gilderick here? How had he possibly gotten in? The last thing Kael remembered before he passed out was looking into his eyes ...

"You're a whisperer — a healer," he said, though he hardly believed himself. Even after Gilderick nodded, he still couldn't grasp it. But then as he thought, the truth began to unravel.

That's why Gilderick never let the mages into the castle: it wasn't because he was trying to keep his slaves under control — it was because he couldn't stand the smell of them. He'd even kept the witch locked up inside the kitchen tower, away from the main rooms.

Kael remembered the story Brend had told him, about how no one could prove that Gilderick tortured the rebel whisperers during the War, because there were never any wounds on their bodies. But he *had* tortured them: after he'd split them open, he just sealed them back up. He must've kept them alive for days, hacking them up and piecing them back together. The rebels must've begged for death ... but they hadn't been allowed to die.

Gilderick wouldn't let them.

Bile rose in Kael's throat at the thought. He might've heaved his scant breakfast out on the floor, but he was too weak to be sick. "The Fallows," he managed to choke out.

"Ah, yes." Gilderick leaned forward excitedly. "Remarkable, are they not? I always knew there must be someway to control the minds of others — to bend their bodies to my will. That's why I asked to rule the plains," he added with a smirk. "The giants are so weak-minded to begin with that I knew they'd be the perfect subjects for my experiments. At first, they were difficult to control. But I found that wounds or sickness helped ... soften them up, for me."

As Gilderick leaned back, his boney hands scraped down the book, dragging behind his wrists like a pair of dead things. "The Fallows are a part of me: my little puppets. And I hold their strings between by fingers. Curious that you should mention them." His mouth twitched slightly. "A few days ago, I felt one of the strings break. I thought my newest Fallow must've perished — that happens sometimes," he mused, his pitiless gaze trailing to the far wall. "Not all of them are strong enough to bear my presence." His eyes roved back to Kael's. "I see now that I was wrong. He didn't die, did he? No ... you set him free.

"You found something of great importance to me — a journal that I plucked from the body of an old friend. Yes, I've read all about it," he said when Kael gasped, tapping the pointed tip of his finger against the book. "It's all right here. I've sent one of my Fallows to retrieve it. I can't let the book slip away from me again. Had it not been for Deathtreader's teachings, I would still be powerless — the weakest class of whisperer. You've been very useful to me, Kael of the Unforgivable Mountains. Now ... what should I do with you?" Gilderick's mouth twisted into an unsettling smile. "It's always nice to meet another healer. We're such a rare breed, after all. Perhaps you might still be useful. I've gotten rather comfortable here," he said, glancing around the room. "Perhaps I'll stay."

Kael's blood ran cold. He didn't want to become a Fallow — to be trapped inside some greasy shadow for the rest of his life, not even free to move his own limbs. He would never see his friends again. He would never see Kyleigh —

The walls around him suddenly groaned, startling him from his thoughts. They creaked, moaning like the underbelly of a ship. A light, tinkling noise came from across the room. Kael looked up above the shelves, and realized that every window in his Sanctum was completely walled up.

They'd been packed full of stone and mortar, sealed shut against the outside. Dark lines ran across them. Moisture struck the floor as they wept.

Somehow, Kael managed to peel his tongue from the roof of his mouth. "What's out there?" he said hoarsely.

Gilderick was staring at the walls, a look of interest on his face. "That depends: what were you feeling, just then?"

"I was afraid," Kael admitted. He didn't see any point in trying to hide it. Besides, if he kept Gilderick talking, it might give his body a chance to recover.

"Then *fear* is what it is," Gilderick murmured. "It's interesting that you would keep your fears so close — most people keep them at a distance. And speaking of interesting things ..."

Gilderick stood up from the desk and trotted down the stairs. He didn't look nearly as weak as Kael. In fact, his body seemed livelier now than it ever had in reality.

He strode out to the stone floor, his boots kicking up thick patches of dust in his wake. "I've only ever read about this," he said, gesturing down to the floor. "People tend keep their foundations clear and open — but yours is hidden."

"My foundation?" Kael said. By now, his body was so weak that he could hardly move. His back slouched over his knees, and his arms hung limply at his sides. His only small chance to live was to keep asking questions.

Gilderick smirked. "Yes, your foundation: the culmination of all your thoughts and beliefs, the one thing you cling to — your great purpose." He crouched and ran his fingers across the ground. "But dust ... in the mind, dust symbolizes the things we have forgotten. Or in your case, perhaps it's something you never even knew. This dust is quite thick, after all. I'm interested to see what you've got hiding under here," he added, grinning up at Kael. "Let's find out together, shall we?"

Gilderick blew across the ground, one small breath. But the dust cleared as if it'd been struck by a tempest's gale: it rose and swirled about the room, spinning across the shelves and trembling the books on their spines. As the dust

544

blew around them, Kael looked down at the floor — and saw a familiar symbol carved into the stone:

An eye with a series of lines crisscrossing through its center, forming three triangles on top, three interlocking triangles on the bottom, and one black triangle in the center.

It was the symbol of the Wright.

"No!" Gilderick said.

He'd taken a hurried step towards Kael when the dust finally broke out of its spin. It roared from the walls and hit Gilderick full in the chest. His body flew into the side of the desk, as if a giant's fist had struck him. He groaned and pressed his arms beneath him.

While Gilderick struggle to rise, the dust fluttered down and stopped in front of Kael. It fell away like a curtain, whispering as it struck the ground.

A man stepped out from behind the dust. His leather armor was tattered — worn down almost to the threads, in places. He carried a humble-looking sword in one hand, and a dented shield in the other. The Wright's symbol stood out on the front of the shield. Kael thought he knew who this man was — who it must've been.

When he forced himself to look up, he saw that he'd been right.

Setheran the Wright stood before him. He looked exactly how he had in Kyleigh's memories: with his bright red hair and lithe frame, even down to the angles of his face. Setheran met Kael with a smile — a smile so kind that it shamed him.

Kael's eyes fell away. He couldn't bear to have a great warrior like Setheran see him like this — to see him weak and beaten, unable even to get to his feet. If he looked up now, would Setheran laugh at him? Would he sneer? Would there be pity in his gaze ... or disappointment?

Kael couldn't look. He couldn't bear it. So he kept his eyes on the floor.

Setheran stepped closer. Kael stared at the scuffs on his boots as they rose and fell. When they were only a few paces apart, Setheran began to speak. His voice rang with a depth that didn't quite match his lithe frame. And Kael felt the familiar words echo inside his soul:

"There are times when death seems certain, and hope is dim. But in those times, I forget my fears. I do not see the storm that rages, or the battle that looms ahead. I close my eyes to the dangers — and in the quiet of the darkness ... what do I see?"

Kael knew the answer. But just as he was about to speak, his face burned and his throat suddenly tightened. No, he wouldn't cry — not in front of Setheran. No matter how ashamed he was, he would speak.

So he forced his chin up, tore his eyes from the ground and gasped: "I see only what must be done."

Setheran crouched in front of him; their faces were even. He smiled hard as he offered his hand. "Then arise, Sir Wright ... and do what you must."

Kael took his hand, and Setheran jerked him onto his feet. A cloud of dust exploded over his body, filling his mouth and nostrils with grit. When the dust finally cleared, Setheran was gone.

Strength surged into Kael's limbs. There was a weapon grasped in his hand. His fingers tightened around the hilt, and he realized that he was carrying Setheran's sword. The dented shield hung from his other arm, and in place of his clothes was Setheran's tattered armor.

"No," Gilderick said again, laughing madly as he pulled himself to his feet. "A *Wright*? Oh, I don't think I could've asked for better! Yes — you'll serve me well. I'll pull your little string, and the whole Kingdom will fall at my feet!" He laughed again as he wiped the dust from his tunic. Then his eyes locked on Kael's. "But first ... I'm going to have to soften you up."

Blackness spilled from Gilderick's pores. It snaked across his body, covering him from head to toe in a protective shell. An axe sprouted from between his boney hands — an axe that was almost as tall and thick as he was. There was no way Gilderick could've carried such a weapon.

But then Kael remembered that they were fighting in the mind. Here, a man could wield whatever he imagined.

"These will be your last free breaths — so be sure to breathe them deeply!" Gilderick called. Then he snapped the guard down over his helmet, and their battle began.

Kael knew Gilderick would be strong. Unfortunately, he didn't know just *how* strong — not until he was already sailing to the other end of the room. His back struck the shelves hard; the sword flew from his hand. He heard the hiss of the axe and threw his shield up instinctively.

His arm shook and his back slammed against the wall. It took all of his concentration to keep Gilderick's blow from crushing him. He imagined that his muscles swelled, and he grew stronger — pushing Gilderick back a few inches. For a moment, it looked like he might actually break free: Gilderick's arms shook against his strength. One hard push was all Kael needed.

Then the axe suddenly burst into flames.

It burned white hot. The heat from its blade began to creep into the iron of Kael's shield. He smelled the singe of leather as the fire reached his armor, and then it bit through his skin.

He cried out as the heat gnawed at him, but forced himself to concentrate. He braced the shield with his other arm and shoved back as hard as he could. Gilderick only moved a step, but that was all Kael needed. He rolled away from the shelves and dove for his sword.

No sooner did he grab the hilt than Gilderick was upon him. Kael had to roll madly as the axe came down. It sparked against the stone floors — where his neck had been only seconds before. He swung blindly for Gilderick's chest and felt the sword tremble when it glanced off his blackened armor.

Kael leapt to his feet. He knew Gilderick was much stronger, but his heavy armor would make him slow. So Kael decided to take a trick out of Noah's book.

He swung for Gilderick in mind-boggling patterns, striking him wherever he could. Not all of his blows landed true — in fact, Gilderick was able to block most of them. But Kael was still hoping to tire him out.

One opening was all he needed. If he could get Gilderick to let his guard down, Kael could deal the ending blow. All he had to do was be patient.

He swung for Gilderick's neck, spinning before the axe could block him, and then cut down for his knees. The sword struck the armor hard, jarring his arm again. But Gilderick's knee buckled under the blow — and Kael saw his chance.

With a cry, he swung for Gilderick's neck. He was shocked when the sword hit his breastplate, instead — so shocked, that he lost his grip. His weapon went sailing to the other side of the room, and the blunt end of the axe knocked him onto his back.

Somehow, Gilderick had grown taller. Now he stood at a giant's height, towering head and shoulders above Kael. His massive foot crunched down into the middle of Kael's chest, pinning him to the floor. He tried to beat Gilderick's boot off of him with his shield, only to have it ripped from his arm and flung after the sword. The axe blade pressed against his throat in warning.

Gilderick raised the guard from his helmet. Beads of sweat dotted the pasty skin around his nose and forehead. "I'm a bit disappointed. I expected a Wright to be more of a challenge, but … ah, well," he tilted the axe against Kael's chin, "let's just finish this cleanly. Your last words, if you please? I collect them," Gilderick explained, tapping the side of his head. "So try to make them worth remembering."

Kael had no intention of giving his last words. He pried his fingers beneath Gilderick's boot, trying to force it off his chest. But the weight only came down harder.

"Take your time," Gilderick said, smiling at him. Then he laughed, and his eyes went to the far wall. "It's odd to use the word *time* in a place where time does not exist. You'll never get out," he added, when Kael tried punching the side of his leg. "So you might as well speak. What words would you have me remember you by, hmm? What can you add to my little collection?"

Kael suddenly realized that it was hopeless. He let his head fall back and heard it thump hollowly against the ground. It was starting to sink in, now: he was going to be trapped here forever — doomed to follow Gilderick around as an empty husk. Would his friends miss him? Would they forget about him? And would Kyleigh ...?

He couldn't even bear to finish the thought. He knew he would never see her again.

The windows groaned as he thought of her, and he watched them dully. Wet lines trickled out from the mortar, running down the sills. He listened to the soft tinkling of the water that dripped onto the cold stone floor.

Perhaps Gilderick was right. Perhaps that *was* his fear out there, waiting to swallow him up. He imagined that it pressed against the sealed windows, that it growled as it tried to claw its way through.

The thing he feared most was the thought of losing Kyleigh. He could've faced anything, even death, as long as she was by his side ...

A mad thought suddenly hit him — so mad that it made the tips of his fingers go cold. But it was almost mad enough to work ... if Kael could force himself to do it. As the walls groaned again, Morris's words filled his head:

Fear can't kill you.

He said this to himself, over and over again — and after a moment, he found the courage to speak: "All right, I'll give you my last words."

"Excellent," Gilderick murmured. "Be sure to speak clearly."

Kael nodded, steeling himself for the mad thing he was about to do. "I love someone," he blurted out. The walls groaned again and the ground trembled slightly, but the windows held firm. Kael knew he would have to dig deeper. "I've loved her for a long while, but I knew she couldn't love me back. And I was afraid ..."

A few pebbles broke from the windows and clattered onto the floor. Water began to leak from the holes in a steady stream. Ice settled in the pit of Kael's stomach. *Fear can't kill you*, he reminded himself. *Fear can't kill you.*

"I was afraid that if I told her how I felt, she would fly across the seas to the Westlands — like Quicklegs did to Iden. I thought I would die of a broken heart, if she ever left me. So I tried to hide my feelings ... but she left me anyways."

More bits of stone struck the floor; the mortar groaned and bowed out, straining like the buttons on a fat man's shirt. But the seals held.

Kael took a deep breath. "I thought she'd figured out that I loved her — I thought she'd left for good. And for a while, I felt dead. But now she's come back ... and I'm afraid that I may have seen her for the last time. I'm terrified that I'll never see her again, that I'll never be able to tell her the truth." A deep rumbling shook the chamber for a moment. It passed behind the windows and sent them bowing out — but it wasn't enough to break them. Kael had to say more. "I love her. No — that's not entirely true: I'm *in* love with her."

He heard the monster groaning behind the windows, pressing them, straining them, but it still wasn't enough. What else could he possibly say?

Gilderick watched in interest. His eyes followed the trail of the water as it leaked from the windows and down the shelves. "In love with *whom*?" he murmured.

Kael nearly laughed.

That was it. *That* was what he had to say. As long as he never said her name, it wouldn't be real. He could keep his heart safe and protected behind these walls, locked away where his feelings could never hurt him. But if he wanted to beat Gilderick, he had to face his fears. He had to admit it out loud — once and for all.

"I'm in love with *her*," he whispered, after a long, quiet breath. "I'm in love with Kyleigh."

That did it.

Stone burst from the windows, and icy water poured in. It fell in torrents down the shelves, swallowing the floor in a matter of seconds. Kael shut his eyes as the water climbed over his head. He felt Gilderick's boot leave his chest; heard the muffled tromping of his steps as he tried to escape the flood.

Kael held his breath. *Fear can't kill you. Fear can't kill you*, he said, as his breath began to run out. *Fear can't kill you!*

Finally, he could hold it no longer. Air burst from his lungs, and he gasped. He expected the icy water to come rushing down his throat ... but it never did. When he opened his eyes, he saw the chamber was completely filled to the brim.

It looked as if he stood at the bottom of the sea, with blues and greens swirling all around him. But the water didn't crush him. He breathed it in as easily as he might've breathed the air. His limbs moved freely as he dragged himself from the ground.

So Morris had been right, then: his fear *couldn't* kill him.

But it could certainly kill Gilderick.

A few steps away, the Lord of the plains hung trapped in the water. Bubbles streamed out between his pasty lips. Though his limbs clawed helplessly for the surface, the weight of his thick armor held him to the ground. His eyes widened in terror when he saw Kael walking towards him.

The world began to wave as Gilderick panicked — and Kael's mind spat them out.

Chapter 46
Braver

Blurry figures swooped by his head. Kael could feel the rush of wind as they passed. Muffled cries filled his ears — thumping as they tried to push through. He shoved the fog away and forced the blurriness from his eyes.

Strong arms wrapped about his middle, carrying him so swiftly that he thought he might be flying.

"Kael!"

His head touched the ground, gently, and then Kyleigh's blazing eyes struck his. Though she glared, her mouth was parted in worry. He felt a dull heat rise in his stomach as she grabbed either side of his face.

"Kael — talk to me! Are you hurt?"

His scalp tingled madly when her fingers ran through his hair. He reached up and managed to grab her wrist. "I'm fine," he whispered. His throat felt raw, as if he'd been screaming for hours on end. He turned towards the blackened throne. "Gilderick ..."

But he realized there was no point in trying to explain what had happened. The giants were now crowded around Gilderick's throne, a wall of filthy bodies hid him from view. Kael allowed himself a smirk.

Good. Brend would take care of Gilderick — he'd give the Lord of the plains exactly what he deserved.

Kael lay back and let his neck rest against the floor, feeling relieved. A few seconds later, the crowd broke from around the throne. One of the giants spun away, pointed his chin towards the door — and that's when Kael got a good look at his eyes.

They were a dead, milky white. His mouth hung slack and drool trailed from his lips. He carried something against his chest. Boney limbs hung out from the cradle of his thick arms, and Kael swore he saw a mop of greasy hair sprouting near the Fallow's elbow.

But it wasn't until the he charged by that Kael knew for certain. As the Fallow ducked under the arch of the doorway, his arms bent open — and Lord Gilderick peered out from between them.

He gave Kael one tiny smirk, one final taunt, and then he was gone. The Fallows crowded out the door, their filthy feet slapped against the hallway as they ran for the courtyard.

Kael tried to shout, but his throat was still too raw. He raised one arm frantically in Gilderick's direction, but Kyleigh didn't look. Her eyes were still on his. She kept asking him if he was all right, demanding that he speak — and behind her, Gilderick was getting away.

It was stubborn will that finally broke the seal across Kael's throat: "Stop them — they've got Lord Gilderick! He's getting away!"

He struggled to crawl out from under Kyleigh, but she held him back, staring at him like he'd just cracked his skull. "What are you —? Quit flailing! You're going to hurt yourself." But Kael didn't give up, and she finally pulled him to his feet. He took a few stumbling steps before his legs gave out. She caught him under the arms and propped him up against her. "What happened to you? Are you all right —?"

"No, I'm blasted not all right!" Kael snapped. He watched the last of the Fallows escaped through the door, and it took every ounce of his self-control to keep from breaking his fist against the wall.

At last, Kyleigh seemed to figure it out. Her eyes swept across the empty throne before they flicked back to the doorway. She loosened her grip for half a moment, as if she was about to charge after Gilderick — but in the end, she seemed to decide against it. Her arms tightened about his middle.

"We'll gut him another day," she promised. "The plains are free, now — and that's the most important thing. Gilderick can rot."

Kael shook his head. "You don't understand … he knows everything."

"Everything about what?"

He told her quickly about what had happened to him, about the battle he'd had with Gilderick — though he didn't tell her *exactly* how he'd managed to win. And when he was finished, she raised her brows.

"Blazes," she whispered. "Gilderick's a *whisperer*?" At first, she looked as if she didn't quite believe it. But as her eyes roved around the room, they hardened. "Well, I suppose that makes sense. Though I don't see how he's managed to keep it a secret." She slung Kael's arm about her shoulder and led him down the hall, shaking her head as she went. "The good news is that I don't think Gilderick will risk going back to Crevan — not after what's happened here. His power is gone, his days as a ruler are finished. If he shows his greasy head again, Crevan won't hesitate to kill him. No, he'll have no choice but to wither away in some dark corner of the Kingdom, alone and beaten."

Kyleigh smiled at him, but he didn't smile back.

Sure, that was the most plausible thing: it would make sense for Gilderick to hide, rather than face the wrath of the King. But then again, Gilderick never did what was plausible. He might be heading straight to Midlan.

And how far would the King go to capture him, once he found out there was a Wright attacking his rulers? Kael's friends wouldn't be safe around him. He would have to leave for good, if Midlan ever discovered him.

Kyleigh seemed to be able to hear the dark thoughts swirling through his head. She squeezed his arm, and her touch pulled him free. "One thing at a time," she said with a smile. "Now, let's go retrieve our favorite pirates."

They found Lysander and Thelred locked up inside one of the castle chambers. The stump of Thelred's leg wasn't bleeding, but it was obvious by how white his face was that he was in a considerable amount of pain. He was madder than Kael had ever seen him — though he seemed to brighten up a bit when he learned that Finks was dead.

"Good. I'm just sorry I wasn't able to do it." He held his hands out to Lysander. "Let's get out of here, Captain. I'm ready to go home."

Lysander looked relieved as he grinned. "Aye, aye, Cousin Red!" Then he pulled Thelred up and led him gingerly to the door.

The numbness had begun to fade from Kael's legs, so he told Kyleigh to lend a hand with Thelred. He walked in front of them, scanning the passageways for any sign of their enemies. But the castle looked completely empty. The Fallows hadn't seemed interested in reclaiming the fortress — only in carrying Gilderick to safety.

When they made it out to the courtyard, they saw that the battle wasn't quite over, yet. A ring of giants blocked them in, circling the two fighters still locked in the middle. Jake met them on the edge of the ring. The little people from the desert trotted along at his heels.

"The ladies have herbs and bandages waiting at the barns," Jake said, his gaze flicking down to Thelred's leg. He glanced at the packed courtyard before waving the pirates back into the castle. "Follow me, I'll take you through the kitchen tower. It's perfectly safe: the witch was already dead when we arrived. We found her bones boiling inside a giant cooking pot." He made a face. "Apparently, Gilderick got to her first. We'd checked the tower for survivors and were on our way out when a whole mob of giants shoved past us," he said, gesturing down to the little people. "We nearly got ourselves trampled, didn't we? I can't imagine why they were in such a rush."

Kael had to grit his teeth to keep from crying out in frustration. The Fallows were gone, then. They'd managed to slip out through the kitchen tower — and because they were dressed like the other slaves, Jake had let them pass. There was no telling where they were headed, and Kael knew he couldn't catch them.

He watched as Lysander and Thelred limped away. Jake led them into the tower, and the little people guarded their backs with silver spears.

There was no point in brooding over Gilderick. He supposed Kyleigh was right: they'd have to gut him another day. Kael shoved his worry to the back of his mind and instead, tried to see what was going on inside the giants' ring.

As he ventured closer, one of the giants caught sight of him. When he snatched Kael by the back of the shirt, he knew what was coming. So he grabbed Kyleigh by the hand and held onto her tightly as the giant hauled them to the front of the circle.

In the middle of the wall of bodies, Declan and Dred still fought. Things looked to be going very poorly for Dred: he had a deep cut on his arm and large chunks of his breastplate were simply missing. He slid backwards on his rump, dragging his pike along behind him, and kept his wounded arm raised protectively over his face.

"Please," he gasped. Sharp, white fear ringed the stony gray of his eyes. The bunched muscles in his arm trembled as he tried to drag himself away from Declan. "Please — I'm your kin! Don't you remember your own brother?"

Declan raised his scythe over his head, as if he meant to drive it straight through Dred's heart — and then, he paused. The wild black sunk out of his eyes, drawn back into his pupils. He looked at Dred calmly; his gaze climbed over the depth of his horrible scar.

"Yeh," Declan said after a moment. "I remember my brother: his name was Dante. And you murdered him."

Before Dred even had a chance to cry out, Declan's scythe came down.

Kael looked away as Dred squirmed. Only after his body went still did he dare to look back. Declan pulled the scythe from the hole in Dred's massive chest and flung it to the ground, a look of disgust on his face. Then his head turned around the giants' circle.

When he saw the many gazes pointed in his direction, his eyes tightened and fell. He ripped the bloodied shirt off his chest and flung it after the scythe. As he marched for the castle gates, the giants parted to let him through.

Kyleigh touched his arm, and Kael realized that he'd been squeezing her fingers very tightly. He hadn't even noticed that he still held her hand.

He dropped it immediately. "Come on," he said, walking towards the maze. "I ought to go help with the healing."

They only made it a few steps in before one of the little people from the desert hopped into their path. Her name was Nadine, and her accent was so thick that Kael had a difficult time understanding everything she said. But from what he could gather, she'd seen the Fallows heading south, through the Spine and towards the desert.

"We tried to stop them, but our legs were not long enough. A few fell to our spears," she added with a rueful smile.

For a moment, Kael's heart leapt. He thought they might have a chance to catch them. But Kyleigh shook her head. "They've likely slipped into the troll tunnels, by now. My powers won't do us much good."

Nadine nodded in agreement. "We could search for years and never find them. And I would not like to face them in such a tight space. Perhaps the trolls will eat them." She smiled at the thought. Then her gaze went to Kael. "You are the Witchslayer, are you not? That is what the men from the seas call you. Others say you are a pirate, or a Wright. I heard one of the giants call you a redheaded rodent, but I do not think that was very nice," she said, pursing her lips. "So what will the mots call you?"

"Just *Kael*," he said, waving his hands. "I don't want any other names."

Nadine's gaze was thoughtful as she nodded. "Just Kael ... yes, that is good. You *are* just — and you have certainly brought justice to these lands today. Very well, you will be known as Just Kael among my people."

That wasn't at all what he'd meant. And when he looked to Kyleigh for help, she only smiled. He could see laughter shining behind her eyes as she said:

"What an excellent name, Nadine. I can't wait to hear what you'll sing about him. *The Ballad of Just Kael* ... that's got quite a nice ring to it, doesn't it?"

He was about to tell her *exactly* how he felt about *The Ballad of Just Kael* when a dark figure dropped down from the rubble behind her. He saw the black mask the figure wore and immediately drew his knife.

"Get back — it's another one!" he cried, jumping between Kyleigh and their masked attacker.

With one swift kick, the masked figure popped the knife out of his hand and caught it deftly as it spun through the air. When the figure pulled the mask down, a forest woman glared out at him. "Another what?" she demanded, cutting the space between them to a sliver. "Have you seen someone else dressed like me —?"

"Careful, Elena," Kyleigh growled.

And under her glaring look, Elena seemed to think better of stepping any closer. She turned the long knife over in her hands — the knife Kael had stolen from the dark rider. She gasped and threw it away from her, as if the weapon had suddenly turned hot.

"Holthan — it's Holthan." Her dark eyes flicked to the castle gates. "I have to get out of here. If he finds me, he'll kill me."

Kyleigh grabbed her arm. "Don't run off just yet — I've got a feeling you won't have to worry about Holthan any longer." Her gaze lighted on Kael, and the look in her eyes made his insides squirm excitedly. "There aren't many fighters who could best this man. I'd wager your nightmare is probably ended."

Kael forced himself to look away from her and back to Elena. "He attacked me, and I killed him." He pointed over the castle walls. "You'll find his body out in the cornfields. I'm sorry," he added, when Elena's glare sharpened. "I know you probably want to kill me —"

"Oh, she wants to kill everybody," Kyleigh said with a wave of her hand.

When Elena still didn't move, Nadine stepped forward and took her gently around the arm. "Come — we will go see him together. You will have to tell me what *corn* is, but we will find him."

Elena's glare melted into a look of worry, and she held Nadine's hand very tightly as they walked away. Kael was still puzzling over the strangeness of it all when Kyleigh nearly knocked him over.

"Thank you," she said, wrapping her arms around his middle. "I know you have no idea what you've done — but thank you."

"You're right, I don't." And perhaps it was the warmth he suddenly felt that made him add: "Though I wish you'd tell me, so I could do it again."

The second the words were out of his mouth, he regretted them.

Kyleigh pulled away. The beginning of a laugh bent her lips, and he prepared himself to be humiliated. But then quite suddenly, her mouth clamped shut and her face went serious. She brushed the wrinkles out of his shirt before she stepped around him and began marching for the gates.

A man stood at the end of the passageway. His chest was bare and he wore a pair of very tight-fitting trousers. As Kyleigh passed, she held a finger to the man's face. "Not one word," she hissed.

He smirked in reply.

His eyes watched Kael with an unnatural focus as he passed, almost as if he could see the blood racing beneath his skin. He couldn't help but think the glow in the man's eyes made them look a bit familiar ... but he couldn't figure out where he'd seen them before.

****

Aerilyn and her archers helped the wounded men limp off the battlefield. Sometimes it would take three or four of them just to help one giant, but they worked tirelessly. When Aerilyn spotted Kael, she waved him over and showed him where the most seriously wounded men were.

Kael stopped their bleeding and sealed up the deepest parts of their wounds. There were so many of them that he knew he would have to save his strength. Once he got a man patched up enough to walk, Kyleigh would lead him to the barns — where the lady giants waited with herbs and bandages.

The afternoon sun burned hot, and smoke trailed up from the ground in places. Kael didn't think he saw a single man without a scrape or a bruise. His stomach dropped and tears pressed against his eyes as he walked among the dead.

He saw faces he recognized: the faces of giants he'd slaved with, of pirates he'd fought beside. He remembered their smiles, the movement of their brows and how their skin had creased about their eyes.

Now, they seemed like masks of the men they once were — with their expressions frozen and their eyes so deadly calm. They were like the statues in Lysander's mansion: noble and cold, with the last lines of their story already written out. All the while he worked, he tried to keep himself focused on the living ... but it was hard to forget the dead.

A line of giants emerged from the barn, with shovels propped over their shoulders, and they began to dig graves on either side of the road. While they worked, others bent to collect the bodies of their friends.

They cradled them gently, holding them in their arms as if they were little more than tired children. The giants' steps were heavy as they carried the dead towards their final rest.

Kael picked his way across the Fields twice over, searching for any wounded men the archers might've missed. He bent and pressed his fingers against every neck he passed, feeling for a pulse. His heart sank a little further each time the coldness answered him.

It was a heavy moment when he realized nothing more could be done. He left the giants to their somber work and dragged himself back to the barns. It was there he heard a voice that lifted his spirits considerably:

"Now, now — I had every intention to pillage and carry on while you were away, but things got complicated!" Uncle Martin insisted.

He stood outside of Eastbarn, leaning on his polished oak cane. At that moment, he seemed to be in the middle of a very heated conversation with Lysander. When he thrust the point of his cutlass under Lysander's nose, the captain had the good sense to lean away from it.

"*Complicated*? You've been sacking ships since before I was born!" Lysander said back. "You know very well what you were supposed to be doing — and don't tell me that you forgot, because I won't believe you. You seemed to remember well enough to hide your ship in a different port —"

"I didn't say I *forgot*," Uncle Martin cut in, waving his sword dangerously close to Lysander's nose. "Forgetting something isn't complicated. It's as simple as downing a cup of grog —"

"You were drunk!" Lysander knocked the sword away from his face as Uncle Martin huffed indignantly. "You got into the cellars again, didn't you?"

"I did no such —"

"You stole the key from Bimply, and you packed your ship full of grog!"

"It was for *morale*." Uncle Martin thrust his sword into its sheath with such vigor that it nearly snapped his belt. "After you left us all behind — bored and heartbroken, I might add — well, I had to do something to get the men's spirits up! And what's better than spirits for lifting spirits? We never actually *meant* to come after you." He looked away and, twirling his moustache thoughtfully, he muttered: "There was a reason we had to come to the plains, but I ... well, I find I can't remember what it was." He marched off across the courtyard, and Lysander followed at a stomp.

"Perhaps you can't remember because you were *drunk*!"

"Accusations!" Uncle Martin barked, waving his cane. "Blind finger-pointing and imputation!"

Kael left them to their argument and slipped inside of Eastbarn, intending to help wherever he could. But the lady giants already had things well in hand: they'd set up the stalls into makeshift hospitals and had the wounded laid out across the pallets. They bandaged scrapes and bruises, mixed poultices from herbs they'd plucked from the Fields — and flatly refused to put up with any sort of heroism.

The giants who'd charged their enemies with such terrible fury were now being made to sit quietly while the women stitched them up. They sat cross-legged and grumbled quite a bit, but if they so much as reached to fuss at their wounds, they'd get their hands slapped away.

"Ho there, wee Kael!" a light voice hailed him.

He turned and saw Clairy walking briskly down the aisle, a roll of clean bandages in her arms. Now that she was awake, Kael thought he could certainly see her resemblance to Brend — particularly in the mischievous glint behind her eyes.

He started to thank her for everything she'd done, but she stopped him. "No, I want to thank *you*, wee thing — for bringing my Jonathan to me." Her fingers almost wrapped the whole way around his arm when she squeezed it. "I'm more than a bit taken with him, and I plan to make him an honest rogue," she added with a wink. "Once that clodded brother of mine sees it, that is."

Then without warning, she bent and kissed him on the cheek. His face burned even after Clairy swept past him.

Jonathan followed along at her heels. His face was swollen and his knees were bent under the weight of a large, steaming pot, but he still managed to give Kael a rather suggestive wink as he passed.

Darrah met him on his way out. She said that Brend had been looking for him, and wanted to speak with him

562

straight away. Kael wasn't sure that he was in the mood to put up with Brend, but he went back to Westbarn, anyways.

When he didn't see Brend in the aisle, he went to check their stall. His pallet had been ripped apart and flung to every end of the room. *Deathtreader* was nowhere to be found. His stomach sank.

So Gilderick had managed to get a hold of the journal, as well.

Just when Kael didn't think things could get any worse, he stepped out of the stall — and was nearly crushed under the weight of a massive arm. A familiar, thick scent filled his nostrils as his head was forced into the depths of Brend's shirt.

"There you are, wee rat! I've been looking for you."

Kael managed to wriggle out of his hold, only to run into Declan — who looked as if he'd just flung himself into the pond. His trousers were dripping wet and moisture clung to his chest and limbs. But at least he'd managed to scrub all of the blood from his face.

He wore a tiny smile as he helped Kael get to his feet. "I didn't think you wee men had much fight in you, but you've proved me wrong. The plains are in giant hands once again."

"I'm glad I could help," Kael muttered as he brushed the dirt off his pants. "What do you plan to do, now? Will your Prince finally show his face?"

The giants weren't fooled: they exchanged quick smirks, but didn't answer him.

Kael thought they'd chosen a rather frustrating time to be clever. "How will I know the plains will be in good hands unless I know who the Prince is?" he countered. "I won't leave until you tell me."

"Well, if it'll get you off of our lands, then I suppose we've got no choice," Brend said with a smirk.

"Who is it, then?"

Brend said nothing — though he *did* break into a rather annoyingly-wide smile. Then he spread his arms out beside him, as if he was daring Kael to guess.

"Oh, for mercy's sake," he groaned, when he saw the answer shining in Brend's eyes. "No — it can't be. It just *can't.*"

"Oh, but it is, wee rat!" Brend said with a laugh. "I'm the son of the Prince's cousin — the last male of his noble line. Most folk would think it was a mightily grand thing to count a Prince among his friends."

"Well, most folk don't know him like I do."

Declan and Brend guffawed loudly at this. Then they grabbed Kael by either shoulder and led him outside. "Come along, wee rodent," Brend said cheerily. "The Prince needs to settle his debts — and you're going to help him."

So Kael spent the rest of the day following Declan and Brend around, helping them repay his friends for their help. And though he hated to admit it, the more he listened to Brend, the more he began to sound like a Prince.

When Nadine told him of the mots' troubles, Brend gave them everything they needed to grow their own food: seed, tools, and training. He arranged for a group of giants to take the mots around the Fields and teach them everything they knew about farming — and Brend himself showed them how to care for the grain.

All Jake asked for was permission to study the plains. He thought he might write a book about them one day, and he wondered if the giants might allow him to come back for a visit. Brend did better than that: he made Jake an official friend of the giants, declaring that wherever he traveled, there would be food and a warm bed waiting for him. And he could come and go as often as he pleased.

Kael thought that Brend was being rather generous, and he was a bit surprised, considering how insufferable he could be. Then they came to Jonathan.

He bowed so deeply that his nose nearly scraped the ground and, without a moment's thought, asked outright for Clairy.

Of course, Brend refused.

"But I swear I won't kill you," he amended, when Clairy glared at him.

They argued for several minutes, bellowing back and forth. It didn't matter how loudly Brend roared, Clairy never backed down. She held Jonathan's head tightly to her chest, threatening to run away with him if Brend didn't see reason. Kael wasn't sure if Jonathan was about to suffocate or have his head ripped off when Darrah finally stepped in.

She dragged Brend aside — and after a good amount of scolding, he returned with his ears burning red.

"Fine, you've got permission to marry my sister, you clod — ah, wee fiddler, " he grumbled, when Darrah shot him a severe look. "But you aren't to take her from me, understood? If you're to marry her, then you'll stay right here. I've only just got her back, and I won't have you carting her off to squat under those great leafy tents of yours any time soon."

Jonathan agreed. Then with a loud whoop, he jumped straight into Clairy's arms — where he kissed her soundly on the lips. Brend looked mad enough to swing for him when Darrah wrapped her hands in his.

It was amazing how quickly he softened.

Once that had been taken care of, Kael led them off to speak to the pirates. At first, Lysander insisted that they didn't want any sort of payment. "You've helped me free my people, and that's more than any of us could've hoped for," he said.

The giants were trying to convince him to ask for something else when Uncle Martin suddenly burst in, shouting from the tops of his lungs. He stepped past the giants and thrust his cane in the middle of Lysander's chest.

"It's all coming back, I remember now — the Duke's been murdered! That's right," he said, when Lysander's mouth dropped open. "I'm afraid your little plan has come thoroughly unraveled. The Duke's been murdered, and the merchants were so furious that they've stripped Colderoy of his office. They've already elected a new high chancellor, and I'll bet you can't guess who it is."

Lysander groaned and slapped a hand to his face. "Please say it isn't —"

"Chaucer," Uncle Martin cut in. "Colderoy's out, and Chaucer's in. And if you think he isn't bitter about your vote-tampering, then you'd better guess again! Chaucer's hardly got the seat warmed on the chancellor's chair, and he's already waged a war on all things pirate. He's convinced the merchants to have their ships travel in fleets — *fleets*, I tell you!"

Lysander groaned again.

"Fleets armed with mercenaries and flaming arrows!"

"Well, I imagine that's put a damper on the pillaging."

"That's right," Uncle Martin went on. "We can hardly stick our heads out of the Bay without having them lopped off. And I expect things will only get worse. How are we going to feed our people, if we can't even raid a merchant's vessel? Hmm? Yes, I'll bet you're wishing you had a stiff pint of grog right now." When Lysander just groaned, Uncle Martin spun to Brend. "And it's not just the pirates who'll have to worry: once those merchants find out the plains are open for trade, they'll pack up your harbors. Food is more valuable than *gold* in the seas. They'll swoop in like locusts, strip your fruit from its vines — and leave you with a mountain of worthless copper to deal with."

Brend didn't seem too concerned. "Well, then I suppose we'll just have to come up with a way to keep your people fed — and to keep those coin-licking clodders off my lands!"

In an hour's time, the deal was official: only the pirates had the rights to trade with the plains, and the giants would kill any other seas men who entered their lands on sight. So if Chaucer and his merchants wanted a share of the crops, they'd have no choice but to stow their weapons and do business with the pirates.

One the pirates were all settled, they went in search of the forest woman named Elena. It took them a bit of time to find her: she seemed to be able to disappear whenever she pleased, and turned up in the most unlikely of places. When they *did* finally manage to catch up with her, she claimed she didn't want anything. And not even Kyleigh could convince her to change her mind.

"It's important for the giants to have some way to pay you back," she insisted, when Elena shook her head. "There must be *something* — some little thing they can give you for fighting for them."

Elena clawed at her sleeve for a moment, and her dark eyes went to the cornfields. "I don't know what I want, anymore. I thought I had a plan — I thought I knew what I was going to do, once I escaped the desert. But ... now I'm not sure." Her gaze trailed to the roads, where Jake was using a spell to help the giants dig their graves. "I suppose I'm freer now than I ever have been. I think I'll just travel for a bit, and let the journey clear my head. Perhaps I'll even find someplace peaceful to live for a while. I've always wondered what it would be like to live in peace."

Declan had been listening quietly, chewing on an apple as Elena talked. But at the word *travel*, he suddenly smiled. "Well, then I think I've got just the thing."

He led them to the Pens, to where the horses roamed. He waved an arm out at the galloping beasts and said that Elena could have her pick. "Yeh, a good horse can carry you anywhere you wish. He'll follow you through every peril, and he'll stand by your side till the end. So, which one will it be?"

Elena's eyes widened. "How should I know? I've never had one of my own before. I always just picked one out of the stables."

"Why don't I choose for you?" Kyleigh said. When Elena nodded, she snatched the half-eaten apple out of Declan's hand and leapt over the fence.

The horses must've been able to smell the predator on her: they galloped away as she walked towards them, their eyes rolling back in terror. Every horse fled for the other side of the pen — save for one.

He had a dapple-gray coat and his mane was cut short. His tail swished in interest, and his brown eyes stayed on the apple. Slowly, he began to walk forward, lumbering on his stocky legs towards Kyleigh. When he reached her, he sniffed her hand in greeting. Then she offered him a bite of the apple.

At Kyleigh's gesture, Elena climbed over the fence and went to join her. She fed the horse the remainder of the apple, stroking him tentatively between the ears. Her dark eyes betrayed nothing, and her glare never wavered. So Kael was rather surprised when she said:

"This one. I choose him."

"*Him?*" Declan glanced at the horse. "But he's a farm horse. He's bred to pull a plow — not to go on travels. I don't want to cheat you. There are other, far grander creatures out here."

"Though none braver," Kyleigh mused.

Elena ran her hand down the horse's dappled neck. "Braver ..." she whispered. Then she grabbed either side of his long face and put her chin to his nose. "What do you say then, Braver? Do you want to go on an adventure?"

He snorted in reply.

Chapter 47
An Unexpected Thing

By evening, the giants had finished taking care of the dead. They piled the bloodtraitors' carcasses in an empty plot of grass and burned them.

"We'll leave no trace of their evil behind," Brend murmured as he watched the fire consume their bodies. He reached over to Declan — who stared with a thick shadow covering his eyes. His shoulders rocked when Brend clasped them, but he made no move to shrug him off. "And those we've lost ... well, they'll rest all the more peaceful for it. Let's leave this filth to their flame, and give our brothers one last goodbye."

They'd buried the pirates and the giants on either side of the road leading up to the castle. Inside one of the damp chambers, they'd found the sapling trees that D'Mere had brought for Lord Gilderick. Some of them were large enough that they already bore fruit, while others were only just starting their leaves.

They planted the trees along the graves, and Brend said they would honor the dead better than any stone marker. "They'll live on in every blossom, in every gift of fruit. We'll hear their whispers in the leaves ... and so our brothers will never be forgotten."

Lysander collected the sheaths from the fallen pirates' swords — while the blades themselves he arranged over their cold chests. He said a few words to each of them, called them by name, and promised he would carry their stories to their families. Though his stormy eyes burned a little redder with every sheath he retrieved, he managed to keep his voice steady ...

Until he came to Noah.

Kael looked away as they wrapped his body in white cloth. He didn't want to see Noah as a mask: he wanted to remember him as the boy he was. Lysander took Noah's sheath and watched in silence as the giants laid him to rest. There was a peach tree planted over his grave, and a small handful of fruit hung in its leaves.

"What'll you do with the sheath?" Declan said to Lysander — who had his arms crossed stubbornly over his chest.

Aerilyn was already crying. She sobbed quietly into the front of Kyleigh's jerkin, and the noise of her tears was making it all the more difficult for Lysander to keep his at bay.

"I'll bring it to his mother," he finally said. "She'll want to hear about the brave thing Noah did."

Declan's eyes went to the sheath. "That's a sorry gift for a mother."

"Well, it's the best I've got," Lysander snapped.

Declan said nothing. Instead, he reached into the tree and grabbed a peach off of one of the limbs. He stared at it for a moment before he stuffed it into his pocket.

"He was a good pirate," Lysander went on. He scowled furiously at the tree, gripping the sheath so tightly that the leather groaned between his hands. "Noah deserved to be buried at sea."

Brend gathered Lysander under his arm, crushing him against his chest — though oddly enough, he didn't try to wriggle free. "We'll take good care of him, Captain," Brend said quietly.

Lysander nodded, but his eyes stayed on the grave. Kael was beginning to think that the darkness might never leave his stare when Kyleigh spoke:

"Well, I think we could all use some good news." She glanced down at Aerilyn, who looked confused beneath her tears.

"News? What sort of news?"

Kyleigh's brows lifted in surprise, and her face turned slightly pink — something it never did. "I'm sorry. I thought you knew ..."

Aerilyn pulled away from her. Her blue eyes were wide with worry as she clutched at the curls of her hair. "Knew what? Oh, please tell me what it is — whatever it is! I don't think I could bear any more shocks. My stomach's already twisting."

Kyleigh's face went pinker. She glanced at the man named Silas — who made a frustrated sound. "Of course she knows," he hissed. "She *must* know. How can you not feel that little thing scratching around inside of you?" He said to Aerilyn, looking pointedly at her belly. "It's no wonder your stomach feels twisty —"

She squealed, and Silas leapt back in fright. He clamped a hand over his ears and glared as Aerilyn threw herself on Kyleigh.

"It's true, I'm afraid," Kyleigh said with a laugh. "I thought you knew —"

"I had no idea." Aerilyn clutched her hands to her chest, an excited smile broke across her lips. "But I suppose it makes sense. I *have* been feeling rather odd, lately. But I just thought ... oh!" She spun to Lysander, her eyes sparkling, and said: "Isn't this exciting? Aren't you thrilled?"

Lysander looked as if he'd just been slapped in the face with a troll's stocking, and therefore didn't know how to feel about it. "What in high tide is going on? Have you been ill?" he said, stepping up to her.

She nodded. "I didn't want to tell you, because I knew you'd only send me back —"

"Blasted right, I would!" Lysander stormed, grabbing her hands. "I won't stand by and let you shrivel away —"

"I thought it was only nerves — but it turns out —"

"— you'll march right back to the ship this instant —"

"— I'm pregnant."

"No wife of mine — what?" Lysander's chin nearly hit his chest as his mouth dropped open. "Did you just say what I think you said?" When Aerilyn nodded, he looked down at her middle. "You mean you're ... *we're*?"

She nodded again, and he stared at her for a long moment, his face unreadable. Then quite suddenly, he snatched her up.

"We're going to have a baby!" he cried, spinning her around in a circle. "I'm going to be a father!"

Aerilyn slapped him across the head. "Put me down, you impossible pirate!"

Neither one of them seemed able to stop grinning. They held each other tightly, and their laughter lightened Kael's steps as they headed back to the barns.

For their gift, Kyleigh, Eveningwing, and Silas had asked for a feast — a dinner where they could eat their fill of meat. And the giants had been only too happy to oblige: they dragged tables from the castle out into the Fields, raided Gilderick's cellars, and left some of their fattest animals in the hands of the lady giants.

Now smoke trailed from the kitchen tower as they worked. One giantess passed them with a massive platter of food in her hands — and normally, Kael would've followed right after her. But tonight, not even the scents wafting off the warm breads or crackling meats could enchant him. His heart was filled with darker things.

Brend's arm fell across his shoulders, jolting him from his thoughts. "I've only got one debt left to settle, then — the debt I owe my favorite little mountain rat. So, what'll it be?" His eyes glinted as he smiled down, and while there was a bit of sharpness left in them, they were mostly soft. "Speak up, now! Nothing you ask will be too great a thing."

For half a breath, Kael's thoughts trailed to Tinnark — to Amos, to Roland, to all of the other villagers who must still be trapped under Titus's hand. If he had the giants on his side, he could free them. No army of men could stand against the giants' fury. And if he asked, they would follow him without thinking.

But *thinking* was precisely the thing that killed the question on his lips.

Kael saw the many faces he'd passed, lying cold and lifeless on the battlefield ... and he couldn't forget them. They'd been carved into the backs of his eyes — even when he closed them, he could still see the emptiness in their stares. The seas were free, the plains were free, the slave trade was ended. If he asked for nothing more, these men could go on to live a life without chains. They could rebuild their homes and raise their children. They could heal, and they could be happy.

But if Kael led them into the mountains ... they might never have that chance. Some might die, frozen and alone in a strange land. While others, like Thelred, might be forced to live with the wounds for the rest of their days.

If Kael asked them to fight, he would steal the happiness from them. And could he bear that weight upon his shoulders? Could he ask his friends to risk their futures in a battle for the mountains — for a land that nobody else cared about? And could he live on, knowing that he'd been responsible for their deaths?

No ... no, he couldn't. And he wouldn't. In fact, he refused to. He still planned to fight for the mountains — but he planned to do it alone.

So he forced himself to smile up at Brend and say: "To know that I have friends in the plains is gift enough." Lysander elbowed him, but he ignored it. "And if I ever find myself in need of friends, I'll be sure to think of the giants."

With that, he shrugged out from under Brend's arm and began to walk away. Lysander grabbed him by the back of the shirt.

"Oh no, you don't. I won't let you do this — you've fought too hard to turn back now. If you won't speak for yourself, then I'll speak for you," he warned, a flinty determination in his stare.

Kael shrugged. "Tell him, then. But it won't change my mind."

This seemed to shock Lysander enough to loosen his grip, and Kael slipped out of his hold. As he walked towards the barns, he could hear Lysander starting in on a tale —

beginning with the moment Kael had first stepped aboard *Anchorgloam*. He had no idea how Lysander would tell his story, though he imagined a good deal of the facts would be lost in the telling. So much had happened that he hadn't meant to; too much of his life had been left to Fate. But that didn't matter, anymore.

All that mattered now was the ending, and Kael intended to write it for himself — starting tonight. He wouldn't leave his fate to chance. He would do what had to be done ... and he would say what had to be said.

****

Kyleigh watched him walk away. There was a determination in Kael's steps that she recognized immediately: the way he lifted his feet was practiced and careful, and he brought them down firmly. He was thinking hard about something — and she wondered what it was. She was about to follow him when she felt Silas's elbow nudge her ribs.

She followed his gaze to the road, where Elena already had Braver saddled and packed. The giants had given her so much food for her journey that the sides bulged out of the bags. It was obvious that she'd been meaning to slip out quietly, but Jake had caught her.

Now they stood together, talking about something. Kyleigh could see the slump of Jake's shoulders and the sharp tilt of Elena's chin. They spoke for only a moment, and then Elena reached behind her and pressed some object into Jake's hand.

Without a second glance, she leapt astride Braver and nudged him into a trot. It wasn't long before they were little more than a smudge in the distance. But Jake never moved: he stared after them, clutching whatever it was that Elena had given him.

"Come on, dragoness," Silas whispered. "Our shaman needs us."

When they arrived, they saw that Jake's face was empty and his stare was hollow. He looked like a man that hadn't slept for weeks. And while he probably *was* exhausted, Kyleigh thought that might've only been part of it.

She stood on one side of him, and Silas stood on the other — as if they could somehow hold him up. They said nothing for a moment, waiting in the quiet of dusk for Jake to speak.

"She gave me her gloves," he finally said, holding them out to Kyleigh. "I'm not sure what I should do with them."

She closed his fingers around the soft, black leather. "Hold onto them, for now. And when it's ready, I expect your heart will tell you what to do."

Jake nodded. Then he stuffed the gloves rather glumly into the folds of his robe.

Silas made an attempt to pat him on the back, but he kept his fingers so stiff that it looked more like he was trying to crush a spider than be comforting. "We should go eat some food — that will cheer you up."

"No, that will cheer *you* up," Jake said with a sigh. "I'm not hungry."

"Nonsense." Kyleigh wrapped an arm about his middle. "You just need to drown your sorrows in a feast. I saw an enormous cake go by a few minutes ago. I swear it must've been four tiers high — covered in sugar and strawberries. What could be more cheerful than that?"

They steered Jake into the courtyard and got him settled at their table. It wasn't long before a nearby giantess spotted him, and she was so shocked by the thinness of his limbs that she made it her personal duty to keep his plate filled at all times.

Other giants crowded in around him, eager to hear his stories and learn more about magic. Jake got so caught up in teaching them that he seemed to forget his troubles. It wasn't long before he was deep into an explanation about why it was such a difficult feat to turn a man into a frog, and a small smile bent his lips.

One of the giants carried Thelred out of the stalls and settled him at a makeshift picnic in the courtyard. They leaned him back against a wall and propped the bandaged stump of his leg on a mountain of bedding, where it could breathe.

He had a steady stream of visitors, including Morris — who promised him that missing a limb wasn't all that bad a thing. "Believe me, lad, there's worse things than missing a leg. At least you'll be able to button your own trousers!"

Uncle Martin certainly did his part to be comforting. He never once left Thelred's side, and talked animatedly throughout the night: about how happy he was that Thelred would have more time to help him brew his grogs, and how he intended to get them a matching set of canes.

"You aren't helping things, father," Thelred grumbled at him.

But Uncle Martin seemed to be helping quite a lot: it wasn't long before a small crowd of lady giants joined them at the picnic, drawn in by his antics. They laughed at Uncle Martin's jokes and fussed over Thelred — whose grumpiness melted a bit under their care.

Across the courtyard, Lysander and Aerilyn sat with Brend. The Prince used one hand to eat, but the other he kept twined in Darrah's. Her face glowed, and she kept an arm resting happily across her belly as she listened to Lysander's tales.

It made Kyleigh smile to think that Darrah's child would grow up freely, and with the protection of a Prince. She didn't know Brend very well, but she could feel the love he had for his people — and she knew he would love Darrah's child as his own.

Lysander chattered on, asking the giants all manner of questions, but Aerilyn seemed more occupied with what was happening on the other side of the table — where Jonathan and Clairy sat together. Or rather, Jonathan sat *in* Clairy's lap, and they spent a great deal more of their time kissing than eating.

Aerilyn watched them with her hands stuck to either side of her face, as if she'd just had a great shock. Kyleigh could read her lips clearly as she muttered to herself:

Oh, dear ... oh, dear.

Not long ago, Kyleigh would've agreed. But now, she found that she envied them. It must be nice to be able to kiss whoever they pleased. She would've given anything to be able to behave so foolishly.

Kyleigh looked away before she could think too much about it, and tried to distract herself with the company of her own benchmates.

Silas and Eveningwing sat on either side of her, gorging themselves on meat. It came in nearly every form they could think of: in legs, wings, slabs, and even wholes. A giantess set an entire roasted hog down in front of them, and when Silas cracked it open, he moaned.

"How do they do it?" He tore off a hunk of flesh and deposited it directly into his mouth. His eyes rolled back as he chewed. "It sings to me!"

Eveningwing snatched a slab of beef from a towering pile and stuck it onto his plate. He held the slab down with either hand, as if he was trying to keep it from running away. His head shot down with lightning quickness, and he ripped a thick chunk of meat from the slab with his teeth. Then he slung his head about — showering them all with splatters of grease.

"For the last time: you don't have to do that," Silas grumped at him, wiping the grease from his eyes. "Your prey is already dead, and the blood is cooked out of it!"

Eveningwing looked up at him sheepishly. "Sorry. I forget," he said around a thick mouthful of meat. "I'm still learning my human manners."

Kyleigh had been forced to behave properly for so long that it was actually rather nice to be able to sit down and eat with people who wouldn't wrinkle their noses at her. There would be plenty of time for manners, later.

She grabbed the leg off a nearby chicken and raised it over her head. "To victory!"

Silas joined her with a chain of sausages. "To food!"

They looked at Eveningwing, who still had his face buried in his meal. "Oh." He quickly grabbed the mangled strip of beef off his plate and held it up. "Yes — to both!"

Then they went back to their feasting. Kyleigh had just torn off a rather large bite when she felt someone tap her shoulder. She turned, and nearly choked when she saw Kael staring back at her.

He said nothing about the fact that she had a chunk of meat hanging out of her mouth. He only smiled.

But it wasn't his usual smile. The crooked ends of his lips trembled a bit, so slightly that she almost didn't see it. She was trying to figure out what that meant when he spoke:

"I was wondering if I might talk to you for a moment." He glanced out around the courtyard. "Someplace quiet, if that's all right."

She immediately dropped the food in her hands and followed him into the night. They walked until they stood just outside of the courtyard, so that the light from the fires still reached them. Kyleigh was trying to make sure she didn't have any of the chicken stuck to her face when Kael's fingers suddenly brushed against her cheek.

She froze.

He hardly ever touched her, and certainly not without some kind of warning. But here he was, with his fingertips balanced against her skin — making her heart beat so wildly that she wondered if he could hear it. She watched his eyes as he wiped a bit of meat off her face, and saw a steady light flickering behind them.

She knew he must have something on his mind, something worth thinking very hard about. His hand fell away and he shoved it into his pocket. The light in his eyes sharpened to a point as he gazed over her shoulder.

"I'm furious with you, I'll have you know."

Kyleigh was surprised. He didn't *feel* furious — well, not at first. But as they stood there in the quiet, she thought she might be able to read it on his face. He wasn't glaring, but his lips were tight. And he certainly wasn't looking at her.

"I'm sorry I let Gilderick get away, but I couldn't leave you. I thought you might be hurt —"

"No, I'm not angry about that," Kael said. He kept staring past her, and the other hand went into his pocket, where they both tightened into fists.

"Kael, whatever it is, just —"

"I'm angry because you left," he said shortly.

A muscle twitched in his jaw — she could see it tightening beneath his skin. Red spread from the bridge of his nose, across his freckles, and Kyleigh knew that he was about to go off on one of his famous rants.

She also knew that she shouldn't laugh. If Kael was angry, then it would be unkind of her to laugh at him. But ... she couldn't help it.

Once the red in his face reached the top of his head, the words would start spilling out. He'd stomp and snort, saying all kinds of ridiculous things — and generally behaving as if the whole earth had turned over on its head. He'd be mad at everybody, and mad at no one in particular. He'd be so busy ranting that he'd forget to look up.

Because had he thought to look up, he would've seen that he was angry over nothing: Kyleigh wasn't gone forever. She'd come back.

It was funny to watch Kael get his knickers in a bunch — especially when it was over something so silly. He could be completely ridiculous, sometimes. He should've *known* that she would come back. Why did he always doubt her?

Those were precisely the words she intended to say, when he started his yelling. But to her great surprise, he didn't yell. He didn't even raise his voice. His brows slipped out of their glare, and he dropped his head.

"I have something to tell you," he said quietly. "But first, I want you to make me a promise."

She would promise him anything. No matter what he said or what he asked, she would do everything in her power to help him. But she thought those words might've been a little too strong for a human. So she simply replied: "All right."

"Promise me you won't leave me again — at least, not without telling me where you're going."

Kyleigh thought that was a fairly reasonable thing to ask. After all, she had no intention of ever leaving him. "Very well, I promise."

"No matter what I say, you won't leave me?"

"You can tell me anything," Kyleigh said firmly. Though by this point, a strange feeling had begun to creep into her gut. Something was about to happen, something that she wasn't ready for. But she pushed the feeling aside. "I promise that nothing you say will drive me off."

He smiled again, that same strange, wavering smile. And then he looked up.

Kael never looked at her, not really. He looked *through* her. The few times he'd met her eyes — *truly* met them — she'd felt as if his gaze sunk through her skin and touched her soul. He never tried to cage her in or figure her out. His eyes didn't paw over her, or measure her up. And he must've seen the wildness in her ... but he never wrinkled his nose.

A dragon and a woman warred inside her heart — always fighting, always trying to decide whether she would be more human or more beast. Sometimes, she wasn't sure what she was. But when Kael looked into her eyes, she saw her reflection shining back clearly:

To him, she was simply *Kyleigh*.

For a long moment, he did nothing more than look at her. Then with a deep breath, he said something that she'd never expected to hear:

"I love you, Kyleigh. I know you can't love me back," he added. "I've read the story of Iden and Quicklegs — I know that shapechangers can't love humans ... but I also know that I can't change what I feel." As he took a step forward, his eyes held her — which was a very good thing, because otherwise she thought she might've lost her footing. "But if you stay, I swear I won't mention it again. I'll hide it so well that you'll forget I ever said it."

Kyleigh doubted that. She doubted it very seriously. Already, his words rang inside her heart:

He loved her. He *loved* her.

She never thought she would care much about love, at least not in the way the humans experienced it. She'd thought it was a rather silly idea, a word that humans seemed to throw around at every opportunity. Sometimes she felt like she'd heard it said so often that it had actually lost its meaning.

But now, quite suddenly, love was more than just a word: it was a true feeling, a deep feeling — one every bit as binding as valtas. She thought she could see it on Kael's face. *That* was the look she'd been trying to figure out, the one she didn't quite understand.

He loved her!

For one impossibly happy moment, her heart soared. She wanted to throw herself in his arms and press her lips to his, to feel his love sink into hers. But then her heart climbed down ... and a reminder rang in her head:

To bond with any but your own is Abomination, and upon all Abomination, Fate will loose her brother — Death.

Shapechangers couldn't bond with humans. Or at least, they weren't supposed to. Was the love she felt for Kael truly an Abomination? If she ran to him now, would she be dragging him to his death?

We have a duty to protect those weaker than us — and unfortunately, that includes the humans.

The words Silas had spoken so long ago stung the insides of her ears. They slid into her chest like a knife, cutting her happiness short. Even if Death didn't take them, Kyleigh knew the sort of path she would lead him down. She knew the emptiness that Kael would have to endure, if she took him as her mate.

She knew the truth ... and because of that, she had a responsibility to protect him.

The burning in her chest was a human emotion, a pain that her dragon half accepted as a fact, but made the human in her ache. "I promise I'll stay — as your ally, and as your friend." She had to fight to keep her face masked as she spoke; she couldn't let Kael see how the words hurt her. "But you would do well to guard your heart."

His eyes dug into hers for a moment, and it took every ounce of her strength to keep the pain from pouring out. When he finally looked away, she felt as if he'd taken a large piece of her heart with him.

"Thank you," he said quietly. As he walked past her, he reached out and clasped her shoulder.

She hadn't been expecting this. The fires in her blood had sealed her wounds quickly: the gashes across her back were scabbed, but still a little sore. When Kael's fingers pressed down upon her wounds, she winced — and he caught her.

"I knew it. I knew it was you." He stepped in front of her, and she looked down to avoid his eyes. "You used that dragon thing to heal me, didn't you?" When she didn't reply, he grabbed her arm. "Well, I won't let you suffer for me. Come on, let's get those wounds sealed up."

"No!" She twisted out of his grasp. When he tried to grab her again, she leapt away.

"Don't be ridiculous —"

"*You're* being ridiculous!"

Kael looked at her incredulously. "How am *I* being ridiculous? I'm trying to help you —!"

"It'll heal on its own," Kyleigh snapped. She didn't know why she was being short with him. All she'd wanted for so long was to be able see him again, to listen to his voice and hear that he loved her back. And now that everything she'd ever hoped for had come to pass — it was all wrong. None of it was right.

She needed some time to be alone ... and to cry. She just needed to cry.

"I'll see you in the morning," she said, striding past him.

Somehow, she managed to make it into the cover of darkness before the tears started rolling down.

Chapter 48
A New Plan

A few days passed as they waited for their companions' wounds to mend. Once the pirates were healed up enough to walk, they began packing for the journey home. And then came a day of farewells.

The mots left with the dawn, their packs heavy with gifts from the plains. Kyleigh watched their backs for a full minute before she realized that Nadine wasn't among them. Instead of returning home, the desert woman had materialized at her side.

"When we left the motlands, Hessa told me we would not see each other again in this life," Nadine explained quietly. Her eyes were light as she watched the mots depart. "I thought it was because I would die in battle, but now I see that it is because she wishes me to find a new life. I have lost Tahir, and Hessa has grown wise beyond my guidance. So my purpose in the motlands is ended. Perhaps in this strange Kingdom of yours, I will find a new purpose." She turned to Kyleigh, and her face brightened with her smile. "Do you need a servant?"

Kyleigh shook her head. "No — but I could always use a friend." She took Nadine about the shoulders and led her over to the shipbuilders. "Listen up, you lot — we're going to have our first guest in Roost. So I expect you all to be on your best behavior."

Shamus grinned. "Oh, of course we will! I'll have a room cleaned out for her first thing. Eh, she might have to stay in the guard's quarters for a bit, just until we can get the roof patched up. But don't you worry, Lady Kyleigh — we'll make sure she's comfortable."

"Why does he call you a lady?" Nadine whispered.

583

"Because I can't convince him to stop," Kyleigh said with a sigh.

She left Nadine and Shamus to discuss her living arrangements and went in search of Kael. She'd spent a few days wandering through the quiet of the Fields, trying to understand all of the many voices crying from her heart. But in the end, she still couldn't figure it out.

How could something so beautiful be an abomination? Was Fate truly that heartless? And if their love was forbidden — why did they share the valtas?

Human love could be explained away as desire, but the valtas was much deeper: it wasn't a conscious choice, nothing she could want with her body or decide upon with her mind. Only her soul understood the valtas. And for whatever reason, her soul had chosen Kael.

Kyleigh didn't know what to do. Had she been a cleverer creature, she might've been able to figure it out. But instead, the facts and feelings were so jumbled together that she knew she had no hope of ever being able to sort them. Perhaps Kael might've been able to tell her what to do ...

But she could never tell him.

If he didn't know she loved him back, then perhaps he would heal. Humans often did that. If they couldn't have one mate, they could always find another. Though it made her sick to think it, she knew she would rather him find love somewhere else, than have to live with a broken heart.

She knew that pain all too well. It was a lonely, miserable sting.

Kyleigh knew she would never get anything accomplished, if she sat around and felt sorry for herself. So instead, she focused on the good things: Kael was here, he was alive. She could speak to him, if she wanted. But first, she had to find him.

After a bit of searching, she stuck her head into one of the barns and found Kael in a heated discussion with Declan and Brend.

"It's too late for that," Brend said with a smirk. "The wee pirate captain's already told me everything. And you said you wanted our friendship — so, you've got it."

Kael glared at him. "Friends don't have to fight for each other. I won't have your people die in my war —"

"You helped us reclaim our lands, and we intend to help you reclaim yours. Though," he added with a snort, "I can't imagine what you'd want them for. Mightily sparse things, the mountains."

"Exactly. So why would you bother fighting —?"

"Because that's what friends do, wee Kael," Declan cut in.

Brend nodded. "Well that, and it's the best way I can think to settle the debt between us." He batted Kael in the shoulder, stumbling him a few steps sideways. "You can count the giants on your side. I'll send my general to you, once you've got everything schemed up."

As he said this, he looked pointedly at Declan — whose deep brows rose in surprise. "You can't mean *me*," he said, when Brend kept staring at him. "I'm not fit to lead — I can't even smell a fight without the whole world going dark! How do you expect me to command an army?"

"Oh, you'll do just fine," Brend said with a wave of his hand. "Our army didn't need to be commanded the other day: it needed courage. And you gave them that. To see one giant stand before an army, with naught but the scythe in his hands ..." He whistled. "Well, that gave us all the orders we needed. They'll follow you to the depths, General." Brend clapped Declan heartily on the shoulder. "Now, let's go and give them the good news!"

The giants made for the door, and Kael stepped aside to let them pass — which Kyleigh thought was rather odd. If Kael ever felt strongly about something, he would never let it go without a fight. He'd defend himself like a badger in his den.

The fact that he'd let the giants go so easily put Kyleigh on edge. "What are you up to?"

Kael didn't always use his mouth to smile: sometimes, she could read the smile in his eyes. Now, it looked as if he smiled rather broadly. "Nothing," he said with a shrug.

It wasn't a very convincing lie. He wasn't very good at lying.

"So, I hear you're the lady of Copperdock. Shamus told me," he explained, when he saw her surprised look. "He told me everything, and it only took a few tankards of ale. You really ought to keep him away from that stuff, if you want to keep any of your secrets."

Kyleigh was deciding whether to be cross or amused when she noticed the look on Kael's face. There had always been a softness to him — something that he tried desperately to keep hidden behind his glares. But it wasn't hidden any longer: she could see it across the angles of his face, down his nose, in the set of his lips.

And she had a difficult time not stepping closer. "Yes, I'm afraid they're trying to turn me into some sort of ruler," she managed to say. She had to look away from him then, or she thought she was in real danger of losing her resolve. "I just came to tell you that I'll be in Copperdock, should you need me. Though I suspect you'll want to stay in the Bay."

She glanced back in time to catch his nod. Now *he* was the one not looking at her. "If we mean to attack Titus, then I've got a lot to plan for. And Morris still has plenty to teach me," he added, with a hard look. "I don't want to make any more mistakes."

Kyleigh could feel him slipping off into his thoughts, but she didn't want to lose him, just yet. So she wrapped her fingers around his wrist. "There'll be time to figure that out later. For now, let's go bid our friends farewell."

One the giants had stuffed their packs full of provisions, they stood in a line to see them off. It was difficult to leave Jonathan behind: he could be a bit ridiculous, but Kyleigh knew she would miss the lightness his spirit brought to their party.

Jonathan let go of Clairy just long enough to give them all a hug goodbye, then his arms went back around her waist.

When Kyleigh saw how they grinned at each other, she knew they'd have many happy years ahead of them — though she cringed to think about the sort of mischief they might get into.

Declan emerged from one of the barns with a small clay pot in his hands, and he went straight for Aerilyn. "I planted one of the seeds from Noah's tree in here. It'll grow better under a woman's care," he explained, when she looked confused. "Peaches need a gentle touch — at least, that's what the Grovers say. I only really know horses." He pressed the pot into her hands. "Give it to Noah's mother ... that way she'll always have a piece of him."

Aerilyn hugged Declan tightly, promising that she would.

They left with the sun rising at their backs: the pirates and the shipbuilders, along with Nadine, Jake, and Silas — who somehow caught wind of their plan to attack the mountains, and seemed to think that he was invited.

"Now you can finally pay me back for all of my work, dragoness," he said as they walked along. "My mountains will be free once again!"

Some of Gilderick's slaves were men and women of the seas, and most were eager to return to their families — though Lysander *did* manage to convince a small number of them to join him as pirates. Much to their surprise, Eveningwing had also insisted on becoming a pirate. Now he soared high above them, screeching happily as he guided them towards the seas. Occasionally, he'd even dip down to bat Lysander across the head.

As they left the plains, Kyleigh wore a wide smile that she could do absolutely nothing about. She didn't know if it was the happiness in the air or her own excitement that made her heart so light: Kael walked beside her the whole way.

He listened intently as she told him about her adventure in the desert — occasionally interjecting that she shouldn't have done one thing or the other. "You were really lucky, you know," he said, when she told him about what had happened to the Baron's castle. "There are so many ways it could've all gone wrong."

"True — but it didn't. So there's no point in worrying about it, is there?"

He shrugged. "I always worry. I can't help it. Especially when it's ..." He clamped his mouth shut.

"When it's what?"

"No — I promised that I wouldn't say anything else about it. And I intend to keep my promise. Now ..." He glanced around them quickly, and then he lowered his voice. "You were right. I *am* up to something."

Kyleigh's stomach flipped when he broke into an unexpected smile. But she forced herself to smile back. "I knew it. And what do you have planned, Kael of the Unforgivable Mountains?"

He shrugged. The lights behind his eyes pulsed as he turned them towards the horizon. "Nothing, yet. But I was hoping you might be able to help me with that."

And she promised she would.

Acknowledgements

I'll never stop thanking God for this opportunity. I've been so blessed with family, friends, and readers who've given me their love and support — and I just want to let y'all know how much it means to me.

Thanks to all my family (you folks in Texas, Oklahoma, Kansas, Arkansas, Indiana, Georgia, and even a few weirdos in Pennsylvania) for supporting me every step of the way. I firmly believe that the reason I've been able to do any of this is because you've kept me in your prayers, kept me in your hearts, and told me constantly how much you believe in me. A wise man once said: "You can pick your nose, but you can't pick your family."

Lucky for me — because I don't think I could've picked a better one!

Special thanks to my beta-readers: Toby, Ashtyn, Gayle, Prudence, Sandra, and of course, Ms. Carmichael. Thanks for trudging through my rough drafts ... and thanks for being gentle!

I'd also like to thank Pam Wiley and Chrystal Houston for hiring me to work that journalism job at Mays.

Pam, you taught me how to comb through my work with an editor's eye. Because of you, I'm not afraid of a little red ink. It's gotten me through the heartache of having to start all over again so many times, because you'd already taught me that a second draft is not an admittance of failure — just the start of something better.

Chrystal, my fellow writer and my friend: I feel like so many of my articles were made more epic by having your LOTR soundtrack playing in the background. I will never forget the day when I stepped into your office and announced that I'd gotten accepted into a business school. You looked at me and said: "Really? Huh. I always thought you'd be a writer."

Well ... fine.

I would also like to thank my friend, Molly — who took time out of her tour of duty in the U.S. Navy to send me a pair of dragon bookends from Japan. I'm sorry that this thanks is so grossly overdue. But I want you to know that both dragons are sitting proudly on my bookshelf, guarding the old tomes that I've rescued from antique shops. And you'll be happy to hear that "Molly" the horse is doing well, too!

Finally, thank *you*, dear Reader, for going on this adventure with me. Time, once spent, cannot be reclaimed. And I thank you for spending your time in my world — walking among the characters I love so dearly, fighting alongside them in every battle, and cheering when good finally triumphs over evil. It has always been my dream to tell a story worth hearing. And you, my readers, make it a story worth telling.

So as you leave the Kingdom and head back into the real world, I want to leave you all with this thought: may your heart find joy, may your soul know peace, and may the sunlight brighten your steps.